THE WAR OF SOULS

VOLUME ONE

DRAGONS OF A FALLEN SUN

Margaret Weis & Tracy Hickman

DRAGONS OF A FALLEN SUN
©2000 Wizards of the Coast, Inc.

Published by Wizards of the Coast. DRAGONLANCE, Wizards of the Coast and their respective logos are trademarks of Wizards of the Coast, Inc., in the U.S.A. and other countries.

Printed in the U.S.A.

Cover art by Matt Stawicki
Cartography by Dennis Kauth
First Printing: March 2000
Library of Congress Catalog Card Number: 99-65606

9 8 7 6

ISBN:978-0-7869-1807-2
620-21807000-001-EN

U.S., CANADA,   EUROPEAN HEADQUARTERS
ASIA, PACIFIC, & LATIN AMERICA   Hasbro UK Ltd
Wizards of the Coast, Inc.   Caswell Way
P.O. Box 707   Newport, Gwent NP9 0YH
Renton, WA 98057-0707   GREAT BRITAIN
+1-800-324-6496   Save this address for your records

Visit our web site at **www.wizards.com**

Dedicated gratefully to Peter Adkison,
who made the magic happen for DRAGONLANCE again.

Mina's Song

The day has passed beyond our power.
The petals close upon the flower.
The light is failing in this hour
Of day's last waning breath.

The blackness of the night surrounds
The distant souls of stars now found,
Far from this world to which we're bound,
Of sorrow, fear and death.

Sleep, love; forever sleep.
Your soul the night will keep.
Embrace the darkness deep.
Sleep, love; forever sleep.

The gathering darkness takes our souls,
Embracing us in chilling folds,
Deep in a Mistress's void that holds
Our fate within her hands.

Dream, warriors, of the dark above
And feel the sweet redemption of
The Night's Consort, and of her love
For those within her bands.

Sleep, love; forever sleep.
Your soul the night will keep.
Embrace the darkness deep.
Sleep, love; forever sleep.

We close our eyes, our minds at rest,
Submit our wills to her behest,
Our weaknesses to her confessed,
And to her will we bend.

The strength of silence fills the sky,
Its depth beyond both you and I.
Into its arms our souls will fly,
Where fear and sorrows end.

Sleep, love; forever sleep.
Your soul the night will keep.
Embrace the darkness deep.
Sleep, love; forever sleep.

BOOK 1

I

The Song of Death

he dwarves named the valley *Gamashinoch*—the Song of Death. None of the living walked here of their own free will. Those who entered did so out of desperation, dire need, or because they had been ordered to do so by their commanding officer.

They had been listening to the "song" for several hours as their advance brought them nearer and nearer the desolate valley. The song was eerie, terrible. Its words, which were never clearly heard, never quite distinguishable—at least not with the ears—spoke of death and worse than death. The song spoke of entrapment, bitter frustration, unending torment. The song was a lament, a song of longing for a place the soul remembered, a haven of peace and bliss now unattainable.

On first hearing the mournful song, the Knights had reined in their steeds, hands reaching for their swords as they stared about them in unease, crying "what is that?" and "who goes there?"

But no one went there. No one of the living. The Knights looked at their commander, who stood up in his stirrups, inspecting the cliffs that soared above them on their right and the left.

"It is nothing," he said at last. "The wind among the rocks. Proceed."

He urged his horse forward along the road, which ran, turning and twisting, through the mountains known as the Lords of Doom. The men under his command followed single file, the pass was too narrow for the mounted patrol to ride abreast.

"I have heard the wind before, my lord," said one Knight gruffly, "and it has yet to have a human voice. It warns us to stay away. We would do well to heed it."

"Nonsense!" Talon Leader Ernst Magit swung around in his saddle to glare at his scout and second-in-command, who walked behind him. "Superstitious claptrap! But then you minotaurs are noted for clinging to old, outmoded ways and ideas. It is time you entered the modern era. The gods are gone, and good riddance, I say. We humans rule the world."

A single voice, a woman's voice, had first sung the Song of Death. Now her voice was joined by a fearful chorus of men, women, and children raised in a dreadful chant of hopeless loss and misery that echoed among the mountains.

At the doleful sound, several of the horses balked, refused to go farther, and, truth told, their masters did little to urge them.

Magit's horse shied and danced. He dug his spurs into the horse's flanks, leaving great bloody gouges, and the horse sulked forward, head lowered, ears twitching. Talon Leader Magit rode about half a mile when it occurred to him that he did not hear other hoof beats. Glancing around, he saw that he was proceeding alone. None of his men had followed.

Furious, Magit turned and galloped back to his command. He found half of his patrol dismounted, the other half looking very ill at ease, sitting astride horses that stood shivering on the road.

"The dumb beasts have more brains than their masters," said the minotaur from his place on the ground. Few horses will allow a minotaur to sit upon their backs and fewer still have the strength and girth to carry one of the huge minotaurs. Galdar was seven feet tall, counting his horns. He kept up with the patrol, running easily alongside the stirrup of his commander.

Magit sat upon his horse, his hands on the pommel, facing his men. He was a tall, excessively thin man, the type whose bones seem to be strung together with steel wire, for he was far stronger than he looked. His eyes were flat and watery blue, without intelligence, without depth. He was noted for his cruelty, his inflexible—many would say mindless—discipline, and his complete and total devotion to a single cause: Ernst Magit.

"You will mount your horses and you will ride after me," said Talon Leader Magit coldly, "or I will report each and every one of you to the groupcommander. I will accuse you of cowardice and betrayal of the Vision and mutiny. As you know, the penalty for even one of those counts is death."

"Can he do that?" whispered a newly made Knight on his first assignment.

"He can," returned the veterans grimly, "and he will."

The Knights remounted and urged their steeds forward, using their spurs. They were forced to circle around the minotaur, Galdar, who remained standing in the center of the road.

"Do you refuse to obey my command, minotaur?" demanded Magit angrily. "Think well before you do so. You may be the protege of the Protector of the Skull, but I doubt if even he could save you if I denounce you to the Council as a coward and an oath-breaker."

Leaning over his horse's neck, Magit spoke in mock confidentiality. "And from what I hear, Galdar, your master might not be too keen on protecting you anymore. A one-armed minotaur. A minotaur whose own kind view him with pity

7

and with scorn. A minotaur who has been reduced to the position of 'scout.' And we all know that they assigned you to that post only because they had to do something with you. Although I did hear it suggested that they turn you out to pasture with the rest of the cows."

Galdar clenched his fist, his remaining fist, driving the sharp nails into his flesh. He knew very well that Magit was baiting him, goading him into a fight. Here, where there would be few witnesses. Here where Magit could kill the crippled minotaur and return home to claim that the fight had been a fair and glorious one. Galdar was not particularly attached to life, not since the loss of his sword arm had transformed him from fearsome warrior to plodding scout. But he'd be damned if he was going to die at the hands of Ernst Magit. Galdar wouldn't give his commander the satisfaction.

The minotaur shouldered his way past Ernst Magit, who watched him with a sneer of contempt upon his thin lips.

The patrol continued toward their destination, hoping to reach it while there was yet sunlight—if one could term the chill gray light that warmed nothing it touched sunlight. The Song of Death wailed and mourned. One of the new recruits rode with tears streaming down his cheeks. The veterans rode hunkered down, shoulders hunched up around their ears, as if they would block out the sound. But even if they had stuffed their ears with tow, even if they had blown out their eardrums, they would have still heard the terrible song.

The Song of Death sang in the heart.

The patrol rode into the valley that was called Neraka.

In a time past memory, the goddess Takhisis, Queen of Darkness, laid in the southern end of the valley a foundation stone, rescued from the blasted temple of the Kingpriest of Istar. The foundation stone began to grow, drawing upon the evil in the world to give it life. The stone grew into a temple, vast and awful; a temple of magnificent, hideous darkness.

Takhisis planned to use this temple to return to the world

from which she'd been driven by Huma Dragonbane, but her way was blocked by love and self-sacrifice. Nevertheless she had great power, and she launched a war upon the world that came near to destroying it. Her evil commanders, like a pack of wild dogs, fell to fighting among themselves. A band of heroes rose up. Looking into their hearts, they found the power to thwart her, defeat her, and cast her down. Her temple at Neraka was destroyed, blasted apart in her rage at her downfall.

The temple's walls exploded and rained down from the skies on that terrible day, huge black boulders that crushed the city of Neraka. Cleansing fires destroyed the buildings of the cursed city, burned down its markets and its slave pens, its numerous guard houses, filling its twisted, mazelike streets with ash.

Over fifty years later, no trace of the original city remained. The splinters of the temple's bones littered the floor of the southern portion of the valley of Neraka. The ash had long since blown away. Nothing would grow in this part of the valley. All sign of life had long been covered up by the swirling sands.

Only the black boulders, remnants of the temple, remained in the valley. They were an awful sight, and even Talon Leader Magit, gazing upon them for the first time, wondered privately if his decision to ride into this part of the valley had been a smart one. He could have taken the long route around, but that would have added two days to his travel, and he was late as it was, having spent a few extra nights with a new whore who had arrived at his favorite bawdyhouse. He needed to make up time, and he'd chosen as his shortcut this route through the southern end of the valley.

Perhaps due to the force of the explosion, the black rock that had formed the outer walls of the temple had taken on a crystalline structure. Jutting up from the sand, the boulders were not craggy, not lumpy. They were smooth-sided, with sharply defined planes culminating in faceted points. Imagine black quartz crystals jutting up from gray sand, some four times the height of a man. Such a man could see his reflection in those glossy black planes, a reflection that was distorted, twisted, yet completely recognizable as being a reflection of himself.

These men had willingly joined up with the army of the Knights of Takhisis, tempted by the promises of loot and slaves won in battle, by their own delight in killing and bullying, by their hatred of elves or kender or dwarves or anyone different from themselves. These men, long since hardened against every good feeling, looked into the shining black plane of the crystals and were appalled by the faces that looked back. For on those faces they could see their mouths opening to sing the terrible song.

Most looked and shuddered and quickly averted their gaze. Galdar took care not to look. At first sight of the black crystals rising from the ground, he had lowered his eyes, and he kept them lowered out of reverence and respect. Call it superstition, as Ernst Magit most certainly would. The gods themselves were not in this valley. Galdar knew that to be impossible; the gods had been driven from Krynn more than thirty years ago. But the ghosts of the gods lingered here, of that Galdar was certain.

Ernst Magit looked at his reflection in the rocks, and simply because he shrank from it inwardly, he forced himself to stare at it until he had stared it down.

"I will not be *cowed* by the sight of my own shadow!" he said with a meaningful glance at Galdar. Magit had only recently thought up this bovine humor. He considered it extremely funny and highly original, and he lost no opportunity to use it. "Cowed. Do you get it, minotaur?" Ernst Magit laughed.

The death song swept up the man's laughter and gave it melody and tone—dark, off key, discordant, opposing the rhythm of the other voices of the song. The sound was so horrible that Magit was shaken. He coughed, swallowed his laughter, much to the relief of his men.

"You have brought us here, Talon Leader," said Galdar. "We have seen that this part of the valley is uninhabited, that no force of Solamnics hides here, prepared to sweep down on us. We may proceed toward our objective safe in the knowledge that we have nothing *from the land of the living* to fear from this direction. Let us now leave this place, and swiftly. Let us turn back and make our report."

The horses had entered the southern valley with such reluctance that in some cases their riders had been forced to dismount again and cover their eyes and guide them, as if from a burning building. Both man and beast were clearly eager to be gone. The horses edged their way back toward the road by which they'd arrived, their riders sidling along with them.

Ernst Magit wanted to leave this place as much as any of them. It was for precisely that reason that he decided they would stay. He was a coward at heart. He knew he was a coward. All his life, he'd done deeds to prove to himself that he wasn't. Nothing truly heroic. Magit avoided danger when at all possible, one reason he was riding patrol duty and not joining with the other Knights of Neraka to lay siege to the Solamnic-controlled city of Sanction. He undertook to perform cheap, petty actions and deeds that involved no risk to himself but that would prove to himself and to his men he wasn't afraid. A deed such as spending the night in this cursed valley.

Magit made a show of squinting up at the sky, which was a pale and unwholesome yellow, a peculiar shade, such as none of the Knights had ever before seen.

"It is now twilight," he announced sententiously. "I do not want to find myself benighted in the mountains. We will make camp here and ride out in the morning."

The Knights stared at their commander incredulously, appalled. The wind had ceased to blow. The song no longer sang in their hearts. Silence settled over the valley, a silence that was at first a welcome change but that they were growing to loathe the longer it lasted. The silence weighed on them, oppressed them, smothered them. None spoke. They waited for their commander to tell them he'd been playing a little joke on them.

Talon Leader Magit dismounted his horse. "We will set up camp here. Pitch my command tent near the tallest of those monoliths. Galdar, you're in charge of setting up camp. I trust you can handle that simple task?"

His words seemed unnaturally loud, his voice shrill and raucous. A breath of air, cold and sharp, hissed through the valley, swept the sand into dust devils that swirled across the barren ground and whispered away.

"You are making a mistake, sir," said Galdar in a soft undertone, to disturb the silence as little as possible. "We are not wanted here."

"Who does not want us, Galdar?" Talon Leader Magit sneered. "These rocks?" He slapped the side of a black crystal monolith. "Ha! What a thick-skulled, superstitious cow!" Magit's voice hardened. "You men. Dismount and begin setting up camp. That is an order."

Ernst Magit stretched his limbs, making a show of being relaxed. He bent double at the waist, did a few limbering exercises. The Knights, sullen and unhappy, did as he commanded. They unpacked their saddle rolls, began setting up the small, two-man tents carried by half the patrol. The others unpacked food and water.

The tents were a failure. No amount of hammering could drive the iron spikes into the hard ground. Every blow of the hammer reverberated among the mountains, came back to them amplified a hundred times, until it seemed as if the mountains were hammering on them.

Galdar threw down his mallet, which he had been awkwardly wielding with his remaining hand.

"What's the matter, minotaur?" Magit demanded. "Are you so weak you can't drive a tent stake?"

"Try it yourself, sir," said Galdar.

The other men tossed down their mallets and stood staring at their commander in sullen defiance.

Magit was pale with anger. "You men can sleep in the open if you are too stupid to pitch a simple tent!"

He did not, however, choose to try to hammer the tent stakes into the rocky floor. He searched around until he located four of the black, crystal monoliths that formed a rough, irregular square.

"Tie my tent to four of these boulders," he ordered. "At least *I* will sleep well this night."

Galdar did as he was commanded. He wrapped the ropes around the bases of the monoliths, all the while muttering a minotaur incantation meant to propitiate the spirits of the restless dead.

The men also endeavored to tie their horses to the monoliths, but the beasts plunged and bucked in panicked terror. Finally, the Knights strung a line between two of the monoliths and tied the horses up there. The horses huddled together, restive and nervous, rolling their eyes and keeping as far from the black rocks as possible.

While the men worked, Ernst Magit drew a map from his saddlebags and, with a final glare around to remind them of their duty, spread the map open and began studying it with a studious and unconcerned air that fooled no one. He was sweating, and he'd done no work.

Long shadows were stealing over the valley of Neraka, making the valley far darker than the sky, which was lit with a flame-yellow afterglow. The air was hot, hotter than when they'd entered, but sometimes eddies of cold wind swirled down from the west, chilling the bones to the marrow. The

Knights had brought no wood with them. They ate cold rations, or tried to eat them. Every mouthful was polluted with sand, everything they ate tasted of ashes. They eventually threw most of their food away. Seated upon the hard ground, they constantly looked over their shoulders, peering intently into the shadows. Each man had his sword drawn. No need to set the watch. No man intended to sleep.

"Ho! Look at this!" Ernst Magit called out with triumph. "I have made an important discovery! It is well that we spent some time here." He pointed at his map and then to the west. "See that mountain range there. It is not marked upon the map. It must be newly formed. I shall certainly bring this to the attention of the Protector. Perhaps the range will be named in my honor."

Galdar looked at the mountain range. He rose slowly to his feet, staring hard into the western sky. Certainly at first glance the formation of iron gray and sullen blue looked very much as if a new mountain had thrust up from the ground. But as Galdar watched, he noticed something that the talon leader, in his eagerness, had missed. This mountain was growing, expanding, at an alarming rate.

"Sir!" Galdar cried. "That is no mountain! Those are storm clouds!"

"You are already a cow, don't be an ass as well," Magit said. He had picked up a bit of black rock and was using it like chalk to add Mount Magit to the wonders of the world.

"Sir, I spent ten years at sea when I was a youth," said Galdar. "I know a storm when I see one. Yet even I have never seen anything like that!"

Now the cloud bank reared up with incredible speed, solid black at its heart, roiling and churning like some many-headed devouring monster, biting off the tops of the mountains as it overtook them, crawling over them to consume them whole. The chill wind strengthened, whipping the sand from the ground into eyes and mouths, tearing at the command tent, which flapped wildly and strained against its bonds.

The wind began to sing again that same terrible song, keening, wailing in despair, shrieking in anguished torment.

Buffeted by the wind, the men struggled to their feet. "Commander! We should leave!" Galdar roared. "Now! Before the storm breaks!"

"Yes," said Ernst Magit, pale and shaken. He licked his lips, spit out sand. "Yes, you are right. We should leave immediately. Never mind the tent! Bring me my horse!"

A bolt of lightning flashed out from the blackness, speared the ground near where the horses were tethered. Thunder exploded. The concussion knocked some of the men flat. The horses screamed, reared, lashed out with their hooves. The men who were still standing tried to calm them, but the horses would have none of it. Tearing free of the rope that held them, the horses galloped away in mad panic.

"Catch them!" Ernst screamed, but the men had all they could do to stand upright against the pummeling wind. One or two took a few staggering steps after the horses, but it was obvious that the chase was a futile one.

The storm clouds raced across the sky, battling the sunlight, defeating it handily. The sun fell, overcome by darkness.

Night was upon them, a night thick with swirling sand. Galdar could see nothing at all, not even his own single hand. The next second all around him was illuminated by another devastating lightning bolt.

"Lie down!" he bellowed, flinging himself to the ground. "Lie flat! Keep away from the monoliths!"

Rain slashed sideways, coming at them like arrows fired from a million bowstrings. Hail pounded on them like iron-tipped flails, cutting and bruising. Galdar's hide was tough, the hail was like stinging ant bites to him. The other men cried out in pain and terror. Lightning walked among them, casting its flaming spears. Thunder shook the ground and boomed and roared.

Galdar lay sprawled on his stomach, fighting against the impulse to tear at the ground with his hand, to burrow into the depths of the world. He was astounded to see, in the next lightning flash, his commander trying to stand up.

"Sir, keep down!" Galdar roared and made a grab for him.

Magit snarled a curse and kicked at Galdar's hand. Head down against the wind, the talon leader lurched over to one of the monoliths. He crouched behind it, used its great bulk to shield him from the lancing rain and the hammering hail. Laughing at the rest of his men, he sat on the ground, placed his back against the stone and stretched out his legs.

The lightning flash blinded Galdar. The blast deafened him. The force of the thunderbolt lifted him up off the ground, slammed him back down. The bolt had struck so close that he had heard it sizzle the air, could smell the phosphorous and the sulphur. He could also smell something else—burned flesh. He rubbed his eyes to try to see through the jagged glare. When his sight was restored, he looked in the direction of the commander. In the next lightning flash, he saw a misshapen mass huddled at the foot of the monolith.

Magit's flesh glowed red beneath a black crust, like a hunk of overcooked meat. Smoke rose from it; the wind whipped it away, along with flecks of charred flesh. The skin of the man's face had burned away, revealing a mouthful of hideously grinning teeth.

"Glad to see you're still laughing, Talon Leader," Galdar muttered. "You were warned."

Galdar scrunched down even closer to the ground, cursed his ribs for being in the way.

The rain fell harder, if that were possible. He wondered how long the raging storm could last. It seemed to have lasted a lifetime, seemed to him that he had been born into this storm and that he would grow old and die in this storm. A hand grabbed hold of his arm, shook him.

"Sir! Look there!" One of the Knights had crawled across

the ground, was right next to him. "Sir!" The Knight put his mouth to Galdar's ear, shouted hoarsely to make himself heard over the lashing rain and pounding hail, the constant thunder and, worse than rain or hail or thunder, the song of death. "I saw something move out there!"

Galdar lifted his head, peered in the direction the Knight pointed, peered into the very heart of the valley of Neraka.

"Wait until the next lightning flash!" the Knight yelled. "There! There it is!"

The next lightning flash was not a bolt but a sheet of flame that lit the sky and the ground and the mountains with a purple white radiance. Silhouetted against the awful glow, a figure moved toward them, walking calmly through the raging storm, seeming untouched by the gale, unmoved by the lightning, unafraid of the thunder.

"Is it one of ours?" Galdar asked, thinking at first that one of the men might have gone mad and bolted like the horses.

But he knew the moment he asked the question that this was not the case. The figure was walking, not running. The figure was not fleeing, it was approaching.

The lightning flared out. Darkness fell, and the figure was lost. Galdar waited impatiently for the next lightning flash to show him this insane being who braved the fury of the storm. The next flash lit the ground, the mountains, the sky. The person was still there, still moving toward them. And it seemed to Galdar that the song of death had transformed into a paean of celebration.

Darkness again. The wind died. The rain softened to a steady downpour. The hail ceased altogether. Thunder rumbled a drumroll, which seemed to mark time with the pace of the strange figure of darkness drawing steadily nearer with each illuminating flare. The storm carried the battle to the other side of the mountains, to other parts of the world. Galdar rose to his feet.

Soaking wet, the Knights wiped water and muck from

their eyes, looked ruefully at sodden blankets. The wind was cold and crisp and chill, and they were shivering except Galdar, whose thick hide and fur pelt protected him from all but the most severe cold. He shook the rain water from his horns and waited for the figure to come within hailing distance.

Stars, glittering cold and deadly as spear points, appeared in the west. The ragged edges of the storm's rear echelon seemed to uncover the stars as they passed. The single moon had risen in defiance of the thunder. The figure was no more than twenty feet away now, and by the moon's argent light Galdar could see the person clearly.

Human, a youth, to judge by the slender, well-knit body and the smooth skin of the face. Dark hair had been shaved close to the skull, leaving only a red stubble. The absence of hair accentuated the features of the face and thrust into prominence the high cheekbones, the sharp chin, the mouth in its bow curve. The youth wore the shirt and tunic of a common foot knight and leather boots, carried no sword upon his hip nor any sort of weapon that Galdar could see.

"Halt and be recognized!" he shouted harshly. "Stop right there. At the edge of camp."

The youth obligingly halted, his hands raised, palms outward to show they were empty.

Galdar drew his sword. In this strange night, he was taking no chances. He held the sword awkwardly in his left hand. The weapon was almost useless to him. Unlike some other amputees, he had never learned to fight with his opposite hand. He had been a skilled swordsman before his injury, now he was clumsy and inept, as likely to do damage to himself as to a foe. Many were the times Ernst Magit had watched Galdar practice, watched him fumble, and laughed uproariously.

Magit wouldn't be doing much laughing now.

Galdar advanced, sword in hand. The hilt was wet and

slippery, he hoped he wouldn't drop it. The youth could not know that Galdar was a washed-up warrior, a has-been. The minotaur looked intimating, and Galdar was somewhat surprised that the youth did not quail before him, did not even really look all that impressed.

"I am unarmed," said the youth in a deep voice that did not match the youthful appearance. The voice had an odd timbre to it, sweet, musical, reminding Galdar strangely of one of the voices he'd heard in the song, the song now hushed and murmuring, as if in reverence. The voice was not the voice of a man.

Galdar looked closely at the youth, at the slender neck that was like the long stem of a lily, supporting the skull, which was perfectly smooth beneath its red down of hair, marvelously formed. The minotaur looked closely at the lithe body. The arms were muscular, as were the legs in their woolen stockings. The wet shirt, which was too big, hung loosely from the slender shoulders. Galdar could see nothing beneath its wet folds, could not ascertain yet whether this human was male or female.

The other knights gathered around him, all of them staring at the wet youth; wet and glistening as a newborn child. The men were frowning, uneasy, wary. Small blame to them. Everyone was asking the same question as Galdar. What in the name of the great horned god who had died and left his people bereft was this human doing in this accursed valley on this accursed night?

"What are you called?" Galdar demanded.

"My name is Mina."

A girl. A slip of a girl. She could be no more than seventeen . . . if that. Yet even though she had spoken her name, a feminine name popular among humans, even though he could trace her sex in the smooth lines of her neck and the grace of her movements, he still doubted. There was something very unwomanly about her.

Mina smiled slightly, as if she could hear his unspoken doubts, and said, "I *am* female." She shrugged. "Though it makes little difference."

"Come closer," Galdar ordered harshly.

The girl obeyed, took a step forward.

Galdar looked into her eyes, and his breath very nearly stopped. He had seen humans of all shapes and sizes during his lifetime, but he'd never seen one, never seen any living being with eyes like these.

Unnaturally large, deep-set, the eyes were the color of amber, the pupils black, the irises encircled by a ring of shadow. The absence of hair made the eyes appear larger still. Mina seemed all eyes, and those eyes absorbed Galdar and imprisoned him, as golden amber holds imprisoned the carcasses of small insects.

"Are you the commander?" she asked.

Galdar flicked a glance in the direction of the charred body lying at the base of the monolith. "I am now," he said.

Mina followed his gaze, regarded the corpse with cool detachment. She turned the amber eyes back to Galdar, who could have sworn he saw the body of Magit locked inside.

"What are you doing here, girl?" the minotaur asked harshly. "Did you lose your way in the storm?"

"No. I found my way in the storm," said Mina. The amber eyes were luminous, unblinking. "I found you. I have been called, and I have answered. You are Knights of Takhisis, are you not?"

"We were once," said Galdar dryly. "We waited long for Takhisis's return, but now the commanders admit what most of us knew long before. She is not coming back. Therefore we have come to term ourselves Knights of Neraka."

Mina listened, considered this. She seemed to like it, for she nodded gravely. "I understand. I have come to join the Knights of Neraka."

At any other time, in any other place, the Knights might

have snickered or made rude remarks. But the men were in no mood for levity. Neither was Galdar. The storm had been terrifying, unlike any he'd ever experienced, and he had lived in this world forty years. Their talon leader was dead. They had a long walk ahead of them, unless by some miracle they could recover the horses. They had no food—the horses had run away with their supplies. No water except what they could wring out of their sodden blankets.

"Tell the silly chit to run back home to mama," said one Knight impatiently. "What do *we* do, Subcommander?"

"I say we get out of here," said another. "I'll walk all night if I have to."

The others muttered their assent.

Galdar looked to the heavens. The sky was clear. Thunder rumbled, but in the distance. Far away, lightning flashed purple on the western horizon. The moon gave light enough to travel. Galdar was tired, unusually tired. The men were hollow-cheeked and gaunt, all of them near exhaustion. Yet he knew how they felt.

"We're moving out," he said. "But first we need to do something with that." He jerked a thumb at the smoldering body of Ernst Magit.

"Leave it," said one of the Knights.

Galdar shook his horned head. He was conscious, all the while, of the girl watching him intently with those strange eyes of hers.

"Do you want to be haunted by his spirit the rest of your days?" Galdar demanded.

The others eyed each other, eyed the body. They would have guffawed at the thought of Magit's ghost haunting them the day before. Not now.

"What do we do with him?" demanded one plaintively. "We can't bury the bastard. The ground's too hard. We don't have any wood for a fire."

"Wrap the body in that tent," said Mina. "Take those

rocks and build a cairn over him. He is not the first to die in the valley of Neraka," she added coolly, "nor will he be the last."

Galdar glanced over his shoulder. The tent they had strung between the monoliths remained intact, though it sagged with an accumulation of rainwater.

"The girl's idea is a good one," he said. "Cut down the tent and use it for a shroud. And be quick about it. The quicker we're finished, the quicker we're away. Strip off his armor," he added. "We're required to take it back to headquarters as proof of his death."

"How?" asked one of the Knights, grimacing. "His flesh is stuck to the metal like a steak seared on a gridiron."

"Cut it off," said Galdar. "Clean it up as best you can. I wasn't that fond of him that I want to be hauling bits of him around."

The men went about their grisly task with a will, eager to be done and away.

Galdar turned back to Mina, found those amber eyes, large, intent upon him.

"You had best go back to your family, girl," he said gruffly. "We'll be traveling hard and fast. We won't have time to coddle you. Besides, you're a female. These men are not very great respecters of women's virtues. You run along home."

"I am home," said Mina with a glance around the valley. The black monoliths reflected the cold light of the stars, summoned the stars to shine pale and chill among them. "And I have found my family. I will become a Knight. That is my calling."

Galdar was exasperated, uncertain what to say. The last thing he wanted was this fey woman-child traveling with them. But she was so self-possessed, so completely in control of herself and in control of the situation that he could not come up with any rational argument.

Thinking the matter over, he made to return his sword to

its sheath. The hilt was wet and slippery, his grip on it awkward. He fumbled, nearly dropped the sword. Managing to hang onto it by a desperate effort, he looked up fiercely, glowering, daring her to so much as smile with either derision or pity.

She watched his struggles, said nothing, her face expressionless.

Galdar shoved the sword into the sheath. "As to joining the Knighthood, the best thing to do is go to your local headquarters and put in your name."

He continued with a recitation of the recruitment policies, the training involved. He launched into a discourse about the years of dedication and self-sacrifice, all the while thinking of Ernst Magit, who had bought his way into the Knighthood, and suddenly Galdar realized that he'd lost her.

The girl was not listening to him. She seemed to be listening to another voice, a voice he could not hear. Her gaze was abstracted, her face smooth, without expression.

His words trailed off.

"Do you not find it difficult to fight one handed?" she asked.

He regarded her grimly. "I may be awkward," he said caustically, "but I can handle a sword well enough to strike your shorn head from your body!"

She smiled. "What are you called?"

He turned away. This conversation was at an end. He looked to see that the men had managed to separate Magit from his armor, were rolling the still-smoking lump of a corpse onto the tent.

"Galdar, I believe," Mina continued.

He turned back to stare at her in astonishment, wondering how she knew his name.

Of course, he thought, one of the men must have spoken it. But he could not recall any of them having done so.

"Give me your hand, Galdar," Mina said to him.

He glowered at her. "Leave this place while you have a chance, girl! We are in no mood for silly games. My commander's dead. These men are my responsibility. We have no mounts, no food."

"Give me your hand, Galdar," said Mina softly.

At the sound of her voice, rough, sweet, he heard again the song singing among the rocks. He felt his hackles rise. A shudder went through him, a thrill flashed along his spine. He meant to turn away from her, but he found himself raising his left hand.

"No, Galdar," said Mina. "Your right hand. Give me your right hand."

"I have no right hand!" Galdar cried out in rage and anguish.

The cry rattled in his throat. The men turned, alarmed, at the strangled sound.

Galdar stared in disbelief. The arm had been cut off at the shoulder. Extending outward from the stump was a ghostly image of what had once been his right arm. The image wavered in the wind, as if his arm were made of smoke and ash, yet he could see it clearly, could see it reflected in the smooth black plane of the monolith. He could feel the phantom arm, but then he'd always felt the arm even when it wasn't there. Now he watched his arm, his right arm, lift; watched his hand, his right hand, reach out trembling fingers.

Mina extended her hand, touched the phantom hand of the minotaur.

"Your sword arm is restored," she said to him.

Galdar stared in boundless astoundment.

His arm. His right arm was once again . . .

His right arm.

No longer a phantom arm. No longer an arm of smoke and ash, an arm of dreams to be lost in the despair of waking. Galdar closed his eyes, closed them tight, and then opened them.

The arm remained.

The other Knights were struck dumb and motionless. Their faces dead white in the moonlight, they stared at Galdar, stared at the arm, stared at Mina.

Galdar ordered his fingers to open and clench, and they obeyed. He reached out with his left hand, trembling, and touched the arm.

The skin was warm, the fur was soft, the arm was flesh and bone and blood. The arm was real.

Galdar reached down the hand and drew his sword. His fingers closed over the hilt lovingly. He was suddenly blinded by tears.

Weak and shivering, Galdar sank to his knees. "Lady," he said, his voice shaking with awe and wonder, "I do not know what you did or how you did it, but I am in your debt for the rest of my days. Whatever you want of me, I grant you."

"Swear to me by your sword arm that you will grant me what I ask," Mina said.

"I swear!" Galdar said harshly.

"Make me your commander," said Mina.

Galdar's jaw sagged. His mouth opened and closed. He swallowed. "I . . . I will recommend you to my superiors . . ."

"Make me your commander," she said, her voice hard as the ground, dark as the monoliths. "I do not fight for greed. I do not fight for gain. I do not fight for power. I fight for one cause, and that is glory. Not for myself, but for my god."

"Who is your god?" Galdar asked, awed.

Mina smiled, a fell smile, pale and cold. "The name may not be spoken. My god is the One God. The One who rides the storm, the One who rules the night. My god is the One God who made your flesh whole. Swear your loyalty to me, Galdar. Follow me to victory."

Galdar thought of all the commanders under whom he'd served. Commanders such as Ernst Magit, who rolled their eyes when the Vision of Neraka was mentioned. The Vision was fake, phony, most of the upper echelon knew it. Commanders such as the Master of the Lily, Galdar's patron, who yawned openly during the recitation of the Blood Oath, who had brought the minotaur into the Knighthood as a joke. Commanders such as the current Lord of the Night, Targonne, whom everyone knew was skimming funds from the knightly coffers to enrich himself.

Galdar raised his head, looked into the amber eyes. "You are my commander, Mina," he said. "I swear fealty to you and to no other."

Mina touched his hand again. Her touch was painful, scalded his blood. He reveled in the sensation. The pain was welcome. For too long now, he'd felt the pain of an arm that wasn't there.

"You will be my second in command, Galdar." Mina turned the amber gaze upon the other Knights. "Will the rest of you follow me?"

Some of the men had been with Galdar when he had lost his arm, had seen the blood spurt from the shattered limb. Four of these men had held him down when the surgeon cut off his arm. They had heard his pleas for death, a death they'd refused to grant him, a death that he could not, in honor, grant himself. These men looked at the new arm, saw Galdar holding a sword again. They had seen the girl walk through the murderous, unnatural storm, walk unscathed.

These men were in their thirties, some of them. Veterans of brutal wars and tough campaigns. It was all very well for Galdar to swear allegiance to this strange woman-child. She had made him whole. But for themselves . . .

Mina did not press them, she did not cajole or argue. She appeared to take their agreement for granted. Walking over to where the corpse of the talon leader lay on the ground beneath the monolith, the body partially wrapped in the tent, Mina picked up Magit's breastplate. She looked at it, studied it, and then, sliding her arms through the straps, she put on the breastplate over her wet shirt. The breastplate was too big for her and heavy. Galdar expected to see her bowed down under the weight.

He gaped to see instead the metal glow red, reform, mold itself to her slender body, embrace her like a lover.

The breastplate had been black with the image of a skull upon it. The armor had been hit by the lightning strike, apparently, though the damage the strike had done was exceedingly strange. The skull adorning the breastplate was split in twain. A lightning bolt of steel sliced through it.

"This will be my standard," said Mina, touching the skull.

She put on the rest of Magit's accoutrements, sliding the bracers over her arms, buckling the shin guards over her legs. Each piece of armor glowed red when it touched her as if newly come from the forge. Each piece, when cooled, fit her as if it had been fashioned for her.

She lifted the helm, but did not put it on her head. She handed the helm to Galdar. "Hold that for me, Subcommander," she said.

He received the helm proudly, reverently, as if it were an artifact for which he had quested all his life.

Mina knelt down beside the body of Ernst Magit. Lifting the dead, charred hand in her own, she bowed her head and began to pray.

None could hear her words, none could hear what she said or to whom she said it. The song of death keened among the stones. The stars vanished, the moon disappeared. Darkness enveloped them. She prayed, her whispered words bringing comfort.

Mina arose from her prayers to find all the Knights on their knees before her. In the darkness, they could see nothing, not each other, not even themselves. They saw only her.

"You are my commander, Mina," said one, gazing upon her as the starving gaze upon bread, the thirsty gaze upon cool water. "I pledge my life to you."

"Not to me," she said. "To the One God."

"The One God!" Their voices lifted and were swept up in the song that was no longer frightening but was exalting, stirring, a call to arms. "Mina and the One God!"

The stars shone in the monoliths. The moonlight gleamed in the jagged lightning bolt of Mina's armor. Thunder rumbled again, but this time it was not from the sky.

"The horses!" shouted one of the knights. "The horses have returned."

Leading the horses was a steed the likes of which none of them had ever seen. Red as wine, red as blood, the horse left the others far behind. The horse came straight to Mina and nuzzled her, rested its head over her shoulder.

"I sent Foxfire for the mounts. We will have need of them," said Mina, stroking the black mane of the blood-colored roan. "We ride south this night and ride hard. We must be in Sanction in three days' time."

"Sanction!" Galdar gaped. "But, girl—I mean, Talon Leader—the Solamnics control Sanction! The city is under siege. Our posting is in Khur. Our orders—"

"We ride this night to Sanction," said Mina. Her gaze turned southward and never looked back.

"But, why, Talon Leader?" Galdar asked.

"Because we are called," Mina answered.

2

Silvanoshei

he strange and unnatural storm laid siege to all of Ansalon. Lightning walked the land; gigantic, ground-shaking warriors who hurled bolts of fire. Ancient trees—huge oaks that had withstood both Cataclysms—burst into flame and were reduced to smoldering ruin in an instant. Whirlwinds raged behind the thundering warriors, ripping apart homes, flinging boards, brick, and stone and mortar into the air with lethal abandon. Torrential cloudbursts caused rivers to swell and overflow their banks, washing away the young green shoots of grain struggling up from the darkness to bask in the early summer sun.

In Sanction, besieger and besieged alike abandoned the ongoing struggle to seek refuge from the terrible storm. Ships on the high seas tried to ride it out, with the result that some went under, never to be seen or heard from again. Others would later limp home with jury-rigged masts, telling tales of sailors swept overboard, the pumps at work day and night.

In Palanthas, innumerable cracks appeared in the roof of the Great Library. The rain poured inside, sending Bertrem and the monks into a mad scramble to staunch the flow, mop the floor and move precious volumes to safety. In Tarsis, the rain was so heavy that the sea which had vanished during the Cataclysm returned, to the wonder and astonishment of all inhabitants. The sea was gone a few days later, leaving behind gasping fish and an ungodly smell.

The storm struck the island of Schallsea a particularly devastating blow. The winds blew out every single window in the Cozy Hearth. Ships that rode at anchor in the harbor were dashed against the cliffs or smashed into the docks. A tidal surge washed away many buildings and homes built near the shoreline. Countless people died, countless others were left homeless. Refugees stormed the Citadel of Light, pleading for the mystics to come to their aid.

The Citadel was a beacon of hope in Krynn's dark night. Trying to fill the void left by the absence of the gods, Goldmoon had discovered the mystical power of the heart, had brought healing back to the world. She was living proof that although Paladine and Mishakal were gone, their power for good lived on in the hearts of those who had loved them.

Yet Goldmoon was growing old. The memories of the gods were fading. And so, it seemed, was the power of the heart. One after another, the mystics felt their power recede, a tide that went out but never returned. Still the mystics of the Citadel were glad to open their doors and their hearts to the storm's victims, provide shelter and succor, and work to heal the injured as best they could.

Solamnic Knights, who had established a fortress on Schallsea, rode forth to do battle with the storm—one of the most fearsome enemies these valiant Knights had ever faced. At risk of their own lives, the Knights plucked people from the raging water and dragged them from beneath smashed buildings, working in the wind and rain and lightning-shattered darkness to save the lives of those they were sworn by Oath and Measure to protect.

The Citadel of Light withstood the storm's rage, although its buildings were buffeted by fierce winds and lancing rain. As if in a last ditch attempt to make its wrath felt, the storm hurled hailstones the size of a man's head upon the citadel's crystal walls. Everywhere the hailstones struck, tiny cracks appeared in the crystalline walls. Rainwater seeped through these cracks, trickled like tears down the walls.

One particularly loud crash came from the vicinity of the chambers of Goldmoon, founder and mistress of the Citadel. The mystics heard the sound of breaking glass and ran in fear to see if the elderly woman was safe. To their astonishment, they found the door to her rooms locked. They beat upon it, called upon her to let them inside.

A voice, low and awful to hear, a voice that was Goldmoon's beloved voice and yet was not, ordered them to leave her in peace, to go about their duties. Others needed their aid, she said. She did not. Baffled, uneasy, most did as they were told. Those who lingered behind reported hearing the sound of sobbing, heartbroken and despairing.

"She, too, has lost her power," said those outside her door. Thinking that they understood, they left her alone.

When morning finally came and the sun rose to shine a lurid red in the sky, people stood about in dazed horror, looking upon the destruction wrought during the terrible night. The mystics went to Goldmoon's chamber to ask for her counsel, but no answer came. The door to Goldmoon's chamber remained closed and barred.

The storm also swept through Qualinesti, an elven kingdom, but one that was separated from its cousins by distance that could be measured both in hundreds of miles and in ancient hatred and distrust. In Qualinesti, whirling winds uprooted giant trees and flung them about like the slender sticks used in *Quin Thalasi*, a popular elven game. The storm shook the fabled Tower of the Speaker of the Sun on its foundation, sent the beautiful stained glass of its storied windows raining down upon the floor. Rising water flooded the lower chambers of the newly constructed fortress of the Dark Knights at Newport, forcing them to do what an enemy army could not—abandon their posts.

The storm woke even the great dragons, slumbering, bloated and fat, in their lairs that were rich with tribute. The storm shook the Peak of Malys, lair of Malystryx, the enormous red dragon who now fashioned herself the Queen of Ansalon, soon to become Goddess of Ansalon, if she had her way. The rain formed rushing rivers that invaded Malys's volcanic home. Rainwater flowed into the lava pools, creating enormous clouds of a noxious-smelling steam that filled the corridors and halls. Wet, half-blind, choking in the fumes, Malys roared her indignation and flew from lair to lair, trying to find one that was dry enough for her to return to sleep.

Finally she was driven to seek the lower levels of her mountain home. Malys was an ancient dragon with a malevolent wisdom. She sensed something unnatural about this storm, and it made her uneasy. Grumbling and muttering to herself, she entered the Chamber of the Totem. Here, on an outcropping of black rock, Malys had piled the skulls of all the lesser dragons she had consumed when she first came to the world. Silver skulls and gold, red skulls and blue stood one atop the other, a monument to her greatness. Malys was comforted by the sight of the skulls. Each brought a memory of a battle won, a foe defeated and devoured. The rain could not penetrate this far down in her mountain home. She could not hear the wind howl. The flashes of lightning did not disturb her slumbers.

Malys gazed upon the empty eyes of the skulls with pleasure, and perhaps she dozed, because suddenly it seemed to her that the eyes of skulls were alive and they were watching her. She snorted, reared her head. She stared closely at the skulls, at the eyes. The lava pool at the heart of the mountain cast a lurid light upon the skulls, sent shadows winking and blinking in the empty eye sockets. Berating herself for an overactive imagination, Malys coiled her body comfortably around the totem and fell asleep.

Another of the great dragons, a Green known grandiosely as Beryllinthranox was also not able to sleep through the storm. Beryl's lair was formed of living trees—ironwoods and redwoods—and enormous, twining vines. The vines and branches of the trees were so thickly interwoven that no raindrop had ever managed to wriggle its way through. But the rain that fell from the roiling black clouds of this storm seemed to make it a personal mission to find a way to penetrate the leaves. Once one had managed to sneak inside, it opened the way for thousands of its fellows. Beryl woke in surprise at the unaccustomed feel of water splashing on her nose. One of the great redwoods that formed a pillar of her lair was struck by a lightning bolt. The tree burst into flames, flames that spread quickly, feeding on rainwater as if it were lamp oil.

Beryl's roar of alarm brought her minions scrambling to douse the flames. Dragons, Reds and Blues who had joined Beryl rather than be consumed by her, dared the flames to pluck out the burning trees and cast them into the sea. Draconians pulled down blazing vines, smothered the flames with dirt and mud. Hostages and prisoners were put to work fighting the fires. Many died doing so, but eventually Beryl's lair was saved. She was in a terrible humor for days afterward, however, convincing herself that the storm had been an attack waged magically by her cousin Malys. Beryl meant to rule someday in Malys's stead. Using her magic to rebuild— a magical power that had lately been dwindling, something else Beryl blamed on Malys—the Green nursed her wrongs and plotted revenge.

Khellendros the Blue (he had abandoned the name Skie for this more magnificent title, which meant Storm over Ansalon), was one of the few of the dragons native to Krynn to have emerged from the Dragon Purge. He was now ruler of Solamnia and all its environs. He was overseer of Schallsea and the Citadel of Light, which he allowed to remain because—according to him—he found it amusing to watch the petty humans struggle futilely against the growing darkness. In truth, the real reason he permitted the citadel to thrive in safety was the citadel's guardian, a silver dragon named Mirror. Mirror and Skie were longtime foes and now, in their mutual detestation of the new, great dragons from afar who had killed so many of their brethren, they had become not friends, but not quite enemies either.

Khellendros was bothered by the storm far more than either of the great dragons, although—strangely enough—the storm did not do his lair much damage. He paced restively about his enormous cave high in the Vingaard mountains, watched the lightning warriors strike viciously at the ramparts of the High Clerist's Tower, and he thought he heard a voice in the wind, a voice that sang of death. Khellendros did not sleep but watched the storm to its end.

The storm lost none of its power as it roared down upon the ancient elven kingdom of Silvanesti. The elves had erected a magical shield over their kingdom, a shield that had thus far kept the marauding dragons from conquering their lands, a shield that also kept out all other races. The elves had finally succeeded in their historic goal of isolating themselves from the troubles of the rest of the world. But the shield did not keep out the thunder and rain, wind and lightning.

Trees burned, houses were torn apart by the fierce winds. The Than-Thalas River flooded, sending those who lived on its banks scrambling to reach higher ground. Water seeped into the palace garden, the Garden of Astarin, where grew the magical tree that was, many believed, responsible for keeping the shield in place. The tree's magic kept it safe. Indeed, when the storm was ended, the soil around the tree was found to be bone dry. Everything else in the garden was drowned or washed away. The elf gardeners and Woodshapers, who bore for their plants and flowers, ornamental trees, herbs, and rose bushes the same love they bore their own children, were heartbroken, devastated to view the destruction.

They replanted after the storm, bringing plants from their own gardens to fill the once wondrous Garden of Astarin. Ever since the raising of the shield, the plants in the garden had not done well, and now they rotted in the muddy soil which could never, it seemed, soak up enough sunlight to dry out.

The strange and terrible storm eventually left the continent, marched away from the war, a victorious army abandoning the field of battle, leaving devastation and destruction behind. The next morning, the people of Ansalon would go dazedly to view the damage, to comfort the bereaved, to bury the dead, and to wonder at the dreadful night's ominous portent.

And yet, there was, after all, one person that night who enjoyed himself. His name was Silvanoshei, a young elf, and he exulted in the storm. The clash of the lightning warriors, the bolts that fell like sparks struck from swords of thunder, beat in his blood like crashing drums. Silvanoshei did not seek shelter from the storm but went out into it. He stood in a clearing in the forest, his face raised to the tumult, the rain drenching him, cooling the burning of vaguely felt wants and desires. He watched the dazzling display of lightning, marveled at the ground-shaking thunder, laughed at the blasts of wind that bent the great trees, making them bow their proud heads.

Silvanoshei's father was Porthios, once proud ruler of the Qualinesti, now cast out by them, termed a "dark elf," one cursed to live outside the light of elven society. Silvanoshei's mother was Alhana Starbreeze, exiled leader of the Silvanesti nation that had cast her out too when she married Porthios. They had meant, by their marriage, to at last reunite the two elven nations, bring them together as one nation, a nation that would have probably been strong enough to fight the cursed dragons and maintain itself in freedom.

Instead, their marriage had only deepened the hatred and mistrust. Now Beryl ruled Qualinesti, which was an occupied land, held in subjugation by the Knights of Neraka. Silvanesti was a land cut off, isolated, its inhabitants cowering under its shield like children hiding beneath a blanket, hoping it will protect them from the monsters who lurk in the darkness.

Silvanoshei was the only child of Porthios and Alhana.

"Silvan was born the year of the Chaos War," Alhana was wont to say. "His father and I were on the run, a target for every elven assassin who wanted to ingratiate himself with either the Qualinesti or the Silvanesti rulers. He was born the day they buried two of the sons of Caramon Majere. Chaos was Silvan's nursemaid, Death his midwife."

Silvan had been raised in an armed camp. Alhana's marriage to Porthios had been a marriage of politics that had deepened to one of love and friendship and utmost respect. Together she and her husband had waged a ceaseless, thankless battle, first against the Dark Knights who were now the overlords of Qualinest, then against the terrible domination of Beryl, the dragon who had laid claim to the Qualinesti lands and who now demanded tribute from the Qualinesti elves in return for allowing them to live.

When word had first reached Alhana and Porthios that the elves of Silvanesti had managed to raise a magical shield over their kingdom, a shield that would protect them from the ravages of the dragons, both had seen this as a possible salvation for their people. Alhana had traveled south with her own forces, leaving Porthios to continue the fight for Qualinesti.

She had tried to send an emissary to the Silvanesti elves, asking permission to pass through the shield. The emissary had not even been able to enter. She attacked the shield with steel and with magic, trying every way possible of breaking through it, without success. The more she studied the shield, the more she was appalled that her people could permit themselves to live beneath it.

Whatever the shield touched died. Woodlands near the shield's boundaries were filled with dead and dying trees. Grasslands near the shield were gray and barren. Flowers wilted, withered, decomposed into a fine gray dust that covered the dead like a shroud.

The shield's magic is responsible for this! Alhana had written to her husband. *The shield is not protecting the land. It is killing it!*

The Silvanesti do not care, Porthios had written in reply. *They are subsumed by fear. Fear of the ogres, fear of the humans, fear of the dragons, fear of terrors they can not even name. The shield is but the outward manifestation of their fear. No wonder anything that comes in contact with it withers and dies!*

These were the last words she had heard from him. For years Alhana had kept in contact with her husband through the messages carried between them by the swift and tireless elven runners. She knew of his increasingly futile efforts to defeat Beryl. Then came the day the runner from her husband did not return. She had sent another, and another vanished. Now weeks had passed and still no word from Porthios. Finally, unable to expend any more of her dwindling manpower, Alhana had ceased sending the runners.

The storm had caught Alhana and her army in the woods near the border of Silvanesti, after yet another futile attempt to penetrate the shield. Alhana took refuge from the storm in an ancient burial mound near the border of Silvanesti. She had discovered this mound long ago, when she had first begun her battle to wrest control of her homeland from the hands of those who seemed intent upon leading her people to disaster.

In other, happier circumstances, the elves would not have disturbed the rest of the dead, but they were being pursued by ogres, their ancient enemy, and were desperately seeking a defensible position. Even so, Alhana had entered the mound with prayers of propitiation, asking the spirits of the dead for understanding.

The elves had discovered the mound to be empty. They found no mummified corpses, no bones, no indication that anyone had ever been buried here. The elves who accompanied Alhana took this for a sign that their cause was just. She did not argue, though she felt the bitter irony that she—the true and rightful Queen of the Silvanesti—was forced to take refuge in a hole in the ground even the dead had abandoned.

The burial mound was now Alhana's headquarters. Her knights, her own personal bodyguard, were inside with her. The rest of the army was camped in the woods around her. A perimeter of elven runners kept watch for ogres, known to be rampaging in this area. The runners, lightly armed, wearing no armor, would not engage the enemy in battle, if they spotted them, but would race back to the picket lines to alert the army of an enemy's presence.

The elves of House Woodshaper had worked long to magically raise from the ground a barricade of thorn bushes surrounding the burial mound. The bushes had wicked barbs that could pierce even an ogre's tough hide. Within the barricade, the soldiers of the elven army found what shelter they could when the torrential storm came. Tents almost immediately collapsed, leaving the elves to hunker down behind boulders or crawl into ditches, avoiding, if possible, the tall trees—targets of the vicious lightning.

Wet to the bone, chilled and awed by the storm, the likes of which not even the longest lived among the elves had ever before seen, the soldiers looked at Silvanoshei, cavorting in the storm like a moonstruck fool, and shook their heads.

He was the son of their beloved queen. They would not say one word against him. They would give their lives defending him, for he was the hope of the elven nation. The elven soldiers liked him well enough, even if they neither admired nor respected him. Silvanoshei was handsome and charming, winning by nature, a boon companion, with a voice so sweet and melodious that he could talk the song-birds out of the trees and into his hand.

In this, Silvanoshei was like neither of his parents. He had none of his father's grim, dour, and resolute nature, and some might have whispered that he was not his father's child, but Silvanoshei so closely resembled Porthios there could be no mistaking the relationship. Silvanoshei, or Silvan, as his mother called him, did not inherit the regal bearing of Alhana Starbreeze. He had something of her pride but little of her com-passion. He cared about his people, but he lacked her undying love and loyalty. He considered her battle to penetrate the shield a hopeless waste of time. He could not understand why she was expending so much energy to return to a people who clearly did not want her.

Alhana doted on her son, more so now that his father appeared to be lost. Silvan's feelings toward his mother were more complex, although he had but an imperfect under-standing of them. Had anyone asked him, he would have said that he loved her and idolized her, and this was true. Yet that love was an oil floating upon the surface of troubled water. Sometimes Silvan felt an anger toward his parents, an anger that frightened him in its fury and intensity. They had robbed him of his childhood, they had robbed him of com-fort, they had robbed him of his rightful standing among his people.

The burial mound remained relatively dry during the downpour. Alhana stood at the entrance, watching the storm, her attention divided between worry for her son—standing bareheaded in the rain, exposed to the murderous lightning and savage winds—and in thinking bitterly that the rain drops could penetrate the shield that surrounded Silvanesti and she, with all the might of her army, could not.

One particularly close lightning strike half-blinded her, its thunderclap shook the cave. Fearful for her son, she ventured a short distance outside the mound's entrance and endeavored to see through the driving rain. Another flash, overspreading the sky with a flame of purple white, revealed him staring upward, his mouth open, roaring back at the thunder in laughing defiance.

"Silvan!" she cried. "It is not safe out there! Come inside with me!"

He did not hear her. Thunder smashed her words, the wind blew them away. But perhaps sensing her concern, he turned his head. "Isn't it glorious, Mother?" he shouted, and the wind that had blown away his mother's words brought his own to her with perfect clarity.

"Do you want me to go out and drag him inside, my queen," asked a voice at her shoulder.

Alhana started, half-turned. "Samar! You frightened me!"

The elf bowed. "I am sorry, Your Majesty. I did not mean to alarm you."

She had not heard him approach, but that was not surprising. Even if there had been no deafening thunder, she would not have heard the elf if he did not want her to hear. He was from House Protector, had been assigned to her by Porthios, and had been faithful to his calling throughout thirty years of war and exile.

Samar was now her second in command, the leader of her armies. That he loved her, she knew well, though he had never spoken a word of it, for he was loyal to her husband Porthios as friend and ruler. Samar knew that she did not love him, that she was faithful to her husband, though they had heard no word of Porthios or from him for months. Samar's love for her was a gift he gave her daily, expecting nothing in return. He walked at her side, his love for her a torch to guide her footsteps along the dark path she walked.

Samar had no love for Silvanoshei, whom he took to be a

spoilt dandy. Samar viewed life as a battle that had to be fought and won on a daily basis. Levity and laughter, jokes and pranks, would have been acceptable in an elf prince whose realm was at peace—an elf prince who, like elf princes of happier times, had nothing to do all day long but learn to play the lute and contemplate the perfection of a rose bud. The ebullient spirits of youth were out of place in this world where the elves struggled simply to survive. Slivanoshei's father was lost and probably dead. His mother expended her life hurling herself against fate, her body and spirit growing more bruised and battered every day. Samar considered Silvan's laughter and high spirits an affront to both, an insult to himself.

The only good Samar saw in the young man was that Silvanoshei could coax a smile from his mother's lips when nothing and no one else could cheer her.

Alhana laid her hand upon Samar's arm. "Tell him that I am anxious. A mother's foolish fears. Or not so foolish," she added to herself, for Samar had already departed. "There is something dire about this storm."

Samar was instantly drenched to the skin when he walked into the storm, as soaked as if he had stepped beneath a waterfall. The wind gusts staggered him. Putting his head down against the blinding torrent, cursing Silvan's heedless foolery, Samar forged ahead.

Silvan stood with his head back, his eyes closed, his lips parted. His arms were spread, his chest bare, his loose-woven shirt so wet that it had fallen from his shoulders. The rainwater poured over his half-naked body.

"Silvan!" Samar shouted into the young man's ear. Grabbing his arm roughly, Samar gave the young elf a good shake. "You are making a spectacle of yourself!" Samar said, his tone low and fierce. He shook Silvan again. "Your mother has worries enough without you adding to them! Get inside with her where you belong!"

Silvan opened his eyes a slit. His eyes were purple, like his mother's, only not as dark; more like wine than blood. The winelike eyes were alight with ecstasy, his lips parted in smile.

"The lightning, Samar! I've never seen anything like it! I can feel it as well as see it. It touches my body and raises the hair on my arms. It wraps me in sheets of flame that lick my skin and set me ablaze. The thunder shakes me to the core of my being, the ground moves beneath my feet. My blood burns, and the rain, the stinging rain, cools my fever. I am in no danger, Samar." Silvan's smile widened, the rain sleeked his face and hair. "I am in no more danger than if I were in bed with a lover—"

"Such talk is unseemly, Prince Silvan," Samar admonished in stern anger. "You should—"

Hunting horns, blowing wildly, frantically, interrupted him. Silvan's ecstatic dream shattered, dashed away by the blasting horns, a sound that was one of the first sounds he remembered hearing as a little child. The sound of warning, the sound of danger.

Silvan's eyes opened fully. He could not tell from what direction the horn calls came, they seemed to come from all directions at once. Alhana stood at the entrance of the mound, surrounded by her knights, peering into the storm.

An elven runner came crashing through the brush. No time for stealth. No need.

"What is it?" Silvan cried.

The soldier ignored him, raced to his commander. "Ogres, sir!" he cried.

"Where?" Samar demanded.

The soldier sucked in a breath. "All around us, sir! They have us surrounded. We didn't hear them. They used the storm to cover their movements. The pickets have retreated back behind the barricade, but the barricade . . ."

The elf could not continue, he was out of breath. He pointed to the north.

A strange glow lit the night purple white, the color of the lightning. But this glow did not strike and then depart. This glow grew brighter.

"What is it?" Silvan shouted, above the drumming of the thunder. "What does that mean?"

"The barricade the Woodshapers created is burning," Samar answered grimly. "Surely the rain will douse the fire—"

"No, sir." The runner had caught his breath. "The barricade was struck by lightning. Not only in one place, but in many."

He pointed again, this time to the east and to the west. The fires could be seen springing up in every direction now, every direction except due south.

"The lightning starts them. The rain has no effect on them. Indeed, the rain seems to fuel them, as if it were oil pouring down from the heavens."

"Tell the Woodshapers to use their magic to put the fire out."

The runner looked helpless. "Sir, the Woodshapers are exhausted. The spell they cast to create the barricade took all their strength."

"How can that be?" Samar demanded angrily. "It is a simple spell— No, never mind!"

He knew the answer, though he continually struggled against it. Of late, in the past two years, the elven sorcerers had felt their power to cast spells ebbing. The loss was gradual, barely felt at first, attributed to illness or exhaustion, but the sorcerers were at last forced to admit that their magical power was slipping away like grains of sand from between clutching fingers. They could hold onto some, but not all. The elves were not alone. They had reports that the same loss was being felt among humans, but this was little comfort.

Using the storm to conceal their movements, the ogres had slipped unseen past the runners and overwhelmed the sentries. The briar-wall barricade was burning furiously in several places at the base of the hill. Beyond the flames stood the tree line, where officers were forming the elven archers into ranks behind the barricade. The tips of their arrows glittered like sparks.

The fire would keep the ogres at bay temporarily, but when it died down, the monsters would come surging across. In the darkness and the slashing rain and the howling wind, the archers would stand little chance of hitting their targets before they were overrun. And when they were overrun, the carnage would be horrible. Ogres hate all other races on Krynn, but their hatred for elves goes back to the beginning of time, when the ogres were once beautiful, the favored of the gods. When the ogres fell, the elves became the favored, the pampered. The ogres had never forgiven them.

"Officers to me!" Samar shouted. "Fieldmaster! Bring your archers into a line behind the lancers at the barrier, and tell them to hold their volley until directed to loose it."

He ran back inside the mound. Silvan followed him, the excitement of the storm replaced by the tense, fierce excitement of the attack. Alhana cast her son a worried glance. Seeing he was unharmed, she turned her complete attention to Samar, as other elven officers crowded inside.

"Ogres?" she asked.

"Yes, my queen. They used the storm for cover. The runner believes that they have us surrounded. I am not certain. I think that the way south may still be open."

"You suggest?"

"That we fall back to the fortress of the Legion of Steel, Your Majesty. A fighting retreat. Your meetings with the human knights went well. It was my thought that—"

Plans and plots, strategy and tactics. Silvan was sick of them, sick of the sound of them. He took the opportunity to slip away. The prince hurried to the back of the mound, where he had laid out his bedroll. Reaching beneath his blanket, he grasped the hilt of a sword, the sword he had purchased in Solace. Silvan was delighted with the weapon, with its shiny newness. The sword had an ornately carved hilt with a griffon's beak. The hilt was admittedly difficult to hold—the beak dug into his flesh—but the sword looked splendid.

Silvanoshei was not a soldier. He had never been trained as a soldier. Small blame to him. Alhana had forbidden it.

"Unlike my hands, these hands"—his mother would take her son's hands in her own, hold them fast—"will not be stained with the blood of his own kind. These hands will heal the wounds that his father and I, against our will, have been forced to inflict. The hands of my son will never spill elven blood."

But this was not elven blood they were talking about spilling. It was ogre blood. His mother could not very well keep him out of this battle. Growing up unarmed and untrained for soldiering in a camp of soldiers, Silvan imagined that the others looked down upon him, that deep inside they thought him a coward. He had purchased the sword in secret, taken a few lessons—until he grew bored with them—and had been looking forward for some time for the chance to show off his prowess.

Pleased to have the opportunity, Silvan buckled the belt around his slender waist and returned to the officers, the sword clanking and banging against his thigh.

Elven runners continued to arrive with reports. The unnatural fire was consuming the barricade at an alarming rate. A few ogres had attempted to cross it. Illuminated by the flames, they had provided excellent targets for the archers. Unfortunately, any arrow that came within range of the fire was consumed by the flames before it could strike its target.

The strategy for retreat settled—Silvan didn't catch much of it, something about pulling back to the south where they would meet up with a force from the Legion of Steel—the officers returned to their commands. Samar and Alhana remained standing together, speaking in low, urgent tones.

Drawing his sword from his sheath with a ringing sound, Silvan gave it a flourish and very nearly sliced off Samar's arm.

"What the—" Samar glared at the bloody gash in his sleeve, glared at Silvan. "Give me that!" He reached out and before Silvan could react, snatched the sword from his grasp.

"Silvanoshei!" Alhana was angry, as angry as he had ever seen her. "This is no time for such nonsense!" She turned her back on him, an indication of her displeasure.

"It is not nonsense, Mother," Silvan retorted. "No, don't turn away from me! This time you will not take refuge behind a wall of silence. This time you will hear me and listen to what I have to say!"

Slowly Alhana turned around. She regarded him intently, her eyes large in her pale face.

The other elves, shocked and embarrassed, did not know where to look. No one defied the queen, no one contradicted her, not even her willful, headstrong son. Silvan himself was amazed at his courage.

"I am a prince of Silvanesti and of Qualinesti," he continued. "It is my privilege, it is my duty to join in the defense of my people. You have no right to try to stop me!"

"I have every right, my son," Alhana returned. She grasped his wrist, her nails pierced his flesh. "You are the heir, the only heir. You are all I have left. . . ." Alhana fell silent, regretting her words. "I am sorry. I did not mean that. A queen has nothing of her own. Everything she has and is belongs to the people. You are all your people have left, Silvan. Now go collect your things," she ordered, her voice tight with the need to control herself. "The knights will take you deeper into the woods—"

"No, Mother, I will not hide anymore," Silvan said, taking care to speak firmly, calmly, respectfully. His cause was lost if he sounded like petulant child. "All my life, whenever danger threatened, you whisked me away, stashed me in some cave, stuffed me under some bed. It is no wonder my people have small respect for me." His gaze shifted to Samar, who was watching the young man with grave attention. "I want to do my part for a change, Mother."

"Well spoken, Prince Silvanoshei," said Samar. "Yet the elves have a saying. 'A sword in the hand of an untrained friend is more dangerous than the sword in the hand of my foe.' One does not learn to fight on the eve of battle, young man. However, if you are serious about this pursuit, I will be pleased to instruct you at some later date. In the meanwhile, there is something you can do, a mission you can undertake."

He knew the response this would bring and he was not wrong. Alhana's arrow-sharp anger found a new target.

"Samar, I would speak with you!" Alhana said, her voice cold, biting, imperious. She turned on her heel, stalked with rigid back and uplifted chin to the rear of the burial mound. Samar, deferential, accompanied her.

Outside were cries and shouts, horns blasting, the deep and terrible ogre war chant sounding like war drums beneath it. The storm raged, unabated, giving succor to the enemy. Silvan stood near the entrance to the burial mound, amazed at himself, proud but appalled, sorry, yet defiant, fearless and terrified all at the same time. The jumble of his emotions confused him. He tried to see what was happening, but the smoke from the burning hedge had settled over the clearing. The shouts and screams grew muted, muffled. He wished he could eavesdrop on the conversation, might have lingered near where he could hear, but he considered that childish and beneath his pride. He could imagine what they were saying anyway. He'd heard the same conversation often enough.

In reality, he was probably not far wrong.

"Samar, you know my wishes for Silvanoshei," Alhana said, when they were out of earshot of the others. "Yet you defy me and encourage him in this wild behavior. I am deeply disappointed in you, Samar."

Her words, her anger were piercing, struck Samar to the heart and drew blood. But as Alhana was queen and responsible to her people, so Samar was also responsible to the people as a soldier. He was committed to providing his people with a present and a future. In that future, the elven nations would need a strong heir, not a milksop like Gilthas, the son of Tanis Half-Elven, who currently played at ruling Qualinesti.

Samar did not speak his true thoughts, however. He did *not* say, "Your Majesty, this is the first sign of spirit I've seen in your son, we should encourage it." He was diplomat as well as soldier.

"Your Majesty," he said, "Silvan is thirty years old—"

"A child—" Alhana interrupted.

Silvan bowed. "Perhaps by Silvanesti standards, my queen. Not by Qualinesti. Under Qualinesti law, he would have attained ranking as a youth. If he were in Qualinesti, he would already be participating in military training. Silvanoshei may be young in years, Alhana," Samar added, dropping the formal title as he did sometimes when they were alone together, "but think of the extraordinary life he has led! His lullabies were war chants, his cradle a shield. He has never known a home. Rarely have his parents been both together in the same room at the same time since the day of his birth. When battle called, you kissed him and rode forth, perhaps to your death. He knew that you might never come back to him, Alhana. I could see it in his eyes!"

"I tried to protect him from all that," she said, her gaze going to her son. He looked so like his father at that moment that her pain overwhelmed her. "If I lose him, Samar, what reason do I have to prolong this bleak and hopeless existence?"

"You cannot protect him from life, Alhana," Samar countered gently. "Nor from the role he is destined to play in life.

Prince Silvanoshei is right. He has a duty to his people. We will let him fulfill that duty *and*"—he laid emphasis on the word—"we will take him out of harm's way at the same time."

Alhana said nothing, but by her look, she gave him reluctant permission to speak further.

"Only one of the runners has returned to camp," Samar continued. "The others are either dead or are fighting for their lives. You said yourself, Your Majesty, that we must send word to the Legion of Steel, warning them of this attack. I propose that we send Silvan to apprise the knights of our desperate need for help. We have only just returned from the fortress, he remembers the way. The main road is not far from the camp and easy to find and follow.

"The danger to him is small. The ogres have not encircled us. He will be safer away from camp than here." Samar smiled. "If I had my way, my Queen, you would go back to the fortress with him."

Alhana smiled, her anger dissipated. "My place is with my soldiers, Samar. I brought them here. They fight my cause. They would lose all trust and respect if I deserted them. Yes, I concede that you are right about Silvan," she added ruefully. "No need to rub salt in my many wounds."

"My queen, I never meant—"

"Yes, you did, Samar," Alhana said, "but you spoke from the heart, and you spoke the truth. We will send the prince upon this mission. He will carry word of our need to the Legion of Steel."

"We will sing his praises when we return to the fortress," said Samar. "And I will purchase him a sword suited to a prince, not a clown."

"No, Samar," said Alhana. "He may carry messages, but he will never carry a sword. On the day he was born, I made my vow to the gods that he would never bear arms against his people. Elven blood would never be spilled because of him."

Samar bowed, wisely remained silent. A skilled commander, he knew when to bring his advance to a halt, dig in, and wait. Alhana walked with stiff back and regal mien to the front of the cave.

"My son," Alhana said and there no emotion in her voice, no feeling. "I have made my decision."

Silvanoshei turned to face his mother. Daughter of Lorac, ill-fated king of the Silvanesti, who had very nearly been his people's downfall, Alhana Starbreeze had undertaken to pay for her father's misdeeds, to redeem her people. Because she had sought to unite them with their cousins, the Qualinesti, because she had advocated alliances with the humans and the dwarves, she was repudiated, cast out by those among the Silvanesti who maintained that only by keeping themselves aloof and isolated from the rest of the world could they and their culture survive.

She was in mature adulthood for the elves, not yet nearing her elder years, incredibly beautiful, more beautiful than at any other time of her life. Her hair was black as the depths of the sea, sunk far below where sunbeams can reach. Her eyes, once amethyst, had deepened and darkened as if colored by the despair and pain which was all they saw. Her beauty was a heartbreak to those around her, not a blessing. Like the legendary dragonlance, whose rediscovery helped bring victory to a beleaguered world, she might have been encased in a pillar of ice. Shatter the ice, shatter the protective barrier she had erected around her, and shatter the woman inside.

Only her son, only Silvan had the power to thaw the ice, to reach inside and touch the living warmth of the woman who was mother, not queen. But that woman was gone. Mother was gone. The woman who stood before him, cold and stern, was his queen. Awed, humbled, aware that he had behaved foolishly, he fell to his knees before her.

"I am sorry, Mother," he said. "I will obey you. I will leave—"

"Prince Silvanoshei," said the queen in a voice he recognized as being her court voice, one she had never used to him. He did not know whether to feel glad or to weep for something irrevocably lost. "Commander Samar has need of a messenger to run with all haste to the outpost of the Legion of Steel. There you will apprise them of our desperate situation. Tell the Lord Knight that we plan to retreat fighting. He should assemble his forces, ride out to meet us at the crossroads, attack the ogres on their right flank. At the moment his knights attack we will halt our retreat and stand our ground. You will need to travel swiftly through the night and the storm. Let nothing deter you, Silvan, for this message must get through."

"I understand, my queen," said Silvan. He rose to his feet, flushed with victory, the thrill of danger flashing like the lightning through his blood. "I will not fail you or my people. I thank you for your trust in me."

Alhana took his face in her hands, hands that were so cold that he could not repress a shiver. She placed her lips upon his forehead. Her kiss burned like ice, the chill struck through to his heart. He would always feel that kiss, from that moment after. He wondered if her pallid lips had left an indelible mark.

Samar's crisp professionalism came as a relief.

"You know the route, Prince Silvan," Samar said. "You rode it only two days before. The road lies about a mile and a half due south of here. You will have no stars to guide you, but the wind blows from the north. Keep the wind at your back and you will be heading in the right direction. The road runs east and west, straight and true. You must eventually cross it. Once you are on the road, travel westward. The storm wind will be on your right cheek. You should make good time. There is no need for stealth. The sound of battle will mask your movements. Good luck, Prince Silvanoshei."

"Thank you, Samar," said Silvan, touched and pleased. For the first time in his life, the elf had spoken to him as an equal, with even a modicum of respect. "I will not fail you or my mother."

"Do not fail your people, Prince," said Samar.

With a final glance and a smile for his mother, a smile she did not return, Silvan turned and left the burial mound, striking out in the direction of the forest. He had not gone far, when he heard Samar's voice raised in a bellowing cry.

"General Aranoshah! Take two orders of swordsmen off to the left flank and send two more to the right. We'll need to keep four units here with Her Majesty in reserve in case they breach the line and break through."

Break through! That was impossible. The line would hold. The line must hold. Silvan halted and looked back. The elves had raised their battle song, its music sweet and uplifting, soaring above the brutish chant of the ogres. He was cheered by the sight and started on, when a ball of fire, blue-white and blinding, exploded on the left side of the hill. The fireball hurtled down the hillside, heading for the burial mounds.

"Shift fire to your left!" Samar called down the slope.

The archers were momentarily confused, not understanding their targets, but their officers managed to turn them in the right direction. The ball of flame struck another portion of the barrier, ignited the thicket, and continued to blaze onward. At first Silvan thought the balls of flame were magical, and he wondered what good archers would do against sorcery, but then he saw that the fireballs were actually huge bundles of hay being pushed and shoved down the hillside by the ogres. He could see their hulking bodies silhouetted black against the leaping flames. The ogres carried long sticks that they used to shove the burning hay stacks.

"Wait for my order!" Samar cried, but the elves were nervous and several arrows were loosed in the direction of the blazing hay.

"No, damn it!" Samar yelled with rage down the slope. "They're not in range yet! Wait for the order!"

A crash of thunder drowned out his voice. Seeing their comrades fire, the remainder of the archer line loosed their first volley. The arrows arched through the smoke-filled night. Three of the ogres pushing the flaming haystacks fell under the withering fire, but the rest of the arrows landed far short of their marks.

"Still," Silvan told himself, "they will soon stop them."

A baying howl as of a thousand wolves converging on their prey cried from the woods close to the elven archers. Silvan stared, startled, thinking that the trees themselves had come alive.

"Shift fire forward!" Samar cried desperately.

The archers could not hear him over the roar of the approaching flames. Too late, their officers noticed the sudden rushing movement in the trees at the foot of the hill. A line of ogres surged into the open, charging the thicket wall that protected the archers. The flames had weakened the barrier. The huge ogres charged into the smoldering mass of burned sticks and logs, shouldering their way through. Cinders fell on their matted hair and sparked in their beards, but the ogres, in a battle rage, ignored the pain of their burns and lurched forward.

Now being attacked from the front and on their flank, the elven archers grappled desperately for their arrows, tried to loose another volley before the ogres closed. The flaming haystacks thundered down on them. The elves did not know which enemy to fight first. Some lost their heads in the chaos. Samar roared orders. The officers struggled to bring their troops under control. The elves fired a second volley, some into the burning hay bales, others into the ogres charging them on the flank.

More ogres fell, an immense number, and Silvan thought that they must retreat. He was amazed and appalled to see the ogres continue forward, undaunted.

"Samar, where are the reserves?" Alhana called out.

"I think they have been cut off," Samar returned grimly. "You should not be out here, Your Majesty. Go back inside where you are safe."

Silvan could see his mother now. She had left the burial mound. She was clad in silver armor, carried a sword at her side.

"I led my people here," Alhana returned. "Will you have me skulk in a cave while my people are dying, Samar?"

"Yes," he growled.

She smiled at him, a tight strained smile, but still a smile. She gripped the hilt of her sword. "Will they break through, do you think?"

"I don't see much stopping them, Your Majesty," Samar said grimly.

The elven archers loosed another volley. The officers had regained control of the troops. Every shot told. The ogres charging from the front fell by the score. Half the line disappeared. Still the ogres continued their advance, the living trampling the bodies of the fallen. In moments they would be within striking range of the archers' position.

"Launch the assault!" Samar roared.

Elven swordsmen rose up from their positions behind the left barricades. Shouting their battle cries, they charged the ogre line. Steel rang against steel. The flaming haystacks burst into the center of the camp, crushing men, setting fire to trees and grass and clothing. Suddenly, without warning, the ogre line turned. One of their number had caught sight of Alhana's silver armor, reflecting the firelight. With guttural cries, they pointed at her and were now charging toward the burial mound.

"Mother!" Silvan gasped, his heart tangled up with his stomach. He had to bring help. They were counting on him, but he was paralyzed, mesmerized by the terrible sight. He couldn't run to her. He couldn't run away. He couldn't move.

"Where are those reserves?" Samar shouted furiously. "Aranosha! You bastard! Where are Her Majesty's swordsmen!"

"Here, Samar!" cried a warrior. "We had to fight our way to you, but we are here!"

"Take them down there, Samar," said Alhana calmly.

"Your Majesty!" He started to protest. "I will not leave you without guards."

"If we don't halt the advance, Samar," Alhana returned. "It won't much matter whether I have guards or not. Go now. Quickly!"

Samar wanted to argue, but he knew by the remote and resolute expression on his queen's face that he would be wasting his breath. Gathering the reserves around him, Samar charged down into the advancing ogres.

Alhana stood alone, her silver armor burning with the reflected flames.

"Make haste, Silvan, my son. Make haste. Our lives rest on you."

She spoke to herself, but she spoke, unknowingly, to her son.

Her words impelled Silvan to action. He had been given an order and he would carry it out. Bitterly regretting the wasted time, his heart swelling with fear for his mother, he turned and plunged into the forest.

Adrenaline pumped in Silvan's veins. He shoved his way through the underbrush, thrusting aside tree limbs, trampling seedlings. Sticks snapped beneath his boots. The wind was cold and strong on his right cheek. He did not feel the pelting rain. He welcomed the lightning that lit his path.

He was prudent enough to keep careful watch for any signs of the enemy and constantly sniffed the air, for the filthy, flesh-eating ogre is usually smelt long before he is seen. Silvan kept his hearing alert, too, for though he himself made what an elf would consider to be an unconscionable amount of noise, he was a deer gliding through the forest compared to the smashing and cracking, ripping and tearing of an ogre.

Silvan traveled swiftly, encountering not so much as a nocturnal animal out hunting, and soon the sounds of battle dwindled behind him. Then it was that he realized he was alone in the forest in the night in the storm. The adrenaline started to ebb. A sliver of fear and doubt pierced his heart. What if he arrived too late? What if the humans—known for their vagaries and their changeable natures—refused to act? What if the attack overwhelmed his people? What if he had left them to die? None of this looked familiar to him. He had taken a wrong turning, he was lost. . . .

Resolutely Silvan pushed forward, running through the forest with the ease of one who has been born and raised in the woodlands. He was cheered by the sight of a ravine on his left hand; he remembered that ravine from his earlier travels to the fortress. His fear of being lost vanished. He took care to keep clear of the rocky edge of the ravine, which cut a large gash across the forest floor.

Silvan was young, strong. He banished his doubts that were a drag on his heart, and concentrated on his mission. A lightning flash revealed the road straight ahead. The sight renewed his strength and his determination. Once he reached the road, he could increase his pace. He was an excellent runner, often running long distances for the sheer pleasure of the feel of the muscles expanding and contracting, the sweat on his body, the wind in his face and the warm suffusing glow that eased all pain.

He imagined himself speaking to the Lord Knight, pleading their cause, urging him to haste. Silvan saw himself leading the rescue, saw his mother's face alight with pride. . . .

In reality, Silvan saw his way blocked. Annoyed, he slid to a halt on the muddy path to study this obstacle.

A gigantic tree limb, fallen from an ancient oak, lay across the path. Leaves and branches blocked his way. Silvan would be forced to circle around it, a move that would bring him close to the edge of the ravine. He was sure on his feet, however. The lightning lit his way. He edged around the end of the severed limb with a good few feet to spare. He was climbing over a single branch, reaching out his hand to steady himself on a nearby pine tree, when a single bolt of lightning streaked out of the darkness and struck the pine.

The tree exploded in a ball of white fire. The concussive force of the blast knocked Silvan over the edge of the ravine. Rolling and tumbling down its rock-strewn wall, he slammed against the stump of a broken tree at the bottom.

Pain seared his body, worse pain seared his heart. He had failed. He would not reach the fortress. The knights would never receive the message. His people could not fight alone against the ogres. They would die. His mother would die with the belief that he had let her down.

He tried to move, to rise, but the pain flashed through him, white hot, so horrible that when he felt consciousness slipping away, he was glad to think he was going to die. Glad to think that he would join his people in death, since he could do nothing else for them.

Despair and grief rose in a great, dark wave, crashed down upon Silvan and dragged him under.

3

AN UNEXPECTED VISITOR

he storm disappeared. A strange storm, it had burst upon Ansalon like an invading army, striking all parts of that vast continent at the same time, attacking throughout the night, only to retreat with the coming of dawn. The sun crawled out from the dark lightning-shot cloudbank to blaze triumphantly in the blue sky. Light and warmth cheered the inhabitants of Solace, who crept out of their homes to see what destruction the tempest had wrought.

Solace did not fare as badly as some other parts of Ansalon, although the storm appeared to have targeted that hamlet with particular hatred. The mighty vallenwoods proved stubbornly resistant to the devastating lightning that struck them time and again. The tops of the trees caught fire and burned, but the fire did not spread to the branches below. The trees' strong arms tossed in the whirling winds but held fast the homes built there, homes that were in their care. Creeks rose and fields flooded, but homes and barns were spared.

The Tomb of the Last Heroes, a beautiful structure of white and black stone that stood in a clearing on the outskirts of town, had sustained severe damage. Lightning had hit one of the spires, splitting it asunder, sending large chunks of marble crashing down to the lawn.

But the worst damage was done to the crude and make-shift homes of the refugees fleeing the lands to the west and south, lands which had been free only a year ago but which were now falling under control of the green dragon Beryl.

Three years ago, the great dragons who had fought for control of Ansalon had come to an uneasy truce. Realizing that their bloody battles were weakening them, the dragons agreed to be satisfied with the territory each had conquered, they would not wage war against each other to try to gain more. The dragons had kept this pact, until a year ago. It was then that Beryl had noticed her magical powers starting to decline. At first, she had thought she was imagining this, but as time passed, she became convinced that something was wrong.

Beryl blamed the red dragon Malys for the loss of her magic—this was some foul scheme being perpetrated by her larger and stronger cousin. Beryl also blamed the human mages, who were hiding the Tower of High Sorcery of Wayreth from her. Consequently, Beryl had begun ever so gradually to expand her control over human lands. She moved slowly, not wanting to draw Malys's attention. Malys would not care if here and there a town was burned or a village plundered. The city of Haven was one such, recently fallen to Beryl's might. Solace remained untouched, for the time being. But Beryl's eye was upon Solace. She had ordered closed the main roads leading into Solace, letting them feel the pressure as she bided her time.

The refugees who had managed to escape Haven and sur-rounding lands before the roads were closed had swelled Solace's population to three times its normal size. Arriving with their belongings tied up in bundles or piled on the back of carts, the refugees were being housed in what the town fathers designated "temporary housing." The hovels were truly meant only to be temporary, but the flood of refugees arriving daily overwhelmed good intentions. The temporary shelters had become, unfortunately, permanent.

The first person to reach the refugee camps the morning after the storm was Caramon Majere, driving a wagon loaded with sacks of food, lumber for rebuilding, dry firewood, and blankets.

Caramon was over eighty—just how far over no one really knew, for he himself had lost track of the years. He was what they term in Solamnia a "grand old man." Age had come to him as an honorable foe, facing him and saluting him, not creeping up to stab him in the back or rob him of his wits. Hale and hearty, his big frame corpulent but unbowed ("I can't grow stooped, my gut won't let me," he was wont to say with a roaring laugh), Caramon was the first of his household to rise, was out every morning chopping wood for the kitchen fires or hauling the heavy ale barrels up the stairs.

His two daughters saw to the day-to-day workings of the Inn of the Last Home—this was the only concession Caramon made to his age—but he still tended the bar, still told his stories. Laura ran the Inn, while Dezra, who had a taste for adventure, traveled to markets in Haven and elsewhere, searching out the very best in hops for the Inn's ale, honey for the Inn's legendary mead, and even hauling dwarf spirits back from Thorbardin. The moment Caramon went outdoors he was swarmed over by the children of Solace, who one and all called him "Grampy" and who vied for rides on his broad shoulders or begged to hear him tell tales of long-ago heroes. He was a friend to the refugees who would have likely had no housing at all had not Caramon donated the wood and supervised the construction. He was currently overseeing a project to build permanent dwellings on the outskirts of

Solace, pushing, cajoling, and browbeating the recalcitrant authorities into taking action. Caramon Majere never walked the streets of Solace but that he heard his name spoken and blessed.

Once the refugees were assisted, Caramon traveled about the rest of Solace, making certain that everyone was safe, raising hearts and spirits oppressed by the terrible night. This done, he went to his own breakfast, a breakfast he had come to share, of late, with a Knight of Solamnia, a man who reminded Caramon of his own two sons who had died in the Chaos War.

In the days immediately following the Chaos War, the Solamnic Knights had established a garrison in Solace. The garrison had been a small one in the early days, intended only to provide Knights to stand honor guard for the Tomb of the Last Heroes. The garrison had been expanded to counter the threat of the great dragons, who were now the acknowledged, if hated, rulers of much of Ansalon.

So long as the humans of Solace and other cities and lands under her control continued to pay Beryl tribute, she allowed the people to continue on with their lives, allowed them to continue to generate more wealth so that they could pay even more tribute. Unlike the evil dragons of earlier ages, who had delighted in burning and looting and killing, Beryl had discovered that burned-out cities did not generate profit. Dead people did not pay taxes.

There were many who wondered why Beryl and her cousins with their wondrous and terrible magicks should covet wealth, should demand tribute. Beryl and Malys were cunning creatures. If they were rapaciously and wantonly cruel, indulging in wholesale slaughter of entire populations, the people of Ansalon would rise up out of desperation and march to destroy them. As it was, most humans found life under the dragon rule to be relatively comfortable. They were content to let well enough alone.

Bad things happened to some people, people who no doubt deserved their fate. If hundreds of kender were killed or driven from their homes, if rebellious Qualinesti elves were being tortured and imprisoned, what did this matter to humans? Beryl and Malys had minions and spies in every human town and village, placed there to foment discord and hatred and suspicion, as well as to make certain that no one was trying to hide so much as a cracked copper from the dragons.

Caramon Majere was one of the few outspoken in his hatred of paying tribute to the dragons and actually refused to do so.

"Not one drop of ale will I give to those fiends," he said heatedly whenever anyone asked, which they rarely did, knowing that one of Beryl's spies was probably taking down names.

He was staunch in his refusal, though much worried by it. Solace was a wealthy town, now larger than Haven. The tribute demanded from Solace was quite high. Caramon's wife Tika had pointed out that their share was being made up by the other citizens of Solace and that this was putting a hardship on the rest. Caramon could see the wisdom of Tika's argument. At length he came up with the novel idea of levying a special tax against himself, a tax that only the Inn paid, a tax whose monies were on no account to be sent to the dragon but that would be used to assist those who suffered unduly from having to pay what was come to be known as "the dragon tax."

The people of Solace paid extra tax, the city fathers refunded them a portion out of Caramon's contribution, and the tribute went to the dragon as demanded.

If they could have found a way to silence Caramon on the volatile subject, they would have done so, for he continued to be loud in his hatred of the dragons, continued to express his views that "if we just all got together we could poke out Beryl's eye with a dragonlance." Indeed, when the city of Haven was attacked by Beryl just a few weeks earlier—ostensibly for defaulting on its payments—the Solace town fathers actually came to Caramon and begged him on bended knee to cease his rabble-rousing remarks.

Impressed by their obvious fear and distress, Caramon agreed to tone down his rhetoric, and the town fathers left happy. Caramon did actually comply, expressing his views in a moderate tone of voice as opposed to the booming outrage he'd used previously.

He reiterated his unorthodox views that morning to his breakfast companion, the young Solamnic.

"A terrible storm, sir," said the Knight, seating himself opposite Caramon.

A group of his fellow Knights were breakfasting in another part of the Inn, but Gerard uth Mondar paid them scant attention. They, in their turn, paid him no attention at all.

"It bodes dark days to come, to my mind," Caramon agreed, settling his bulk into the high-backed wooden booth, a booth whose seat had been rubbed shiny by the old man's backside. "But all in all I found it exhilarating."

"Father!" Laura was scandalized. She slapped down a plate of beefsteak and eggs for her father, a bowl of porridge for the Knight. "How can you say such things? With so many people hurt. Whole houses blown, from what I hear."

"I didn't mean that," Caramon protested, contrite. "I'm sorry for the people who were hurt, of course, but, you know, it came to me in the night that this storm must be shaking Beryl's lair about pretty good. Maybe even burned the evil old bitch out. *That's* what I was thinking." He looked worriedly at the young Knight's bowl of porridge. "Are you certain that's enough to eat, Gerard? I can have Laura fry you up some potatoes—"

"Thank you, sir, this is all I am accustomed to eat for

breakfast," Gerard said as he said every day in response to the same question.

Caramon sighed. Much as he had come to like this young man, Caramon could not understand any one who did not enjoy food. A person who did not relish Otik's famous spiced potatoes was a person who did not relish life. Only one time in his own life had Caramon ever ceased to enjoy his dinner and that was following the death several months earlier of his beloved wife Tika. Caramon had refused to eat a mouthful for days after that, to the terrible worry and consternation of the entire town, which went on a cooking frenzy to try to come up with something that would tempt him.

He would eat nothing, do nothing, say nothing. He either roamed aimlessly about the town or sat staring dry-eyed out the stained glass windows of the Inn, the Inn where he had first met the red-haired and annoying little brat who had been his comrade in arms, his lover, his friend, his salvation. He shed no tears for her, he would not visit her grave beneath the vallenwoods. He would not sleep in their bed. He would not hear the messages of condolence that came from Laurana and Gilthas in Qualinesti, from Goldmoon in the Citadel of Light.

Caramon lost weight, his flesh sagged, his skin took on a gray hue.

"He will follow Tika soon," said the townsfolk.

He might have, too, had not one day a child, one of the refugee children, happened across Caramon in his dismal roamings. The child placed his small body squarely in front of the old man and held out a hunk of bread.

"Here, sir," said the child. "My mother says that if you don't eat you will die, and then what will become of us?"

Caramon gazed down at the child in wonder. Then he knelt down, gathered the child into his arms, and began to sob uncontrollably. Caramon ate the bread, every crumb, and that night he slept in the bed he had shared with Tika. He placed flowers on her grave the next morning and ate a breakfast that would have fed three men. He smiled again and laughed, but there was something in his smile and in his laughter that had not been there before. Not sorrow, but a wistful impatience.

Sometimes, when the door to the Inn opened, he would look out into the sunlit blue sky beyond and he would say, very softly, "I'm coming, my dear. Don't fret. I won't be long."

Gerard uth Mondar ate his porridge with dispatch, not really tasting it. He ate his porridge plain, refusing to flavor it with brown sugar or cinnamon, did not even add salt. Food fueled his body, and that was all it was good for. He ate his porridge, washing down the congealed mass with a mug of tar-bean tea, and listened to Caramon talk about the awful wonders of the storm.

The other Knights paid their bill and left, bidding Caramon a polite good-day as they passed, but saying nothing to his companion. Gerard appeared not to notice, but steadfastly spooned porridge from bowl to mouth.

Caramon watched the Knights depart and interrupted his story in mid-lightning bolt. "I appreciate the fact that you share your time with an old geezer like me, Gerard, but if you want to have breakfast with your friends—"

"They are not my friends," said Gerard without bitterness or rancor, simply making a statement of fact. "I much prefer dining with a man of wisdom and good, common sense." He raised his mug to Caramon in salute.

"It's just that you seem . . ." Caramon paused, chewed steak vigorously. "Lonely," he finished in a mumble, his mouth full. He swallowed, forked another piece. "You should have a girlfriend or . . . or a wife or something."

Gerard snorted. "What woman would look twice at a man with a face like this?" He eyed with dissatisfaction his own reflection in the highly polished pewter mug.

Gerard was ugly; there was no denying that fact. A

childhood illness had left his face cragged and scarred. His
nose had been broken in a fight with a neighbor when he was
ten and had healed slightly askew. He had yellow hair—not
blond, not fair, just plain, straw yellow. It was the consistency
of straw, too, and would not lie flat, but stuck up at all sorts of
odd angles if allowed. To avoid looking like a scarecrow,
which had been his nickname when he was young, Gerard
kept his hair cut as short as possible.

His only good feature were his eyes, which were of a startling, one might almost say, alarming blue. Because there was
rarely any warmth behind these eyes and because these eyes
always focused upon their objective with unblinking intensity, Gerard's blue eyes tended to repel more people than they
attracted.

"Bah!" Caramon dismissed beauty and comeliness with a
wave of his fork. "Women don't care about a man's looks.
They want a man of honor, of courage. A young Knight your
age . . . How old are you?"

"I have seen twenty-eight years, sir," Gerard replied. Fin-
ishing his porridge, he shoved the bowl to one side. "Twenty-
eight boring and thoroughly wasted years."

"Boring?" Caramon was skeptical. "And you a Knight? I
was in quite a few wars myself. Battles were lots of things, as
I recall, but boring wasn't one of them—"

"I have never been in battle, sir," said Gerard and now his
tone was bitter. He rose to his feet, placed a coin upon the
table. "If you will excuse me, I am on duty at the tomb this
morning. This being Midyear Day, and consequently a holiday, we expect an influx of rowdy and destructive kender. I
have been ordered to report to my post an hour early. I wish
you joy of the day, sir, and I thank you for your company."

He bowed stiffly, turned on his heel as if he were already
performing the slow and stately march before the tomb, and
walked out the door of the Inn. Caramon could hear his
booted feet ringing on the long staircase that led down from

the Inn, perched high in the branches of Solace's largest vallenwood.

Caramon leaned back comfortably in the booth. The sunshine streamed in through the red and green windows, warming him. His belly full, he was content. Outside, people were cleaning up after the storm, gathering up the branches that had fallen from the vallenwoods, airing out their damp houses, spreading straw over the muddy streets. In the afternoon, the people would dress in their best clothes, adorn their hair with flowers, and celebrate the longest day of the year with dancing and feasting. Caramon could see Gerard stalking stiff-backed and stiff-necked through the mud, paying no heed to anything going on around him, making his way to the Tomb of the Last Heroes. Caramon watched as long as he could see the Knight, before finally losing sight of him in the crowd.

"He's a strange one," said Laura, whipping away the empty bowl and pocketing the coin. "I wonder how you can eat alongside him, Father. His face curdles the milk."

"He cannot help his face, Daughter," Caramon returned sternly. "Are there any more eggs?"

"I'll bring you some. You've no idea what a pleasure it is to see you eating again." Laura paused in her work to kiss her father tenderly on his forehead. "As for that young man, it's not his face that makes him ugly. I've loved far uglier in looks in my time. It's his arrogance, his pride that drives people away. Thinks he's better than all the rest of us, so he does. Did you know that he comes from one of the wealthiest families in all of Palanthas? His father practically funds the Knighthood, they say. And he pays well for his son to be posted here in Solace, away from the fighting in Sanction and other places. It's small wonder the other Knights have no respect for him."

Laura flounced off to the kitchen to refill her father's plate.

Caramon stared after his daughter in astonishment. He'd

been eating breakfast with this young man every day for the past two months, and he had no notion of any of this. They'd developed what he considered a close relationship, and here was Laura, who'd never said anything to the young Knight beyond, "Sugar for your tea?" knowing his life's history.

"Women," Caramon said to himself, basking in the sunlight. "Eighty years old and I might as well be sixteen again. I didn't understand them then, and I don't understand them now."

Laura returned with a plate of eggs piled high with spiced potatoes on the side. She gave her father another kiss and went about her day.

"She's so much like her mother, though," Caramon said fondly and ate his second plate of eggs with relish.

Gerard uth Mondar was thinking about women, as well, as he waded through the ankle-deep mud. Gerard would have agreed with Caramon that women were creatures not to be understood by men. Caramon liked women, however. Gerard neither liked them nor trusted them. Once when he had been fourteen and newly recovered from the illness that had destroyed his looks, a neighbor girl had laughed at him and called him "pock face."

Discovered in gulping tears by his mother, he was comforted by his mother, who said, "Pay no attention to the stupid chit, my son. Women will love you one day." And then she had added, in a vague afterthought, "You are very rich, after all."

Fourteen years later, he would wake in the night to hear the girl's shrill, mocking laughter, and his soul would cringe in shame and embarrassment. He would hear his mother's counsel and his embarrassment would burn away in anger, an anger that burned all the hotter because his mother had proved a prophetess. The "stupid chit" had thrown herself at Gerard when they were both eighteen and she had come to realize that money could make the ugliest weed beautiful as a rose. He had taken great pleasure in scornfully snubbing her. Ever since that day, he had suspected that any woman who looked at him with any interest whatsoever was secretly calculating his worth, all the while masking her disgust for him with sweet smiles and fluttering lashes.

Mindful of the precept that the best offense is a good defense, Gerard had built a most excellent fortress around himself, a fortress bristling with sharp barbs, its walls stocked with buckets of acidic comments, its high towers hidden in a cloud of dark humors, the entire fortress surrounded by a moat of sullen resentment.

His fortress proved extremely good at keeping out men, as well. Laura's gossip was more accurate than most. Gerard uth Mondar did indeed come from one of the wealthiest families in Palanthas, probably one of the wealthiest in all of Ansalon. Prior to the Chaos War, Gerard's father, Mondar uth Alfric, had been the owner of the most successful shipyard in Palanthas. Foreseeing the rise of the Dark Knights, Sir Mondar had wisely converted as much of his property into good solid steel as possible and moved his family to Southern Ergoth, where he started his shipbuilding and repairing business anew, a business which was now thriving.

Sir Mondar was a powerful force among the Knights of Solamnia. He contributed more money than any other Knight to the support and maintenance of the Knighthood. He had seen to it that his son became a Knight, had seen to it that his son had the very best, the safest posting available. Mondar had never asked Gerard what he wanted from life. The elder Knight took it for granted that his son wanted to be a Knight and the son had taken it for granted himself until the very night he was holding vigil before the ceremony of knighthood. In that night, a vision came to him, not a vision of glory and honor won on the battlefield, but a vision of a sword rusting away in its scabbard, a vision of running errands and posting guard detail over dust and ashes that didn't need guarding.

Too late to back out. To do so would break a family tradition that supposedly extended back to Vinas Solamnus. His father would renounce him, hate him forever. His mother, who had sent out hundreds of invitations to a celebratory party, would take to her bed for a month. Gerard had gone through with the ceremony. He had taken his vow, a vow he considered meaningless. He had donned the armor that had become his prison.

He had served in the Knighthood now for seven years, one of which had been spent in the "honorary" duty of guarding a bunch of corpses. Before that, he'd brewed tarbean tea and written letters for his commanding officer in Southern Ergoth. He had requested posting to Sanction and had been on the verge of leaving, when the city was attacked by the armies of the Knights of Neraka and his father had seen to it that his son was sent instead to Solace. Returning to the fortress, Gerard cleaned the mud from his boots and left to join the fellow of his watch, taking up his hated and detested position of honor before the Tomb of the Last Heroes.

The tomb was a simple structure of elegant design, built by dwarves of white marble and black obsidian. The tomb was surrounded by trees, that had been planted by the elves, and which bore fragrant flowers all year long. Inside lay the bodies of Tanis Half-elven, fallen hero of the battle of the High Clerist's Tower, and Steel Brightblade, son of Sturm Brightblade and the hero of the final battle against Chaos. Here also were the bodies of the knights who had fought the Chaos god. Above the door of the tomb was written a single name, Tasslehoff Burrfoot, the kender hero of the Chaos war.

Kender came from all over Ansalon to pay tribute to their hero, feasting and picnicking on the lawns, singing songs of Uncle Tas and telling stories about his brave deeds.

Unfortunately, some years after the tomb had been built, the kender took it into their heads to each come away with a piece of the tomb for luck. To this end, they began to attack the tomb with chisels and hammers, forcing the Solamnic knights to erect a wrought-iron fence around the tomb that was starting to have the appearance of being nibbled by mice.

The sun blazing down on him, his armor baking him slowly as Laura was slowly baking her beef roast, Gerard marched with slow and solemn step the one hundred paces that took him from the left of the tomb to the center. Here he met his fellow who had marched an equal distance. They saluted one another. Turning, they saluted the fallen heroes. Turning, they marched back, each guard's motions mirroring exactly the motions of the guard opposite.

One hundred paces back. One hundred paces forth.

Over and over and over.

An honor to some, such as the Knight who stood watch this day with Gerard. This Knight had purchased this posting with blood, not with money. The veteran Knight walked his beat with a slight limp, but he walked it proudly. Small blame to him that every time he came face to face with Gerard, he regarded him with lip-curling enmity.

Gerard marched back and forth. As the day progressed, crowds gathered, many having traveled to Solace especially for this holiday. Kender arrived in droves, spreading lunches on the lawn, eating and drinking, dancing and playing games of goblin ball and kender-keep-away. The kender loved to watch the Knights, loved to annoy them. The kender danced around the Knights, tried to make them smile, tickled them, rapped on their armor, called them "Kettle Head" and "Canned Meat," offered them food, thinking they might be hungry.

Gerard uth Mondar disliked humans. He distrusted elves. He hated kender. Actively hated them. Detested them. He hated all kender equally, including the so-called "afflicted" kender, whom most people now viewed with pity. These

71

kender were survivors of an attack by the great dragon Malys on their homeland. They were said to have seen such acts of violence and cruelty that their merry, innocent natures had been forever altered, leaving them much like humans: suspicious, cautious, and vindictive. Gerard didn't believe this "afflicted" act. To his mind, it was just another sneaky way for kender to get their grubby little hands into a man's pockets.

Kender were like vermin. They could flatten their boneless little bodies and crawl into any structure made by man or dwarf. Of this Gerard was firmly convinced, and so he was only a little surprised when, sometime nearing the end of his watch, drawing on late afternoon, he heard a shrill voice hallooing and hollering. The voice came from inside the tomb.

"I say!" cried the voice. "Could someone let me out? It's extremely dark in here, and I can't find the door handle."

The partner of Gerard's watch actually missed a step. Halting, he turned to stare. "Did you hear that?" he demanded, regarding the tomb with frowning concern. "It sounded like someone was in there."

"Hear what?" Gerard said, though he himself had heard it plainly. "You're imagining things."

But they weren't. The noise grew louder. Knocking and pounding were now added to the hallooing and hollering.

"Hey, I heard a voice inside the tomb!" shouted a kender child, who had dashed forward to retrieve a ball that had bounced off Gerard's left foot. The kender put his face to the fence, pointed inside at the tomb's massive and sealed doors. "There's someone trapped in the tomb! And it *wants out!*"

The crowd of kender and other residents of Solace who had come to pay their respects to the dead by swilling ale and munching cold chicken forgot their suppers and their games. Gasping in wonder, they crowded around the fence, nearly overrunning the Knights.

"They buried someone alive in there!" a girl screamed.

The crowd surged forward.

"Keep back!" Gerard shouted, drawing his sword. "This is holy ground! Any who desecrates it will be arrested! Randolph, go and get reinforcements! We need to clear this area."

"I suppose it could be a ghost," his fellow Knight speculated, his eyes glowing with awe. "A ghost of one of the fallen Heroes come back to warn us of dire peril."

Gerard snorted. "You've been listening to too many bards' tales! It's nothing more than one of these filthy little vermin who's got himself inside there and can't get out. I have the key to the fence, but I have no idea how to open the tomb."

The banging on the door was growing louder.

The Knight cast Gerard a disgusted glance. "I will go fetch the provost. He'll know what to do."

Randolph pelted off, holding his sword to his side to keep it from clanking against his armor.

"Get away! Move aside!" Gerard ordered in firm tones.

He drew out the key and, putting his back against the gate, keeping his face to the crowd, he fumbled around behind his back until he managed to fit the key into the lock. Hearing it click, he opened the gate, much to the delight of the crowd, several of whom endeavored to push through. Gerard walloped the boldest with the flat of his sword, drove them back a few moments, time enough for him to hastily dodge inside the fence gate and slam it shut behind him.

The crowd of humans and kender pressed in around the fence. Children poked their heads through the bars, promptly got their heads stuck, and began to wail. Some climbed the bars in a futile attempt to crawl over, while others thrust their hands and arms and legs inside for no logical reason that Gerard could see, which only went to prove what he'd long suspected—that his fellow mortals were ninnies.

The Knight made certain the gate was locked and secure and then walked over to the tomb, intending to post himself at the entrance until the Provost came with some means of breaking the seal.

He was climbing the marble and obsidian stairs when he heard the voice say cheerfully, "Oh, never mind. I've got it!"

A loud snick, as of a lock being tripped, and the doors to the tomb began to slowly creak open.

The crowd gasped in thrilled horror and crowded nearer the fence, each trying to get the best view possible of the Knight being ripped apart by hordes of skeletal warriors.

A figure emerged from the tomb. It was dusty, dirty, its hair windswept, its clothes in disarray and singed, its pouches rather mangled and worse for wear. But it wasn't a skeleton. It wasn't a blood-sucking vampire or an emaciated ghoul.

It was a kender.

The crowd groaned in disappointment.

The kender peered out into the bright sunlight and blinked, half-blinded. "Hullo," he said. "I'm—" The kender paused to sneeze. "Sorry. It's extremely dusty in there. Someone should really do something about that. Do you have a handkerchief? I seem to have mislaid mine. Well, it actually belonged to Tanis, but I don't suppose he'll be wanting it back now that he's dead. Where am I?"

"Under arrest," said Gerard. Laying firm hands upon the kender, the Knight hauled him down the stairs.

Understandably disappointed that they weren't going to witness a battle between the Knight and the undead, the crowd returned to their picnics and playing goblin ball.

"I recognize this place," said the kender, staring about instead of watching where he was going and consequently tripping himself. "I'm in Solace. Good! That's where I meant to come. My name is Tasslehoff Burrfoot, and I'm here to speak at the funeral of Caramon Majere, so if you could just take me to the Inn quickly, I really do have to get back. You see, there's this giant foot about to come down—blam! right on top of me, and that's something I don't want to miss, and now then—"

Gerard put the key into the gate lock, turned it, and opened the gate. He gave the kender a shove that sent him sprawling. "The only place you're going is off to jail. You've done enough mischief already."

The kender picked himself up cheerfully, not at all angry or disconcerted. "Awfully nice of you to find me a place to spend the night. Not that I'll be here that long. I've come to speak . . ." He paused. "Did I mention that I was Tasslehoff Burrfoot?"

Gerard grunted, not interested. He took firm hold of the kender and stood waiting with him until someone came to take the little bastard off his hands.

"*The* Tasslehoff," said the kender.

Gerard cast a weary glance out over the crowd and shouted, "Everyone named Tasslehoff Burrfoot raise his hand!"

Thirty-seven hands shot up in the air, and two dogs barked.

"Oh, my!" said the kender, clearly taken aback.

"You can see why I'm not impressed," said Gerard and searched hopefully for some sign that relief was on the way.

"I don't suppose it would matter if I told you that I was the original Tasslehoff . . . No, I guess not." The kender sighed and stood fidgeting in the hot sun. His hand, strictly out of boredom, found its way into Gerard's money pouch, but Gerard was prepared for that and gave the kender a swift and nasty crack across the knuckles.

The kender sucked his bruised hand. "What's all this?" He looked around at the people larking and frolicking upon the lawn. "What are these people doing here? Why aren't they attending Caramon's funeral? It's the biggest event Solace has ever seen!"

"Probably because Caramon Majere is not dead yet," said Gerard caustically. "Where *is* that good-for-nothing provost?"

"Not dead?" The kender stared. "Are you sure?"

"I had breakfast with him myself this very morning," Gerard replied.

"Oh, no!" The kender gave a heartbroken wail and slapped himself on the forehead. "I've gone and goofed it up *again!* And I don't suppose that now I've got time to try it a third time. What with the giant foot and all." He began to rummage about in his pouch. "Still, I guess I had better try. Now, where did I put that device—"

Gerard glowered around as he tightened his grip on the collar of the kender's dusty jacket. The thirty-seven kender named Tasslehoff had all come over to meet number thirty-eight.

"The rest of you, clear out!" Gerard waved his hand as if he were shooing chickens.

Naturally, the kender ignored him. Though extremely disappointed that Tasslehoff hadn't turned out to be a shambling zombie, the kender were interested to hear where he'd been, what he'd seen and what he had in his pouches.

"Want some Midyear Day's cake?" asked a pretty female kender.

"Why, thank you. This is quite good. I—" The kender's eyes opened wide. He tried to say something, couldn't speak for the cake in his mouth, and ended up half choking himself. His fellow kender obligingly pounded him on the back. He bolted the cake, coughed, and gasped out, "*What* day is this?"

"Midyear's Day!" cried everyone.

"Then I haven't missed it!" the kender shouted triumphantly. "In fact, this is better than I could have hoped! I'll get to tell Caramon what I'm going to say at his funeral tomorrow! He'll probably find it extremely interesting."

The kender looked up into the sky. Spotting the position of the sun, which was about half-way down, heading for the horizon, he said, "Oh, dear. I don't have all that much time. If you'll just excuse me, I had best be running."

And run he did, leaving Gerard standing flat-footed on the grassy lawn, a kender jacket in his hand.

Gerard spent one baffled moment wondering how the imp had managed to wriggle out of his jacket, yet still retain all his pouches, which were jouncing and bouncing as he ran, spilling their contents to the delight of the thirty-seven Tasslehoffs. Concluding that this was a phenomenon that, much like the departure of the gods, he would never understand, Gerard was about to run after the errant kender, when he remembered that he could not leave his post unguarded.

At this juncture, the provost came into sight, accompanied by an entire detail of Solamnic Knights solemnly arrayed in their best armor to welcome back the returning Heroes, for this is what they had understood they were going to be meeting.

"Just a kender, sir," Gerard explained. "Somehow he managed to get himself locked inside the tomb. He let himself out. He got away from me, but I think I know where he's headed."

The provost, a stout man who loved his ale, turned very red in the face. The Knights looked extremely foolish—the kender were now dancing around them in a circle—and all looked very black at Gerard, whom they clearly blamed for the entire incident.

"Let them," Gerard muttered, and dashed off after his prisoner.

The kender had a good head start. He was quick and nimble and accustomed to fleeing pursuit. Gerard was strong and a swift runner, but he was encumbered by his heavy, ceremonial armor, which clanked and rattled and jabbed him uncomfortably in several tender areas. He would likely have never even caught sight of the felon had not the kender stopped at several junctures to look around in amazement, demanding loudly to know, "Where did *this* come from?" staring at a newly built garrison, and, a little farther on, "What are all these doing here?" This in reference to the refugee housing. And "Who put *that* there?" This to a large sign posted by the town fathers proclaiming that Solace was a town in good standing and had paid its tribute to the dragon and was therefore a safe place to visit.

The kender seemed extremely disconcerted by the sign. He stood before it, eyeing it severely. "That can't stay there," he said loudly. "It will block the path of the funeral procession."

Gerard thought he had him at this point, but the kender gave a bound and a leap and dashed off again. Gerard was forced to halt to catch his breath. Running in the heavy armor in the heat caused his head to swim and sent little shooting stars bursting across his vision. He was close to the Inn, however, and he had the grim satisfaction of seeing the kender dash up the stairs and through the front door.

"Good," Gerard thought grimly. "I have him."

Removing his helm, he tossed it to the ground, and leaned back against the signpost until his breathing returned to normal, while he watched the stairs to make certain the kender didn't depart. Acting completely against regulations, Gerard divested himself of the pieces of armor that were chafing him the worst, wrapped them in his cloak, and stashed the bundle in a dark corner of the Inn's woodshed. He then walked over to the community water barrel and plunged the gourd deep into the water. The barrel stood in a shady spot beneath one of the vallenwoods. The water was cool and sweet. Gerard kept one eye on the door of the Inn and, lifting the dipper, dumped the water over his head.

The water trickled down his neck and breast, wonderfully refreshing. He took a long drink, slicked back his hair, wiped his face, picked up his helm and, tucking it beneath his arm, made the long ascent up the stairs to the Inn. He could hear the kender's voice quite clearly. Judging by his formal tones and unnaturally deep voice, the kender appeared to be making a speech.

" 'Caramon Majere was a very great hero. He fought dragons and undead and goblins and hobgoblins and ogres and draconians and lots of others I can't remember. He traveled back in time with this very device—right here, this very device—' " The kender resumed normal speech for a moment to say, "Then I show the crowd the device, Caramon. I'd show you that part, but I can't quite seem to find it right now. Don't worry, I won't let anyone touch it. Now, where was I?"

A pause and the sound of paper rustling.

Gerard continued climbing the stairs. He had never truly noticed just how many stairs there were before. His legs, already aching and stiff from running, burned, his breath came short. He wished he'd taken off all his armor. He was chagrined to see how far he'd let himself go. His formerly strong athlete's body was soft as a maiden's. He stopped on the landing to rest and heard the kender launch back into his speech.

" 'Caramon Majere traveled back in time. He saved Lady Crysania from the Abyss.' She'll be here, Caramon. She'll fly here on the back of a silver dragon. Goldmoon will be here, too, and Riverwind will come and their beautiful daughters and Silvanoshei, the king of the United Elven Nations, will be here, along with Gilthas, the new ambassador to the United Human Nations, and, of course, Laurana. Even Dalamar will be here! Think of that, Caramon! The Head of the Conclave coming to your funeral. He'll be standing right over there next to Palin, who's head of the White Robes, but then I guess you already know that, him being your son and all. At least, I think that's where they were standing. The last time I was here for your funeral I came after it was all over and everyone was going home. I heard about it later from Palin, who said that they were sorry. If they'd known I was coming they would have waited. I felt a bit insulted, but Palin said that they all thought I was dead, which I am, of course, only not at the moment. And because I missed your funeral the first time, that's why I had to try to hit it again."

Gerard groaned. Not only did he have to deal with a kender, he had to deal with a mad kender. Probably one of those who claimed to be "afflicted." He felt badly for Caramon, hoped the old man wasn't too upset by this incident. Caramon would probably be understanding. For reasons passing Gerard's comprehension, Caramon seemed to have a soft spot for the little nuisances.

"So anyway my speech goes on," the kender said. " 'Caramon Majere did all these things and more. He was a great hero and a great warrior, but do you know what he did best?' " The kender's voice softened. " 'He was a great friend. He was my friend, my very best friend in all of the world. I came back—or rather I came forward—to say this because I think it's important, and Fizban thought it was important, too, which is why he let me come. It seems to me that being a great friend is more important than being a great hero or a great warrior. Being a good friend is the most important thing there is. Just think, if everyone in the world were great friends, then we wouldn't be such terrible enemies. Some of you here are enemies now—' I look at Dalamar at this point, Caramon. I look at him very sternly, for he's done some things that haven't been at all nice. And then I go on and say, 'But you people are here today because you were friends with this one man and he was your friend, just like he was mine. And so maybe when we lay Caramon Majere to rest, we will each leave his grave with friendlier feelings toward everyone. And maybe that will be the beginning of peace.' And then I bow and that's the end. What do you think?"

Gerard arrived in the doorway in time to see the kender jump down off a table, from which vantage point he'd been delivering his speech, and run over to stand in front of Caramon. Laura was wiping her eyes on the corners of her apron. Her gully dwarf helper blubbered shamelessly in a corner, while the Inn's patrons were applauding wildly and banging their mugs on the table, shouting, "Hear, hear!"

Caramon Majere sat in one of the high-backed booths. He was smiling, a smile touched by the last golden rays of the sun, rays that seem to have slipped into the Inn on purpose just to say goodnight.

"I'm sorry this had to happen, sir," said Gerard, walking inside. "I didn't realize he would trouble you. I'll take him away now."

Caramon reached out his hand and stroked the kender's topknot, the hair of which was standing straight up, like the fur of a startled cat.

"He's not bothering me. I'm glad to see him again. That part about friendship was wonderful, Tas. Truly wonderful. Thank you."

Caramon frowned, shook his head. "But I don't understand the rest of what you said, Tas. All about the United Elven Nations and Riverwind coming to the Inn when he's been dead these many years. Something's peculiar here. I'll have to think about it." Caramon stood up from the booth and headed toward the door. "I'll just be taking my evening walk, now, Laura."

"Your dinner will be waiting when you come back, Father," she said. Smoothing her apron, she shook the gully dwarf, ordered him to pull himself together and get back to work.

"Don't think about it too long, Caramon," Tas called out. "Because of . . . well, you know."

He looked up at Gerard, who had laid a firm hand on the kender's shoulder, getting a good grip on flesh and bone this time.

"It's because he's going to be dead pretty soon," Tas said in a loud whisper. "I didn't like to mention that. It would have been rude, don't you think?"

"I think you're going to spend the next year in prison," said Gerard sternly.

Caramon Majere stood at the top of the stairs. "Yes, Tika, dear. I'm coming," he said. Putting his hand over his heart, he pitched forward, headfirst.

The kender tore himself free of Gerard, flung himself to the floor, and burst into tears.

Gerard moved swiftly, but he was too late to halt Caramon's fall. The big man tumbled and rolled down the stairs of his beloved Inn. Laura screamed. The patrons cried out in shock and alarm. People in the street, seeing Caramon falling, began to run toward the Inn.

Gerard dashed down the stairs as fast as ever he could and was the first to reach Caramon. He feared to find the big man in terrible pain, for he must have broken every bone in his body. Caramon did not appear to be suffering however. He had already left mortal cares and pain behind, his spirit lingering only long enough to say good-bye. Laura threw herself beside him on the ground. Taking hold of his hand, she held it pressed to her lips.

"Don't cry, my dear," he said softly, smiling. "Your mother's here with me. She'll take good care of me. I'll be fine."

"Oh, Daddy!" Laura sobbed. "Don't leave me yet!"

Caramon's eyes glanced around at the townspeople who had gathered. He smiled and gave a little nod. He continued to search through the crowd and he frowned.

"But where's Raistlin?" he asked.

Laura looked startled, but said, brokenly, "Father, your brother's been dead a long, long time—"

"He said he would wait for me," Caramon said, his voice beginning strong, but growing fainter. "He should be here. Tika's here. I don't understand. This is not right. Tas . . . What Tas said . . . A different future . . ."

His gaze came to Gerard. He beckoned the Knight to come near.

"There's something you must . . . do," said Caramon, his breath rasping in his chest.

Gerard knelt beside him, more touched by this man's death than he could have imagined possible. "Yes, sir," he said. "What is it?"

"Promise me . . ." Caramon whispered. "On your honor . . . as a Knight."

"I promise," said Gerard. He supposed that the old man was going to ask him to watch over his daughters or to take care of his grandchildren, one of whom was also a Solamnic Knight. "What would you have me do, sir?"

"Dalamar will know. . . . Take Tasslehoff to Dalamar," Caramon said and his voice was suddenly strong and firm. He looked intently at Gerard. "Do you promise? Do you swear that you will do this?"

"But, sir," Gerard faltered, "what you ask of me is impossible! No one has seen Dalamar for years. Most believe that he is dead. And as for this kender who calls himself Tasslehoff . . ."

Caramon reached out his hand, a hand that was bloody from his fall. He grasped hold of Gerard's most unwilling hand and gripped it tightly.

"I promise, sir," said Gerard.

Caramon smiled. He let out his breath and did not draw another. His eyes fixed in death, fixed on Gerard. The hand, even in death, did not relinquish its grip. Gerard had to pry the old man's fingers loose and was left with a smear of blood on his palm.

"I'll be happy to go with you to see Dalamar, Sir Knight, but I can't go tomorrow," said the kender, snuffling and wiping his tear-grimed face with the sleeve of his shirt. "I have to speak at Caramon's funeral."

4

A Strange Awakening

ilvan's arm was on fire. He couldn't put out the blaze, and no one would come help him. He called out for Samar and for his mother, but his calls went unanswered. He was angry, deeply angry, angry and hurt that they would not come, that they were ignoring him. Then he realized that the reason they were not coming was that they were angry with him. He had failed them. He had let them down, and they would come to him no more. . . .

With a great cry, Silvan woke himself. He opened his eyes to see above him a canopy of gray. His vision was slightly blurred, and he mistook the gray mass above him for the gray ceiling of the burial mound. His arm pained him, and he remembered the fire. Gasping, he shifted to put out the flames. Pain lanced through his arm and hammered in his head. He saw no flames, and he realized dazedly that the fire had been a dream. The pain in his left arm was not a dream, however. The pain was real. He examined the arm as best he could, though every movement of his head cost him a gasp.

Not much doubt. The arm was broken just above the

wrist. The flesh was swollen so that it looked like a monster arm, a strange color of greenish purple. He lay back down and stared around him, feeling sorry for himself, and wondered very much that his mother did not come to him when he was in such agony. . . .

"Mother!" Silvan sat up so suddenly that the pain coiled round his gut and caused him to vomit.

He had no idea how he came to be here or even where here was. He knew where he was supposed to be, knew he had been dispatched to bring help to his beleaguered people. He looked around, trying to gain some sense of the time. Night had passed. The sun shone in the sky. He had mistaken a canopy of gray leaves for the ceiling of the burial mound. Dead gray leaves, hanging listlessly from dead branches. Death had not come naturally, as with the fall of the year, causing them to release their hold on life and drift in a dream of reds and golds upon the crisp air. The life had been sucked from leaves and branches, trunk and roots, leaving them desicated, mummified but still standing, a husk, an empty mockery of life.

Silvan had never seen a blight of this kind attack so many trees before, and his soul shrank from the sight. He could not take time to consider it, however. He had to complete his mission.

The sky above was a pearl gray with a strange kind of shimmer that he put down to the aftereffects of the storm. Not so many hours have passed, he told himself. The army could hold out this long. I have not failed them utterly. I can still bring help.

He needed to splint his arm, and he searched through the forest undergrowth for a strong stick. Thinking he'd found what he sought, he put out his hand to grasp it. The stick disintegrated beneath his fingers, turned to dust. He stared, startled. The ash was wet and had a greasy feel to it. Repulsed, he wiped his hand on his shirt, wet from the rain.

All around him were gray trees. Gray and dying or gray and dead. The grass was gray, the weeds gray, the fallen branches gray, all with that look of having been sucked dry.

He'd seen something like this before or heard of something like this. . . . He didn't recall what, and he had no time to think. He searched with increasingly frantic urgency among the gray-covered undergrowth for a stick and found one eventually, a stick that was covered with dust but had not been struck with the strange blight. Placing the stick on his arm, gasping at the pain, he gritted his teeth against it. He ripped off a shred of his shirttail and tied the splint in place. He could hear the broken ends of the bone grind together. The pain and the hideous sound combined to nearly make him pass out. He sat hunched over, his head down, fighting the nausea, the sudden heat that swept over his body.

Finally, the star bursts cleared from his vision. The pain eased somewhat. Holding his injured left arm close to his body, Silvan staggered to his feet. The wind had died. He could no longer feel its guiding touch upon his face. He could not see the sun itself for the pearl gray clouds, but the light shone brightest in one portion of the sky, which meant that way must be east. Silvan put his back to the light and looked to the west.

He did not remember his fall or what had occurred just prior to the fall. He began to talk to himself, finding the sound of his voice comforting.

"The last thing I remember, I was within sight of the road I needed to take to reach Sithelnost," he said. He spoke in Silvanesti, the language of his childhood, the language his mother favored.

A hill rose up above him. He was standing in the bottom of a ravine, a ravine he vaguely remembered from the night before.

"Someone either climbed or fell down into the ravine," he said, eyeing a crooked trail left in the gray ash that covered the hillside. He smiled ruefully. "My guess would be that someone was me. I must have taken a misstep in the darkness, tumbled down the ravine. Which means," he added, heartened, "the road must lie right up there. I do not have far to go."

He began to climb back up the steep sides of the ravine, but this proved more difficult than he'd supposed. The gray ash had formed a silt with the rain and was slippery as goose grease. He slid down the hill twice, jarring his injured arm, causing him almost to lose consciousness.

"This will never do," Silvan muttered.

He stayed at the bottom of the ravine where the walking was easier, always keeping the top of the hill in sight, hoping to find an outcropping of rock that would act as a staircase up the slippery slope.

He stumbled over the uneven ground in a haze of pain and fear. Every step brought a jolt of pain to his arm. He pushed himself on, however, trudging through the gray mud that seemed to try to drag him down among the dead vegetation, searching for a way out of this gray vale of death that he grew to loathe as a prisoner loathes his cell.

He was parched with thirst. The taste of ash filled his mouth, and he longed for a drink of water to wash it away. He found a puddle once, but it was covered with a gray film, and he could not bring himself to drink from it. He staggered on.

"I have to reach the road," he said and repeated it many times like a mantra, matching his footfalls to its rhythm. "I have to go on," he said to himself dreamily, "because if I die down here, I will turn into one of the gray mummies like the trees and no one will ever find me."

The ravine came to a sudden end in a jumble of rock and fallen trees. Silvan straightened, drew in a deep breath and wiped chill sweat from his forehead. He rested a moment, then began to climb, his feet slipping on the rocks, sending him scrabbling backward more than once. Grimly, he pressed on, determined to escape the ravine if it proved to be the last act of his life. He drew nearer and nearer the top, up to the point where he thought he should have been able to see the road.

He peered out through the boles of the gray trees, certain the road must be there but unable to see it due to some sort of strange distortion of the air, a distortion that caused the trees to waver in his sight.

Silvan continued to climb.

"A mirage," he said. "Like seeing water in the middle of the road on a hot day. It will disappear when I come near it."

He reached the top of the hill and tried to see through the trees to the road he knew must lie beyond. In order to keep moving, moving through the pain, he had concentrated his focus upon the road until the road had become his one goal.

"I have to reach the road," he mumbled, picking up the mantra. "The road is the end of pain, the road will save me, save my people. Once I reach the road, I am certain to run into a band of elven scouts from my mother's army. I will turn over my mission to them. Then I will lie down upon the road and my pain will end and the gray ash will cover me . . ."

He slipped, nearly fell. Fear jolted him out of his terrible reverie. Silvan stood trembling, staring about, prodding his mind to return from whatever comforting place it had been trying to find refuge. He was only a few feet from the road. Here, he was thankful to see, the trees were not dead, though they appeared to be suffering from some sort of blight. The leaves were still green, though they drooped, wilting. The bark of the trunks had an unhealthy look to it, was staring to drop off in places.

He looked past them. He could see the road, but he could not see it clearly. The road wavered in his vision until he grew dizzy to look at it. He wondered uneasily if this was due to his fall.

"Perhaps I am going blind," he said to himself.

Frightened, he turned his head and looked behind him. His vision cleared. The gray trees stood straight, did not shimmer. Relieved, he looked back to the road. The distortion returned.

"Strange," he muttered. "I wonder what is causing this?"

His walk slowed involuntarily. He studied the distortion closely. He had the oddest impression that the distortion was like a cobweb spun by some horrific spider strung between him and the road, and he was reluctant to come near the shimmer. The disquieting feeling came over him that the shimmering web would seize him and hold him and suck him dry as it had sucked dry the trees. Yet beyond the distortion was the road, his goal, his hope.

He took a step toward the road and came to a sudden halt. He could not go on. Yet there lay the road, only a few steps away. Gritting his teeth, he shoved forward, cringing as if he expected to feel sticky web cling to his face.

Silvan's way was blocked. He felt nothing. No physical presence halted him, but he could not move. Rather, he could not move forward. He could move sideways, he could move backward. He could not move ahead.

"An invisible barrier. Gray ash. Trees dead and dying," he murmured.

He reached into the swirling depths of pain and fear and despair and brought forth the answer.

"The shield. This is the shield!" he repeated, aghast.

The magical shield that the Silvanesti had dropped over their homeland. He had never seen it, but he'd heard his mother describe it often enough. He had heard others describe the strange shimmer, the distortion in the air produced by the shield.

"It can't be," Silvan cried in frustration. "The shield cannot be here. It is south of my position! I was on the road, traveling west. The shield was south of me." He twisted, looked up to find the sun, but the clouds had thickened, and he could not see it.

The answer came to him and with it bitter despair. "I'm turned around," he said. "I've come all this way . . . and it's been the wrong way!"

Tears stung his eyelids. The thought of descending this hill, of going back down into the ravine, of retracing his steps, each step that had cost him so dearly in pain, was almost too much to bear. He sank down to the ground, gave way to his misery.

"Alhana! Mother," he said in agony, "forgive me! I have failed you! What have I ever done in life but fail you . . . ?"

"Who are you who speaks the name that is forbidden to speak?" said a voice. "Who are you who speaks the name Alhana?"

Silvan leaped to his feet. He dashed the tears from his eyes with a backhand smear, looked about, startled, to see who had spoken.

At first he saw only a patch of vibrant, living green, and he thought that he had discovered a portion of the forest untouched by the disease that had stricken the rest. But then the patch moved and shifted and revealed a face and eyes and mouth and hands, revealed itself to be an elf.

The elf's eyes were gray as the forest around him, but they were only reflecting the death he saw, revealing the grief he felt for the loss.

"Who am I who speaks my mother's name?" Silvan asked impatiently. "Her son, of course." He took a lurching step forward, hand outstretched. "But the battle . . . Tell me how the battle went! How did we fare?"

The elf drew back, away from Silvan's touch. "What battle?" he asked.

Silvan stared at the man. As he did so, he noted movement behind him. Three more elves emerged from the woods. He would have never seen them had they not stirred, and he wondered how long they had been there. Silvan did not recognize them, but that wasn't unusual. He did not venture out much among the common soldiers of his mother's forces. She did not encourage such companionship for her son, who was someday destined to be king, would one day be their ruler.

"The battle!" Silvan repeated impatiently. "We were attacked by ogres in the night! Surely, you must . . ."

Realization dawned on him. These elves were not dressed for warfare. They were clad in clothes meant for traveling. They might well not know of any battle.

"You must be part of the long-range patrol. You've come back in good time." Silvan paused, concentrated his thoughts, trying to penetrate the smothering fog of pain and despair. "We were attacked last night, during the storm. An army of ogres. I . . ." He paused, bit his lip, reluctant to reveal his failure. "I was sent to fetch aid. The Legion of Steel has a fortress near Sithelnost. Down that road." He made a feeble gesture. "I must have fallen. My arm is broken. I came the wrong way and now I must backtrack, and I don't have the strength. I can't make it, but you can. Take this message to the commander of the legion. Tell him that Alhana Starbreeze is under attack. . . ."

He stopped speaking. One of the elves had made a sound, a slight exclamation. The elf in the lead, the first to approach Silvan, raised his hand to impose silence.

Silvan was growing increasingly exasperated. He was mortifyingly aware that he cut but a poor figure, clutching his wounded arm to his side like a hurt bird dragging a wing. But he was desperate. The time must be midmorning now. He could not go on. He was very close to collapse. He drew himself up, draped in the cloak of his title and the dignity it lent him.

"You are in the service of my mother, Alhana Starbreeze," he said, his voice imperious. "She is not here, but her son,

Silvanoshei, your prince, stands before you. In her name and in my own, I command you to bear her message calling for deliverance to the Legion of Steel. Make haste! I am losing patience!"

He was also rapidly losing his grip on consciousness, but he didn't want these soldiers to think him weak. Wavering on his feet, he reached out a hand to steady himself on a tree trunk. The elves had not moved. They were staring at him now in wary astonishment that widened their almond eyes. They shifted their gazes to the road that lay beyond the shield, looked back at him.

"Why do you stand there staring at me?" Silvan cried. "Do as you are commanded! I am your prince!" A thought came to him. "You need have no fear of leaving me," he said. "I'll be all right." He waved his hand. "Just go! Go! Save our people!"

The lead elf moved closer, his gray eyes intent upon Silvan, looking through him, sifting, sorting.

"What do you mean that you went the wrong way upon the road?"

"Why do you waste time with foolish questions?" Silvan returned angrily. "I will report you to Samar! I will have you demoted!" He glowered at the elf, who continued to regard him steadily. "The shield lies to the south of the road. I was traveling to Sithelnost. I must have gotten turned around when I fell! Because the shield . . . the road . . ."

He turned around to stare behind him. He tried to think this through, but his head was too muzzy from the pain.

"It can't be," he whispered.

No matter what direction he would have taken, he must have still been able to reach the road, which lay outside the shield.

The road still lay outside the shield. *He* was the one who was inside it.

"Where am I?" he asked.

"You are in Silvanesti," answered the elf.

Silvan closed his eyes. All was lost. His failure was complete. He sank to his knees and pitched forward to lie face down in the gray ash. He heard voices but they were far away and receding rapidly.

"Do you think it is truly him?"

"Yes. It is."

"How can you be sure, Rolan? Perhaps it is a trick!"

"You saw him. You heard him. You heard the anguish in his voice, you saw the desperation in his eyes. His arm is broken. Look at the bruises on his face, his torn and muddy clothes. We found the trail in ash left by his fall. We heard him talking to himself when he did not know we were close by. We saw him try to reach the road. How can you possibly doubt?"

Silence, then, in a piercing hiss, "But how did he come through the shield?"

"Some god sent him to us," said the lead elf, and Silvan felt a gentle hand touch his cheek.

"What god?" The other was bitter, skeptical. "There are no gods."

Silvan woke to find his vision clear, his senses restored. A dull ache in his head made thinking difficult, and at first he was content to lie quite still, take in his surroundings, while his brain scrambled to make sense of what was happening. He remembered the road . . .

Silvan struggled to sit up.

A firm hand on his chest arrested his movement.

"Do not move too hastily. I have set your arm and wrapped it in a poultice that will speed the healing. But you must take care not to jar it."

Silvan looked at his surroundings. He had the thought at first that it had all been a dream, that he would wake to find himself once again in the burial mound. He had not been dreaming, however. The boles of the trees were the same as he remembered—ugly gray, diseased, dying. The bed of leaves on which he lay was a deathbed of rotting vegetation. The young trees and plants and flowers that carpeted the forest floor drooped and languished.

Silvanoshei took the elf's counsel and lay back down, more to give himself time to sort out the confusion over what had happened to him than because he needed the rest.

"How do you feel?" The elf's tone was respectful.

"My head hurts a little," Silvan replied. "But the pain in my arm is gone."

"Good," said the elf. "You may sit up then. Slowly, slowly. Otherwise you will pass out."

A strong arm assisted Silvan to a seated position. He felt a brief flash of dizziness and nausea, but he closed his eyes until the sick feeling passed.

The elf held a wooden bowl to Silvan's lips.

"What's this?" he asked, eying with suspicion the brown liquid the bowl contained.

"An herbal potion," replied the elf. "I believe that you have suffered a mild concussion. This will ease the pain in your head and promote the healing. Come, drink it. Why do you refuse?"

"I have been taught never to eat or drink anything unless I know who prepared it and I have seen others taste it first," Silvanoshei replied.

The elf was amazed. "Even from another elf?"

"*Especially* from another elf," Silvanoshei replied grimly.

"Ah," said the elf, regarding him with sorrow. "Yes, of course. I understand."

Silvan attempted to rise to his feet, but the dizziness assailed him again. The elf put the bowl to his own lips and drank several mouthfuls. Then, politely wiping the edge of the bowl, he offered it again to Silvanoshei.

"Consider this, young man. If I wanted you dead, I could have slain you while you were unconscious. Or I could have simply left you here." He cast a glance around at the gray and withered trees. "Your death would be slower and more painful, but it would come to you as it has come to too many of us."

Silvanoshei thought this over as best he could through the throbbing of his head. What the elf said made sense. He took the bowl in unsteady hands and lifted it to his lips. The liquid was bitter, smelled and tasted of tree bark. The potion suffused his body with a pleasant warmth. The pain in his head eased, the dizziness passed.

Silvanoshei saw that he had been a fool to think this elf was a member of his mother's army. This elf wore a cloak strange to Silvan, a cloak made of leather that had the appearance of leaves and sunlight and grass and brush and flowers. Unless the elf moved, he would blend into his forest surroundings so perfectly that he would never be detected. Here in the midst of death, he stood out; his cloak retaining the green memory of the living forest, as if in defiance.

"How long have I been unconscious?" Silvan asked.

"Several hours from when we found you this morning. It is Midyear's Day, if that helps you in your reckoning."

Silvan glanced around. "Where are the others?" He had the thought that they might be in hiding.

"Where they need to be," the elf answered.

"I thank you for helping me. You have business elsewhere, and so do I." Silvan rose to his feet. "I must go. It may be too late. . . ." He tasted bitter gall in his mouth, took a moment to choke it down. "I must still fulfill my mission. If you will show me the place I can use to pass back through the shield . . ."

The elf regarded him with that same strange intensity. "There is no way through the shield."

"But there has to be!" Silvan retorted angrily. "I came through, didn't I?" He glanced back at the trees standing near the road, saw the strange distortion. "I'll go back to the point where I fell. I'll pass through there."

Grimly, he started off, retracing his steps. The elf said no word to halt him but accompanied him, following after him in silence.

Could his mother and her army have held out against the ogres this long? Silvan had seen the army perform some incredible feats. He had to believe the answer was yes. He had to believe there was still time.

Silvan found the place where he must have entered the shield, found the trail his body had left as it rolled down the ravine. The gray ash had been slippery when he'd first tried to climb back up, but it had dried now. The way was easier. Taking care not to jar his injured arm, Silvan clambered up the hill. The elf waited in the bottom of the ravine, watching in silence.

Silvan reached the shield. As before, he was loathe to touch it. Yet here, this place, was where he'd entered it before, however unknowingly. He could see the gouge his boot heel had made in the mud. He could see the fallen tree crossing the path. Some dim memory of attempting to circumvent it returned.

The shield itself was not visible, except as a barely perceptible shimmer when the sun struck it at exactly the correct angle. Other than that, the only way he could tell the shield was before him was by its effect on his view of the trees and plants beyond it. He was reminded of heat waves rising from a sun-baked road, causing everything visible behind the waves to ripple in a mockery of water.

Gritting his teeth, Silvan walked straight into the shield.

The barrier would not let him pass. Worse, wherever he touched the shield, he felt a sickening sensation, as if the shield had pressed gray lips against his flesh and was seeking to suck him dry.

Shuddering, Silvan backed away. He would not try that again. He glared at the shield in impotent fury. His mother had worked for months to penetrate that barrier and for months she had failed. She had thrown armies against it, only to see them flung back. At peril to her own life, she had ridden her griffon into it without success. What could he do against it, one elf.

"Yet," Silvan argued in frustration, "I am inside it! The shield let me in. It will let me out! There must be a way. The elf. It must have something to do with the elf. He and his cohorts have entrapped me, imprisoned me."

Silvan whipped around to find the elf still standing at the bottom of the ravine. Silvan scrambled down the slope, half-falling, slipping and sliding on the rain-wet grass. The sun was sinking. Midyear's Day was the longest day of the year, but it must eventually give way to night. He reached the bottom of the ravine.

"You brought me in here!" Silvan said, so angry that he had to suck in a huge breath to even force the words out. "You *will* let me out. You *have* to let me out!"

"That was the bravest thing I ever saw a man do." The elf cast a dark glance at the shield. "I myself cannot bear to come near it, and I am no coward. Brave, yet hopeless. You cannot pass. None can pass."

"You lie!" Silvan raged. "You dragged me inside here. Let me out!"

Without really knowing what he was doing, he reached out his hand to seize the elf by the throat and choke him, force him to obey, frighten him into obeying.

The elf caught hold of Silvan's wrist, gave it an expert twist, and before he knew what was happening, Silvan found himself on his knees on the ground. The elf immediately released him.

"You are young, and you are in trouble. You do not know me. I make allowances. My name is Rolan. I am one of the kirath. My companions and I found you lying at the bottom of the ravine. That is the truth. If you know of the kirath, you know that we do not lie. I do not know how you came through the shield."

Silvan had heard his parents speak of the kirath, a band of elves who patrolled the borders of Silvanesti. The kirath's duty was to prevent the entrance of outsiders into Silvanesti.

Silvan sighed and lowered his head to his hands.

"I have failed them! Failed them, and now they will die!"

Rolan came near, put his hand upon the young elf's shoulder. "You spoke your name before when we first found you, but I would ask that you give it to me again. There is no need to fear and no reason to keep your identity a secret, unless, of course," he added delicately, "you bear a name of which you are ashamed."

Silvan looked up, stung. "I bear my name proudly. I speak it proudly. If my name brings about my death, so be it." His voice faltered, trembled. "The rest of my people are dead, by now. Dead or dying. Why should I be spared?"

He blinked the tears from his eyes, looked at his captor. "I am the son of those you term 'dark elves' but who are, in truth, the only elves to see clearly in the darkness that covers us all. I am the son of Alhana Starbreeze and Porthios of the Qualinesti. My name is Silvanoshei."

He expected laughter. Disbelief, certainly.

"And why do you think your name would bring death to you, Silvanoshei of the House of Caldaron?" Rolan asked calmly.

"Because my parents are dark elves. Because elven assassins have tried more than once to kill them," Silvan returned.

"Yet Alhana Starbreeze and her armies have tried many times to penetrate the shield, to enter into this land where she is outlaw. I have myself seen her, as I and my fellows walked the border lands."

"I thought you were forbidden to speak her name," Silvan muttered sullenly.

"We are forbidden to do many things in Silvanesti," Rolan added. "The list grows daily, it seems. Why does Alhana Starbreeze want to return to a land that does not want her?

"This is her home," Silvan answered. "Where else would she come?"

"And where else would her son come?" Rolan asked gently.

"Then you believe me?" Silvan asked.

"I knew your mother and your father, Your Highness," Rolan replied. "I was a gardener for the unfortunate King Lorac before the war. I knew your mother when she was a child. I fought with your father Porthios against the dream. You favor him in looks, but there is something of her inside you that brings her closer to the mind. Only the faithless do not believe. The miracle has occurred. You have returned to us. It does not surprise me that, for you, Your Highness, the shield would part."

"Yet it will not let me out," said Silvan dryly.

"Perhaps because you are where you are supposed to be, Your Highness. Your people need you."

"If that is true, then why don't you lift the shield and let my mother return to her kingdom?" Silvanoshei demanded. "Why keep her out? Why keep your own people out? The elves who fight for her are in peril. My mother would not now be battling ogres, would not be trapped—"

Rolan's face darkened. "Believe me, Your Majesty. If we, the kirath, could take down this accursed shield, we would. The shield casts a pall of despair on those who venture near it. It kills every living thing it touches. Look! Look at this, Your Majesty."

Rolan pointed to the corpse of a squirrel lying on the ground, her young lying dead around her. He pointed to golden birds buried in the ash, their song forever silenced.

"Thus our people are slowly dying," he said sadly.

"What is this you say?" Silvan was shocked. "Dying?"

"Many people, young and old, contract a wasting sickness for which there is no cure. Their skin turns gray as the skin of these poor trees, their limbs wither, their eyes dull. First they cannot run without tiring, then they cannot walk, then they cannot stand or sit. They waste away until death claims them."

"Then why don't you take down the shield?" Silvan demanded.

"We have tried to convince the people to unite and stand against General Konnal and the Heads of House, who decided to raise the shield. But most refuse to heed our words. They say the sickness is a plague brought to us from the outside. The shield is all that stands between them and the evils of the world. If it is removed, we all will die."

"Perhaps they are right," Silvan said, glancing back through the shield, thinking of the ogres attacking in the night. "There is no plague striking down elves, at least none that I have heard of. But there are other enemies. The world is fraught with danger. In here, at least you are safe."

"Your father said that we elves had to join the world, become a part of it," Rolan replied with a grim smile. "Otherwise we would wither away and die, like a branch that is cut from the tree or the—"

"—rose stripped from the bush," Silvan said and smiled in remembrance. "We haven't heard from my father in a long time," he added, looking down at the gray ash and smoothing it with the toe of his boot. "He was fighting the great dragon Beryl near Qualinesti, a land she holds in thrall. Some believe he is dead—my mother among them, although she refuses to admit it."

"If he died, he died fighting for a cause he believed in," Rolan said. "His death has meaning. Though it may seem pointless now, his sacrifice will help destroy the evil, bring back the light to drive away the darkness. He died a living man! Defiant, courageous. When our people die," Rolan continued, his voice taking on increasing bitterness, "one hardly notices their passing. The feather flutters and falls limp."

He looked at Silvan. "You are young, vibrant, alive. I feel

the life radiate from you, as once I felt it radiate from the sun. Contrast yourself with me. You see it, don't you: the fact that I am withering away? That we are all slowly being drained of life? Look at me, Your Highness. You can see I am dying."

Silvan did not know what to say. Certainly the elf was paler than normal, his skin had a gray tinge to it, but Silvan had put that down to age, perhaps, or to the gray dust. He recalled now that the other elves he had seen bore the same gaunt, hollow-eyed look.

"Our people will see you, and they will see by contrast what they have lost," Rolan pursued. "This is the reason you have been sent to us. To show them that there is no plague in the world outside. The only plague is within." Rolan laid his hand on his heart. "Within us! You will tell the people that if we rid ourselves of this shield, we will restore our land and ourselves to life."

Though my own has ended, Silvan said to himself. The pain returned. His head ached. His armed throbbed. Rolan regarded him with concern.

"You do not look well, Your Highness. We should leave this place. We have lingered near the shield too long already. You must come away before the sickness strikes you, as well."

Silvanoshei shook his head. "Thank you, Rolan, but I cannot leave. The Shield may yet open and let me out as it has let me in."

"If you stay here, you will die, Your Majesty," said Rolan. "Your mother would not want that. She would want you to come to Silvanost and to claim your rightful place upon the throne."

You will someday sit upon the throne of the United Elven Nations, Silvanoshei. On that day, you will right the wrongs of the past. You will purge our people of the sins we elves have committed, the sin of pride, the sin of prejudice, the sin of hatred. These sins have brought about our ruin. You will be our redemption.

His mother's words. He remembered the very first time

she had spoken them. He had been five or six. They were camping in the wilderness near Qualinesti. It was night. Silvan was asleep. Suddenly a cry pierced his dreams, brought him wide awake. The fire burned low, but by its light he could see his father grappling with what seemed a shadow. More shadows surrounded them. He saw nothing else because his mother flung her body over his, pressed him to the ground. He could not see, he could not breathe, he could not cry out. Her fear, her warmth, her weight crushed and smothered him.

And then it was all over. His mother's warm, dark weight was lifted from him. Alhana held him in her arms, cradling him, weeping and kissing him and asking him to forgive her if she hurt him. She had a bloody gash on her thigh. His father bore a deep knife wound in his shoulder, just missing the heart. The bodies of three elves, clad all in black, lay around the fire. Years later Silvanoshei woke suddenly in the night with the cold realization that one of those assassins had been sent to murder him.

They dragged away the bodies, left them to the wolves, not considering them worthy of proper burial rites. His mother rocked him to sleep, and she spoke those words to him to comfort him. He would hear them often, again and again.

Perhaps now she was dead. His father dead. Their dream lived, however, lived in him.

He turned away from the shield. "I will come with you," he said to Rolan of the kirath.

5

The Holy Fire

In the old days, the glory days, before the War of the Lance, the road that led from Neraka to the port city of Sanction had been well maintained, for that road was the only route through the mountains known as the Lords of Doom. The road—known as the Hundred Mile Road, for it was almost one hundred miles long, give or take a furlong or two—was paved with crushed rock. Thousands of feet had marched over the crushed rock during the intervening years; booted human feet, hairy goblin feet, clawed draconian feet. So many thousand that the rock had been pounded into the ground and was now deeply embedded.

During the height of the War of the Lance, the Hundred Mile Road had been clogged with men, beasts, and supply wagons. Anyone who had need of speed took to the air, riding on the backs of the swift-flying blue dragons or traversing the skies in floating citadels. Those forced to move along the road could be delayed for days, blocked by the hundreds of foot soldiers who slogged along its torturous route, either marching to the city of Neraka or marching away from it. Wagons lurched and jolted along the road. The grade was steep, descending from the high mountain valley all the way to sea level, making the journey a perilous one.

Wagons loaded with gold, silver, and steel, boxes of stolen jewels, booty looted from people the armies had conquered, were hauled by fearsome beasts known as mammoths, the only creatures strong enough to drag the heavily laden wagons up the mountain road. Occasionally one of the wagons would tip over and spill its contents or lose a wheel, or one of the mammoths would run berserk and trample its keepers and any one else unfortunate enough to be in its path. At these times, the road was shut down completely, bringing everything to a halt while officers tried to keep their men in order and fumed and fretted at the delay.

The mammoths were gone, died out. The men were gone too. Most of them now old. Some of them now dead. All of them now forgotten. The road was empty, deserted. Only the wind's whistling breath blew across the road, which, with its smooth, inlaid gravel surface, was considered one of the man-made wonders of Krynn.

The wind was at the backs of the Dark Knights as they galloped down the winding, twisting snake's back that was the Hundred Mile Road. The wind, a remnant of the storm, howled among the mountain tops, an echo of the Song of Death they had heard in Neraka, but only an echo, not as terrible, not as frightening. The Knights rode hard, rode in a daze, rode without any clear idea of why they rode or where they were heading. They rode in an ecstasy, an excitement that was unlike anything they had ever before experienced.

Certainly Galdar had felt nothing like it. He loped along at Mina's side, running with new-found strength. He could have run from here to Ice Wall without pause. He might have credited his energy to pure joy at regaining his severed limb, but he saw his awe and fervor reflected in the faces of the men who made that exhilarating, mad dash alongside him. It was as if they brought the storm with them—hooves thundering among the mountain walls, the iron shoes of the horses striking lightning bolts from the rock surface.

Mina rode at their head, urging them on when they would have stopped from fatigue, forcing them to look into themselves to find just a bit more strength than they knew they possessed. They rode through the night, their way lit by lightning flashes. They rode through the day, halting only to water the horses and eat a quick bite standing.

When it seemed the horses must founder, Mina called a halt. The Knights had traversed well over half the distance. As it was, her own roan, Foxfire, could have continued on. He appeared to actually resent the stop, for the horse stamped and snorted in displeasure, his irritated protests splitting the air and bouncing back from the mountain tops.

Foxfire was fiercely loyal to his mistress and to her alone. He had no use for any other being. During their first brief rest stop, Galdar had made the mistake of approaching the horse to hold Mina's stirrup as she dismounted, as he had been trained to do for his commander and with much better grace than he'd used for Ernst Magit. Foxfire's lip curled back over his teeth, his eyes gleamed with a wild, wicked light that gave Galdar some idea of how the beast had come by his name. Galdar hastily backed away.

Many horses are frightened by minotaurs. Thinking this might be the problem, Galdar ordered one of the others to attend the commander.

Mina countermanded his order. "Stay back, all of you. Foxfire has no love for any being other than myself. He obeys only my commands and then only when my commands agree with his own instincts. He is very protective of his rider, and I could not prevent him from lashing out at you if you came too near."

She dismounted nimbly, without aid. Removing her own saddle and bridle, she led Foxfire to drink. She fed him and brushed him down with her own hands. The rest of the soldiers tended to their own weary mounts, saw them safely settled for the night. Mina would not allow them to build a campfire. Solamnic eyes might be watching, she said. The fire would be visible a long distance.

The men were as tired as the horses. They'd had no sleep for two days and a night. The terror of the storm had drained them, the forced march left them all shaking with fatigue. The excitement that had carried them this far began to ebb. They looked like prisoners who have wakened from a wonderful dream of freedom to find that they still wear their shackles and their chains.

No longer crowned by lightning and robed with thunder, Mina looked like any other girl, and not even a very attractive girl, more like a scrawny youth. The Knights sat hunched over their food in the moonlit darkness, muttering that they'd been led on a fool's errand, casting Mina dark looks and angry glances. One man even went so far as to say that any of the dark mystics could have restored Galdar's arm, nothing so special in that.

Galdar could have silenced them by pointing out that no dark mystic had restored his arm, though he had begged them often enough. Whether they refused because their powers were not strong or because he lacked the steel to pay them, it was all the same to him. The dark mystics of the Knights of Neraka had not given him an arm. This strange girl had and he was dedicated to her for life. He kept quiet, however. He was ready to defend Mina with his life, should that become necessary, but he was curious to see how she would handle the increasingly tense situation.

Mina did not appear to notice that her command was slowly slipping away. She sat apart from the men, sat above them, perched on an enormous boulder. From her vantage point, she could look out across the mountain range, jagged black teeth taking a bite out of the starry sky. Here and there, fires from the active volcanoes were blots of orange against the black. Withdrawn, abstracted, she was absorbed in her thoughts to the point that she seemed totally unaware of the rising tide of mutiny at her back.

"I'll be damned if I'm riding to Sanction!" said one of the Knights. "You know what's waiting for us there. A thousand of the cursed Solamnics, that's what!"

"I'm off to Khur with the first light," said another. "I must have been thunderstruck to have come this far!"

"I'll not stand first watch," a third grumbled. "She won't let us have a fire to dry out our clothes or cook a decent meal. Let her stand first watch."

"Aye, let her stand first watch!" The others agreed.

"I intend to," said Mina calmly. Rising from her seat, she descended to the road. She stood astride it, her feet planted firmly. Arms crossed over her chest, she faced the men. "I will stand all the watches this night. You will need your rest for the morrow. You should sleep."

She was not angry. She was not sympathetic. She was certainly not pandering to them, did not seem to be agreeing with them in hope of gaining their favor. She was making a statement of fact, presenting a logical and rational argument. The men would need their rest for the morrow.

The Knights were mollified, but still angry, behaving like children who've been made the butt of a joke and don't like it. Mina ordered them to make up their beds and lie down.

The Knights did as they were told, grumbling that their blankets were still wet and how could she expect them to sleep on the hard rock? They vowed, one and all, to leave with the dawn.

Mina returned to her seat upon the boulder and looked out again at the stars and the rising moon. She began to sing.

The song was not like the Song of Death, the terrible dirge sung to them by the ghosts of Neraka. Mina's song was a battle song. A song sung by the brave as they march upon the foe, a song meant to stir the hearts of those who sing it, a song meant to strike terror into the hearts of their enemies.

> Glory calls us
> With trumpet's tongue,
> calls us do great deeds
> on the field of valor,
> calls us to give our blood
> to the flame,
> to the ground,
> the thirsty ground,
> the holy fire.

The song continued, a paean sung by the victors in their moment of triumph, a song of reminiscence sung by the old soldier telling his tale of valor.

Closing his eyes, Galdar saw deeds of courage and bravery, and he saw, thrilling with pride, that he was the one performing these heroic feats. His sword flared with the purple white of the lightning, he drank the blood of his enemies. He marched from one glorious battle to the next, this song of victory on his lips. Always Mina rode before him, leading him, inspiring him, urging him to follow her into the heart of the battle. The purple white glow that emanated from her shone on him.

The song ended. Galdar blinked, realized, to his astonishment and chagrin, that he had fallen asleep. He had not meant to, he had intended to stand watch with her. He rubbed his eyes, wished she would start singing again. The night was cold and empty without the song. He looked around to see if the others felt the same.

They slumbered deeply and peacefully, smiles on their lips. They had laid their swords within reach on the ground beside them. Their hands closed over the hilts as if they would leap up and race off to the fray in an instant. They were sharing Galdar's dream, the dream of the song.

Marveling, he looked at Mina to find her looking at him.

He rose to his feet, went to join her upon her rock.

"Do you know what I saw, Commander?" he asked.

Her amber eyes had caught the moon, encased it. "I know," she replied.

"Will you do that for me, for us? Will you lead us to victory?"

The amber eyes, holding the moon captive, turned upon him. "I will."

"Is it your god who promises you this?"

"It is," she replied gravely.

"Tell me the name of this god, that I may worship him," said Galdar.

Mina shook her head slowly, emphatically. Her gaze left the minotaur, went back to the sky, which was unusually dark, now that she had captured the moon. The light, the only light, was in her eyes. "It is not the right time."

"When will it be the right time?" Galdar pursued.

"Mortals have no faith in anything anymore. They are like men lost in a fog who can see no farther than their own noses, and so that is what they follow, if they follow anything at all. Some are so paralyzed with fear that they are afraid to move. The people must acquire faith in themselves before they are ready to believe in anything beyond themselves."

"Will you do this, Commander? Will you make this happen."

"Tomorrow, you will see a miracle," she said.

Galdar settled himself upon the rock. "Who are you, Commander?" he asked. "Where do you come from?"

Mina turned her gaze upon him and said, with a half-smile, "Who are you, Subcommander? Where do you come from?"

"Why, I'm a minotaur. I was born in—"

"No." She shook her head gently. "Where before that?"

"Before I was born?" Galdar was confused. "I don't know. No person does."

"Precisely," said Mina and turned away.

Galdar scratched his horned head, shrugged in his turn. Obviously she did not want to tell him, and why should she? It was none of his business. It made no difference to him. She was right. He had not believed in anything before this moment. Now he had found something in which to believe. He had found Mina.

She confronted him again, said abruptly, "Are you still tired?"

"No, Talon Leader, I am not," Galdar replied. He had slept only a few hours, but the sleep had left him unusually refreshed.

Mina shook her head. "Do not call me 'Talon Leader.' I want you to call me 'Mina.' "

"That is not right, Talon Leader," he protested. "Calling you by your name does not show proper respect."

"If the men have no respect for me, will it matter what they call me?" she returned. "Besides," she added with calm conviction, "the rank I hold does not yet exist."

Galdar really thought she was getting a bit above herself now, needed taking down a notch or two. "Perhaps you think you should be the 'Lord of the Night,' " he suggested by way of a joke, naming the highest rank that could be held by the Knights of Neraka.

Mina did not laugh. "Someday, the Lord of the Night will kneel down before me."

Galdar knew Lord Targonne well, had difficulty imagining the greedy, grasping, ambitious man kneeling to do anything unless it might be to scoop up a dropped copper. Galdar didn't quite know what to say to such a ludicrous concept and so fell silent, returning in his mind to the dream of glory, reaching for it as a parched man reaches out to water. He wanted so much to believe in it, wanted to believe it was more than mirage.

"If you are certain you are not tired, Galdar," Mina continued, "I want to ask a boon of you."

"Anything, Tal— Mina," he said, faltering.

"Tomorrow we ride into battle." A little frown line marred Mina's smooth complexion. "I have no weapon, nor have I ever been trained in the use of one. Have we time to do so tonight, do you think?"

Galdar's jaw went slack. He wondered if he'd heard correctly. He was so stunned, he could at first make no reply. "You . . . you've never wielded a weapon?"

Mina shook her head calmly.

"Have you ever been in battle, Mina?"

She shook her head again.

"Have you ever seen a battle?" Galdar was feeling desperate.

"No, Galdar." Mina smiled at him. "That is why I am asking for your help. We will go a little ways down the road to practice, so that we will not disturb the others. Do not worry. They will be safe. Foxfire would warn me if an enemy approached. Bring along whatever weapon you think would be easiest for me to learn."

Mina walked off down the road to find a suitable practice field, leaving an amazed Galdar to search through the weapons he and the others carried, to find one suitable for her, a girl who had never before held a weapon and who was, tomorrow, going to lead them into battle.

Galdar cudgeled his brain, tried to knock some common sense back into his head. A dream seemed reality, reality seemed a dream. Drawing his dagger, he stared at it a moment, watched the moonlight flow like quicksilver along the blade. He jabbed the point of the dagger into his arm, the arm Mina had restored to him. Stinging pain and the warm flow of blood indicated that the arm was real, confirmed that he was indeed awake.

Galdar had given his promise, and if he had one thing left to him in this life that he hadn't sold, battered, or flung away, it was his honor. He slid the dagger back into its sheath upon his belt and looked over the stock of weapons.

A sword was out of the question. There was no time to train her properly in its use, she would do more damage to herself or those around than to a foe. He could find nothing that he deemed suitable, and then he noticed the moonlight shining on one weapon in particular, as if it were trying to bring it to his attention—the weapon known as a morning star. Galdar eyed it. Frowning thoughtfully, he hefted it in his hand. The morning star is a battlehammer adorned with spikes on the end, spikes the fanciful said give it the look of a star, hence its name. The morning star was not heavy, took relatively little skill to learn to use, and was particularly effective against knights in armor. One simply bashed one's opponent with the morning star until his armor cracked like a nutshell. Of course, one had to avoid the enemy's own weapon while one was doing the bashing. Galdar picked up a small shield and, armed with these, trudged off down the road, leaving a horse to stand watch.

"I've gone mad," he muttered. "Stark, staring mad."

Mina had located an open space among the rocks, probably used as a wayside camping place for those long-ago armies that had marched along the road. She took hold of the morning star, eyed it critically, hefted it to test its weight and balance. Galdar showed her how to hold the shield, where to position it for best advantage. He instructed her in the use of the morning star, then gave her some simple exercises so that she could accustom herself to the feel of the weapon.

He was gratified (and relieved) to learn that Mina was a quick study. Though her frame was thin, she was well-muscled. Her balance was good, her movements were graceful and fluid. Galdar raised his own shield, let her take a few practice blows. Her first strike was impressive, her second drove him backward, her third put a great dent in his shield and jarred his arm to the marrow.

"I like this weapon, Galdar," she said approvingly. "You have chosen well."

Galdar grunted, rubbed his aching arm, and laid down his shield. Drawing his broadsword from its sheathe, he wrapped the sword in a cloak, bound the cloth around it tightly with rope, and took up a fighting stance.

"Now we go to work," he said.

At the end of two hours, Galdar was astonished at his pupil's progress.

"Are you certain you have never trained as a soldier?" he asked, pausing to catch his breath.

"I have never done so," said Mina. "Look, I will show you." Dropping her weapon, she held out the hand that had been wielding the morning star to the moonlight. "Judge my truthfulness."

Her soft palm was raw and bloody from opened blisters. Yet she had never once complained, never flinched in her strikes, though the pain of her wounds must have been excruciating.

Galdar regarded her with undisguised admiration. If there is one virtue the minotaurs prize, it is the ability to bear pain in stoic silence. "The spirit of some great warrior must live in you, Mina. My people believe that such a thing is possible. When one of our warriors dies courageously in battle, it is the custom in my tribe to cut out his heart and eat it, hoping that his spirit will enter our own."

"The only hearts I will eat will be those of my enemies," said Mina. "My strength and my skill are given to me by my god." She bent to pick up the morning star.

"No, no more practice this night," said Galdar, snatching it out from under her fingers. "We must tend to those blisters. Too bad," he said, eyeing her. "I fear that you will not be able to even set your hand to your horses' reins in the morning, much less hold a weapon. Perhaps we should wait here a few days until you are healed."

"We must reach Sanction tomorrow," said Mina. "So it is ordered. If we arrive a day late, the battle will be finished. Our troops will have suffered a terrible defeat."

"Sanction has long been besieged," Galdar said, disbelieving. "Ever since the foul Solamnics made a pact with that bastard who rules the city, Hogan Bight. We cannot dislodge them, and they do not have the strength to drive us back. The battle is at a stalemate. We attack the walls every day and they defend. Civilians are killed. Parts of the city catch fire. Eventually they'll grow weary of this and surrender. The siege has lasted for well over a year now. I don't see that a single day will make any difference. Stay here and rest."

"You do not see because your eyes are not yet fully open," Mina said. "Bring me some water to wash my hands and some cloth to wipe them clean of blood. Have no fear. I will be able to ride and to fight."

"Why not heal yourself, Mina?" Galdar suggested, testing her, hoping to see another miracle. "Heal yourself as you healed me."

Her amber eyes caught the light of the coming dawn, just starting to brighten the sky. She looked into the dawn and the thought came to his mind that she was already seeing tomorrow's sunset.

"Many hundreds will die in terrible agony," she said in a soft voice. "The pain I bear, I bear in tribute to them. I give it as gift to my god. Rouse the others, Galdar. It is time."

Galdar expected more than half the soldiers to depart, as they had threatened to do in the night. He found on his return to camp that the men were already up and stirring. They were in excellent spirits, confident, excited, speaking of the bold deeds they would do this day. Deeds that they said had come to them in dreams more real than waking.

Mina appeared among them, carrying her shield and her morning star in hands that still bled. Galdar watched her with concern. She was weary from her exercise and from the previous day's hard ride. Standing upon the road, isolated, alone, she seemed suddenly mortal, fragile. Her head drooped, her shoulders sagged. Her hands must burn and sting, her muscles ache. She sighed deeply and looked heavenward, as if questioning whether or not she truly had the strength to carry on.

At sight of her, the Knights lifted their swords, clashed them against their shields in salute.

"Mina! Mina!" they chanted and their chants bounded back from the mountains with the stirring sound of a clarion's call.

Mina lifted her head. The salute was wine to her flagging spirits. Her lips parted, she drank it in. Weariness fell from her like cast-off rags. Her armor shone red in the lurid light of the rising sun.

"Ride hard. We ride this day to glory," she told them, and the Knights cheered wildly.

Foxfire came at her command. She mounted and grasped the reins firmly in her bleeding, blistered hands. It was then that Galdar, taking his place alongside her, running at her stirrup, noted that she wore around her neck a silver medallion upon a silver chain. He looked at it closely, to see what the medallion might have engraved upon its surface.

The medallion was blank. Plain silver, without mark. Strange. Why should anyone wear a blank medallion? He had no chance to ask her, for at that instant Mina struck her spurs to her horse's flank.

Foxfire galloped down the road.

Mina's Knights rode behind her.

6

The Funeral of Caramon Majere

t the rising of the sun—a splendid dawn of gold and purple with a heart of deep, vibrant red—the people of Solace gathered outside the Inn of the Last Home in silent vigil, offering their love and their respect for the brave, good and gentle man who lay inside.

There was little talk. The people stood in silence presaging the great silence that will fall eventually upon us all. Mothers quieted fretful children, who stared at the Inn, ablaze with lights, not understanding what had happened, only sensing that it was something great and awful, a sensation that impressed itself upon their unformed minds, one they would remember to the end of their own days.

"I'm truly sorry, Laura," Tas said to her in the quiet hour before dawn.

Laura stood beside the booth where Caramon was accustomed to have his breakfast. She stood there doing nothing, staring at nothing, her face pale and drawn.

"Caramon was my very best friend in all the world," Tas told her.

"Thank you." She smiled, though her smile trembled. Her eyes were red from weeping.

"Tasslehoff," the kender reminded her, thinking she had forgotten his name.

"Yes." Laura appeared uneasy. "Er . . . Tasslehoff."

"I *am* Tasslehoff Burrfoot. The original," the kender added, recalling his thirty-seven namesakes—thirty-nine counting the dogs. "Caramon recognized me. He gave me a hug and said he was glad to see me."

Laura regarded him uncertainly. "You certainly do *look* like Tasslehoff. But then I was just a little girl the last time I remember seeing him, and all kender look alike anyway, and it just doesn't make sense! Tasslehoff Burrfoot's been dead these thirty years!"

Tas would have explained—all about the Device of Time Journeying and Fizban having set the device wrong the first time so that Tas had arrived at Caramon's first funeral too late to give his speech, but there was a lump of sadness caught in the kender's gullet, a lump so very big that it prevented the words from coming out.

Laura's gaze went to the stairs of the Inn. Her eyes filled again with tears. She put her head in her hands.

"There, there," Tas said, patting her shoulder. "Palin will be here soon. He knows who I am, and he'll be able to explain everything."

"Palin won't be here," Laura sobbed. "I can't get word to him. It's too dangerous! His own father dead and him not able to come to the burial. His wife and my dear sister trapped in Haven, since the dragon's closed the roads. Only me here to say good-bye to father. It's too hard! Too hard to bear!"

"Why, of course, Palin will be here," Tas stated, wondering what dragon had closed the roads and why. He meant to ask, but with all the other thoughts in his mind, this one couldn't battle its way to the front. "There's that young wizard staying here in the Inn. Room Seventeen. His name is . . . well, I forget his name, but you'll send him to the Tower of High Sorcery in Wayreth, where Palin is Head of the Order of White Robes."

"What tower in Wayreth?" Laura said. She had stopped crying and was looking puzzled. "The tower's gone, disappeared, just like the tower in Palanthas. Palin was head of the Academy of Sorcery, but he doesn't even have that, anymore. The dragon Beryl destroyed the academy a year ago, almost to this date. And there is no Room Seventeen. Not since the Inn was rebuilt the second time."

Tas, busy with remembering, wasn't listening. "Palin will come right away and he'll bring Dalamar, too, and Jenna. Palin will send the messengers to Lady Crysania in the Temple of Paladine and to Goldmoon and Riverwind in Queshu and Laurana and Gilthas and Silvanoshei in Silvanesti. They'll all be here soon so we . . . we . . ."

Tas's voice trailed off.

Laura was staring at him as if he'd suddenly sprouted two heads. Tas knew because he'd felt that same expression on his own face when he'd been in the presence of a troll who had done that very thing. Slowly, keeping her eyes on Tas, Laura edged away from him.

"You sit right down here," she said, and her voice was very soft and very gentle. "Sit right here, and I'll . . . I'll bring you a big plate of—"

"Spiced potatoes?" Tas asked brightly. If anything could get rid of the lump in his throat, it was Otik's spiced potatoes.

"Yes, a big, heaping dish of spiced potatoes. We haven't lit the cook fires yet this morning, and Cook was so upset I gave her the day off, so it may take me awhile. You sit down and promise you won't go anywhere," Laura said, backing away from the table. She slid a chair in between her and Tas.

"Oh, I won't go anywhere at all," Tas promised, plopping himself down. "I have to speak at the funeral, you know."

"Yes, that's right." Laura pressed her lips tightly together with the result that she wasn't able to say anything for a few moments. Drawing in a deep breath, she added, "You have to speak at the funeral. Stay here, that's a good kender."

"Good" and "kender" being two words that were rarely, if ever, linked, Tasslehoff spent the time sitting at the table, thinking about what a good kender might be and wondering if he was one himself. He assumed he probably was, since he was a hero and all that. Having settled this question to his satisfaction, he took out his notes and went over his speech, humming a little tune to keep himself company and to help the sadness work its way down his windpipe.

He heard Laura talking to a young man, perhaps the wizard in Room Seventeen, but Tas didn't really pay much attention to what she was saying, since it seemed to involve a poor person who was afflicted, a person who had gone crazy and might be dangerous. At any other time, Tas would have been interested to see a dangerous, afflicted, crazy person, but he had his speech to worry about, and since that was the reason he'd made this trip in the first place—or rather, in the second place—he concentrated on that.

He was still concentrating on it, along with a plate of potatoes and a mug of ale, when he became aware that a tall person was standing over him wearing a grim expression.

"Oh, hullo," Tas said, looking up smiling to see that the tall person was actually his extremely good friend, the Knight who'd arrested him yesterday. Since the Knight was an extremely good friend, it was a pity Tas couldn't recall his name. "Please, sit down. Would you like some potatoes? Maybe some eggs?"

The Knight refused all offers of anything to eat or drink. He took a seat opposite Tas, regarded the kender with a stern expression.

"I understand that you have been causing trouble," the Knight said in a cold and nasty flat tone of voice.

It just so happened that at that moment Tasslehoff was

rather proud of himself for *not* causing any trouble. He'd been sitting quietly at the table, thinking sad thoughts of Caramon's being gone and happy thoughts of the wonderful time they'd spent together. He hadn't once looked to see if there might be something interesting in the wood box. He had foregone his usual inspection of the silver chest, and he had only acquired one strange purse, and while he didn't exactly remember how he had come by that, he had to assume that someone had dropped it. He'd be sure to return it after the funeral.

Tas was therefore justifiably resentful of the Knight's implication. He fixed the Knight with a stern eye—dueling stern eyes, as it were. "I'm sure you don't mean to be ugly," Tas said. "You're upset. I understand."

The young Knight's face took on a very peculiar color, going extremely red, almost purple. He tried to say something, but he was so angry that when he opened his mouth, only sputters came out.

"I see the problem," Tas said, correcting himself. "No wonder you didn't understand me. I didn't mean 'ugly' as in 'ugly.' I was referring to your disposition, not your face, which is, however, a remarkably ugly one. I don't know when I've seen one uglier. Still, I know you can't mend your face, and perhaps you can't mend your disposition either, being a Solamnic Knight and all, but you have made a mistake. I have *not* been causing trouble. I have been sitting at this table eating potatoes—they're really quite good, are you sure you won't have some? Well, if you won't, I'll just finish up these last few. Where was I? Oh, yes. I've been sitting here eating and working on my speech. For the funeral."

When the Knight was finally able to speak without sputters, his tone was even colder and nastier, if such a thing were possible. "Mistress Laura sent word through one of the customers that you were scaring her with your outlandish and irrational statements. My superiors sent me to bring you back to jail. They would also like to know," he added, his tone grim, "how you managed to get out of jail this morning."

"I'll be very happy to come back to the jail with you. It was a very nice jail," Tas answered politely. "I've never seen one that was kender-proof before. I'll go back with you right after the funeral. I missed the funeral once, you see. I can't miss it again. Oops! No, I forgot." Tas sighed. "I can't go back to the jail with you." He really wished he could remember the Knight's name. He didn't like to ask. It wasn't polite. "I have to return to my own time right away. I promised Fizban I wouldn't go gallivanting. Perhaps I could visit your jail another time."

"Maybe you should let him stay, Sir Gerard," Laura said, coming up to stand beside them, twisting her apron in her hands. "He seems very determined, and I wouldn't want him to cause any trouble. Besides"—her tears started to flow—"maybe he's telling the truth! After all, Father thought he was Tasslehoff."

Gerard! Tas was vastly relieved. Gerard was the knight's name.

"He did?" Gerard was skeptical. "He said so?"

"Yes," Laura said, wiping her eyes with her apron. "The kender walked into the Inn. Daddy was sitting here in his usual place. The kender walked right up to him and said, 'Hullo, Caramon! I've come to speak at your funeral. I'm a little bit early, so I thought you might like to hear what I'm going to say,' and Daddy looked at him in surprise. At first I don't think he believed him, but then he looked at him closer and cried out, 'Tas!' And he gave him a big hug."

"He did." Tas felt a snuffle coming on. "He hugged me, and he said he was glad to see me and where had I been all this time? I said that it was a very long story and time was the one thing he didn't have a lot of so I should really let him hear the speech first." Giving way to the snuffle, Tas mopped his dribbling nose with his sleeve.

"Perhaps we could let him stay for the funeral," Laura urged. "I think it would have pleased Daddy. If you could . . . well . . . just keep an eye on him."

Gerard was clearly dubious. He even ventured to argue with her, but Laura had made up her mind, and she was very much like her mother. When her mind was made up, an army of dragons would not move her.

Laura opened the doors to the Inn to let in the sunshine, to let in life and to let in the living who came to pay their respects to the dead. Caramon Majere lay in a simple wooden casket in front of the great fireplace of the Inn he loved. No fire burned, only ashes filled the grate. The people of Solace filed past, each pausing to offer something to the dead—a silent farewell, a quiet blessing, a favorite toy, fresh-picked flowers.

The mourners noted that his expression was peaceful, even cheerful, more cheerful than they had seen him since his beloved Tika died. "Somewhere, they're together," people said and smiled through their tears.

Laura stood near the door, accepting condolences. She was dressed in the clothes she wore for work—a snowy white blouse, a clean fresh apron, a pretty skirt of royal blue with white petticoats. People wondered that she wasn't draped head to toe in black.

"Father would not have wanted me to," was her simple reply.

People said it was sad that Laura was the only member of the family to be present to lay their father to rest. Dezra, her sister, had been in Haven purchasing hops for the Inn's famous ale, only to be trapped there when the dragon Beryl attacked the city. Dezra had managed to smuggle word to her sister that she was safe and well, but she dared not try to return; the roads were not safe for travelers.

As for Caramon's son, Palin, he was gone from Solace on yet another of his mysterious journeys. If Laura knew where he was, she didn't say. His wife, Usha, a portrait painter of some renown, had traveled to Haven as company for Dezra. Since Usha had painted the portraits of families of some of the commanders of the Knights of Neraka, she was involved in negotiations to try to win a guarantee of safe passage for herself and for Dezra. Usha's children, Ulin and Linsha, were off on adventures of their own. Linsha, a Solamnic Knight, had not been heard from in many months. Ulin had gone away after hearing a report of some magical artifact and was believed to be in Palanthas.

Tas sat in a booth, under guard, the Knight Gerard at his side. Watching the people file in, the kender shook his head.

"But I tell you this isn't the way Caramon's funeral's supposed to be," Tasslehoff repeated insistently.

"Shut your mouth, you little fiend," Gerard ordered in a low, harsh tone. "This is hard enough on Laura and her father's friends without you making matters worse with your foolish chatter." To emphasize his words, he gripped the kender's shoulder hard, gave him a good shake.

"You're hurting me," Tas protested.

"Good," Gerard growled. "Now just keep quiet, and do as you're told."

Tas kept quiet, a remarkable feat for him, but one that was easier at this moment than any of his friends might have had reason to expect. His unaccustomed silence was due to the lump of sadness that was still stuck in his throat and that he could not seem to swallow. The sadness was all mixed up with the confusion that was muddling his mind and making it hard to think.

Caramon's funeral was not going at all the way it was meant to go. Tas knew this quite well because he'd been to Caramon's funeral once already and remembered how it went. This wasn't it. Consequently, Tas wasn't enjoying himself nearly as much as he'd expected.

Things were wrong. All wrong. Utterly wrong. Completely and irretrievably wrong. None of the dignitaries were here who were supposed to be here. Palin hadn't arrived, and Tas began to think that perhaps Laura was right and he wasn't going to arrive. Lady Crysania did not come. Goldmoon and Riverwind were missing. Dalamar did not suddenly appear, materializing out of the shadows and giving everyone a good scare. Tas discovered that he couldn't give his speech. The lump was too big and wouldn't let him. Just one more thing that was wrong.

The crowds were large—the entire population of Solace and surrounding communities came to pay their final respects and to extol the memory of the beloved man. But the crowds were not as large as they had been at Caramon's first funeral.

Caramon was buried near the Inn he loved, next to the graves of his wife and sons. The vallenwood sapling Caramon had planted in honor of Tika was young and thriving. The vallenwoods he had planted for his fallen sons were full-grown trees, standing tall and proud as the guard provided by the Knights of Solamnia, who accorded Caramon the honor rarely performed for a man who was not a Knight: escorting his coffin to the burial site. Laura planted the vallenwood in her father's memory, planted the tree in the very heart of Solace, near the tree she had planted for her mother. The couple had been the heart of Solace for many years, and everyone felt it was fitting.

The sapling stood uneasily in the fresh-turned earth, looking lost and forlorn. The people said what was in their hearts, paid their tribute. The Knights sheathed their swords with solemn faces, and the funeral was over. Everyone went home to dinner.

The Inn was closed for the first time since the red dragon had picked it up and hurled it out of its tree during the War of the Lance. Laura's friends offered to spend the first lonely nights with her, but she refused, saying that she wanted to have her cry in private. She sent home Cook, who was in such a state that when she finally did come back to work, she did not need to use any salt in the food for the tears she dripped into it. As for the gully dwarf, he had not moved from the corner into which he'd collapsed the moment he heard of Caramon's death. He lay in a huddled heap wailing and howling dismally until, to everyone's relief, he cried himself to sleep.

"Good-bye, Laura," said Tas, reaching out his hand. He and Gerard were the last to leave; the kender having refused to budge until everyone was gone and he was quite certain that nothing was going to happen the way it was intended to happen. "The funeral was very nice. Not as nice as the other funeral, but then I guess you couldn't help that. I really do *not* understand what is going on. Perhaps that's why Caramon told Sir Gerard to take me to see Dalamar, which I would, except that I think Fizban might consider that to be gallivanting. But, anyway, good-bye and thank you."

Laura looked down at the kender, who was no longer jaunty and cheerful but looking very forlorn and bereft and downcast. Suddenly, Laura knelt beside him and enfolded him in her arms.

"I do believe you're Tasslehoff!" she said to him softly, fiercely. "Thank you for coming." She hugged the breath from his small body and then turned and ran through the door leading to the family's private quarters. "Lock up, will you, Sir Gerard?" she called out over her shoulder and shut and locked the door behind her.

The Inn was quiet. The only sound that could be heard was the rustling of the leaves of the vallenwood tree and the creaking of the branches. The rustling had a weepy sound to it, and it seemed that the branches were lamenting. Tas had never seen the Inn empty before. Looking around, he remembered the night they had all met here after their five-year separation. He could see Flint's face and hear his gruff complaining, he could see Caramon standing protectively near his twin brother, he could see Raistlin's sharp eyes keeping watch over everything. He could almost hear Goldmoon's song again.

> The staff flares in blue light
> And both of them vanish;
> The grasslands are faded, and autumn is here.

"Everyone's vanished," Tas said to himself softly, and felt another snuffle coming on.

"Let's go," said Gerard.

Hand on the kender's shoulder, the Knight steered Tas toward the door, where he brought the kender to a halt to remove several articles of a valuable nature, which had happened to tumble into his pouches. Gerard left them on the bar for their owners to reclaim. This done, he took down the key that hung from a hook on the wall near the door, and locked the door. He hung the key on a hook outside the Inn, placed there in case anyone needed a room after hours, and then marched the kender down the stairs.

"Where are we going?" Tas asked. "What's that bundle you're carrying? Can I look inside? Are you going to take me to see Dalamar? I haven't seen him in a long time. Did you ever hear the story of how I met Dalamar? Caramon and I were—"

"Just shut up, will you?" Gerard said in a nasty, snapping sort of way. "Your chatter is giving me a headache. As to where we're going, we're returning to the garrison. And speaking of the bundle I'm carrying, if you touch it I'll run you through with my sword."

The Knight would say nothing more than that, although Tas asked and asked and tried to guess and then asked if he'd guessed right and if not, could Gerard give him a clue. Was what was in the bundle bigger than a breadbox? Was it a cat? Was it a cat in a breadbox? All to no avail. The Knight said nothing. His grip on the kender was firm.

The two of them arrived at the Solamnic garrison. The guards on duty greeted the Knight distantly. Sir Gerard did not return their greetings but said that he needed to see the Lord of Shields. The guards, who were members of the Lord of Shield's own personal retinue, replied that his lordship had just returned from the funeral and left orders not to be disturbed. They wanted to know the nature of Gerard's request.

"The matter is personal," the knight said. "Tell his lordship that I seek a ruling on the Measure. My need is urgent."

A guardsman departed. He returned a moment later to say, grudgingly, that Sir Gerard was to go in.

Gerard started to enter with Tasslehoff in tow.

"Not so fast, sir," the guard said, blocking their way with his halberd. "The Lord of Shields said nothing about a kender."

"The kender is in my custody," said Gerard, "as ordered by the lord himself. I have not been given leave to release him from my care. I would, however, be willing to leave him here with you if you will guarantee that he does no harm during the time I am with His Lordship—which may be several hours, my dilemma is complex—and that he will be here when I return."

The Knight hesitated.

"He will be pleased to tell you his story of how he first met the wizard Dalamar," Gerard added dryly.

"Take him," said the Knight.

Tas and his escort entered the garrison, passing through the gate that stood in the center of a tall fence made of wooden poles, each planed to a sharp point at the top. Inside the garrison were stables for the horses, a small training field with a target set up for archery practice, and several buildings. The garrison was not a large one. Having been established to house those who guarded the Tomb of the Heroes, it had been expanded to accommodate the Knights who would make what would probably be a last-stand defence of Solace if the dragon Beryl attacked.

Gerard had been thinking with some elation that his days of guarding a tomb might be drawing to a close, that battle with the dragon was imminent, though he and all the Knights were under orders not mention this to anyone. The Knights had no proof that Beryl was preparing to sweep down on Solace and they did not want to provoke her into attacking. But the Solamnic commanders were quietly making plans.

Inside the stockade, a long, low building provided sleeping quarters for the Knights and the soldiers under their command. In addition, there were several outbuildings used for storage and an administrative building, where the head of the garrison had his own lodgings. These doubled as his office.

His lordship's aide-de-camp met Gerard and ushered him inside. "His lordship will be with you shortly, Sir Gerard," said the aide.

"Gerard!" called out a woman's voice. "How good to see you! I thought I heard your name."

Lady Warren was a handsome woman of about sixty years with white hair and a complexion the color of warm tea. Throughout their forty years of marriage, she had accompanied her husband on all his journeys. As gruff and bluff as any soldier, she presently wore an apron covered with flour. She kissed Gerard on his cheek—he stood stiffly at attention, his helm beneath his arm—and glanced askance at the kender.

"Oh, dear," she said. "Midge!" she called to the back of the house in a voice that might have rung across the battlefield, "lock up my jewels!"

"Tasslehoff Burrfoot, ma'am," said Tas, offering his hand.

"Who isn't these days?" Lady Warren returned and promptly thrust her flour-covered hands that sparkled with several interesting looking rings beneath her apron. "And how are your dear father and mother, Gerard?"

"Quite well, I thank you, ma'am," said Gerard.

"You naughty boy." Lady Warren scolded, shaking her finger at him. "You know nothing about their health at all. You haven't written to your dear mother in two months. She writes to my husband to complain and asks him, most pathetically, if you are well and keeping your feet dry. For shame. To worry your good mother so! His lordship has promised that you shall write to her this very day. I wouldn't be surprised if he didn't sit you down and have you compose the letter while you are in there with him."

"Yes, ma'am," said Gerard.

"Now I must go finish the baking. Midge and I are taking one hundred loaves of bread to Laura to help keep the Inn going, poor thing. Ah, it's a sad day for Solace." Lady Warren wiped her face with her hand, leaving a smear of flour behind.

"Yes, ma'am," said Gerard.

"You may go in now," said the aide and opened a door leading from the main lodging to the lord's personal quarters.

Lady Warren took her leave, asking to be remembered to Gerard's dear mother. Gerard promised, his voice expressionless, that he would do so. Bowing, he left to follow the aide.

A large man of middle years with the black skin common to the people of Southern Ergoth greeted the young man warmly, a greeting the young Knight returned with equal and unusual warmth.

"I'm glad you stopped by, Gerard!" said Lord Warren. "Come and sit down. So this is the kender, is it?"

"Yes, sir. Thank you, sir. I'll be with you in a moment." Gerard led Tas to a chair, plunked him down, and took out a length of rope. Acting so swiftly that Tas did not have time to protest, the Knight tied the kender's wrists to the chair's arms. He then brought out a gag and wrapped it around Tas's mouth.

"Is that necessary?" Lord Warren asked mildly.

"If we want to have any semblance of a rational conversation, it is, sir," Gerard replied, drawing up a chair. He placed the mysterious bundle on the floor at his feet. "Otherwise you would hear stories about how this was the second time Caramon Majere had died. The kender would tell you how this funeral differed from Caramon Majere's first funeral. You would hear a recitation of who attended the first time and who wasn't at this one."

"Indeed." Lord Warren's face took on a softened, pitying look. "He must be one of the afflicted ones. Poor thing."

"What's an afflicted one?" Tas asked, except that due to the gag the words came out all gruff and grumbly, sounding as if he were speaking dwarven with a touch of gnome thrown in for good measure. Consequently no one understood him, and no one bothered to answer.

Gerard and Lord Warren began to discuss the funeral. Lord Warren spoke in such warm tones about Caramon that the lump of sadness returned to Tas's throat with the result that he didn't need the gag at all.

"And now, Gerard, what can I do for you?" Lord Warren asked, when the subject of the funeral was exhausted. He regarded the young Knight intently. "My aide said you had a question about the Measure."

"Yes, my lord. I require a ruling."

"You, Gerard?" Lord Warren raised a graying eyebrow. "Since when do you give a damn about the dictates of the Measure?"

Gerard flushed, looked uncomfortable.

Lord Warren smiled at the Knight's discomfiture. "I've heard you express yourself quite clearly regarding what you consider to be the 'old-fashioned, hidebound' way of doing things—"

Gerard shifted in his chair. "Sir, I may have, on occasion, expressed my doubts about certain precepts of the Measure—"

Lord Warren's eyebrow twitched even higher.

Gerard considered that it was time to change the subject. "My lord, an incident occurred yesterday. There were several civilians present. There will be questions asked."

Lord Warren looked grave. "Will this require a Knight's Council?"

"No, my lord. I hold you in the highest esteem, and I will respect your decision concerning this matter. A task has been given me, and I need to know whether or not I should pursue it or if I may, in honor, refuse."

"Who gave you this task? Another Knight?" Lord Warren appeared uneasy. He knew of the rancor that existed between Gerard and the rest of the Knights in the garrison. He had long feared that some quarrel would break out, perhaps resulting in some foolish challenge on the field of honor.

"No, sir," Gerard answered evenly. "The task was given to me by a dying man."

"Ah!" said Lord Warren. "Caramon Majere."

"Yes, my lord."

"A last request?"

"Not so much a request, my lord," said Gerard. "An assignment. I would almost say an order, but Majere was not of the Knighthood."

"Not by birth, perhaps," said Lord Warren gently, "but in spirit there was no better Knight living."

"Yes, my lord." Gerard was silent a moment, and Tas saw, for the first time, that the young man was truly grieved at Caramon's death.

"The last wishes of the dying are sacred to the Measure, which states such wishes must be fulfilled if it be mortally possible. The Measure makes no distinction if the dying person be of the Knighthood, if it be male or female, human, elf, dwarf, gnome, or kender. You are honor bound to take this task, Gerard."

"If it be mortally possible," Gerard countered.

"Yes," said Lord Warren. "So reads the Measure. Son, I see you are deeply troubled by this. If you break no confidence, tell me the nature of Caramon's last wish."

"I break no confidence, sir. I must tell you in any case, for if I am to undertake it I will need your permission to be absent from my post. Caramon Majere asked me to take this kender I have here with me, a kender who claims to be Tasslehoff Burrfoot, dead these thirty years, to Dalamar."

"The wizard Dalamar?" Lord Warren was incredulous.

"Yes, my lord. This is what happened. As he lay dying, Caramon spoke of being reunited with his dead wife. Then he appeared to be searching for someone in the crowd of people gathered around him. He said, 'But where's Raistlin?'"

"That would be his twin brother," Lord Warren interrupted.

"Yes, sir. Caramon added, 'He said he would wait for me'—meaning Raistlin had agreed to wait for him before leaving this world for the next, or so Laura told me. Caramon often said that since they were twins, one could not enter into the blessed realm without the other."

"I would not think that Raistlin Majere would be permitted to enter a 'blessed realm' at all," Lord Warren said dryly.

"True, sir." Gerard gave a wry smile. "If there is even a blessed realm, which I doubt, then . . ."

He paused, coughed in embarrassment. Lord Warren was frowning and looking very stern. Gerard apparently decided to skip the philosophical discussion and continue with his story.

"Caramon added something to effect that 'Raistlin should be here. With Tika. I don't understand. This is not right. Tas . . . What Tas said . . . A different future . . . Dalamar will know. . . . Take Tasslehoff to Dalamar.' He was very upset, and it seemed to me that he would not die in peace unless I promised to do as he asked. So I promised."

"The wizard Raistlin has been dead over fifty years!" Lord Warren exclaimed.

"Yes, sir. The so-called hero Burrfoot has been dead over thirty years, so this cannot possibly be him. And the wizard Dalamar has disappeared. No one has seen or heard of him since the Tower of High Sorcery vanished. It is rumored that he has been declared legally dead by the members of the Last Conclave."

"The rumors are true. I had it as fact from Palin Majere. But we have no proof of that, and we have a man's dying wish to consider. I am not certain how to rule."

Gerard was silent. Tas would have spoken up but for the gag and the realization that nothing he said could or would or should make a difference. To be quite truthful, Tasslehoff himself didn't know what to do. He had been given strict orders by Fizban to go to the funeral and to hurry right back. "Don't go gallivanting!" had been the old wizard's exact words, and he'd looked very fierce when he'd said them. Tas sat in the chair, chewing reflectively on the gag and pondering the exact meaning of the word, "gallivanting."

"I have something to show you, my lord," Gerard said. "With your permission . . ."

Lifting the bundle, Gerard placed it on Lord Warren's desk and began to untie the string at the top.

In the interim, Tas managed to wriggle his hands free of their bonds. He could remove the gag now, and he could go off to explore this truly interesting room, which had several very fine swords hanging on the wall, a shield, and a whole case of maps. Tas looked longingly at the maps, and his feet very nearly carried him that direction, but he was extremely curious to see what was in the Knight's bundle.

Gerard was taking a long time to open it; he seemed to be having difficulty with the knots.

Tas would have offered to help but thus far every time he had offered to be of help, Gerard had not seemed to appreciate it much. Tas occupied himself by watching the grains of sand fall from the top of an hourglass into the bottom and trying to count them as they fell. This proved a challenge, for the sand grains fell quite rapidly and just when he had them sorted out, one after the other, two or three would fall all in a heap and ruin his calculations.

Tas was somewhere between five thousand seven hundred and thirty-six and five thousand seven hundred and thirty-eight when the sands ran out. Gerard was still fumbling with the knots. Lord Warren reached over and turned the glass. Tas began to count again. "One, two, threefourfive . . ."

"Finally!" Gerard muttered and released the ties of the bundle.

Tas left off counting sand grains and sat up as straight as he possibly could in order to get a good view.

Gerard pressed the folds of the sack down around the object, taking care—Tas saw—not to touch the object itself. Jewels flashed and sparkled in the rays of the setting sun. Tas was so excited that he jumped out of his chair and tore the gag from his mouth.

"Hey!" he cried, reaching for the object. "That's just like mine! Where did you get it? Say!" he said, taking a good, close look. "That *is* mine!"

Gerard closed his hand over the kender's hand that was just inches away from the bejeweled object. Lord Warren stared at the object, openmouthed.

"I found this in the kender's pouch, sir," said Gerard. "Last night, when we searched him before locking him up in our prison. A prison that, I might add, is not as kender-proof as we thought. I'm not certain—I am no mage, my lord—but the device appears to be to be magical. *Quite* magical."

"It *is* magical," Tasslehoff said proudly. "That's the way I came here. It used to belong to Caramon, but he was always worried for fear someone would steal it and misuse it—I can't imagine who would do such a thing, myself. I offered to take care of it for him, but Caramon said, no, he thought it should go somewhere where it would be truly safe, and Dalamar said he'd take it, so Caramon gave it to him and he . . ." Tas quit talking because he didn't have an audience.

Lord Warren had withdrawn his hands from the desk. The object was about the size of an egg, encrusted with jewels that sparkled and glowed. Close examination revealed it to be made up of a myriad small parts that looked as if they could be manipulated, moved about. Lord Warren eyed it warily. Gerard kept fast hold of the kender.

The sun sank down toward the horizon and now shone brightly through the window. The office was cool and shadowed. The object glittered and gleamed, its own small sun.

"I have never seen the like of it," said Lord Warren, awed.

"Nor have I, sir," said Gerard. "But Laura has."

Lord Warren looked up, startled.

"She said that her father had an object like this. He kept it locked in a secret place in a room in the Inn that is dedicated to the memory of his twin brother Raistlin. She remembers well the day, some months prior to the Chaos War, when he removed the object from its secret hiding place and gave it to . . ." Gerard paused.

"Dalamar?" said Lord Warren, astounded. He stared at the device again. "Did her father say what it did? What magic it possessed?"

"He said that the object had been given to him by Par-Salian and that he had traveled back in time by means of its magic."

"He did, too," Tasslehoff offered. "I went with him. That's how I knew how the device worked. You see, it occurred to me that I might not outlive Caramon—"

Lord Warren said a single word, said it with emphasis and sincerity. Tas was impressed. Knights didn't usually say words like that.

"Do you think it's possible?" Lord Warren had shifted his gaze. He began staring at Tas as if he'd sprouted two heads.

Obviously he's never seen a troll. These people should really get out more, Tas thought.

"Do you think this is the real Tasslehoff Burrfoot?"

"Caramon Majere believed it was, my lord."

Lord Warren looked back at the strange device. "It is obviously an ancient artifact. No wizard has the ability to make magical objects like this these days. Even I can feel its power, and I'm certainly no mage, for which I thank fate." He looked back at Tas. "No, I don't believe it's possible. This kender stole it, and he has devised this outlandish tale to conceal his crime.

"We must return the artifact to the wizards, of course, though not, I would say, to the wizard Dalamar." Lord Warren frowned. "At the very least the device should be kept out of the hands of the kender. Where is Palin Majere? It seems to me that he is the one to consult."

"But you can't stop the device from coming back to my hands," Tas pointed out. "It's meant to always come back to me, and it will, sooner or later. Par-Salian—the great Par-Salian, I met him once, you know. He was very respectful to kender. Very." Tas fixed Gerard with a stern eye, hoping the Knight would take the hint. "Anyhow, Par-Salian told Caramon that the device was magically designed to always return to the person who used it. That's a safety precaution, so that you don't end up stranded back in time with no way of going back home. It's come in quite handy, since I have a tendency to lose things. I once lost a woolly mammoth. The way it happened was—"

"I agree, my lord," Gerard said loudly. "Be silent, kender. Speak when you are spoken to."

"Excuse me," said Tas, beginning to be bored. "But if you're not going to listen to me, may I go look at your maps? I'm very fond of maps."

Lord Warren waved his hand. Tas wandered off and was soon absorbed in reading the maps, which were really lovely, but which, the more he looked at them, he found very puzzling.

Gerard dropped his voice so low that Tas had a difficult

time hearing him. "Unfortunately, my lord, Palin Majere is on a secret mission to the elven kingdom of Qualinesti, to consult with the elven sorcerers. Such meetings have been banned by the dragon Beryl, and if his whereabouts became known to her, she would exact terrible retribution."

"Yet, it seems to me that he must know of this immediately!" Lord Warren argued.

"He must also know of his father's death. If you will grant me leave, my lord, I will undertake to escort the kender and this device to Qualinesti, there to put both of them in the hands of Palin Majere and also to impart the sad news about his father. I will relate to Palin his father's dying request and ask him to judge whether or not it may undertaken. I have little doubt but that he will absolve me of it."

Lord Warren's troubled expression eased. "You are right. We should put the matter into the hands of the son. If he declares his father's last request impossible to fulfill, you may, with honor, decline it. I wish you didn't have to go to Qualinesti, however. Wouldn't it be more prudent to wait until the wizard returns?"

"There is no telling when that will be, my lord. Especially now that Beryl has closed the roads. I believe this matter to be of the utmost urgency. Also"—Gerard lowered his voice—"we would have difficulty keeping the kender here indefinitely."

"Fizban told me to come right back to my own time," Tas informed them. "I'm not to go gallivanting. But I *would* like to see Palin and ask him why the funeral was all wrong. Do you think that could be considered 'gallivanting'?"

"Qualinesti lies deep in Beryl's territory," Lord Warren was saying. "The land is ruled by the Knights of Neraka, who would be only too pleased to lay their hands on one of our order. And if the Knights of Neraka don't seize you and execute you as a spy, the elves will. An army of our Knights could not enter that realm and survive."

"I do not ask for an army, my lord. I do not ask for any escort," Gerard said firmly. "I would prefer to travel on my own. *Much* prefer it," he added with emphasis. "I ask you for leave from my duties for a time, my lord."

"Granted, certainly." Lord Warren shook his head. "Though I don't know what your father will say."

"He will say that he is proud of his son, for you will tell him that I am undertaking a mission of the utmost importance, that I do it to fulfill the last request of a dying man."

"You are putting yourself in danger," said Lord Warren. "He would not like that at all. And as for your mother—" He frowned ominously.

Gerard stood straight and tall. "I have been ten years a Knight, my lord, and all I have to show for it is the dust of a tomb on my boots. I have earned this, my lord."

Lord Warren rose to his feet. "Here is my ruling. The Measure holds the final wishes of the dying to be sacred. We are bound in honor to fulfill them if it be mortally possible. You will go to Qualinesti and consult with the sorcerer Palin. I have found him to be a man of good judgment and common sense—for a mage, that is. One must not expect too much. Still, I believe that you can rely on him to help you determine what is right. Or, at the very least, to take the kender and this stolen magical artifact off our hands."

"Thank you, my lord." Gerard looked extremely happy.

Of course he's happy, Tasslehoff thought. He gets to travel to a land ruled by a dragon who's closed all the roads, and maybe he'll be captured by Dark Knights who'll think he's a spy, and if that doesn't work out he gets to go to the elven kingdom and see Palin and Laurana and Gilthas.

The pleasant tingle so well known to kender, a tingle to which they are seriously addicted, began in the vicinity of Tasslehoff's spine. The tingle burned its way right down to his feet, which started to itch, shot through his arms into his fingers, which started to wriggle, and up into his head. He could feel his hair beginning to curl from the excitement.

The tingle wound up in Tasslehoff's ears and, due to the rushing of the blood in his head, he noticed that Fizban's admonition to return *soon* was starting to get lost amidst thoughts of Dark Knights and spies and, most important of all, The Road.

Besides, Tas realized suddenly, Sir Gerard is counting on me to go with him! I can't let a Knight down. And then there's Caramon. I can't let him down either, even if he did hit his head one too many times on the stairs on the way down.

"I'll go with you, Sir Gerard," Tas announced magnanimously. "I've thought it over quite seriously, and it doesn't seem to me to be gallivanting. It seems to me to be a quest. And I'm sure Fizban won't mind if I went on a little quest."

"I will think of something to tell your father to placate him," Lord Warren was saying. "Is there any thing I can provide you for this mission? How will you travel? You know that according to the Measure you may not disguise your true identity."

"I will travel as a Knight, my lord," Gerard replied with a slight quirk of his eyebrow. "I give you my word on that."

Lord Warren eyed him speculatively. "You're up to something. No, don't tell me. The less I know about this the better." He glanced down at the device, glittering on the table, and heaved a sigh. "Magic and kender. It seems to me to be a fatal combination. My blessing go with you."

Gerard wrapped the device carefully in the bundle. Lord Warren left his desk to accompany Gerard to the door of the office, collecting Tasslehoff on the way. Gerard removed several of the smaller maps that had just happened to find their way down the front of the kender's shirt.

"I was taking them to be fixed," said Tas, looking at Lord Warren accusingly. "You really hire very poor mapmakers. They've made several serious mistakes. The Dark Knights aren't in Palanthas any more. We drove them out two years after the Chaos War. And why's that funny little circle like a bubble drawn around Silvanesti?"

The Knights were deep in a private discussion of their own, a discussion that had something to do with Gerard's mission, and they paid no attention. Tas pulled out another map that he had managed somehow to stuff itself down his trousers and that was at the moment pinching a sensitive portion of his anatomy. He transferred the map from his pants to his pouch and, while doing so, his knuckles brushed across something hard and sharp and egg-shaped.

The Device of Time Journeying. The device that would take him back to his own time. The device had come back to him, as it was bound to do. It was once more in his possession. Fizban's stern command seemed to ring loudly in his ears.

Tas looked at the device, thought about Fizban, and considered the promise he'd made to the old wizard. There was obviously only one thing to be done.

Taking firm hold of the device, careful not to accidentally activate it, Tasslehoff crept up behind Gerard, who was engrossed in his conversation with Lord Warren, and by dint of working loose a corner of the bundle, working nimbly and quietly as only a kender can work, Tasslehoff slipped the device back inside.

"And stay there!" he told it firmly.

7

Beckard's Cut

ocated on the shore of New Sea, Sanction was the major port city for the northeastern part of Ansalon. The city was an ancient one, established long before the Cataclysm. Nothing much is known for certain about its history except that prior to the Cataclysm, Sanction had been a pleasant place to live.

Many have wondered how it came by its odd name. Legend has it that there was once in the small village a human woman of advanced years whose opinions were well-known and respected far and wide. Disputes and disagreements over everything from ownership of boats to marriage contracts were brought before the old woman. She listened to all parties and then rendered her verdict, verdicts noted for being fair and impartial, wise and judicious. "The old 'un sanctioned it," was the response to her judgments, and thus the small village in which she resided became known as a place of authority and law.

When the gods in their wrath hurled the fiery mountain at the world, the mountain struck the continent of Ansalon and broke it asunder. The water of the Sirrion Ocean poured into the newly formed cracks and crevices creating a new sea, aptly named, by the pragmatic, New Sea. The volcanoes of the Doom Range flared into furious life, sending rivers of lava flowing into Sanction.

Mankind being ever resilient, quick to turn disaster to advantage, those who had once tilled the soil harvesting crops of beans and barley turned from the plow to the net, harvested the fruit of the sea. Small fishing villages sprang up along the coast of New Sea.

The people of Sanction moved to the beaches, where the offshore breeze blew away the fumes of the volcanoes. The town prospered, but it did not grow significantly until the tall ships arrived. Adventurous sailors out of Palanthas took their ships into New Sea, hoping to find quick and easy passage to the other side of the continent, avoiding the long and treacherous journey through the Sirrion Sea to the north. The explorers' hopes were dashed. No such passage existed. What they did discover, however, was a natural port in Sanction, an overland passage that was not too difficult, and markets waiting for their goods on the other side of the Khalkhist Mountains.

The town began to thrive, to expand, and, like any growing child, to dream. Sanction saw itself another Palanthas: famous, staid, stolid, and wealthy. Those dreams did not materialize, however. Solamnic Knights watched over Palanthas, guarded the city, ruled it with the Oath and the Measure. Sanction belonged to whoever had the might and the power to hold onto it. The city grew up headstrong and spoiled, with no codes, no laws, and plenty of money.

Sanction was not choosy about its companions. The city welcomed the greedy, the rapacious, the unscrupulous. Thieves and brigands, con men and whores, sell-swords and assassins called Sanction home.

The time came when Takhisis, Queen of Darkness, tried to

return to the world. She raised up armies to conquer Ansalon in her name. Ariakas, general of these armies, recognized the strategic value of Sanction to the Queen's holy city of Neraka and the military outpost of Khur. Lord Ariakas marched his troops into Sanction, conquered the city, which put up little resistance. He built temples to his Queen in Sanction and made his headquarters there.

The Lords of Doom, the volcanoes that ringed Sanction, felt the heat of the Queen's ambition stirring beneath them and came again to life. Streams of lava flowed from the volcanoes, lighting Sanction with a lurid glow by night. The ground shook and shivered from tremors. The inns of Sanction lost a fortune in broken crockery and began to serve food on tin plates and drink in wooden mugs. The air was poisonous, thick with sulphurous fumes. Black-robed wizards worked constantly to keep the city fit for habitation.

Takhisis set out to conquer the world, but in the end she could not overcome herself. Her generals quarreled, turned on each other. Love and self-sacrifice, loyalty and honor won the day. The stones of Neraka lay blasted and cursed in the shadowed valley leading to Sanction.

The Solamnic Knights marched on Sanction. They seized the city after a pitched battle with its inhabitants. Recognizing Sanction's strategic as well as financial importance to this part of Ansalon, the Knights established a strong garrison in the city. They tore down the temples of evil, set fire to the slave markets, razed the brothels. The Conclave of Wizards sent mages to continue to cleanse the poisonous air.

When the Knights of Takhisis began to accumulate power, some twenty years later, Sanction was high on the list of priorities. The Knights might well have captured it. Years of peace had made the Solamnic Knights sleepy and bored. They dozed at their posts. But before the Dark Knights could attack Sanction, the Chaos War diverted the attention of the Dark Knights and woke up the Solamnics.

The Chaos War ended. The gods departed. The residents of Sanction came to realize that the gods were gone. Magic— as they had known it—was gone. The people who had survived the war now faced death by asphyxiation from the noxious fumes. They fled the city, ran to the beaches to breathe the clean sea air. And so for a time, Sanction returned to where it had begun.

A strange and mysterious wizard named Hogan Bight not only restored Sanction to its former glory but helped the city surpass itself. He did what no other wizard had been able to do: He not only cleansed the air, he diverted the lava away from the city. Water, cool and pure, flowed from the snowy mountain tops. A person could actually step outside and take a deep breath and not double over coughing and choking.

Older and wiser, Sanction became prosperous, wealthy, and respectable. Under Bight's protection and encouragement, good and honest merchants moved into the city. Both the Solamnic Knights and the Knights of Neraka approached Bight, each side offering to move into Sanction and provide protection from the other.

Bight trusted neither side, refused to allow either to enter. Angry, the Knights of Neraka argued that Sanction was part of the land given to them by the Council in return for their service during the Chaos War. The Knights of Solamnia continued to try to negotiate with Bight, who continued to refuse all their offers of aid.

Meanwhile the Dark Knights, now calling themselves Knights of Neraka, were growing in strength, in wealth, and in power—for it was they who collected the tribute due the dragons. They watched Sanction as the cat watches the mouse hole. The Knights of Neraka had long coveted the port that would allow them a base of operations from which they could sail forth and gain a firm hold on all the lands surrounding New Sea. Seeing that the mice were busy biting and clawing each other, the cat pounced.

The Knights of Neraka laid siege to Sanction. They expected the siege to be a long one. As soon as the Dark Knights attacked the city, its fractured elements would unite in its defense. The Knights were patient, however. They could not starve the city into submission; blockade runners continued to bring supplies into Sanction. But the Knights of Neraka could shut down all overland trade routes. Thus the Knights of Neraka effectively strangled the merchants and brought Sanction's economy to ruin.

Pressured by the demands of the citizens, Hogan Bight had agreed within the last year to permit the Solamnic Knights to send in a force to bolster the city's flagging defenses. At first, the Knights were welcomed as saviors. The people of Sanction expected the Knights would put an immediate end to the siege. The Solamnics replied that they had to study the situation. After months of watching the Knights study, the people again urged the Solamnics to break the siege. The Knights replied that their numbers were too few. They needed reinforcements.

Nightly the besiegers bombarded the city with boulders and fiery bales of hay flung from catapults. The burning hay bales started blazes, the boulders knocked holes in buildings. People died, property was destroyed. No one could get a good night's sleep. As the leadership of the Knights of Neraka had calculated, the excitement and fervor of Sanction's residents, which had burned hot when first defending their city against the foe, cooled as the siege dragged out month after month. They found fault with the Solamnics, called them cowards. The Knights retorted that the citizens were hot-heads who would have them all die for nothing. Hearing reports from their spies that the unity was starting to crack, the Knights of Neraka began to build up their forces for an all-out, major assault. Their leadership waited only for a sign that the cracks had penetrated to the enemy's heart.

A large valley known as Zhakar Valley lay to the east of Sanction. Early in the siege, the Knights of Neraka had gained control of this valley and all of the passes that led from Sanction into the valley. Hidden in the foothills of the Zhakar Mountains, the valley was being used by the Knights as a staging area for their armies.

"The Zhakar Valley is our destination," Mina told her Knights. But when asked why, what they would do there, she would say nothing other than, "We are called."

Mina and her forces arrived at noon. The sun was high in a cloudless sky, seeming to stare down upon all below with avid expectation, an expectation that sucked up the wind, left the air still and hot.

Mina brought her small command to a halt at the entrance to the valley. Directly opposite them, across the valley, was a pass known as Beckard's Cut. Through the cut, the Knights could see the besieged city, see a small portion of the wall that surrounded Sanction. Between the Knights and Sanction lay their own army. Another city had sprung up in the valley, a city of tents and campfires, wagons and draft animals, soldiers and camp followers.

Mina and her Knights had arrived at a propitious time, seemingly. The camp of the Knights of Neraka rang with cheers. Trumpets blared, officers bellowed, companies formed on the road. Already the lead forces were marching through the cut, heading toward Sanction. Others were quickly following.

"Good," said Mina. "We are in time."

She galloped her horse down the steep road, her Knights followed after. They heard in the trumpets the melody of the song they had heard in their sleep. Hearts pounded, pulses quickened, yet they had no idea why.

"Find out what is going on," Mina instructed Galdar.

The minotaur nabbed the first officer he could locate,

questioned the man. Returning to Mina, the minotaur grinned and rubbed his hands.

"The cursed Solamnics have left the city!" he reported. "The wizard who runs Sanction has thrown the Solamnic Knights out on their ears. Kicked them in the ass. Sent them packing. If you look"—Galdar turned, pointed through Beckard's Cut—"you can see their ships, those little black dots on the horizon."

The Knights under Mina's command began to cheer. Mina looked at the distant ships, but she did not smile. Foxfire stirred restlessly, shook his mane and pawed the ground.

"You brought us here in good time, Mina," Galdar continued with enthusiasm. "They are preparing to launch the final assault. This day, we'll drink Sanction's blood. This night, we'll drink Sanction ale!"

The men laughed. Mina said nothing, her expression indicated neither elation nor joy. Her amber eyes roved the army camp, seeking something and not finding what she wanted, apparently, for a small frown line appeared between her brows. Her lips pursed in displeasure. She continued her search and finally, her expression cleared. She nodded to herself and patted Foxfire's neck, calming him.

"Galdar, do you see that company of archers over there?"

Galdar looked, found them, indicated that he did.

"They do not wear the livery of the Knights of Neraka."

"They are a mercenary company," Galdar explained. "In our pay, but they fight under their own officers."

"Excellent. Bring their commander to me."

"But, Mina, why—"

"Do as I have ordered, Galdar," said Mina.

Her Knights, gathered behind her, exchanged startled glances, shrugging, wondering. Galdar was about to argue. He was about to urge Mina to let him join in the final drive toward victory instead of sending him off on some fool's errand. A jarring, tingling sensation numbed his right arm, felt as if he'd struck his "funny bone." For one terrifying moment, he could not move his fingers. Nerves tingled and jangled. The feeling went away in a moment, leaving him shaken. Probably nothing more than a pinched nerve, but the tingling reminded him of what he owed her. Galdar swallowed his arguments and departed on his assignment.

He returned with the archer company's commander, an older human, in his forties, with the inordinately strong arms of a bowman. The mercenary officer's expression was sullen, hostile. He would not have come at all, but it is difficult to say no to a minotaur who towers over you head, shoulders, and horns and who is insistent upon your coming.

Mina wore her helm with the visor raised. A wise move, Galdar thought. The helm shadowed her youthful, girl's face, kept it hidden.

"What are you orders, Talon Leader?" Mina asked. Her voice resonated from within the visor, cold and hard as the metal.

The commander looked up at the Knight with a certain amount of scorn, not the least intimidated.

"I'm no blasted 'talon leader,' Sir Knight," he said and he laid a nasty, sarcastic emphasis on the word 'sir.' "I hold my rank as captain of my own command, and we don't take orders from your kind. Just money. We do whatever we damn well please."

"Speak politely to the talon leader," Galdar growled and gave the officer a shove that staggered him.

The man wheeled, glowered, reached for his short sword. Galdar grasped his own sword. His fellow soldiers drew their blades with a ringing sound. Mina did not move.

"What are your orders, Captain?" she asked again.

Seeing he was outnumbered, the officer slid his sword back into its sheath, his movement slow and deliberate, to show that he was still defiant, just not stupid.

"To wait until the assault is launched and then to fire at the guards on the walls. Sir," he said sulkily, adding in sullen tones, "We'll be the last ones into the city, which means all the choice pickings will already be gone."

Mina regarded him speculatively. "You have little respect for the Knights of Neraka or our cause."

"What cause?" The office gave a brief, barking laugh. "To fill your own coffers? That's all you care about. You and your foolish visions." He spat on the ground.

"Yet you were once one of us, Captain Samuval. You were once a Knight of Takhisis," Mina said. "You quit because the cause for which you joined was gone. You quit because you no longer believed."

The captain's eyes widened, his face muscles went slack. "How did—" He snapped his mouth shut. "What if I was?" he growled. "I didn't desert, if that's what you're thinking. I bought my way out. I have my papers—"

"If you do not believe in our cause, why do you continue to fight for us, Captain?" Mina asked.

Samuval snorted. "Oh, I believe in your cause now, all right," he said with a leer. "I believe in money, same as the rest of you."

Mina sat her horse, who was still and calm beneath her hand, and gazed through Beckard's Cut, gazed at the city of Sanction. Galdar had a sudden, strange impression that she could see through the walls of the city, see through the armor of those defending the city, see through their flesh and their bones to their very hearts and minds, just as she had seen through him. Just as she had seen through the captain.

"No one will enter Sanction this day, Captain Samuval," said Mina softly. "The carrion birds will be the ones who find 'choice pickings.' The ships that you see sailing away are not filled with Solamnic Knights. The troops that line their decks are in reality straw dummies wearing the armor of Solamnics Knights. It is a trap."

Galdar stared, aghast. He believed her. Believed as surely

as if he had seen inside the ships, seen inside the walls to the enemy army hiding there, ready to spring.

"How do you know this?" the captain demanded.

"What if I gave you something to believe in, Captain Samuval?" she asked instead of answering. "What if I make you the hero of this battle? Would you pledge your loyalty to me?" She smiled slightly. "I have no money to offer you. I have only this sure knowledge that I freely share with you— fight for me and on this day you will come to know the one true god."

Captain Samuval gazed up at her in wordless astonishment. He looked dazed, lightning-struck.

Mina held out her raw and bleeding hands, palms open. "You are offered a choice, Captain Samuval. I hold death in one hand. Glory in the other. Which will it be?"

Samuval scratched his beard. "You're a strange one, Talon Leader. Not like any of your kind I've ever met before."

He looked back through Beckard's Cut.

"Rumor has spread among the men that the city is abandoned," Mina said. "They have heard it will open its gates in surrender. They have become a mob. They run to their own destruction."

She spoke truly. Ignoring the shouts of the officers, who were vainly endeavoring to maintain some semblance of order, the foot soldiers had broken ranks. Galdar watched the army disintegrate, become in an instant an undisciplined horde rampaging through the cut. Eager for the kill, eager for spoils. Captain Samuval spat again in disgust. His expression dark, he looked back at Mina.

"What would you have me do, Talon Leader?"

"Take your company of archers and post them on that ridge there. Do you see it?" Mina pointed to a foothill overlooking Beckard's Cut.

"I see it," he said, glancing over his shoulder. "And what do we do once we're there?"

"My Knights and I will take up our positions there. Once arrived, you will await my orders," Mina replied. "When I give those orders, you will obey my commands without question."

She held out her hand, her blood-smeared hand. Was it the hand that held death or the hand that held life? Galdar wondered.

Perhaps Captain Samuval wondered as well, for he hesitated before he finally took her hand into his own. His hand was large, callused from the bowstring, brown and grimy. Her hand was small, its touch light. Her palm was blistered, rimed with dried blood. Yet it was the captain who winced slightly.

He looked down at his hand when she released him, rubbed it on his leather corselet, as if rubbing away the pain of sting or burn.

"Make haste, Captain. We don't have much time," Mina ordered.

"And just who are you, Sir Knight?" Captain Samuval asked. He was still rubbing his hand.

"I am Mina," she said.

Grasping the reins, she pulled sharply. Foxfire wheeled. Mina dug in her spurs, galloped straight for the ridge above Beckard's Cut. Her Knights rode alongside her. Galdar ran at her stirrup, legs pumping to keep up.

"How do you know that Captain Samuval will obey you, Mina?" the minotaur roared over the pounding of horses' hooves.

She looked down on him and smiled. Her amber eyes were bright in the shadow of the helm.

"He will obey," she said, "if for no other reason now than to demonstrate his disdain for his superiors and their foolish commands. But the captain is a man who hungers, Galdar. He yearns for food. They have given him clay to fill his belly. I will give him meat. Meat to nourish his soul."

Mina leaned over her horse's head and urged the animal to gallop even faster.

Captain Samuval's Archer Company took up position on the ridgeline overlooking Beckard's Cut. They were several hundred strong, well-trained professional bowmen who had fought in many of Neraka's wars before now. They used the elven long bow, so highly prized among archers. Taking up their places, they stood foot to foot, packed tightly together, with not much room to maneuver, for the ridgeline was not long. The archers were in a foul mood. Watching the army of the Knights of Neraka sweep down on Sanction, the men muttered that there would be nothing left for them—the finest women carried off, the richest houses plundered. They might as well go home.

Above them clouds thickened; roiling gray clouds that bubbled up over the Zhakar Mountains and began to slide down the mountain's side.

The army camp was empty, now, except for the tents and supply wagons and a few wounded who had been unable to go with their brethren and were cursing their ill luck. The clamor of the battle moved away from them. The surrounding mountains and the lowering clouds deflected the sounds of the attacking army. The valley was eerily silent.

The archers looked sullenly to their captain, who looked impatiently to Mina.

"What are your orders, Talon Leader?" he asked.

"Wait," she said.

They waited. The army washed up against the walls of Sanction, pounded against the gate. The noise and commotion was far away, a distant rumbling. Mina removed her helm, ran her hand over her shorn head with its down of dark red hair. She sat straight-backed upon her horse, her chin lifted. Her gaze was not on Sanction but on the blue sky above them, blue sky that was rapidly darkening.

The archers stared, astounded at her youth, amazed at her strange beauty. She did not heed their stares, did not hear their coarse remarks that were swallowed by the silence welling up out of the valley. The men felt something ominous about the silence. Those who continued to make remarks did so out of bravado and were almost immediately hushed by their uneasy comrades.

An explosion rocked the ground around Sanction, shattered the silence. The clouds boiled, the sunlight vanished. The Neraka army's gloating roars of victory were abruptly cut off. Shouts of triumph shrilled to screams of panic.

"What is happening?" demanded the archers, their tongues loosed. Everyone talked at once. "Can you see?"

"Silence in the ranks!" Captain Samuval bellowed.

One of the Knights, who had been posted as observer near the cut, came galloping toward them.

"It was a trap!" He began to yell when he was still some distance away. "The gates of Sanction opened to our forces, but only to spew forth the Solamnics! There must be a thousand of them. Sorcerers ride at their head, dealing death with their cursed magicks!"

The Knight reined in his excited horse. "You spoke truly, Mina!" His voice was awed, reverent. "A huge blast of magical power killed hundreds of our troops at the outset. Their bodies lie smoldering on the field. Our soldiers are fleeing! They are running this way, retreating through the cut. It is a rout!"

"All is lost, then," said Captain Samuval, though he looked at Mina strangely. "The Solamnic forces will drive the army into the valley. We will be caught between the anvil of the mountains and the hammer of the Solamnics."

His words proved true. Those in the rear echelons were already streaming back through Beckard's Cut. Many had no idea where they were going, only that they wanted to be far away from the blood and the death. A few of the less confused and more calculating were making for the narrow road that ran through the mountains to Khur.

"A standard!" Mina said urgently. "Find me a standard!"

Captain Samuval took hold of the grimy white scarf he wore around his neck and handed it up to her. "Take this and welcome, Mina."

Mina took the scarf in her hands, bowed her head. Whispering words no one could hear, she kissed the scarf and handed it to Galdar. The white fabric was stained red with blood from the raw blisters on her hand. One of Mina's Knights offered his lance. Galdar tied the bloody scarf onto the lance, handed the lance back to Mina.

Wheeling Foxfire, she rode him up the rocks to a high promontory and held the standard aloft.

"To me, men!" she shouted. "To Mina!"

The clouds parted. A mote of sunlight jabbed from the heavens, touched only Mina as she sat astride her horse on the ridgeline. Her black armor blazed as if dipped in flame, her amber eyes gleamed, lit from behind with the light of battle. Her redound, a clarion call, brought the fleeing soldiers to a halt. They looked to see from whence the call came and saw Mina outlined in flame, blazing like a beacon fire upon the hillside.

The fleeing soldiers halted in their mad dash, looked up, dazzled.

"To me!" Mina yelled again. "Glory is ours this day!"

The soldiers hesitated, then one ran toward her, scrambling, slipping and sliding up the hillside. Another followed and another, glad to have purpose and direction once again.

"Bring those men over there to me," Mina ordered Galdar, pointing to another group of soldiers in full retreat. "As many as you can gather. See that they are armed. Draw them up in battle formation there on the rocks below."

Galdar did as he was commanded. He and the other Knights blocked the path of the retreating soldiers, ordered them to join their comrades who were starting to form a dark pool at Mina's feet. More and more soldiers were pouring through the cut, the Knights of Neraka riding among them, some of the officers making valiant attempts to halt the retreat, others joining the footmen in a run for their lives. Behind them rode Solamnic Knights in their gleaming silver armor, their white-feathered crests. Deadly, silver light flashed, and everywhere that light appeared, men withered and died in its magical heat. The Solamnic Knights entered the cut, driving the forces of the Knights of Neraka like cattle before them, driving them to slaughter.

"Captain Samuval," cried Mina, riding her horse down the hill, her standard streaming behind her. "Order your men to fire."

"The Solamnics are not in bow range," he said to her, shaking his head at her foolishness. "Any fool can see that."

"The Solamnics are not your target, Captain," Mina returned coolly. She pointed to the forces of the Knights of Neraka streaming through the cut. "Those are your targets."

"Our own men?" Captain Samuval stared at her. "You are mad!"

"Look upon the field of battle, Captain," Mina said. "It is the only way."

Captain Samuval looked. He wiped his face with his hand, then he gave the command. "Bowmen, fire."

"What target?" demanded one.

"You heard Mina!" said the captain harshly. Grabbing a bow from one of his men, he nocked an arrow and fired.

The arrow pierced the throat of one of the fleeing Knights of Neraka. He fell backward off his horse and was trampled in the rush of his retreating comrades.

Archer Company fired. Hundreds of arrows—each shot with deliberate, careful aim at point-blank range—filled the air with a deadly buzz. Most found their targets. Foot soldiers clutched their chests and dropped. The feathered shafts struck through the raised visors of the helmed Knights or took them in the throat.

"Continue firing, Captain," Mina commanded.

More arrows flew. More bodies fell. The panic-stricken soldiers realized that the arrows were coming from in front of them now. They faltered, halted, trying to discover the location of this new enemy. Their comrades crashed into them from behind, driven mad by the approaching Solamnic Knights. The steep walls of Beckard's Cut prevented any escape.

"Fire!" Captain Samuval shouted wildly, caught up in the fervor of death-dealing. "For Mina!"

"For Mina!" cried the archers and fired.

Arrows hummed with deadly accuracy, thunked into their targets. Men screamed and fell. The dying were starting to pile up like hideous cordwood in the cut, forming a blood-soaked barricade.

An officer came raging toward them, his sword in his hand. "You fool!" he screamed at Captain Samuval. "Who gave you your orders? You're firing on your own men!"

"I gave him the order," said Mina calmly.

Furious, the Knight accosted her. "Traitor!" He raised his blade.

Mina sat unmoving on her horse. She paid no attention to the Knight, she was intent upon the carnage below. Galdar brought down a crushing fist on the Knight's helm. The Knight, his neck broken, went rolling and tumbling down the hillside. Galdar sucked bruised knuckles and looked up at Mina.

He was astounded to see tears flowing unchecked down her cheeks. Her hand clasped the medallion around her neck. Her lips moved, she might have been praying.

Attacked from in front, attacked from behind, the soldiers inside Beckard's Cut began milling about in confusion. Behind them, their comrades faced a terrible choice. They could either be speared in the back by the Solamnics or they could turn and fight. They wheeled to face the enemy, battling with the ferocity of the desperate, the cornered.

The Solamnics continued to fight, but their charge was slowed and, at length, ground to a halt.

"Cease fire!" Mina ordered. She handed her standard to Galdar. Drawing her morning star, she held it high over her head. "Knights of Neraka! Our hour has come! We ride this day to glory!"

Foxfire gave a great leap and galloped down the hillside, carrying Mina straight at the vanguard of the Solamnic Knights. So swift was Foxfire, so sudden Mina's move, that she left her own Knights behind. They watched, openmouthed, as Mina rode to what must be her doom. Then Galdar raised the white standard.

"Death is certain!" the minotaur thundered. "But so is glory! For Mina!"

"For Mina!" cried the Knights in grim, deep voices and they rode their horses down the hill.

"For Mina!" yelled Captain Samuval, dropping his bow and drawing his short sword. He and the entire Archer Company charged into the fray.

"For Mina!" shouted the soldiers, who had gathered around her standard. Rallying to her cause, they dashed after her, a dark cascade of death rumbling down the hillside.

Galdar raced down the hillside, desperate to catch up to Mina, to protect and defend her. She had never been in a battle. She was unskilled, untrained. She must surely die. Enemy faces loomed up before him. Their swords slashed at him, their spears jabbed at him, their arrows stung him. He struck their swords aside, broke their spears, ignored their arrows. The enemy was an irritant, keeping him from his goal. He lost her and then he found her, found her completely surrounded by the enemy.

Galdar saw one knight try to impale Mina on his sword. She turned the blow, struck at him with the morning star. Her first blow split open his helm. Her next blow split open his head. But while she fought him, another was coming to attack her from behind. Galdar bellowed a warning, though he knew with despair that she could not hear him. He battled ferociously to reach her, cutting down those who stood between him and his commander, no longer seeing their faces, only the bloody streaks of his slashing sword.

He kept his gaze fixed on her, and his fury blazed, and his heart stopped beating when he saw her pulled from her horse. He fought more furiously than ever, frantic to save her. A blow struck from behind stunned him. He fell to his knees. He tried to rise, but blow after savage blow rained down on him, and he knew nothing more.

The battle ended sometime near twilight. The Knights of Neraka held, the valley was secure. The Solamnics and soldiers of Sanction were forced to retreat back into the walled city, a city that was shocked and devastated by the crushing defeat. They had felt the victory wreath upon their heads, and then the wreath had been savagely snatched away, trampled in the mud. Devastated, disheartened, the Solamnic Knights dressed their wounds and burned the bodies of their dead. They had spent months working on this plan, deemed it their only chance to break the siege of Sanction. They wondered over and over how they could have failed.

One Solamnic Knight spoke of a warrior who had come upon him, so he said, like the wrath of the departed gods. Another had seen this warrior, too, and another and another after that. Some claimed it was a youth, but others said that no, it was a girl, a girl with a face for which a man might die. She had ridden in the front of the charge, smote their ranks like a thunderclap, battling without helm or shield, her weapon a morning star that dripped with blood.

Pulled from her horse, she fought alone on foot.

"She must be dead," said one angrily. "I saw her fall."

"True, she fell, but her horse stood guard over her," said another, "and struck out with lashing hooves at any who dared approach."

But whether the beautiful destructor had perished or survived, none could tell. The tide of battle turned, came to meet her, swept around her, and rolled over the heads of the Solamnic Knights, carried them in a confused heap back into their city.

"Mina!" Galdar called hoarsely. "Mina!"

There came no answer.

Desperate, despairing, Galdar searched on.

The smoke from the fires of the funeral pyres hung over the valley. Night had not yet fallen, the twilight was gray and thick with smoke and orange cinders. The minotaur went to the tents of the dark mystics, who were treating the wounded, and he could not find her. He looked through the bodies that were being lined up for the burning, an arduous task. Lifting one body, he rolled it over, looked closely at the face, shook his head, and moved on to the next.

He did not find her among the dead, at least, not those who had been brought back to camp thus far. The work of removing the bodies from that blood-soaked cut would last all night and into the morrow. Galdar's shoulders sagged. He was wounded, exhausted, but he was determined to keep searching. He carried with him, in his right hand, Mina's standard. The white cloth was white no longer. It was brownish red, stiff with dried blood.

He blamed himself. He should have been at her side. Then at least if he had not been able to protect her, he could have died with her. He had failed, struck down from behind. When he had finally regained consciousness, he found that the battle was over. He was told that their side had won.

Hurt and dizzy, Galdar staggered over to the place he had last glimpsed her. Bodies of her foes lay heaped on the ground, but she was nowhere to be found.

She was not among the living. She was not among the dead. Galdar was starting to think that he had dreamed her, created her out of his own hunger to believe in someone or something when he felt a touch upon his arm.

"Minotaur," said the man. "Sorry, I never did catch your name."

Galdar could not place the soldier for a moment—the face was almost completely obscured by a bloody bandage. Then he recognized the captain of Archer Company.

"You're searching for her, aren't you?" Captain Samuval asked. "For Mina?"

For Mina! The cry echoed in his heart. Galdar nodded. He was too tired, too dispirited to speak.

"Come with me," said Samuval. "I have something to show you."

The two trudged across the floor of the valley, heading for the battlefield. Those soldiers who had escaped the battle uninjured were busy rebuilding the camp, which had been wrecked during the chaos of the retreat. The men worked with a fervor unusual to see, worked without the incentive of the whip or the bullying cries of the masters-at-arms. Galdar had seen these same men in past battles crouched sullenly over their cooking fires, licking their wounds, swilling dwarf spirits, and boasting and bragging of their bravery in butchering the enemy's wounded.

Now, as he passed the groups of men hammering in tent stakes or pounding the dents out of breastplate and shield or picking up spent arrows or tending to countless other chores, he listened to them talk. Their talk was not of themselves, but of her, the blessed, the charmed. Mina.

Her name was on every soldier's lips, her deeds recounted time and again. A new spirit infused the camp, as if the lightning storm out of which Mina had walked had sent jolts of energy flashing from man to man.

Galdar listened and marveled but said nothing. He accompanied Captain Samuval, who appeared disinclined to talk about anything, refused to answer all Galdar's questions. In another time, the frustrated minotaur might have smashed the human's skull into his shoulders, but not now. They had shared in a moment of triumph and exaltation, the likes of which neither had ever before experienced in battle. They had both been carried out of themselves, done deeds of bravery and heroism they had never thought themselves capable of doing. They had fought for a cause, fought together for a cause, and against all odds they had won.

When Captain Samuval stumbled, Galdar reached out a steadying arm. When Galdar slipped in a pool of blood, Captain Samuval supported him. The two arrived at the edge of the battlefield. Captain Samuval peered through the smoke that hung over the valley. The sun had disappeared behind the mountains. Its afterglow filled the sky with a smear of pale red.

"There," said the captain, and he pointed.

The wind had lifted with the setting of the sun, blowing the smoke to rags that swirled and eddied like silken scarves. These were suddenly whisked away to reveal a horse the color of blood and a figure kneeling on the field of battle only a few feet away from him.

"Mina!" Galdar breathed. Relief weakened all the muscles in his body. A burning stung his eyes, a burning he attributed to the smoke, for minotaurs never wept, could not weep. He wiped his eyes. "What is she doing?" he asked after a moment.

"Praying," said Captain Samuval. "She is praying."

Mina knelt beside the body of a soldier. The arrow that had killed him had gone clean through his breast, pinned him to the ground. Mina lifted the hand of the dead man, placed the hand to her breast, bent her head. If she spoke, Galdar could not hear what she said, but he knew Samuval was right. She was praying to this god of hers, this one, true god. This god who had foreseen the trap, this god who had led her here to turn defeat into glorious victory.

Her prayers finished, Mina laid the man's hand atop the

terrible wound. Bending over him, she pressed her lips to the cold forehead, kissed it, then rose to her feet.

She had barely strength to walk. She was covered with blood, some of it her own. She halted, her head drooped, her body sagged. Then she lifted her head to the heavens, where she seemed to find strength, for she straightened her shoulders and with strong step walked on.

"Ever since the battle was assured, she has been going from corpse to corpse," said Captain Samuval. "In particular, she finds those who fell by our own arrows. She stops and kneels in the blood-soaked mud and offers prayer. I have never seen the like."

"It is right that she honors them," Galdar said harshly. "Those men bought us victory with their blood."

"*She* bought us victory with their blood," Captain Samuval returned with a quirk of the only eyebrow visible through the bandage.

A sound rose behind Galdar. He was reminded of the *Gamashinoch,* the Song of Death. This song came from living throats, however; starting low and quiet, sung by only a few. More voices caught it up and began to carry it forward, as they had caught up their dropped swords and run forward into battle.

"Mina . . . Mina . . ."

The song swelled. Begun as a soft, reverent chant, it was now a triumphal march, a celebratory paean accompanied by a timpani of sword clashing against shield, of stomping feet and clapping hands.

"Mina! Mina! Mina!"

Galdar turned to see the remnants of the army gathering at the edge of the battlefield. The wounded who could not walk under their own power were being supported by those who could. Bloody, ragged, the soldiers chanted her name.

Galdar lifted his voice in a thunderous shout and raised Mina's standard. The chanting became a cheer that rolled among the mountains like thunder and shook the ground mounded high with the bodies of the dead.

Mina had started to kneel down again. The song arrested her. She paused, turned slowly to face the cheering throng. Her face was pale as bone. Her amber eyes were ringed with ash-like smudges of fatigue. Her lips were parched and cracked, stained with the kisses of the dead. She gazed upon the hundreds of living who were shouting, singing, chanting her name.

Mina raised her hands.

The voices ceased in an instant. Even the groans and screams of the wounded hushed. The only sound was her name echoing from the mountainside, and eventually that died away as silence settled over the valley.

Mina mounted her horse, so that all the multitude who had gathered at the edge of the field of the battle, now being called "Mina's Glory," could better see and hear her.

"You do wrong to honor me!" she told them. "I am only the vessel. The honor and the glory of this day belong to the god who guides me along the path I walk."

"Mina's path is a path for us all!" shouted someone.

The cheering began again.

"Listen to me!" Mina shouted, her voice ringing with authority and power. "The old gods are gone! They abandoned you. They will never return! One god has come in their place. One god to rule the world. One god only. To that one god, we owe our allegiance!"

"What is the name of this god?" one cried.

"I may not pronounce it," Mina replied. "The name is too holy, too powerful."

"Mina!" said one. "Mina, Mina!"

The crowd picked up the chant and, once started, they would not be stopped.

Mina looked exasperated for a moment, even angry. Lifting her hand, she clasped her fingers over the medallion she wore round her neck. Her face softened, cleared.

"Go forth! Speak my name," she cried. "But know that you speak it in the name of my god."

The cheers were deafening, jarred rocks from the mountain sides.

His own pain forgotten, Galdar shouted lustily. He looked down to see his companion grimly silent, his gaze turned elsewhere.

"What?" Galdar bellowed over the tumult. "What's wrong?"

"Look there," said Captain Samuval. "At the command tent."

Not everyone in camp was cheering. A group of Knights of Neraka were gathered around their leader, a Lord of the Skull. They looked on with black gazes and scowls, arms crossed over their chests.

"Who is that?" Galdar asked.

"Lord Milles," Samuval replied. "The one who ordered this disaster. As you see, he came well out of the fray. Not a speck of blood on his fine, shiny armor."

Lord Milles was attempting to gain the soldiers' attention. He waved his arms, shouted out words no one could hear. No one paid him any heed. Eventually he gave it up as a bad job.

Galdar grinned. "I wonder how this Milles likes seeing his command pissing away down the privy hole."

"Not well, I should imagine," said Samuval.

"He and the other Knights consider themselves well rid of the gods," Galdar said. "They ceased to speak of Takhisis's return long ago. Two years past, Lord of the Night Targonne changed the official name to Knights of Neraka. In times past, when a Knight was granted the Vision, he was given to know his place in the goddess's grand plan. After Takhisis fled the world, the leadership tried for some time to maintain the Vision through various mystical means. Knights still undergo the Vision, but now they can only be certain of what Targonne and his ilk plant in their minds."

"One reason I left," said Samuval. "Targonne and officers like this Milles enjoy being the ones in charge for a change, and they will not be pleased to hear that they are in danger of being knocked off the top of the mountain. You may be certain Milles will send news of this upstart to headquarters."

Mina climbed down from her horse. Leading Foxfire by the reins, she left the field of battle, walked into the camp. The men cheered and shouted until she reached them, and then, as she came near, moved by something they did not understand, they ceased their clamor and dropped to their knees. Some reached out their hands to touch her as she passed, others cried for her to look upon them and grant them her blessing.

Lord Milles watched this triumphant procession, his face twisted in disgust. Turning on his heel, he reentered his command tent.

"Bah! Let them skulk and plot!" Galdar said, elated. "She has an army now. What can they do to her?"

"Something treacherous and underhanded, you can be sure," said Samuval. He cast a glance heavenward. "It may be true that there is One who watches over her from above. But she needs friends to watch over her here below."

"You speak wisely," said Galdar. "Are you with her then, Captain?"

"To the end of my time or the world's, whichever comes first," said Samuval. "My men as well. And you?"

"I have been with her always," said Galdar, and it truly seemed to him that he had.

Minotaur and human shook hands. Galdar proudly raised Mina's standard and fell in beside her as she made her victory march through the camp. Captain Samuval walked behind Mina, his hand on his sword, guarding her back. Mina's Knights rode to her standard. Every one of those who had followed her from Neraka had suffered some wound, but none had perished. Already, they were telling stories of miracles.

"An arrow came straight toward me," said one. "I knew I was dead. I spoke Mina's name, and the arrow dropped to the ground at my feet."

"One of the cursed Solamnics held his sword to my throat," said another. "I called upon Mina, and the enemy's blade broke in twain."

Soldiers offered her food. They brought her wine, brought her water. Several soldiers seized the tent of one of Milles's officers, turned him out, and prepared it for Mina. Snatching up burning brands from the campfires, the soldiers held them aloft, lighting Mina's progress through the darkness. As she passed, they spoke her name as if it were an incantation that could work magic.

"Mina," cried the men and the wind and the darkness. "Mina!"

8

UNDER the Shield

The Silvanesti elves have always revered the night.

The Qualinesti delight in the sunlight. Their ruler is the Speaker of the Sun. They fill their homes with sunlight, all business is conducted in the daylight hours, all important ceremonies such as marriage are held in the day so that they may be blessed by the light of the sun.

The Silvanesti are in love with the star-lit night.

The Silvanesti's leader is the Speaker of the Stars. Night had once been a blessed time in Silvanost, the capital of the elven state. Night brought the stars and sweet sleep and dreams of the beauty of their beloved land. But then came the War of the Lance. The wings of evil dragons blotted out the stars. One dragon in particular, a green dragon known as Cyan Bloodbane, laid claim to the realm of Silvanesti. He had long hated the elves and he wanted to see them suffer. He could have slaughtered them by the thousands, but he was cruel and clever. The dying suffer, that is true, but the pain is fleeting and is soon forgotten as the dead move from this reality to the next. Cyan wanted to inflict a pain that nothing could ease, a pain that would endure for centuries.

The ruler of Silvanesti at the time was an elf highly skilled in magic. Lorac Caladon foresaw the coming of evil to Ansalon. He sent his people into exile, telling them he had the power to keep their realm safe from the dragons. Unbeknownst to anyone, Lorac had stolen one of the magical dragon orbs from the Tower of High Sorcery. He had been warned that an attempt to use the orb by one who was not strong enough to control its magic could result in doom. In his arrogance, Lorac believed that he was strong enough to wrest the orb to his will. He looked into the orb and saw a dragon looking back. Lorac was caught and held in thrall.

Cyan Bloodbane had his chance. He found Lorac in the Tower of the Stars, as he sat upon his throne, his hand held fast by the orb. Cyan whispered into Lorac's ear a dream of Silvanesti, a terrible dream in which lovely trees became hideous, deformed monstrosities that attacked those who had once loved them. A dream in which Lorac saw his people die, one by one, each death painful and terrible to witness. A dream in which the Thon-Thalas river ran red with blood.

The War of the Lance ended. Queen Takhisis was defeated. Cyan Bloodbane was forced to flee Silvanesti, but he left smugly satisified with the knowledge that he had accomplished his goal. He had inflicted upon the Silvanesti a tortured dream from which they would never awaken. When the elves returned to their land after the war was over, they discovered to their shock and horror that the nightmare was reality. Lorac's dream, given to him by Cyan Bloodbane, had hideously altered their once beautiful land.

The Silvanesti fought the dream and, under the leadership of a Qualinesti general, Porthios, the elves eventually managed to defeat it. The cost was dear, however. Many elves fell victim to the dream, and even when it was finally cast out of the land, the trees and plants and animals remained horribly deformed. Slowly, the elves coaxed their forests back to beauty, using newly discovered magicks to heal the wounds left by the dream, to cover over the scars.

Then came the need to forget. Porthios, who had risked his life more than once to wrest their land from the clutches of the dream, became a reminder of the dream. He was no longer a savior. He was a stranger, an interloper, a threat to the Silvanesti who wanted to return to their life of isolation and seclusion. Porthios wanted to take the elves into the world, to make them one with the world, to unify them with their cousins, the Qualinesti. He had married Alhana Starbreeze, daughter of Lorac, with this hope in mind. Thus if war came again, the elves would not struggle alone. They would have allies to fight on their side.

The elves did not want allies. Allies who might decide to gobble up Silvanesti land in return for their help. Allies who might want to marry Silvanesti sons and daughters and dilute the pure Silvanesti blood. These isolationists had declared Porthios and his wife, Alhana, "dark elves" who could never, under penalty of death, return to their homelands.

Porthios was driven out. General Konnal took control of the nation and placed it under martial law "until such time as a true king can be found to rule the Silvanesti." The Silvanesti ignored the pleas of their cousins, the Qualinesti, for help to free them from the rule of the great dragon Beryl and the Knights of Neraka. The Silvanesti ignored the pleas of those who fought the great dragons and who begged the elves for their help. The Silvanesti wanted no part of the world. Absorbed in their own affairs, their eyes looked at the mirror of life and saw only themselves. Thus it was that while they gazed with pride at their own reflections, Cyan Bloodbane, the green dragon who had been their bane, came back to the land he had once nearly destroyed. Or so at least, it was reported by the kirath, who kept watch on the borders.

"Do not raise the shield!" the kirath warned. "You will trap us inside with our worst enemy!"

The elves did not listen. They did not believe the rumors. Cyan Bloodbane was a figure out of the dark past. He had died in the Dragon Purge. He must have died. If he had returned, why had he not attacked them? So fearful were the elves of the world outside that the Heads of House were unanimous in their approval of the magical shield. The people of Silvanesti could now be said to have gained their dearest wish. Under the magical shield, they were truly isolated, cut off from everyone. They were safe, protected from the evil of the outside world.

"And yet, it seems to me that we have not so much as shut the evil out," Rolan said to Silvan, "as that we have locked the evil in."

Night had come to Silvanesti. The darkness was welcome to Silvan, even as it was a grief to him. They had traveled by day through the forest, covering many miles until Rolan deemed they were far enough from the ill effects of the shield to stop and rest. The day had been a day of wonder to Silvanoshei.

He had heard his mother speak with longing, regret, and sorrow of the beauty of her homeland. He remembered as a child when he and his exiled parents were hiding in some cave with danger all about them, his mother would tell him tales of Silvanesti to quiet his fears. He would close his eyes and see, not the darkness, but the emerald, silver and gold of the forest. He would hear not the howls of wolf or goblin but the melodious chime of the bell flower or the sweetly sorrowful music of the flute tree.

His imagination paled before the reality, however. He could not believe that such beauty existed. He had spent the day as in a waking dream, stumbling over rocks, tree roots, and his own feet as wonders on every side brought tears to his eyes and joy to his heart.

Trees whose bark was tipped with silver lifted their branches to the sky in graceful arcs, their silver-edged leaves shining in the sunlight. A profusion of broad-leafed bushes lined the path, every bush ablaze with flame-colored flowers that scented the air with sweetness. He had the impression he did not walk through a forest so much as through a garden, for there were no fallen branches, no straggling weeds, no thickets of brambles. The Woodshapers permitted only the beautiful, the fruitful, and the beneficial to grow in their forests. The Woodshapers' magical influence extended throughout the land, with the exception of the borders, where the shield cast upon their handiwork a killing frost.

The darkness brought rest to Silvan's dazzled eyes. Yet the night had its own heart-piercing beauty. The stars blazed with fierce brilliance, as if defying the shield to try to shut them out. Night flowers opened their petals to the starlight, scented the warm darkness with exotic perfumes, while their luminescent glow filled the forest with a soft silvery white light.

"What do you mean?" Silvan asked. He could not equate evil with the beauty he'd witnessed.

"The cruel punishment we inflicted on your parents, for one, Your Majesty," said Rolan. "Our way of thanking your father for his aid was to try to stab him in the back. I was ashamed to be Silvanesti when I heard of this. But there has come a reckoning. We are being made to pay for our shame and our dishonor, for cutting ourselves off from the rest of the world, for living beneath the shield, protected from the dragons while others suffer. We pay for such protection with our lives."

They had stopped to rest in a clearing near a swift-flowing stream. Silvan was thankful for the respite. His injuries had started to pain him once more, though he had not liked to say anything. The excitement and shock of the sudden change in his life had drained him, depleted his energy.

Rolan found fruit and water with a sweetness like nectar for their dinner. He tended to Silvan's wounds with a respectful, solicitous care that the young man found quite pleasant.

Samar would have tossed me a rag and told me to make the best of it, Silvanoshei thought.

"Perhaps Your Majesty would like to sleep for a few hours," Rolan suggested after their supper.

Silvan had thought he was dropping from fatigue but found that he felt much better after eating, refreshed and renewed.

"I would like to know more about my homeland," he said. "My mother has told me some, but, of course, she could not know what has been happening since she . . . she left. You spoke of the shield." Silvan glanced about him. The beauty took his breath away. "I can understand why you would want to protect this"—he gestured to the trees whose boles shone with an iridescent light, to the star flowers that sparkled in the grass—"from the ravages of our enemies."

"Yes, Your Majesty," said Rolan and his tone softened. "There are some who say that no price is too high to pay for such protection, not even the price of our own lives. But if all of us are dead, who will be left to appreciate the beauty? And if we die, I believe that eventually the forests will die, too, for the souls of the elves are bound up in all things living."

"Our people number as the stars," said Silvan, amused, thinking that Rolan was being overly dramatic.

Rolan glanced up at the heavens. "Erase half those stars, Your Majesty, and you will find the light considerably diminished."

"Half!" Silvanoshei was shocked. "Surely not *half!*"

"Half the population of Silvanost alone has perished from the wasting sickness, Your Majesty." He paused a moment, then said, "What I am about to tell you would be considered treason, for which I would be severely punished."

"By punished, you mean cast out?" Silvan was troubled. "Exiled? Sent into darkness?"

"No, we do not do that anymore, Your Majesty," Rolan replied. "We cannot very well cast people out, for they could not pass through the shield. Now people who speak against Governor General Konnal simply disappear. No one knows what happens to them."

"If this is true, why don't the people rebel?" Silvan asked, bewildered. "Why don't they overthrow Konnal and demand that the shield be brought down?"

"Because only a few know the truth. And those of us who do have no evidence. We could stand in the Tower of the Stars and say that Konnal has gone mad, that he is so fearful of the world outside that he would rather see us all dead than be a part of that world. We could say all that, and then Konnal would stand up and say, 'You lie! Lower the shield and the Dark Knights will enter our beloved woods with their axes, the ogres will break and maim the living trees, the Great Dragons will descend upon us and devour us.' That is what he will say, and the people will cry, 'Save us! Protect us, dear Governor General Konnal! We have no one else to turn to!' and that will be that."

"I see," said Silvan thoughtfully. He glanced at Rolan, who was gazing intently into the darkness.

"Now the people will have someone else to turn to, Your Majesty," said Rolan. "The rightful heir to the Silvanesti throne. But we must proceed carefully, cautiously." He smiled sadly. "Else you, too, might 'disappear.'"

The lovely song of the nightingale throbbed in the darkness. Rolan pursed his lips and whistled back. Three elves materialized, emerging from the shadows. Silvan recognized them as the three who had first accosted him near the shield this morning.

This morning! Silvan marveled. Was it only this morning? Days, months, years had gone by since then.

Rolan stood to greet the three, clasping the elves by the hand and exchanging the ritual kiss on the cheek.

The elves wore the same cloak as did Rolan, and even though Silvan knew that they had entered the clearing, he was having a difficult time seeing them, for they seemed to be wrapped in darkness and starlight.

Rolan questioned them about their patrol. They reported

that the border along the Shield was quiet, "deathly quiet" one said with terrible irony. The three turned their attention back to Silvan.

"So have you questioned him, Rolan?" asked one, turning a stern gaze upon Silvanoshei. "Is he what he claims?"

Silvan scrambled to his feet, feeling awkward and embarrassed. He started to bow politely to his elders, as he had been taught, but then the thought came to him that he was king, after all. It was they who should bow to him. He looked at Rolan in some confusion.

"I did not 'question' him," Rolan said sternly. "We discussed certain things. And yes, I believe him to be Silvanoshei, the rightful Speaker of the Stars, son of Alhana and Porthios. Our king has returned to us. The day for which we have been waiting has arrived."

The three elves looked at Silvan, studied him up and down, then turned back to Rolan.

"He could be an imposter," said one.

"I am certain he is not," Rolan returned with firm conviction. "I knew his mother when she was his age. I fought with his father against the dreaming. He has the likeness of them both, though he favors his father. You, Drinel. You fought with Porthios. Look at this young man. You will see the father's image engraven on the son's."

The elf stared intently at Silvanoshei, who met his gaze and held it.

"See with your heart, Drinel," Rolan urged. "Eyes can be blinded. The heart cannot. You heard him when we followed him, when he had no idea we were spying on him. You heard what he said to us when he believed us to be soldiers of his mother's army. He was not dissembling. I stake my life on it."

"I grant you that he favors his father and that there is something of his mother in his eyes. By what miracle does the son of our exiled queen walk beneath the shield?" Drinel asked.

"I don't know how I came to be inside the shield," Silvan

said, embarrassed. "I must have fallen through it. I don't remember. But when I sought to leave, the shield would not let me."

"He threw himself against the shield," Rolan said. "He tried to go back, tried to leave Silvanesti. Would an imposter do that when he had gone to so much trouble to enter? Would an imposter admit that he did not know how he came through the shield? No, an imposter would have a tale to hand us, logical and easy to believe."

"You spoke of seeing with my heart," said Drinel. He glanced back at the other elves. "We are agreed. We want to try the truth-seek on him."

"You disgrace us with your distrust!" Rolan said, highly displeased. "What will he think of us?"

"That we are wise and prudent," Drinel answered dryly. "If he has nothing to hide, he will not object."

"It is up to Silvanoshei," Rolan replied. "Though I would refuse, if I were him."

"What is it?" Silvan looked from one to another, puzzled. "What is this truth-seek?"

"It is a magical spell, Your Majesty," Rolan answered and his tone grew sad. "Once there was a time when the elves could trust each other. Trust each other implicitly. Once there was a time when no elf could possibly lie to another of our people. That time came to an end during Lorac's dream. The dream created phantasms of our people, false images of fellow elves that yet seemed very real to those who looked on them and touched them and spoke to them. These phantasms could lure those who believed in them to ruin and destruction. A husband might see his wife beckoning to him and plunge headlong over a cliff in an effort to reach her. A mother might see a child perishing in flames and rush into the fire, only to find the child vanished.

"We kirath developed the truth-seek to determine if these phantasms were real or if they were a part of the dream. The phantasms were empty inside, hollow. They had no memories, no thoughts, no feelings. A touch of a hand upon the heart and we would know if we dealt with living person or the dream.

"When the dream ended, the need for the truth-seek ended, as well," Rolan said. "Or so we hoped. A hope that proved forlorn. When the dream ended, the twisted, bleeding trees were gone, the ugliness that perverted our land departed. But the ugliness had entered the hearts of some of our people, turned them as hollow as the hearts of those created by the dream. Now elf can lie to elf and does so. New words have crept into the elven vocabulary. Human words. Words like distrust, dishonest, dishonor. We use the truth-seek on each other now and it seems to me that the more we use it, the more the need to use it." He looked very darkly upon Drinel, who remained resolute, defiant.

"I have nothing to hide," said Silvan. "You may use this truth-seek on me and welcome. Though it would grieve my mother deeply to hear that her people have come to such a pass. She would never think to question the loyalty of those who follow her, as they would never think to question her care of them."

"You see, Drinel," said Rolan, flushing. "You see how you shame us!"

"Nevertheless, I will know the truth," Drinel said stubbornly.

"Will you?" Rolan demanded. "What if the magic fails you again?"

Drinel's eyes flashed. He cast a dark glance at his fellow. "Curb your tongue, Rolan. I remind you that as yet we know nothing about this young man."

Silvanoshei said nothing. It was not his place to interject himself into this dispute. But he stored up the words for future thought. Perhaps the elf sorcerers of his mother's army were not the only people who had found their magical power starting to wane.

Drinel approached Silvan, who stood stiffly, eyeing the elf

askance. Drinel reached out his left hand, his heart hand, for that is the hand closest to the heart, and rested his hand upon Silvan's breast. The elf's touch was light, yet Silvan could feel it strike through to his soul, or so it seemed.

Memory flowed from the font of his soul, good memories and bad, bubbling up from beneath surface feelings and thoughts and pouring into Drinel's hand. Memories of his father, a stern and implacable figure who rarely smiled and never laughed. Who never made any outward show of his affection, never spoke approval of his son's actions, rarely seemed to notice his son at all. Yet within that glittering flow of memory, Silvanoshei recalled one night, when he and his mother had narrowly escaped death at the hands of someone or other. Porthios had clasped them both in his arms, had held his small son close to his breast, had whispered a prayer over them in Elvish, an ancient prayer to gods who were no longer there to hear it. Silvanoshei remembered cold wet tears touching his cheek, remembered thinking to himself that these tears were not his. They were his father's.

This memory and others Drinel came to hold in his mind, as he might have held sparkling water in his cupped hands.

Drinel's expression altered. He looked at Silvan with new regard, new respect.

"Are you satisfied?" Silvan asked coldly. The memories had opened a bleeding gash in his being.

"I see his father in his face, his mother in his heart," Drinel replied. "I pledge you my allegiance, Silvanoshei. I urge others to do the same."

Drinel bowed deeply, his hand over his breast. The other two elves added their words of acceptance and allegiance. Silvan returned gracious thanks, all the while wondering a bit cynically just what all this kowtowing was truly worth to him. Elves had pledged allegiance to his mother, as well, and Alhana Starbreeze was little better than a bandit skulking in the woods.

If being the rightful Speaker of the Stars meant more

nights hiding in burial mounds and more days dodging assassins, Silvan could do without it. He was sick of that sort of life, sick to death of it. He had never fully admitted that until now. For the first time he admitted to himself that he was angry—hotly, bitterly angry—at his parents for having forced that sort of life upon him.

He was ashamed of his anger the next moment. He reminded himself that perhaps his mother was either dead or captive, but, irrationally, his grief and worry increased his anger. The conflicting emotions, complicated further by guilt, confused and exhausted him. He needed time to think, and he couldn't do that with these elves staring at him like some sort of stuffed curiosity in a mageware shop.

The elves remained standing, and Silvan eventually realized that they were waiting for him to sit down and rest themselves. He had been raised in an elven court, albeit a rustic one, and he was experienced at courtly maneuverings. He urged the other elves to be seated, saying that they must be weary, and he invited them to eat some of the fruit and water. Then Silvan excused himself from their company, explaining that he needed to make his ablutions.

He was surprised when Rolan warned him to be careful, offered him the sword he wore.

"Why?" Silvan was incredulous. "What is there to fear? I thought the shield kept out all our enemies."

"With one exception," Rolan answered dryly. "There are reports that the great green dragon, Cyan Bloodbane, was—by a 'miscalculation' on the part of General Konnal—trapped inside the shield."

"Bah! That is nothing but a story Konnal puts about in order to distract us," Drinel asserted. "Name me one person who has seen this monster! No one. The dragon is rumored to be here. He is rumored to be there. We go here and we go there and never find a trace of him. I think it odd, Rolan, that this Cyan Bloodbane is always sighted just when Konnal feels himself under pressure to answer to the leaders of the House-holds about the state of his rule."

"True, no one has seen Cyan Bloodbane," Rolan agreed. "Nevertheless, I confess I believe that the dragon is in Sil-vanesti somewhere. I once saw tracks I found very difficult to explain otherwise. Be careful, therefore, Your Majesty. And take my sword. Just in case."

Silvan refused the sword. Thinking back to how he had almost skewered Samar, Silvan was ashamed to let the others know he could not handle a weapon, ashamed to let them know that he was completely untrained in its use. He assured Rolan that he would keep careful watch and walked into the glittering forest. His mother, he recalled, would have sent an armed guard with him.

For the first time in my life, Silvan thought suddenly, I am free. Truly free.

He washed his face and hands in a clear, cold stream, raked his fingers through his long hair, and looked long at his reflection in the rippling water. He could see nothing of his father in his face, and he was always somewhat irritated by those who claimed that they could. Silvan's memories of Por-thios were of a stern, steel-hard warrior who, if he had ever known how to smile, had long since abandoned the practice. The only tenderness Silvan ever saw in his father's eyes was when they turned their gaze to his mother.

"You are king of the elves," Silvan said to his reflection. "You have accomplished in a day what your parents could not accomplish in thirty years. Could not . . . or would not."

He sat down on the bank. His reflection stirred and shim-mered in the light of the newly risen moon. "The prize they sought is within your grasp. You didn't particularly want it before, but now that it is offered, why not take it?"

Silvan's reflection rippled as a breath of wind passed over the surface of the water. Then the wind stilled, the water smoothed, and his reflection was clear and unwavering.

"You must walk carefully. You must think before you speak, think of the consequences of every word. You must consider your actions. You must not be distracted by the least little thing.

"My mother is dead," he said, and he waited for the pain.

Tears welled up inside him, tears for his mother, tears for his father, tears for himself, alone and bereft of their comfort and support. Yet, a tiny voice whispered deep inside, when did your parents ever support you? When did they ever trust you to do anything? They kept you wrapped in cotton wool, afraid you'd break. Fate has offered you this chance to prove yourself. Take it!

A bush grew near the stream, a bush with fragrant white flowers shaped like tiny hearts. Silvan picked a cluster of flowers, stripped the blossoms from the leafy stems. "Honor to my father, who is dead," he said and scattered the blossoms in the stream. They fell upon the reflection that broke apart in the spreading ripples. "Honor to my mother, who is dead."

He scattered the last of the blossoms. Then, feeling cleansed, empty of tears and empty of emotion, he returned to the camp.

The elves started to rise, but he asked them to remain seated and not disturb themselves on his account. The elves appeared pleased with his modesty.

"I hope my long absence did not worry you," he said, knowing well that it had. He could tell they had been talking about him. "These changes have all been so drastic, so sudden. I needed time to think."

The elves bowed in acquiescence.

"We have been discussing how best to advance Your Majesty's cause," said Rolan.

"You have the full support of the kirath, Your Majesty," Drinel added.

Silvan acknowledged this with a nod. He thought on

where he wanted this conversation to go and how best to take it there and asked mildly, "What is the 'kirath'? My mother spoke of many things in her homeland but not of this."

"There is no reason why she should," Rolan replied. "Your father created our order to fight the dream. We kirath were the ones who entered the forest, searching for the parts that were still held in thrall by the dream. The work took its toll on body and on mind, for we had to enter the dream in order to defeat it.

"Other kirath served to defend the Woodshapers and clerics who came into the forest to heal it. For twenty years we fought together to restore our homeland, and eventually we succeeded. When the dream was defeated we were no longer needed, and so we disbanded, returned to the lives we had led before the war. But those of us in the kirath had forged a bond closer than brothers and sisters. We kept in touch, passing news and information.

"Then the Dark Knights of Takhisis came to try to conquer the continent of Ansalon, and after that came the Chaos War. It was during this time that General Konnal took control of Silvanesti, saying that only the military could save us from the forces of evil at work in the world.

"We won the Chaos War, but at a great cost. We lost the gods, who, so it is said, made the ultimate sacrifice—withdrawing from the world so that Krynn and its people might continue on. With them went the magic of Solinari and healing powers. We grieved long for the gods, for Paladine and Mishakal, but we had to go on with our lives.

"We worked to continue to rebuild Silvanesti. Magic came to us again, a magic of the land, of living things. Though the war was over, General Konnal did not relinquish control. He said that now the threat came from Alhana and Porthios, dark elves who wanted only to avenge themselves on their people."

"Did you believe this?" Silvan asked indignantly.

"Of course not. We knew Porthios. We knew the great sacrifices he had made for this land. We knew Alhana and how much she loved her people. We did not believe him."

"And so you supported my father and mother?" Silvan asked.

"We did," Rolan replied.

"Then why didn't you aid them?" Silvan demanded, his tone sharpening. "You were armed and skilled in the use of arms. You were, as you have said, in close contact with one another. My mother and father waited on the borders, expecting confidently that the Silvanesti people would rise up and protest the injustice that had been done to them. They did not. You did nothing. My parents waited in vain."

"I could offer you many excuses, Your Majesty," Rolan said quietly. "We were weary of fighting. We did not want to start a civil war. We believed that over time this breach could all be made right by peaceful means. In other words"—he smiled faintly, sadly—"we pulled the blankets over our heads and went back to sleep."

"If it is any comfort to you, Your Majesty, we have paid for our sins," Drinel added. "Paid most grievously. We realized this when the magical shield was erected, but by that time it was too late. We could not go out. Your parents could not come within."

Understanding came to Silvan in a flash, dazzling and shocking as the lightning bolt that had struck right in front of him. All had been darkness before and in the next thudding heartbeat all was lit brighter than day, every detail clear cut and stark in the white-hot light.

His mother claimed to hate the shield. In truth the shield was her excuse, keeping her from leading her army into Silvanesti. She could have done so anytime during the years before the shield was raised. She and her father could have marched an army into Silvanesti, they would have found support among the people. Why hadn't they?

The spilling of elven blood. That was the excuse they gave then. They did not want to see elf killing elf. The truth was that Alhana had expected her people to come to her and lay the crown of Silvanesti at her feet. They had not done so. As Rolan had said, they wanted only to go back to sleep, wanted to forget Lorac's nightmare in more pleasant dreams. Alhana had been the cat yowling beneath the window, disturbing their rest.

His mother had refused to admit this to herself and thus, though she railed against the raising of the shield, in reality the shield had been a relief to her. Oh, she had done all she could to try to destroy it. She had done all she could to prove to herself that she wanted desperately to penetrate the barrier. She had thrown her armies against the shield, thrown herself against it. But all the while, secretly, in her heart, she did not want to enter and perhaps that was the reason the shield had been successful in keeping her out.

Drinel and Rolan and the rest of the elves were inside it for the very same reason. The shield was in place, the shield existed, because the elves wanted it. The Silvanesti had always yearned to be kept safe from the world, safe from the contamination of the crude and undisciplined humans, safe from the dangers of ogre and goblin and minotaur, safe from the dragons, safe amidst ease and luxury and beauty. That was why his mother had wanted to find a way inside—so that she too could finally sleep in warmth and in safety, not in burial mounds.

He said nothing, but he realized now what he had to do.

"You pledge your allegiance to me. How do I know that when the path grows dark you will not abandon me as you abandoned my parents?"

Rolan paled. Drinel's eyes flashed in anger. He started to speak, but his friend laid a calming hand on his arm.

"Silvanoshei is right to rebuke us, my friend. His Majesty is right to ask this question of us." Rolan turned to face

Silvan. "Hand and heart, I pledge myself and my family to Your Majesty's cause. May my soul be held in thrall on this plane of existence if I fail."

Silvan nodded gravely. It was a terrible oath. He shifted his gaze to Drinel and the other two members of the kirath. Drinel was hesitant.

"You are very young," he said harshly. "How old are you? Thirty years? You are considered an adolescent among our people."

"But not among the Qualinesti," Silvanoshei returned. "And I ask you to think of this," he added, knowing that the Silvanesti were not likely to be impressed by comparisons with their more worldly (and therefore more corrupt) cousins. "I have not been raised in a pampered, sheltered Silvanesti household. I have been raised in caves, in shacks, in hovels—wherever my parents could find safe shelter. I can count on my two hands the number of nights I have slept in a room in a bed. I have been twice wounded in battles. I bear the scars upon my body."

Silvan did not add that he had not received his wounds while fighting in those battles. He did not mention that he had been injured while his body guards were hustling him off to a place of safety. He would have fought, he thought to himself, if anyone had given him a chance. He was prepared to fight now.

"I make the same pledge to you that I ask of you," Silvan said proudly. "Heart and hand, I pledge to do everything in my power to regain the throne that is mine by right. I pledge to bring wealth, peace, and prosperity back to our people. May my soul be held in thrall on this plane of existence if I fail."

Drinel's eyes sifted, searched that soul. The elder elf appeared satisfied with he saw. "I make my pledge to you, Silvanoshei, son of Porthios and Alhana. By aiding the son, may we make restitution for our failures in regard to the parents."

"And now," said Rolan. "We must make plans. We must find a suitable hiding place for His Majesty—"

"No," said Silvan firmly. "The time for hiding is past. I am the rightful heir to the throne. I have a lawful claim. I have nothing to fear. If I go sneaking and skulking about like a criminal, then I will be perceived as a criminal. If I arrive in Silvanost as a king, I will be perceived as a king."

"Yet, the danger—" Rolan began.

"His Majesty is right, my friend," Drinel said, regarding Silvan with now marked respect. "He will be in less danger by making a great stir than he would be if he were to go into hiding. In order to placate those who question his rule, Konnal has stated many times that he would gladly see the son of Alhana take his rightful place upon the throne. He could make such a promise easily enough, for he knew—or thought he knew—that with the shield in place, the son could not possibly enter.

"If Your Majesty arrives triumphantly in the capital, with the people cheering on all sides, Konnal will be forced to make some show of keeping his promise. He will find it difficult to make the rightful heir disappear, as have others in the past. The people would not stand for it."

"What you say has merit. Yet we must never underestimate Konnal," said Rolan. "Some believe he is mad, but if so, his is a cunning, calculating madness. He is dangerous."

"So am I," said Silvan. "As he will soon discover."

He sketched out his plan. The others listened, voiced their approval, offered changes he accepted, for they knew his people best. He listened gravely to the discussion of possible danger, but in truth, he paid little heed.

Silvanoshei was young, and the young know they will live forever.

9

Gallivanting

he same night that Silvanoshei accepted the rulership of the Silvanesti, Tasslehoff Burrfoot slept
soundly and peacefully—much to his disappointment.

The kender was deposited for safekeeping in a room
inside the Solamnic garrison in Solace. Tas had offered to
return to the wonderful kender-proof Solace jail, but his
request was firmly denied. The garrison room was clean and
neat, with no windows, no furniture except a stern-looking
bed with iron railings and a mattress so stiff and rigid that it
could have stood at attention with the best of the Knights.
The door had no lock at all, which might have provided some
light after-dinner amusement but was held in place by a
wooden bar across the outside.

"All in all," Tas said to himself as he sat disconsolately on
his bed, kicking his feet against the iron railings and looking
wistfully about, "this room is the single most boring place
I've ever been in my life with the possible exception of the
Abyss."

Gerard had even taken away his candle, leaving Tas alone in the dark. There seemed nothing to do but go to sleep.

Tasslehoff had long thought that someone would do a very good service to mankind by abolishing sleep. Tas had mentioned this to Raistlin once, remarking that a wizard of his expertise could probably find a way around sleep, which took up a good portion of one's time with very little benefit that Tas could see. Raistlin had replied that the kender should be thankful someone had invented sleep for this meant that Tasslehoff was quiet and comatose for eight hours out of a day and this was the sole reason that Raistlin had not yet strangled him.

Sleep had one benefit and that was dreams, but this benefit was almost completely nullified by the fact that one woke from a dream and was immediately faced with the crushing disappointment that it had been a dream, that the dragon chasing one with the intent of biting off one's head was not a real dragon, that the ogre trying to bash one into pulp with a club was not a real ogre. Add to this the fact that one always woke up at the most interesting and exciting part of the dream—when the dragon had one's head in his mouth, for example, or the ogre had hold of the back of one's collar. Sleep, as far as Tas was concerned, was a complete waste of time. Every night saw him determined to fight sleep off, and every morning found him waking up to discover that sleep had sneaked up on him unawares and run away with him.

Tasslehoff didn't offer sleep much of a fight this night. Worn out from the rigors of travel and the excitement and snuffles occasioned by Caramon's funeral, Tas lost the battle without a struggle. He woke to find that not only had sleep stolen in on him but that Gerard had done the same. The Knight stood over him, glaring down with his customary grim expression, which looked considerably grimmer by lantern light.

"Get up," said the Knight. "Put these on."

Gerard handed Tas some clothes that were clean and well-made, drab, dull and—the kender shuddered—serviceable.

"Thank you," said Tas, rubbing his eyes. "I know you mean well, but I have my own clothes—"

"I won't travel with someone who looks as if he had been in a fight with a Maypole and lost," Gerard countered. "A blind gully dwarf could see you from six miles off. Put these on, and be quick about it."

"A fight with a Maypole," Tas giggled. "I actually saw one of those once. It was at this Mayday celebration in Solace. Caramon put on a wig and petticoats and went out to dance with the young virgins, only his wig slipped over his eye—"

Gerard held up a stern finger. "Rule number one. No talking."

Tas opened his mouth to explain that he wasn't really talking, not talking as in talking, but talking as in telling a story, which was quite a different thing altogether. Before Tas was able to get a word out, Gerard displayed the gag.

Tasslehoff sighed. He enjoyed traveling, and he was truly looking forward to this adventure, but he did feel that he might have been granted a more congenial traveling companion. He sadly relinquished his colorful clothes, laying them on the bed with a fond pat, and dressed himself in the brown knickers, the brown wool socks, the brown shirt, and brown vest Gerard had laid out for him. Tas, looking down at himself, thought sadly that he looked exactly like a tree stump. He started to put his hands in his pockets when he discovered there weren't any.

"No pouches, either," said Gerard, picking up Tasslehoff's bags and pouches and preparing to add them to the pile of discarded clothing.

"Now, see here—" Tas began sternly.

One of the pouches fell open. The light from the lantern glittered merrily on the gleaming, winking jewels of the Device of Time Journeying.

"Oops," said Tasslehoff as innocently as ever he could and indeed he was innocent, this time at least.

"How did you get this away from me?" Gerard demanded.

Tasslehoff shrugged and, pointing to his sealed lips, shook his head.

"If I ask you a question, you may answer," Gerard stated, glowering. "When did you steal this from me?"

"I didn't steal it," Tas replied with dignity. "Stealing is extremely bad. I told you. The device keeps coming back to me. It's not my fault. *I* don't want it. I had a stern talk with it last night, in fact, but it doesn't seem to listen."

Gerard glared, then, muttering beneath his breath—something to the effect that he didn't know why he bothered—he thrust the magical device in a leather pouch he wore at his side. "And it had better *stay* there," he said grimly.

"Yes, you'd better do what the Knight says!" Tas added loudly, shaking his finger at the device. He was rewarded for his help by having the gag tied around his mouth.

The gag in place, Gerard snapped a pair of manacles over Tas's wrists. Tas would have slipped right out of ordinary manacles, but these manacles were specially made for a kender's slender wrists, or so it appeared. Tas worked and worked and couldn't free himself. Gerard laid a heavy hand on the kender's shoulder and marched him out of the room and down the hall.

The sun had not yet made an appearance. The garrison was dark and quiet. Gerard allowed Tas time to wash his face and hands—he had to wash around the gag—and do whatever else he needed to do, keeping close watch on him all the time and not allowing the kender a moment's privacy. He then escorted him out of the building.

Gerard wore a long, enveloping cloak over his armor. Tas couldn't see the armor beneath the cloak, and he knew the Knight was wearing armor only because he heard it clank and rattle. Gerard did not wear a helm or carry a sword. He walked the kender back to the Knights' quarters, where Gerard picked up a large knapsack and what could have been a sword wrapped up in a blanket tied with rope.

Gerard then marched Tasslehoff, bound and gagged, to the front of the garrison. The sun was a tiny sliver of light on the horizon and then it was swallowed by a cloudbank, so that it seemed as if the sun were starting to rise and had suddenly changed its mind and gone back to bed.

Gerard handed a paper to the Captain of the Guard. "As you can see, sir, I have Lord Warren's permission to remove the prisoner."

The captain glanced at it and then at the kender. Gerard, Tas noticed, was careful to keep out of the light of the flaring torches mounted on the wooden posts on either side of the gate. Instantly the idea came to Tas that Gerard was trying to hide something. The kender's curiosity was aroused, an occurrence that often proves fatal to the kender and also to those who happen to be a kender's companions. Tas stared with all his might, trying to see what was so interesting beneath the cloak.

He was in luck. The morning breeze came up. The cloak fluttered slightly. Gerard caught it quickly, held it fastened in front of him, but not before Tasslehoff had seen the torchlight shine on armor that was gleaming black.

Under normal circumstances Tas would have demanded loudly and excitedly to know why a Solamnic Knight was wearing black armor. The kender probably would have tugged on the cloak in order to obtain a better view and pointed out this odd and interesting fact to the captain of the guard. The gag prevented Tas from saying any of this except in muffled and incoherent squeaks and "*mfrts*," which was all he could manage.

On second thought—and it was due solely to the gag that Tasslehoff actually had a second thought—the kender realized that perhaps Gerard might not want anyone to know he was wearing black armor. Thus, the cloak.

Quite charmed by this new twist to the adventure, Tasslehoff kept silent, merely letting Gerard know with several cunning winks that he, the kender, was in on the secret.

"Where are you taking the little weasel?" the captain asked, handing the paper back to Gerard. "And what's wrong with his eye? He hasn't got pink eye, has he?"

"Not to my knowledge, sir. Begging the captain's pardon, but I can't tell you where I'm ordered to deliver the kender, sir. That information is secret," Gerard replied respectfully. Lowering his voice, he added, "He's the one who was caught desecrating the tomb, sir."

The captain nodded in understanding. He glanced askance at the bundles the Knight was carrying. "What's that?"

"Evidence, sir," Gerard replied.

The captain looked very grim. "Did a lot of damage, did he? I trust they'll make an example of him."

"I should think they might, sir," Gerard replied evenly.

The captain waved Gerard and Tas through the gate, paid no further attention to them. Gerard hustled the kender away from the garrison and out onto the main road. Although the morning itself wasn't quite awake yet, many people were. Farmers were bringing in their goods to market. Wagons were rolling out to the logging camps in the mountains. Anglers were heading for Crystalmir Lake. People cast a few curious glances at the cloaked Knight—the morning was already quite warm. Busy with their own cares, they passed by without comment. If he wanted to swelter, that was his concern. None of them so much as looked twice at Tasslehoff. The sight of a bound and gagged kender was nothing new.

Gerard and Tas took the road south out of Solace, a road that meandered alongside the Sentinel range of mountains and would eventually deposit them in South Pass. The sun had finally decided to crawl out of bed. Pink light spread in a colorful wash across the sky. Gold gilded the tree leaves, and diamonds of dew sparkled on the grass. A fine day for adventuring, and Tas would have enjoyed himself immensely but for the fact that he was hustled along and harried and not permitted to stop to look at anything along the road.

Although encumbered with the knapsack, which appeared quite heavy, and the sword in a blanket, Gerard set a fast pace. He carried both objects in one hand, keeping the other to prod Tasslehoff in the back if he started to slow down or to grab hold of his collar if he started to wander off or jerk him backward if he made a sudden dart across the road.

One would not have guessed it from looking at him, but Gerard, for all that he was of average height and medium build, was extremely strong.

The Knight was a grim and silent companion. He did not return the cheerful "good mornings" of those heading into Solace, and he coldly rebuffed a traveling tinker who was going in their direction and offered them a seat on his wagon.

He did at least remove the gag from the kender's mouth. Tas was thankful. Not as young as he used to be—something he would freely admit—he found that between the fast pace set by the Knight and the constant prodding, tugging, and jerking, he was doing more breathing than his nose alone could manage.

Tas immediately asked all the questions he had been storing up, starting with, "Why is your armor black? I've never seen black armor before. Well, yes, I have but it wasn't on a Knight of Solamnia," and ending with, "Are we going to walk all the way to Qualinesti, and if we are would you mind not seizing hold of my shirt collar in that very energetic way you have because it's starting to rub off all my skin."

Tas soon found out that he could ask all the questions he liked, just so long as he didn't expect any answers. Sir Gerard made no response except, "Keep moving."

The Knight was young, after all. Tas felt compelled to point out to him the mistake he was making.

"The very best part of questing," the kender said, "is seeing the sights along the way. Taking time to enjoy the view and investigating all the interesting things you find along the road and talking to all the people. If you stop to think about it, the goal of the quest, such as fighting the dragon or rescuing the woolly mammoth, takes up only a small bit of time, and although it's always very exciting, there's a whole lot more time stacked up in front of it and behind it—the getting there and the coming back—which can be very dull if you don't work at it."

"I am not interested in excitement," said Gerard. "I want simply to be done with this and to be done with you. The sooner I am finished the sooner I can do something to achieve my goal."

"And what's that?" Tas asked, delighted that the Knight was finally talking to him.

"To join the fighting in defense of Sanction," Gerard answered, "and when that is done, to free Palanthas from the scourge of the Knights of Neraka."

"Who are they?" Tas asked, interested.

"They used to be known as the Knights of Takhisis, but they changed their name when it grew clear to them that Takhisis wasn't coming back anymore."

"What do you mean, not coming back. Where did she go?" Tas asked.

Gerard shrugged. "With the other gods, if you believe what people say. Personally I think claiming that the bad times are a result of the gods leaving us is just an excuse for our own failures."

"The gods left!" Tas's jaw dropped. "When?"

Gerard snorted. "I'm not playing games with you, kender."

Tas pondered all that Gerard had told him.

"Don't you have this whole Knight business backward?" Tas asked finally. "Isn't Sanction being held by the Dark Knights and Palanthas by your Knights?"

"No, I do not have it backward. More's the pity," Gerard said.

Tas sighed deeply. "I'm extremely confused."

Gerard grunted and prodded the kender, who was slowing down a bit, his legs not being as young as they used to be either. "Hurry up," he said. "We don't have much farther."

"We don't?" Tas said meekly. "Did they move Qualinesti, too?"

"If you must know, kender, I have two mounts waiting for us at the Solace bridge. And before you can ask yet another question, the reason we walked from the garrison and did not ride is that the horse I am using is not my customary mount. The animal would have occasioned comment, would have required explanation."

"I have a horse? A horse of my own! How thrilling! I haven't ridden a horse in ever so long." Tasslehoff came to a halt, looked up at the Knight. "I'm terribly sorry I misjudged you. I guess you do understand about adventuring, after all."

"Keep moving." Gerard gave him a shove.

A thought occurred to the kender—a truly astonishing thought that took away what little breath he had remaining. He paused to find his breath again and then used it to ask the question the thought had produced.

"You don't like me, do you, Sir Gerard?" Tas said. He wasn't angry or accusing, just surprised.

"No," said Gerard, "I do not." He took a drink of water from a waterskin and handed the skin to Tas. "If it is any consolation, there is nothing personal in my dislike. I feel this way about all your kind."

Tas considered this as he drank the water, which was quite tepid and tasted of the waterskin. "Maybe I'm wrong, but it seems to me that I'd much rather be disliked for being me than to be disliked just because I'm a kender. I can do something about me, you see, but I can't do much about being a kender because my mother was a kender and so was my father and that seems to have a lot to do with me being a kender.

"I might have wanted to be a Knight," Tas continued, warming to his subject. "In fact, I'm pretty sure I probably did, but the gods must have figured that my mother, being small, couldn't very well give birth to someone as big as you, not without considerable inconvenience to herself, and so I came out a kender. Actually, no offense, but I take that back about being a Knight. I think what I really wanted to be was a draconian—they are so very fierce and scaly, and they have wings. I've always wanted wings. But, of course, that would have been *extremely* difficult for my mother to have managed."

"Keep moving," was all Gerard said in reply.

"I could help you carry that bundle if you'd take off these manacles," Tas offered, thinking that if he made himself useful, the Knight might come to like him.

"No," Gerard returned, and that was that. Not even a thank you.

"*Why* don't you like kender?" Tas pursued. "Flint always said he didn't like kender, but I know deep down he did. I don't think Raistlin liked kender much. He tried to murder me once, which gave me sort of a hint as to his true feelings. But I forgave him for that, although I'll never forgive him for murdering poor Gnimsh, but that's another story. I'll tell you that later. Where was I? Oh, yes. I was about to add that Sturm Brightblade was a Knight, and he liked kender, so I was just wondering what you have against us."

"Your people are frivolous and heedless," said Gerard, his voice hard. "These are dark days. Life is serious business and should be taken seriously. We do not have the luxury for joy and merriment."

"But if there's no joy and merriment, then of course the days will be dark," Tas argued. "What else do you expect?"

"How much joy did you feel, kender, when you heard the

news that hundreds of your people in Kendermore had been slaughtered by the great dragon Malystryx?" Gerard asked grimly, "and that those who survived were driven from their homes and now seem to be under some sort of curse and are called afflicted because they now know fear and they carry swords, not pouches. Did you laugh when you heard that news, kender, and sing 'tra la, how merry we are this day'?"

Tasslehoff came to a stop and rounded so suddenly that the Knight very nearly tripped over him.

"Hundreds? Killed by a dragon?" Tas was aghast. "What do you mean hundreds of kender died in Kendermore? I never heard that. I never heard anything like that! It's not true. You're lying. . . . No," he added miserably. "I take that back. You can't lie. You're a Knight, and while you may not like me you're honor bound not to lie to me."

Gerard said nothing. Putting his hand on Tas's shoulder, he turned the kender around bodily and started him, once again, on his way.

Tas noticed a queer feeling in the vicinity of his heart, a constricting kind of feeling, as if he'd swallowed one of the more ferocious constricting snakes. The feeling was uncomfortable and not at all pleasant. Tas knew in that moment that the Knight had indeed spoken truly. That hundreds of his people had died most horribly and painfully. He did not know how this had happened, but he knew it was true, as true as the grass growing along the side of the road or the tree branches overhead or the sun gleaming down through the green leaves.

It was true in this world where Caramon's funeral had been different from what he remembered. But it hadn't been true in that other world, the world of Caramon's first funeral.

"I feel sort of strange," Tas said in a small voice. "Kind of dizzy. Like I might throw up. If you don't mind, I think I'm going to be quiet for awhile."

"Praise be," said the Knight, adding, with another shove. "Keep walking."

They walked in silence and eventually, about mid-morning, reached Solace Bridge. The bridge spanned Solace Stream, an easy-going, meandering brook that wandered around the foothills of the Sentinel Mountains and then tumbled blithely through South Pass until it reached the White Rage River. The bridge was wide in order to accommodate wagons and teams of horses as well as foot traffic.

In the old days, the bridge had been free for the use of the traveler, but as traffic increased over the bridge, so did the maintenance and the upkeep of the span. The Solace city fathers grew weary of spending tax money to keep the bridge in operation and so they erected a tollgate and added a toll-taker. The fee required was modest. Solace Stream was shallow, you could walk across it in places, and travelers could always cross at other fords along the route. However, the banks through which the stream ran were steep and slippery. More than one wagon load of valuable merchandise had ended up in the water. Most travelers elected to pay the toll.

The Knight and the kender were the only ones crossing this time of day. The toll-taker was eating breakfast in his booth. Two horses were tied up beneath a stand of cottonwood trees that grew along the bank. A young lad who looked and smelled like a stable hand dozed on the grass. One of the horses was glossy black, his coat gleamed in the sunlight. He was restive, pawed the ground and occasionally gave a jerk on the reins as a test to see if he could free himself. The other mount was a small pony, dapple gray, with a bright eye and twitching ears and nose. Her hooves were almost completely covered by long strands of fur.

The constricting snake around Tas's heart eased up a good deal at the sight of the pony, who seemed to regard the kender with a friendly, if somewhat mischievous, eye.

"Is she mine?" Tas asked, thrilled beyond belief.

"No," said Gerard. "The horses have been hired for the journey, that is all."

He kicked at the stable hand, who woke up and, yawning and scratching at himself, said that they owed him thirty steel for the horses, saddles, and blankets, ten of which would be given back to them upon the animals' safe return. Gerard took out his money purse and counted out the coin. The stable hand—keeping as far from Tasslehoff as possible—counted the money over again distrustfully, deposited it in a sack and stuffed the sack in his straw-covered shirt.

"What's the pony's name?" asked Tasslehoff, delighted.

"Little Gray," said the stable hand.

Tas frowned. "That doesn't show much imagination. I think you could have come up with something more original than that. What's the black horse's name?"

"Blackie," replied the stable hand, picking his teeth with a straw.

Tasslehoff sighed deeply.

The tollbooth keeper emerged from his little house. Gerard handed him the amount of the toll. The keeper raised the gate. This done, he eyed the Knight and kender with intense curiosity and seemed prepared to spend the rest of the morning discussing where the two were headed and why.

Gerard answered shortly, "yay" or "nay" as might be required. He hoisted Tasslehoff onto the pony, who swiveled her head to look back at him and winked at him as if they shared some wonderful secret. Gerard placed the mysterious bundle and the sword wrapped in the blanket on the back of his own horse, tied them securely. He took hold of the reins of Tas's pony and mounted his own horse, then rode off, leaving the toll-taker standing on the bridge talking to himself.

The Knight rode in front, keeping hold of the pony's reins. Tas rode behind, his manacled hands holding tight to the pommel of the saddle. Blackie didn't seem to like the gray pony much better than Gerard liked the kender. Perhaps Blackie was resentful of the slow pace he was forced to set to accommodate the pony or perhaps he was a horse of a stern and serious nature who took umbrage at a certain friskiness exhibited by the pony. Whatever the reason, if the black horse caught the gray pony doing a little sideways shuffle for the sheer fun of it, or if he thought she might be tempted to stop and nibble at some buttercups on the side of the road, he would turn his head and regard her and her rider with a cold eye.

They had ridden about five miles when Gerard called a halt. He stood in his saddle, looked up and down the road. They had not met any travelers since they had left the bridge, and now the road was completely empty. Dismounting, Gerard removed his cloak and rolling it up, he stuffed it in his bedroll. He was wearing the black breastplate decorated with skulls and the death lily of a Dark Knight.

"What a great disguise!" Tas exclaimed, charmed. "You told Lord Warren you were going to be a Knight and you didn't lie. You just didn't tell him what sort of Knight you were going to become. Do I get to be disguised as a Dark Knight? I mean a Neraka Knight? Oh, no, I get it! Don't tell me. I'm going to be your prisoner!" Tasslehoff was quite proud of himself for having figured this out. "This is going to be more fun—er, interesting—than I'd expected."

Gerard did not smile. "This is not a joy ride, kender," he said and his voice was stern and grim. "You hold my life and your own in your hands, as well as the fate of our mission. I must be a fool, to trust something so important to one of your kind, but I have no choice. We will soon be entering the territory controlled by the Knights of Neraka. If you breathe a word about my being a Solamnic Knight, I will be arrested and executed as a spy. But first, before they kill me, they will torture me to find out what I know. They use the rack to torture people. Have you ever seen a man stretched upon the rack, kender?"

"No, but I saw Caramon do calisthenics once, and he said that was torture. . . ."

Gerard ignored him. "They tie your hands and feet to the rack and then pull them in opposite directions. Your arms and legs, wrists and elbows, knees and ankles are pulled from their sockets. The pain is excruciating, but the beauty of the torture is that though the victim suffers terribly, he doesn't die. They can keep a man on the rack for days. The bones never return to their proper place. When they take a man off the rack, he is a cripple. They have to carry him to the scaffold, put him in a chair in order to hang him. That will be my fate if you betray me, kender. Do you understand?"

"Yes, Sir Gerard," said Tasslehoff. "And even though you don't like me, which I have to tell you really hurts my feelings, I wouldn't want to see you stretched on the rack. Maybe someone else—because I never saw anyone's arm pulled out of its socket before—but not you."

Gerard did not appear impressed by this magnanimous offer. "Keep a curb on your tongue for your sake as well as mine."

"I promise," said Tas, putting his hand to his topknot and giving it a painful yank that brought tears to his eyes. "I *can* keep a secret, you know. I've kept any number of secrets—important secrets, too. I'll keep this one. You can depend on me or my name's not Tasslehoff Burrfoot."

This appeared to impress Gerard even less. Looking very dour, he returned to his horse, remounted and rode forward—a Dark Knight leading his prisoner.

"How long will it take us to reach Qualinesti?" Tas asked.

"At this pace, four days," Gerard replied.

Four days. Gerard paid no more attention to the kender. The Knight refused to answer a single question. He was deaf to Tasslehoff's very best and most wonderful stories, and did not bother to respond when Tas suggested that he knew a most exciting short cut through Darken Wood.

"Four days of this! I don't like to complain," Tas said, talking to himself and the pony since the Knight wasn't listening, "but this adventure is turning out to be dull and boring. Not really an adventure at all, more of a drudge, if that is a word, which whether it is or not certainly fits the situation."

He and the pony plodded along, looking forward to four days with no one to talk to, nothing to do, nothing to see except trees and mountains, which would have been interesting if Tas could have spent some time exploring them, but, as he couldn't, he'd seen plenty of trees and mountains at a distance before. So bored was the kender that the next time the magical device came back to him, appearing suddenly in his manacled hands, Tasslehoff was tempted to use it. Anything, even getting squished by a giant, would be better than this.

If it hadn't been for the pony ride, he would have.

At that moment, the black horse looked around to regard the pony balefully and perhaps some sort of communication passed between horse and rider for Gerard turned around too.

Grinning sheepishly and shrugging, Tas held up the Device of Time Journeying.

His face fixed and cold as that of the skull on his black breastplate, Gerard halted, waited for the pony to plod up beside him. He reached out his hand, snatched the magical device from Tas's hands, and, without a word, thrust the device in a saddlebag.

Tasslehoff sighed again. It was going to be a long four days.

10

Lord of the Night

he Order of the Knights of Takhisis was born in a dream of darkness and founded upon a remote and secret island in Krynn's far north, an island known as Storm's Keep. But the island headquarters had been severely damaged during the Chaos War. Boiling seas completely submerged the fortress—some said due to the sea goddess Zeboim's grief at the death of her son, the Knights' founder, Lord Ariakan. Although the waters receded, no one ever returned to it. The fortress was now deemed too remote to be of practical use to the Knights of Takhisis, who had emerged from the Chaos War battered and bruised, bereft of their Queen and her Vision, but with a sizeable force, a force to be reckoned with.

Thus it was that a Knight of the Skull, Mirielle Abrena, attending the first Council of the Last Heroes, felt confident enough to demand that the remnant of the Knighthood that remained be granted land on the continent of Ansalon in return for their heroic deeds during the war. The council allowed the Knights to keep territory they had captured, mainly Qualinesti (as usual, few humans cared much about the elves) and also the land in the northeastern part of Ansalon that included Neraka and its environs. The Dark Knights accepted this region, blasted and cursed though parts of it were, and set about building up their Order.

Many on that first council hoped the Knights would suffocate and perish in the sulphur-laden air of Neraka. The Dark Knights not only survived, but thrived. This was due in part to the leadership of Abrena, Lord of the Night, who added to that military title the political title of governor-general of Neraka. Abrena instituted a new recruitment policy, a policy that was not so choosy as the old policy, not so nice, not so restrictive. The Knights had little problem filling their ranks. In the dark days following the Chaos War, the people felt alone and abandoned. What might be called the Ideal of the Great "I" arose on Ansalon. Its main precept: "No one else matters. Only I."

Embracing this precept, the Dark Knights were clever in their rule. They did not permit much in the way of personal freedoms, but they did encourage trade and promote business. When Khellendros, the great blue dragon, captured the city of Palanthas, he placed the Dark Knights in charge. Terrified at the thought of these cruel overlords ravishing their city, the people of Palanthas were amazed to find that they actually prospered under the rulership of the Dark Knights. And although the Palanthians were taxed for the privilege, they were able to keep enough of their profits to believe that life under the dictatorial rule of the Dark Knights wasn't all that bad. The knights kept law and order, they waged continuous war against the Thieves Guild, and they sought to rid the city of the gully dwarves residing in the sewers.

The dragon purge that followed the arrival of the great dragons at first appalled and angered the Knights of Takhisis, who lost many of their own dragons in the slaughter. In vain the Knights fought against the great Red, Malys, and her cousins. Many of the Knights' order died, as did many of their chromatic dragons. Mirielle's cunning leadership managed to turn even this near disaster into a triumph. The Dark Knights made secret pacts with the dragons, agreeing to work for them to collect tribute and maintain law and order in lands ruled by the dragons. In return, the dragons would give the Dark Knights a free hand and cease preying upon their surviving dragons.

The people of Palanthas, Neraka, and Qualinesti knew nothing of the pact made between the Knights and the Dragons. The people saw only that once again the Dark Knights had defended them against a terrible foe. The Knights of Solamnia and the mystics of the Citadel of Light knew or guessed of these pacts but could not prove anything.

Although there were some within the ranks of the Dark Knights who still held to the beliefs of honor and self-sacrifice expounded by the late Ariakan, they were mostly the older members, who were considered out of touch with the ways of the modern world. A new Vision had come to replace the old. This new Vision was based on the mystical powers of the heart developed by Goldmoon in the Citadel of Light and stolen by several Skull Knights, who disguised themselves and secretly entered the Citadel to learn how to use these powers for their own ambitious ends. The Dark Knight mystics came away with healing skills and, more frightening, the ability to manipulate their followers' thoughts.

Armed with the ability to control not only the bodies of those who entered the Knighthood but their minds as well, the Skull Knights rose to prominence within the ranks of the Dark Knights. Although the Dark Knights had long and loudly maintained that Queen Takhisis was going to return, they had ceased to believe it. They had ceased to believe in anything except their own power and might, and this was reflected in the new Vision. The Skull Knights who administered the new Vision were adept at probing a candidate's mind, finding his most secret terrors and playing upon those, while at the same time promising him his heart's desire—all in return for strict obedience.

So powerful did the Skull Knights grow through the use of the new Vision that those closest to Mirielle Abrena began to look upon the Skull Knights with distrust. In particular, they warned Abrena against the leader, the Adjudicator, a man named Morham Targonne.

Abrena scoffed at these warnings. "Targonne is an able administrator," she said. "I grant him that much. But, when all is said and done, what *is* an able administrator? Nothing more than a glorified clerk. And that is Targonne. He would never challenge me for leadership. The man grows queasy at the sight of blood! He refuses to attend the jousts or tourneys but keeps himself locked up in his dingy little cabinet, absorbed in his debits and his credits. He has no stomach for battle."

Abrena spoke truly. Targonne had no stomach for battle. He would have never dreamed of challenging Abrena for the leadership in honorable combat. The sight of blood really did make him sick. And so he had her poisoned.

As Lord of the Skull Knights, Targonne announced at Abrena's funeral that he was the rightful successor. No one stood to challenge him. Those who might have done so, friends and supporters of Abrena's, kept their mouths shut, lest they ingest the same "tainted meat" that had killed their leader. Eventually Targonne killed them too, so that by now he was firmly entrenched in power. He and those Knights who were trained in mentalism used their powers to delve into the minds of their followers to ferret out traitors and malcontents.

Targonne came from a wealthy family with extensive holdings in Neraka. The family's roots were in Jelek, a city north of what had formerly been the capital city of Neraka. The Targonne family's motto was the Great "I," which could have been entwined with the Great "P" for profit. They had risen to wealth and power with the rise of Queen Takhisis, first by supplying arms and weapons to the leaders of her armies, then, when it appeared that their side was losing, by supplying arms and weapons to the armies of Takhisis's enemies. Using the wealth obtained from the sale of weapons, the Targonnes bought up land, particularly the scarce and valuable agricultural land in Neraka.

The scion of the Targonne family had even had the incredible good fortune (he claimed it was foresight) to pull his money out of the city of Neraka only days before the Temple exploded. After the War of the Lance, during the days when Neraka was a defeated land, with roving bands of disenfranchised soldiers, goblins, and draconians, he was in sole possession of the two things people needed desperately: grain and steel.

It had been Abrena's ambition to build a fortress for the Dark Knights in southern Neraka, near the location of the old temple. She had the plans drawn up and sent in crews to start building. Such was the terror inspired by the accursed valley and its eerie and haunting Song of Death that the crews immediately fled. The capital city was shifted to the northern part of the Neraka valley, a site still too close to the southern part for the comfort of some.

One of Targonne's first orders of business was to move the capital city. The second was to change the name of the Knighthood. He established the headquarters of the Knights of Neraka in Jelek, close to the family business. Much closer to the family business than most of the Neraka Knights ever knew.

Jelek was now a highly prosperous and bustling city located at the intersection of the two major highways that ran through Neraka. Either by great good fortune or crafty dealing the city had escaped the ravages of the great dragons. Merchants from all over Neraka, even as far south as Khur, hastened to Jelek to start new businesses or to expand existing ones. So long as they made certain to stop by to pay the requisite fees to the Knights of Neraka and offer their respects to Lord of the Night and Governor-General Targonne, the merchants were welcome.

If respect for Targonne had a cold, substantial feel to it and made a fine clinking sound when deposited together with other demonstrations of respect in the Lord of the Night's large money box, the merchants knew better than to complain. Those who did complain or those who considered that verbal marks of respect were sufficient found that their businesses suffered severe and sudden reverses of fortune. If they persisted in their misguided notions, they were generally found dead in the street, having accidentally slipped and fallen backward onto a dagger.

Targonne personally designed the Neraka Knights' fortress that loomed large over the city of Jelek. He had the fortress built on the city's highest promontory with a commanding view of the city and the surrounding valley.

The fortress was practical in shape and design—innumerable squares and rectangles stacked one on top of the other, with squared-off towers. What windows there were—and there weren't many—were arrow-slits. The exterior and interior walls of the fortress were plain and unadorned. So stark and grim was the fortress that it was often mistaken by visitors for either a prison or a countinghouse. The sight of black-armored figures patrolling the walls soon corrected their first impression, which wasn't, after all, so very far wrong. The below-ground level of the fortress housed an extensive dungeon and, two levels below that and more heavily guarded, was the Knights' Treasury.

Lord of the Night Targonne had his headquarters and his living quarters in the fortress. Both were economical in design, strictly functional, and if the fortress was mistaken for a countinghouse, its commander was often mistaken for a clerk. A visitor to the Lord of the Night was led into a small, cramped office with bare walls and a sparse scattering of furniture, there to wait while a small, bald, bespectacled man dressed in somber, though well-made clothes, completed his work of copying figures in a great leather-bound ledger.

Thinking that he was in the presence of some minor functionary, who would eventually take him to the Lord of the Night, the visitor would often roam restlessly about the room, his thoughts wandering here and there. Those thoughts were snagged in midair, like butterflies in a web, by the man behind the desk. This man used his mentalist powers to delve into every portion of the visitor's mind. After a suitable length of time had passed, during which the spider had sucked his captive dry, the man would raise his bald head, peer through his spectacles, and acquaint the appalled visitor with the fact that he was in the presence of Lord of the Night Targonne.

The visitor who sat in the lord's presence this day knew very well that the mild looking man seated across from him was his lord and governor. The visitor was second in command to Lord Milles and, although Sir Roderick had not yet met Targonne, he had seen him in attendance at certain formal functions of the Knighthood. The Knight stood at attention, holding himself straight and stiff until his presence should be acknowledged. Having been warned about Targonne's mentalist capabilities, the Knight attempted to keep his thoughts stiffly in line as well, with less success. Before Sir Roderick even spoke, Lord Targonne knew a great deal of what had happened at the siege of Sanction. He never liked to exhibit his powers, however. He asked the Knight, in a mild voice, to be seated.

Sir Roderick, who was tall and brawny and could have lifted Targonne off the floor by the coat collar with very little exertion, took a seat in the only other chair in the office and sat on the chair's edge, tense, rigid.

Perhaps due to the fact that he had come to resemble what he most loved, the eyes of Morham Targonne resembled nothing so much as two steel coins—flat, shining, and cold. One looked into those eyes and saw not a soul, but numbers and figures in the ledger of Targonne's mind. Everything he looked upon was reduced to debits and credits, profits and loss, all weighed in the balance, counted to the penny, and chalked up into one column or another.

Sir Roderick saw himself reflected in the shining steel of those cold eyes and felt himself being moved into a column of unnecessary expenditures. He wondered if it was true that the spectacles were artifacts salvaged from the ruins of Neraka and that they gave the wearer the ability to see into one's brain. Roderick began to sweat in his armor, though the fortress with its massive stone and concrete walls was always cool, even during the warmest months of the summer.

"My aide tells me you have come from Sanction, Sir Roderick," said Targonne, his voice the voice of a clerk, mild and pleasant and unassuming. "How goes our siege of the city?"

It should be noted here that the Targonne family had extensive holdings in the city of Sanction, holdings they had lost when the Knights of Neraka lost Sanction. Targonne had made the taking of Sanction one of the top priorities for the Knighthood.

Sir Roderick had rehearsed his speech on the two-day ride from Sanction to Jelek and he was prepared with his answer.

"Excellency, I am here to report that on the day after Midyear Day, an attempt was made by the accursed Solamnics to break the siege of Sanction and to try to drive off our armies. The foul Knights endeavored to trick my commander, Lord Milles, into attacking by making him think they had abandoned the city. Lord Milles saw through their plot and he, in turn, led them into a trap. By launching an attack against the city of Sanction, Lord Milles lured the Knights out of hiding. He then faked a retreat. The Knights took the bait and pursued our forces. At Beckard's Cut, Lord Milles ordered our troops to turn and make a stand. The Solamnics were summarily defeated, many of their number killed or wounded. They were forced to retreat back inside Sanction. Lord Milles is pleased to report, Excellency, that the valley in which our armies are encamped remains safe and secure."

Sir Roderick's words went into Targonne's ears. Sir Roderick's thoughts went into Targonne's mind. Sir Roderick was recalling quite vividly fleeing for his life in front of the rampaging Solamnics, alongside Lord Milles who, commanding from the rear, had been caught up in the retreating stampede. And elsewhere in the mind of the Knight was a picture Targonne found very interesting, also rather disturbing. That picture was that of a young woman in black armor, exhausted and stained with blood, receiving the homage and accolades of Lord Milles's troops. Targonne heard her name resound in Roderick's mind: "Mina! Mina!"

With the tip of his pen the Lord of the Night scratched the thin mustache that covered his upper lip. "Indeed. It sounds a great victory. Lord Milles is to be congratulated."

"Yes, Excellency." Sir Roderick smiled, pleased. "Thank you, Excellency."

"It would have been a greater victory if Lord Milles had actually captured the city of Sanction as he has been ordered, but I suppose he will attend to that little matter when he finds it convenient."

Sir Roderick was no longer smiling. He started to speak, coughed, and spent a moment clearing his throat. "In point of fact, Excellency, we most likely would have been able to capture Sanction were it not for the mutinous actions of one of our junior officers. Completely contrary to Lord Milles's command, this officer pulled an entire company of archers from the fray, so that we had no covering fire necessary for us to launch an attack upon Sanction's walls. Not only that, but in her panic, this officer ordered the archers to shoot their arrows while our own soldiers were yet in the line of fire. The casualties we sustained were due completely to this officer's incompetence. Therefore Lord Milles felt it would not be wise to proceed with the attack."

"Dear, dear," Targonne murmured. "I trust this young officer has been dealt with summarily."

Sir Roderick licked his lips. This was the tricky part. "Lord Milles would have done so, Excellency, but he felt it would be best to consult with you first. A situation has arisen that makes it difficult for his lordship to know how to proceed. The young woman exerts some sort of magical and uncanny influence over the men, Excellency."

"Indeed?" Targonne appeared surprised. He spoke somewhat dryly. "The last I heard, the magical powers of our wizards were failing. I did not know any of our mages were this talented."

"She is not a magic-user, Excellency. Or at least, so she says. She claims to be a messenger sent by a god—the One, True God."

"And what is the name of this god?" Targonne asked.

"Ah, there she is quite clever, Excellency. She maintains that the name of the god is too holy to pronounce."

"Gods have come, and gods have gone," Targonne said impatiently. He was seeing a most astonishing and disquieting sight in Sir Roderick's mind, and he wanted to hear it from the man's lips. "Our soldiers would not be sucked in by such claptrap."

"Excellency, the woman does not make use of words alone. She performs miracles—miracles of healing the likes of which we have not seen in recent years due to the weakening of our mystics. This girl restores limbs that have been hacked off. She places her hands upon a man's chest, and the gaping hole in it closes over. She tells a man with a broken back that he can stand up, and he stands up! The only miracle she does not perform is raising the dead. Those she prays over."

Sir Roderick heard the creaking of a chair, looked up to see Targonne's steel eyes gleaming unpleasantly.

"Of course"—Sir Roderick hastened to correct his mistake—"Lord Milles knows that these are not miracles, Excellency. *He* knows that she is a charlatan. It's just that we can't seem to figure out how she does it," he added lamely. "And the men are quite taken with her."

Targonne understood with alarm that all of the foot soldiers and most of the Knights had mutinied, were refusing to obey Milles. They had transferred their allegiance to some shaven-headed chit in black armor.

"How old is this girl?" Targonne asked, frowning.

"She is reputed to be no more than seventeen, Excellency," Sir Roderick replied.

"Seventeen!" Targonne was aghast. "Whatever induced Milles to make her an officer in the first place?"

"He did not, Excellency," said Sir Roderick. "She is not part of our wing. None of us had ever seen her before her arrival in the valley just prior to the battle."

"Could she be a Solamnic in disguise?" Targonne wondered.

"I doubt that, Excellency. It was due to her that the Solamnics lost the battle," Sir Roderick replied, completely unconscious that the truth he had just now spoken accorded ill with the fabrications he'd pronounced earlier.

Targonne noted the inconsistency but was too absorbed in the clicking abacus of his mind to pay any attention to them, beyond marking down that Milles was an incompetent bungler who should be replaced as speedily as possible. Targonne rang a silver bell that stood upon his desk. The door to the office opened, and his aide entered.

"Look through the rolls of the Knighthood," Targonne ordered. "Locate a—What is her name?" he asked Roderick, though he could hear it echo in the Knight's mind.

"Mina, Excellency."

"Meenaa," Targonne repeated, holding the name in his mouth as if he were tasting it. "Nothing else? No surname?"

"Not to my knowledge, Excellency."

The aide departed, dispatched several clerks to undertake the task. The two Knights sat in silence while the search was being conducted. Targonne took advantage of the time to continue to sift through Roderick's mind, which affirmed his surmise that the siege against Sanction was being handled by a nincompoop. If it hadn't been for this girl, the siege might well have been broken, the Dark Knights defeated, annihilated, the Solamnics in triumphant and unhindered possession of Sanction.

The aide returned. "We find no knight named 'Mina' on the rolls, Excellency. Nothing even close."

Targonne made a dismissive gesture, and the aide departed.

"Brilliant, Excellency!" Sir Roderick exclaimed. "She is an imposter. We can have her arrested and executed."

"Hunh." Targonne grunted. "And just what do you think your soldiers will do in that instance, Sir Roderick? Those she has healed? Those she has led to victory against the detested foe? The morale among Milles's troops was not that good to begin with." Targonne flipped a hand at a stack of ledgers. "I've read the reports. The desertion rate is five times higher among Milles's troops than with any other commander in the army.

"Tell me this"—Targonne eyed the other Knight shrewdly—"are you capable of having this Mina girl arrested? Do you have guards who will obey your order? Or will they most likely arrest Lord Milles instead?"

Sir Roderick opened his mouth and shut it again without replying. He looked around the room, looked at the ceiling, looked anywhere but into those steel eyes, horribly magnified by the thick glass of the spectacles, but still he seemed to see them boring into his skull.

Targonne clicked the beads upon his mental abacus. The

girl was an imposter, masquerading as a Knight. She had arrived at the moment she was most needed. In the face of terrible defeat, she had achieved stunning victory. She performed "miracles" in the name of a nameless god.

Was she an asset or a liability?

If liability, could she be turned into an asset?

Targonne abhorred waste. An excellent administrator and a shrewd bargainer, he knew where and how every steel coin was spent. He was not a miser. He made certain that the Knighthood had the best quality weapons and armor, he made certain that the recruits and mercenaries were paid well. He was adamant that his officers keep accurate records of monies paid out to them.

The soldiers wanted to follow this Mina. Very well. Let them follow her. Targonne had that very morning received a message from the great dragon Malystryx wanting to know why he permitted the Silvanesti elves to defy her edicts by maintaining a magical shield over their land and refusing to pay her tribute. Targonne had prepared a letter to send in return explaining to the dragon that attacking Silvanesti would be a waste of time and manpower that could be used elsewhere to more profit. Scouts sent to investigate the magical shield had reported that the shield was impossible to penetrate, that no weapon—be it steel or sorcery—had the slightest effect on the shield. One might hurl an entire army at it—so said his scouts—and one would achieve nothing.

Add to this the fact that an army heading into Silvanesti must first travel through Blöde, the homeland of the ogres. Former allies of the Dark Knights, the ogres had been infuriated when the Knights of Neraka expanded southward, taking over the ogres' best land and driving them into the mountains, killing hundreds in the process. Reports indicated that the ogres were currently hounding the dark elf Alhana Starbreeze and her forces somewhere near the shield. But if the Knights advanced into ogre lands, the ogres would be quite happy to leave off attacking elves—something they could do any time—to take vengeance on the ally who had betrayed them.

The letter was on his desk, awaiting his signature. It had been on his desk for several days. Targonne was fully aware that this letter of refusal would infuriate the dragon, but he was much better prepared to face Malys's fury than throw away valuable resources in a hopeless cause. Reaching for the letter, Targonne picked it up and slowly and thoughtfully tore it into small pieces.

The only god Targonne believed in was a small, round god that could stacked up in neat piles in his treasure room. He did not believe for a moment that this girl was a messenger from the gods. He did not believe in her miracles of healing or in the miracle of her generalship. Unlike the wretched and imbecilic Sir Roderick, Targonne didn't feel a need to explain how she had done what she had done. All he needed to know was that she was doing it for the benefit of the Knights of Neraka—and that which benefitted the Knights benefitted Morham Targonne.

He would give her a chance to perform a "miracle." He would send this imposter Knight and her addle-pated followers to attack and capture Silvanesti. By making a small investment of a handful of soldiers, Targonne would please the dragon, keep Malys happy. The dangerous Mina girl and her forces would be wiped out, but the loss would be offset by the gain. Let her die in the wilderness somewhere, let some ogre munch on her bones for his supper. That would be an end to the chit and her "nameless" god.

Targonne smiled upon Sir Roderick and even left his desk to walk the Knight to the door. He watched until the black-armored figure had marched down the echoing, empty hallways of the fortress, then summoned his aide to his office.

He dictated a letter to Malystryx, explaining his plan for the capture of Silvanesti. He issued an order to the com-

mander of the Knights of Neraka in Khur to march his forces
west to join the siege of Sanction, take over command from
Lord Milles. He issued an order commanding Talon Leader
Mina and a company of hand-picked soldiers to march south,
there to attack and capture the great elven nation of Silvanesti.

"And what of Lord Milles, Excellency?" his aide asked. "Is
he to be reassigned? Where is he to be sent?"

Targonne considered the matter. He was in an excellent
humor, a feeling which normally came with the closing of an
extremely good business deal.

"Send Milles to report in person to Malystryx. He can tell
her the story of his great 'victory' over the Solamnics. I'm sure
she will be very interested to hear how he fell into an enemy
trap and in so doing came close to losing all that we have
fought so hard to gain."

"Yes, Excellency." The aide gathered up his papers and
prepared to return to his desk to execute the documents.
"Shall I take Lord Milles off the rolls?" he asked, as an afterthought.

Targonne had returned to his ledger. He adjusted the spectacles carefully on his nose, picked up his pen, waved a neg-
ligent hand in acquiescence, and returned to his credits and
debits, his additions and subtractions.

II

The Song of Lorac

hile Tasslehoff was near dying of boredom on the road to Qualinesti and while Sir Roderick was returning to Sanction, blissfully unaware that he had just delivered his commander into the jaws of the dragon, Silvanoshei and Rolan of the kirath began their journey to place Silvanoshei upon the throne of Silvanesti. Rolan's plan was to move close to the capital city of Silvanost, but not to enter it until word spread through the city that the true head of House Royal was returning to claim his rightful place as Speaker of the Stars.

"How long will that take?" Silvan asked with the impatience and impetuosity of youth.

"The news will travel faster than we will, Your Majesty," Rolan replied. "Drinel and the other kirath who were with us two nights ago have already left to spread it. They will tell every other kirath they meet and any of the Wildrunners they feel that they can trust. Most of the soldiers are loyal to General Konnal, but there are a few who are starting to doubt him. They do not openly state their opposition yet, but Your

Majesty's arrival should do much to change that. The Wild-drunners have always sworn allegiance to House Royal. As Konnal himself will be obliged to do—or at least make a show of doing."

"How long will it take us to reach Silvanost, then?" Silvanoshei asked.

"We will leave the trail and travel the Thon-Thalas by boat," Rolan responded. "I plan to take you to my house, which is located on the outskirts of the city. We should arrive in two days time. We will take a third day to rest and to receive the reports that will be coming in by then. Four days from now, Your Majesty, if all goes well, you will enter the capital in triumph."

"Four days!" Silvan was skeptical. "Can so much be accomplished that fast?"

"In the days when we fought the dream, we kirath could send a message from the north of Silvanesti into the far reaches of the south in a single day. I am not exaggerating, Your Majesty," Rolan said, smiling at Silvanoshei's obvious skepticism. "We accomplished such a feat many times over. We were highly organized then, and there were many more of us than there are now. But I believe that Your Majesty will be impressed, nevertheless."

"I am already impressed, Rolan," Silvanoshei replied. "I am deeply indebted to you and the others of the kirath. I will find some way of repaying you."

"Free our people from this dreadful scourge, Your Majesty," Rolan answered, his eyes shadowed with sorrow, "and that will be payment enough."

Despite his praise, Silvanoshei still harbored doubts, though he kept them to himself. His mother's army was well organized, yet even she would make plans, only to see them go awry. Ill luck, miscommunication, bad weather, any one of these or a host of other misfortunes could turn a day that had seemed meant for victory into disaster.

"No plan ever survives contact with the enemy," was one of Samar's dictums, a dictum that had proven tragically true.

Silvan anticipated disasters, delays. If the boat Rolan promised even existed, it would have a hole in it or it would have been burned to cinders. The river would be too low or too high, run too swift or too slow. Winds would blow them upstream instead of down or down when they wanted to travel up.

Silvan was vastly astonished to find the small boat at the river landing where Rolan had said it would be, perfectly sound and in good repair. Not only that, but the boat had been filled with food packed in waterproof sacks and stowed neatly in the prow.

"As you see, Your Majesty," Rolan said, "the kirath have been here ahead of us."

The Thon-Thalas River was calm and meandering this time of year. The boat, made of tree bark, was small and light and so well balanced that one would have to actively work to tip it over. Well knowing that Rolan would never think of asking the future Speaker of the Stars to help row, Silvan volunteered his assistance. Rolan at first demurred, but he could not argue with his future ruler and so at last he agreed and handed Silvanoshei a paddle. Silvan saw that he had earned the elder elf's respect by this act, a pleasant change for the young man, who, it seemed, had always earned Samar's disrespect.

Silvan enjoyed the exercise that burned away some of his pent-up energy. The river was placid, the forests through which it flowed were green and verdant. The weather was fine, but Silvan could not say that the day was beautiful. The sun shone through the shield. He could see blue sky through the shield. But the sun that shone on Silvanesti was not the same fiercely burning orb of orange fire that shone on the rest of Ansalon. The sun Silvan looked upon was a pale and sickly yellow, the yellow of jaundiced skin, the yellow of an ugly bruise. It was as if he were looking at a reflection of the sun, floating facedown, drowned in a pool of stagnant, oily water. The yellow sun altered the color of the sky from azure blue to a hard metallic blue-green. Silvan did not look long at the sun but instead shifted his gaze to the forest.

"Do you know a song to ease our labors?" he called out to Rolan who was seated in the front of the boat.

The kirath paddled with quick, strong strokes, digging his paddle deep into the water. The far-younger Silvan was hard pressed to keep pace with his elder.

Rolan hesitated, glanced back over his shoulder. "There is a song that is a favorite of the kirath, but I fear it may displease His Majesty. It is a song that tells the story of your honored grandfather, King Lorac."

"Does it start out, 'The Age of Might it was, the Age of the Kingpriest and his minions?' " Silvan asked, singing the melody tentatively. He had only heard the song once before.

"That is the beginning, Your Majesty," Rolan replied.

"Sing it for me," Silvan said. "My mother sang it once to me on the day I turned thirty. That was the first time I had ever heard the story of my grandfather. My mother never spoke of him before, nor has she spoken of him since. To honor her, none of the other elves speak of him either."

"I, too, honor your mother, who gathered roses in the Garden of Astarin when she was your age. And I understand her pain. We share in that pain every time we sing this song, for as Lorac was snared by his own hubris into betraying his country, so we who took the easy way out, who fled our land and left him to do battle alone, were also at fault.

"If all our people had stayed to fight, if all our people— those of House Royal to House Servitor, those of House Protector, House Mystic, House Mason—if we had all joined together and stood shoulder to shoulder, regardless of caste, against the dragonarmies, then I believe that we could have saved our land.

"But you shall hear the full tale in the song.

Song of Lorac

The Age of Might it was,
the Age of the Kingpriest and
his minions.
Jealous of the wizards, the Kingpriest
said, "You will hand over your high Towers
to me and you will fear me and obey me."
The wizards gave over their High Towers, the last
the Tower of Palanthas.

Comes to the Tower Lorac Caladon, King of the
    Silvanesti,
to take his Test in magic before the closing of the
    Tower.
In his Test, one of the dragon orbs,
fearful of falling into the hands
of the Kingpriest and his minions,
speaks to Lorac.
"You must not leave me here in Istar.
If you do, I will be lost and the world will perish."
Lorac obeys the voice of the dragon orb,
hides the orb away.
carries it with him from the Tower,
carries the orb back to Silvanesti,
holds the orb in secret, hugging his secret to him,
never telling anyone.

Comes the Cataclysm. Comes Takhisis, Queen of
    Darkness,
with her dragons, mighty and powerful.
Comes war. War to Silvanesti.
Lorac summons all his people, orders them to flee
    their homelands
Orders them away.

Says to them,
"I alone will be the savior of the people."
"I alone will stop the Queen of Darkness."

Away the people.
Away the loved daughter, Alhana Starbreeze.
Alone, Lorac hears the voice of the dragon orb,
calling his name, calling to him to come to the
    darkness.
Lorac heeds the call.
Descends into darkness.
Puts his hands upon the dragon orb and
the dragon orb puts its hands upon Lorac.
Comes the dream.
Comes the dream to Silvanesti,
dream of horror,
dream of fear,
dream of trees that bleed the blood of elvenkind,
dream of tears forming rivers,
dream of death.

Comes a dragon,
Cyan Bloodbane,
minion of Takhisis,
to hiss into Lorac's ear the terrors of the dream.
To hiss the words, "I alone have the power to save the
    people.
I alone." To mock the words, "I alone have the power
    to save."
The dream enters the land,
kills the land,
twists the trees, trees that bleed,
fills the rivers with the tears of the people,
the tears of Lorac,
held in thrall by the orb and by Cyan Bloodbane,

minion of Queen Takhisis,
minion of evil,
who alone has the power.

"I can understand why my mother does not like to hear that song," Silvan said when the last long-held, sweet, sad note drifted over the water, to be echoed by a sparrow. "And why our people do not like to remember it."

"Yet, they should remember it," said Rolan. "The song would be sung daily, if I had my way. Who knows but that the song of our own days will be just as tragic, just as terrible? We have not changed. Lorac Caladon believed that he was strong enough to wield the dragon orb, though he had been warned against it by all the wise. Thus he was snared, and thus he fell. Our people, in their fear, chose to flee rather than to stand and fight. And thus in fear today we cower under this shield, sacrificing the lives of some of our people in order to save a dream."

"A dream?" Silvan asked. He was thinking of Lorac's dream, the dream of the song.

"I do not refer to the whispers of the dragon," said Rolan. "That dream is gone, but the sleeper refuses to wake and thus another dream has come to take its place. A dream of the past. A dream of the glories of days that have gone. I do not blame them," Rolan added, sighing. "I, too, love to think upon what has gone and long to regain it. But those of us who fought alongside your father know that the past can never be recovered, nor should it be. The world has changed, and we must change with it. We must become a part of it, else we will sicken and die in the prison house in which we have locked ourselves."

Rolan ceased paddling for a moment. He turned in the boat to face Silvan. "Do you understand what I am saying, Your Majesty?"

"I think so," said Silvan cautiously. "I am of the world, so to speak. I come from the outside. I am the one who can lead our people out into the world."

"Yes, Your Majesty." Rolan smiled.

"So long as I avoid the sin of hubris," Silvan said, ceasing his paddling, thankful for the rest. He grinned when he said it for he meant it teasingly, but on reflection, he became more serious. "Pride, the family failing," Silvan said, half to himself. "I am forewarned, and that is forearmed, they say."

Picking up his paddle, he fell to work with a will.

The pallid sun sank down behind the trees. Day languished, as if it too was one of the victims of the wasting sickness. Rolan watched the bank, searching for a suitable site to moor for the night. Silvan watched the opposite shore and so he saw first what the kirath missed.

"Rolan!" Silvan whispered urgently. "Pull for the western shore! Quickly!"

"What is it, Your Majesty?" Rolan was quick to take alarm. "What do you see?"

"There! On the eastern bank! Don't you see them? Hurry! We are nearly within arrow range!"

Rolan halted his rapid stroking. He turned around to smile sympathetically at Silvan. "You are no longer among the hunted, Your Majesty. Those people you see gathered on that bank are your own. They have come to look upon you and do you honor."

Silvan was astonished. "But . . . how do they know?"

"The kirath have been here, Your Majesty."

"So soon?"

"I told Your Majesty that we would spread the word rapidly."

Silvan blushed. "I am sorry, Rolan. I did not mean to doubt you. It's just that . . . My mother uses runners. They travel in secret, carrying messages between my mother and her sister by marriage, Laurana, in Qualinesti. Thus we are kept apprised of what is happening with our people in that realm. But it would take them many days to cover the same number of miles. . . . I had thought—"

"You thought I was exaggerating. You need make no apology for that, Your Majesty. You are accustomed to the world beyond the shield, a world that is large and filled with dangers that wax and wane daily, like the moon. Here in Silvanesti, we kirath know every path, every tree that stands on that path, every flower that grows beside it, ever squirrel that crosses it, every bird that sings in every branch, so many times have we run them. If that bird sings one false note, if that squirrel twitches its ears in alarm, we are aware of it. Nothing can surprise us. Nothing can stop us."

Rolan frowned. "That is why we of the kirath find it troubling that the dragon Cyan Bloodbane has so long eluded us. It is not possible that he should. And yet it is possible that he has."

The river carried them within sight of the elves standing on the western shoreline. Their houses were in the trees, houses a human would have probably never seen, for they were made of the living tree, whose branches had been lovingly coaxed into forming walls and roofs. Their nets were spread out upon the ground to dry, their boats pulled up onto the shore. There were not many elves, this was only a small fishing village, and yet it was apparent that the entire population had turned out. The sick had even been carried to the river's edge, where they lay wrapped in blankets and propped up with pillows.

Self-conscious, Silvan ceased paddling and rested his oar at the bottom of the boat.

"What do I do, Rolan?" he asked nervously.

Rolan looked back, smiled reassuringly. "You need only be yourself, Your Majesty. That is what they expect."

Rolan steered closer to the bank. The river seemed to run faster here, rushed Silvan toward the people before he was quite ready. He had ridden on parade with his mother to review the troops and had experienced the same uneasiness and sense of unworthiness that assailed him now.

The river brought him level with his people. He looked at them and nodded slightly and raised his hand in a shy wave. No one waved back. No one cheered, as he had been half-expecting. They watched him float upon the river in silence, a silence that was poignant and touched Silvan more deeply than the wildest cheering. He saw in their eyes, he heard in their silence, a wistful hopefulness, a hope in which they did not want to believe, for they had felt hope before and been betrayed.

Profoundly moved, Silvan ceased his waving and stretched out his hand to them, as if he saw them sinking and he could keep them above the water. The river bore him away from them, took him around a hill, and they were lost to his sight.

Humbled, he huddled in the stern and did not move nor speak. For the first time, he came to the full realization of the crushing burden he had taken upon himself. What could he do to help them? What did they expect of him? Too much, perhaps. Much too much.

Rolan glanced back every now and again in concern, but he said nothing, made no comment. He continued to paddle alone until he found a suitable place to beach the boat. Silvan roused himself and jumped into the water, helped to drag the boat up onto the bank. The water was icy cold and came as a pleasant shock. He submerged his worries and fears of his own inadequacies in the Thon-Thalas, was glad to have something to do to keep himself busy.

Accustomed to living out of doors, Silvan knew what needed to be done to set up camp. He unloaded the supplies, spread out the bedrolls, and began to prepare their light supper of fruit and flatbread, while Rolan secured the boat. They ate for the most part in silence, Silvan still subdued by the enormity of the responsibility he had accepted so blithely just two nights before and Rolan respecting his ruler's wish for quiet. The two made an early night of it. Wrapping themselves in their blankets, they left the woodland animals and night birds to stand watch over their slumbers.

Silvan fell asleep much sooner than he'd anticipated. He was wakened in the night by the hooting of an owl and sat up in fear, but Rolan, stirring, said the owl was merely calling to a neighbor, sharing the gossip of the darkness.

Silvan lay awake, listening to the mournful, haunting call and its answer, a solemn echo in some distant part of the forest. He lay awake long, staring up at the stars that shimmered uneasily above the shield, the Song of Lorac running swift like the river water through his mind.

> The tears of Lorac,
> held in thrall by the orb and by Cyan Bloodbane,
> minion of Queen Takhisis,
> minion of evil,
> who alone has the power.

The words and melody of the song were at this moment being echoed by a minstrel singing to entertain guests at a party in the captial city of Silvanost.

The party was being held in the Garden of Astarin on the grounds of the Tower of the Stars, where the Speaker of the Stars would live had there been a Speaker. The setting was beautiful. The Tower of the Stars was magically shaped of marble, for the elves will not cut or otherwise harm any part of the land, and thus the Tower had a fluid, organic feel to it, looking almost as if someone had formed it of melted wax. During Lorac's dream, the Tower had been hideously transformed, as were all the other structures in Silvanost. Elven mages worked long years to reshape the dwelling. They replaced the myriad jewels in the walls of the tall building, jewels which had once captured the light of the silver moon, Solinari, and the red moon, Lunitari, and used their blessed moonlight to illuminate the Tower's interior so that it seemed bathed in silver and in flame. The moons were gone now. A single moon only shone on Krynn and for some reason that the wise among the elves could not explain, the pale light of this single moon glittered in each jewel like a staring eye, bringing no light at all to the Tower, so that the elves were forced to resort to candles and torches.

Chairs had been placed among the plants in the Garden of Astarin. The plants appeared to be flourishing. They filled the air with their fragrance. Only Konnal and his gardeners knew that the plants in the garden had not grown there but had been carried there by the Woodshapers from their own private gardens, for no plants lived long now in the Garden of Astarin. No plants except one, a tree. A tree surrounded by a magical shield. A tree known as the Shield Tree, for from its root was said to have sprung the magical shield that protected Silvanesti.

The minstrel was singing the Song of Lorac in answer to a request from a guest at the party. The minstrel finished, ending the song on its sad note, her hand brushing lightly the strings of her lute.

"Bravo! Well sung! Let the song be sung again," came a lilting voice from the back row of seats.

The minstrel looked uncertainly at her host. The elven audience was much too polite and too well bred to indicate overt shock at the request, but a performer comes to know the mood of the audience by various subtle signs. The minstrel noted faintly flushed cheeks and sidelong embarrassed glances cast at their host. Once around for this song was quite enough.

"Who said that?" General Reyl Konnal, military governor of Silvanesti, twisted in his seat.

"Whom do you suppose, Uncle?" his nephew replied with a dark glance for the seats behind them. "The person who requested it be sung in the first place. Your friend, Glaucous."

General Konnal rose abruptly to his feet, a move that ended the evening's musical entertainment. The minstrel bowed, thankful to be spared so arduous a task as singing that song again. The audience applauded politely but without enthusiasm. A sigh that might have been expressive of relief joined the night breeze in rustling the trees whose intertwined branches formed a barren canopy above them, for many of the leaves had dropped off. Lanterns of silver filigree hung from the boughs, lighting the night. The guests left the small amphitheater, moved to a table that had been set up beside a reflecting pool, there to dine on sugared fruits and buttery shortbreads and to drink chilled wine.

Konnal invited the minstrel to partake of a late night morsel and personally escorted the woman to the table. The elf named Glaucous who had requested the song was already there, a cup of wine in his hand. Raising a toast to the minstrel, he was lavish in her praise.

"A pity you were not permitted to sing the song again," he said, glancing in the general's direction. "I never tire of that particular melody. And the poetry! My favorite part is when—"

"Might I offer you food and drink, Madame?" the nephew asked, responding to a nudge from his uncle.

The minstrel cast him a grateful glance and accepted his invitation. He led her to the table, where she was graciously received by the other guests. The grassy area on which Glaucous and the general stood was soon empty. Although many of the guests would have been pleased to bask in the the presence of the charming and attractive Glaucous and pay their share of flattery to General Konnal, they could tell at a glance that the general was angry.

"I don't know why I invite you to these parties, Glaucous," Konnal said, seething. "You always do something to embarrass me. It was bad enough you requested she sing that piece, and then to ask for it a second time!"

"Considered in light of the rumors I heard today," Glaucous returned languidly, "I thought the song of Lorac Caladon most appropriate."

Konnal shot his friend a sharp glance from beneath

lowered brows. "I heard . . ." He paused, glanced at his guests. "Come, walk with me around the pond."

The two moved away from the other guests. Now free of the constraint of the general's presence, the elves gathered in small groups, their voices sibilant with suppressed excitement, eager to discuss the rumors that were the talk of the capital.

"We need not have left," Glaucous observed, looking back upon the refreshment table. "Everyone has heard the same thing."

"Yes, but they speak of it as rumor. I have confirmation," Konnal said grimly.

Glaucous halted. "You know this for a fact?"

"I have my sources among the kirath. The man saw him, spoke to him. The young man is said to be the image of his father. He is Silvanoshei Caladon, son of Alhana Starbreeze, grandson of the late and unlamented King Lorac."

"But that is impossible!" Glaucous stated. "The last we heard of the whereabouts of that accursed witch, his mother, she was lurking about outside the shield and her son was with her. He could not have come through the shield. Nothing and no one can penetrate the shield." Glaucous was quite firm on that point.

"Then his arrival must be a miracle, as they are claiming," Konnal said dryly, with a wave of his hand at his whispering guests.

"Bah! It is some imposter. You shake your head." Glaucous regarded the governor in disbelief. "You have actually swallowed this!"

"My source is Drinel. As you know, he has the skill of truthseek," Konnal replied. "There can be no doubt. The young man passed the test. Drinel saw into his heart. He knows more about what happened to him than the young man does, apparently."

"So what *did* happen to him?" Glaucous asked with a slight lift of a delicate eyebrow.

"The night of that terrible storm, Alhana and her rebels

were preparing to launch an all-out assault on the shield when their camp was overrun by ogres. The young man went running to the Legion of Steel to beg the help of the humans—witness how low this woman has sunk—when he was dazzled by a lightning bolt. He slipped and fell down an embankment. He lost consciousness. Apparently, when he awoke, he was inside the shield."

Glaucous stroked his chin with his hand. The chin was well-formed, the face handsome. His almond eyes were large and penetrating. He could make no move that was not graceful. His complexion was flawless, his skin smooth and pale. His features were perfectly molded.

To human eyes, all elves are beautiful. The wise say this accounts for the animosity between the two races. Humans—even the most beautiful among them—cannot help but feel that they are ugly by comparison. The elves, who worship beauty, see gradations of beauty among their own kind, but they always see beauty. In a land of beauty, Glaucous was the most beautiful.

At this moment, Glaucous's beauty, his perfection, irritated Konnal beyond measure.

The general shifted his gaze to his pond. Two new swans glided over its mirrorlike surface. He wondered how long these two would live, hoped it would be longer than the last pair. He was spending a fortune in swans, but the pond was bleak and empty without them.

Glaucous was a favorite at court, which was odd considering that he was responsible for many members of the elven court losing their positions, influence, and power. But then, no one ever blamed Glaucous. They blamed Konnal, the one responsible for their dismissal.

Yet, what choice do I have? Konnal would ask himself. These people were untrustworthy. Some of them even plotting against me! If it hadn't been for Glaucous, I might have never known.

Upon first being introduced into the general's retinue, Glaucous had ferreted out something bad about every person Konnal had ever trusted. One minister had been heard defending Porthios. Another was said to have once, when she was a youth, been in love with Dalamar the Dark. Still another was called to account because he had disagreed with Konnal over a matter of taxation. Then came the day when Konnal woke to the realization that he had only one advisor left and that advisor was Glaucous.

The exception was Konnal's nephew Kiryn. Glaucous made no secret of his affection for Kiryn. Glaucous flattered the young man, brought him little gifts, laughed heartily at his jokes, and was effusive in his attention to him. Courtiers who courted Glaucous's favor were intensely jealous of the young man. Kiryn himself would have much preferred Glaucous's dislike. Kiryn distrusted Glaucous, though the young man could give no reason why.

Kiryn dared say no word against Glaucous, however. No one dared say anything against him. Glaucous was a powerful wizard, the most powerful wizard the Silvanesti had ever known among their kind, even counting the dark elf Dalamar.

Glaucous had arrived in Silvanost one day shortly after the dragon purge began. He was, he said, a representative of those elves who served in the Tower of Shalost, a monument in western Silvanesti, where lay the body of the druid Waylorn Wyvernsbane. Although the gods of magic had departed, the enchantment remained around the crystal bier on which the hero of the elves lay enshrined. Careful not to disturb the rest of the dead, the elven sorcerers, desperate to regain their magic, had attempted to capture and use some of the enchantment.

"We succeeded," Glaucous had reported to the general. "That is," he had added with becoming modesty, "I succeeded."

Fearing the great dragons that were decimating the rest of Ansalon, Glaucous had worked with the Woodshapers to devise a means by which Silvanesti could be protected from the ravages of the dragons. The Woodshapers, acting under Glaucous's direction, had grown the tree now known as the Shield Tree. Surrounded by its own magical barrier through which nothing could penetrate to do it harm, the tree was planted in the Garden of Astarin and was much admired.

When Glaucous had proposed to the governor-general that he could raise a magical shield over all of Silvanesti, Konnal had experienced an overwhelming sense of thankfulness and relief. He had felt a weight lifted from his shoulders. Silvanesti would be safe, truly safe. Safe from dragons, safe from ogres, safe from humans, dark elves, safe from the rest of the world. He had put the matter to a vote by the Heads of House. The vote had been unanimous.

Glaucous had raised the shield and become the hero of the elves, some of whom were already talking about building him his own monument. Then plants in the Garden of Astarin began to die. Reports came that trees and plants and animals that lived within the borders touched by the magical shield were also dying. People in Silvanost and other elven villages started to die of a strange wasting sickness. The kirath and other rebels said it was the shield. Glaucous said it was a plague brought to their land by humans before the raising of the shield and that only the shield kept the rest of the populace from dying.

Konnal could not do without Glaucous now. Glaucous was his friend, his trusted adviser, his only trusted adviser. Glaucous's magic was responsible for placing the shield over Silvanesti and Glaucous could use his magic to remove the shield anytime he wanted. Remove the shield and leave the Silvanesti open to the terrors of the world beyond.

"Mmmm? I beg your pardon? What were you saying?" General Konnal tore his attention from his swans, returned it to Glaucous, who had been speaking all this time.

"I said, 'You are not listening to me,' " Glaucous repeated with a sweet smile.

"No, I am sorry. There is one thing I want to know, Glaucous. How did this young man come through the shield?" He lowered his voice to a whisper, though there was no one within earshot. "Is the shield's magic failing, too?"

Glaucous's expression darkened. "No," he replied.

"How can you be certain?" Konnal demanded. "Tell me honestly—have you not felt a weakening of your power over the past year? All other wizards have."

"That may be. I have not," Glaucous said coldly.

Konnal gazed at his friend intently. Glaucous refused to meet his gaze and Konnal guessed that the wizard was lying.

"Then what explanation do we have for this phenomenon?"

"A very simple one," Glacous returned, unperturbed. "I brought him through."

"You?" Konnal was so shocked he shouted the word. Many in the crowd halted their conversations to turn and stare.

Glaucous smiled at them reassuringly and took hold of his friend's arm, led him to a more secluded area of the garden.

"Why would you do this? What do you plan to do with this young man, Glaucous?" Konnal demanded.

"I will do what you should have done," Glaucous said, smoothing back the flowing sleeves of his white robes. "I will put a Caladon on the throne. I remind you, my friend, that if you had proclaimed your nephew Speaker as I recommended there would be no problem with Silvanoshei."

"You know perfectly well that Kiryn refused to accept the position," Konnal returned.

"Due to misguided loyalty to his Aunt Alhana." Glaucous sighed. "I have tried to counsel him on this matter. He refuses to listen to me."

"He will not listen to me, either, if that is what you are implying, my friend," Konnal said. "And might I point out that it is your insistence on maintaining the right of the Caladon family to rule Silvanesti that has landed us in this stew. I am of House Royal myself—"

"You are not a Caladon, Reyl," Glaucous murmured.

"I can trace my lineage back beyond the Caladons!" Konnal said indignantly. "Back to Quinari, wife of Silvanos! I have as much right to rule as the Caladons. Perhaps more."

"I know that, my dear friend," said Glaucous softly, placing a soothing hand upon Konnal's arm. "But you would have a difficult time persuading the Heads of House."

"Lorac Caladon plunged this nation into ruin," Konnal continued bitterly. "His daughter Alhana Starbreeze took us from ruination to near destruction with her marriage to Porthios, a Qualinesti. If we had not acted quickly to rid ourselves of both these vipers, we would have found Silvanesti under the heel of that half-breed, dim-witted Speaker of Suns Gilthas, son of Tanis. Yet the people continue to argue that a Caladon should sit upon the throne! I do not understand it!"

"My friend," Glaucous said gently, "that bloodline has ruled Silvanesti for hundreds of years. The people would be content to accept another Caladon as ruler without a murmur. But if you put yourself forward as a ruler, there would be months or even years of endless arguments and jealousies, researchings of family histories, perhaps even rival claims to the throne. Who knows but that some powerful figure might arise who would oust you and seize control for himself? No, no. This is the best possible solution. I remind you again that your nephew is a Caladon and that he would be the perfect choice. The people would be quite willing to see your nephew take the position. His mother, your sister, married into the Caladon family. It is a compromise the Heads of House would accept.

"But this is all water beneath the bridge. In two days time, Silvanoshei Caladon will be in Silvanost. You have proclaimed publicly that you would support a member of the Caladon family as Speaker of the Stars."

"Because you advised that I do so!" Konnal returned.

"I have my reasons," Glaucous said. He glanced at the

guests, who continued to talk, their voices rising in their excitement. The name "Silvanoshei" could be heard now, coming to them through the starlit darkness. "Reasons that will become clear to you someday, my friend. You must trust me."

"Very well, what do you recommend that I do about Silvanoshei?"

"You will make him Speaker of the Stars."

"What are you saying?" Konnal was thunderstruck. "This . . . this son of dark elves . . . Speaker of the Stars . . ."

"Calm yourself, my dear friend," Glaucous admonished in placating tones. "We will borrow a leaf out of the book of the Qualinesti. Silvanoshei will rule in name only. You will remain the general of the Wildrunners. You will retain control over all the military. You will be the true ruler of Silvanesti. And in the interim, Silvanesti will have a Speaker of the Stars. The people will be joyful. Silvanoshei's ascension to the throne will put a stop to the unrest that has developed of late. Once their goal is achieved, the militant factions among our people—most notably the kirath—will cease to cause trouble."

"I cannot believe you are serious, Glaucous." Konnal was shaking his head.

"Never more serious in my life, dear friend. The people will bring their cares and woes to the king now instead of you. You will be free to accomplish the real work of ruling Silvanesti. Someone must be proclaimed regent, of course. Silvanoshei is young, very young for such a vast responsibility."

"Ah!" Konnal looked quite knowing. "I begin to see what you have in mind. I suppose that I—"

He stopped. Glaucous was shaking his head.

"You cannot be regent and general of the Wildrunners," he said.

"And whom do *you* suggest?" Konnal asked.

Glaucous bowed with graceful humility. "I offer myself. I will undertake to counsel the young king. You have found my advice useful from time to time, I believe."

"But you have no qualifications!" Konnal protested. "You are not of House Royal. You have not served in the Senate. Before this you were a wizard serving in the Tower of Shalost," he stated brusquely.

"Oh, but you yourself will recommend me," said Glaucous, resting his hand on Konnal's arm.

"And what am I to say by way of recommendation?"

"Only this—you will remind them that the Shield Tree grows in the Garden of Astarin, a garden that I oversee. You will remind them that I am the one who helped plant the Shield Tree. You will remind them that I am the one currently responsible for keeping the shield in place."

"A threat?" Konnal glowered.

Glaucous gazed long at the general, who began to feel uncomfortable. "It is my fate never to be trusted," Glaucous said at last. "To have my motives questioned. I accept that, a sacrifice I make to serve my people."

"I am sorry," Konnal said gruffly. "It's just that—"

"Apology accepted. And now," Glaucous continued, "we should make preparations to welcome the young king to Silvanost. You will declare a national holiday. We will spare no expense. The people need something to celebrate. We will have that minstrel who sang tonight sing something in honor of our new Speaker. What a lovely voice she has."

"Yes," Konnal agreed absently, abstracted. He was beginning to think that this plan of Glaucous's wasn't a bad plan after all.

"Ah, how very sad, my friend," Glaucous said, pointing to the pond. "One of your swans is dying."

12

Marching Orders

he first day after the siege of Sanction, Mina tried to leave her tent to go stand in line with the other soldiers waiting for food. She was mobbed, surrounded by soldiers and camp followers who wanted to touch her for luck or who wanted her to touch them. The soldiers were respectful, awed in her presence. Mina spoke to each one, always in the name of the One, True God. But the press of men, women and children was overwhelming. Seeing that Mina was about to drop from exhaustion, her Knights, led by Galdar, drove the people away. Mina returned to her tent. Her Knights stood guard over her rest. Galdar brought her food and drink.

The next day, Mina held a formal audience. Galdar ordered the soldiers to form ranks. She passed among them, speaking to many by name, recalling their bravery in battle. They left her presence dazzled, her name upon their lips.

After the review, she visited the tents of the dark mystics. Her Knights had spread the story of how Mina had restored Galdar's arm. Miracles of healing such as this had once been common in the Fourth Age, but not anymore.

The mystic healers of the Knights of Neraka, healers who had stolen the means of healing from the Citadel of Light, had in years past been able to perform healing miracles that rivaled those the gods themselves had granted in the Fourth Age. But recently, the healers had noticed that they were losing some of their mystical powers. They could still heal, but even simple spells drained them of energy to the point where they found themselves near collapse.

No one could explain this strange and dire occurrence. At first, the healers blamed the mystics of the Citadel of Light, saying that they had found a way to prevent the Knights of Neraka from healing their soldiers. But they soon heard reports from their spies within the Citadel that the mystics on Schallsea and in other locations throughout Ansalon were encountering the very same phenonmena. They, too, sought answers, but thus far, in vain.

Overwhelmed by the number of casualties, forced to conserve their energy, the healers had aided Lord Milles and his staff first, for the army needed its commanders. Even then, they could do nothing for critical wounds. They could not restore hacked off limbs, they could not stop internal bleeding, they could not mend a cracked skull.

The eyes of the wounded fixed on Mina the moment she entered the healers' tent. Even those who had been blinded, whose eyes were covered with bloody bandages, turned their sightless gaze instinctively in her direction, as a plant languishing in shadow seeks the sunlight.

The healers continued their work, pretending not to notice Mina's entry. One did pause, however, to look up. He seemed about to order her out, then saw Galdar, who stood behind her and who had placed his hand upon the hilt of his sword.

"We are busy. What do you want?" the healer demanded churlishly.

"To help," Mina replied. Her amber-eyed gaze roved

swiftly about the tent. "What is that area back there? The place you have screened off?"

The healer cast a glance in that direction. Groans and moaning sounds came from behind the blanket which had been hastily strung up in the back end of the large hospital tent.

"The dying," he said, cold, casual. "We can do nothing for them."

"You do not give them anything for the pain?" Mina asked.

The healer shrugged. "They are of no more use to us. Our supplies are limited and must go to help those who have a chance to return to the battle."

"You will not mind, then, if I give them my prayers?"

The healer sniffed. "By all means, go 'pray' over them. I'm sure they'll appreciate it."

"I'm sure they will," she said gravely.

She walked to the back of the tent, passing along the rows of cots where lay the wounded. Many stretched out their hands to her or called out her name, begging her to notice them. She smiled upon them and promised to return. Reaching the blankets behind which lay the dying, Mina reached out her hand, parted the blankets and let them fall behind her.

Galdar took his place in front of the blankets, turned, hand on his sword, to keep an eye on the healers. They made a fine show of paying no attention, but they cast sidelong glances in the direction of the blankets and then exchanged those glances with each other.

Galdar listened to what was happening behind him. He could smell the stench of death. A look cast back through the curtain showed him seven men and two women. Some lay on cots, but others lay on the crude stretchers, which had been used to carry them from the battle field. Their wounds were horrendous, at least so Galdar perceived in that quick glance. Flesh cleaved open, organs and bone exposed. Blood dripped on the floor, forming gruesome pools. One man's intentestines spewed out of him like a string of grotesque sausages. A woman Knight was missing half her face, the eyeball dangling hideously from beneath a blood-soaked bandage.

Mina came to the first of the dying, the woman who had lost her face. Her one good eye was closed. Her breathing was labored. She seemed to have already started on her long journey. Mina rested her hand on the horrible wound.

"I saw you fight in the battle, Durya," Mina said softly. "You fought bravely, held your ground though those around you panicked and retreated. You must stay your journey, Durya. The One God has need of you."

The woman breathed easier. Her mangled face moved slowly toward Mina, who bent and kissed her.

Galdar heard murmuring behind him, turned back quickly. The healer's tent had grown quiet. All had heard Mina's words. The healers made no more pretense of working. Everyone was watching, waiting.

Galdar felt a hand touch him on the shoulder. Thinking it was Mina, he turned. He saw instead the woman, Durya, who had lain dying. Her face was covered with blood, she would always bear a hideous scar, but the flesh was whole, the eye back in its place. She walked, she smiled, she drew a tremulous breath.

"Mina brought me back," Durya said, her tone awed, wondering. "She brought me back to serve her. And I will. I will serve her all her days."

Exalted, her face radiant, Durya left the tent. The wounded cheered and began to chant, "Mina, Mina!" The healers started after Durya in shocked disbelief.

"What is she doing in there?" demanded one, seeking to enter.

"Praying," Galdar said gruffly, blocking the way. "You gave her permission, remember?"

The healer glowered and swiftly departed. Galdar saw the man hot-footing his way to Lord Milles's tent.

"Yes, you tell Lord Milles what you've witnessed," Galdar advised the man silently, gleefully. "Tell him and add yet another twist of the knife that rankles in his chest."

Mina healed them all, healed every one of the dying. She healed a Talon commander who had taken a Solamnic spear in his gut. She healed a foot soldier who had been trampled by the slashing hooves of a battle horse. One by one, the dying rose from their beds and walked out to cheers from the other wounded. They thanked her and praised her, but Mina turned all their gratitude aside.

"Offer your thanks and your loyalty to the One True God," she told them. "It is by the god's power that you are restored."

Indeed, it seemed that she was given divine assistance, for she did not grow weary or faint, no matter how many of the injured she treated. And that was many. When she came from helping the dying, she moved from one of the wounded to another, laying her hands upon them, kissing them, praising their deeds in battle.

"The power of healing does not come from me," she told them. "It comes from the God who has returned to care for you."

By midnight, the healer's tent was empty.

Under orders from Lord Milles, the dark mystics kept close watch on Mina, trying to figure out her secret so as to discredit her, denounce her as a charlatan. They said that she must be resorting to tricks or sleight-of-hand. They poked pins into limbs she had restored, trying to prove they were illusion, only to see real blood flow. They sent patients to her suffering from horrible contagious diseases, patients the healers themselves feared to approach. Mina sat beside these sufferers, laid her hands upon their open sores and oozing pustules and bid them be well in the name of the One God.

The grizzled veterans whispered that she was like the clerics of old, who were given wondrous powers by the gods.

Such clerics, they said, had once been able to raise the dead. But that miracle, Mina either would not or could not perform. The dead received special attention from her, but she did not restore them to life, though she was often begged to do so.

"We are brought into this world to serve the One True God," Mina said. "As we serve the True God in this world, the dead do important service in the next. It would be wrong to bring them back."

By her command, the soldiers had carried all the bodies from the field—bodies of friend and foe alike—and arranged them in long rows on the bloodstained grass. Mina knelt beside each corpse, prayed over each no matter which side the person had fought on, commended the spirit of each to the nameless god. Then she ordered them to be buried in a mass grave.

At Galdar's insistence, the third day after the siege Mina held counsel with the Neraka Knights' commanders. They now included almost all the officers who had formerly reported to Lord Milles, and to a man these officers urged Mina to take up the siege of Sanction, to lead them to what must be a resounding victory over the Solamnics.

Mina refused their entreaties.

"Why?" Galdar demanded this morning, the morning of the fifth day, when he and Mina were alone. He was frustrated at her refusal. "Why will you not launch an attack? If you conquer Sanction, Lord Targonne will not be able to touch you! He will be forced to recognize you as one of his most valued Knights!"

Mina was seated at a large table she had ordered be brought into her tent. Maps of Ansalon were spread out upon it. She had studied the maps every day, moving her lips as she went over them, speaking silently the names of the towns and cities and villages to herself, memorizing their locations. Ceasing her work, she looked up at the minotaur.

"What do you fear, Galdar?" she asked mildly.

The minotaur scowled, the skin between his eyes, above his snout, creased into folds. "My fear is for you, Mina. Those who are deemed a threat to Targonne disappear from time to time. No one is safe from him. Not even our former leader, Mirielle Abrena. It was put about that she died after eating spoiled meat, but everyone knows the truth."

"And that truth is?" Mina asked in abstracted tones. She was looking again at the map.

"He had her poisoned, of course," Galdar returned. "Ask him yourself if you ever chance to meet him. He will not deny it."

Mina sighed. "Mirielle is fortunate. She is with her God. Though the Vision she proclaimed was false, she now knows the truth. She has been punished for her presumption and is now performing great deeds in the name of the One who shall be nameless. As for Targonne"—Mina lifted her gaze again—"he serves the One True God in this world, and so he will be permitted to remain for the time being."

"Targonne?" Galdar gave a tremendous snort. "He serves a god all right, the god of currency."

Mina smiled a secret, inward smile. "I did not say that Targonne knows he is serving the One, Galdar. But serve he does. That is why I will not attack Sanction. Others will fight that battle. Sanction is not our concern. We are called to greater glory."

"Greater glory?" Galdar was astonished. "You do not know what you are saying, Mina! What could be greater than seizing Sanction? Then the people would see that the Knights of Neraka are once again a powerful force in this world!"

Mina traced a line on the map with her finger, a line that came to rest near the southern portion of the map. "What about the conquering of the great elven kingdom of Silvanesti?"

"Hah! Hah!" Galdar roared his laughter. "You have me there, Mina. I concede. Yes, that would be a magnificent victory. And it would be magnificent to see the moon drop out of the sky and land on my breakfast plate, which is just about as likely to happen."

"You will see, Galdar," Mina said quietly. "Bring me word the moment the messenger arrives. Oh, and Galdar . . ."

"Yes, Mina?" The minotaur had turned to go.

"Take care," she said to him, her amber eyes piercing him through, as if they had been sharpened to arrow points. "Your mockery offends the God. Do not make that mistake again."

Galdar felt a throbbing pain in his sword arm. The fingers went numb.

"Yes, Mina," he mumbled. Massaging the arm, he ducked out of the tent, leaving Mina to study her map.

Galdar calculated it would take two days for one of Lord Milles's flunkies to ride to the Knights' headquarters in Jelek, a day to report to Lord of the Night Targonne, two days to ride back. They should hear something today. After he left Mina's tent, the minotaur roamed about the outskirts of camp, watching the road for riders.

He was not alone. Captain Samuval and his Archer Company were there, as well as many of the soldiers of Milles's command. They stood with weapons ready. They had sworn among themselves that they would stop anyone who tried to take Mina from them.

All eyes were on the road. The pickets who were supposed to be watching Sanction kept looking behind them, instead of ahead at the besieged city. Lord Milles, who had made one experimental foray out of his tent following the siege and who had been harried back inside by a barrage of horse turds, cat-calls and jeers, parted the tent flaps to glare impatiently up that road, never doubting but that Targonne would come to his commander's aide by sending troops to help him put down the mutiny.

The only eyes in camp who did not turn to the road were Mina's. She remained in her tent, absorbed in studying her maps.

"And that is the reason she gave for not attacking Sanction? That we are going to attack Silvanesti?" Captain Samuval said to Galdar as the two stood in the road, awaiting the arrival of the messenger. The captain frowned. "What nonsense! You don't suppose she could be afraid, do you?"

Galdar glowered. Placing his hand on the hilt of his sword, he drew it halfway from its sheath. "I should cut out your tongue for saying such a thing! You saw her ride alone into the front ranks of the enemy! Where was her fear then?"

"Peace, Minotaur," Samuval said. "Put away your sword. I meant no disrespect. You know as well as I that when the blood burns hot in battle, a man thinks himself invincible and he does deeds he would never dream of doing in cold blood. It is only natural she should be a little frightened now that she has taken a good long look at the situation and realized the enormity of the task."

"There is no fear in her," Galdar growled, sheathing his blade. "How can there be fear in one who speaks of death with a wistful, impatient look in her eyes, as if she would rush to embrace it if she could and is constrained to continue living against her will."

"A man may fear many things besides death," Samuval argued. "Failure, for one. Perhaps she fears that if she leads these worshipers of hers into battle and fails, they will turn against her as they did against Lord Milles."

Galdar twisted his horned head, looked back over his shoulder, back to where Mina's tent stood by itself upon a small rise, the bloody standard hanging before it. The tent was surrounded by people standing silent vigil, waiting, watching, hoping to catch a glimpse of her or hear her voice.

"Would you leave her now, Captain?" Galdar asked.

Captain Samuval followed the minotaur's gaze. "No, I would not," he said at last. "I don't know why. Perhaps she has bewitched me."

"I'll tell you why," Galdar said. "It's because she offers us something to believe in. Something besides ourselves. I mocked that something just now," he added humbly, rubbing his arm, which still tingled unpleasantly. "And I am sorry I did so."

A trumpet call rang out. The pickets placed at the entrance to the valley were letting those in camp know that the expected messenger approached. Every person in camp stopped what they were doing and looked up, ears pricked to hear, necks craned to see. A large crowd blocked the road. They parted to let the messenger on his steaming horse gallop past. Galdar hastened to take the news to Mina.

Lord Milles emerged from his command tent at precisely the same moment Mina left hers. Confident that the messenger was here to bring word of Targonne's anger and the promise of a force of armed Knights to seize and execute the imposter, Lord Milles glared triumphantly at Mina. He felt certain that her downfall was imminent.

She did not so much as glance at him. She stood outside her tent, awaiting developments with calm detachment, as if she already knew the outcome.

The messenger slid down from his horse. He looked in some astonishment at the crowd of people gathered around Mina's tent, was alarmed to see them regarding him with a baleful and threatening air. The messenger kept glancing backward at them over his shoulder as he went to deliver a scroll case to Lord Milles. Mina's followers did not take their eyes from him, nor did they take their hands from the hilts of their swords.

Lord Milles snatched the scroll case from the messenger's hand. So certain was he of its contents that he did not bother to retreat to the privacy of his tent to read it. He opened the plain and unadorned leather-bound case, removed the scroll, broke the seal and unfurled it with a snap. He had even filled his lungs to make the announcement that would cause the upstart female to be arrested.

The breath whistled from him as from a deflated pig's bladder. His complexion went sallow, then livid. Sweat beaded his forehead, his tongue passed several times over his lips. He crumpled the missive in his hand and, stumbling as one blind, he fumbled at the tent flaps, trying vainly to open them. An aide stepped forward. Lord Milles shoved the man aside with a savage snarl and entered the tent, closing the flaps behind him and tying them shut.

The messenger turned to face the crowd.

"I seek a Talon leader named 'Mina,' " he said, his voice loud and carrying.

"What is your business with her?" roared a gigantic minotaur, who stepped out of the crowd and confronted the messenger.

"I bear orders for her from Lord of the Night Targonne," the messenger replied.

"Let him come forward," called Mina.

The minotaur acted as escort. The crowd that had barred the messenger's way cleared a path leading from Lord Milles's tent to Mina's.

The messenger walked along the path that was bounded by soldiers, all keeping their weapons to hand, regarding him with not very friendly looks. He kept his gaze forward, though that was not very comfortable for him since he stared squarely at the back, shoulders, and bull neck of the enormous minotaur. The messenger continued on his way, mindful of his duty.

"I am sent to find a *knight officer* called 'Mina,' " the messenger repeated laying emphasis on the words. He stared at the young girl who confronted him in some confusion. "You are nothing but a child!"

"A child of battle. A child of war. A child of death. I am Mina," said the girl, and there was no doubting her air of authority, the calm consciousness of command.

The messenger bowed and handed over a second scroll

case. This one was bound in elegant black leather, the seal of a skull and lily graven upon it in silver. Mina opened the case and drew forth the scroll. The crowd hushed, seemed to have stopped breathing. The messenger looked about, his astonishment growing. He would later report to Targonne that he felt as if he were in a temple, not a military camp.

Mina read the missive, her face expressionless. When she finished, she handed it to Galdar. He read it. His jaw dropped so that his sharp teeth glistened in the sun, his tongue lolled. He read and reread the message, turned his amazed gaze upon Mina.

"Forgive me, Mina," he said softly, handing the piece of parchment back to her.

"Do not ask my forgiveness, Galdar," she said. "I am not the one you doubted."

"What does the message say, Galdar?" Captain Samuval demanded impatiently, and his question was echoed by the crowd.

Mina raised her hand and the soldiers obeyed her unspoken command instantly. The templelike hush fell over them again.

"My orders are to march south, invade, seize, and hold the elven land of Silvanesti."

A low and angry rumble, like the rumble of thunder from an approaching storm, sounded in the throats of the soldiers.

"No!" several shouted, incensed. "They can't do this! Come with us, Mina! To the Abyss with Targonne! We'll march on Jelek! Yes, that's what we'll do! We'll march on Jelek!"

"Hear me!" Mina shouted above the clamor. "These orders do not come from General Targonne! His is but the hand that writes them. The orders come from the One God. It is our God's will that we attack Silvanesti in order to prove the God's return to all the world. We will march on Silvanesti!" Mina's voice raised in a stirring cry. "And we will be victorious!"

"Hurrah!" The soldiers cheered and began to chant, "Mina! Mina! Mina!"

The messenger stared about him in dazed astoundment. The entire camp, a thousand voices, were chanting this girl's name. The chant echoed off the mountains and thundered to the heavens. The chant was heard in the town of Sanction, whose residents trembled and whose Knights grimly gripped their weapons, thinking this portended some terrible doom for their besieged city.

A horrible, bubbling cry rose above the chanting, halting some of it, though those on the outskirts of the crowd continued on, unhearing. The cry came from the tent of Lord Milles. So awful was that cry that those standing near the tent backed away, regarded it in alarm.

"Go and see what has happened," Mina ordered.

Galdar did as commanded. The messenger accompanied him, knowing that Targonne would be interested in the outcome. Drawing his sword, Galdar sliced through the leather strings that held the flap shut. He went inside and came back out a instant later.

"His lordship is dead," he reported, "by his own hand."

The soldiers began to cheer again, and many jeered and laughed.

Mina rounded upon those near her in anger that lit the amber eyes with a pale fire. The soldiers ceased their cheering, quailed before her. Mina said no word but walked past them, her chin set, her back rigid. She came to the entrance of the tent.

"Mina," said Galdar, holding up the bloodstained message. "This wretch tried to have you hanged. The proof is here in Targonne's response."

"Lord Milles stands before the One God, now, Galdar," Mina said, "where we will all stand one day. It is not for us to judge him."

She took the bloody bit of paper, tucked it into her belt,

and walked inside the tent. When Galdar started to go with her, she ordered him away, closed the tent flaps behind her.

Galdar put an eye to the flap. Shaking his head, he turned and mounted guard upon the entrance.

"Go about your business," the minotaur commanded the soldiers who were milling about in front of the tent. "There's work to be done if we're marching to Silvanesti."

"What is she doing in there?" asked the messenger.

"Praying," Galdar said shortly.

"Praying!" the messenger repeated to himself in wonder. Mounting his horse, he rode off, anxious not to lose a moment in reporting the day's astonishing events to the Lord of the Night.

"So what happened?" Captain Samuval asked, coming to stand next to Galdar.

"To Milles?" Galdar grunted. "He fell on his sword." He handed over the message. "I found this in his hand. As we guessed he would, he sent a pack of lies to Targonne, all about how Mina nearly lost the battle and Milles saved it. Targonne may be a murdering, conniving bastard, but he's not stupid." Galdar spoke with grudging admiration. "He saw through Milles's lies and ordered him to report word of his 'victory' directly to the great dragon Malystryx."

"No wonder he chose this way out," Samuval commented. "But why send Mina south to Silvanesti? What happens to Sanction?"

"Targonne has ordered General Dogah to leave Khur. He will take over the siege of Sanction. As I said, Targonne's not stupid. He knows that Mina and her talk of One True God is a threat to him and the phony 'Visions' he's been handing out. But he also knows that he will start a rebellion among the troops if he tries to have her arrested. The great dragon Malystryx has long been annoyed by Silvanesti and the fact that the elves have found a way to thwart her by hiding beneath their magical shield. Targonne can placate Malystryx on the one hand by telling her he has sent a force to attack Silvanesti, and he can rid himself of a dangerous threat to his authority at the same time."

"Does Mina know that in order to reach Silvanesti we must march through Blöde?" Captain Samuval demanded. "A realm held by the ogres? They are already angry that we have taken some of their land. They will resent any further incursion into their territory." Samuval shook his head. "This is suicidal! We will never even see Silvanesti. We must try to talk her out of this act of folly, Galdar."

"It is not my place to question her," said the minotaur. "She knew we were going to Silvanost this morning before the messenger arrived. Remember, Captain? I told you of it myself."

"Did you?" Captain Samuval mused. "In all the excitement, I had forgotten. I wonder how she found out?"

Mina emerged from Milles's tent. She was very pale.

"His crimes have been forgiven. His soul has been accepted." She sighed, glanced about, appeared disappointed to find herself back among mortals. "How I envy him!"

"Mina, what are your orders?" Galdar asked.

Mina looked at him without recognition for a moment, the amber still seeing wondrous sights not given to other mortals. Then she smiled bleakly, sighed again, and came back to her surroundings.

"Assemble the troops. Captain Samuval, you will address them. You will tell them truthfully that the assignment is dangerous one. Some might say 'suicidal.' " She smiled at Samuval. "I will order no man to make this march. Any who come do so of their own free will."

"They will all come, Mina," said Galdar softly.

Mina gazed at him, her eyes luminous, radiant. "If that be true, then the force will be too large, too unwieldy. We must move fast and we must keep our movement secret. My own Knights will accompany me, of course. You will select five hundred of the best of the foot soldiers, Galdar. The remainder will stay behind with my blessing. They must continue to besiege Sanction."

Galdar blinked. "But, Mina, didn't you hear? Targonne has given orders that General Dogah is to take over the siege of Sanction."

Mina smiled. "General Dogah will receive new orders telling him that he is to turn his forces south and march with all possible haste upon Silvanesti."

"But . . . where will these orders come from?" Galdar asked, gaping. "Not Targonne. He is ordering us to Silvanesti simply to get rid of us, Mina!"

"As I told you, Galdar, Targonne acts for the One God, whether he knows it or not." Mina reached into her belt, where she had tucked the orders Milles had received from Targonne. She held the parchment to the sunlight. Targonne's name loomed large and black at the bottom, his seal gleamed red. Mina pointed her finger to the words on the page, a page that was stained with Milles's blood.

"What does it say, Galdar?"

Mystified, Galdar looked at the words and began to read them, read exactly what he had read before.

Lord Milles is hereby commanded . . .

The words suddenly began to writhe and twist in his vision. Galdar closed his eyes, rubbed them, opened them. The words continued to writhe and now they began to crawl over the page, the black of the ink mingling with the red of Milles's blood.

"What does it say, Galdar?" Mina asked again.

Galdar felt his breath catch in his throat. He tried to speak, could only whisper huskily, "General Dogah is hereby commanded to shift his forces south and march with all possible speed to Silvanesti. Signed in Targonne's name."

The handwriting was Targonne's. There could be no doubt. His signature was in place, as was his seal.

Mina rolled the parchment neatly and tucked it back into the scroll case.

"I want you to deliver these orders yourself, Galdar. Then catch up with us on the road south. I will show you the route of our march. Samuval, you will be second in command until Galdar rejoins us."

"You can count on me and on my men, Mina," said Captain Samuval. "We would follow you into the Abyss."

Mina regarded him thoughtfully. "The Abyss is no more, Captain. She who ruled there has left, never to return. The dead have their own realm now—a realm in which they are permitted to continue their service to the One God."

Her gaze shifted focus, encompassed the mountains, the valley, the soldiers who were even now busy striking camp. "We will depart in the morning. The march will take us two weeks. Issue the necessary commands. I'll want two supply wagons to accompany us. Let me know when we are ready."

Galdar ordered his officers to call the men to assembly. Entering Mina's tent, he found her bent over one of her maps, placing small pebbles upon it at various locations. Galdar looked to see that the pebbles were all concentrated in an area designated "Blöde."

"You will meet us here," she said, indicating a place on the map marked with a pebble. "I calculate that it will take you two days to meet up with General Dogah and another three days to rejoin us. The One God speed you, Galdar."

"The One God be with you until we meet again, Mina," said Galdar.

He meant to leave. He could yet cover many miles before daylight waned. But he found the leaving difficult. He could not imagine a day going by without seeing her amber eyes, hearing her voice. He felt as bereft as if he were suddenly shorn of all his fur, left in the world shivering and weak as a newborn calf.

Mina laid her hand upon his, upon the hand she had given

him. "I will be with you wherever you go, Galdar," she said.

He fell to one knee, pressed her hand to his forehead. Keeping the memory of her touch an amulet in his mind, he turned and ran from the tent.

Captain Samuval entered next, coming to report that, as he had foreseen, every single soldier in the camp had volunteered to come. He had chosen the five hundred he considered the best. These soldiers were now the envy of the rest.

"I fear that those left behind may desert to follow you, Mina," Captain Samuval said.

"I will speak to them," she said. "I will explain to them that they must continue to hold Sanction without any expectation of reinforcements. I will explain to them how it can be done. They will see their duty."

She continued to put the small stones upon the map.

"What is that?" Samuval asked curiously.

"The location of the ogre forces," Mina replied. "Look, Captain, if we march this way, directly east out of the Khalkist Mountains, we can make much better time heading southward across the Plains of Khur. We will avoid the largest concentration of their troops, which are down here in the southern end of the mountain range, fighting the Legion of Steel and the forces of the elf-witch, Alhana Starbreeze. We will attempt to steal a march on them by traveling along this route, the Thon-Thalas River. I fear that at some point we must fight the ogres, but if my plan works, we will fight only a diminished force. With the God's blessing, most of us will reach our destination."

And what happened when that destination was reached? How did she intend to break through a magical shield that had thus far baffled all attempts to enter it? Samuval did not ask her. Nor did he ask how she knew the position of the ogre forces or how she knew they were fighting the Legion of Steel and the dark elves. The Knights of Neraka had sent scouts into ogre lands but none had ever returned alive to tell what they saw. Captain Samuval did not ask Mina how she intended to hold Silvanesti with such a small force, a force that would be decimated by the time they reached their destination. Samuval asked her none of this.

He had faith. If not necessarily in this One God, he had faith in Mina.

13

The Scourge of Ansalon

he odd occurrence that befell Tasslehoff Burrfoot on the fifth night of his journey to Qualinesti in the custody of Sir Gerard can best be explained by the fact that although the days had been sunny and warm and fine for traveling, the nights had been cloudy and overcast, with a drizzly rain. Up until this night. This night the sky was clear, the air was soft and warm and alive with the sounds of the forest, crickets and owls and the occasional wolf howling.

Far north, near Sanction, the minotaur Galdar ran along the road that led to Khur. Far south, in Silvanesti, Silvanoshei entered Silvanost as he had planned, in triumph and with fanfare. The entire population of Silvanost came out to welcome him and stare at him and marvel over him. Silvanoshei was shocked and troubled by how few elves remained in the city. He said nothing to anyone however and was greeted with appropriate ceremony by General Konnal and a whiterobed elven wizard whose charming manners endeared him to Silvanoshei at once.

While Silvanoshei dined on elven delicaces off plates of

gold and drank sparkling wine from goblets of crystal, and while Galdar munched on dried peas as he marched, Tas and Gerard ate their customary boring and tasteless meal of flatbread and dried beef washed down with nothing more interesting than plain, ordinary water. They had ridden south as far as Gateway, where they passed several inns, whose innkeepers were standing in the doors with pinched faces. These innkeepers would have barred the door against a kender before the roads were closed by the dragon. Now they had come running out to offer them lodging and a meal for the unheard-of price of a single steel.

Sir Gerard had paid no attention to them. He had ridden past without a glance. Tasslehoff had sighed deeply and looked back longingly at the inns dwindling in the distance. When he had hinted that a mug of cold ale and a plate of hot food would be a welcome change, Gerard had said no, the less attention they called to themselves the better for all concerned.

So they continued on south, traveling along a new road that ran near the river, a road Gerard said had been built by the Knights of Neraka to maintain their supply lines into Qualinesti. Tas wondered at the time why the Knights of Neraka were interested in supplying the elves of Qualinesti, but he assumed that this must be some new project the elven king Gilthas had instituted.

Tas and Gerard had slept outdoors in a drizzling rain for the last four nights. This fifth night was fine. As usual, sleep sneaked up on the kender before he was quite ready for it. He woke up in the night, jolted from his slumbers by a light shining in his eyes.

"Hey! What's that?" he demanded in a loud voice. Throwing off his blanket, he leaped to his feet and grabbed Gerard by the shoulder, shaking him and pummeling him.

"Sir Gerard! Wake up!" Tasslehoff shouted. "Sir Gerard!"

The Knight was up and awake in an instant, his sword in

his hand. "What?" He stared around, alert for danger. "What is it? Did you hear something? See something? What?"

"That! That right there!" Tasslehoff clutched the Knight's shirt and pointed.

Sir Gerard regarded the kender with an extremely grim look. "Is this your idea of a joke?"

"Oh, no," Tas stated. "My idea of a joke is this. I say, 'Knock, knock,' and you say, 'Who's there?' and I say, 'Minotaur,' and you say 'Minotaur who,' and I say, 'So *that's* what you stepped in.' That's my idea of a joke. This has to do with that strange light in the sky."

"That's the moon," said Sir Gerard through gritted teeth.

"No!" Tasslehoff was astonished. "Really? The moon?"

He looked back at it. The thing did appear to have certain moonlike qualities: it was orb-shaped, and it was in the sky alongside the stars, and it glowed. But that was where the resemblance ended.

"If that's Solinari," Tas said, eyeing the moon skeptically. "Then what happened to him? Is he sick?"

Sir Gerard did not answer. He lay back down on his blanket, placed his sword within hand's reach, and, grabbing hold of a corner of his blanket, rolled himself up in it. "Go to sleep," he said coldly, "and stay that way until morning."

"But I want to know about the moon!" Tas persisted, hunkering down beside the Knight, nothing daunted by the fact that Gerard's back was turned and his head covered up by the blanket and that he was still obviously extremely irate at having been violently wakened for nothing. Even his back looked angry. "What happened to make Solinari look so pale and sickly? And where's lovely red Lunitari? I guess I'd wonder where Nuitari was if I'd been able to see the black moon in the first place, which I couldn't, so it might be there and I just wouldn't know it—"

Sir Gerard flipped over quite suddenly. His head emerged from the blanket, revealing a stern and unfriendly eye. "You know perfectly well that Solinari has not been seen in the skies these past thirty-odd years, ever since the end of the Chaos War. Lunitari either. So you can stop this ridiculous nonsense. I am now going to sleep. I am to be awakened for nothing less than an invasion of hobgoblins. Is that clear?"

"But the moon!" Tas argued. "I remember when I came to Caramon's first funeral Solinari shown so very brightly that it was like day only it was night. Palin said this was Solinari's way of honoring his father and—"

Gerard flipped over again and covered his head.

Tas continued talking until he heard the Knight start to snore. Tas gave the Knight an experimental poke in the shoulder, to no avail. The kender thought that he might try prying open one of Gerard's eyelids to see if he was really asleep or just shamming, a trick which had never been known to fail with Flint, although it usually ended with the irate dwarf chasing the kender around the room with the poker.

Tas had other things to think about, however, and so he left the Knight alone and returned to his own blanket. Lying down, he put his hands beneath his head and gazed at the strange moon, which gazed back at him without the slightest hint of recognition. This gave Tas an idea. Abandoning the moon, he shifted his gaze to the stars, searched for his favorite constellations.

They were gone, as well. The stars he looked at now were cold and distant and unfamiliar. The only understanding star in the night sky was a single red star burning brightly not far from the strange moon. The star had a warm and comforting glow about it, which made up for the empty cold feeling in the pit of Tas's stomach, a feeling he had once thought, when he was a young kender, meant he needed something to eat but that he now knew, after years of adventuring, was his inside's way of telling him that something was wrong. In fact, he'd felt pretty much this same way just about the time the giant's foot had been poised over his head.

Tas kept his gaze on the red star, and after awhile the cold, empty feeling didn't hurt so much anymore. Just when he was feeling more comfortable and had put the thoughts of the strange moon and the unfriendly stars and the looming giant out of his mind, and just when he was starting to enjoy the night, sleep crept up and nabbed him again.

The kender wanted to discuss the moon the next day, and discuss it he did, but only with himself. Sir Gerard never responded to any of Tasslehoff's innumerable questions, never turned around, just rode along at a slow pace, the reins of Tas's pony in his hands.

The Knight rode in silence, though he was watchful and alert, constantly scanning the horizon. The entire world seemed to be riding in silence today, as well, once Tasslehoff quit talking, which he did after a couple of hours. It wasn't so much that he was bored with talking to himself, it was the answering himself that grew old fast. They met no one on the road, and now even the sounds of other living creatures came to an end. No bird sang. No squirrel scampered across the path. No deer walked among the shadows or ran from them, white tail flashing an alarm.

"Where are the animals?" Tas asked Gerard.

"They are in hiding," the Knight answered, the first words he'd spoken all morning. "They are afraid."

The air was hushed and still, as if the world held its breath, fearful of being heard. Not even the trees rustled and Tas had the feeling that if they had been able to make the choice, they would have dragged their roots out of the ground and run away.

"What are they afraid of?" Tasslehoff asked with interest, looking around in excitement, hoping for a haunted castle or a crumbling manor or, at the very least, a spooky cave.

"They fear the great green dragon. Beryl. We are in the West Plains now. We have crossed over into her realm."

"You keep talking about this green dragon. I've never heard of her. The only green dragon I knew was named Cyan Bloodbane. Who is Beryl? Where did she come from?"

"Who knows?" Gerard said impatiently. "From across the sea, I suppose, along with the great red dragon Malystryx and others of their foul kind."

"Well, if she isn't from around these parts, why doesn't some hero just go stick a lance into her?" Tas asked cheerfully.

Gerard halted his horse. He tugged on the reins of Tasslehoff's pony, who had been trudging behind, her head down, every bit as bored as the kender. She came plodding up level with the black, shaking her mane and eyeing a patch of grass hopefully.

"Keep your voice down!" Gerard said in a low voice. He looked as grim and stern as the kender had ever seen him. "Beryl's spies are everywhere, though we do not see them. Nothing moves in her realm but she is aware of it. Nothing moves here without her permission. We crossed into her realm an hour ago," he added. "I will be very surprised if someone doesn't come to take a look at us— Ah, there. What did I tell you?"

He had shifted in his saddle, to gaze intently to the east. A large speck of black in the sky was growing steadily larger and larger and larger with every passing moment. As Tas watched, he saw the speck develop wings and a long tail, saw a massive body—a massive green body.

Tasslehoff had seen dragons before, he'd ridden dragons before, he'd fought dragons before. But he had never seen or hoped to see a dragon this immense. Her tail seemed as long as the road they traveled; her teeth, set in slavering jaws, could have served as the high, crenellated walls of a formidable fortress. Her wicked red eyes burned with a hotter fire than the sun and seemed to illuminate all they looked upon with a glaring light.

"As you have any regard for your life or mine, kender,"

Gerard said in a fierce whisper, "do or say nothing!"

The dragon flew directly over them, her head swiveling to study them from all angles. The dragonfear slid over them like the dragon's shadow, blotting out the sunshine, blotting out reason and hope and sanity. The pony shook and whimpered. The black whinnied in terror and kicked and plunged. Gerard clung to the bucking horse's back, unable to calm the animal, prey to the same fear himself. Tasslehoff stared upward in open-mouthed astonishment. He felt a most unpleasant sensation come over him, a stomach-shriveling, spine-watering, knee-buckling, hand-sweating sort of feeling. As feelings went, he didn't much like it. For making a person miserable, it ranked right up there with a bad, sniffly cold in the head.

Beryl circled them twice and, seeing nothing more interesting than one of her own Knight allies with a kender prisoner in tow, she left them alone, flying lazily and unhurriedly back to her lair, her sharp eyes taking note of everything that moved upon her ground.

Gerard slid off his horse. He stood next to the shivering animal, leaned his head against its heaving flanks. He was exceedingly pale and sweating, a tremor shook his body. He opened and shut his mouth several times and at one point looked as if he might be sick, but he recovered himself. At length his breathing evened out.

"I have shamed myself," he said. "I did not know I could experience fear like that."

"*I* wasn't afraid," Tas announced in voice that seemed to have developed the same shakiness as his body. "I wasn't afraid one bit."

"If you had any sense, you would have been," Gerard said dourly.

"It's just that while I've seen some hideous dragons in my time I've never seen one quite that . . ."

Tasslehoff's words shriveled under Gerard's baleful stare.

"That . . . imposing," the kender said loudly, just in case any of the dragon's spies were listening. "Imposing," he whispered to Gerard. "That's a sort of compliment, isn't it?"

The Knight did not reply. Having calmed himself and his horse, he retrieved the reins to Tasslehoff's pony and, holding them in his hand, remounted the black. He did not set off immediately, but continued to sit some time in the middle of the road, gazing out to the west.

"I had never seen one of the great dragons before," he said quietly. "I did not think it would be that bad."

He sat quite still for several more moments, then, with a set jaw and pale face, he rode forward.

Tasslehoff followed along behind because he couldn't do anything else except follow along behind, what with the Knight holding onto the pony's reins.

"Was that the same dragon who killed all the kender?" Tasslehoff asked in a small voice.

"No," Gerard replied. "That was an even bigger dragon. A red dragon named Malys."

"Oh," said Tas. "Oh, my."

An even bigger dragon. He couldn't imagine it, and he very nearly said that he would like to see an even bigger dragon when it came to him quite forcibly that, in all honesty, he wouldn't.

"What is the matter with me?" Tasslehoff wailed in dismay. "I must be coming down with something. I'm *not* curious! I don't *want* to see a red dragon that might be bigger than Palanthas. This is just not like me."

Which led to an astounding thought, a thought so astounding Tas almost tumbled off the pony.

"Maybe I'm not me!"

Tasslehoff considered this. After all, no one else believed he was him except Caramon, and he was pretty old and almost dead at the time so perhaps he didn't count. Laura had *said* that she thought Tasslehoff was Tasslehoff but she was probably only being polite, so he couldn't count on that either. Sir Gerard had said that he couldn't possibly be Tasslehoff Burrfoot and Lord Warren had said the same thing, and they were Solamnic Knights, which meant that they were smart and most likely knew what they were talking about.

"That would explain everything," said Tasslehoff to himself, growing cheerier the more he thought about it. "That would explain why nothing that happened to me the first time I went to Caramon's funeral happened the second time, because it wasn't me it was happening to. It was someone else entirely. But if that's the case," he added, becoming rather muddled, "if I'm not me, I wonder who I am?"

He pondered on this for a good half-mile.

"One thing is certain," he said. "I can't keep calling myself Tasslehoff Burrfoot. If I meet the real one, he would be highly annoyed that I'd taken his name. Just the way I felt when I found out that there were thirty-seven other Tasslehoff Burrfoots in Solace—thirty-nine counting the dogs. I suppose I'll have to give him back the Device of Time Journeying, too. I wonder how I came to have it? Ah, of course. He must have dropped it."

Tas kicked his pony in the flanks. The pony perked up and trotted forward until Tas had caught up with the knight.

"Excuse me, Sir Gerard," Tas said.

The Knight glanced at him and frowned. "What?" he asked coldly.

"I just wanted to tell you that I made a mistake," Tas said meekly. "I'm not the person I said was."

"Ah, now there's a surprise!" Gerard grunted. "You mean you're not Tasslehoff Burrfoot, who's been dead for over thirty years?"

"I thought I was," Tas said wistfully. He found the notion more difficult to give up than he'd imagined. "But I can't be. You see, Tasslehoff Burrfoot was a hero. He wasn't afraid of anything. And I don't think he would have felt all strange the way I felt when that dragon flew over us. But I know what's wrong with me."

He waited for the Knight to ask politely but the Knight didn't. Tas volunteered the information.

"I have magnesia," he said solemnly.

This time Gerard said, "What?" only he didn't say it very politely.

Tas put his hand to his forehead, to see if he could feel it. "Magnesia. I'm not sure how a person gets magnesia. I think it has something to do with milk. But I remember that Raistlin said he knew someone with it once and that person couldn't remember who he was or why he was or where he'd left his spectacles or anything. So I must have magnesia, because that's my situation entirely."

This solved, Tasslehoff—or rather, the kender who used to think he was Tasslehoff—felt extremely proud to know he had come down with something so important.

"Of course," he added with a sigh, "a lot of people like you who expect me to be Tasslehoff are going to be in for a sad disappointment when they find out I'm not. But they'll just have to come to grips with it."

"I'll try to bear up," Gerard said dryly. "Now why don't you think really hard and see if you can 'remember' the truth about who you are."

"I wouldn't mind remembering the truth," Tas said. "I have the feeling that the truth doesn't want to remember me."

The two rode on in silence through a silent world until at last, to Tasslehoff's relief, he heard a sound, the sound of water, angry water of a river that foamed and seethed as if it resented being held prisoner within its rocky banks. Humans named the river the White-rage River. It marked the northern border of the elven land of Qualinesti.

Gerard slowed his horse. Rounding a bend in the road, they came within sight of the river, a broad expanse of white foaming water falling over and around glistening black rocks.

They had arrived at the end of the day. The forest was shadowed with the coming of darkness. The river held the light still, the water shining in the afterglow, and by that light they could see in the distance a narrow bridge spanning the river. The bridge was guarded by a lowered gate and guards wearing the same black armor as Gerard.

"Those are Dark Knights," said Tasslehoff in astonishment.

"Keep your voice down!" Gerard ordered sternly. Dismounting, he removed the gag from his belt and approached the kender. "Remember, the only way we're going to be able to see your alleged friend Palin Majere is if they let us past."

"But why are there Dark Knights here in Qualinesti?" Tas asked, talking quickly before Gerard had time to put the gag in place.

"The dragon Beryl rules the realm. These Knights are her overseers. They enforce her laws, collect the taxes and the tribute the elves pay to stay alive."

"Oh, no," said Tas, shaking his head. "There must be some mistake. The Dark Knights were driven out by the combined forces of Porthios and Gilthas in the year— Ulp!"

Gerard stuffed the gag in the kender's mouth, fastened it securely in a knot at the back of his head. "Keep saying things like that and I won't have to gag you. Everyone will just think you're crazy."

"If you'd tell me what has happened," Tas said, pulling the gag from his mouth and peering around at Gerard, "then I wouldn't have to ask questions."

Gerard, exasperated, put the gag back in place. "Very well," he said crossly. "The Knights of Neraka took Qualinesti during the Chaos War and they have never relinquished their hold on it," he said as he tied the knot. "They were prepared to go to war against the dragon, when she demanded that they cede the land to her. Beryl was clever enough to realize that she didn't need to fight. The Knights could be of use to her. She formed an alliance with them. The elves pay tribute, the Knights collect it and turn over a percentage—a large percentage—to the dragon. The Knights keep the rest. They prosper. The dragon prospers. It's the elves who are out of luck."

"I guess that must have happened when I had magnesia," Tas said, tugging one corner of the gag loose.

Gerard fastened the knot even tighter and added, irritably, "The word is 'amnesia,' damn it. And just keep quiet!"

He remounted his horse, and the two rode toward the gate. The guards were alert and had probably been on the watch for them, warned of their coming by the dragon, for they did not appear surprised to see the two emerge from the shadows. Knights armed with halberds stood guard at the gate, but it was an elf, clad all in green cloth and glittering chain mail, who walked up to question them. He was followed by an officer of the Knights of Neraka, who stood behind the elf, observing.

The elf regarded the two, particularly the kender, with disdain.

"The elven realm of Qualinesti is closed to all travelers by orders of Gilthas, Speaker of the Sun," said the elf, speaking Common. "What is your business here?"

Gerard smiled to indicate that he appreciated the joke. "I have urgent news for Marshal Medan," he said, and reaching into his black leather gauntlet he brought out a well-worn paper which he handed over with bored air of one who has done this many times before.

The elf did not even glance at the paper, but passed it to the officer of the Neraka Knights. The officer paid more attention to it. He studied it closely and then studied Gerard. The officer returned the paper to Gerard, who retrieved it and placed it back inside his glove.

"What business have you with Marshal Medan, Captain?" the officer inquired.

"I have something he wants, sir," Gerard replied. He jerked a thumb. "This kender."

The officer raised his eyebrows. "What does Marshal Medan want with a kender?"

"There is a warrant for the little thief, sir. He stole an important artifact from the Knights of the Thorn. A magical artifact that once purportedly belonged to Raistlin Majere."

The elf's eyes flickered at this. He regarded them with more interest.

"I've heard nothing of any bounty," the officer stated, frowning. "Or any robbery, for that matter."

"That is not surprising, sir, considering the Gray Robes," Gerard said with a wry smile and a covert glance around.

The officer nodded and twitched an eyebrow. The Gray Robes were sorcerers. They worked in secret, reporting to their own officers, working to forward their own goals and ambitions, which might or might not coincide with the rest of the Knighthood. As such, they were widely distrusted by the warrior Knights, who viewed the Knights of the Thorn with the same suspicion that men of the sword have viewed men of the staff for centuries.

"Tell me of this crime," the officer said. "When and where was it committed?"

"As you know, the Gray Robes have been combing the Forest of Wayreth, searching for the magical and elusive Tower of High Sorcery. It was during this search that they uncovered this artifact. I do not know how or where, sir. That information was not provided to me. The Gray Robes were transporting the artifact to Palanthas for further study, when they stopped at an inn for some refreshment along the way. It was there the artifact was stolen. The Gray Robes missed it the next morning when they awoke," Gerard added with a meaningful roll of his eyes. "This kender had stolen it."

"So that's how I got it!" Tas said to himself, fascinated. "What a perfectly wonderful adventure. Too bad I can't remember it."

The officer nodded his head. "Damn Gray Robes. Dead

drunk, no doubt. Carrying a valuable artifact. Just like their arrogance."

"Yes, sir. The criminal fled with his booty to Palanthas. We were told to be on the lookout for a kender who might try to fence stolen artifacts. We watched the mageware shops, and that was how we caught him. And a weary journey I've had of it to bring him back here, guarding the little fiend day and night."

Tas attempted to look quite fierce.

"I can imagine." The officer was sympathetic. "Was the artifact recovered?"

"I am afraid not, sir. He claims to have 'lost' it, but the fact that he was discovered in the mageware shop led us to believe that he has stashed it somewhere with the intent to produce it when he had closed a bargain. The Thorn Knights plan to question him regarding its whereabouts. Otherwise, of course"—Gerard shrugged—"we could have spared ourselves the trouble. We would have simply hung the thieving nit."

"The headquarters for the Thorns is down south. They're still looking for that damned tower. A waste of time, if you ask me. Magic is gone from the world again and I say good riddance."

"Yes, sir," Gerard replied. "I was instructed to report to Marshal Medan first, this being under his jurisdiction, but if you think I should proceed directly—"

"Report to Medan, by all means. If nothing else, he will get a good laugh out of the story. Do you need help with the kender? I have a man I could spare—"

"Thank you, sir. As you can see, he is well-secured. I anticipate no trouble."

"Ride on, then, Captain," said the officer, indicating with a wave of his hand that the gate was to be lifted. "Once you've delivered the vermin, ride back this way. We'll open a bottle of dwarf spirits, and you will tell me of the news from Palanthas."

"I will do that, sir," said Gerard, saluting.

He rode through the gate. Tasslehoff, bound and gagged, followed. The kender would have waved his manacled hands in a friendly good-bye, but he considered that this might not be in keeping with his new identity—Highwayman, Stealer of Valuable Magical Artifacts. He quite liked this new persona and decided he should try to be worthy of it. Therefore, instead of waving, he scowled defiantly at the knight as they rode past.

The elf had been standing in the road all this time, maintaining a deferential and bored silence. He did not even wait until the gate was lowered to go back to the gatehouse. The twilight had deepened to night and torches were being lit. Tasslehoff, peering over his shoulder as the pony clattered across the wooden bridge, saw the elf squat down beneath a torch and draw out a leather bag. A couple of the Knights knelt down in the dirt and they began a game of dice. The last Tas saw of them, the officer had joined them, bringing with him a bottle. Few travelers passed this way since the dragon now patrolled the roads. Their watch was a lonely one.

Tasslehoff indicated by various grunts and squeaks that he would be interested in talking about their successful adventure at the gate—in particular he wanted to hear more details about his daring theft—but Gerard paid no attention to the kender. He did not ride off at a gallop, but, once he was out of sight of the bridge he urged Blackie to increase his pace markedly.

Tasslehoff assumed that they would ride all night. They were not far from Qualinost, or at least so he remembered from his previous journeys to the elven capital. A couple of hours would find them in the city. Tas was eager to see his friends once again, eager to ask them if they had any idea who he was, if he wasn't himself. If anyone could cure magnesia, it would be Palin. Tasslehoff was extremely surprised when Gerard suddenly reined in his horse and, professing himself exhausted by the long day, announced that they would spend the night in the forest.

They made camp, building a fire, much to the kender's astonishment, for the Knight had refused to build a fire prior to this, saying that it was too dangerous.

"I guess he figures we're safe now that we're inside the borders of Qualinesti." Tasslehoff spoke to himself, for he was still wearing the gag. "I wonder why we stopped though? Maybe he doesn't know how close we are."

The Knight fried some salt pork. The aroma spread throughout the forest. He removed Tasslehoff's gag so that the kender could eat and was instantly sorry he'd done so.

"How did I steal the artifact?" Tas asked eagerly. "That's so exciting. I've never stolen anything before, you know. Stealing is extremely wrong. But I guess in this case it would be all right, since the Dark Knights are bad people. What inn was it? There are quite a few on the road to Palanthas. Was it the Dirty Duck? That's a great place. Everyone stops there. Or maybe the Fox and the Unicorn? They don't much like kender, so probably not."

Tasslehoff talked on, but he couldn't induce the Knight to tell him anything. That didn't really matter much to Tas, who was perfectly capable of making up the entire incident himself. By the time they had finished eating and Gerard had gone to wash the pan and the wooden bowls in a nearby stream, the bold kender had stolen not one but a host of wondrous magical artifacts, snatching them out from under the very noses of six Thorn Knights, who had threatened him with six powerful magicks, but who had, all six, been dispatched by a skilled blow from the kender's hoopak.

"And that must have been how I came down with magnesia!" Tas concluded. "One of the Thorn Knights struck me severely on the headbone! I was unconscious for several days. But, no," he added in disappointment. "That couldn't be true for otherwise I wouldn't have escaped." He pondered on this for a considerable time. "I have it," he said at last, looking with triumph at Gerard. "You hit me on the head when you arrested me!"

"Don't tempt me," Gerard said. "Now shut up and get some sleep." He spread out his blanket near the fire, which had been reduced to a pile of glowing embers. Pulling the blanket over himself, he turned his back to the kender.

Tasslehoff relaxed on his blanket, gazed up at the stars. Sleep wasn't going to catch him tonight. He was much too busy reliving his life as the Scourge of Ansalon, the Menace of Morgash, the Thug of Thorbardin. He was quite a wicked fellow. Women would faint and strong men would blanch at the mere sound of his name. He wasn't certain exactly what blanching entailed, but he had heard that strong men were subject to it when faced with a terrible foe, so it seemed suitable in this instance. He was just picturing his arrival in a town to find all the women passed out in their laundry tubs and the strong men blanching left and right when he heard a noise. A small noise, a twig snapping, nothing more.

Tas would not have noticed it except that he was used to not hearing any noises at all from the forest. He reached out his hand and tugged on the sleeve of Gerard's shirt.

"Gerard!" Tas said in a loud whisper. "I think someone's out there!"

Gerard snuffled and snorted, but didn't wake up. He hunched down deeper in his blanket.

Tasslehoff lay quite still, his ears stretched. He couldn't hear anything for a moment, then he heard another sound, a sound that might have been made by a boot slipping on a loose rock.

"Gerard!" said Tasslehoff. "I don't think it's the moon this time." He wished he had his hoopak.

Gerard rolled over at that moment and faced Tasslehoff, who was quite amazed to see by the dying fire that the Knight was not asleep. He was only playing possum.

"Keep quiet!" Gerard said in a hissing whisper. "Pretend you're asleep!" He shut his eyes.

Tasslehoff obediently shut his eyes, though he opened them again the next instant so as to be sure not to miss anything. Which was good, otherwise he would have never seen the elves creeping up on them from the darkness.

"Gerard, look out!" Tas started to shout, but a hand clapped down over his mouth and cold steel poked him in the neck before he could stammer out more than "Ger—"

"What?" Gerard mumbled sleepily. "What's—"

He was wide awake the next moment, trying to grab the sword that lay nearby.

One elf stomped down hard on Gerard's hand—Tas could hear bones crunch and he winced in sympathy. A second elf picked up the sword and moved it out of the Knight's reach. Gerard tried to stand up, but the elf who had stomped on his hand now kicked him viciously in the head. Gerard groaned and rolled over on his back, unconscious.

"We have them both, Master," said one of the elves, speaking to the shadows. "What are your orders?"

"Don't kill the kender, Kalindas," said a voice from the darkness, a human's voice, a man's voice, muffled, as if he were speaking from the depths of a hood. "I need him alive. He must tell us what he knows."

The human was not very woods-crafty apparently. Although Tas couldn't see him—the human had remained in the shadows—Tas could hear his booted feet mashing dry leaves and breaking sticks. The elves, by contrast, were as quiet as the night air.

"What about the Dark Knight?" the elf asked.

"Slay him," said the human indifferently.

The elf placed a knife at the Knight's throat.

"No!" Tas squeaked and wriggled. "You can't! He's not really a Dark—ulp!"

"Keep silent, kender," said the elf, who held onto Tas. He

shifted the point of his knife from the kender's throat to his head. "Make another sound and I will cut off your ears. That will not affect your usefulness to us."

"I wish you wouldn't cut off my ears," said Tas, talking desperately, despite feeling the knife blade nick his skin. "They keep my hair from falling off my head. But if you have to, you have to, I guess. It's just that you're about to make a terrible mistake. We've come from Solace, Gerard's not a Dark Knight, you see. He's a Solamnic—"

"Gerard?" said the human suddenly from the darkness. "Hold your hand, Kellevandros! Don't kill him yet. I know a Solamnic named Gerard from Solace. Let me take a look."

The strange moon had risen again. Its light was intermittent, coming and going as dark clouds glided across its empty, vacuous face. Tas tried to catch a glimpse of the human, who was apparently in charge of this operation, for the elves deferred to him in all that was done. The kender was curious to see him, because he had a feeling he'd heard that voice before, although he couldn't quite place it.

Tas was doomed to disappointment. The human was heavily cloaked and hooded. He knelt beside Gerard. The Knight's head lolled to one side. Blood covered his face. His breathing was raspy. The human studied his face.

"Bring him along," he ordered.

"But, Master—" The elf called Kellevandros started to protest.

"You can always kill him later," said the human. Rising, he turned on his heel and walked back into the forest.

One of the elves doused the fire. Another elf went to calm the horses, particularly the black, who had reared in alarm at the sight of the intruders. A third elf put a gag in Tas's mouth, pricking Tas's right ear with the tip of the knife the moment the kender even looked as if he might protest.

The elves handled the Knight with efficiency and dispatch. They tied his hands and feet with leather cord, thrust a gag into his mouth, and fixed a blindfold around his eyes. Lifting the comatose Knight from the ground, they carried him to his horse and threw him over the saddle. Blackie had been alarmed by the sudden invasion of the camp, but he now stood quite calm and placid under an elf's soothing hand, his head over the elf's shoulder, nuzzling his ear. The elves tied Gerard's hands to his feet, passing the rope underneath the horse's belly, securing the Knight firmly to the saddle.

The human looked at the kender, but Tas couldn't get a glimpse of his face because at that moment an elf popped a gunny sack over his head and he couldn't see anything except gunny sack. The elves bound his feet together. Strong hands lifted him, tossed him headfirst over the saddle, and the Scourge of Ansalon, his head in a sack, was carried off into the night.

14
The Masquerade

s the Scourge of Ansalon was being hauled off in ignominy and a sack, only a few miles away in Qualinost the Speaker of the Sun, ruler of the Qualinesti people, was hosting a masquerade ball. The masquerade was something relatively new to the elves—a human custom, brought to them by their Speaker, who had some share of human blood in him, a curse passed on by his father, Tanis Half-Elven. The elves generally disdained human customs as they disdained humans, but they had taken to the masquerade, which had been introduced by Gilthas in the year 21 to celebrate his ascension to the throne twenty years previously. Each year on this date he had given a masquerade, and it was now the social highlight of the season.

Invitations to this important event were coveted. The members of House Royal, the Heads of Household, the Thalas-Enthia—the elven Senate—were invited, as well as the top ranking leaders of the Dark Knights, Qualinesti's true rulers. In addition, twenty elf maidens were chosen to attend, hand-picked by Prefect Palthainon, a former member of the elven

Senate and now the chief magistrate newly appointed by the Knights of Neraka to oversee Qualinesti. Palthainon was nominally Gilthas's advisor and counselor. Around the capital he was jocularly referred to as the "Puppeteer."

The young ruler Gilthas was not yet married. There was no heir to the throne nor any prospect of one. Gilthas had no particular aversion to being married, but he simply could not quite make up his mind to go through with it. Marriage was an immense decision, he told his courtiers, and should not be entered into without due consideration. What if he made a mistake and chose the wrong person? His entire life could be ruined, as well as the life of the unfortunate woman. Nothing was ever said of love. It was not expected that the king should be in love with his wife. His marriage would be for political purposes only; this had been determined by Prefect Palthainon, who had chosen several eligible candidates from among the most prominent (and the most wealthy) elven families in Qualinesti.

Every year for the past five years, Palthainon had gathered together twenty of these hand-chosen elven women and presented them to the Speaker of the Sun for his approbation. Gilthas danced with them all, professed to like them all, saw good qualities in them all, but could not make up his mind. The prefect controlled much of the life of the Speaker— disparagingly termed "the puppet king" by his subjects—but Palthainon could not force his majesty to take a wife.

Now the time was an hour past midnight. The Speaker of the Sun had danced with each of the twenty in deference to the prefect, but Gilthas had not danced with any one of the elven maidens more than once—for a second dance would be seen as making a choice. After the close of every dance, the king retired to his chair and sat looking upon the festivities with a brooding air, as if the decision over which of the lovely women to dance with next was a weight upon him that was completely destroying his pleasure in the party.

The twenty maidens glanced at him out of the corners of their eyes, each hoping for some sign that he favored her above all the others. Gilthas was handsome to look upon. The human blood was not much apparent in his features, except, as he had matured, to give him a squareness of jaw and chin not usually seen in the male elf. His hair, of which he was said to be vain, was shoulder-length and honey-colored. His eyes were large and almond-shaped. His face was pale; it was known that he was in ill health much of the time. He rarely smiled and no one could fault him for that for everyone knew that the life he led was that of a caged bird. He was taught words to speak, was told when to speak them. His cage was covered up with a cloth when the bird was to be silent.

Small wonder then that Gilthas was known to be indecisive, vacillating, fond of solitude and of reading and writing poetry, an art he had taken up about three years previous and in which he showed undeniable talent. Seated on his throne, a chair of ancient make and design, the back of which was carved into the image of a sun and gilded with gold, Gilthas watched the dancers with a restive air and looked as if he could not wait to escape back to the privacy of his quarters and the happiness of his rhymes.

"His Majesty seems in unusually high spirits tonight," observed Prefect Palthainon. "Did you notice the way he favored the eldest daughter of the guildmaster of the Silver-smiths?"

"Not particularly," returned Marshal Medan, leader of the occupation forces of the Knights of Neraka.

"Yes, I assure you, it is so," Palthainon argued testily. "See how he follows her with his eyes."

"His Majesty appears to me to be staring either at the floor or his shoes," Medan remarked. "If you are going to ever see an heir to the throne, Palthainon, you will have to make the marriage yourself."

"I would," Palthainon said, grumbling, "but elven law dictates that only the family may arrange a marriage, and his mother adamantly refuses to become involved unless and until the king makes up his mind."

"Then you had better hope His Majesty lives a long, long time," said Medan. "I should think he would, since you watch over him so closely and attend to his needs so assiduously. You can't really fault the king, Palthainon," the marshal added, "His Majesty is, after all, exactly what you and the late Senator Rashas have made him—a young man who dares not even take a piss without looking to you for permission."

"His Majesty's health is fragile," Palthainon returned stiffly. "It is my duty to remove from him from the burden of the cares and responsibilities of the ruler of the elven nation. Poor young man. He can't help dithering. The human blood, you know, Marshal. Notoriously weak. And now, if you will excuse me, I will go pay my respects to His Majesty."

The marshal, who was human, bowed wordlessly as the prefect, whose mask was, most appropriately, that of a stylized bird of prey, went over to peck at the young king. Politically, Medan found Prefect Palthainon extremely useful. Personally, Medan thought Palthainon utterly detestable.

Marshal Alexius Medan was fifty-five years old. He had joined the Knights of Takhisis under the leadership of Lord Ariakan prior to the Chaos War that had ended the Fourth Age of Krynn and brought in the Fifth. Medan had been the commander responsible for attacking Qualinesti over thirty years ago. He had been the one to accept the surrender of the Qualinesti people and had remained in charge ever since. Medan's rule was strict, harsh where it needed to be harsh, but he was not wantonly cruel. True, the elves had few personal freedoms anymore, but Medan did not view this lack as a hardship. To his mind, freedom was a dangerous notion, one that led to chaos, anarchy, the disruption of society.

Discipline, order, and honor—these were Medan's gods,

now that Takhisis, with a complete lack of discipline and of honor, had turned traitor and run away, leaving her loyal Knights looking like utter fools. Medan imposed discipline and order on the Qualinesti. He imposed discipline and order on his Knights. Above all, he imposed these qualities on himself.

Medan watched with disgust as Palthainon bowed before the king. Well knowing that Palthainon's humility was all for show, Medan turned away. He could almost pity the young man Gilthas.

The dancers swirled about the marshal, elves dressed as swans and bears and every other variety of bird or woodland creature. Jesters and clowns clad in gay motley were in abundance. Medan attended the masquerade because protocol required it, but he refused to wear a mask or a costume. Years ago, the marshal had adopted the elven dress of loose flowing robes draped gracefully over the body as being most comfortable and practicable in the warm and temperate climate of Qualinesti. Since he was the only person in elven dress attending the masquerade, the human had the odd distinction of looking more like an elf than any other elf in the room.

The marshal left the hot and noisy dance floor and escaped, with relief, into the garden. He brought no body guards with him. Medan disliked being trailed about by Knights in clanking armor. He was not overly fearful for his safety. The Qualinesti had no love for him, but he had outlived a score of assassination attempts. He could take care of himself, probably better care than any of his Knights. Medan had no use for the men being taken into the Knighthood these days, considering them to be an undisciplined and surly lot of thieves, killers, and thugs. In truth, Medan trusted elves at his back far more than his own men.

The night air was soft and perfumed with the scents of roses and gardenias and orange blossoms. Nightingales sang in the trees, their melodies blending with the music of harp and lute. He recognized the music. Behind him, in the Hall of the Sky, lovely elf maidens were performing a traditional dance. He paused and half-turned, tempted to go back by the beauty of the music. The maidens were performing the *Quanisho*, the Awakening Promenade, a dance said to drive elf men wild with passion. He wondered if it would have any effect on the king. Perhaps he might be moved to a write a poem.

"Marshal Medan," said a voice at his elbow.

Medan turned. "Honored Mother of our Speaker," he said and bowed.

Laurana extended her hand, a hand that was white and soft and fragrant as the flower of the camellia. Medan took her hand, brought the hand to his lips.

"Come now," she said to him, "we are by ourselves. Such formal titles need not be observed between those of us who are—how should I describe us? 'Old enemies'?"

"Respected opponents," said Medan, smiling. He relinquished her hand, not without some reluctance.

Marshal Medan was not married, except to his duty. He did not believe in love, considered love a flaw in a man's armor, a flaw that left him vulnerable, open to attack. Medan admired Laurana and respected her. He thought her beautiful, as he thought his garden beautiful. He found her useful in assisting him to find his way through the sticky mass of fine-spun cobweb that was the elven version of government. He used her and he was well aware that in return she used him. A satisfactory and natural arrangement.

"Believe me, madam," he said quietly, "I find your dislike of me much preferable to other people's friendship."

He glanced meaningfully back into the palace, where Palthainon was standing at the young king's side, whispering into his ear.

Laurana followed his gaze. "I understand you, Marshal," she replied. "You are a representative of an organization I believe to be wholly given over to evil. You are the conqueror of my people, our subjugator. You are allied with our worst enemy, a dragon who is intent upon our total destruction. Yet, I trust you far more than I trust that man."

She turned away abruptly. "I do not like this view, sir. Would you mind if we walked to the arboretum?"

Medan was quite willing to spend a lovely moonlit night in the most enchanting land on Ansalon in company with the land's most enchanting woman. They walked side by side in companionable silence along a walkway of crushed marble that glittered and sparkled as if it would mimic the stars. The scent of orchids was intoxicating.

The Royal Arboretum was a house made of crystal, filled with plants whose fragile and delicate natures could not survive even the relatively mild winters of Qualinesti. The arboretum was some distance from the palace. Laurana did not speak during their long walk. Medan did not feel that it was his place to break this peaceful silence, and so he said nothing. In silence, the two approached the crystal building, its many facets reflecting the moon so that it seemed there must be a hundred moons in the sky instead of just one.

They entered through a crystal door. The air was heavy with the breath of the plants, which stirred and rustled as if in welcome.

The sound of the music and the laughter was completely shut out. Laurana sighed deeply, breathed deeply of the perfume that scented the warm, moist air.

She placed her hand upon an orchid, turning it to the moonlight.

"Exquisite," said Medan, admiring the plant. "My orchids thrive—especially those you have given me—but I cannot produce such magnificent blossoms."

"Time and patience," Laurana said. "As in all things. To continue our earlier conversation, Marshal, I will tell you why I respect you more than Palthainon. Though your words are not easy for me to hear sometimes I know that when you speak, you speak from your heart. You have never lied to me, even when a lie might have served your purpose better than the truth. Palthainon's words slide out of his mouth and fall to the ground, then slither away into the darkness."

Medan bowed to acknowledge the compliment, but he would not enter into further disparagement of the man who helped him keep Qualinesti under control. He changed the subject.

"You have left the revelries at an early hour, madam. I hope you are not unwell," he said politely.

"The heat and the noise were too much to bear," Laurana replied. "I came out into the garden for some quiet."

"Have you dined?" the marshal asked. "Could I send the servants for food or wine?"

"No, thank you, Marshal. I find I have very little appetite these days. You can serve me best by keeping me company for a while, if your duties do not call you away."

"With such a charming companion, I do not think that death himself could call me away," the Marshal returned.

Laurana glanced at him from beneath lowered lashes, smiled slightly. "Humans are not generally given to such pretty speeches. You have been around elves much too long, Marshal. In fact, I believe you are more elf than human now. You wear our clothes, you speak our language flawlessly, you enjoy our music and our poetry. You have issued laws that protect our woodlands, laws stronger than those we might have passed ourselves. Perhaps I was wrong," she added lightly. "Perhaps you are the conquered and we are, in truth, your conquerors."

"You make sport of me, madam," Medan returned, "and you will probably laugh when I say that you are not far wrong. I was blind to nature before I came to Qualinesti. A tree was a thing I used to build a wall for a fortress or a handle for my battle-axe. The only music I enjoyed was the martial beating of the war drum. The only reading in which I took pleasure were dispatches from headquarters. I freely admit that I laughed when I first entered this land to see an elf speaking respectfully to a tree or talking gently to a flower. And then, one spring, after I had been living here about seven years, I was amazed to find myself eagerly awaiting the return of the flowers to my garden, wondering which would blossom first, wondering if the new rosebush the gardener had planted last year would bloom. At about the same time, I discovered the songs of the harpist running through my mind. I began to study the poetry to learn the words.

"In truth, Madam Lauralanthalasa, I do love your land. That is why," Medan added, his expression darkening, "I do my best to keep this land safe from the wrath of the dragon. That is why I must harshly punish those of your people who rebel against my authority. Beryl wants only an excuse to destroy you and your land. By persisting in resistance, by committing acts of terror and sabotage against my forces, the misguided rebels among your people threaten to bring destruction down upon you all."

Medan had no idea how old Laurana must be. Hundreds of years, perhaps. Yet she was as beautiful and youthful as the days when she had been the Golden General, leading the armies of light against the forces of Queen Takhisis during the War of the Lance. He had met old soldiers who spoke still of her courage in battle, her spirit that rallied the flagging spirits of the crumbling armies and led them to victory. He wished he could have known her then, though they would have been on opposite sides. He wished he could have seen her riding to battle on the back of her dragon, her golden hair a shining banner for her troops to follow.

"You say that you trust in my honor, madam," he continued and he took hold of her hand in his earnestness. "Then you must believe me when I tell you that I am working day and night to try to save Qualinesti. These rebels do not make my task easy. The dragon hears of their attacks and their defiance and grows extremely angry. She wonders aloud why she wastes her time and money ruling over such troublesome subjects. I do my best to placate her, but she is fast losing patience."

"Why do you tell me this, Marshal Medan?" Laurana asked. "What has this to do with me?"

"Madam, if you have any influence over these rebels, please stop them. Tell them that while their acts of terror may do some harm to myself and my troops, in the long run, the rebels are harming only their own people."

"And what makes you think that I, the Queen Mother, have anything to do with rebels?" Laurana asked. A flush came to her cheeks. Her eyes glittered.

Medan regarded her in silent admiration for a moment, then replied, "Let us say that I find it difficult to believe that someone who fought the Dark Queen and her minions so tenaciously over fifty years ago during the War of the Lance has ceased to do battle."

"You are wrong, Marshal," Laurana protested. "I am old, too old for such matters. No, Sir"—she forestalled his speaking—"I know what you are going to say. You are going to say that I look as young as a maiden at her first dance. Save your pretty compliments for those who desire to hear them. I do not. I have no heart left for battle, for defiance. My heart is in the tomb where my dear husband, Tanis, lies buried. My family is all that matters to me now. I want to see my son happily married, I want to hold grandchildren in my arms. I want our land to be at peace and I am willing to pay tribute to the dragon for our land to remain at peace."

Medan regarded her skeptically. He heard the ring of truth in her voice, but she was not telling him the entire truth. Laurana had been a skilled diplomat in the days following the war. She was accustomed to telling people what they wanted to hear while subtly swaying them to believe what she wanted them to believe. Still, it would have been extremely impolite to openly doubt her words. And if she meant them, Medan pitied her. The son on whom she doted was a spineless jellyfish who took hours to decide whether to have strawberries or blueberries for luncheon. Gilthas was not likely to ever take such an important step as making up his mind to wed. Unless, of course, someone else picked out his bride for him.

Laurana averted her head but not before Medan had seen the tears welling in her almond eyes. He changed the subject back to orchids. He was attempting to grow some in his own garden and was having minimal success. He discussed orchids for a long while, giving Laurana a chance to regain her composure. A quick touch of her hand to her eyes and she was once more in control. She recommended her own gardener, a master with orchids.

Medan accepted the offer with pleasure. The two of them lingered another hour in the arboretum, discussing strong roots and waxen flowers.

"Where is my honored mother, Palthainon?" Gilthas, Speaker of the Sun, asked. "I have not seen her this past half-hour."

The king was dressed in the costume of an elven ranger, all in greens and browns, colors that were becoming to him. Gilthas looked quite impressive, though few elven rangers were likely to go about their duties attired in the finest silken hose and shirts, or a hand-tooled and gold-embossed leather vest with matching boots. He held a cup of wine in his hand, but he only sipped at it out of politeness. Wine gave him a headache, everyone knew.

"I believe that your mother is walking in the garden, Your Majesty," said Prefect Palthainon, who missed nothing of the comings and goings of the House Royal. "She spoke of needing air. Would you have me send for her? Your Majesty does not look well."

"I am not well," Gilthas said. "Thank you for your kind offer, Palthainon, but do not disturb her." His eyes darkened, he looked out upon the throng of dancers with sadness and wistful envy. "Do you think anyone would take it amiss if I were to retire to my room, Prefect?" he asked in a low voice.

"Perhaps a dance would cheer Your Majesty," Palthainon said. "There, look at how the lovely Amiara smiles at you." The prefect leaned near the king to whisper, "Her father is one of the wealthiest elves in all of Qualinesti. Silversmith, you know. And she is perfectly charming—"

"Yes, she is," said Gilthas in disinterested agreement. "But I do not feel equal to dancing. I am feeling faint and nauseated. I believe that I really must retire."

"By all means, if Your Majesty is truly not well," said Palthainon reluctantly. Medan was right. Having robbed the king of a spine, the prefect could not very well fault the young man for crawling about on his hands and knees. "Your Majesty should rest in bed tomorrow. I will take care of the affairs of state."

"Thank you, Palthainon," Gilthas said quietly. "If I am not needed, I will spend the day working on the twelfth canto in my new poem."

He rose to his feet. The music came to a sudden halt. The dancers ceased in mid-whirl. Elven men bowed, elven women curtsied. The elven maidens looked up in expectation. Gilthas seemed embarrassed by the sight of them. Ducking his head, he stepped down off the dais and walked quickly toward the door that led to his private chambers. His personal servant accompanied him, walking ahead of the king, bearing a glowing candelabra to light His Majesty's way. The elven maidens shrugged and glanced about demurely for new partners. The music began again. The dancing continued.

Prefect Palthainon, muttering imprecations, headed for the refreshment table.

Gilthas, glancing back before he left the room, smiled to himself. Turning, he followed the soft glow of the candlelight through the darkened hallways of his palace. Here no courtiers flattered and fawned, here no one was permitted to enter without first obtaining permission from Palthainon, who lived in constant fear that some day someone else might wrest away the marionette's strings. Kagonesti guards stood at every entrance.

Freed from the music and the lights, the twittering laughter and the whispering conversations, Gilthas breathed a sigh of relief as he walked the well-guarded corridors. The newly built palace of the Speaker of the Sun was a large and airy dwelling of living trees that had been magically altered and lovingly transformed into ceilings and walls. The tapestries were made of flowers and plants coaxed to form beautiful works of art that changed daily depending on what was in bloom. The floors of some of the rooms of the palace, such as the dancing room and the audience chambers, were made of marble. Most of the private rooms and the hallways that wound among the boles of the trees were carpeted with fragrant plants.

The palace was considered something of a marvel among the Qualinesti people. Gilthas had insisted that all the trees standing on the land be utilized in the shapes and positions in which the trees had grown naturally. He would not permit the Woodshapers to coax them into bending themselves into unnatural poses to accommodate a staircase or shifting their branches to provide more light. Gilthas intended this as a sign of honor to the trees, who were pleased, it seemed, for they flourished and thrived. The result was, however, an irregular maze of leafy corridors, where those new to the palace would often lose themselves for hours on end.

The king did not speak, but walked with his head bowed and his hands clasped behind him. He was often to be seen in this attitude, roaming restlessly the halls of the palace. It was known that at these times he was mulling over some rhyme or trying to work out the rhythm of a stanza. The servants knew better than to interrupt him. Those who passed bowed low and said nothing.

The palace was quiet this night. The music of the dance could be heard, but it was soft and muted by the gentle rustling of the thickly entangled leaves that formed the high ceiling of the corridor through which they walked. The king lifted his head, glanced about. Seeing no one, Gilthas moved a step closer to his servant.

"Planchet," said Gilthas in a low voice, speaking the human language which few elves spoke, "where is Marshal Medan? I thought I saw him go into the garden."

"He did, Your Majesty," his servant replied, answering in the same language, soft and low, not turning around to look at the king lest someone should be watching them. Palthainon's spies were everywhere.

"That's unfortunate," said Gilthas, frowning. "What if he's still hanging about out there?"

"Your mother noticed and followed after him immediately, Your Majesty. She will keep him occupied."

"You are right," said Gilthas with a smile, a smile only a trusted few ever saw. "Medan will not bother us this night. Is everything ready?"

"I have packed food enough for a day's journeying, Your Majesty. The knapsack is hidden in the grotto."

"And Kerian? Does she know where to meet me?"

"Yes, Your Majesty. I left the message in the usual spot. It was gone the next morning when I went to check. A red rose was in its place."

"You have done well, as always, Planchet," Gilthas said. "I do not know what I would do without you. I want that rose, by the way."

"The rose is with Your Majesty's knapsack," said Planchet.

The two ceased talking. They had arrived at the Speaker's

personal chambers. The king's Kagonesti guards—ostensibly body guards, but in reality, prison guards—saluted as His Majesty approached. Gilthas paid them no heed. The guards were in Palthainon's pay, they reported every movement the king made to the prefect. Servants waited in the king's bedroom to assist His Majesty in undressing and preparing for bed.

"His Majesty is not feeling well," Planchet announced to the servants as he placed the candelabra upon a table. "I will attend him. You have leave to go."

Gilthas, pale and languishing, dabbed his lips with his lace handkerchief and went immediately to lie down upon his bed, not even bothering to take off his boots. Planchet would see to that for him. The servants, who were accustomed to the king's ill health and his desire for solitude, had expected nothing else after the rigors of a party. They bowed and departed.

"No one is to disturb His Majesty," Planchet said, shutting the door and locking it. The guards also had keys, but they rarely used them now. In the past, they had checked upon the young king on a frequent basis. They always found him where he was supposed to be, sick in bed or dreaming over his pen and paper, and at last they'd stopped checking.

Planchet listened at the door a moment, waited to hear the guards relax and return to their games of chance with which they whiled away the long and boring hours. Satisfied, he crossed the room, threw open the doors that led to the balcony, and looked out into the night.

"All is well, Your Majesty."

Gilthas jumped from the bed and headed for the window. "You know what to do?"

"Yes, Your Majesty. The pillows are prepared that will take your place in the bed. I am to keep up the pretense that you are in the room. I will not permit anyone to visit you."

"Very good. You need not worry about Palthainon. He will

not put in an appearance until tomorrow morning. He will be too busy signing my name and affixing my seal to important documents."

Gilthas stood by the balustrade of the balcony. Planchet affixed a rope to the balustrade, held it fast. "A profitable journey, Your Majesty. When do you return?"

"If all goes well, Planchet, I will be back by midnight tomorrow night."

"All will go well," said the elf. He was several years older than Gilthas, hand-picked by Laurana to serve her son. Prefect Palthainon had approved the choice. Had the prefect bothered to check Planchet's background, which included many years of loyal service to the dark elf Porthios, the prefect might not have. "Fate smiles upon Your Majesty."

Gilthas had been looking into the garden, searching for signs of movement. He glanced back quickly. "There was a time I could have argued with that statement, Planchet. I used to believe myself the unluckiest person in this world, snared by my own vanity and conceit, imprisoned by my own fear. There was a time I used to see death as my only escape."

Impulsively, he reached out and grasped the hand of his servant. "You forced me to look away from the mirror, Planchet. You forced me to stop staring into my own reflection, to turn and look upon the world. When I did, I saw my people suffering, crushed beneath the heel of black boots, living in the shadows of dark wings, facing a future of despair and certain destruction."

"No longer do they live without hope," said Planchet, gently withdrawing his hand, embarrassed by the king's regard. "Your Majesty's plan will succeed."

Gilthas sighed. "Let us hope so, Planchet. Let us hope that Fate smiles on more than me. Let us hope she smiles upon our people."

He descended the rope nimbly, hand over hand, and

dropped lightly into the garden. Planchet watched from the balcony until the king had disappeared into the night. Planchet then shut the doors and walked back over to the bed. He placed the pillows on it and arranged the coverlet convincingly about them so that if anyone looked, they would see what appeared to be a body in the bed.

"And now, Your Majesty," Planchet said loudly, picking up a small harp and running his hands over the strings, "take your sleeping draught and I will play some soft music to lull you into slumber."

15

Tasslehoff, the One and Only

espite being in pain and extreme discomfort, Sir Gerard was satified with the way things were going thus far. He had a throbbing headache from where the elf had kicked him. He was tied to his horse, dangling head down over the saddle. The blood pounded in his temples, his breastplate jabbed into his stomach and constricted his breathing, leather cords cut into his flesh, and he had lost all feeling in his feet. He did not know his captors, he'd been unable to see them in the darkness, and now, blindfolded, he could see nothing at all. They had very nearly killed him. He had the kender to thank for keeping him alive.

Yes, things were going as planned.

They traveled for a considerable distance. The journey seemed endless to Gerard, who began to think after awhile that they had been riding for decades, long enough to have circumnavigated Krynn itself at least six times. He had no idea how the kender was faring, but judging by the occasional indignant squeaks emanating from somewhere behind him Gerard assumed that Tasslehoff was relatively intact. Gerard must have dozed, either that or he'd passed out, for he woke suddenly when the horse came to a halt.

The human was speaking, the human whom Gerard took to be the leader. He was speaking in Elvish, a language Gerard did not understand. But it seemed that they had reached their destination for the elves were cutting loose the bindings holding him on the saddle. One of the elves grabbed him by the back of the breastplate, pulled him off the horse's back and dumped him on the ground.

"Get up, swine!" the elf said harshly in Common. "We are not going to carry you." The elf removed the Knight's blind-fold. "Into that cave over there. March."

They had traveled through the night. The sky was pink with the coming of dawn. Gerard saw no cave, only thick and impenetrable forest, until one of the elves picked up what appeared to be a stand of young trees and moved it. A dark cavern in the side of a rock wall came into view. The elf placed the screen of trees to one side.

Staggering to his feet, Gerard limped forward. The sky was growing brighter, now fiery orange and sea-blue. He looked about for his companion, saw the kender's feet sticking out of a sack that was a bulky shape on the pony's back. The human leader stood near the cave entrance, keeping watch. He was cloaked and hooded, but Gerard caught a glimpse of dark robes beneath the cloak, robes such as a magic-user might wear. The Knight was becoming more and more certain that his plan had worked. Now he just had to hope that the elves would not kill him before he had a chance to explain himself.

The cave was set in a small hill in a heavily forested area. Gerard had the impression that they were not in some isolated patch of wilderness but close to a community. He could hear on the distant breeze the sound of the bell flowers elves liked to plant around the windows of their dwellings, flowers whose blossoms rang musically when the wind's breath touched them. He could also smell the scent of fresh-baked bread. Glancing in the direction of the rising sun, he confirmed that they had traveled due west during the night. If he was not actually in the city of Qualinost, he must be very close by.

The human entered the cavern. Two of the elves followed, one of them carrying the squirming kender trussed up in his sack, the other walking behind Gerard, prodding him in the back with a sword. The other elves who had accompanied them did not enter the cave but vanished into the woods, taking the pony and the Knight's horse with them. Gerard hesitated a moment before stepping into the cave. The elf shoved him in the back and he stumbled forward.

A dark, narrow passage opened up into a smallish chamber lit by a flame floating on a bowl of sweet-smelling oil. The elf carrying the kender dropped the sack to the floor, where the kender began to squeak and squeal and wriggle inside the sack. The elf gave the sack a nudge with his foot, told the kender to be silent; they would let him out in good time, and then only if he behaved himself. The elf guarding Gerard prodded him again in the back.

"On your knees, swine," said the elf.

Gerard sank to his knees and lifted his head. Now he had a good view of the human's face, for he could look up into it. The man in the cloak looked down grimly at Gerard.

"Palin Majere," said Gerard with a sigh of relief. "I have come a long way in search of you."

Palin brought the torch close. "Gerard uth Mondar. I thought that was you. But since when did you become a Knight of Neraka? You had best explain and quickly." He frowned. "As you know, I have no love for that accursed Knighthood."

"Yes, sir." Gerard glanced uncertainly at the elves. "Do they speak the human language, sir?"

"And Dwarvish and Common," Palin answered. "I can order them to kill you in any number of languages. I say again, explain yourself. You have one minute."

"Very well, sir," Gerard replied. "I wear this armor of necessity, not by choice. I bear important news for you and, finding out from your sister Laura that you were in Qualinesti, I disguised myself as one of the enemy so that I could safely reach you."

"What news?" Palin asked. He had not removed the dark hood, but spoke from its shadowy depths. Gerard could not see his face. His voice was deep and stern and cold.

Gerard thought of what people in Solace were saying about Palin Majere these days. He was changed since the Academy had been destroyed. He had changed and not for the better. He had veered off the sunlit road to walk a dark path, a path his uncle Raistlin had walked before him.

"Sir," said Gerard, "your honored father is dead."

Palin said nothing. His expression did not alter.

"He did not suffer," the Knight hastened to assure Palin. "Death took your father swiftly. He walked out the door of the Inn, looked into the sunset, spoke your mother's name, pressed his hand over his heart, and fell. I was with him when he died. He was at peace, in no pain. We held his funeral the next day. He was laid to rest at your mother's side."

"Did he say anything?" Palin asked at last.

"He made a request of me, which I will tell you about in due time."

Palin regarded Gerard in silence for long moments. Then he said, "And how is everything else in Solace?"

"Sir?" Gerard was astonished, appalled.

The kender in the sack gave a wail, but no one paid any attention.

"Did you not hear—?" Gerard began.

"My father is dead. I heard," Palin replied. He threw back his cowl, regarded Gerard with an unwavering gaze. "He was an old man. He missed my mother. Death is a part of life. Some might say"—his voice hardened—"the best part."

Gerard stared. He had last seen Palin Majere a few months ago, when he had attended the funeral of his mother, Tika. Palin had not remained in Solace long. He had left almost immediately on yet another search for ancient magical artifacts. With the Academy destroyed, Solace held nothing for Palin anymore. And with rumors running rife that wizards all over the world were losing their magical powers, people guessed that Palin was no different. It seemed, so they whispered, that life held nothing more for him. His marriage was not the happiest. He had grown careless, reckless of his safety, especially if the slightest chance offered of obtaining a magical artifact from the Fourth Age. For these artifacts had not lost their power and such power could be leeched by a skilled wizard.

Gerard had thought Palin looked unwell at the funeral. This trip had done nothing to improve the mage's health. If anything, he was more gaunt, more pallid, his manner more restive, his gaze furtive, distrustful.

Gerard knew a great deal about Palin. Caramon had been fond of talking about his only surviving son, and he had been a topic of conversation at almost every breakfast.

Palin Majere, the youngest son of Caramon and Tika, had been a promising young mage when the gods left Krynn, taking magic with them. Although he grieved the loss of the godly magic, Palin had not given up, as did so many wizards of his generation. He had brought together mages from all over Ansalon in an effort to learn to use the magic he believed remained in the world, wild magic that was of the world itself. Such magic had been part of the world before the coming of the gods, and, so he had supposed, would remain in the world even after the departure of the gods. His efforts had been successful. He had established the Academy of Sorcery in Solace, a center of learning for magic. The Academy had grown and prospered. He had used his skills to fight the great dragons and was renowed throughout Abanasinia as a hero.

Then the tapestry of his life had begun to unravel.

Extraordinarily sensitive to the wild magic, he had been among the first, two years ago, to notice that its powers were starting to weaken. At first, Palin thought this might be nothing more than a symptom of advancing age. He was past fifty, after all. But then his students began to report similar problems. Even the young were finding spell-casting more difficult. Obviously age was not a factor.

The spells would work, but they required more and more effort on the part of the magic-user to cast them. Palin compared it once to putting a jar over a lighted candle. The flame will burn only so long as there is air trapped within the jar. When the air is gone, the flame will falter, flicker, and die.

Was magic finite, as some were saying? Could it dry up like a pond in the desert? Palin didn't think so. The magic was there. He could feel it, see it. But it was as if the desert pond was being drunk dry by a vast multitude.

Who or what was draining the magic? Palin suspected the great dragons. He was forced to change his mind when the great green dragon Beryl grew more threatening, became more aggressive, sent her armies to seize more territory. Qualinesti spies reported that this was happening because the dragon was feeling her own magical powers on the decrease. Beryl had long sought to find the Tower of High Sorcery at Wayreth. The magical forest had kept the Tower hidden from her and from the Knights of the Thorn who had been searching for it. Her need for the Tower and its magic became more urgent. Angry and uneasy, she began to extend her reach over as much of Abanasinia as was possible without drawing down on herself the wrath of her cousin Malys.

The Knights of the Thorn, the magic-wielding arm of the

Knights of Neraka, were also feeling their magical powers on the wane. They blamed Palin and his mages of the Academy of Sorcery. In a daring raid on the Academy, they kidnapped Palin, while Beryl's dragon minions destroyed it.

After months of "questioning," the Gray Robes had released Palin. Caramon had not wanted to go into details about the torment his son had endured, and Gerard had not pressed him. The residents of Solace discussed the matter at length, however. In their opinion, the enemy had not only twisted Palin's Majere's fingers, they had twisted his soul as well.

Palin's face was haggard, hollow-cheeked, with dark splotches beneath the eyes as if he slept little. He had few wrinkles; the skin was pulled taut, stretched over the fine bones. The deep lines around his mouth, which had marked the track of smiles, were beginning to fade away from disuse. His auburn hair had gone completely gray. The fingers of his hands, once supple and slender, were now twisted, cruelly deformed.

"Cut his bindings," Palin ordered the elves. "He is a Solamnic Knight, as he claims."

The two elves were dubious, but they did as they were told, though they continued to keep a close watch on him. Gerard rose to his feet, flexed his arms, and stretched his aching muscles.

"So you came all this way, disguised, risking your life to bring me this news," said Palin. "I must confess that I fail to see the need for the kender. Unless the story I heard is true, that this kender really did steal a powerful magical artifact. Let us have a look at him."

Palin knelt down beside the sack where the kender wriggled. He stretched out his hand, started to try to untie the knots, but his deformed fingers could not manage. Gerard looked at the wizard's fingers, looked quickly away, not wanting to seem to pity him.

"Does the sight distress you?" Palin asked with a sneer.

Standing up, he covered his hands with the sleeves of his robes. "I'll take care not to trouble you."

"It does distress me, sir," Gerard said quietly. "It distresses me to see any good man suffer as you have suffered."

"Suffered, yes! I was a prisoner of the Thorn Knights for three months. Three months! And not a day passed when they did not torment me in some way. Do you know why? Do you know what they wanted? They wanted to know why their magical power was waning! They thought *I* had something to do with it!" Palin gave a bitter laugh. "And do you want to know why they let me go? Because they realized I was not a threat! Just a broken old man who could do nothing to harm them or hinder them."

"They might have killed you, sir," Gerard said.

"It would have been better if they had," Palin returned.

The two were silent. Gerard looked down at the floor. Even the kender was quiet, subdued. He had quit wriggling.

Palin gave a soft sigh. Reaching out his broken hand, he touched Gerard's arm.

"Forgive me, Sir Knight," he said in a quieter tone. "Pay no heed to what I said. I am quick to take offense these days. And I have not yet even thanked you for bringing me news of my father. I do thank you. I am sorry for his death, but I cannot grieve for him. As I said, he has gone to a better place.

"And now," Palin added with a shrewd look at the young Knight, "I am beginning to think that this sad news alone has not brought you all this way. Wearing this disguise puts you in great danger, Gerard. If the Dark Knights were to discover the truth, you would endure torment far worse than what I suffered, and then you would be executed."

Palin's thin lips formed a bitter smile. "What other news do you have for me? It can't be good. No one would risk his life to bring me good news. And how could you know that you would find me?"

"I did not find you, sir," Gerard said. "You found me."

Palin looked puzzled, at first, then he nodded. "Ah, I understand. The mention of the artifact that once belonged to my Uncle Raistlin. You knew that would pique my interest."

"I hoped it would do so, sir," said Gerard. "My guess was that either the elf posted at the bridge would be part of the resistance movement or the bridge itself would be under observation. I trusted that the mention of an artifact coupled with the name Majere would be carried to you."

"You ran a great risk in trusting yourself to the elves. As you found out, there are those who would have no compunction in slaying one of your kind."

Gerard glanced at the two elves, Kalindas and Kelevandros, if he had heard the names right. They had not shifted their eyes from him once, kept their hands on the hilts of their swords.

"I am aware of that, sir," said Gerard. "But this seemed the only way to reach you."

"So I take it there is no artifact?" Palin said, adding in a tone of bitter disappointment. "It was all a ruse."

"On the contrary, sir, there *is* an artifact. That is part of the reason I came."

At this, the kender's squeaks started up again, louder and more insistent. He began to drum his feet on the floor, and he rolled about wildly in his sack.

"For mercy's sake, shut him up," Palin ordered irritably. "His screeching will summon every Dark Knight in Qualinesti. Carry him inside."

"We should leave him in the sack, Master," said Kalindas. "We do not want him finding his way back here."

"Very well," Palin agreed.

One of the elves picked up the kender, sack and all. The other elf glared sternly at Gerard and asked a question.

"No," Palin answered. "We do not need to blindfold him. He belongs to the old school of Knights: those who still believe in honor."

The elf carrying the kender walked toward the back of the

cave and, to Gerard's intense astonishment, continued right through solid stone. Palin followed, placing his hand on Gerard's arm and propelling the Knight forward. The illusion of stone was so convincing that it was all Gerard could do to keep from wincing as he walked into what looked like a wall of sharp and jagged rocks.

"Some magic still works apparently," Gerard said, impressed.

"Some," Palin said. "But it is erratic. The spell can fail at any moment and must be constantly renewed."

Gerard emerged from the wall to find himself in a garden of wondrous beauty, shaded by trees whose branches and thick leaves formed a solid curtain above and around them. Kalindas carried the bagged kender through the wall, deposited him on the flagstone walk of the garden. Chairs made of bent willow branches and a table made of crystal stood beside a shining pool of clear water.

Palin said something to Kelevandros. Gerard caught the name, "Laurana." The elf departed, running lightly through the garden.

"You have loyal guardians, sir," said Gerard, looking after the elf.

"They belong to the household of the Queen Mother," Palin replied. "They have been in Laurana's service for years, ever since her husband died. Sit down."

He made a motion with his crooked hands and a fall of water began, streaming down in front of the illusionary wall to splash into the pool below.

"I have sent to inform the Queen Mother of your arrival. You are now a guest in her house. Or rather, one of the gardens in her house. Here, you are safe, as safe as anyone is in these dark times."

Thankfully, Gerard removed the heavy breastplate and rubbed his bruised ribs. He laved his face with the cool water and drank deeply.

"Let the kender out now," Palin ordered.

Kalindas untied the sack and the kender emerged, flushed and indignant, his long hair covering his face. He sucked in a huge breath and wiped his forehead.

"Whew! I was getting really sick of smelling nothing but sack."

Flipping his topknot back over his head, the kender looked around with interest.

"My," he said. "This garden is pretty. Are there fish in that pool? Could I catch one, do you think? It was certainly stuffy in that sack, and I much prefer riding a horse sitting up on the saddle instead of lying down. I have a sort of pain here in my side where something poked me. I would introduce myself," he said contritely, apparently realizing that he wasn't conforming to the mores of polite society, "but I'm suffering from"—he caught Gerard's eye and said, with emphasis, "I am suffering *from a severe bump on the head* and I'm not quite certain who I am. You look awfully familiar to me. Have we met?"

Palin Majere had said nothing through this diatribe. His face had gone livid. He opened his mouth, but no words came out.

"Sir." Gerard reached out a supporting hand. "Sir, you should sit down. You don't look well."

"I have no need of your support," Palin snapped, shoving aside Gerard's hand. He stared at the kender.

"Quit the nonsense," he said coldly. "Who are you?"

"Who do you think I am?" the kender parried.

Palin seemed about to make an angry rejoinder, but he closed his lips over the words and, after drawing in a deep breath, he said tightly, "You look like a kender I once knew named Tasslehoff Burrfoot."

"And you look sort of like a friend of mine named Palin Majere." The kender was gazing at Palin with interest.

"I am Palin Majere. Who are—"

"Really?" The kender's eyes opened wide. "You're Palin?

What *happened* to you? You look *terrible!* Have you been sick? And your poor hands. Let me see them. You said the Dark Knights did that to you? How? Did they smash your finger bones with a hammer, 'cause that's what it looks like—"

Palin drew his sleeves over his hands, moved away from the kender. "You say you know me, kender? How?"

"I just saw you at Caramon's *first* funeral. You and I had a nice long chat, all about the Tower of High Sorcery at Wayreth and you being head of the White Robes, and Dalamar was there, and he was Head of the Conclave, and his girl friend Jenna was Head of the Red Robes, and—"

Palin frowned, looked at Gerard. "What is he talking about?"

"Don't pay any attention to him, sir. He's been acting crazy ever since I found him." Gerard looked strangely at Palin. "You said he resembled 'Tasslehoff.' That's who he claimed to be, until he started all this nonsense about having amnesia. I know it sounds odd, but your father also thought he was Tasslehoff."

"My father was an old man," Palin said, "and like many old men, he was probably reliving the days of his youth. And yet," he added softly, almost to himself, "he certainly does look like Tasslehoff!"

"Palin?" A voice called to him from the far end of the garden. "What is this Kelevandros tells me?"

Gerard turned to see an elven woman, beautiful as a winter's twilight, walking toward them along the flagstones. Her hair was long and the color of honey mingled with sunlight. She was dressed in robes of a pearly diaphanous material, so that she seemed to be clothed in mist. Catching sight of Gerard, she regarded him in disbelief, too outraged at first to pay any attention to the kender, who was jumping up and down and waving his hand in excitement.

Gerard, confused and awe-struck, made an awkward bow.

"You have brought a Dark Knight *here*, Palin!" Laurana turned on him in anger. "To our hidden garden! What is the reason for this?"

"He is not a Dark Knight, Laurana," Palin explained tersely, "as I told Kelevandros. Apparently, he doubts me. This man is Gerard uth Mondar, Knight of Solamnia, a friend of my father's from Solace."

Laurana looked at Gerard skeptically. "Are you certain, Palin? Then why is he wearing that foul armor?"

"I wear the armor for disguise only, my lady," Gerard said. "And, as you see, I have taken the first opportunity I could to cast it aside."

"This was the only way he could enter Qualinesti," Palin added.

"I beg your pardon, Sir Knight," Laurana said, extending a hand that was white and delicate. Yet, when he took it, he felt the calluses on her palm from her days when she had carried a shield and wielded a sword, the days when she had been the Golden General. "Forgive me. Welcome to my home."

Gerard bowed again in profound respect. He wanted to say something graceful and correct, but his tongue felt too big for his mouth, just as his hands and feet felt big and clumsy. He flushed deeply and stammered something that died away in a muddle.

"Me, Laurana! Look at me!" The kender called out.

Laurana turned now to take a good look at the kender and appeared astonished at what she saw. Her lips parted, her jaw went slack. Putting her hand to her heart, she fell back a step, staring all the while at the kender.

"*Alshana, Quenesti-Pah!*" she whispered. "It cannot be!"

Palin was watching her closely. "You recognize him, as well."

"Why, yes! It's Tasslehoff!" Laurana cried dazedly. "But how—Where—"

"I am Tasslehoff?" The kender looked anxious. "Are you certain?"

"What makes you think you're not?" Laurana asked.

"I always thought I was," Tas said solemnly. "But no one else did, and so I thought perhaps I'd made a mistake. But if you say I am Tasslehoff, Laurana, I suppose that settles it. You of all people wouldn't be likely to make a mistake. Would you mind if I gave you a hug?"

Tas flung his arms around Laurana's waist. She looked confusedly over his head from Palin back to Gerard, asking silently for an explanation.

"Are you in earnest?" Gerard demanded. "Begging your pardon, my lady," he added, flushing, realizing he'd come close to calling the Queen Mother a liar, "but Tasslehoff Burrfoot has been dead for over thirty years. How could this be possible? Unless—"

"Unless what?" Palin asked sharply.

"Unless his whole wild tale is somehow true." Gerard fell silent, pondering this unforeseen development.

"But, Tas, where have you been?" Laurana asked, removing one of her rings from his hand just as the ring was disappearing down his shirt front. "As Sir Gerard said, we thought you were dead!"

"I know. I saw the tomb. Very nice." Tas nodded. "That's where I met Sir Gerard. I do think you might work to keep the grounds cleaner—all the dogs you know—and the tomb itself is not in good repair. It was hit by lightning when I was inside it. I heard the most tremendous boom, and some of the marble fell off. And it was awfully dark inside. A few windows would sort of brighten the place—"

"We should go somewhere to talk, Palin," Gerard interrupted urgently. "Some place private."

"I agree. Laurana, the Knight has brought other sad news. My father is dead."

"Oh!" Laurana put her hand to her mouth. Tears filled her

eyes. "Oh, I am sorry, Palin. My heart grieves for him, yet grief seems wrong. He is happy now," she added in wistful envy. "He and Tika are together. Come inside," she added, glancing about the garden where Tasslehoff was now wading in the ornamental pond, displacing the water lilies and terrorizing the fish. "We should not discuss this out here." She sighed. "I fear that even my garden is not safe anymore."

"What happened, Laurana?" Palin demanded. "What do you mean the garden is not safe?"

Laurana sighed, a line marred her smooth forehead. "I spoke to Marshal Medan at the masquerade last night. He suspects me of having dealings with the rebels. He urged me to use my influence to make them cease their acts of terror and disruption. The dragon Beryl is grown paranoid lately. She threatenes to send her armies to attack us. We are not yet prepared if she should."

"Pay no heed to Medan, Laurana. He is concerned only with saving his own precious skin," said Palin.

"I believe that he means well, Palin," Laurana returned. "Medan has no love for the dragon."

"He has no love for anyone except himself. Don't be fooled by his show of concern. Medan avoids trouble for Medan, that is all. He is caught in a quandary. If the attacks and sabotage continue, his superiors will relieve him of his command, and from what I've heard of their new Lord of the Night Targonne, Medan might well be relieved of his head. Now, if you will excuse me, I will go divest myself of this heavy cloak. I will meet you in the atrium."

Palin departed, the folds of his black traveling cloak sweeping behind him. His stance was straight, his walk quick and firm. Laurana looked after him, troubled.

"Madam," said Gerard, finding his tongue at last. "I agree with Palin. You must not trust this Marshal Medan. He is a Dark Knight, and although they speak of honor and sacrifice their words are empty and hollow as their souls."

"I know you are right," Laurana said. "Still, I have seen the seed of good fall in the darkest swamp to grow strong and beautiful though it was poisoned by the most noxious miasma. And I have seen the same seed, nurtured by the softest rains and the brightest sunshine, grow twisted and ugly, to bear a bitter fruit."

She continued to gaze after Palin. Sighing, she shook her head and turned around. "Come along, Tas. I would like you and Gerard to see the rest of the wonders I have in my house."

Cheerfully dripping, Tasslehoff climbed out of the pond. "You go ahead, Gerard. I want to talk to Laurana alone for a moment. It's a secret," he added.

Laurana smiled at the kender. "Very well, Tas. Tell me your secret. Kalindas," she said to the elf who had been waiting silently all this time, "escort Gerard to the house. Show him to one of the guest rooms."

Kalindas did as commanded. As he showed Gerard the way to the house, the elf's tone was gracious, but he kept his hand on the hilt of his sword.

When they were alone, Laurana turned to the kender.

"Yes, Tas," she said. "What is it?"

Tas looked extremely anxious. "This is very important, Laurana. Are you *sure* I'm Tasslehoff? Are you extremely sure?"

"Yes, Tas, I'm sure," Laurana said, smiling indulgently. "I don't know how or why, but I am quite certain you are Tasslehoff."

"It's just that I don't *feel* like Tasslehoff," Tas continued earnestly.

"You don't seem yourself, Tas, that is true," Laurana replied. "You are not as joyful as I remember you to be. Perhaps you are grieving for Caramon. He led a full life, Tas, a life of love and wonder and joy. He had his share of sorrow and trouble, but the dark days only made the days of light shine brighter. You were his good friend. He loved you. Don't be sad. He wouldn't want you to be unhappy."

"That's not what's making me unhappy," Tas protested. "That is, I was unhappy when Caramon died because it was so unexpected, even though I was expecting it. And I still sometimes have a lump of unhappiness right here in my throat when I think about him being gone, but I can manage a lump. It's the other feeling I can't manage, because I never felt anything like it before."

"I see. Perhaps we could talk about this later, Tas," Laurana said and started toward the house.

Tas caught hold of her sleeve, hung on for dear life. "It's the feeling that came to me when I saw the dragon!"

"What dragon?" Laurana stopped, turned back. "When did you see a dragon?"

"While Gerard and I were riding into Qualinesti. The dragon came around to take a look at us. I was . . ." Tas paused, then said in a awful whisper, "I think I was . . . scared." He gazed at Laurana with round eyes, expecting to see her reel backward into the pond, stunned with the shock and horror of this unnatural occurrence.

"You were wise to be scared, Tas," Laurana replied, taking the terrible news quite calmly. "The dragon Beryl is a loathsome, fearsome beast. Her claws are stained with blood. She is a cruel tyrant, and you are not the first to be afraid in her presence. Now, we should not keep the others waiting."

"But it's *me*, Laurana! Tasslehoff Burrfoot! Hero of the Lance!" Tas pounded himself frantically on his chest. "I'm not afraid of anything. There's a giant in the other time who's about to step on me and probably squash me flat, and that gives me a sort of squirmy feeling in my stomach when I think about it, but this is different." He sighed deeply. "You must be mistaken. I *can't* be Tasslehoff and be afraid."

The kender was truly upset, that much was obvious. Laurana regarded him thoughtfully. "Yes, this is different. This is very strange. You have been around dragons before, Tas."

"All sorts of dragons," Tas said proudly. "Blues and reds and greens and blacks, bronze and copper and silver and gold. I even flew on the back of one. It was glorious."

"And you never felt dragonfear?"

"I remember thinking that dragons were beautiful in an awful kind of way. And I felt afraid, but that was for my friends, never for myself. Much."

"This must have been true of the other kender, as well," Laurana mused, "the kender we now call 'afflicted.' Some of them must have experienced dragonfear years ago, during the War of the Lance and after. Why would these experiences be different? I never thought about it."

"Lots of times people don't think about us," Tas said in an understanding tone. "Don't feel bad."

"But I do feel badly," Laurana sighed. "We should have done something to help the kender. It's just that there's been so much happening that was more important. Or at least it seemed more important. If this fear is different from dragonfear, I wonder what it could be? A spell, perhaps?"

"That's it!" Tas shouted. "A spell! A curse!" He was thrilled. "I'm under a curse from the dragon. Do you truly think so?"

"I really don't know—" Laurana began, but the kender was no longer listening.

"A curse! I'm cursed!" Tasslehoff gave a blissful sigh. "Dragons have done lots of things to me but I've never before had one curse me! This is almost as good as the time Raistlin magicked me into a duck pond. Thank you, Laurana," he said, fervently shaking her hand and accidently removing the last of her rings. "You have no idea what a weight you have taken off my mind. I can be Tasslehoff now. A *cursed* Tasslehoff! Let's go tell Palin!

"Say, speaking of Palin," Tas added in a piercing whisper, "when did he become a Black Robe? The last I saw him, he was Head of the Order of White Robes! What made him change? Was it like Raistlin? Is someone else inhabit—habitat—habitating Palin's body?"

"Black robes, white robes, red robes, the distinction between one and the other is now gone, Tas," Laurana said. "Palin wore black robes because he wanted to blend in with the night." She looked at the kender oddly. "Palin was never Head of the Order of White Robes. What made you think that?"

"I'm beginning to wonder," Tasslehoff said. "I don't mind telling you, Laurana, but I'm *extremely confused*. Maybe someone's inhabitating my body," he added, but without much hope.

With all the strange feelings and lumps, there just didn't seem to be room for anyone else in there.

16

Tasslehoff's Tale

he Queen Mother's house was built on the side of a cliff overlooking Qualinesti. Like all elven structures, the house blended with nature, seemed a part of the landscape, as, indeed, much of it was. The elven builders had constructed the house so as to utilize the cliff-face in the design. Seen from a distance, the house appeared to be a grove of trees growing on a broad ledge that jutted out from the cliff. Only when one drew closer, did one see the path leading up to the house and then one could tell that the trees were in reality walls, their branches the roof and that cliff was also used for many of the walls of the house.

The north wall of the atrium was made of the rocky slope of the cliff face. Flowers and small trees blossomed, birds sang in the trees. A stream of water ran down the cliff, splashing into many small pools along the way. As each pool varied in depth, the sound of the falling water differed from pool to pool, producing a wondrous harmony of musical sound.

Tasslehoff was quite enchanted with the fact that there was a real waterfall inside the house and he climbed upon the rocks, slipping perilously on the slippery surface. He loudly exclaimed over the wonder of every bird's nest, uprooted a rare plant while trying to pick its flower and was forcibly removed by Kalindas when the kender insisted on trying to climb clear up to the ceiling.

This *was* Tasslehoff. The more Palin watched, the more he remembered and the more he became convinced that this kender was the kender he had known well over thirty years ago. He noted that Laurana watched Tas, as well. She watched him with a bewilderment tinged with wonder. Palin supposed it was perfectly plausible that Tasslehoff could have been wandering the world for thirty-eight years and had finally taken it into his head to drop by for a chat with Caramon.

Palin discarded the notion. Another kender might have done so, but not Tasslehoff. He was a unique kender, as Caramon liked to say. Or perhaps, not so unique as all that. Perhaps if they had taken time to come to know another kender, they might have discovered that they were all loyal and compassionate friends. But if Tas had not been roaming the world for almost forty years, than where had he been?

Palin listened attentively to the Knight's story of Tas's appearance in the tomb the night of the storm (most remarkable, Palin made a mental note of this occurrence), Caramon's recognition, his subsequent death and his last words to Sir Gerard.

"Your father was upset that he could not find his brother Raistlin. He said that Raistlin had promised to wait for him. And then came your father's dying request, sir," said Gerard in conclusion. "He asked me to take Tasslehoff to Dalamar. I would have to assume that to be the wizard, Dalamar, of infamous repute?"

"I suppose so," said Palin evasively, determined to betray nothing of his thoughts.

"According to the Measure, sir, I am honor bound to fulfill

a request made by the dying. But since the wizard Dalamar has disappeared and no one has heard from him in many years, I'm not quite certain what to do."

"Nor am I," Palin said.

His father's final words intrigued Palin. He was well aware of his father's firmly held belief that Raistlin would not depart this mortal plane until his twin had joined him.

"We're twins, Raist and I," Caramon would say. "And because we're twins, one of us can't leave this world and move on to the next without the other. The gods granted Raist peace in sleep, but then they woke him up during the Chaos War and it was then that he told me he would wait for me."

Raistlin had indeed returned from the dead during the Chaos War. He had gone to the Inn of the Last Home and had spent some time with Caramon. During that time, Raistlin had, according to Caramon, sought his brother's forgiveness. Palin had never questioned his father's faith in his faithless brother, though he had privately thought that Caramon was indulging in wishful thinking.

Still Palin did not feel he had the right to try to dissuade Caramon of his belief. After all, none could say for certain what happened to the souls of those who died.

"The kender maintains that he traveled forward in time and that he came here with the help of the magical device." Gerard shook his head, smiled. "At least it's the most original excuse I've heard from one of the little thieves."

"It's not an excuse," Tas said loudly. He had attempted to interrupt Gerard at several key points in the story, until finally the knight had threatened to gag him again if he wasn't quiet. "I *didn't* steal the device. Fizban gave it to me. And I *did* travel forward in time. Twice. The first time I was late and the second time I . . . don't know what happened."

"Let me see the magical artifact, Sir Gerard," Palin said. "Perhaps that will help us arrive at an answer."

"I'll show you!" Tas offered eagerly. He fumbled about in his pockets, looked down his shirtfront, felt all about his pant legs. "I know it's here somewhere . . ."

Palin looked accusingly at the knight. "If this artifact is as valuable as you describe, sir, why did you allow it to remain in the kender's possession? If it is still *in* his possession—"

"I didn't, sir," Gerard said defensively. "I've taken it away from him I don't know how many times. The artifact keeps going back to him. He says that's how it works."

Palin's heartbeat quickened. His blood warmed. His hands, that seemed always cold and numb, tingled with life. Laurana had risen involuntarily to her feet.

"Palin! You don't suppose . . ." she began.

"I found it!" Tas announced in triumph. He dragged the artifact out of his boot. "Would you like to hold it, Palin? It won't hurt you or anything."

The artifact had been small enough to fit inside the kender's small boot. Yet as Tas held it out, the kender had to hold the device with both hands. Yet Palin had not seen it change shape or enlarge. It was as if it was always the shape and size it was meant to be, no matter what the circumstances. If anything changed, it was the viewer's perception of the artifact, not the artifact itself.

Jewels of antiquity—rubies, sapphires, diamonds and emeralds—sparkled and glittered in the sunlight, catching the sunbeams and transforming them into smears of rainbow light splashed on the walls and the floor and shining up from the kender's cupped hands.

Palin started to reach out his own crippled hands to hold the device, then he hesitated. He was suddenly afraid. He did not fear that the artifact might do him some harm. He knew perfectly well it wouldn't. He had seen the artifact when he was a boy. His father had shown it off proudly to his children. In addition, Palin recognized the device from his studies when he was a youth. He had seen drawings of it in the books in the

Tower of High Sorcery. This was the Device of Time Journeying, one of the greatest and most powerful of all the artifacts ever created by the masters of the Towers. It would not harm him, yet it would do him terrible, irrevocable damage.

Palin knew from experience the pleasure he would feel when he touched the artifact: he would sense the old magic, the pure magic, the loved magic, the magic that came to him untainted, freely given, a gift of faith, a blessing from the gods. He would sense the magic, but only faintly, as one senses the smell of rose leaves, pressed between the pages of a book, their sweet fragrance only a memory. And because it was only a memory, after the pleasure would come the pain—the aching, searing pain of loss.

But he could not help himself. He said to himself, "Perhaps this time I will be able to hold onto it. Perhaps this time with this artifact, the magic will come back to me."

Palin touched the artifact with trembling, twisted fingers.

Glory . . . brilliance . . . surrender . . .

Palin cried out, his broken fingers clenched over the artifact. The jewels cut into the flesh of his hand.

Truth . . . beauty . . . art . . . life . . .

Tears burned his eyelids, slid down his cheeks.

Death . . . loss . . . emptiness . . .

Palin sobbed harshly, bitterly for what was lost. He wept for his father's death, wept for the three moons that had vanished from the sky, wept for his broken hands, wept for his own betrayal of all that he had believed in, wept for his own inconstancy, his own desperate need to try to find the ecstasy again.

"He is ill. Should we do something?" Gerard asked uneasily.

"No, Sir Knight. Leave him be," Laurana admonished gently. "There is nothing we can do for him. There is nothing we *should* do for him. This is necessary to him. Though he suffers now, he will be better for this release."

"I'm sorry, Palin," Tasslehoff cried remorsefully. "I didn't think it would hurt you. Honestly, I didn't! It never hurt me."

"Of course it would not hurt you, wretched kender!" Palin returned, the pain a living thing inside him, twisting and coiling around his heart so that it fluttered in his chest like a frantic bird caught by the snake. "To you it is nothing but a pretty toy! To me it is an opiate that brings blissful, wondrous dreams." His voice cracked. "Until the effect wears off. The dreams end and I must wake again to drudgery and despair, wake to the bitter, mundane reality."

He clenched his hand over the device, quenched the light of its jewels. "Once," he said, his voice tight, "I might have crafted a marvelous and powerful artifact such as this. Once I might have been what you claim I was—Head of the Order of White Robes. Once I might have had the future my uncle foresaw for me. Once I might have been a wizard, gifted, puissant, powerful. I look at this device and that is what I see. But I look into a mirror and I see something far different."

He opened his hand. He could not see the device for his bitter tears. He could see only the light of its magic, glinting and winking, mocking. "My magic dwindles, my powers grow weaker every day. Without the magic, there is one hope left for us—to hope that death is better than this dismal life!"

"Palin, you must not speak like that!" Laurana said sternly. "So we thought in the dark days before the War of the Lance. I remember Raistlin saying something to the effect that hope was the carrot dangled before the nose of the cart horse to fool him into plodding forward. Yet we did plod forward and, in the end, we were rewarded."

"We were," said Tas. "I ate the carrot."

"We were rewarded all right," Palin said, sneering. "With this wretched world in which we find ourselves!"

The artifact was painful to his touch—indeed, he had clutched so tightly that the sharp-edged jewels had cut him. But still he held it fast, carressing it covetously. The pain was so much preferable to the feeling of numbness.

Gerard cleared his throat, looked embarrassed.

"I take it, sir, that I was right," he said diffidently. "This is a powerful artifact of the Fourth Age?"

"It is," Palin answered.

They waited for him to say more, but he refused to indulge them. He wanted them to leave. He wanted to be alone. He wanted to sort out his thoughts that were running hither and yon like rats in a cave when someone lights a torch. Scuttling down dark holes, crawling into crevices and some staring with glittering, fascinated eyes at the blazing fire. He had to endure them, their foolishiness, their inane questions. He had to hear the rest of Tasslehoff's tale.

"Tell me what happened, Tas," Palin said. "None of your woolly mammoth stories. This is very important."

"I understand," Tas said, impressed. "I'll tell the truth. I promise. It all started one day when I was attending the funeral of an extremely good kender friend I'd met the day before. She'd had an unfortunate encounter with a bugbear. What happened was—er—"— Tas caught sight of Palin's brows constricting—"never mind, as the gnomes say. I'll tell you that story later. Anyhow during her funeral, it occurred to me that very few kender ever live long enough to be what you might call old. I've already lived a lot longer than most kender I know and I suddenly realized that Caramon was likely to live a lot longer than I was. The one thing I really, really wanted to do before I was dead was to tell everyone what a good friend Caramon had been to me. It seemed to me that the best time to do this would be at his funeral. But if Caramon outlived me, then me going to his funeral would be something of a problem.

"Anyway, I was talking to Fizban one day and I explained this and he said that he thought what I wanted to do was a fine and noble thing and he could fix it up. I could speak at

Caramon's funeral by traveling to the time when the funeral was taking place. And he gave me this device and told me how it worked and gave me strict instructions to just jump ahead, talk at the funeral, and come straight back. 'No gallivanting,' he said. By the way," Tas asked anxiously, "you don't think he'd consider this trip 'gallivanting,' do you? Because I'm finding that I really am enjoying seeing all my friends again. It's much more fun than being stepped on by a giant."

"Go on with the story, Tas," Palin said tersely. "We'll discuss that later."

"Yes, right. So I used the device and I jumped forward in time, but, well, you know that Fizban gets things a bit muddled now and then. He's always forgetting his name or where his hat is when it's right on his head or forgetting how to cast a fireball spell and so I guess he just miscalculated. Because when I jumped forward in time the first time, Caramon's funeral was over. I'd missed it. I arrived just in time for refreshments. And while I did have a nice visit visiting with everyone and the cream cheese puffs Jenna made were truly scrumptious, I wasn't able to do what I'd meant to do all along. Remembering that I'd promised Fizban no gallivanting, I went back.

"And, to be honest"—Tas hung his head and shuffled his foot—"after that, I forgot all about speaking at Caramon's funeral. I had a really good reason. The Chaos War came and we were fighting shadow wights and I met Dougan and Usha, your wife, you know, Palin. It was all immensely interesting and exciting. And now the world is about to come to an end and there's this horrible giant about to smash me flat and it was at that precise moment that I remembered that I hadn't spoken at Caramon's funeral. So I activated the device really quickly and came here to say what a good friend Caramon was before the giant steps on me."

Gerard was shaking his head. "This is ridiculous."

"Excuse me," said Tas, stern in his turn. "It's not polite to interrupt. So anyway I came here and ended up in the Tomb and Gerard found me and took me to see Caramon. And I was able to tell him what I was going to say about him at the funeral, which he enjoyed immensely, only nothing was like I remembered it the first time. I told that to Caramon, too, and he seemed really worried, but he dropped dead before he had time to do anything about it. And then he couldn't find Raistlin when he knew that Raistlin would never go on to the next life without his twin. Which is why I think he said I was to talk to Dalamar." Tas drew in a deep breath, having expended most of his air on his tale. "And that's why I'm here."

"Do you believe this, my lady?" Gerard demanded.

"I don't know what to believe," Laurana said softly. She glanced at Palin, but he carefully avoided her gaze, pretended to be absorbed in examining the device, almost as if he expected to find the answers engraved upon the shining metal.

"Tas," he said mildly, not wanting to reveal the direction of his thoughts, "tell me everything you remember about the first time you came to my father's funeral."

Tasslehoff did so, talking about how Dalamar attended and Lady Crysania and Riverwind and Goldmoon, how the Solamnic Knights sent a representative who traveled all the way from the High Clerist's Tower and Gilthas came from the elven kingdom of Qualinesti and Silvanoshei from his kingdom of Silvanesti and Porthios and Alhana came and she was as beautiful as ever. "And you were there, Laurana, and you were so happy because you said you'd lived to see your dearest dream come true, the elven kingdoms united in peace and brotherhood."

"It's just a story he's made up," Gerard said impatiently. "One of those tales of 'what might have been.'"

"What might have been," Palin said, watching the sunlight sparkle on the jewels. "My father had a story of what might have been." He looked at Tas. "You and my father traveled forward in time together once, didn't you?"

"It wasn't my fault," Tas said quickly. "We overshot our mark. You see, we were trying to go back to our own time which was 356 but due to a miscalculation we ended up in 358. Not the 358 which was 358, but a really horrible 358 where we found Tika's tomb and poor Bupu dead in the dust and Caramon's corpse, a 358 which thank goodness never happened because Caramon and I went back in time to make sure that Raistlin didn't become a god."

"Caramon once told me that story," Gerard said. "I thought—Well, he was getting on in years and he did like to tell tales, so I never really took him seriously."

"My father believed that it happened," Palin said and that was all he said.

"Do you believe it, Palin?" Laurana asked insistently. "More important, do you believe that Tas's story is true. That he really did travel through time? Is that what you are thinking?"

"What I am thinking is that I need to know much more about this device," he replied. "Which is, of course, why my father urged that the device be taken to Dalamar. He is the only person in this world who was actually present during the time my father worked the magic of the device."

"I was there!" Tas reminded them. "And now I'm here."

"Yes," said Palin with a cool, appraising glance. "So you are."

In his mind, an idea was forming. It was only a spark, a tiny flash of flame in a vast and empty darkness. Yet it had been enough to send the rats scurrying.

"You cannot ask Dalamar," Laurana said practically. "No one's seen him since his return from the Chaos War."

"No, Laurana, you are wrong," Palin said. "One person saw him before his mysterious disappearance—his lover, Jenna. She always claimed that she had no idea where he went, but I never believed her. And she would be the one person who might know something about this artifact."

"Where does this Jenna live?" Gerard asked. "Your father gave me the task of taking the kender and the device to Dalamar. I may not be able to do that, but I could at least escort you, sir, and the kender—"

Palin was shaking his head. "That will not be possible, Sir Knight. Mistress Jenna lives in Palanthas, a city under the control of the Dark Knights."

"So is Qualinesti, sir," Gerard pointed out, with a slight smile.

"Slipping unnoticed across the heavily wooded borders of Qualinesti is one thing," Palin observed. "Entering the walled and heavily guarded city of Palanthas is quite another. Besides the journey would take far too long. It would be easier to meet Jenna half way. Perhaps in Solace."

"But can Jenna leave Palanthas?" Laurana asked. "I thought the Dark Knights had restricted travel out of the city as well as into it."

"Such restrictions may apply to ordinary people," Palin said drily. "Not to Mistress Jenna. She made it her business to get on well with the knights when they took over the city. Very well, if you take my meaning. Youth is lost to her, but she is still an attractive woman. She is also the wealthiest woman in Solamnia and one of the most powerful mages. No, Laurana, Jenna will have no difficulty traveling to Solace." He rose to his feet. He needed to be alone, to think.

"But aren't her powers abating like yours, Palin?" Laurana asked.

He pressed his lips together in displeasure. He did not like speaking of his loss, as another might not like speaking of a cancerous growth. "Jenna has certain artifacts which continue to work for her, as I have some which continue to work for me. It is not much," he added caustically, "but we make do."

"Perhaps this is the best plan," Laurana agreed. "But how will you return to Solace? The roads are closed—"

Palin bit his lip, bit back bitter words. Would they never quit yammering at him?

"Not to one of the Dark Knights," Gerard was saying. "I offer myself as escort, sir. I came here with a kender prisoner. I will leave with a human one."

"Yes, yes, a good plan, Sir Knight," Palin said impatiently. "You work out the details." He started to walk off, eager to escape to the silence of his room, but he thought of one more important question. Pausing, he turned to ask it. "Does anyone else know of the discovery of this artifact?"

"Probably half of Solace by now, sir," Gerard answered dourly. "The kender was not very secretive."

"Then we must not waste time," Palin said tersely. "I will contact Jenna."

"How will you do that?" Laurana asked him.

"I have my ways," he said, adding, with a curl of his lip, "Not much, but I make do."

He left the room, left abruptly, without looking back. He had no need. He could feel her hurt and her sorrow accompany him like a gentle spirit. He was momentarily ashamed, half-turned to go back to apologize. He was her guest, after all. She was putting her very life in danger to host him. He hesitated, and then he kept walking.

No, he thought grimly. Laurana can't understand. Usha doesn't understand. That brash and arrogant knight doesn't understand. They can't any of them understand. They don't know what I've been through, what I've suffered. They don't know my loss.

Once, he cried in silent anguish, once I touched the minds of gods!

He paused, listening in the stillness, to see if he could by chance hear a faint voice answering his grieving cry.

He heard, as he always heard, only the empty echo.

They think I've been freed from prison. They think my torment is ended.

They are wrong.

My confinement endures day after dreary day. The torture goes on indefinitely. Gray walls surround me. I squat in my own filth. The bones of my spirit are cracked and splintered. My hunger is so great that I devour myself. My thirst so great that I drink my own waste. This is what I've become.

Reaching the sanctuary of his room, he shut the door and then dragged a chair across to lean against it. No elf would dream of disturbing the privacy of one who has shut himself away, but Palin didn't trust them. He didn't trust any of them.

He sat down at a writing desk, but he did not write to Jenna. He placed his hand on a small silver earring he wore in his ear lobe. He spoke the words to the spell, words that perhaps didn't matter anymore, for there was no one to hear them. Sometimes artifacts worked without the ritual words, sometimes they only worked with the words, sometimes they didn't work at all under any circumstances. That was happening more and more often these days.

He repeated the words and added "Jenna" to them.

A hungry wizard had sold her the six silver earrings. He was evasive about where he had found them, mumbled something to the effect that they had been left to him by a dead uncle.

Jenna had told Palin, "Certainly, the dead once owned these earrings. But they were not willed to him. He stole them."

She did not pursue the matter. Many once respectable wizards—including Palin himself—had turned to grave robbery in their desperate search for magic. The wizard had described what the earrings did, said he would not have sold them but that dire necessity drove him to it. She had paid him a handsome sum and, instead of placing the earrings in her shop, she had given one to Palin and one to Ulin, his son. She had not told Palin who wore the others.

He had not asked. Once there had been a time when the mages of the Conclave had trusted each other. In these dark days, with the magic dwindling, each now looked sidelong at the others wondering, "Does he have more than I do? Has he found something I have not? Has the power been given to him and not to me?"

Palin heard no response. Sighing, he repeated the words and rubbed the metal with his finger. When he was first given the earrings, the spell had worked immediately. Now it would take him three or four tries and there was always the nagging fear that this might be the time it would fail altogether.

"Jenna!" he whispered urgently.

Something wispy and delicate brushed across his face, like the touch of a fly's wings. Annoyed, he waved it away hurriedly, his concentration broken. He looked for the insect, to shoo it off, but couldn't find it. He was settling down to try the magic once again, when Jenna's thoughts answered his.

"Palin . . ."

He focused his thoughts, keeping the message short, in case the magic failed midway. "Urgent need. Meet me in Solace. Immediately."

"I will come at once." Jenna said nothing more, did not waste time or the her own magic with questions. She trusted him. He would not send for her unless he had good reason.

Palin looked down at the device that he cherished in his broken hands.

Is this the key to my cell? he asked himself. Or nothing but another lash of the whip?

"He is very changed," said Gerard, after Palin had left the atrium. "I would not have recognized him. And the way he spoke of his father . . ." He shook his head.

"Wherever Caramon is, I am certain he understands," Laurana said. "Palin is changed, yes, but then who would not be changed after such a terrible experience. I don't think any of us will ever know what torment he endured at the hands of the Gray Robes. Speaking of them, how do you plan to travel to Solace?" she asked, skillfully turning the subject away from Palin to more practical considerations.

"I have my horse, the black one. I thought that perhaps Palin could ride the smaller horse I brought for the kender."

"And then I could ride the black horse with you!" Tas announced, pleased. "Although I'm not sure Little Gray will really like Palin, but perhaps if I talk to her—"

"You are not going," Gerard said flatly.

"Not going!" Tas repeated, stunned. "But you need me!"

Gerard ignored this statement, which, of all statements ever made in the course of history, could be ranked as most likely to be ignored. "The journey will take many days, but that can't be helped. It seems the only course—"

"I have another suggestion," Laurana said. "Griffons could fly you to Solace. They brought Palin here and they will carry him back and you along with them. My falcon Brightwing will take a message to them. The griffons could be here the day after tomorrow. You and Palin will be in Solace by that evening."

Gerard had a brief, vivid image of flying on griffon back or perhaps it would be more accurate to say he had a brief vivid image of falling off a griffon's back and smashing headfirst into the ground. He flushed and fumbled for an answer that didn't make him out to be a craven coward.

"I couldn't possibly impose . . . We should leave at once . . ."

"Nonsense. The rest will do you good," Laurana replied, smiling as if she understood the real reason behind his reluctance. "This will save you over a week's time and, as Palin said, we must move swiftly before Beryl discovers such a valuable magical device is in her lands. Tomorrow night, after dark, Kalindas will guide you to the meeting place."

"I've never ridden a griffon," Tas said, hinting. "At least, not that I can remember. Uncle Trapspringer did once. He said . . ."

"No," Gerard cut in firmly. "Absolutely not. You will stay with the Queen Mother, if she'll have you. This is already dangerous enough without—" His words died away.

The magical device was once again in the kender's possession. Tasslehoff was, even now, stuffing the device down the front of his shirt.

Far from Qualinesti, but not so far that she couldn't keep an eye watching and an ear listening, the great green dragon Beryl lay in her tangled, overgrown, vine-ridden bower and chafed at the wrongs which had been done to her. Wrongs which itched and stung her like a parasitic infestation and, like a parasite, she could scratch here and scratch there, but the itch seemed to move so that she was never quite rid of it.

At the heart of all her trouble was a great red dragon, a monstrous wyrm that Beryl feared more than anything else in this world, though she would have allowed her green wings to be pulled off and her enormous green tail to be tied up in knots before she admitted it. This fear was the main reason Beryl had agreed to the pact three years ago. She had seen in her mind her own skull adorning Malys's totem. Besides the fact that she wanted to keep her skull, Beryl had resolved that she would never give her bloated red cousin that satisfaction.

The pact of peace between the dragons had seemed a good idea at the time. It ended the bloody Dragon Purge, during which the dragons had fought and killed not only mortals, but each other, as well. The dragons who had emerged alive and powerful divided up parts of Ansalon, each claiming a portion to rule and leaving some previously disputed lands, such as Abanasinia, untouched.

The peace had lasted about a year before it started to crumble. When Beryl felt her magical powers start to seep away, she blamed the elves, she blamed the humans, but in her heart she knew full well where the real blame lay. Malys was stealing her magic. No wonder her red cousin had no more need to kill her own kind! She had found some way to drain the other dragons of their power. Beryl's magic had been a major defense against her stronger cousin. Without that magic, the green dragon would be as helpless as a gully dwarf.

Night fell while Beryl was musing. Darkness wrapped around her bower like another, larger vine. She fell asleep, lulled by the lullaby of her scheming and plotting. She was dreaming that she had found at last the legendary Tower of High Sorcery at Wayreth. She wrapped her huge body around the tower and felt the magic flow into her, warm and sweet as the blood of a gold dragon. . . .

"Exalted One!" A hissing voice woke her from her pleasant dream.

Beryl blinked and snorted, sending fumes of poisonous gas roiling among the leaves. "Yes, what is it?" she demanded, focusing her eyes on the source of the hiss. She could see quite well in the darkness, had no need of light.

"A messenger from Qualinost," said her draconian servant. "He claims his news is urgent, else I would not have disturbed you."

"Send him in."

The draconian bowed and departed. Another draconian appeared in his place. A baaz named Groul, he was one of Beryl's favorites, a trusted messenger who traveled between her lair and Qualinesti. Draconians were created during the War of the Lance when black robed wizards and evil clerics loyal to Takhisis stole the eggs of good dragons and gave them hideous life in the form of these winged lizard-men. Like all his kind, the baaz walked upright on two powerful legs, but he could run on all fours, using his wings to increase his movement over the ground. His body was covered with scales that had a dull metallic sheen. He wore little in the way of clothing, which would have hampered his movements. He was a messenger and so he was armed only lightly, with a short sword that he wore strapped to his back, in between his wings.

Beryl wakened more fully. Normally a laconic creature, who rarely evinced any type of emotion, Groul appeared quite pleased with himself this night. His lizard eyes glittered with excitement, his fangs were prominent in a wide grin. The tip of his flickered in his mouth.

Beryl shifted and rolled her huge body, wallowing deeper in the muck to increase her comfort, gathering her vines around her like a writhing blanket.

"News from Qualinost?" Beryl asked casually. She did not want to seem too eager.

"Yes, Exalted One," said Groul, moving forward to stand near one of the gigantic claws of her front foot. "Most interesting news involving the Queen Mother, Laurana."

"Indeed? Is that fool knight Medan still enamored of her?"

"Of course." Groul dismissed this as old news. "According to our spy, he shields and protects her. But that is not such a bad thing, Mistress. The Queen Mother believes herself to be invulnerable and thus we are able to discover what the elves are plotting."

"True," Beryl agreed. "So long as Medan remembers where his true loyalties lie, I permit his little flirtation. He has served me well thus far and he is easily removed. What else? There is something else, I believe . . ."

Beryl rested her head on the ground, to put herself level with the draconian, gazed intently at him. His excitement was catching. She could feel it quiver through her. Her tail twitched, her claws dug deep into the oozing mud.

Groul drew closer still. "I reported to you several days ago that the human mage, Palin Majere, was hiding out in the Queen Mother's house. We wondered at the reason for this visit. You suspected he was there searching for magical artifacts."

"Yes," Beryl said. "Go on."

"I am pleased to report, Exalted One, that he found one."

"Indeed?" Beryl's eyes gleamed, casting an eerie green light over the draconian. "And what is the artifact he found? What does it do?"

"According to our elven spy, the artifact may have something to do with traveling through time. The artifact is in the possession of a kender, who claims that he came from another time, a time prior to the Chaos War."

Beryl snorted, filling her lair with noxious fumes. The draconian choked and coughed.

"Those vermin will say anything. If this is all—"

"No, no, Exalted One," Groul hastened to add when he could speak. "The elven spy reports that Palin Majere was tremendously excited over this find. So excited that he has made arrangements to leave Qualinost with the artifact immediately, in order to study it."

"Is that so?" Beryl relaxed, settled herself more comfortably. "He was excited by it. The artifact *must* be powerful, then. He has a nose for these things, as I said to the Gray Robes when they would have slain him. 'Let him go,' I told them. 'He will lead us to magic as a pig to truffles.' How may we acquire this?"

"The day after this day, Exalted One, the mage and the kender will depart Qualinesti. They will be met by a griffon who will fly them from there to Solace. That would be the best time to capture them."

"Return to Qualinost. Inform Medan—"

"Pardon me, Exalted One. I am not permitted into the marshal's presence. He finds me and my kind distasteful."

"He is becoming more like an elf every day," Beryl growled. "Some morning he will wake with pointed ears."

"I can send my spy to report to him. That is the way I usually operate. Thus my spy keeps me informed of what is going on in Medan's household as well."

"Very well. Here are my orders. Have your spy tell Marshal Medan that I want this mage captured and delivered alive. He is to be brought to *me*, mind you. Not those worthless Gray Robes."

"Yes, Exalted One." Groul started to leave, then turned back. "Do you trust the marshal with a matter of this importance?"

"Certainly not," Beryl said disdainfully. "But I will make my own arrangements. Now go!"

Marshal Medan was taking his breakfast in his garden, where he liked to watch the sun rise. He had placed his table and chair on a rock ledge beside a pond so covered with water lilies that he could barely see the water. A nearby snowfall bush filled the air with tiny white blossoms. Having finished his meal, he read the morning dispatches, which had just arrived, and wrote out his orders for the day. Every so often he paused in his work to toss bread crumbs to the fish who were so accustomed to his routine that every morning at this time they came to the surface in anticipation of his arrival.

"Sir." Medan's aide approached, irritably brushing the falling blossoms from his black tunic. "An elf to see you, sir. From the household of the Queen Mother."

"Our traitor?"

"Yes, sir."

"Bring him to me at once."

The aide sneezed, gave a sullen response and departed.

Medan drew his knife from the sheath he wore on a belt around his waist, placed the knife on the table, and sipped at his wine. He would not ordinarily have taken such precautions. There had been one assassination attempt against him long ago, when he had first arrived to take charge of Qualinesti. Nothing had come of it. The perpetrators had been caught and hanged, drawn and quartered; the pieces of their bodies fed to the carrion birds.

Recently, however, the rebel groups were becoming bolder, more desperate. He was concerned about one in particular, a female warrior whose personal beauty, courage in battle and daring exploits were making her a heroine to the subjugated elves. They called her "Lioness," for her mane of shining hair. She and her band of rebels attacked supply trains, harried patrols, ambushed messengers and generally made Medan's formerly quiet and peaceful life among the Qualinesti elves increasingly difficult.

Someone was feeding the rebels information on troop movements, the timing of patrols, the locations of baggage trains. Medan had clamped down tightly on security, removing all elves (except his gardener) from his staff and urging Prefect Palthainon and the other elven officials who were known to collaborate with the knights to watch what they said and where they said it. But security was difficult in a land where a squirrel sitting eating nuts on your windowsill might be taking a look at your maps, noting down the disposition of your forces.

Medan's aide returned, still sneezing, with the elf following along behind, bearing a slip of a branch in his hand.

Medan dismissed his aide with a recommendation that he drink some catnip tea to help his cold. The Marshal sipped his morning wine slowly, enjoying it. He loved the flavor of elven wine, could taste the flowers and the honey from which it was made.

"Marshal Medan, my mistress sends this lilac cutting to you for your garden. She says that your gardener will know how to plant it."

"Put it here," said Medan, indicating the table. He did not look at the elf, but continued to toss crumbs to the fish. "If that is all, you have leave to go."

The elf coughed, cleared his throat.

"Something more?" Medan asked casually.

The elf cast a furtive glance all around the garden.

"Speak. We are alone," Medan said.

"Sir, I have been ordered to relay information to you. I told you previously that the mage, Palin Majere, was visiting my mistress."

Medan nodded. "Yes, you were assigned to keep watch on him and report to me what he does. I must assume from the fact that you are here that he has done something."

"Palin Majere has recently come into possession of an extremely valuable artifact, a magical artifact from the Fourth Age. He is going to transport that artifact out of Qualinost. His plan is to take it to Solace."

"And you reported the discovery of this artifact to Groul who reported it to the dragon," said Medan with an inward sigh. More trouble. "And, of course, Beryl wants it."

"Majere will be traveling by griffon. He is to meet the griffin tomorrow morning at dawn in a clearing located about twenty miles north of Qualinost. He travels in company with a kender and a Solamnic Knight—"

"A Solamnic Knight?" Medan was amazed, more interested in the knight than in the magic-user. "How did a Solamnic Knight manage to enter Qualinesti without being discovered?"

"He disguised himself as one of your knights, my lord. He pretended that the kender was his prisoner, that he had stolen a magical artifact and that he was taking the prisoner to the Gray Robes. Word reached Majere of the artifact and he waylaid the knight and the kender, as the Knight had planned, and brought them to the home of the queen mother."

"Intelligent, courageous, resourceful." Medan threw crumbs to the fish. "I look forward to meeting this paragon."

"Yes, my lord. As I said, the Knight will be with Majere in the forest, along with the kender. I can provide you with a map—"

"I am certain you can," said Medan. He made a dismissive gesture. "Give the details to my aide. And remove your treacherous carcass from my garden. You poison the air."

"Excuse me, sir," the elf said boldly. "But there is the matter of payment. According to Groul, the dragon was extremely pleased with the information. That makes it worth a considerable amount. More than usual. Shall we say, double what I usually receive?"

Medan cast the elf a contemptuous glance, then reached for quill and paper.

"Give this to my aide. He will see that you are paid." Medan wrote slowly and deliberately, taking his time. He hated this business, considered the use of spies sordid and demeaning. "What are you doing with all this money we have paid you to betray your mistress, Elf?" He would not dignify the wretch with a name. "Do you plan to enter the Senate? Perhaps take over from Prefect Palthainon, that other monument to treachery."

The elf hovered near, his eyes on the paper and the figures the Marshal was writing, his hand waiting to pluck it away. "It is easy for you to talk, Human," the elf said bitterly. "You were not born a servant as I was, given no chance to better myself. 'You should be honored with your lot in life,' they tell me. 'After all, your father was a servant to the House Royal. Your grandfather was a servant in that household as was his grandfather before him. If you try to leave or raise yourself, you will bring about the downfall of elven society!' Hah!

"Let my brother demean himself. Let him bow and scrape and grovel to the mistress. Let him fetch and carry for her. Let him wait to die with her on the day the dragon attacks and destroys them all. I mean to do something better with my life. As soon as I have saved money enough, I will leave this place and make my own way in the world."

Medan signed the note, dripped melted wax beneath his signature, and pressed his seal ring into the wax. "Here, take this. I am pleased to be able to contribute to your departure."

The elf snatched the note, read the amount, smiled and, bowing, departed in haste.

Medan tossed the remainder of the bread into the pond and rose to his feet. His enjoyment of the day had been ruined by that contemptible creature, who, out of greed, was now informing on the woman he served, a woman who trusted him.

At least, Medan thought, I will capture this Palin Majere outside of Qualinost. There will be no need to bring Laurana into it. Had I been forced to apprehend Majere in the queen mother's house, I would have had to arrest the queen mother for harboring a fugitive.

He could imagine the uproar over such an arrest. The queen mother was immensely popular; her people having apparently forgiven her for marrying a half-human and for having a brother who was in exile, termed a "dark elf," one who is cast from the light. The Senate would be in a clamor. The population, already in an excited state, would be incensed. There was even the remote possibility that news of his mother's arrest would cause her worthless son to grow a backbone.

Much better this way. Medan had been waiting for just such an opportunity. He would turn Majere and his artifact over to Beryl and be done with it.

The marshal left the garden to put his lilac slip into water, so that it would not dry out.

17

Gilthas and the Lioness

ilthas, Laurana's "worthless son," was at that moment resting his quite adequate backbone against a chair in an underground room of a tavern owned and run by gully dwarves. The tavern was called the Gulp and Belch—this being, as near as the gully dwarves could ascertain, the only thing humans did in a tavern.

The Gulp and Belch was located in a small habitation of gully dwarves (one could not dignify it by terming it a "village") located near the fortress of Pax Tharkas. The tavern was the only building in the habitation. The gully dwarves who ran the tavern lived in caves in the hills behind the tavern, caves that could be reached only by tunnels located beneath the tavern.

The gully dwarf community was located some eighty miles straight as the griffon flies from Qualinost, longer—far longer—if one traveled by road. Gilthas had flown here on the back of a griffon, one whose family was in the service of House Royal. The beast had landed the king and his guide in the forest and was now awaiting their return with less impatience than might have been expected. Kerian had made certain to provide the griffon with a freshly killed deer to make the long hours of waiting pass pleasantly and to ensure that the beast didn't dine on any of their hosts.

The Gulp and Belch was surprisingly popular. Or perhaps not surprising, considering that the prices were the lowest in Ansalon. Two coppers could buy anything. The business had been started by the same gully dwarf who had been a cook in the household of the late Dragon Highlord, Verminaard.

People who know gully dwarves, but who have never tasted gully dwarf cooking, find it impossible to even imagine eating anything a gully dwarf might prepare. Considering that a favorite delicacy of gully dwarf is rat meat, some equate the idea of having a gully dwarf for a cook with a death wish.

Gully dwarves are the outcasts of dwarfdom. Although they are dwarves, the dwarves do not claim them and will go to great lengths to explain why gully dwarves are dwarves in name only. Gully dwarves are extremely stupid, or so most people believe. Gully dwarves cannot count past two, their system of numbering being "one", "two." The very smartest gully dwarf, a legend among gully dwarves, whose name was Bupu, actually once counted past two, coming up with the term "a whole bunch."

Gully dwarves are not noted for their interest in higher mathematics. They are noted for their cowardice, for their filth, their love of squalor and—oddly enough—their cooking. Gully dwarves make extremely good cooks, so long as the diner sets down rules about what may and may not be served at the table and refrains from entering the kitchen to see how the food is prepared.

The Gulp and Belch served up an excellent roast haunch of venison smothered in onions and swimming in rich brown gravy. The ale was adequate—not as good as in many establishments, but the price was right. The dwarf spirits made the tavern's reputation. They were truly remarkable. The gully dwarves distilled their own from mushrooms cultivated in their bedrooms. Those drinking the brew are advised not to dwell on that fact for too long.

The tavern was frequented mainly by humans who could afford no better, by kender who were glad to find a tavern-keeper who did not immediately toss them out into the street, and by the lawless, who were quick to discover that the Knights of Neraka rarely patrolled the wagon ruts termed a road leading to the tavern.

The Gulp and Belch was also the hideout and head-quarters for the warrior known as the Lioness, a woman who was also, had anyone known it, queen of Qualinesti, secret wife of the Speaker of the Sun, Gilthas.

The elven king sat in the chair in the semidarkness of the tavern's back room, trying to curb his impatience. Elves are never impatient. Elves, who live for hundreds of years, know that the water will boil, the bread will rise, the acorn will sprout, the oak will grow and that all the fuming and watching and attempts to hurry it make only for an upset stomach. Gilthas had inherited impatience from his half-human father, and although he did his best to hide it, his fingers drummed on the table and his foot tapped the floor.

Kerian glanced over at him, smiled. A single candle stood on the table between them. The candle's flame was reflected in her brown eyes, shone warmly on smooth, brown skin, glinted in the burnished gold of her mane of hair. Kerian was a Kagonesti, a Wilder elf, a race of elves who, unlike their city-dwelling cousins, the Qualinesti and the Silvanesti, live with nature. Since they do not try to alter nature or shape it, the Wilder elves are looked upon as barbarians by their more sophisticated cousins, who have also gone so far as to enslave the Kagonesti and force them to serve in wealthy elven households—all for the Kagonesti's own good, of course.

Kerian had been a slave in the household of Senator

Rashas. She had been present when Gilthas was first brought to that house, ostensibly as a guest, in reality a prisoner. The two had fallen in love the first moment they had seen each other, although it was months, even years, before they actually spoke of their feelings, exchanged their secret vows.

Only two other people, Planchet and Gilthas's mother, Laurana, knew of the king's marriage to the girl who had once been a slave and who was now known as the Lioness, fearless leader of the Khansari, the Night People.

Catching Kerian's eye, Gilthas realized immediately what he was doing. He clenched the tapping fingers to a fist and crossed his booted feet to keep them quiet. "There," he said ruefully. "Is that better?"

"You will fret yourself into a sickness if you're not careful," Kerian scolded, smiling. "The dwarf will come. He gave his word."

"So much depends on this," said Gilthas. He stretched out his legs to ease the kinks of the unaccustomed exercise "Perhaps our very survival as a—" He halted, stared down at the floor. "Did you feel that?"

"The shaking? Yes. I've felt it the last couple of hours. It's probably just the gully dwarves adding to their tunnels. They love to dig in the dirt. As to what you were saying, there is no 'perhaps' about our ultimate destruction," Kerian returned crisply.

Her voice with its accent that civilized elves considered uncouth was like the song of the sparrow, of piercing sweetness with a note of melancholy.

"The Qualinesti have given the dragon everything she has demanded. They have sacrificed their freedom, their pride, their honor. They have, in some instances, even sacrificed their own—all in return for the dragon's permission to live. But the time will come when Beryl will make a demand your people will find impossible to fulfill. When that day comes and she finds her will thwarted, she will destroy the Qualinesti."

"Sometimes I wonder why you care," Gilthas said, looking gravely at his wife. "The Qualinesti enslaved you, took you from your family. You have every right to feel vengeful. You have every right to steal away into the wilderness and leave those who hurt you to the fate they so richly deserve. Yet you do not. You risk your life on a daily basis fighting to force our people to look at the truth, no matter how ugly, to hear it, no matter how unpleasant."

"That is the problem," she returned. "We must stop thinking of the elven people as 'yours' and 'mine.' Such division and isolation is what has brought us to this pass. Such division gives strength to our enemies."

"I don't see it changing," Gilthas said grimly. "Not unless some great calamity befalls us and forces us to change, and perhaps not even then. The Chaos War, which might have brought us closer, did nothing but further fragment our people. Not a day goes by but that some senator makes a speech telling of how our cousins the Silvanesti have shut us out of their safe haven beneath the shield, how they want us all to die so that they can take over our lands. Or someone starts a tirade against the Kagonesti, how their barbaric ways will bring down all that we have worked over the centuries to build. There are actually those who approve of the fact that the dragon has closed the roads. We will do better without contact with the humans, they say. The Knights of Neraka urge them on, of course. They love such rantings. It makes their task far easier."

"From the rumors I hear, the Silvanesti may be finding that their vaunted magical shield is in reality a tomb."

Gilthas looked startled, sat upright. "Where did you hear this? You have not told me."

"I have not seen you in a month," Kerian replied with a touch of bitterness. "I only heard this a few days ago, from the runner Kelevandros your mother sends regularly to keep in touch with your aunt Alhana Starbreeze. Alhana and her forces have settled on the border of Silvanesti, near the shield.

They are allied with the humans who belong to the Legion of Steel. Alhana reports that the land around the shield is barren, trees sicken and die. A horrible gray dust settles over everything. She fears that this same malaise may be infecting all of Silvanesti."

"Then why do our cousins maintain the shield?" Gilthas wondered.

"They are afraid of the world beyond. Unfortunately, they are right in some instances. Alhana and her forces fought a pitched battle with ogres only a short time ago, the night of that terrible thunderstorm. The Legion of Steel came to their rescue or they would have been wiped out. As it was, Alhana's son Silvanoshei was captured by ogres, or so she believes. She could find no trace of him when the battle was ended. Alhana grieves for him as for the dead."

"My mother has said nothing of this to me," Gilthas stated, frowning.

"According to Kelevandros, Laurana fears Marshal Medan's heightened watchfulness. She trusts only those in her household. She dare not trust anyone outside it. Whenever the two of you are together, she is certain that you are spied upon. She does not want the Dark Knights to find out that she is in constant contact with Alhana."

"Mother is probably right," Gilthas admitted. "My servant Planchet is the only person I trust and that is because he has proven his loyalty to me time and again. So Silvanoshei is dead, killed by ogres. Poor young man. His death must have been a cruel one. Let us hope he passed swiftly."

"Did you ever meet him?"

Gilthas shook his head. "He was born in the Inn of the Last Home in Solace during the time Alhana was exiled. I never saw her after that. My mother told me that the boy favored my Uncle Porthios in looks."

"His death makes you heir to both kingdoms," Kerian observed. "The Speaker of the Sun and Stars."

"Which Senator Rashas always wanted," Gilthas said caustically. "In reality, it seems I will be nothing more than the Speaker of the Dead."

"Speak no words of ill omen!" Kerian said and made the sign against evil with her hand, drawing a circle in the air to encompass the words and keep them trapped. "You— Yes, what is it, Silverwing?"

She turned to speak to an elf who had entered the secret room. The elf started to say something but was interrupted by a gully dwarf, who appeared to be in a state of extreme excitement, to judge by the smell.

"Me tell!" the gully dwarf cried indignantly, jostling the elf. "Me lookout! Her say so!" He pointed at Kerian.

"Your Majesty." The elf made a hurried bow to Gilthas, before he turned to Kerian, his commander, with his information. "The high king of Thorbardin has arrived."

"Him here," the gully dwarf announced loudly. Although he did not speak Elvish, he could guess at what was being said. "Me bring in?"

"Thank you, Ponce." Kerian rose to her feet, adjusted the sword she wore at her waist. "I will come to meet him. It would be better if you remained here, Your Majesty," she added. Their marriage was a secret, even from the elves under Kerian's command.

"Big muckity-muck dwarf. Him wear hat!" Ponce was impressed. "Him wear shoes!" The gully dwarf was doubly impressed. "Me never see dwarf wear shoes."

"The high king has brought four guards with him," the elf told Kerian. "As you ordered, we have watched their movements ever since they left Thorbardin."

"For their safety, as well as ours, Your Majesty," Kerian was quick to add, seeing Gilthas's expression darken.

"They met with no one," the elf continued, "and they were not followed—"

"Except by us," Gilthas said sardonically.

"It never hurts to be cautious, Your Majesty," Kerian said. "Tarn Bellowgranite is the new high king of the clans of Thorbardin. His rule is secure among his people, but dwarves have traitors living among them, as do we elves."

Gilthas sighed deeply. "I wish the day would come when this was not so. I trust the dwarves did not notice that we were dogging them?"

"They saw the starlight, Your Majesty," said the elf proudly. "They heard the wind in the trees. They did not see or hear us."

"Him say he like our dwarf spirits," Ponce said importantly, his face shining, though this might have been due to the fact that it was smeared with grease from the goose he had been basting. "Him say we make fine dwarf spirits. You want try?" he asked Gilthas. "Put hair up your nose."

Kerian and the elf departed, taking the gully dwarf with them. Gilthas sat watching the candle flame flicker with the stirring of the air. Beneath his feet came that strange shivering in the ground, as if the very world trembled. All around him was darkness. The candle's flame was the only light, and it could be extinguished in a breath. So much could go wrong. Even now, Marshal Medan might be entering Gilthas's bedroom. The Marshal might be ripping up the pillows from the bed, arresting Planchet, demanding to know the whereabouts of the king.

Gilthas was suddenly very tired. He was tired of this duplicitous life, tired of the lies and the deceptions, tired of the fact that he was constantly performing. He was always on stage, never allowed a moment to rest in the wings. He could not even sleep well at night, for he was afraid he might say something in his sleep that would bring about his downfall.

Not that he would be the one to suffer. Prefect Palthainon would see to that. So would Medan. They needed Gilthas on the throne, jerking and twitching to the strings they pulled. If they found out that he'd cut those strings, they would simply reattach them. He would remain on the throne. He would remain alive. Planchet would die, tortured until he was forced to reveal all he knew. Laurana might not be executed but she would certainly be exiled, deemed a dark elf like her brother. Kerian might well be captured, and Medan had proclaimed publicly the terrible death the Lioness would suffer should she ever fall into his hands.

Gilthas would not suffer, except that he would be forced to watch those he loved most in the world suffer and know he was powerless to help them. That would be, perhaps, the greatest torment of all.

Out of the darkness crept his old companions: fear, self-doubt, self-hatred, self-loathing. He felt them lay their cold hands upon him and reach inside and twist his gut and wring the icy sweat from his shivering body. He heard their wailing voices cry to him warnings of doom, shout prophecies of death and destruction. He was not equal to this task. He dared not continue this course of action. It was foolhardy. He was putting his people at risk. He was certain they had been discovered. Medan knew everything. Perhaps if Gilthas went back now, he could make it all right. He would crawl into his bed and they would never know he had been gone. . . .

"Gilthas," said a stern voice.

Gilthas started. He looked wildly into a face he did not know.

"My husband," Kerian said gently.

Gilthas shut his eyes, a shudder passed through his body. Slowly he unclenched the hands that had tightened to fists. He made himself relax, forced the tension to ease from his body, forced himself to quit shaking. The darkness that had momentarily blinded him retreated. The candle's flame that was Kerian burned brightly, steadily. He drew in a deep, shivering breath.

"I am well, now," he said.

"Are you certain?" Kerian asked. "The thane waits in the adjacent room. Should I stall him?"

"No, the attack has passed," Gilthas said, swallowing to rid his mouth of the taste of bile. "You drove away the demons. Give me a moment to make myself presentable. How do I look?"

"As if you had seen a wraith," said Kerian. "But the dwarf will not notice anything amiss. All elves seem pasty-faced to them."

Gilthas caught hold of his wife, held her close.

"Stop it!" she protested, half-laughing and half in earnest. "There's no time for this now. What if someone saw us?"

"Let them," he said, casting caution aside. "I am tired of lying to the world. You are my strength, my salvation. You saved my life, my sanity. When I think back to what I was, a prisoner to those same demons, I wonder how you ever came to love me."

"I looked through the cell bars and saw the man locked inside," Kerian replied, relaxing in her husband's arms, if only for a moment. "I saw his love for his people. I saw how he suffered because they suffered and he felt helpless to prevent their pain. Love was the key. All I did was put it into the door and turn the lock. You have done all the rest."

She slid out of his embrace and was, once again, the warrior queen. "Are you ready? We should not keep the high king waiting longer."

"I am ready," Gilthas said.

He took in another deep breath, shook back his hair and, walking straight and tall, entered the room.

"His Majesty, Speaker of the Sun, Gilthas of the House of Solostaran," Kerian announced formally.

The dwarf, who was enjoying a mug of dwarf spirits, placed the mug on a table and lowered his head in a gesture of respect. He was tall for a dwarf and looked far older than his true age, for his hair had gone prematurely gray, his beard was gray streaked with white. His eyes were bright and clear and youthful, his gaze sharp and penetrating. He kept his gaze fixed on Gilthas, seemed to bore through the elf's breastbone as if he would see straight into his heart.

"He has heard rumors of me," Gilthas said to himself. "He wonders what to believe. Am I a weak dish rag to be wrung out by every hand? Or am I truly the ruler of my people as he is the ruler of his?"

"The High King of the Eight Clans," said Kerian, "Tarn Bellowgranite."

The dwarf was himself a half-breed. Much as Gilthas, who had human blood in his veins, Tarn was a product of a liaison between a Hylar dwarf—the nobles of dwarfdom— and a Daergar, the dark dwarves. After the Chaos War, the Thorbardin dwarves had worked with humans to rebuild the fortress of Pax Tharkas. It seemed that the Thorbardin dwarves might actually once more begin to interact with the other races, including their brethren, the hill dwarves, who, due to a feud that dated back to the Cataclysm, had long been shut out of the great dwarven kingdom beneath the mountain.

But with the coming of the great dragons and the death and destruction they brought, the dwarves had gone back underground. They had sealed up the gates of Thorbardin once again, and the world had lost contact with them. The Daergar had taken advantage of the turmoil to try to seize the rulership of Thorbardin, plunging that nation into a bloody civil war. Tarn Bellowgranite was a hero of the war, and when it came time to pick up the pieces, the thanes had turned to him for leadership. He had found a people divided, a kingdom tottering on the edge of ruin when he came to his rule. He had placed that kingdom upon a firm foundation. He had united the warring clans behind his leadership. Now he was about to contemplate another step that would be something new in the annals of the dwarves of Thorbardin.

Gilthas stepped forward and bowed deeply, with sincere respect. "High King," he said speaking flawless Dwarvish, a language he had learned from his father. "I am honored to meet you at last. I know you do not like to leave your home beneath the mountain. Your journey was a long one and perilous, as are all journeys made in the world during these dark times. I thank you for making the journey, for undertaking to meet me here this day to close and formally seal our agreement."

The high king nodded his head, tugging on his beard, a sign that he was pleased with the words. The fact that the elf spoke Dwarvish had already impressed Tarn. Gilthas had been right. The dwarf king had heard stories of the elf king's weak and indecisive nature. But Tarn had learned over the years that it was never wise to judge a man until, as the dwarves would say, you had seen the color of his beard.

"The journey was pleasant. It is good to breathe the air above the ground for a change," Tarn replied. "And now, let us get down to business." He looked at Gilthas shrewdly. "I know how you elves love to palaver. I believe that we can dispense with the niceties."

"I am part human," Gilthas replied with a smile. "The impatient part, or so they tell me. I must be back in Qualinost before tomorrow's dawning. Therefore I will begin. This matter has been under negotiation for a month. We know where we stand, I believe? Nothing has changed?"

"Nothing has changed with us," said Tarn. "Has anything changed with you?"

"No, it has not. We are in agreement then." Gilthas dropped the formal tone. "You have refused to accept any payment, sir. I would not permit this, but that I know there is not wealth enough in all of Qualinesti to compensate you and your people for what you are doing. I know the risks that you run. I know that this agreement has caused controversy among your people. I guess that it has even threatened your rule. And I can give you nothing in return except for our thanks—our eternal and undying thanks."

"Nay, lad," said Tarn, flushing in embarrassment. Dwarves dislike being praised. "What I do will bring good to my people as well as yours. Not all of them can see that at this point, but they will. Too long we have lived hidden away from the world beneath the mountain. The notion came to me when civil war erupted in Thorbardin, that we dwarves might well kill each other off and who would ever know? Who would grieve for us? None in this world. The caverns of Thorbardin might fall silent in death, darkness overtake us, and there would be none to speak a word to fill that silence, none to light a lamp. The shadows would close over us, and we would be forgotten.

"I determined I would not allow that to happen. We dwarves would return to the world. The world would enter Thorbardin. Of course," Tarn said, with a wink and sip of dwarf spirits, "I could not thrust such change upon my people overnight. It has taken me long years to bring them around to my way of thinking, and even then many are still wagging their beards and stamping their feet over it. But we are doing the right thing. Of that I am convinced. We have already started work on the tunnels," he added complacently.

"Have you? Before the papers were signed?" Gilthas asked amazed.

Tarn took a long gulp, belched contentedly, and grinned. "Bah! What are papers? What are signatures? Give me your hand, King Gilthas. That will seal our bargain."

"I give you my hand, King Tarn, and I am honored to do so," Gilthas replied, deeply touched. "Is there any point on which I can reassure you? Do you have any questions to ask of me?"

"Just one, lad," said Tarn, putting down his mug and wiping his chin with his sleeve. "Some of the thanes, most notably the Neidar—a suspicious lot if I do say so—have said repeatedly that if we allow elves to enter Thorbardin, they will turn on us and seize our realm and make it their new home. You and I know that will not happen," Tarn added, raising his hand to forestall Gilthas's quick protest, "but what would you say to my people to convince them that this tragedy would not come about?"

"I would ask the thanes of the Neidar," said Gilthas, smiling, "if they would build their homes in trees. What would be their answer, do you think, sir?"

"Hah, hah! They would as soon think of hanging themselves by their beards," Tarn said, chuckling.

"Then, by the same token, we elves would as soon think of hanging ourselves by our *ears* as to live in a hole in the ground. No insult to Thorbardin intended," Gilthas added politely.

"None taken, lad. I will tell the Neidar exactly what you have said. That should blow the foam off their ale!" Tarn continued to chuckle.

"To speak more clearly, I vow on my honor and my life that the Qualinesti will use the tunnels only for the purpose of removing those in peril from the dragon's wrath. We have made arrangements with the Plains people to shelter the refugees until such time as we can welcome them back to their own homeland."

"May that day be quick to dawn," said Tarn gravely, no longer laughing. He regarded Gilthas intently. "I would ask why you do not send your refugees to the land of your cousins, the realm of Silvanesti, but I hear that it is closed and barred to you. The elves there have placed some sort of magical fortress around it."

"The forces of Alhana Starbreeze continue to try to find some way to enter the shield," Gilthas said. "We must hope that they will eventually find a way, not only for our sakes, but for the sake of our cousins, as well. How long do you believe the work will take for the tunnel to reach Qualinost?"

"A fortnight, not more," said Tarn easily.

"A fortnight, sir! To dig a tunnel over sixty-five miles

through solid rock? I know the dwarves are master stonecutters," Gilthas said, "but I must confess that this astounds me."

"As I said, we had already started working. And we have help," said Tarn. "Have you ever heard of the Urkhan? No? I'm not surprised. Few outsiders know anything about them. The Urkhan are gigantic worms that eat rock. We harness them up, and they gnaw through granite as if it were fresh-baked bread. Who do you think built the thousands of miles of tunnels in Thorbardin?" Tarn grinned. "The Urkhan, of course. The worm does all the work, and we dwarves take all the credit!"

Gilthas expressed his admiration for the remarkable worms and listened politely to a discussion of the Urkhan's habits, its docile nature, and what happened to the rock after it passed through the worm's system.

"But enough of this. Would you like to see them in action?" Tarn asked suddenly.

"I would, sir," Gilthas said, "but perhaps some other time. As I mentioned earlier, I must return to Qualinost by morning light—"

"You shall, lad, you shall," the dwarf replied, grinning hugely. "Watch this." He stomped his booted foot twice on the floor.

A momentary pause and then two thumps resonated loudly, coming from the ground.

Gilthas looked at Kerian, who was looking angered and alarmed. Angry that she had not thought to investigate the strange rumblings, alarmed because, if this was a trap, they had just fallen neatly into it.

Tarn laughed loudly at their discomfiture.

"The Urkhan!" he said by way of explanation. "They're right beneath us!"

"Here? Is that true?" Gilthas gasped. "They have come so far? I know that I felt the ground shake—"

Tarn was nodding his head, his beard wagging. "And we have gone farther. Would you come below?"

Gilthas looked at his wife. "In all the rest of Qualinesti I am king, but the Lioness is in charge here," he said, smiling. "What do you say, madam? Shall we go see these wonderful worms?"

Kerian made no objection, although this unforeseen turn of events had made her wary. She said nothing outright that might offend the dwarves, but Gilthas noted that every time she encountered one of her Wilder elves, she gave him a signal with either a look, a tilt of the head, or a slight gesture of her hand. The elves disappeared, but Gilthas guessed that they had not gone far, were watching and waiting, their hands on their weapons.

They left the Gulp and Belch, some of Tarn's escort departing with every show of reluctance, wiping their lips and heaving sighs laced with the pungent smell of dwarf spirits. Tarn walked no trail but shouldered and trampled his way through the brush, thrusting or pushing aside anything that happened to be in his path. Gilthas, looking back, saw the dwarves had cut a large swath through the woods, a trail of broken limbs, trampled grass, dangling vines, and crushed grass.

Kerian cast a glance at Gilthas and rolled her eyes. He knew exactly what she was thinking. No need to worry about the dwarves hearing some trace of sound from shadowing elves. The dwarves would have been hard put to hear a thunderclap over their stomping and crashing. Tarn slowed his pace. He appeared to be searching for something. He said something in Dwarvish to his companions, who also began to search.

"He's looking for the tunnel entrance," Gilthas said softly to Kerian. "He says that his people were supposed to have left one here, but he can't find it.

"He won't, either," Kerian stated grimly. She was still irritated over being hoodwinked by the dwarves. "I know this land. Every inch of it. If there had been any sort of—"

She stopped, stared.

"Tunnel entrance," Gilthas finished, teasing. "You would have discovered it?"

They had come to a large outcropping of granite some thirty feet high jutting up through the forest floor. The striations on the rock ran sideways. Small trees and patches of wild flowers and grass grew between the layers. A large mass of boulders, parts of the outcropping that had broken off and tumbled down the side, lay at the foot of the outcropping. The boulders were huge, some came to Gilthas's waist, many were larger than the dwarves. He watched in astonishment as Tarn walked up to one of these boulders, placed his hand on it, and give it a shove. The boulder rolled aside as if it were hollow.

Which, in fact, it was.

Tarn and his fellows cleared the boulder fall, revealing a large and gaping hole in the outcropping.

"This way!" Tarn bellowed, waving his hand.

Gilthas looked at Kerian, who simply shook her head and gave a wry smile. She stopped to investigate the boulder, the inside of which had been hollowed out like a melon at a feast.

"The worms did this?" she asked, awed.

"The Urkhan," said Tarn proudly, gesturing with his hand. "The little ones," he added. "They nibble. The bigger ones would have gulped down the boulder whole. They're not very bright, I'm afraid. And they're always very hungry."

"Look at it this way, my dear," said Gilthas to Kerian as the passed from the moonlit night into the coolness of the dwarf-made cavern. "If the dwarves managed to hide the tunnel entrance from you and your people, they will have no trouble at all hiding it from the cursed Knights."

"True," Kerian admitted.

Inside the cavern, Tarn stomped twice again on what appeared to be nothing but a dirt floor. Two knocks greeted him from below. Cracks formed in the dirt, and a trapdoor, cunningly hidden, popped open. The head of dwarf poked out. Light streamed upward.

"Visitors," said Tarn in Dwarvish.

The dwarf nodded, and his head vanished. They could hear his thick boots clumping down the rungs of a ladder.

"Your Majesty," said Tarn, gesturing politely.

Gilthas went immediately. To hesitate would imply that he did not trust the high thane and Gilthas had no intention of alienating this new ally. He climbed nimbly down the sturdy ladder, descending about fifteen feet and coming to rest on a smooth surface. The tunnel was well-lit by what Gilthas first took to be lanterns.

Strange lanterns, though, he thought, drawing close to one. They gave off no heat. He looked closer and saw to his amazement that the light came not from burning oil but from the body of what appeared to be a large insect larvae. The larva lay curled up in a ball at the bottom of an iron cage that hung from a hook on the tunnel wall. A cage hung every few feet. The glow from the body of the slumbering larva lit the tunnels as bright as day.

"Even the offspring of the Urkhan work for us," Tarn said, arriving at the bottom of the ladder. "The larva glow like this for a month, and then they go dark. By that time, they are too big to fit into the cages anyway, and so we replace them. Fortunately, there is always a new crop of Urkhan to be harvested. But you must see them. This way. This way."

He led them along the tunnels. Rounding a bend, they came upon an astonishing sight. An enormous, undulating, slime-covered body, reddish brown in color, took up about half the tunnel. Dwarven handlers walked alongside the worm, guiding it by reins attached to straps wrapped around its body, slapping it with their hands or with sticks if the body of the worm started to veer off course or perhaps roll over and crush the handlers. Half the tunnel had been cleared already by a worm up ahead, so Tarn told them. This second worm came behind, widening what had already been built.

The huge worm moved incredibly fast. Gilthas and Kerian marveled at its size. The worm's body was as big around as Gilthas was tall and, according to Tarn, this worm was thirty feet in length. Piles of chewed and half-digested rock littered the floor behind the worm. Dwarves came along to shovel it to one side, keeping a sharp eye out for gold nuggets or unrefined gemstones as they cleared the rubble.

Gilthas walked the worm's length, finally reaching its head. It had no eyes, for it had no need of eyes, spending its life burrowing beneath the ground. Two horns protruded from the top of its head. The dwarves had placed a leather harness over these horns. Reins extended from the harness back to a dwarf who sat in a large basket strapped to the worm's body. The dwarf guided the worm from the basket, pulling the head in the direction he wanted to go.

The worm seemed not to even know the dwarf was there. Its one thought was to eat. It spewed liquid onto the solid rock in front of it, liquid that must have been some sort of acid, for it hissed when it hit the rock, which immediately started to bubble and sizzle. Several large chunks of rock split apart. The worm's maw opened, seized a chunk, and gulped it down.

"Most impressive!" Gilthas said with such utter sincerity that the high thane was immensely pleased, while the other dwarves looked gratified.

There was only one drawback. As the worm gnawed its way through the rock, its body heaved and undulated, causing the ground to shake. Being accustomed to it, the dwarves paid no attention to the motion but walked with the ease of sailors on a canting deck. Gilthas and Kerian had slightly more difficulty, stumbling into each other or falling against the wall.

"The Dark Knights will notice this!" Kerian observed,

shouting to be heard over the worm's rending of the rock and the dwarven handlers' yelling and cursing. "When Medan's bed starts to bounce across the room and he hears shouts coming from beneath his floor, he's going to be suspicious."

"Tarn, this shaking and rumbling," Gilthas said, speaking directly into the dwarf's ear. "Can anything be done to quiet it? The Dark Knights are sure to hear it or at least feel it."

Tarn shook his head. "Impossible!" he bellowed. "Look at it this way, lad, the worms are far quieter than a work force of dwarves going at it with hammer and pick."

Gilthas looked dubious. Tarn motioned, and they followed him back down the tunnel, leaving the worms and the worst of the commotion behind. Climbing the ladder, they emerged out into a night that was far less dark than it had been when they went underground. Dawn was coming. Gilthas would have to leave soon.

"My thought was that we would not tunnel under Qualinost itself," Tarn explained, as they walked back to the Gulp and Belch. "We're about forty miles away now. We will run our tunnels to within five miles of the city limits. That should be far enough so that the Neraka Knights have no idea what we are about. Also they'll be less likely to discover the entrances."

"What would happen if they did discover it?" Gilthas asked. "They could use the tunnels to invade Thorbardin."

"We'd collapse it first," Tarn said bluntly. "Bring it down on top of them and, likely, on top of a few of us, too."

"More and more I understand the risks you run for us," Gilthas said. "There is no way to thank you."

Tarn Bellowgranite waved aside the words, looked uncomfortable and embarrassed. Gilthas thought it best to change the subject.

"How many tunnels will there be altogether, sir?"

"Given time enough, we can build three fine ones," the dwarf replied. "As it is, we have one this far. You can begin to evacuate some of your people soon. Not many, for the walls are not completely shored up yet, but we can manage a few. As for the other two tunnels, we will need at least two months."

"Let us hope we have that long," Gilthas said quietly. "In the meanwhile, there are people in Qualinost who have run afoul of the Neraka Knights. The punishment of the Knights for lawbreakers is swift and cruel. The smallest infraction of one of their many laws can result in imprisonment or death. With this tunnel, we will be able to save some who otherwise would have perished.

"Tell me, Thane," Gilthas asked, knowing the answer, but needing to hear it for himself, "would it be possible to evacuate the entire city of Qualinost through that one tunnel?"

"Yes, I think so," said the High Thane, "given a fortnight to do it."

A fortnight. If the dragon and the Neraka Knights attacked, they would have hours at most to evacuate the people. At the end of a fortnight, there would be no one left alive to evacuate. Gilthas sighed deeply.

Kerian drew closer, put her hand on his arm. Her fingers were strong and cool, and their touch reassured him. He had been granted more than he had ever expected. He was not a baby, to cry for the stars when he had been given the moon.

He looked meaningfully at Kerian. "We will have to lay low and not antagonize the dragon for at least a month."

"My warriors will not roll over and play dead!" Kerian returned sharply, "if that is what you have in mind. Besides, if we suddenly ceased all our attacks, the Knights would grow suspicious that we were up to something, and they would start searching for it. This way, we will keep them distracted."

"A month," Gilthas said softly, silently, praying to whatever was out there, if anything was out there. "Just give me a month. Give my people a month."

18
Dawn in a Time of Darkness

orning came to Ansalon, too fast for some, too slow for others. The sun was a red slit in the sky, as if someone had drawn a knife across the throat of the darkness. Gilthas slipped hurriedly through the shadowy garden that surrounded his prison palace, returning somewhat late to take up the dangerous role he must continue to play.

Planchet was lurking upon the balcony, watching anxiously for the young king, when a knock on the door announced Prefect Palthainon, come for his morning string-jerking. Planchet could not plead His Majesty's indisposition this day as he had the last. Palthainon, an early riser, was here to bully the king, exercise his power over the young man, make a show of his puppeteering to the rest of the court.

"Just a moment, Prefect!" Planchet shouted. "His Majesty is using the chamber pot." The elf caught sight of movement in the garden. "Your Majesty!" he hissed as loudly as he dared. "Make haste!"

Gilthas stood under the balcony. Planchet lowered the rope. The king grasped it, climbed up nimbly, hand over hand.

The knocking resumed, louder and more impatient.

"I insist upon seeing His Majesty!" Palthainon demanded.

Gilthas clambered over the balcony. He made a dive for his bed, climbed in between the sheets fully dressed. Planchet tossed the blankets over the king's head and answered the door with his finger on his lips.

"His Majesty was ill all night. This morning he is unable to keep down so much as a bit of dry toast," Planchet whispered. "I had to help him back to bed."

The prefect peered over Planchet's shoulder. He saw the king raise his head, peering at the senator with bleary eyes.

"I am sorry His Majesty has been ill," said the prefect, frowning, "but he would be better up and doing instead of lying about feeling sorry himself. I will be back in an hour. I trust His Majesty will be dressed to receive me."

Palthainon departed. Planchet closed the door. Gilthas smiled, stretched his arms over his head, and sighed. His parting from Kerian had been wrenching. He could still smell the scent of the wood smoke that clung to her clothing, the rose oil she rubbed on her skin. He could smell the crushed grass on which they had lain, wrapped in each others arms, loathe to say good-bye. He sighed again and then climbed out of bed, going to his bath, reluctantly washing away all traces of his clandestine meeting with his wife.

When the prefect entered an hour later, he found the king busy writing a poem, a poem—if one could believe it—about a dwarf. Palthainon sniffed and told the young man to leave off such foolishness and return to business.

Clouds rolled in over Qualinesti, blotting out the sun. A light drizzle began to fall.

The same morning sunshine that had gleamed down upon Gilthas shone on his cousin, Silvanoshei, who had also been awake all night. He was not dreading the morning, as was

Gilthas. Silvanoshei waited for the morning with an impatience and a joy that still left him dazed and disbelieving.

This day, Silvanoshei was to be crowned Speaker of the Stars. This day, beyond all hope, beyond all expectation, he was to be proclaimed ruler of his people. He would succeed in doing what his mother and his father had tried to do and failed.

Events had happened so fast, Silvanoshei was still dazed by it all. Closing his eyes, he relived it all again.

He and Rolan, arriving yesterday on the outskirts of Silvanost, were confronted by a group of elf soldiers.

"So much for my kingship," Silvanoshei thought, more disappointed than afraid. When the elf soldiers drew their swords, Silvan expected to die. He waited, braced, weaponless. At least he would meet his end with dignity. He would not fight his people. He would be true to what his mother wanted from him.

To Silvan's amazement, the elf soldiers lifted their swords to the sunlight and began to cheer, proclaiming him Speaker of the Stars, proclaiming him king. This was not an execution squad, Silvan realized. It was an honor guard.

They brought him a horse to ride, a beautiful white stallion. He mounted and rode into Silvanost in triumph. Elves lined the streets, cheering and throwing flowers so that the street was covered with them. Their perfume scented the air.

The soldiers marched on either side, keeping the crowd back. Silvan waved graciously. He thought of his mother and father. Alhana had wanted this more than anything in the world. She had been willing to give her life to attain it. Perhaps she was watching from wherever the dead go, perhaps she was smiling to see her son fulfill her dearest dream. He hoped so. He was no longer angry at his mother. He had forgiven her, and he hoped that she had forgiven him.

The parade ended at the Tower of the Stars. Here a tall and stern-looking elf with graying hair met them. He introduced himself as General Konnal. He introduced his nephew, Kiryn, who—Silvan was delighted to discover—was a cousin. Konnal then introduced the Heads of House, who would have to determine if Silvanoshei was indeed the grandson of Lorac Caladon (his mother's name was not mentioned) and therefore rightful heir to the Silvanesti throne. This, Konnal assured Silvanoshei in an aside, was a mere formality.

"The people want a king," Konnal said. "The Heads of House are quite ready to believe you are a Caladon, as you claim to be."

"I *am* a Caladon," Silvanoshei said, offended by the implication that whether he was or he wasn't, the Heads would approve him anyhow. "I am the grandson of Lorac Caladon and the son of Alhana Starbreeze." He spoke her name loudly, knowing quite well that he wasn't supposed to speak the name of one deemed a dark elf.

And then an elf had walked up to him, one of the most beautiful of his people that Silvanoshei had ever seen. This elf, who was dressed in white robes, stood looking at him intently.

"I knew Lorac," the elf said at last. His voice was gentle and musical. "This is indeed his grandson. There can be no doubt." Leaning forward, he kissed Silvanoshei on both cheeks. He looked at General Konnal and said again, "There can be no doubt."

"Who are you, sir?" Silvan asked, dazzled.

"My name is Glaucous," said the elf, bowing low. "I have been named regent to aid you in the coming days. If General Konnal approves, I will make arrangements for your coronation to be held tomorrow. The people have waited long years for this joyful day. We will not make them wait longer."

Silvan lay in bed, a bed that had once belonged to his grandfather, Lorac. The bedposts were made of gold and of silver twined together to resemble vines, decorated with flowers formed of sparkling jewels. Fine sheets scented with lavender covered the mattress that was stuffed with swan's down. A silken coverlet of scarlet kept the night's chill from him. The ceiling above him was crystal. He could lie in his bed and give audience every night to the moon and the stars, come to pay homage.

Silvanoshei laughed softly to himself for the delight of it all. He thought that he should pinch his flesh to wake himself from this wonderful dream, but he decided not to risk it. If he were dreaming, let him never wake. Let him never wake to find himself shivering in some dank cave, eating dried berries and waybread, drinking brackish water. Let him never wake to see elf warriors drop dead at his feet, pierced by ogre arrows. Let him never wake. Let this dream last the remainder of his life.

He was hungry, wonderfully hungry, a hunger he could enjoy because he knew it would be satiated. He imagined what he would order for breakfast. Honeyed cakes, perhaps. Sugared rose petals. Cream laced with nutmeg and cinnamon. He could have anything he wanted, and if he didn't like it, he would send it away and ask for something else.

Reaching out his hand lazily for the silver bell that stood on an ornate gold and silver nightstand, Silvanoshei rang for his servants. He lay back to await the deluge of elf attendants to flood the room, wash him out of his bed to be bathed and dressed and combed and brushed and perfumed and bejeweled, made ready for his coronation.

The face of Alhana Starbreeze, his mother's face, came to Silvan's mind. He wished her well, but this was his dream, a dream in which she had no part. He had succeeded where she had failed. He would make whole what she had broken.

"Your Majesty. Your Majesty. Your Majesty."

The elves of House Servitor bowed low before him. He acknowledged them with a charming smile, allowed them to fluff up his pillows and smooth the coverlet. He sat up in bed and waited languidly to see what they would bring him for breakfast.

"Your Majesty," said an elf who had been chosen by the Regent Glaucous to serve in the capacity of chamberlain, "Prince Kiryn waits without to pay you honor on this day."

Silvanoshei turned from the mirror in which he'd been admiring his new finery. Seamstresses had worked all yesterday and all today in a frantic hurry to stitch the young king's robes and cape he would wear for the ceremony.

"My cousin! Please, let him enter without delay."

"Your Majesty should never say, 'Please,' the chamberlain chided with a smile. "When Your Majesty wants something done, speak it and it will be done."

"Yes, I will. Thank you." Silvan saw his second mistake and flushed. "I guess I'm not supposed to say, 'Thank you' either, am I?"

The chamberlain shook his head and departed. He returned with an elf youth, several years older than Silvan. They had met only briefly the day before. This was the first time they had been alone together. Both young men regarded each other intently, searching for some sign of relationship and, pleasing to both, finding it.

"How do you like all this, Cousin?" Kiryn asked, after the many niceties and polite nothings had been given and received. "Excuse me. I meant to say, 'Your Majesty.' " He bowed.

"Please, call me 'cousin,' " Silvan said warmly. "I never had a cousin before. That is, I never knew my cousin. He is the king of Qualinesti, you know. At least, that's what they call him."

"Your cousin Gilthas. The son of Lauralanthalasa and the half-human, Tanis. I know of him. Porthios spoke of him. He said that Speaker Gilthas was in poor health."

"You needn't be polite, Cousin. All of us know that he is melancholy mad. Not his fault, but there you have it. Is it proper for me to call you 'cousin'?"

"Perhaps not in public, Your Majesty," Kiryn replied with a smile. "As you may have noted, we in Silvanesti love formalities. But in private, I would be honored." He paused a moment, then added quietly, "I heard of the deaths of your father and mother. I want to say how deeply grieved I am. I admired both of them very much."

"Thank you," Silvan said and, after a decent interval, he changed the subject. "To answer your earlier question, I must admit that I find all this rather daunting. Wonderful, but daunting. A month ago I was living in a cave and sleeping on the ground. Now I have this bed, this beautiful bed, a bed in which my grandfather slept. The Regent Glaucous arranged for the bed to be brought to this chamber, thinking it would please me. I have these clothes. I have whatever I want to eat and drink. It all seems a dream."

Silvan turned back to regarding himself again in the mirror. He was enchanted with his new clothing, his new appearance. He was clean, his hair perfumed and brushed, his fingers adorned with jewels. He was not flea bitten, he was not stiff from sleeping with a rock for a pillow. He vowed, in his heart, never again. He did not notice that Kiryn appeared grave when Silvan spoke of the regent.

His cousin's gravity deepened as Silvan continued speaking. "Talking of Glaucous, what an estimable man he is! I am quite pleased with him as regent. So polite and condescending. Asking my opinion about everything. At first, I don't mind telling you, Cousin, I was a little put out at General Konnal for suggesting to the Heads of House that a regent be appointed to guide me until I am of age. I am already considered of age by Qualinesti standards, you see."

Silvan's expression hardened. "And I am determined not to be a puppet king like my poor cousin Gilthas. However, the Regent Glaucous gave me to understand that he will not be the ruler. He will be the person to smooth the way so that my wishes and commands are carried out."

Kiryn was silent, made no answer. He looked around the room as if making up his mind to something. Drawing a step nearer Silvan, he said, in a low voice, "May I suggest that Your Majesty dismiss the servants?"

Silvan regarded Kiryn in troubled astonishment, suddenly wary, suspicious. Glaucous had told him that Kiryn himself had designs upon the throne. What if this were a ploy to catch him alone and helpless. . . .

Silvan looked at Kiryn, who was slender and delicate of build, with the soft, smooth hands of the scholar. Silvan compared his cousin to himself, whose body was hardened, well-muscled. Kiryn was unarmed. He could hardly represent a threat.

"Very well," Silvan said and sent away the servants, who had been tidying the room and laying out the clothes he would wear at the formal dance given in his honor this evening.

"There, Cousin. We are alone. What is it you have to say to me?" Silvan's voice and manner were cool.

"Your Majesty, Cousin," Kiryn spoke earnestly, keeping his voice low, despite the fact that the two of them were alone in the large and echoing room, "I came here today with one fixed purpose and that is to warn you against this Glaucous."

"Ah," said Silvan, with a knowing air. "I see."

"You don't seem surprised, Your Majesty."

"I am not, Cousin. Disappointed, I confess, but not surprised. Glaucous himself warned me that you might be jealous of both him and of me. He told me quite candidly that you seemed to dislike him. The feeling is not mutual. Glaucous speaks of you with the highest regard and is deeply saddened that the two of you cannot be friends."

"I am afraid I cannot return the compliment," Kiryn said. "The man is not worthy to be regent, Your Majesty. He is not of House Royal. He is . . . or was . . . a wizard who tended the

Tower of Shalost. I know that my Uncle Konnal suggested him, but . . ."

He stopped talking, as if he found it difficult to proceed. "I tell you what I have never told anyone else, Your Majesty. I believe that Glaucous has some sort of strange hold upon my uncle.

"My uncle is a good man, Your Majesty. He fought bravely during the War of the Lance. He fought the dream alongside Porthios, your father. What he saw during those awful times has caused him to live in constant fear, unreasoning fear. He is terrified of the evil days returning. He believes that this shield will save the Silvanesti from the coming darkness. Glaucous controls the magic of the shield and through threats of lowering it, he controls my uncle. I would not want to see Glaucous control you in the same way."

"Perhaps you think, Cousin, that I am already under his control. Perhaps you think that you would be a better Speaker of Stars?" Silvan asked with mounting anger.

"I could have been Speaker, Cousin," Kiryn said with quiet dignity. "Glaucous sought to make me Speaker. I refused. I knew your mother and your father. I loved them both. The throne is yours by right. I would not usurp it."

Silvan felt he deserved the rebuke. "Forgive me, Cousin. I spoke before my brain had time to guide my tongue. But I believe that you are mistaken about Glaucous. He has only the best interests of the Silvanesti at heart. The fact that he has risen to his high estate from a low one is to his credit and to the credit of your uncle for seeing his true worth and not being blinded by class as we elves have been in the past. My mother said often that we have harmed ourselves by keeping people of talent from fulfilling their true potential by judging a person only by birth and not by ability. One of my mother's most trusted advisers was Samar, who began life as a soldier in the ranks."

"If Glaucous had come to us with expertise in the governing of our people, I would be the first to support him, no matter what his background. But all he has done is to plant a magical tree," Kiryn said wryly, "and cause a shield to be raised over us."

"The shield is for our protection," Silvanoshei argued.

"Just as prisoners in their jail cells are protected," Kiryn returned.

Silvan was thoughtful. He could not doubt his cousin's sincerity and his earnestness. Silvan did not want to hear anything against the regent. Quite honestly, Silvan was overwhelmed by the new responsibilities that had been thrust so suddenly upon him. He found it comforting to think that someone like Glaucous was there to advise and counsel him. Someone as formal and polite and charming as Glaucous.

"Let us not quarrel over this, Cousin," Silvan said. "I will consider your words, and I thank you for speaking from your heart, for I know that this cannot have been an easy task for you." He extended his hand.

Kiryn took his cousin's hand with true goodwill and pressed it warmly. The two talked of other matters, of the ceremonies of the forthcoming coronation, of the current fashions in elven dancing. Kiryn then took his leave, promising to return to escort his cousin to his crowning.

"I will be wearing the crown that last graced the head of my grandfather," said Silvan.

"May it bring you better fortune than it brought him, Your Majesty," said Kiryn. With a grave expression, he took his departure.

Silvan was sorry to see his cousin leave, for he was very pleased with Kiryn's warm friendliness and lively nature, even though he felt rather resentful at Kiryn for spoiling the morning. On this day of all days, a new king should experience nothing but joy.

"He is just envious," Silvan said to himself. "Perfectly

natural. I am sure I would feel the same."

"Your Majesty," said one of his servants, "I grieve to report that it is starting to rain."

"Well, and what do you think of our new king?" General Konnal asked his companion as they ascended the stairs of the royal palace to pay homage to His Majesty on the morning of his coronation. The rain was steady and heavy now, had drawn a curtain of gray over the sun.

"I find him to be intelligent, modest, unaffected," Glaucous replied, smiling. "I am extremely pleased with him. You?"

"He is an adolescent puppy," said Konnal, shrugging. "He will give us no trouble." His tone softened. "Your advice was right, my friend. We did well to place him on the throne. The people adore him. I have not seen them so happy in a long time. The entire city has turned out to celebrate. The streets are decked with flowers, everyone is dressed in his or her finest clothes. There will be parties that last for days. They are calling his coming a miracle. It is being said that those afflicted with the wasting sickness feel life restored to their limbs. There will be no more talk of lifting the shield. No reason to do so now."

"Yes, we have uprooted the weed of rebellion the kirath were attempting to plant in our lovely garden," Glaucous replied. "The kirath imagine they have defeated you by placing Lorac's grandson on the throne. Do nothing to disillusion them. Let them celebrate. They have their king. They will trouble us no more."

"And if by some unfortunate chance the shield should fail us," Konnal stated with a meaningful look at the wizard, "we have settled his mother, as well. She will rush in with her troops, armed to the teeth, to save her country and find it in the hands of her very own son. It would almost be worth it just to see the expression on her face."

"Yes, well, perhaps." Glaucous did not seem to find this

idea all that amusing. "I, for one, can do very well without ever seeing the witch's face again. I do not believe for a moment that she would let her son remain on the throne. She wants that prize for herself. Fortunately," he said smiling, his good humor restored, "she is unlikely to ever find her way inside. The shield will keep her out."

"Yet the shield admitted her son," said Konnal.

"Because I wanted it to do so," Glaucous reminded the general.

"So you say."

"Do you doubt me, my friend?"

Glaucous halted, turned to face the general. The wizard's white robes rippled around him.

"Yes," Konnal replied evenly. "Because I sense that you doubt yourself."

Glaucous started to reply, closed his mouth on his words. Clasping his hands behind him, he walked on.

"I am sorry," Konnal began.

"No, my friend." Glaucous halted, turned. "I am not angry. I am hurt, that is all. Saddened."

"It's just that—"

"I will explain myself. Perhaps then you will believe me."

Konnal sighed. "You purposefully misunderstand me. But, very well, I will hear your explanation."

"I will tell you how it came about. But not here. Too many people." Glaucous indicated a servant carrying a large wreath of laurel leaves. "Come into the library where we may talk privately."

A large room lined with shelves of dark, polished wood filled with books and scrolls, the library was quiet, the books seeming to absorb the sounds of anyone who spoke, as if noting them down for future reference.

"When I said that the shield acted according to my wishes," Glaucous explained, "I did not mean that I gave the shield a specific command to admit this young man. The magic of the shield emanates from the tree in the Garden of Astarin. Acting on my direction, the Woodshapers planted and nurtured the Shield Tree. I instructed them in the magic that caused the tree to grow. The magic is very much a part of me. I devote an immense amount of my strength and energy to maintaining the magic and keeping the shield in place. I feel sometimes," Glaucous added softly, "as if I *am* the shield. The shield that keeps our people safe."

Konnal said nothing, waited to hear more.

"I have suspected before now that the shield has been reacting to my unspoken wishes," Glaucous continued, "wishes I did not even know I was making. I have long wanted a king to sit upon the throne. The shield knew that unconscious desire of mine. Thus when Silvanoshei happened to be near it, the shield embraced him."

The general wanted to believe this, but his doubts lingered. Why has Glaucous said nothing of this before? Konnal wondered. Why do his eyes avoid mine when he speaks of it? He knows something. He is keeping something from me.

Konnal turned to Glaucous. "Can you assure me that no one else will enter the shield?"

"I can assure you of that, my dear General," Glaucous answered. "I stake my life upon it."

19

The Blind Beggar

ina's troops left Sanction in good spirits, roaring out songs to keep the cadence of the march and speaking of the bold deeds they would do in Silvanesti in the name of their idolized commander. Whenever Mina came in sight, riding her blood-red horse, the soldiers cheered wildly, often breaking ranks (braving the ire of their commanding officers) to cluster round her and touch her for luck.

Galdar was gone. He had left several days earlier for Khur, bearing Mina's orders to General Dogah. Captain Samuval was in command in the minotaur's absence. His command was easy at this point. The sun shone. The summer days were warm. The marching at this stage was safe and easy, for the Knights were only a few days out of Sanction and still in friendly territory. Soon they would enter the land of the ogres—once allies and now bitter enemies. The thought of fighting even those savage monsters could not cloud their spirits. Mina lit their shadows like a cold, pale sun.

A veteran campaigner, Samuval knew that when the weather broke and the rain set in, when the road narrowed, the wind howled and the enemy nipped at their heels, the soldiers would begin to have second thoughts about this venture. They would start to grouse and grumble, and a few might take it into their heads to start trouble. But, for now, his duties were light. He marched at Mina's side—the envy of all in the column. He stood next to her as she sat on her horse reviewing the troops as they passed by. He was in her tent every night, studying the map and marking out the next day's route. He slept near her tent, wrapped in his cloak, his hand on his sword hilt, ready to rush to her defense should she have need of him.

He did not fear any of the men would try to harm her. Lying on his cloak one night, he stared into the stars in the clear sky and wondered about that. She was a young woman—a very attractive young woman. He was a man who loved women, all kinds of women. He could not begin to count the number he had bedded. Usually the sight of a young slip of a maid as pretty as Mina would have had his blood bubbling, his loins aching. But he felt no twinge of desire in Mina's presence and, listening to the talk around the campfires, he knew the other men in the ranks felt the same. They loved her, they adored her. They were awestruck, reverent. But he did not want her and he could not name anyone who did.

The next morning's march began the same as those before it. Samuval calculated that if all went well with Galdar's business in Khur, the minotaur would catch up to them in another two days. Prior to this, Samuval had never had much use for minotaurs, but he was actually looking forward to seeing Galdar again. . . .

"Sir! Stop the men!" a scout shouted.

Samuval halted the column's march and walked forward to meet the scout.

"What is it?" the captain demanded. "Ogres?"

"No, sir." The scout saluted. "There's a blind beggar on the path ahead, sir."

Samuval was irate. "You called a halt for a blasted beggar?"

"Well, sir"—the scout was discomfited—"he's blocking the path."

"Shove him out of the way then!" Samuval said, infuriated.

"There's something strange about him, sir." The scout was uneasy. "He's no ordinary beggar. I think you should come talk to him, sir. He said . . . he said he is waiting for Mina." The soldier's eyes were round.

Samuval rubbed his chin. He was not surprised to hear that word of Mina had spread abroad, but he was considerably surprised and not particularly pleased to hear that knowledge of their march and the route they were taking had also apparently traveled ahead of them.

"I'll see to this," he said and started to leave with the scout. Samuval planned to question this beggar to find out what else he knew and how he knew it. Hopefully, he would be able to deal with the man before Mina heard about it.

He had taken about three steps when he heard Mina's voice behind him.

"Captain Samuval," she said, riding up on Foxfire, "what is the problem? Why have we stopped?"

Samuval was about to say that the road ahead was blocked by a boulder, but, before he could open his mouth, the scout had blurted out the truth in a loud voice that could be heard up and down the column.

"Mina! There's a blind beggar up ahead. He says he's waiting for you."

The men were pleased, nodding and thinking it only natural that Mina should rate such attention. Fools! One would think they were parading through the streets of Jelek!

Samuval could envision the road ahead lined with the poxed and the lame from every measly village on their route, begging Mina to cure them.

"Captain," said Mina, "bring the man to me."

Samuval went to stand by her stirrup. "Listen a moment,

Mina," he argued. "I know you mean well, but if you stop to heal every wretched cripple between here and Silvanost, we'll arrive in the elf kingdom in time to celebrate Yule with 'em. That is if we arrive at all. Every moment we waste is another moment the ogres have to gather their forces to come meet us."

"The man asks for me. I will see him," Mina said and slid down off her horse. "We have marched long. The men could do with a rest. Where he is, Rolof?"

"He's right up ahead," said the scout, pointing. "About half a mile. At the top of the hill."

"Samuval, come with me," Mina said. "The rest of you, wait here."

Samuval saw the man before they reached him. The road they were following led up and down small hillocks and, as the scout had said, the beggar was waiting for them at the top of one of these. He sat on the ground, his back against a boulder; a long, stout staff in his hand. Hearing their approach, he rose to his feet and turned slowly and sightlessly to face them.

The man was younger than the captain had expected. Long hair that shimmered with a silver sheen in the morning sunshine fell over his shoulders. His face was smooth and youthful. Once it might have been handsome. He was dressed in robes that were pearl gray in color, travel-worn and frayed at the hem, but clean. All this, Samuval noted later. For now, all he could do was stare at the hideous scar that disfigured the man's face.

The scar looked to be a burn mark. The hair on the right side of the man's head had been singed off. The scar slanted across the man's face from the right side of his head to below the left side of his chin. He wore a rag tied around his right eye socket. Samuval wondered with morbid curiosity if the eye was still there or if it was destroyed, melted in the terrible heat that had seared the flesh and burned away the hair to the roots. The left eye remained, but it was useless seemingly, for it held no light. The horrible wound was fresh, not a month old. The man must be in pain from the injury, but if so he did not reveal it. He stood waiting for them silently and, though he could not see her, his face turned toward Mina. He must have picked out the sound of her lighter steps from Samuval's heavier footfalls.

Mina paused, just a moment, and Samuval saw her stiffen, as if she were taken by surprise. Then, shrugging, she continued to walk toward the beggar. Samuval came behind, his hand on his sword hilt. Despite the fact that the man was blind, Samuval sensed him to be a threat. As the scout had said, there was something strange about this blind beggar.

"You know me, then," the man said, his sightless eye gazing over her head.

"Yes, I know you," she replied.

Samuval found it hard to look at the beggar's horrid wounds. Yellow puss oozed from beneath the rag. The skin around the burn was fiery red, swollen and inflamed. The captain could smell the stink of putrefying flesh.

"When did this happen to you?" Mina asked.

"The night of the storm," he replied.

She nodded gravely, as if she had expected that answer. "Why did you venture out into the storm?"

"I heard a voice," he replied. "I wanted to investigate."

"The voice of the One God," Mina said.

The beggar shook his head, disbelieving. "I could hear the voice over the roaring of the wind and the crashing thunder, but I could not hear the words it spoke. I traveled far through rain and the hail in search of the voice, and I was near the source, I think. I was almost in Neraka when a lightning bolt struck me. I remember nothing after that."

"You take this human form," she said abruptly. "Why?"

"Can you blame me, Mina?" he asked, his tone rueful. "I

am forced to walk through the land of my enemies." He gestured with his staff. "This is the only way I am able to travel now—on two feet, with my stick to guide me."

"Mina"—Samuval spoke to her, but he kept his eyes on the blind man—"we have many more miles to march this day. Say the word and I will rid both the path and the world of this fellow."

"Easy, Captain," Mina said quietly, resting her hand on his arm. "This is an old acquaintance. I will be only a moment longer. How did you find me?" she asked the blind man.

"I have heard the stories of your deeds everywhere I go," the beggar answered. "I knew the name, and I recognized the description. Could there be another Mina with eyes the color of amber? No, I said to myself. Only one—the orphan girl who, years ago, washed up on the shores of Schallsea. The orphan girl who was taken in by Goldmoon and who won the First Master's heart. She grieves for you, Mina. Grieves for you these three years as for one dead. Why did you run away from her and the rest of us who loved you?"

"Because she could not answer my questions," Mina replied. "None of you could."

"And have you found the answer, Mina?" the man asked and his voice was stern.

"I have," she said steadily.

The beggar shook his head. He did not seem angry, only sorrowful.

"I could heal you," Mina offered, and she took a step toward him, her hand outstretched.

Swiftly the beggar stepped backward. In the same movement, he shifted the staff from one hand to two and held it out in front of his body, barring her way. "No!" he cried. "As much as my wound pains me now, that pain is physical. It does not strike to my soul as would the pain of your so-called healing touch. And though I walk in darkness, my darkness is not so deep as the darkness in which you now walk, Mina."

She smiled at him, her smile calm, radiant.

"You heard the voice, Solomirathnius," she said. "You hear it still. Don't you?"

He did not reply. He lowered his staff slowly, stared at her long moments. He stared so long that Samuval wondered suspiciously if the man could see out of that one milky white eye.

"Don't you?" she pressed him.

Abruptly, angrily, the man turned away from her. Tapping the ground with his staff, he left the path and entered the woods. The end of his staff knocked brutally against the boles of trees and thrust savagely into bushes. His hand groped to feel his way.

"I don't trust him," Samuval said. "He has the stink of a Solamnic about him. Let me skewer him."

Mina turned away. "You could do him no harm, Captain. He may look feeble, but he is not."

"What is he then? A wizard?" Samuval asked with a slight sneer.

"No, he is much more powerful than any wizard," Mina replied. "In his true form, he is the silver dragon known to most as Mirror. He is the Guardian of the Citadel of Light."

"A dragon!" Samuval stopped dead in the path, stared back into the brush. He could no longer see the blind beggar, and that worried him more now than ever. "Mina," he said urgently, "let me take a squadron of men after him! He will surely try to kill us all!"

Mina smiled slightly at Samuval's fears. "We are safe, Captain. Order the men to resume the march. The path ahead is clear. Mirror will not trouble us."

"Why not?" Samuval was frowning, doubtful.

"Because once, many years ago, every night, Goldmoon, the First Master of the Citadel of Light, brushed my hair," Mina said softly.

Reaching up her hand, she touched, very lightly, her shaven head.

20

Betrayed

he days of waiting had passed pleasantly for Gerard. The queen mother's house was a sanctuary of peace and serenity. Every room was a bower of green and growing plants and flowers. The sounds of falling water soothed and relaxed. He was not in possession of the supposed time travel device, yet he had the feeling that here time was suspended. The sunlit hours melted into dusk that melted into night and back to sunlight again with no one seeming to notice the change of one day to next. No hourglass dropped its sands into elven lives, or so Gerard imagined. He was jolted back into harsh reality when, on the afternoon of the day they were to leave, he walked in the garden and saw, quite by chance, sunlight flash off shining black armor.

The Neraka Knight was distant, but he was plainly keeping watch on the house. Gerard ducked back into the doorway, his idyll of peace shattered. He waited tensely for the Neraka Knights to come beating on the door, but hours passed and no one disturbed them. He trusted, at last, that he had not been seen. He took care not to venture outside after that, not until nightfall, when they were ready to depart.

Gerard had seen little of Palin Majere, for which he was not sorry. He deplored the mage's rudeness to everyone in the household, but most particularly to Laurana. Gerard tried to make allowances. Palin Majere had suffered a great deal, the Knight reminded himself. But the mage's dark moods cast a shadow that dimmed the brightest sunlight. Even the two servant elves tiptoed around, afraid of making a sound that would bring down on them the mage's irrational anger. When Gerard mentioned this to Laurana, making some comment on what he considered boorish human behavior, she smiled and urged him to be patient.

"I was a prisoner once," she said, her eyes dark with memory, "a prisoner of the Dark Queen. Unless you have been a prisoner, Sir Knight; until you have been shut away in darkness, alone in pain and in fear, I don't believe you can understand."

Gerard accepted the gentle rebuke and said nothing more.

He had seen little of the kender, as well, for which the Knight was extremely grateful. Palin Majere kept Tasslehoff closeted away for hours at a time, having the kender relate in detail his ridiculous stories over and over. No torture devised by the cruelest Neraka Knight could match being forced to endure the kender's shrill voice for hours on end.

The night they were to leave Qualinesti came all too soon. The world beyond, the world of humans, seemed a hurried, grasping, sordid sort of place. Gerard was sorry to be returning to it. He had come to understand why the elves were loathe to travel outside their beautiful, serene realm.

Their elven guide stood waiting. Laurana kissed Tas, who, feeling a snuffle coming on, was quiet for all of three minutes. She thanked Gerard graciously for his help and gave him her hand to kiss, which he did with respect and admiration and a true feeling of loss. She spoke last to Palin, who had remained aloof, off to one side. He was obviously impatient to be gone.

"My friend," she said to him, placing her hand on his arm, "I believe that I know something of what you are thinking."

He frowned at this and shook his head slightly.

Laurana continued, "Be careful, Palin. Think long and well before you act."

He made no answer but kissed her as was the elven custom between old friends and told her, rather curtly, not to worry. He knew what he was about.

As he followed their elven guide into the night, Gerard looked back at the house on the cliff. Its lights shone brilliant as stars, but, like the stars, they were too small to bring day to night.

"Yet without the darkness," said Palin suddenly, "we would never be aware that the stars exist."

So that's how you rationalize evil, Gerard thought. He made no comment, and Palin did not speak again. The mage's morose silence was more than made up for by Tasslehoff.

"One would think that a cursed kender would talk less," Gerard grumbled.

"The curse isn't on my tongue," Tasslehoff pointed out. "It's on my insides. It made them go all squirmy. Have you ever been cursed like that?"

"Yes, the moment I set eyes on you," Gerard retorted.

"You are all making noise enough to wake a drunken gully dwarf!" their elven guide said irritably, speaking Common. Gerard had no idea if this was Kalindas or Kelevandros. He could never keep the two brothers straight. They were as alike as twins, although one was older than the other, or so he had been told. Their elven names, both beginning with K, blurred in his mind. He might have asked Palin, but the mage was disinclined to talk, appeared absorbed in his own dark thoughts.

"The kender's chatter is like the twittering of birds compared to the rattle and clank of your armor, Sir Knight," the elf added. "Not that it would be much different if you were naked. You humans cannot even draw a breath without making noise. I could hear the huffing and bellowing of your breathing a mile distant."

"We've been on the move through this forest for hours," Gerard countered. "Are we anywhere near our destination?"

"Quite near," the elf replied. "The clearing where you will meet the griffon is straight ahead at the end of this trail. If you had elven sight you could see it from here. In fact, this would be a good place to halt, if you would like to rest. We should keep under cover until the last possible moment."

"Don't worry. I'm not going anywhere," Gerard said gratefully. Dropping his pack, he sank down at the base of a tall aspen tree, leaned his back against it, closed his eyes and stretched his legs. "How long until morning?"

"An hour. And now I must leave you for a while to go hunting. We should be prepared to offer the griffons fresh meat. They will be hungry from their long flight and will appreciate the courtesy. You should be safe here, provided none of you wander off." The elf looked at the kender as he spoke.

"We will be fine," Palin said the first words he had spoken in hours. He did not sit down, but paced beneath the trees, restless and impatient. "No, Tas. You stay here with us. Where is the device? You still have it, don't you? No, don't bring it out. I just want to know it's safe."

"Oh, it's safe," the kender said. "It couldn't be unsafe, if you know what I mean."

"Damn funny time to go hunting," Gerard observed, watching the elf slip off into the darkness.

"He leaves on my orders," Palin said. "The griffons will be in a much better humor when they have eaten, and we will have a safer ride. I was once on the back of a griffon who decided that her empty belly was more important than her rider. Spying a deer on the ground, she swooped down upon it. I could do nothing but cling to her in terror. Fortunately we all came out of it alive, including the deer, who heard my cries to the griffon to stop and dashed off into the forest. The griffon was in a foul mood, however, and refused to carry me farther. Since then, I have always made certain that I brought a gift of food."

"Then why didn't the elf do that before we left instead of waiting to go hunting now?"

"Probably because he did not want to walk for miles lugging a deer carcass over his shoulder," Palin said sardonically. "You must take into account the fact that the smell of fresh-killed meat makes many elves sick to their stomachs."

Gerard said nothing, fearing to say too much. By the mage's tone, Palin took the Knight for an idiot. Perhaps he had not meant it that way, but that was how Gerard understood it.

"By the way, Sir Gerard," Palin said stiffly, "I want you to know that I consider that you have done your part in fulfilling my father's dying request. I will take up the matter from here. You need no longer concern yourself with it."

"As you wish, sir," Gerard returned.

"I want to thank you for what you have done," Palin added after a pause during which the chill in the air could have caused snow to start falling in midsummer. "You have performed a great service at the risk of your own life. A great service," he repeated softly. "I will recommend to Lord Warren that you be given a commendation."

"Thank you, sir," Gerard said. "But I'm only doing my duty by your father, a man I much admired."

"As opposed to his son, is that it?" Palin asked. He turned and walked off a few paces, his head bowed, his arms folded in the sleeves of his dark-colored robes. He obviously considered their conversation at an end.

Tasslehoff settled himself down beside Gerard, and because a kender's hands must always be busy doing something, he turned out all the pockets in the new shirt he'd persuaded

Laurana to sew for him. The shirt was a riot of color and gave Gerard eyestrain just to look it. By the lambent light of a half-moon and many thousand stars, Tas sorted through the interesting things he'd picked up while in Laurana's house.

No doubt about it. Gerard would be extremely glad to deposit the mage and the kender in Solace and be done with them both.

The sky above them gradually grew lighter, the stars faded away, the moon paled, but the elf did not return.

Marshal Medan and his escort reached the rendezvous appointed by the elf about an hour before dawn. He and the two Knights with him reined in their horses. Medan did not dismount. Rebel elves were known to inhabit this part of the forest. He looked intently into the shadows and the swirling mists and thought that this would make an excellent place for an ambush.

"Subcommander," Medan said. "Go see if you can find our traitor. He said he would be waiting by those three white rocks over there."

The subcommander dismounted. Keeping his hand on his sword, half-drawing it from its scabbard, he moved slowly forward, making as little noise as possible. He wore only his breastplate, no other metal armor.

The marshal's horse was restive. The animal snorted and blew and pricked his ears. Medan patted the horse on the neck. "What is it, boy?" he asked softly. "What's out there?"

The subcommander disappeared in the shadows, reappeared again as a shadowy silhouette against the backdrop of the three large white boulders. Medan could hear the man's harsh whisper. He could not hear if there was a reply but assumed there must have been, for the subcommander nodded and returned to make his report.

"The traitor says the three are not far from here, near a clearing, where they are to meet the griffon. He will lead us there. We should walk, he says. The horses make too much noise."

The marshal dismounted and dropped the reins with a single spoken word of command. The horse would remain where it was, would not move from the spot until ordered. The other Knight dismounted, taking from his saddle a short bow and a quiver of arrows.

Medan and his escorts crept through the forest.

"And this is what I've been reduced to," Medan muttered to himself, shoving aside tree branches, stepping carefully through the undergrowth. He could barely see the man in front of him. Only the three white rocks showed up clearly and they were sometimes obscured by the dank mists. "Skulking about the woods at night like a blasted thief. Relying on the word of an elf who thinks nothing of betraying his mistress for a handful of steel. And all for what? To ambush some wretch of a wizard!"

"Did you say something, sir?" the subcommander whispered.

"Yes," Medan returned. "I said I would rather be on the field of honorable battle lying dead with a spear through my heart than here at this moment. What about you, Subcommander?"

"Sir?" The subcommander stared at him. The man had no clue what his marshal was talking about.

"Never mind," Medan grated. "Just keep going." He waved his hand.

The traitor elf appeared, a glimmer of a pale face in the darkness. He raised a pallid hand, motioned for Medan to join him. The marshal drew forward, eyed the elf grimly.

"Well? Where are they?" Medan did not use the elf's name. In Medan's mind, the elf was not worthy of a name.

"There!" The elf pointed. "Beneath that tree. You cannot see it from here, but there is a clearing a hundred paces beyond. They plan to meet the griffon there."

The sky was graying with the dawn. Medan could see

nothing at first and then the mists swirled apart, revealing three shadowy figures. One appeared to be wearing dark armor, for though Medan could not see it clearly, he could hear it rattle and clank.

"Sir," said the traitor, sounding nervous, "have you further need of me? If not, I should be going. My absence may be noted."

"Leave, by all means," said Medan.

The elf slipped away into the woods.

The marshal motioned for the knight with the bow to come forward.

"Remember, the dragon wants them alive," Medan said. "Aim high. Shoot to cripple. Fire on my order. Not before."

The Knight nodded and took his place in the brush. He fit an arrow to his bow string and looked to the marshal.

Medan watched and waited.

Gerard heard a flapping sound, as of immense wings. He'd never before seen a griffon, but this sounded like what he expected a griffon would sound like. He jumped to his feet.

"What is it?" Palin lifted his head, startled by the Knight's sudden movement.

"I think I hear the griffon, sir," Gerard replied.

Palin drew back his hood to hear better, looked toward the clearing. They could not see the griffon yet. The beast was still among the treetops, but the wind from its wings was starting to scatter dead leaves and kick up dust.

"Where? Where?" Tasslehoff cried, hastily gathering up all his valuables and stuffing them into whatever location presented itself.

The griffon came into view, huge wings stilled now, floating on the air currents to a smooth landing. Gerard forgot his irritation with the mage and his annoyance at the kender in wonder at the sight of the strange beast. Elves ride griffons as humans ride horses, but few humans did. Griffons have always had a distrust of humans, who were known to hunt and kill them.

Gerard had tried not to dwell on the fact that he would soon be trusting his life to a beast that had little reason to love him, but now he was forced to confront the idea of actually riding on the back of one of these creatures, riding it not over a road but into the air. High in the air, so that any mischance would send him plummeting to a horrible death.

Gerard steeled himself, faced this as he faced any other daunting task. He noted the proud eagle head with its white feathers, the shining black eyes, and the hooked beak that could, or so he'd heard, snap a man's spine in two or rip his head from his neck. The front legs were those of an eagle, with rending talons; the back legs and body were those of a lion, covered in a soft brown fur. The wings were large and snow white underneath, brown on top. The griffon was taller than Gerard by at least head and shoulders.

"There is only one of them," Gerard reported coolly, as if meeting one were an everyday occurrence with him. "At least so far. And no sign of the elf."

"Strange," Palin said, glancing about. "I wonder where he went? This is not like him."

The griffon flapped its wings and turned its head, searching for its riders. The wind of the enormous wings whipped up a gale that sent wisps of morning fog swirling and lashed the tree branches. They waited another few moments, but no other griffon appeared.

"It seems there is to be only one, sir," Gerard said, trying not to sound relieved. "You and the kender go ahead. I'll see you off safely. Don't worry about me. I'll find my own way out of Qualinesti. I have my horse. . . ."

"Nonsense," said Palin crisply, displeased at any change in plans. "The griffon can carry all three of us. The kender counts as nothing."

"I do, too, count for something!" Tasslehoff stated, offended.

"Sir, I really don't mind," Gerard began.

An arrow thunked into the tree beside him. Another arrow whizzed over his head. Gerard dropped to the ground, grabbing hold of the kender on the way down.

"Sir! Take cover!" he yelled at Palin.

"Rebel elves," Palin said, peering through the shadows. "They have seen your armor. We are friends!" he called out in elven and lifted his hand to wave.

An arrow tore through the sleeve of his robe. He stared at the hole in angry astonishment. Gerard leaped to his feet, caught hold of the mage and pulled him to cover behind a large oak tree.

"They're not elves, sir!" he said and he pointed grimly to one of the arrows. The tip was steel and the arrow was fletched in black feathers. "They're Knights of Neraka."

"But so are you," said Palin, eyeing Gerard's breastplate, adorned with the skull and the death lily. "At least for all they know."

"Oh, they know all right," Gerard answered grimly. "You notice the elf never returned. I think we've been betrayed."

"It's not possible—" Palin began.

"I see them!" Tasslehoff cried, pointing. "Over there in those bushes. Three of them. They're wearing black armor."

"You have sharp eyes, kender," Gerard conceded. He couldn't see a thing in the shadows and mists of early dawn.

"We cannot stay here. We must make a run for the griffon!" Palin said, and started to stand up.

Gerard pulled the mage back down.

"Those archers rarely miss, sir. You'll never make it alive!"

"True, they don't miss," Palin retorted. "And yet they have fired three arrows at us and we live. If we have been betrayed, they know we carry the artifact! That's what they want. They mean to capture us alive and interrogate us." He gripped Gerard's arm hard, his cruelly deformed fingers driving the chain mail painfully into the knight's flesh. "I won't give up the device. And I won't be taken alive! Not again! Do you hear me? I won't!"

Two more arrows thudded into the tree, causing the kender, who had poked his head up to see, to duck back down.

"Whew!" he said, feeling his top-knot anxiously. "That was close! Do I still have my hair?"

Gerard looked at Palin. The mage's face was pale, his lips a thin, tight line. Laurana's words came back to Gerard. *Until you have been a prisoner, you cannot understand.*

"You go on, sir. You and the kender."

"Don't be a fool," said Palin. "We leave together. They want me alive. They have a use for me. They don't need you at all. You will be tortured and killed."

Behind them, the griffon's harsh cry sounded loud and raucous and impatient.

"I am not the fool, sir," Gerard said, looking the mage in the eye. "You are, if you don't listen to me. I can distract them, and I can defend myself properly. You cannot, unless you have some magical spell at your fingertips?"

He knew by Majere's pale, pinched face that he did not.

"Very well," said Gerard. "Take the kender and your precious magical artifact and get out of here!"

Palin hesitated a moment, staring at the direction of the enemy. His face was set, rigid, corpselike. Slowly, he withdrew his hand from Gerard's arm. "This is what I have become," he said. "Useless. Wretched. Forced to run instead of facing my enemies . . ."

"Sir, if you're going, go now," Gerard said, drawing his sword with a ringing sound. "Keep low and use the trees for cover. Fast!"

He rose from his hiding position. Brandishing his sword, he charged unhesitatingly at the Knights crouched in the brush, shouting his battle challenge, drawing their fire.

Palin rose to his feet. Crouching low, he grabbed hold of Tasslehoff's shirt collar, jerked the kender to a standing position. "You're coming with me," he ordered.

"But what about Gerard?" Tas hung back.

"You heard him," Palin said, dragging the kender forward. "He can take care of himself. Besides, the Knights must not capture the artifact!"

"But they *can't* take the device away from me!" Tas protested, tugging at his shirt to free it from Palin's grasp. "It will always come back to me!"

"Not if you're dead," Palin said harshly, biting the words.

Tas stopped suddenly and turned around. His eyes went wide.

"Do . . . do you see a dragon anywhere?" he asked nervously.

"Quit stalling!" Palin seized hold of the kender by the arm this time and, using strength borne of adrenaline, hauled Tasslehoff bodily through the trees toward the griffon.

"I'm not stalling. I feel sick," Tas asserted. "I think the curse is working on me again."

Palin paid no attention to the kender's whining. He could hear Gerard yelling, shouting challenges to his enemies. Another arrow whistled past, but it fell spent about a yard away from Palin. His dark robes blended into the forest, he was a running target moving through the mists and dim light, keeping low, as Gerard had recommended, and putting the trunks of the trees between him and the enemy whenever possible.

Behind him, Palin heard steel clash against steel. The arrows ceased. Gerard was fighting the Knights. Alone.

Palin plunged grimly ahead, dragging the protesting kender along with him. The mage was not proud of himself. His fear and his shame rankled in him, more painful than one of the arrows if it had happened to hit. He risked a glance backward but could see nothing for the shadows and the fog.

He was near the griffon. He was near escape. His steps slowed. He hesitated, half-turned . . .

A blackness came over him. He was once again in the prison cell in the Gray Robes' encampment on the border of Qualinesti. He crouched at the bottom of a deep, narrow pit dug into the ground. The walls of the pit were smooth. He could not climb up them. An iron grating was placed over the top. A few holes in the grate permitted the air to filter down into the pit, along with the rain that dripped monotonously and filled the bottom of the pit with water.

He was alone, forced to live in his own filth. Forced to eat whatever scraps they tossed down to him. No one spoke to him. He had no guards. None were necessary. He was trapped, and they knew it. He rarely even heard the sound of a human voice for days on end. He almost came to welcome those times when his captors threw down a ladder and brought him up for "questioning."

Almost.

The bright blazing pain seared through him again. Breaking his fingers, slowly, one by one. Ripping out his fingernails. Flailing his back with leather cords that cut through his flesh to the bone.

A shudder ran through him. He bit his tongue, tasted blood and bile that surged up from his clenching stomach. Sweat trickled down his face.

"I'm sorry, Gerard!" he gasped. "I'm sorry!"

Catching hold of Tasslehoff by the scruff of his neck, Palin lifted the kender and tossed him bodily onto the griffon's back. "Hold on tightly!" he ordered the kender.

"I think I'm going to throw up," Tas cried, squirming. "Let's wait for Gerard!"

Palin had no time for any kender ploys. "Leave at once!" he ordered the griffon. Palin pulled himself into the saddle that was strapped onto the griffon's back, between the feathery wings. "The Knights of Neraka surround us. Our guard is holding them off, but I doubt he can last for long."

The griffon glared back at the mage with bright, black eyes.

"Do we leave him behind, then?" the griffon asked.

"Yes," said Palin evenly. "We leave him behind."

The griffon did not argue. He had his orders. The strange habits of humans were not his concern. The beast lifted his great wings and leaped into the air, his powerful lion legs driving into the ground. He circled the clearing, striving to gain altitude and avoid the trees. Palin peered down, trying to find Gerard. The sun had cleared the horizon, was burning away the mists and lighting the shadows. Palin could see flashes of steel and hear ringing blows.

Miraculously, the Knight was still alive.

Palin turned away. He faced into the rushing wind. The sun vanished suddenly, overtaken by huge, rolling gray storm clouds that boiled up over the horizon. Lightning flickered amid the churning clouds. Thunder rumbled. A chill wind, blowing from the storm, cooled the sweat that had drenched his robes and left his hair wringing wet. He shivered slightly and drew his dark cloak close around him. He did not look back again.

The griffon rose high above the trees. Feeling the air currents beneath his wings, the beast soared into the blue sky.

"Palin!" Tasslehoff cried, tugging urgently on the back of his robes. "There's something flying behind us!"

Palin twisted to look.

The green dragon was distant, but it was moving at great speed, its wings slicing the air, its clawed feet pressed up against its body, its green tail streaming out behind. It was not Beryl. One of her minions, out doing her bidding.

Of course. She would not trust the Knights of Neraka to bring her this prize. She would send one of her own kind to fetch it. He leaned over the griffon's shoulder.

"A dragon!" he shouted. "East of us!"

"I see it!" the griffon snarled.

Palin shaded his eyes to view the dragon, trying not to blink in case he should miss a single beat of the immense wings.

"The dragon has spotted us," he reported. "It is coming straight for us."

"Hang on!" The griffon veered sharply, made a steep, banking turn. "I'm going to fly into the storm. The ride will be rough!"

Tall, spiring clouds formed a wall of gray and purple-black on the horizon. The clouds had the look of a fortress, massive and impenetrable. Lightning flared from breaks in the clouds, like torchlight through windows. Thunder rolled and boomed.

"I do not like the looks of that storm!" Palin cried out to the griffon.

"Do you like the insides of the dragon's belly better?" the griffon demanded. "The beast gains on us. We cannot outfly it."

Palin looked back, hoping that the griffon might have misjudged. Huge wings beat the air, the dragon's jaws parted. Palin met the dragon's eyes, saw the single-minded purpose in them, saw them intent on him.

Grasping the reins with one hand and taking firm hold of a shouting Tas with the other, Palin bent low over the griffon's neck, keeping his head and body down so that the rushing wind did not blow him off the griffon's back. The first few drops of rain pelted his face, stinging.

The clouds rose to immense heights, towering spires of lightning-shot gray-black, taller than the mighty fortress of Pax Tharkas. Palin looked up in awe, his head bent so that his neck ached and still he could not see the top. The griffon swooped nearer. Tasslehoff was still shouting something, but the wind took his words and whipped them away behind him, as it whipped his topknot.

Palin looked back. The dragon was almost on them. The claws of the dragon twitched now in anticipation of the capture. She would breathe her lethal gas on them, then seize them all three in one of her huge clawed feet and hurl them to the ground. With luck, the fall would kill them. The dragon would devour the griffon and then, at her leisure, she would rip their bodies apart, searching for the device.

Palin averted his eyes, stared ahead into the storm and urged the griffon to fly faster.

The cloud fortress rose before them. A flash of lightning blinded him. Thunder rolled, sounding like enormous cables turning a gigantic cog wheel. A solid bank of clouds suddenly parted, revealing a dark, lightning-lit hallway curtained by driving rain.

The griffon plunged into the cloud bank. Rain lashed at them in stinging torrents, deluged them. Wiping the water from his eyes, Palin stared in awe. Row after row of columns of gray cloud rose from a mottled gray floor to support a ceiling of boiling black.

Clouds shrouded them, wrapped around them. Palin could see nothing for the woolly grayness. He could not even see the griffon's head. Lightning sizzled near him. He could smell the brimstone, thunder crashed, nearly stopping his heart.

The griffon flew a zigzag course among the columns, soaring up and diving down, rounding and circling, then doubling back. Sheets of rain hung like silver tapestries, drenching them as they flew beneath. Palin could not see the dragon, though he could hear the discordant horn blast of its frustration as it tried desperately to find them.

The griffon left the cavernous halls of the fortress of storm clouds and flew out into the sunshine. Palin looked back, waited tensely for the dragon to appear. The griffon chortled, pleased. The dragon was lost somewhere in the storm clouds.

Palin told himself that he'd had no choice in the matter, he had acted logically in escaping. He had to protect the magical artifact. Gerard had practically ordered the mage to leave. If he had stayed, he could have accomplished nothing. They would have all died, and the artifact would have been in Beryl's possession.

The artifact was safe. Gerard was either dead or a prisoner. There was nothing that could be done to save him now.

"Best to forget it," Palin said to himself. "Put it out of my mind. What's done is done and can't be undone."

He dropped remorse and guilt into a dark pit, a deep pit in his soul and covered them with the iron grating of necessity.

"Sir," reported Medan's subcommander, "the Knight is attacking—alone. The magic-user and the kender are escaping. What are your orders?"

"Attacking alone. So he is," Medan replied, astonished.

The Solamnic came crashing through the underbrush, brandishing his sword and shouting the Solamnic battle-cry, a cry Marshal Medan had not heard in many years. The sight took the marshal back to the days when knights in shining silver and gleaming black clashed headlong on the field of battle; when champions came forward to duel to the death while armies looked on, their fates in the hands of heroes; when combatants saluted each other with honor before commencing with the deadly business at hand.

Here was Medan, crouched in a bush, safely ensconced behind a large tree stump, taking potshots at a washed-up mage and a kender.

"Can I sink any lower?" he muttered to himself.

The archer was drawing his bow. Having lost sight of the mage, he shifted his aim to the Knight, going for the legs, hoping for a crippling shot.

"Belay that," Medan snapped, resting his hand on the bowman's arm.

The subcommander looked around. "Sir? Your orders?"

The Solamnic was closing in. The magic-user and the kender were out of range, lost in the trees and the mists.

"Sir, should we pursue them?" the subcommander asked.

"No," Medan answered and saw a look of amazement cross the man's face.

"But our orders," he ventured.

"I know our orders," Medan snapped. "Do you want to be remembered in song as the Knight who slew a kender and a broken-down old mage, or as a Knight who fought a battle with an equal?"

The subcommander evidently did not want to be remembered in song. "But our orders," he persisted.

Damn the man for a thick-headed lout! Medan glowered at him.

"You *have* your orders, Subcommander. Don't make me repeat them."

The forest grew dark again. The sun had risen only to have its warmth and light cut off by storm clouds. Thunder rumbled in the distance, a few drops of rain pelted down. The kender and the mage had disappeared. They were on the back of the griffon and heading away from Qualinesti. Away from Laurana. Now, with luck, he could shield her from any involvement with the mage.

"Go meet the Knight," Medan said, waving his hand. "He challenges you to combat. Fight him."

The subcommander rose from his place, sword drawn. The archer dropped his bow. He held a dagger in his hand, ready to strike from behind while the subcommander attacked from the front.

"Single combat," Medan added, holding the bowman back. "Face him one on one, Subcommander."

"Sir?" The man was incredulous. He looked back to see if the marshal was joking.

What had the subcommander been before he became a

Knight? Sell-sword? Thief? Thug? Well, this day, he would have a lesson in honor.

"You heard me," Medan said.

The subcommander exchanged dour glances with his fellow, then walked forward without enthusiasm to meet the Solamnic's crashing charge. Medan rose to his feet. Crossing his arms over his chest, he leaned back against one of the white boulders to watch the encounter.

The subcommander was a powerfully built man with a bull neck, thick shoulders and muscular arms. He was accustomed to relying on his strength and low cunning in battle, hacking and slashing at his opponent until either a lucky cut or sheer brute force wore the enemy down.

The subcommander charged head-on like a snorting bison, swinging his sword with murderous strength. The Solamnic parried the blow, met it with such force that sparks glittered on the steel blades. The subcommander held on, swords locked, trying to drive his opponent into the ground. The Solamnic was no match for such strength. He recognized this and changed tactics. He staggered backward, leaving himself temptingly open.

The subcommander fell for the ruse. He leaped to the attack, slashing with his blade, thinking to make a quick kill. He managed to wound the knight in the left upper arm, cutting through the leather armor to open a great bleeding gash.

The Solamnic took the blow and never winced. He held his ground, watched for his opportunity and coolly drove his sword into the subcommander's belly.

The subcommander dropped his sword and doubled over with a horrible, gurgling cry, clutching himself, trying to hold his insides in. The Solamnic yanked his sword free. Blood gushed from the man's mouth. He toppled over.

Before Medan could stop him, the bowman had lifted his bow, shot an arrow at the Solamnic. The arrow plunged deep into the Knight's thigh. He cried out in agony, stumbled, off-balance.

"You cowardly bastard!" Medan swore. Snatching the bow, he slammed it against the rock, smashing it.

The archer then drew his sword and ran to engage the wounded Solamnic. Medan considered halting the battle, but he was interested to see how the Solamnic handled this new challenge. He watched dispassionately, glorying in a battle-to-the-death contest such as he had not witnessed in years.

The archer was a shorter, lighter man, a cagier fighter than the subcommander. He took his time, testing his opponent with jabbing strikes of his short sword, searching for weaknesses, wearing him down. He caught the Solamnic a glancing blow to the face beneath the raised visor. The wound was not serious, but blood poured from it, running into the Solamnic's eye, partially blinding him. The Solamnic blinked the blood out of his eye and fought on. Crippled and bleeding, he grimaced every time he was forced to put weight on his leg. The arrow remained lodged in his thigh. He had not had time to yank it out. Now he was on the offensive. He had to end this fight soon, or he would not have any strength to pursue it.

Lightning flashed. The rain fell harder. The men struggled together over the corpse of the subcommander. The Solamnic jabbed and slashed, his sword seeming to be everywhere like a striking snake. Now it was the archer who was hard-pressed. He had all he could do to keep that snake's fang from biting.

"Well struck, Solamnic," Medan said softly more than once, watching with pleasure the sight of such skill, such excellent training.

The archer slipped in the rain-wet grass. The Solamnic lunged forward on his wounded leg and drove his sword into the man's breast. The archer fell, and so did the Solamnic, collapsing on his knees onto the forest floor, gasping for breath.

Medan left his boulder, walked out into the open. The

Solamnic, hearing him coming, staggered to his feet with a wrenching cry of pain. His wounded leg gave out beneath him. Limping, the Solamnic placed his back against a tree trunk to provide stability and raised his sword. He looked at death. He knew he could not win this last battle, but at least he would die upright, not on his knees.

"I thought the flame had gone out in the hearts of the Knighthood, but it lives on in one man seemingly," said Medan, facing the Solamnic. The marshal rested his hand on the hilt of his sword, but he did not draw it.

The Solamnic's face was a mask of blood. Eyes of a startling, arresting blue color regarded Medan without hope, but without fear.

He waited for Medan to strike.

The marshal stood in the mud and the rain, straddling the bodies of his two dead subordinates, and waited.

The Solamnic's defiance began to waver. He realized suddenly what Medan was doing, realized that he was waiting for the Solamnic to collapse, waiting to capture him alive.

"Fight, damn you!" The Solamnic lurched forward, lashed out with his sword.

Medan stepped to one side.

The Solamnic forgot, put his weight on his bad leg. The leg gave way. He lost his balance, fell to the forest floor. Even then, he made one last opportunity to try to struggle to his feet, but he was too weak. He had lost too much blood. His eyes closed. He lay face down in the muck alongside the bodies of his foes.

Medan rolled the Knight over. Placing his hand on the Knight's thigh for leverage, the marshal took hold of the arrow and yanked it out. The Knight groaned with the pain, but did not regain consciousness. Medan took off his cloak, cut the material into strips with his sword, and made a battlefield tourniquet to staunch the bleeding. He then wrapped the Knight warmly in what remained of the cloak.

"You have lost a lot of blood," Medan said, returning his sword to its sheath, "but you are young and strong. We will see what the healers can do for you."

Rounding up the two horses of his subordinates, Medan threw the bodies unceremoniously over their saddles, tied them securely. Then the marshal whistled to his own horse. The animal came trotting over in response to his master's summons to stand quietly at Medan's side.

Medan lifted the Solamnic in his arms, eased the wounded Knight into the saddle. He examined the wound, was pleased to see that the tourniquet had stopped the flow of blood. He relaxed the tourniquet a notch, not wanting to cut off the blood flow to the leg completely, then climbed into the saddle. Seating himself behind the injured Knight, Medan put his arm around the man and held him gently but firmly in the saddle. He took hold of the reins of the other two horses and, leading them behind, began the long ride back to Qualinost.

21

The Device of Time Journeying

he wild and terrifying flight from the dragon ended in blue sky and sunshine. The flight took longer than usual, for the griffon had been blown off course by the storm. The beast made landfall somewhere in the wilds of the Kharolis Mountains to feed on a deer, a delay Palin chafed at, but all his pleas for haste went unheeded. After dining, the griffon took a nap, while Palin paced back and forth, keeping a firm grip on Tasslehoff. When night fell, the creature stated that it would not fly after dark. The griffon and Tasslehoff slept. Palin sat fuming and waiting for the sun to rise.

They continued their journey the next day. The griffon landed Palin and Tasslehoff at midmorning in an empty field not far from what had once been the Academy of Sorcery. The stone walls of the academy still stood, but they were black and crumbling. The roof was a skeleton of charred beams. The tower that had once been a symbol of hope to the world, hope that magic had returned, was nothing but a pile of rubble, demolished by the blast that had torn out its heart.

Palin had once planned to rebuild the academy, if for no

other reason than to show his defiance for Beryl. When he began to lose the magic, began to feel it slip away from him like water falling from cupped palms, he discarded the idea. It was a waste of time and effort. Better far to spend his energies searching for artifacts of the Fourth Age, artifacts that still held the magic inside and could still be used by those who knew how.

"What is that place?" Tasslehoff asked, sliding down from the griffon's back. He stared with interest at the destroyed walls with their gaping, empty windows. "And what happened to it?"

"Nothing. Never mind," Palin said, not wanting to enter into long explanations involving the death of a dream. "Come along. We have no time to was—"

"Look!" Tas cried, pointing. "Someone's walking around there. I'm going to go look!"

He was off, his bright shirt tail fluttering behind him, his topknot bouncing with glee.

"Come back—" Palin began and then realized he might as well save his breath.

Tas was right. Someone was indeed walking around the ruins of the academy and Palin wondered who it might be. The residents of Solace considered the place cursed and never went there for any reason. The person was wearing long robes; Palin caught a glimpse of crimson fabric beneath a gold-trimmed beige cloak. This could, of course, be some former student, come back to gaze in nostalgia at his wrecked place of learning, but Palin doubted it. By the graceful walk and the rich dress, he realized that this was Jenna.

Mistress Jenna of Palanthas had been a powerful red-robed wizardess in the days before the Chaos War. An extraordinarily beautiful woman, she was reputed to have been the lover of Dalamar the Dark, pupil of Raistlin Majere and once Master of the Tower of High Sorcery at Palanthas. Jenna had earned her living by running a mageware shop in

Palanthas. Her shop had done moderately well during the Fourth Age, when magic had been a gift granted to people by the three gods, Solinari, Lunitari, and Nuitari. She carried the usual assorted spell components: bat guano, butterfly wings, sulphur, rose leaves (whole and crushed), spider eggs, and so forth. She had a good supply of potions and was known to have the best collection of spell scrolls and books outside the Tower of Wayreth, all to be had for a price. She was particularly renowned for her collection of magical artifacts: rings, bracers, daggers, swords, pendants, charms, amulets. These were the artifacts on display. She had other, more potent, more dangerous, more powerful artifacts, which she kept hidden away, to be shown only to serious customers and that by appointment.

When the Chaos War came, Jenna had joined Dalamar and a white-robed mage on a perilous mission to help defeat the rampaging Father of the Gods. She never spoke of what befell them on that terrible journey. All Palin knew was that on their return Dalamar had been critically wounded. He had lain near death in his tower for many long weeks.

Jenna had been his constant companion and nurse until the day when she walked out of the tower, never to return. For on that night, the Tower of High Sorcery at Palanthas was destroyed in a magical blast. No one ever saw Dalamar again. After many years had passed and he had not returned, the Conclave pronounced him officially dead. Mistress Jenna reopened her mageware shop and discovered that she was sitting on a treasure trove.

With the magic of the gods vanished, desperate mages had sought ways to hold onto their power. They discovered that magical artifacts crafted in the Fourth Age retained their power. The only drawback was that sometimes this power was erratic, did not act as expected. A magical sword, once an artifact of good, suddenly began to slay those it was meant to protect. A ring of invisibility failed its owner at a critical moment, landing the thief five years in a Sanction dungeon. No one knew the reason. Some said the unreliability was due to the fact that the gods no longer had influence over them, others said that it had nothing to do with the gods. Artifacts were always known to be tricky objects to handle.

Buyers were more than willing to take the risk, however, and the demand for Fourth Age artifacts soared higher than a gnomish steam-driven mechanical flapjack-flipping device. Mistress Jenna's prices rose to match. She was now, at the age of sixty-something, one of the wealthiest women in Ansalon. Still beautiful, though her beauty had ripened, she had retained her influence and power even under the rule of the Knights of Neraka, whose commanders found her charming, fascinating, mysterious, and accommodating. She paid no attention to those who termed her "collaborator." Jenna had long been accustomed to playing both ends against the middle, knew how to fool the middle and the ends into thinking each was getting the best of the bargain.

Mistress Jenna was also the acknowledged expert in Ansalon on Fourth Age magical artifacts.

Palin could not go immediately to greet her. The griffon complained again of hunger. The beast was, in fact, eyeing the kender avariciously, obviously considering Tas a toothsome morsel. Palin promised he would send back a haunch of venison. This satisfied the griffon, who began to preen herself, pleased at having reached her destination.

Palin went off in pursuit of Tasslehoff, who was happily picking his way through the rubble, turning over rocks to see what was underneath and exclaiming over every find.

Jenna had been strolling around the grounds of the ruined academy. Curious herself to see what the kender had discovered, she walked over to look.

Tas lifted his head, stared at the mage for long moments and then, with a glad cry, he jumped up and ran straight for her with arms outstretched.

Jenna quickly extended both hands, palms outward. Light flashed from one of several rings she wore, and Tas stumbled backward as if he'd run headlong into a brick wall.

"Keep your distance, Kender," she said calmly.

"But, Jenna!" Tas cried, rubbing his nose and eyeing the rings with interest, "don't you recognize me? It's Tasslehoff! Tasslehoff Burrfoot. We met in Palanthas during the Chaos War, only a few days ago for me, but I guess for you it's been years and years 'cause you're a lot older now. A *lot* older," he added with emphasis. "I came to your mageware shop and . . ." Tas prattled on.

Jenna kept her hands stretched outward, regarding the kender with amusement—a pleasant distraction. She obviously did not believe a word he was saying.

Hearing footsteps crunch on rock, Jenna turned her head quickly. "Palin!" She smiled to see him.

"Jenna." He bowed in respect. "I am pleased you could find the time to come."

"My dear, if what you intimated to me is true, I would not have missed this for all the treasure in Istar. You will excuse me if I do not shake hands, but I am keeping this kender at bay."

"How was your journey?"

"Long." She rolled her eyes. "My ring of teleportation"—she indicated a large ring of sparkling amethyst set in silver that she wore on her thumb—"used to take me from one end of the continent to another in a flash. Now it takes me two days to travel from Palanthas to Solace."

"And what are you doing here at the academy?" Palin asked, glancing around. "If you're looking for artifacts, don't bother. We salvaged what we could."

Jenna shook her head. "No, I was just taking a walk. I stopped by your house," she added with an arch glance. "Your wife was there, and she was not overly pleased to see me. Finding the reception a bit chilly indoors, I decided I would prefer a walk in the sunshine." She looked around in her turn, shook her head sadly. "I had not been here since the destruction. They did a thorough job. You're not going to rebuild?"

"Why should I?" Palin shrugged. His tone was bitter. "What use does anyone have for an Academy of Sorcery if there is no more sorcery? Tas," he said abruptly, "Usha is at home. Why don't you go surprise her?" Turning, he pointed to a large house which could barely be seen for the tall trees surrounding it. "There is our house—"

"I know!" Tasslehoff said excitedly. "I was there the first time I went to Caramon's funeral. Does Usha paint wonderful pictures like she did then?"

"Why don't you go ask her yourself?" Palin said irritably.

Tas glanced at the rubble and appeared undecided.

"Usha would be very hurt if you didn't go to see her," Palin added.

"Yes, you're right," Tas replied, making up his mind. "I wouldn't do anything to hurt her. We are *great* friends. Besides, I can always come back here later. Good-bye, Jenna!" He started to extend his hand, thought better of it. "And thanks for magicking me. That hasn't happened to me in a long time. I really enjoyed it."

"Odd little fellow," remarked Jenna, gazing after Tas, who was running pell-mell down the hillside. "He looks and talks very much like the kender I knew as Tasslehoff Burrfoot. One would almost think he *is* Tasslehoff."

"He is," said Palin.

Jenna shifted her gaze to him. "Oh, come now." She scrutinized him more closely. "By the lost gods, I believe that you are serious. Tasslehoff Burrfoot died—"

"I know!" Palin said impatiently. "Thirty-odd years ago. Or thereabouts. I'm sorry, Jenna." He sighed. "It's been a long night. Beryl found out about the artifact. We were ambushed by Neraka Knights. The kender and I barely escaped with our lives, and the Solamnic who brought Tas to me didn't escape at all. Then we were attacked in the air by one of Beryl's greens. We escaped the dragon only by making a harrowing flight into a thunderstorm."

"You should get some sleep," Jenna advised, regarding him with concern.

"I can't sleep," Palin returned, rubbing his eyes, which were red-rimmed and burning. "My thoughts are in turmoil, they give me no rest. We need to talk!" he added in a kind of frantic desperation.

"That's why I am here, my friend," Jenna said. "But you should at least eat something. Let us go to your house and drink a glass of wine. Say hello to your wife, who has just returned herself from what I gather was a very harrowing journey herself."

Palin grew calmer. He smiled at her wanly. "Yes, you are right, as usual. It's just . . ." He paused, thinking what to say and how to say it. "That is the real Tasslehoff, Jenna. I'm convinced of it. And he has been to a future that is not ours, a future in which the great dragons do not exist. A future where the world is at peace. He has brought with him the device he used to travel to that future."

Jenna gazed at him searchingly and intently. Seeing that he was in earnest, utterly serious, her eyes darkened, narrowed with interest.

"Yes," she said at last. "We do need to talk." She took his arm, they walked side by side.

"Tell me everything, Palin," she said.

The Majeres' house was a large structure that had once belonged to a Master Theobald, the man who had taught Raistlin Majere magic. Caramon had purchased the house at the master's death, in memory of his brother, and had given the house as gift to Palin and Usha when they were married. Here their children had been born and grown up, going off on adventures of their own. Palin had transformed the classroom where the young Raistlin had once droned through his lessons into a studio for his wife, a portrait painter of some renown throughout Solamnia and Abanasinia. He continued to use the master's old laboratory for his studies.

Tasslehoff had spoken truly when he told Palin that he remembered the house from Caramon's first funeral. He did remember the house—*it* hadn't changed. But Palin certainly had.

"I suppose having your fingers all mangled would give you a mangled view of life," Tas was saying to Usha as he sat with her in the kitchen, eating a large bowl of oatmeal. "That must be the reason, because at Caramon's first funeral, Palin's fingers were just fine and so was he. He was cheerful and happy. Well, maybe not happy, because poor Caramon had just died and no one could feel truly happy. But Palin was happy underneath. So that when he was over being sad, I knew he would be happy again. But now he's terribly unhappy, so unhappy that he can't even be sad."

"I . . . I suppose so," Usha murmured.

The kitchen was a large one with a high, beamed ceiling and an enormous stone fireplace, charred and blackened with years of use. A pot hung from a black chain in the center of the fireplace. Usha sat across from the kender at a large, butcher-block table used for chopping the heads off chickens and such, or so Tas supposed. Right now it was washed clean, no headless chickens lying about. But then it was only mid-morning. Dinnertime was a long way off.

Usha was staring at him just like all the rest of them—as if he'd grown two heads or maybe was headless altogether, like the chickens. She had been staring at him that way ever since his arrival, when he had thrown open the front door (remembering to knock afterward), and cried out, "Usha! It's me, Tas! I haven't been stepped on by the giant yet!"

Usha Majere had been a lovely young woman. Age had

enhanced her good looks, although, Tas thought, she doesn't have quite the same prettiness she had when I came back here for Caramon's funeral the first time. Her hair shone with the same silver sheen, her eyes glinted with the same gold, but the gold lacked warmth, the silver was dull and tarnished. She looked faded and tired.

She's unhappy, too, Tas realized suddenly. It must be catching. Like measles.

"That will be Palin now!" Usha said, hearing the front door open and close. She sounded relieved.

"And Jenna," Tas mumbled, his mouth full.

"Yes. Jenna," Usha repeated, her voice cool. "You can stay here, if you like, er . . . Tas. Finish your oatmeal. There's more in the pot."

She rose to her feet and left the kitchen. The door swung shut behind her. Tas ate his oatmeal and eavesdropped with interest on the conversation being held in the entry hall. Ordinarily he would not have listened in on someone else's conversation, because that wasn't polite, but they were talking about him when he wasn't there, which wasn't polite, either, and so he felt justified.

Besides, Tas was starting not to like Palin very much. The kender felt badly about this, but he couldn't help the feeling. He'd spent a considerable amount of time with the mage when they were at Laurana's, relating over and over everything he could remember about Caramon's first funeral. The kender added the usual embellishments, of course, without which no kender tale is considered complete. Unfortunately, instead of entertaining Palin, these embellishments—which shifted from story to story—appeared to irritate him to no end. Palin had a way of looking at him—Tas—not as if he had two heads, but more as if the mage would like to rip off the kender's single head and open it up to see what was inside.

"Not even Raistlin looked at me like that," Tas said to himself, scraping the oatmeal out of the bowl with his finger. "He looked at me as if he'd like to kill me sometimes, but never like he wanted to turn me inside out first."

Usha's voice came floating through the door ". . . *claims* he's Tasslehoff . . ."

"He *is* Tasslehoff, my dear," Palin returned. "You know Mistress Jenna, I believe, Usha? Mistress Jenna will be spending a few days with us. Will you make up the guest room?"

There was a silence that sounded as if it had been mashed through a sieve, then Usha's voice, cold as the oatmeal had grown by now. "Palin, may I see you in the kitchen?"

Palin's voice, colder than the oatmeal. "Please excuse us, Mistress Jenna."

Tasslehoff sighed and, thinking he should look as if he hadn't been listening, began to hum loudly to himself and started to rummage through the pantry, searching for something else to eat.

Fortunately, neither Palin nor Usha paid any attention to the kender at all, except for Palin to snap at him to stop that infernal racket.

"What is *she* doing here?" Usha demanded, her hands on her hips.

"We have important matters to discuss," Palin answered evasively.

Usha fixed him with a look. "Palin, you promised me! This trip to Qualinesti would be your last! You know how dangerous this search for artifacts has become—"

"Yes, my dear, I do know," Palin interrupted, his tone cool. "That is why I think it would be best if you left Solace."

"Left!" Usha repeated, astonished. "I've just come back home after being away for three months! Your sister and I were virtual prisoners in Haven. Did you know that?"

"Yes, I knew—"

"You knew! And you didn't say anything? You weren't worried? You didn't ask how we escaped—"

"My dear, I haven't had time—"

"We couldn't even come back for your father's funeral!" Usha continued. "We were permitted to leave only because I agreed to paint a portrait of the magistrate's wife. She has a face that would have been ugly on a hobgoblin. Now you want me to leave again."

"It's for your own safety."

"What about your safety?" she demanded.

"I can take care of myself."

"Can you, Palin?" Usha asked. Her voice was suddenly gentle. She reached out, tried to take hold of his hands in her own.

"Yes," he snapped and snatched his crippled hands away, folded them in the sleeves of his robes.

Tasslehoff, feeling extremely uncomfortable, wished he could crawl inside the pantry and shut the door. Unfortunately, there was no room, not even after he'd cleared out a space by stashing several interesting-looking objects in his pockets.

"Very well, if that's how you feel. I'm not to touch you apparently"—Usha folded her arms across her chest—"but I do think you owe me an explanation. What is going on? Why did you send this kender here claiming to be Tas! What are you up to?"

"We're keeping Mistress Jenna waiting—"

"I'm sure she won't mind. I am your wife, in case you've forgotten!" Usha tossed her silver hair. "I wouldn't be surprised if you had. We never see each other anymore."

"Don't start that again!" he shouted angrily and turned away toward the door.

"Palin!" Usha reached out her hand impulsively. "I love you! I want to help you!"

"You can't help me!" he cried, rounding on her. "No one can." He lifted his hands, held them to the light, the fingers crooked and turned inward like the claws of a bird. "No one can," he repeated.

More silence. Tas recalled the time he'd been a prisoner in the Abyss. He had felt very alone then, desolate and unhappy. Strangely, he was feeling the same now sitting in his friends' kitchen. He lacked the spirit to even give the lock on the silver cabinet a second glance.

"I am sorry, Usha," Palin said stiffly. "You are right. You deserve an explanation. This kender *is* Tasslehoff."

Usha shook her head.

"Do you remember my father telling the story about how he and Tas traveled back in time?" Palin continued.

"Yes," she answered, her voice tight.

"They did so by means of a magical artifact. Tasslehoff used that same device to jump forward in time so he could speak at Caramon's funeral. He was here once, but he over-shot the mark. He arrived too late. The funeral was over, so he came back a second time. In this instance, he was on time. Only everything was different. The other future he saw was a future of hope and happiness. The gods had not gone away. I was head of the Order of White Robes. The elven kingdoms were united—"

"And you *believe* all this?" Usha asked, amazed.

"I do," Palin said stubbornly. "I believe it because I have seen the device, Usha. I've held it in my hands. I've felt its power. That's why Mistress Jenna is here. I need her advice. And that's why it's not safe for you to stay in Solace. The dragon knows I have the device. I'm not sure how she found out, but I fear someone in Laurana's household may be a trai-tor. If so, Beryl may already be aware that I have brought the device to Solace. She'll send her people to try to—"

"You're going to use it!" Usha gasped, pointed her finger at Palin.

He made no response

"I know you, Palin Majere," Usha said. "You're planning to use the device yourself! To try to go back in time and . . . and . . . who knows what else!"

"I've only been thinking about it," he returned, uneasily. "I haven't made up my mind. That's why I needed to speak to Mistress Jenna."

"You planned to speak to her and not to me? Your wife?"

"I was going to tell you," Palin said.

"*Tell* me? Not ask me? Not ask me what I thought about this insanity? Not ask my opinion? No." She answered her own question. "You intend to do this whether I want you to or not. No matter how dangerous. No matter that you could be killed!"

"Usha," he said, after a moment, "it's so very important. The magic . . . if I could . . ." He shook his head, unable to explain. His voice trailed away.

"The magic is dead, Palin," Usha cried, her voice choked with tears. "Good riddance, I say. What did it ever do for you? Nothing except destroy you and ruin our marriage."

He reached out his hand, but this time she was the one who pulled away. "I'm going to the Inn," she said, not looking at him. "Let me know if . . . if you want me to come home."

Turning away from him, she walked over to Tas. Usha looked him over long and hard. "You really are Tas, aren't you?" she said, awed.

"Yes, Usha," Tas said miserably. "But I wish right now I wasn't."

She leaned down, kissed him on the forehead. He could see the unshed tears shimmer in her golden eyes.

"Good-bye, Tas. It was nice to see you again."

"I'm sorry, Usha," he wailed. "I didn't mean to make a mess of things. I just came back to speak at Caramon's funeral."

"It's not your fault, Tas. Things were a mess long before you came."

Usha left the kitchen, walking past Palin without glancing at him. He stood where she had left him, staring at nothing, his expression dark, his face pale. Tas heard Usha say something to

Jenna, something he couldn't quite catch. He heard Jenna respond, but he couldn't catch that either. Usha left the house. The front door shut with a bang. The house was silent, except for Jenna's restive pacing. Still Palin did not move.

Tas reached into several of his pockets and at last located the device. He removed some string that had become tangled around it, dusted off the lint from his pocket and some crumbs from a biscuit he'd meant to eat two days ago.

"Here, Palin," Tas said, holding out the device. "You can have it."

Palin stared at him, uncomprehending.

"Go on," Tas said, pushing the device at him. "If you want to use it, like Usha said you did, I'll let you. Especially if you can go back and make things the way they're supposed to be. That's what you're thinking, isn't it? Here," Tas said insistently and he gave the device a shake, which caused its jewels to wink.

"Take it!" Jenna said.

Tas was startled. He had been so intent on Palin, he hadn't heard Jenna come into the kitchen. She stood in the doorway, the door partially ajar.

"Take it!" she repeated urgently. "Palin, you were worried about overcoming the geas laid on the device, the spell that would always return the device to the person who uses it. Such a geas would protect the owner if the device was ever stolen or lost, but if the device is *freely given*, this act may break the geas!"

"I don't know anything about gewgaws," said Tas, "but I know that I'll let you use the device if you want to."

Palin lowered his head. His gray hair fell forward, covering his face, but not before Tas had seen the pain that contorted and twisted it into a face he did not recognize. Reaching out, Palin took hold of the device, his crooked fingers wrapping around it lovingly.

Tas watched the device go with something akin to relief.

Whenever the device was in his possession, he could always hear Fizban's voice reminding him in irritable tones that he wasn't supposed to be off having adventures. He was supposed to go back to his own time. And while this adventure certainly left a lot to be desired as far as adventures go—what with being cursed and having to see Usha cry and discovering that he didn't like Palin anymore—Tas was starting to think that even a bad adventure was probably better than being stepped on by a giant.

"I can tell you how it works," Tas offered.

Palin placed the device on the kitchen table. He sat there staring at it, not saying a word.

"There's a rhyme that goes with it and stuff you have to do to it," Tas added, "but it's pretty easy to learn. Fizban said I had to know it so that I could recite it standing on my head and I could, so I'm sure you probably can, too."

Palin was only half-listening. He looked up at Jenna. "What do you think?"

"It is the Device of Time Journeying," she said. "I saw it at the Tower of High Sorcery when your father brought it to Dalamar for safekeeping. He studied it, of course. I believe he had some of your uncle's notes regarding it. He never used it that I know of, but he has more knowledge about it than anyone now living. I never heard that the device went missing. However, as I recall, we *did* find Tasslehoff in the Tower right before the Chaos War. He might have taken it then."

Jenna eyed the kender quite sternly.

"I did not take it!" Tas said, insulted. "Fizban gave it to me! He told me—"

"Hush, Tas." Palin leaned across the table, lowered his voice. "I don't suppose there is any way you could contact Dalamar."

"I do not practice necromancy," Jenna returned coolly.

Palin's eyes narrowed. "Come now, you don't believe he's dead. Do you?"

Jenna relaxed back in her chair. "Perhaps I don't. But he might as well be. I have not heard a word from him in more than thirty years. I don't know where he may have gone."

Palin looked dubious, as if he did not quite believe her. Jenna spread her bejeweled hands on the table's surface, fingers apart. "Listen to me, Palin. You do not know him. No one knows him as I know him. You did not see him at the end, when he came back from the Chaos War. I did. I was with him. Day and night. I nursed him to health. If you could call it that."

She sat back, her expression dark and frowning.

"I am sorry if I offended you," Palin said. "I never heard. . . . You never told me."

"It is not something I enjoy talking about," Jenna said tersely. "You know that Dalamar was gravely wounded during our battle against Chaos. I brought him back to the Tower. For weeks he hovered between the realm of the living and that of the dead. I left my home and my shop and moved into the Tower to care for him. He survived. But the loss of the gods, the loss of godly magic, was a terrible blow, one from which he never truly recovered. He changed, Palin. Do you remember how he used to be?"

"I didn't know him very well. He supervised my Test in the Tower, the Test during which my Uncle Raistlin took him by surprise, turning what Dalamar had intended as illusion into reality. I'll never forget the look on his face when he saw I had been given my uncle's staff." Palin sighed deeply, regretfully. The memories were sweet, yet painful. "All I remember of Dalamar is that I thought him sharp-tongued and sarcastic, self-centered and arrogant. I know that my father had a better opinion of him. My father said Dalamar was a very complicated man, whose loyalty was to magic, rather than to the Dark Queen. From what little I knew of Dalamar, I believe that to be true."

"He was excitable," Tas chimed in. "He used to get very

excited when I started to touch anything that belonged to him. Jumpy, too."

"Yes, he was all that. But he could also be charming, soft-spoken, wise . . ." Jenna smiled and sighed. "I loved him, Palin. I still do, I suppose. I have never met any other man to equal him." She was quiet a moment, then she shrugged and said, "But that was long ago."

"What happened between you two?" Palin asked.

She shook her head. "After his illness, he withdrew into himself, became sullen and silent, morose and isolated. I have never been a particularly patient person," Jenna admitted. "I couldn't stomach his self-pity and I told him so. We quarreled, I walked out, and that was the last I saw of him."

"I can understand how he felt," Palin said. "I know how lost I felt when I realized the gods were gone. Dalamar had practiced the arcane art far longer than I. He had sacrificed so much for it. He must have been devastated."

"We all were," Jenna said bluntly, "but we dealt with it. You went on with your life, and so did I. Dalamar could not. He fretted and fumed until I feared that his frustration would do what his wounds could not. I honestly thought he would die of it. He could not eat or sleep. He spent hours locked up in his laboratory searching desperately for what had been lost. He had the key to it, he once told me during one of the rare times he actually spoke to me. He said the key had come to him during his sickness. Now he had only to find the door. It's my belief," Jenna added wryly, "that he found it."

"So you do not think he destroyed himself when he destroyed the Tower," Palin said.

"The Tower's gone?" Tas was stunned. "That great big Tower of High Sorcery in Palanthas? What happened to it?"

"I am not even convinced he blew up the Tower," Jenna said, continuing the conversation as if the kender wasn't there. "Oh, I know what people say. That he destroyed the Tower for fear the dragon Khellendros would seize it and use its magic.

I saw the pile of rubble that was left. People found all sorts of magical artifacts in the ruins. I bought many of them and resold them later for five times what I paid for them. But I know something I've never told anyone. The truly valuable artifacts that were in the Tower were never found. Not a trace. The scrollbooks, the spellbooks, those belonging to Raistlin and Fistandantilus, Dalamar's own spellbooks—those were gone, too. People thought they were destroyed in the blast. If so," she added with fine irony, "the blast was extremely selective. It took only what was valuable and important, left the trinkets behind."

She eyed Palin speculatively. "Tell me, my friend, would you take this device to Dalamar if you had the chance?"

Palin stirred restlessly. "Probably not, now that I think of it. If he knew I had it, the device would not remain long in my possession."

"Do you truly intend to use it?" she asked.

"I don't know." Palin was evasive. "What do you think? Would it be dangerous?"

"Yes, very," she answered.

"But the kender used it—"

"*If* you believe him, he used it in his own time," she said. "And that was the time of the gods. The artifact is now in *this* time. You know as well as I do that the magic of the artifacts from the Fourth Age is erratic in nature. Some artifacts behave perfectly predictably and others go haywire."

"So I won't really find out until I try," Palin said. "What do you suppose *could* happen?"

"Who knows!" Jenna lifted her hands, the jewels on her fingers glittered. "The journey alone might kill you. You might be stranded back in time, unable to return. You might accidently do something to change the past and, in so doing, obliterate the present. You might blow up this house and everything around it for a twenty-mile radius. I would not risk it. Not for a kender tale."

"Yet I would like to go back to before the Chaos War. Go back simply to look. Perhaps I could see the moment where destiny veered off the path it should have taken. Then we would know how to steer it back on the right course."

Jenna snorted. "You speak of time as if it were a horse and cart. For all you know, this kender has made up this nonsensical story of a future in which the gods never left us. He is a kender, after all."

"But he is an unusual kender. My father believed him, and Caramon knew something about traveling through time."

"Your father also said the kender and the device were to be given to Dalamar," Jenna reminded him.

Palin frowned. "I think we have to find out the truth for ourselves," he argued. "I believe that it is worth the risk. Consider this, Jenna. If there is another future, a better future for our world, a future in which the gods did not depart, no price would be too great to pay for it."

"Even your life?" she asked.

"My life!" Palin was bitter. "Of what value is my life to me now? My wife is right. The old magic is gone, the new magic is dead. I am nothing without the magic!"

"I do not believe that the new magic is dead," Jenna said gravely. "Nor do I believe those who say that we 'used it all up.' Does one use up water? Does one use up air? The magic is a part of this world. We could not consume it."

"Then what has happened to it?" Palin demanded impatiently. "Why do our spells fail? Why do even simple spells require so much energy that one has to go to bed for a week after casting them?"

"Do you remember that old test they used to give us in school?" Jenna asked. "The one where they put an object on the table and tell you to move it without touching it. You do, and then they put the object on a table behind a brick wall and tell you to move it. Suddenly, it's much more difficult. Since you can't see the object, it's difficult to focus your magic on it. I feel the same when I try to cast a spell—as if something is in the way. A brick wall, if you will. Goldmoon told me her healers were experiencing similar feelings—"

"Goldmoon!" Tas cried eagerly. "Where is Goldmoon? If anyone could fix things around here, it's Goldmoon." He was on his feet, as if he would run out the door that instant. "She'll know what to do. Where is she?"

"Goldmoon? Who brought up Goldmoon? What does she have to do with anything?" Palin glowered at the kender. "Please sit down and be quiet! You've interrupted my thoughts!"

"I'd really like to see Goldmoon," Tas said, but he said it quietly, under his breath, so as not to disturb Palin.

The mage lifted the device carefully in his hand, turned it over, examined it, caressed it.

"Your wife was right," Jenna stated. "You're going to use the device, aren't you, Palin?"

"Yes, I am," he replied, closing his hands over it.

"No matter what I say?"

"No matter what anyone says." He glanced at her, appeared embarrassed. "Thank you for your help. I'm certain my sister can find you a room at the Inn. I'll send word."

"Did you really think I would leave and miss this?" Jenna asked, amused.

"It's dangerous. You said—"

"These days, walking across the street is dangerous." Jenna shrugged. "Besides, you will need a witness. Or at the very least," she added lightly, "you'll need someone to identify your body."

"Thank you very much," Palin said, but he managed a smile, the first Tas had seen the mage wear. Palin drew in a deep breath, let it out slowly. His hands holding the device trembled.

"When should we try this?" he asked

"No *time* like the present," Jenna said and grinned.

22

The Journey Back

nd that's the rhyme," said Tasslehoff. "Do you want
me to repeat it again?"

"No, I have it memorized," Palin said.

"Are you sure?" Tas was anxious. "You'll need to recite it
to return to this time. Unless you want to take me with you?"
he added excitedly. "Then I could bring us."

"I am quite sure I have the spell memorized," Palin said
firmly. And, indeed, the words were emblazoned in his mind.
It seemed to him that he could see their fiery images on the
backs of his eyes. "And, no, I'm *not* taking you with me. Someone needs to stay here and keep Mistress Jenna company."

"And to identify the body," Tas said, nodding and settling
down in his chair, kicking his feet against the rungs. "Sorry, I
forgot about that. I'll stay here. You won't be gone long
anyway. Unless you don't come back at all," he mentioned, as
an afterthought. Twisting in his chair, he looked at Jenna, who
had dragged her chair to a far corner in the kitchen. "Do you
really think he'll blow up?"

Palin carefully ignored the kender.

"I will chant the magic that activates the device. If the spell works, I believe that I will vanish from your sight. As the kender says, I should not be gone long. I do not plan to stay in the past. I am going to my father's first funeral where, hopefully, I will be able talk to Dalamar. Perhaps I'll even talk to myself." He smiled grimly. "I'll try to find out what went wrong—"

"Take no action, Palin," Jenna warned. "If you do find out anything useful, return and report. We will need to think long and hard before acting upon it."

"Who is 'we'?" Palin demanded, frowning.

"I suggest a gathering of the wise," Jenna said. "The elven king Gilthas, his mother Laurana, Goldmoon, Lady Crysania—"

"And while we are spreading the word of what we've found far and wide and waiting for all these people to come together, Beryl murders us and steals the device," Palin said acerbically. "She uses it, and we're all dead."

"Palin, you are talking about altering the past," Jenna said in stern rebuke. "We have no idea what the ramifications would be to those of us living in the present."

"I know," he said, after a moment. "I understand. I will return and report. But we must be prepared to act rapidly after that."

"We will. How long do you think you will be gone?"

"According to Tasslehoff, hundreds of days will pass for me for each second of time that passes for you. I estimate that I may be gone an hour or two marked by our time."

"Good fortune on your journey," Jenna said quietly. "Kender, come over here and stand beside me."

Palin took hold of the device, moved to the center of the kitchen. The jewels glinted and sparkled in the sunshine.

He closed his eyes. He stood for long moments in deep thought and concentration. His hands cherished the device. He delighted in the feel of the magic. He began to give himself to the magic, let it cherish him, caress him. The dark years slipped away like receding waves, leaving memory's shore-line smooth and clean. Palin was, for a moment, young and filled with hope and promise. Tears blurred his vision.

"Holding the pendant in my hand, I repeat the first verse, turning the face of the device up toward myself." Palin recited the first words of the spell: " 'Thy time is thy own.' " Acting as he had been instructed, he twisted the face plate of the device.

"Next, at the second verse, I move the face plate from the right to the left." He moved the face of the device in the direction indicated and recited the second verse of the chant: " 'Though across it you travel.' "

"At the recitation of the third verse, the back plate drops to form two spheres connected by rods. " 'Its expanses you see.' "

Palin gave the device another twist and smiled with pleasure when it performed as designed. He no longer held an egg-shaped bauble in his hand but something that resembled a scepter. "At the fourth verse, twist the top clockwise—a chain will drop down."

Palin repeated the fourth verse: " 'Whirling across forever.' "

The chain dropped as Tas had foretold. Palin's heartbeat increased with excitement and exultation. The spell was working.

"The fifth verse warns me to make certain that the chain is clear of the mechanism. As the sixth verse instructs, I hold the device by each sphere and rotate the spheres forward, while reciting the seventh verse. The chain will wind itself into the body. I hold the device over my head, repeating the final verse, and summon a clear vision of where I want to be and the time I want to be there."

Palin drew in a deep breath. Manipulating the device as instructed, he recited the rest of the chant: " 'Obstruct not its flow. Grasp firmly the end and the beginning. Turn them forward upon themselves. All that is loose shall be secure. Destiny will be over your own head.' "

He held the device over his head and brought to mind a

vision of the Chaos War, his own part in it. His part and Tasslehoff's.

Closing his eyes, Palin focused on the vision and gave himself to the magic. He surrendered himself to his longtime mistress. She proved faithful to him.

The floor of the kitchen elongated, scrolled up into the air. The ceiling slid underneath the floor, the dishes on the shelves melted and trickled down the walls, the walls merged with the floor and the ceiling, and all began to roll into themselves, forming an enormous spiral. The spiral sucked in the house and then the woods beyond. Trees and grass wrapped around Palin, then the blue sky, and the ball in which he was the center started to revolve, faster and faster.

His feet left the floor. He was suspended in the center of a whirling, spinning kaleidoscope of places and people and events. He saw Jenna and Tas whirl past, saw the blur of their faces, and then they disappeared. He was moving very slowly but the people around him were moving fast, or perhaps he was the one speeding past them while they walked by him as slowly if they were walking under water.

He saw forests and mountains. He saw villages and cities. He saw the ocean and ships on the ocean, and all of them were drawn up to form part of the great ball in the middle of which he drifted.

The spiral wound down. The spinning slowed, slowed . . . he could see people, objects more clearly . . .

He saw Chaos, the Father of All and of Nothing, a fearsome giant with beard and hair of flame, standing taller than the tallest mountain, the top of his head brushing eternity, his feet extending to the deepest part of the Abyss. Chaos had just smashed his foot down on the ground, presumably killing Tasslehoff but inflicting his death blow upon himself, for Usha would catch a drop of his blood in the Chaos jewel and banish him.

The spinning continued, carrying Palin on past that moment into . . .

Blackness. Utter darkness. A darkness so vast and deep that Palin feared he'd been struck blind. And then he saw light behind him, blazing firelight.

He glanced back into fire, looked ahead into darkness. Looked into nothing.

Panic-stricken, he closed his eyes. "Go back beyond the Chaos War!" he said, half-suffocated with fear. "Go back to my childhood! Go back to my father's childhood! Go back to Istar! Go back to the Kingpriest! Go back to Huma! Go back . . . go back . . ."

He opened his eyes.

Darkness, emptiness, nothing.

He took another step and realized that he had taken a step too far. He had stepped off the precipice.

He screamed, but no sound came from his throat. Time's rushing wind carried it away from. He experienced the sickening sensation of falling that one feels in a dream. His stomach dropped. Cold sweat bathed him. He tried desperately to wake himself, but then came the horrible knowledge that he would never wake.

Fear seized him, paralyzed him. He was falling, and he would continue to fall and fall and keep falling into time's well of darkness.

Time's empty well.

Having been the one using the device to travel back through time, Tasslehoff had never actually seen what happened to himself when he used it. He had always rather regretted this and had once tried to go back to watch himself going back, but that hadn't worked. He was extremely gratified, therefore, to watch Palin using the device and quite charmed to see the mage disappear before his very eyes.

All that was interesting and exciting, but it lasted only a few moments. Then Palin was gone, and Tasslehoff and Jenna were alone in the Majere's kitchen.

"We didn't explode," Tas observed.

"No, we didn't," Jenna agreed. "Disappointed?"

"A little. I've never seen anything explode before, not counting the time Fizban tried to boil water to cook an egg. Speaking of eggs, would you like something to eat while we wait? I could heat up some oatmeal." Tas felt it incumbent upon himself to act as host in Usha's and Palin's absence.

"Thank you," Jenna replied, glancing at the remains of the congealed oatmeal in the pot and making a slight grimace, "but I think not. If you could find some brandy, now, I believe I could use a drink—"

Palin materialized in the room. He was ashen, disheveled, and he clutched the device in a hand that shook so he could barely hold it.

"Palin!" Jenna cried, rising from her chair in amazement and consternation. "Are you hurt?"

He stared at her wildly, without recognition. Then he shuddered, gave a gasping sigh of relief. Staggering, he very nearly fell. His hand went limp. The device tumbled to the floor and bounced away in a flash of jewels. Tas chased after it, caught it before it rolled into the fireplace.

"Palin, what went wrong?" Jenna ran to him. "What happened? Tas, help me!"

Palin started to crumple. Between the two of them, Tas and Jenna eased the mage to the floor.

"Go fetch blankets," Jenna ordered.

Tasslehoff dashed out of the kitchen, pausing only a moment to deposit the device in a pocket. He returned moments later, tottering under a load of several blankets, three pillows, and a feather mattress that he had dragged off the master bed.

Palin lay on the floor, his eyes closed. He was too weak to move or speak. Jenna put her hand on his wrist, felt his pulse racing. His breathing was rapid, rasping, his body chilled. He was shivering so that his teeth clicked together. She wrapped two of the blankets snugly around him.

"Palin!" she called urgently.

He opened his eyes, stared at her. "Darkness. All darkness."

"Palin, what do you mean? What did you see in the past?"

He grasped her hand, hard, hurting her. He held fast to her as if he were being swept away by a raging river and she was his only salvation.

"There is no past!" he whispered through pallid lips. He sank back, exhausted.

"Darkness," he murmured. "Only darkness."

Jenna sat back on her heels, frowning.

"That doesn't make any sense. Brandy," she said to Tas.

She held the flask to Palin's lips. He drank a little, and some color came to his pale cheeks. The shivering eased. Jenna took a swallow of the brandy herself, then handed the flask to the kender. Tas helped himself, just to be sociable.

"Put it back on the table," Jenna ordered.

Tas removed the flask from his pocket and, after several more sociable gulps, he placed it on the table.

The kender looked down at Palin in remorseful concern. "What's wrong? Was this my fault? I didn't mean it, if it was."

Palin's eyes flared open again. "Your fault!" he cried hoarsely. Flinging off the blankets, he sat up. "Yes, it's your fault!"

"Palin, keep calm," Jenna said, alarmed. "You'll make yourself ill again. Tell me what you saw."

"I'll tell you what I saw, Jenna." Palin said, his voice hollow. "I saw nothing. Nothing!"

"I don't understand," Jenna said.

"I don't either." Palin sighed, concentrated, tried to order his thoughts. "I traveled back in time and as I did so, time unrolled before me, like a vast parchment. I saw all that has passed in the Fifth Age. I saw the coming of the great dragons. I saw the dragon purge. I saw the building of this Citadel. I saw the raising of the shield over Silvanesti. I saw the dedication of the Tomb of the Last Heroes. I saw the defeat of Chaos, and that is where it all ends. Or begins."

"Ends? Begins?" Jenna repeated, baffled. "But that can't be, Palin. What of the Fourth Age? What of the War of the Lance? What of the Cataclysm?"

"Gone. All of it. I stood amidst the ether and saw the battle with Chaos, but when I tried to see beyond, when I looked into the past, I saw only darkness. I took a step and . . ." He shuddered. "I fell into the darkness. A void where no light shines, no light has ever shone. Darkness that is eternal, everlasting. I had the feeling that I was falling through centuries of time and that I would continue to fall until death took me, and then my corpse would keep falling. . . ."

"If that is true, what does it mean?" Jenna pondered.

"I'll tell you what it means," Palin said raggedly. He pointed at Tasslehoff. "This is Tas's fault. Everything that has happened is his fault."

"Why? What does he have to do with it?"

"Because *he's not dead!*" Palin said, hissing the words through clenched teeth. "He changed time by *not* dying! The future he saw was the future that happened because he died and by his death, we were able to defeat Chaos. But he's not dead! We didn't defeat Chaos. The Father of All and Nothing banished his children, the gods, and these past forty years of death and turmoil have been the result!"

Jenna looked at Tas. Palin was looking at Tas, this time as if he'd grown five heads, wings and a tail.

"Let's all have another drink of brandy," Tas suggested, taking his own advice. "Just to make us feel better. *Clear our heads,*" he added pointedly.

"You could be right, Palin," Jenna said thoughtfully.

"I know I'm right!" he said grimly.

"And we all know that two rights make a wrong," Tas observed helpfully. "Would anyone like oatmeal?"

"What other explanation could there be?" Palin continued, ignoring the kender.

"I'm not sure," said Tas, backing up a few steps toward the

kitchen door, "but if you give me a moment, I'll bet I could think of several."

Palin threw off the blanket and rose to his feet. "We have to send Tas back to die."

"Palin, I'm not so sure . . ." Jenna began, but he wasn't listening to her.

"Where's the device?" he demanded feverishly. "What happened to it?"

"While it is true," Tas said, "that I had promised Fizban I would go back in time for the giant to step on me, the more I think about that part of it, the less I like it. For while being stepped on by a giant might be extremely interesting, it would be interesting for only a few seconds at most, and then as you said I would be dead."

Tas bumped up against the kitchen door.

"And while I've never been dead," he continued, "I've seen people being dead before, and I must say that it looks like about the most uninteresting thing that could happen to a person."

"Where is the device?" Palin demanded.

"It rolled into the ashes!" Tas cried and pointed at the fireplace. He took another gulp of brandy.

"I'll look," Jenna offered. Seizing the poker, she began to sift through the ashes.

Palin peered over her shoulder. "We *must* find it!"

Tasslehoff put his hand in his pocket and, taking hold of the Device of Time Journeying, he began to turn it and twist it and slide it, all the while speaking the rhyme under his breath.

" 'Thy time is thy own, though across it you travel . . .' "

"Are you sure it went under here, Tas?" Jenna asked. "Because I can't see anything except cinders—"

Tas spoke faster, his nimble fingers working swiftly.

" 'Whirling across forever. Obstruct not its flow,' " he whispered.

This was going to be the tricky part.

Palin's head jerked up. Turning around, he made a diving leap for the kender.

Tas whipped the device out of his pocket and held it up. "Destiny be over your own head!" he cried, and he was pleased to realize, as time rolled up the kitchen, the brandy flask, and him along with it, that he had just made a very pithy remark.

"The little weasel," said Jenna, looking at the empty place on the floor where the kender had once been standing. "So he had the device all along."

"My gods!" Palin gasped. "What have I done?"

"Scared the oatmeal out of him, unless I'm much mistaken," Jenna returned. "Which is quite an accomplishment, considering he's a kender. I don't blame him," she added, scrubbing her soot-covered hands vigorously on a towel. "If you had shouted at me like that, I would have run, too."

"I'm not a monster," Palin said, exasperated. "I am scared! I don't mind admitting it." He pressed his hand over his heart. "The fear is here, worse than anything I've ever known, even during the dark days of my captivity. Something strange and terrible has happened to the world, Jenna, and I don't understand what!" His fists clenched. "The kender is the cause. I'm sure of it!"

"If so, we better find him," said Jenna practically. "Where do you think he would have gone? Not back in time?"

"If he has, we'll never locate him. But I don't think he would," Palin said, pondering. "He wouldn't go back because if he did, he'd wind up exactly where he doesn't want to be—dead. I believe he's still in the present. Then where would he go?"

"To someone who would protect him from you," said Jenna bluntly.

"Goldmoon," said Palin. "He talked about wanting to see her only moments before he left. Or Laurana. He's already been to see Laurana. Knowing Tas, though, he'd want some new adventure. I will travel to the Citadel of Light. I would like to discuss what I have seen with Goldmoon anyhow."

"I'll loan you one of my magical rings to speed you across the miles," Jenna said, tugging the ring off her finger. "Meanwhile, I will send a message to Laurana, warning her to watch for the kender and if he shows up on her doorstep, to hang onto him."

Palin accepted the ring. "Warn her to be cautious of what she says and does," he added, his expression troubled. "I believe that there may be a traitor in her household. Either that or the Neraka Knights have found some way to spy on her. Will you . . ." He paused, swallowed. "Will you stop by the Inn and tell Usha . . . tell her . . ."

"I'll tell her you're not a monster," said Jenna, patting his arm with a smile. She looked at him intently, frowning in anxiety. "Are you certain you are well enough for this?"

"I was not injured. Only shocked. I can't say that's wearing off, but I'll be well enough to make the journey." He looked curiously at the ring. "How does this work?"

"Not all that well anymore," Jenna wryly. "It will take you two or three jumps to reach your destination. Place the ring on the middle finger of your left hand. That's close enough," she added, seeing Palin struggle to ease it over a swollen joint. "Put your right hand over the ring and conjure up the image of where you want to be. Keep that image in your mind, repeat it to yourself over and over again. I want that ring back, by the way."

"Certainly." He smiled at her wanly. "Farewell, Jenna. Thank you for your help. I'll keep you informed."

He placed his hand over the ring and began to picture in his mind the crytal rainbow domes of the Citadel of Light.

"Palin," Jenna said suddenly, "I haven't been entirely honest with you. I may have an idea where to find Dalamar."

"Good," Palin replied. "My father was right. We need him."

23

The Hedge Maze

he gnome was lost in the hedge maze.

This was nothing unusual. The gnome was frequently lost in the hedge maze. In fact, whenever anyone in the Citadel of Light wanted the gnome (which wasn't often) and asked where he was, the response was invariably, "Lost in the hedge maze."

The gnome did not wander the hedge maze aimlessly. Far from it. He entered the hedge maze daily with a set purpose, a mission, and that was to make a map of the maze. The gnome, who belonged to the Guild of PuzzlesRiddlesEnigmasRebus-LogogriphsMonogramsAnagramsAcrosticsCrosswordsMazes-LabyrinthsParadoxesScrabbleFeminineLogicandPoliticians, otherwise known as P3 for short, knew of a certainty that if he could map the hedge maze, he would find in that map the key to the Great Mysteries of Life, among these being: Why Is It That When You Wash Two Socks You Only End Up With One? Is There Life After Death? and Where Did The Other Sock Go? The gnome was convinced that if you found the answer to the second question you would also find the answer to the third.

In vain the mystics of the Citadel attempted to explain to him that the hedge maze was magical. Those who entered it with minds troubled or sad found their cares eased, their burdens lifted. Those who entered it seeking solitude and peace were not disturbed, no matter how many other people walked the fragrant hedgerows at the same moment. Those who entered seeking a solution to a problem found that their thoughts grew centered, their minds cleared of clutter. Those who entered on their mystical journey to climb the Silver Stair that stood in the center of the maze found that they did not journey through a maze of shrubbery, but through the maze of their hearts.

Those who entered the hedge maze with the firm resolve to map out the hedge maze, to try to define it in terms of X number of rows and left and right turnings and longitudes and latitudes and degrees of angles and radiuses and circumferences discovered that here mathematics need not apply. The hedge maze shifted beneath the compass, skittered out from underneath the ruler, defied all calculation.

The gnome, whose name (the short version) was Conundrum, refused to listen. He entered the hedge maze every day, convinced that this would be the day he solved the mystery. This would be the day he would achieve his Life Quest and produce the definitive map of the hedge maze, a map he would then copy and sell to tour groups.

With one quill pen stuck behind his ear and another through the bosom of his robe, rather as if he'd been stabbed, the gnome would enter the hedge maze in the morning and work feverishly all during the hours of sunlight. He would measure and count his steps, note down the elevation of the hedge at Point A, indicate where Point A converged with Point B, and cover himself in ink and perspiration. He would emerge at the end of the day glowing with pride, with bits of the hedge stuck in his hair and beard, and produce for the edification of any poor unfortunate he could coerce into viewing his project an ink-spattered and sweat-stained map of the hedge maze.

He would then spend the night copying the map so that it was perfect, absolutely perfect, not a twig missing. Next morning he would take the map into the hedge maze and become immediately and hopelessly lost. He would manage to find his way out about noontime, which just gave him daylight enough to redraw his map—and so forth and so on daily for about a year now.

On this day Conundrum had worked his way through the hedge maze to about the halfway point. He was down on his knees, tape in hand, measuring the angle between a zig and a zag when he noted a foot blocking his way. The foot was encased in a boot that was attached to a leg that was attached— on looking up—to a kender.

"Excuse me," said the kender politely, "but I'm lost and I was wondering—"

"Lost! Lost!" Conundrum scrambled to his feet, overturning his ink jar, which left a large purple stain on the grassy path. Sobbing, the gnome flung his arms around the kender. "How gratifying! I'm so glad! So glad! You can't know!"

"There, there," said the kender, patting the gnome on the back. "I'm certain that whatever it is, it will be all right. Have you a hankie? Here, borrow mine. Actually, it's Palin's, but I don't suppose he'd care."

"Thank you," said the gnome, blowing his nose.

Generally gnomes talk extremely fast and mash all their words together, one on top of the other, in the belief that if you don't reach the end of a sentence quickly you might never reach it all. Conundrum had lived among humans long enough to have learned to slow his speech pattern. He now talked very slowly and haltingly, which led other gnomes he encountered to consider him quite stupid.

"I'm sorry I fell apart like that." The gnome sniffed. "It's just, I've been working so long, and no one has been kind enough to get lost before . . ." He started to weep again.

"Glad I could oblige," said the kender hurriedly. "Now

that I am lost, I was wondering if you could show me the way out. You see, I have just arrived through magical means"—the kender was quite proud of this and repeated it to make certain the gnome was impressed—"magical means that are quite secret and mysterious, otherwise I'd tell you about them. Anyhow my business is extremely urgent. I'm looking for Goldmoon. I have a feeling she must be here because I thought about her very hard just as the magic happened. My name is Tasslehoff Burrfoot, by the way."

"Conundrum Solitaire," replied the gnome, and the two shook hands, after which Tasslehoff completed the ruin of Palin's handkerchief by using it to wipe the residual ink left on his fingers.

"I can show you the way out!" the gnome added eagerly. "I have drawn this map, you see."

Proudly, with a flourish of his hand, Conundrum presented the map to Tasslehoff's view. Drawn on an immense piece of parchment, the map lay on the ground, covering the path between the two hedge rows, overlapping on the edges. The map was bigger than the gnome, who was a smallish, misty-eyed, dimly smiling gnome with a nut-brown complexion and a long wispy beard that had probably once been white but was now stained purple due to the fact that the gnome invariably dragged his beard through the wet ink as he bent on hands and knees over the map.

The map was quite complicated, with Xs and Arrows and Do Not Enters and Turn Left Heres scrawled all over it in Common. Tasslehoff looked down at the map. Looking up, he saw the end of the row in which they were standing. The hedge opened up and he could see the sun shining on several very beautiful crystalline domed structures that caught the sunlight and turned it into rainbows. Two golden dragons formed an immense archway. The grounds were green and filled with flowers. People dressed in white robes strolled around, talking in low voices.

"Oh, that must be the way out!" said Tasslehoff. "Thanks all the same."

The gnome looked at his map and looked at what was undeniably the exit from the hedge maze.

"Drat," he said and began to stomp on the map.

"I'm extremely sorry," said Tas, feeling guilty. "It was a really nice map."

"Hah!" Conundrum jumped up and down on the map.

"Well, excuse me, but I've got to go," Tasslehoff said, inching toward the exit. "But once I have talked to Goldmoon, I'll be glad to come back and get lost again, if that will help."

"Bah!" cried the gnome, kicking the ink jar into the hedge.

The last Tasslehoff saw of Conundrum, he was back at the beginning of the hedge maze, measuring his foot with the tape in preparation to pace off the precise distance between the first turning and the second.

Tas walked a good distance, leaving the hedge maze far behind. He was about to wander into a lovely building made of sparkling crystal when he heard footsteps behind him and felt a hand on his shoulder.

"Have you business in the Citadel of Light, kender?" asked a voice, speaking Common.

"The where?" said Tasslehoff. "Oh, yes. Of course."

Quite accustomed to having the heavy hand of the law fall on his shoulder, he was not surprised to find himself in the custody of a tall young woman of stern expression wearing a helm of silver chain mail and a chain-mail shirt that glittered in the sun. She wore a long tabard marked with the symbol of the sun and carried a sword in a silver scabbard, girded around her waist.

"I'm here to see Goldmoon, ma'am," Tasslehoff said politely. "My business is urgent. Quite urgent. If you could just show me where—"

"What do you have here, Guardian?" asked another voice. "Trouble?"

Tasslehoff twisted his head to see another woman clad in armor, except that she was wearing the armor of a Solamnic Knight. Two more Solamnic Knights walked on either side of her as she proceeded up the walkway.

"I am not certain, Lady Camilla," replied the guard, saluting. "This kender has asked to see Goldmoon."

The two exchanged glances and it seemed to Tas that a shadow crossed the face of the lady Knight. "What does a kender want of the First Master?"

"The who?" Tas wondered.

"Goldmoon, the First Master."

"I'm an old friend of hers," Tas said. He held out his hand. "My name is . . ." He paused. He was growing extremely tired of people staring at him oddly whenever he said his name. He withdrew his hand. "It's not important. If you'll just tell me where to find Goldmoon . . ."

Neither of the women answered, but Tas, watching closely, saw the Solamnic Knight glance in the direction of the largest crystal dome. He guessed at once that this was where he needed to be.

"You both look very busy," he said, edging away. "I'm sorry to have bothered you. If you'll excuse me . . ." He made a dash for it.

"Should I go after him, sir?" he heard the guard ask the Knight.

"No, leave him be," Lady Camilla replied. "The First Master has a soft spot in her heart for kender."

"But he might disturb her solitude," the guard said.

"I would give him thirty steel pieces, if he could," Lady Camilla replied.

The lady Knight was fifty years old, a handsome woman, hale and hearty, though her black hair was streaked with silver. Stern of countenance, grim and stoic, she did not appear to be the sort of person given to displays of emotion. Yet, Tas heard her say this with a sigh.

Tas reached to the door of the crystal dome and halted, fully expecting someone to come out and tell him he shouldn't be there. Two white-robed men did emerge, but they only smiled at him and wished him a good afternoon.

"And a good afternoon to you, sirs," Tas said, bowing. "By the way, I'm lost. What building is this?"

"The Grand Lyceum," said one.

"Oh," said Tas, looking wise, although he hadn't a clue what a lyceum was. "I'm so glad I've found it. Thank you."

Bidding the gentlemen good-bye, the kender entered the Grand Lyceum. After a thorough exploration of the area, an exploration involving opening doors and interrupting classes, asking innumerable questions, and eavesdropping on private conversations, the kender discovered that he was inside the Grand Hall, a popular meeting place for the people who lived and worked and studied in the Citadel of Light.

This being afternoon, the Grand Hall was quiet, with only a few people reading or talking together in small groups. At night, the Grand Hall would be crowded, for it served as the dining hall for the Citadel, and here everyone—teachers and students alike—gathered for their evening meal.

The rooms inside the crystal dome glowed with sunshine. Chairs were numerous and comfortable. Long wooden tables stood at one end of the enormous room. The smell of baking bread wafted from the kitchen that was located on a level below. The reception rooms were at the far end, some of them occupied by students and their masters.

Tasslehoff had no difficulty gathering information about Goldmoon. Every conversation he overheard and half those he interrupted were centered on the First Master. Everyone, it seemed, was very worried about her.

"I cannot believe that the Masters have allowed this to go on this long," one woman said to a visitor. "Permitting the First Master to remain sealed up in her room like this! She might be in danger. She might be ill."

"Has no one made any attempt to try to talk to her?"

"Of course, we have tried to talk to her!" The woman shook her head. "We are all of us worried about her. Ever since the night of the storm, she has refused to see or speak to anyone, even those closest to her. Food and water are left for her on a tray during the night. The tray is always found empty in the morning. She leaves us notes on the tray assuring us that she is well, but she begs that we will respect her privacy and not disturb her."

"I won't disturb her," Tasslehoff said to himself. "I'll tell her very quickly what's happened, and then I'll leave."

"What are we to do?" the woman continued. "The handwriting on the notes is her own. We are all agreed on that."

"That proves nothing. She may be a prisoner. She may be writing those notes under duress, especially if she fears she will bring down harm upon others in the Citadel."

"But with what motive? If she were taken hostage, we would expect a ransom request or that some demand be made in return for her well-being. Nothing has been asked of us. We have not been attacked. The island remains as peaceful as anywhere in this dark time. Ships come and go. Refugees arrive daily. Our lives continue apace."

"What of the silver dragon?" the second woman asked. "Mirror is one of the guardians of Schallsea Isle and of the Citadel of Light. I would think that the dragon, with his magic, would be able to discover if some evil had taken possession of the First Master."

"He undoubtedly could, but Mirror has vanished as well," her friend returned helplessly. "He took flight during the worst of the storm. No one has seen him since."

"I knew a silver dragon once," Tas said, barging in on the conversation. "Her name was Silvara. I couldn't help overhearing you talk about Goldmoon. She's a very good friend of mine. I'm deeply worried about her. Where did you say her rooms were?"

"At the very top of the Lyceum. Up those stairs," said one.

"Thank you," said Tas and turned that direction.

"But no one's allowed up there," the woman added sternly.

Tas turned back again. "Oh, sure. I understand. Thanks."

The two women walked off, continuing their conversation. Tasslehoff loitered in the area, admiring a large statue of a silver dragon that occupied an honored place in the center of the hall. When the women were gone, Tas glanced about. Seeing that one was watching him, he began to climb the stairs.

Goldmoon's chambers were located at the very top of the Grand Lyceum. A spiral staircase of many hundred steps led upward through the various levels. The climb was long, the stairs built for the tall legs of humans, not the short legs of kender. Tas had begun bounding up the stairs enthusiastically, but after stair number seventy-five, he was forced to sit down and take a brief rest.

"Whew!" he said, panting. "I wish I were a silver dragon. At least then I'd have wings."

The sun was starting to dip down into the sea, by the time Tasslehoff—after a few more rests—reached the top.

The staircase ended, so Tas presumed he'd arrived at the level where Goldmoon lived. The hallway was peaceful and quiet, or so it seemed at first. A door decorated with sheaves of wheat and vines and fruit and flowers stood at the end of the corridor. As Tas moved closer to the door, he detected the faint sound of someone weeping.

The tender-hearted kender forgot his own trouble. He knocked gently on the door. "Goldmoon," he called out. "It's me, Tasslehoff. Is anything wrong? Maybe I can help."

The sound of weeping ceased immediately, replaced by silence.

"Goldmoon," Tas began. "I really need to talk to—"

A hand grasped hold of his shoulder. Startled, Tas jumped and banged his head against the door. He looked wildly around.

Palin gazed down at him sternly.

"I thought I might find you here," he stated.

"I'm not going back," Tas said, rubbing his head. "Not yet. Not until I talk to Goldmoon." He looked up at Palin with suspicion. "Why are you here?"

"We were worried about you," Palin replied.

"I'll bet," Tas muttered. Sidling away from Palin, he turned back to the door. "Goldmoon!" He knocked again on the door. "Let me in! It's me, Tasslehoff!"

"First Master," Palin added, "I am here with Tas. Something very strange has happened. We would like your wise counsel."

A moment's silence, then a voice, muffled from crying, came back, "You must excuse me, Palin, but I am seeing no one at present."

"Goldmoon," Palin said, after a moment. "I have very sad news. My father is dead."

Another moment's silence, then the voice, strained and hushed. "Caramon dead?"

"He died several weeks ago. His end was peaceful."

"I came in time to speak at his funeral, Goldmoon," Tasslehoff added. "It's too bad you missed my speech. But I could give it again if you—"

A terrible cry burst from behind the door. "Oh, fortunate man! Oh, lucky, lucky man!"

Palin looked grim. "Goldmoon!" he called out. "Please let me in!"

Tasslehoff, very subdued and solemn, put his nose to the doorknob.

"Goldmoon," he said, speaking through the key hole, "I'm very sorry to hear that you've been sick. And I was sorry to hear that Riverwind was dead. But I heard he died being a hero and saving my people from the dragon when there were probably quite a few who said that we kender weren't worth saving. I want you to know that I'm grateful and that I was proud to call Riverwind my friend."

"This is a shabby trick you play upon me, Palin," said the voice angrily from inside. "You have inherited your uncle's gift of mimickry. Everyone knows that Tasslehoff Burrfoot is dead."

"No, I'm not," Tas returned. "And that's the problem. At least it is for *some* people." He gave Palin a stern look. "It's really me, Goldmoon," Tas continued. "If you put your eye to the keyhole you can see me."

He waved his hand.

A lock clicked. Slowly, the door opened. Goldmoon stood framed within. Her room was lit by many candles, their glow cast a halo of light around her. The corridor into which she stepped was dark, except for the light of a single red star. She was cloaked in shadows. Tas could not see her.

"First Master . . ." Palin stepped forward, his hand outstretched.

Goldmoon turned, allowed the light from her room to touch her face. "Now, you see . . ." she said softly.

The light of the candles gleamed on hair that was thick and golden and luxuriant, on a face that was soft and smooth, on eyes that, though red with weeping, were blue as the morning sky and shone with the luster of youth. Her body was strong as the days when the Chieftain's Daughter had first fallen in love with a young warrior named Riverwind. The years Goldmoon had lived in the world numbered ninety, but her body, her hair, her eyes, her voice, her lips and hands were those of the young woman who had carried the blue crystal staff into the Inn of the Last Home.

Beautiful, she stood sorrowfully before them, her head drooping like the bud of a cut rose.

"What miracle is this?" Palin cried, awed.

"No miracle," said Goldmoon bitterly. "A curse."

"Are you cursed?" said Tas with interest. "So am I!"

Goldmoon turned to the kender, looked him up and down. "It *is* you!" she murmured. "I recognized your voice. Why are you here? Where have you been? Why have you come?"

Tasslehoff extended his hand, shook hers politely. "I'd love to tell you all about everything, Goldmoon. All about Caramon's first funeral and then his second funeral and how I'm cursed. But right now Palin is trying to murder me. I came to see if you would tell him to stop. So if you'll just speak to him, I'll be going."

Tas made a break for it. He had very nearly reached the stairs and was just about to dash down them when Palin's hand snaked out and snagged him by the collar of his shirt.

Tas wriggled and writhed, trying various kender tricks developed through years of practice at escaping the long arm of irritated sheriffs and irate shopkeepers. He used the old Twist and Bite and the always effective Stomp and Kick, but Palin was proof against them. At last, truly desperate, Tas tried the Lizard. He endeavored to slide his arms out of his shirt sleeves, regretful at having to leave his shirt behind, but, like the lizard who leaves part of his tail in the hand of the would-be captor, he would be free. Unfortunately, the new shirt proved a bit snug, and this didn't work. Palin was thin, but he was strong and, in addition, he had a strong incentive to hold onto the kender.

"What is he talking about?" Goldmoon asked, staring at Tas in bewilderment. She shifted her gaze to Palin. "*Are* you trying to murder him?"

"Of course not," Palin said impatiently.

"Are too!" Tas muttered, squirming.

"Listen to me, Tas. I'm truly sorry about what happened back there," Palin said.

He seemed about to continue, then sighed and lowered his head. He looked old, older than Tas remembered, and he'd seen him only a few moments ago. The lines in his face had deepened, darkened, pulled taut; the skin stretched tight across the bones. He blinked his eyes too frequently and often rubbed them, as if trying to see through a film or mist covering them. Tas—who was set to run—was touched by Palin's obvious trouble. The kender decided he could at least stay to listen.

"I'm sorry, Tas," Palin said finally, and his voice was tight as the lines on his face. "I was upset. I was frightened. Jenna was quite angry with me. After you left, she said she didn't blame you for running. She was right. I should have explained things to you calmly and rationally. I shouldn't have yelled at you. After what I saw, I panicked."

He looked down at Tas and sighed deeply. "Tas, I wish there was some other way. You have to understand. I'll try to explain this as best I can. You were meant to die. And because you haven't died, it is possible that this is the reason all these terrible things that have happened to the world have happened. To put it another way, if you were dead, the world might be the world you saw the first time you came back to my father's funeral. Do you understand?"

"No," said Tas.

Palin regarded the kender with obvious disappoinment. "I'm afraid I can't explain it any better than that. Perhaps you and Goldmoon and I should discuss it. You don't need to run away again. I won't force you to go back."

"I don't want to hurt your feelings, Palin," Tas returned, "but you can't force me to do anything. I have the device, and you don't."

Palin regarded the kender with deepening gravity, then suddenly and unexpectedly he smiled. The smile was not quite a whole smile, more a quarter-smile, for it lifted the corners of his thin lips and didn't come anywhere near his unhappy eyes, but it was a start.

"That is true, Tas," he said. "You do have the device. You know yourself what is right. You know that you made a promise to Fizban and that he trusted you to keep that promise."

Palin paused, then said quietly. "Were you aware, Tas, that Caramon spoke at *your* funeral?"

"He did?" Tas was astonished. "I didn't even know I had

a funeral! I just figured there probably wouldn't be much of me left, except a bit of goo between the giant's toes. What did Caramon say? Was there a big turnout? Did Jenna bring cheese puffs?"

"There was an immense turnout," Palin said. "People came from all over Ansalon to pay their respects to a heroic kender. As for my father, he called you 'a kender among kender.' He said that you exemplifed all that was best in the kender race: you were noble, self-sacrificing, brave, and, above all, honorable."

"Maybe Caramon was wrong about me," Tas said uneasily, glancing at Palin out of the corner of his eyes.

"Maybe he was," Palin said.

Tas didn't like the way Palin was looking at him, as if he were shriveling into something icky, like a squished cockroach. He didn't know what to do or say—an unusual feeling for him. He couldn't recall ever having had this feeling before, and he hoped he never would again. The silence grew stretched, until Tas was afraid that if one of them let loose, the silence would snap back and smack someone in the face. He was therefore quite thankful when a commotion sounded on the stairs, distracting Palin and easing the tense silence.

"First Master!" Lady Camilla called. "We thought we heard your voice. Someone said they saw a kender come up here—"

Reaching the head of the stairs, she caught sight of Goldmoon.

"First Master!" The Knight stopped dead in her tracks and stared. The Citadel guards bunched up behind her, staring and gaping.

This was Tas's opportunity to head for freedom again. No one would try to stop him. No one was paying the least attention to him. He could slip past them all and run away. Almost certainly the gnome Conundrum had some sort of sailing vessel. Gnomes always had sailing vessels. Sometimes they had flying vessels, as well, and sometimes they had vessels that both flew and sailed, although this generally resulted in an explosion.

Yes, thought Tas, eyeing the stairs and the people standing there with their mouths open. That's what I'll do. I'll go. Right now. I'm running. Any moment now. My feet will start to run.

But his feet had other ideas, apparently, because they stayed pretty much firmly attached to the floor.

Perhaps his feet were thinking the same thing as his head. His head was thinking about what Caramon had said. Those words were almost the very same words he'd heard people say about Sturm Brightblade, about Tanis Half-Elven. And they'd said those words about him! Tasslehoff Burrfoot! He felt a warm glow in the vicinity of his heart, and, at the same time, he felt another kind of glow around his stomach. A much more uncomfortable glow, a sort of gurgling glow, as if he'd eaten something that disagreed with him. He wondered if it could be the oatmeal.

"Excuse me, Goldmoon," Tas said, interrupting the gaping and staring and general stupidity that was taking place around him. "Do you think I could go inside your room and lie down? I'm not feeling very well."

Goldmoon drew herself up. Her face was pale, cold. Her voice was bitter. "I knew it would be like this. I knew you would look upon me as some sort of sideshow at a fair."

"Forgive me, First Master," Lady Camilla said, her own face crimson with shame. She lowered her gaze. "I beg your pardon. It's just . . . this miracle . . ."

"It is *not* a miracle!" Goldmoon said in sharp tones. She lifted her head and something of her regal presence, her noble spirit, flashed from her. "I am sorry for all the trouble I have caused, Lady Camilla. I know that I have brought pain to many. Please carry word to all in the Citadel that they need worry for me no longer. I am well. I will come among them presently, but first I want to speak to my friends in private."

"Of course, I will be happy to do whatever you ask, First Master," Lady Camilla said, and though she tried her best not to stare, she could not help but gaze with astonishment at the amazing change that had come over Goldmoon.

Palin coughed meaningfully.

Lady Camilla blinked. "I am sorry, First Master. It's just—"

She shook her head, helpless to put her confused thoughts into words. Turning away, yet with one more backward glance, as if to reassure herself that what she saw was real, she hastened down the spiral stairs. The Citadel guards, after a moment's hesitation, turned to run down after the Knight. Tas could hear their voices loudly exclaiming over the "miracle."

"They will all be like that," Goldmoon said in anguish, returning thoughtfully to her chambers. "They will all stare at me and exclaim and wonder." She shut the door swiftly behind them, leaned against it.

"You can hardly blame them, First Master," said Palin.

"Yes. I know. That's one reason I kept myself locked inside this room. I had hoped that when the change first happened it would be . . . temporary." Goldmoon gestured. "Please sit down. We have much to discuss, it seems."

Her chambers were plainly furnished, contained a bed made of a simple wood frame, a writing desk, handwoven rugs upon the floor, and a large number of soft cushions scattered about. A lute stood in one corner. The only other article of furniture—a tall standing mirror—lay toppled on the floor. The broken glass had been swept into a neat pile.

"What happened to you, First Master?" Palin asked. "Was this transformation magical in nature?"

"I don't know! I wish I could find an explanation!" she said helplessly. "The transformation occurred the night of the thunderstorm."

"The storm," Palin murmured and glanced at Tas. "Many strange things happened during that storm, seemingly. The kender arrived the night of the storm."

"The rain drummed on the roof," Goldmoon continued, as if she hadn't heard. "The wind howled and beat against the crystal as if it would smash it in. A brilliant lightning flash lit up the entire room more brightly than the brightest sunshine. It was so bright that it blinded me. For a time, I could see nothing at all. The blindness passed in a moment. I saw my reflection in the mirror.

"I . . . I thought a stranger was in the room. I turned, but there was no one there. It was then, when I turned back, that I recognized myself. Not as I had been, not gray and wrinkled and old, but young. Young as on my wedding day . . ."

She closed her eyes. Tears rolled down her cheeks.

"The crash they heard below," Palin said. "You broke the mirror."

"Yes!" Goldmoon cried, her fists clenched. "I was so close to reaching him, Palin! So near! Riverwind and I would have been together soon. He has waited so patiently. He knew that I had important tasks to perform, but my work is done now and I could hear him calling to me to join him. We would be together forever. I was going to walk again with my beloved at last and . . . and now . . . this!"

"You truly have no idea how this happened?" Palin hesitated, frowning. "Perhaps a secret wish of your heart . . . some potion . . . or magical artifact . . ."

"In other words, did I ask for this?" Goldmoon returned, her voice cool. "No, I did not. I was content. My work is finished. Others have the strength and heart and will to carry on. I want only to rest in my husband's arms again, Palin. I want to walk with him into the next stage of being. Riverwind and I used to speak of that next step on our great journey. I was given a glimpse of it during the time I was with Mishakal, the time she gave me the staff. The beauty of that far distant place . . . I can't describe it.

"I am tired. So very tired. I look young, but I don't feel young, Palin. This body is like a costume for the masquerade, the face a mask. Except that I can't take it off! I've tried and I can't!"

Goldmoon put her hands to her cheeks, pressed on them. Her face was scarred and now Tas, shocked, knew the cause. In her desperation, she had endeavored to claw away the smooth, supple flesh.

"Inside I am still old, Palin," Goldmoon said, her voice hollow and ragged. "I have lived my allotted life span. My husband has traveled on before me, my friends are gone. I am alone. Oh, I know." She raised her hand to forestall his objections. "I know that I have friends here. But they are not of my time. They . . . don't sing the same songs."

She turned to Tasslehoff with a smile that was sweet but so sad that the kender's eyes filled with tears.

"*Is* this my fault, Goldmoon?" Tas asked mournfully. "I didn't mean to make you unhappy! I didn't!"

"No, kenderken." Goldmoon soothed him with her gentle touch. "You have brought me cheer. And a puzzle." She turned to Palin. "How does he come to be here? Has he been roaming the world these thirty years when we thought him dead?"

"The kender came the night of the storm by using a magical device, Goldmoon," Palin said in a low voice. "The Device of Time Journeying. A device that once belonged to my father. Do you remember hearing the story of how Caramon traveled back in time with Lady Crysania—"

"Yes, I remember," Goldmoon said, flushing. "I must say that I found your father's story very difficult to believe. If it hadn't been for Lady Crysania's account—"

"There is no need to apologize," Palin said. "I admit that I myself found the story difficult to credit. I was able to speak to Dalamar about it years ago, before the Chaos War. And I talked to Tanis Half-Elven. Both confirmed my father's tale. In addition, I read Par-Salian's notes, which spoke of how the decision to send my father back into time came to be made. And I have a friend, Mistress Jenna, who was present in the Tower of High Sorcery when my father handed over the device to Dalamar for safekeeping. She had seen the device before and she recognized it. Above all, I have my account to serve as witness. Tasslehoff has with him the magical device my father used to transport himself through time. I know because I used it myself."

Goldmoon's eyes widened. She drew in a breath, soft as a sigh.

"Are you saying that the kender has come to us from the past? That he has traveled through time? That *you* traveled through time?"

"Tasslehoff," Palin said, "tell Goldmoon what you told me about Caramon's funeral. The first one. Be brief and concise as possible."

Since neither the word "brief" nor the word "concise" are in the kender vocabulary, Tasslehoff's story was considerably involved and extended, taking many little detours and side trips, and once losing himself completely in a morass of words from which he had to be patiently extricated. Goldmoon was a most attentive listener, however, seating herself next to him on the floor amongst the cushions and never saying a word.

When Tas spoke of how she and Riverwind had attended Caramon's first funeral together; her husband gray and stooped, the proud chieftain of the united tribes of the Plains, accompanied by his son and daughters, grandchildren and great-grandchildren, Goldmoon's tears flowed again. She wept silently, however, and never took her rapt gaze from the kender.

Tasslehoff came to a halt, mainly because his voice gave out. He was given a restorative glass of water and lay back down on the cushions.

"Well, what do you think of his tale, First Master?" Palin asked.

"A time in which Riverwind did *not* die," Goldmoon murmured. "A time in which we grow old together. Is it possible?"

"I used the device," Palin said. "I went back into the past, hoping to find the moment in time when we traded one future for the other. I had hoped to find such a moment, thinking that I might be able to effect a change."

"That would be very dangerous," Goldmoon said, her tone sharp-edged.

"Yes, well, it doesn't matter if it was or it wasn't," Palin returned, "because I did not find such a moment in our past."

"That is just as well," Goldmoon began.

Palin interrupted her. "First Master," he said, "I found no past at all."

"What do you mean? No past?"

"I went back in time," Palin said. "I saw the end of the Chaos War. I witnessed the departure of the gods. When I looked beyond that, when I tried to see the beginning of the Chaos War, when I tried to see events that had come before that, I saw nothing but a vast and empty darkness, like looking down into an enormous well."

"What does this mean?" Goldmoon asked.

"I don't know, First Master." Palin looked at Tasslehoff. "What I do know is this: Many years ago, Tasslehoff Burrfoot died. At least, he was supposed to die. As you see, here he sits, very much alive."

"That is why you wanted to send him back to die," Goldmoon murmured, looking sorrowfully at Tas.

"Perhaps I am wrong. Perhaps that wouldn't make any difference. I am the first to admit that I do not understand time journeying," Palin said ruefully. "Only one of our order does, and that is Dalamar. But none know if he is dead or alive or how to find him if he is alive."

"Dalamar!" Goldmoon's expression darkened. "When I heard of his disappearance and that of the Tower of High Sorcery, I remember thinking how wonderful it was that some good had come out of the evil of these times. I know others liked and trusted him—Tanis, for example, and your father. But every time I saw him, I saw that he walked in shadow, and more than that, that he liked the shadow. He wrapped it around him, hiding his deeds. I believe Tanis and Caramon were deceived by him and I, for one, hope he has left this world. Bad as things are, they are better than if he were here. I trust," she added sharply, "that you will have nothing to do with him, should he happen to reappear."

"There seems little likelihood Dalamar will enter into this at all," Palin returned impatiently. "If he is not dead, he is where we are not likely to ever find him. Now that I have spoken to you, First Master, what I find most singular is that all these strange events happened the night of the storm."

"There was a voice in that storm," Goldmoon said, shivering. "It filled me with terror, though I could not understand what it said." She looked again at Tas. "The question is, what do we do now?"

"That is up to Tas," Palin replied. "The fate of the world in the hands of a kender." He looked very grim.

Tas rose, with dignity, to his feet. "I'll give the matter serious thought," he announced. "The decision isn't easy. I have lots of things to consider. But before I go away to think and to help Conundrum map the hedge maze, which I promised I would do before I left, I want to say one thing. If you people had left the fate of the world in the hands of kender all along, you probably wouldn't be in this mess."

Leaving that shot to rankle in Palin's bosom, Tasslehoff Burrfoot left the room.

24

Sleep, Love; Forever Sleep

ver a week had passed since Mina had received her orders to march on Silvanesti. During that time, Silvanoshei had been crowned king of the Silvanesti kingdom that slumbered beneath its protective shield, unaware of doom marching nearer.

Galdar had spent three days racing to Khur to deliver Mina's orders to General Dogah. He had spent another three days traveling south from Khur, eager to meet up with Mina and her troops, following the route she'd shown him on her map. Finding them was easy. He could see signs of their passing all along the way—wheel ruts, footprints, abandoned equipment. If he could find the army this easily, so could the ogres.

Galdar marched with bowed head, slogging through the mud, rain running into his eyes, dripping from his muzzle. The rain had been falling for two days straight now, ever since Galdar's return, with no letup in sight. Not a soft drizzly summer shower, either, but a lancing, wind-driven rain that chilled the spirit and cast a gloom over the soul.

The men were wet through, cold, and miserable. The trail

was slick with mud that was either so slippery no man could stand on it or was so sticky that it nearly sucked the men's boots off their feet. The heavily laden supply wagons were mired in the mud at least thrice daily, requiring the men to put poles beneath the wheels and heave them out. Galdar's strength was called upon during these mishaps. The minotaur's back and shoulders ached with the strain, for he often had to lift the wagon to free the wheel.

The soldiers began to actively hate the rain, to view it as the enemy, never mind ogres. The rain beating on the soldiers' helms sounded like someone constantly drumming on a tin pot, or so one grumbled. Captain Samuval and his archers worried that the feathers with which the arrows were fletched were so wet and bedraggled that the arrows would not fly accurately.

Mina required the men to be up and marching with the dawn, always supposing there was a dawn, which there hadn't been for the last few days. They marched until the twilight grew so gloomy that the officers feared the wagon masters would drive off the road in the darkness. The wood was too wet for even the most experienced fire-builder to have any success. Their food tasted of mud. They slept in the mud, with mud for a pillow and rain for a blanket. The next morning they were up and marching again. Marching to glory with Mina. So all firmly believed. So all knew.

According to the mystics, the soldiers would have no chance to penetrate the magical shield. They would be caught between the anvil of the shield to their front and the hammer of the ogres to their back. They would perish ignominiously. The soldiers scoffed at the mystics. Mina could raise the shield, Mina could batter it down with a touch of her hand. They believed in her, and so they followed her. Not a man deserted during that long and arduous march.

They did complain—complained bitterly—about the mud and the rain and the poor food and the lack of sleep. Their grumblings grew louder. Mina could not help but hear them.

"What I want to know is this," one man said loudly, his voice sounding above the squelching of boots in the mud. "If the God we follow wants us to win, then why doesn't the Nameless One send us sunshine and a dry road?"

Galdar marched in his accustomed place at Mina's side. He glanced up at her. She had heard the grumblings before now and had ignored them. But this was the first man who had dared question her god.

Mina reined in her horse, wheeled the animal. She galloped back along the column, searching for the man who had spoken. None of his comrades pointed him out, but Mina found him. She fixed the man with her amber eyes.

"Subcommander Paregin, is it not?" she said.

"Yes, Mina," he replied, defiant.

"You took an arrow in the chest. You were dying. I restored you to life," Mina said. She was angry. The men had never seen her angry. Galdar shivered, recalled suddenly the appalling storm of lightning and thunder that had given her birth.

Paregin's face went red with shame. He mumbled a reply, lowered his gaze before her.

"Listen to me, Subcommander," Mina said and her voice was cold and sharp. "If we marched in dry weather under the blazing sun, it would not be rain drops that pierce your armor but ogre lances. The gray gloom is a curtain that hides us from the sight of our enemy. The rain washes away all trace of our passing. Do not question the God's wisdom, Paregin, especially since it seems you have little of your own."

Paregin's face was pale. "Forgive me, Mina," he said through pallid lips. "I meant no disrespect. I honor the God. I honor you." He looked at her in adoration. "Would that I had a chance to prove it!"

Mina's expression softened. Her amber eyes glowed, the only color in the gray gloom. "You will have that chance, Paregin," she said gently, "I promise it to you."

Wheeling her horse, she galloped back to the head of the column, mud flying from the horse's hooves.

The men lowered their heads against the rain and prepared to march on.

"Mina!" a voice cried from the rear. A figure was slipping and sliding, hastening toward the front of the line.

Mina halted her steed, turned to see what was amiss. "One of the rearguard," Galdar reported.

"Mina!" The man arrived panting and out of breath. "Blue dragons!" he gasped. "From the north." He looked back, frowned. "I swear, Mina! I saw them. . . ."

"There!" Galdar said, pointing.

Blue dragons, five of them, emerged from the clouds, their scales glistening with the rain. The ragged column of men slowed and shuffled to a stop, all staring in alarm.

The dragons were immense creatures, beautiful, awful. The rain gleamed on scales that were blue as the ice of a frozen lake beneath a clear winter sky. They rode the storm winds without fear, their immense wings barely moving to keep the dragons aloft. They had no fear of the jagged lightning, for their breath was lightning, could blast a stone tower to rubble or kill a man as he stood on the ground far below.

Mina said nothing, gave no orders. She calmed her horse, who shied at the sight of the dragons, and gazed up at them in silence. The blue dragons flew nearer, and now Galdar could see riders clad in black armor. One by one, in formation, each of the blue dragons swooped low over the ragged column of marching men. The dragonriders and their mounts took a good long look, then the blue dragons flapped their wings and lifted back up among the gray clouds.

The dragons were lost to sight, but their presence could still be felt, oppressing the heart, sapping courage.

"What's going on?" Captain Samuval slogged through the mud. At the sight of the dragons, his archers had drawn their bows, fitted their arrows. "What was that all about?"

"Targonne's spies," Galdar growled. "By now he must know that you countermanded his order and sent General Dogah an order of your own, Mina. That's treason. He'll have you drawn and quartered, your head on a spike."

"Then why didn't he attack us?" Captain Samuval demanded, with a grim glance skyward. "His dragons could have incinerated us where we stood."

"Yes, but what would that gain him?" Mina answered. "He does not profit by killing us. He does profit if we succeed. He is a short-sighted, avaricious, grasping, covetous man. A man like Targonne has never been loyal to anyone in his life, cannot believe anyone else can be loyal. A man who believes in nothing except the clink of steel coins mounting one on top of the other cannot understand another's faith. Judging all people by himself, he cannot understand what is happening here, and consequently he does not know how to deal with it. I will give him what he wants. Our victory will earn him the wealth of the Silvanesti nation and Malystryx's favor."

"Are you so certain we will win, Mina?" Galdar asked. "It's not that I'm doubting," he added hastily. "But five hundred against the entire Silvanesti nation? And we have yet to march through ogre lands."

"Of course, we will win, Galdar," Mina replied. "The One God has decreed it."

Child of battle, child of war, child of death, she rode forward, and the men followed after her through the steadily falling rain.

Mina's army marched southward, following the Thon-Thalas River. The rain finally stopped. The sun returned, its heat welcome to the soldiers, though they had to pay for warmth and dry clothes by redoubling their patrols. They were deep in ogre lands now.

The ogres were now threatened from the south by the cursed elves and the Legion of Steel and from the north by their former allies. Finding they could not dislodge the

Knights of Neraka from the north, the ogres had lately pulled their armies from that front and sent them south, concentrating their attacks against the Legion of Steel, believing that they were the weaker foe and would thus more readily fall.

Mina sent out scouting parties daily. Long-range scouts returned to report that a large army of ogres was gathering around the fortress of the Legion of Steel, near the border of Silvanesti. The Legion of Steel and an army of elves, believed to be under the leadership of the dark elf Alhana Starbreeze, were inside the fort preparing to stave off the ogre attack. The battle had not yet begun. The ogres were waiting for something—more manpower, perhaps, or favorable omens.

Mina heard the scouts' reports in the morning, prior to setting out on the day's march. The men were packing their gear, complaining as usual but in better spirits since the rain had quit. The blue dragons that dogged them kept their distance. Occasionally someone would catch sight of dark wings and the flash of sunlight off blue scales, but the dragons did not fly closer. The men ate their meager breakfast, waited for the orders to move out.

"You bring good news, gentlemen," Mina said to the scouts, "but we must not relax our vigilance. How close are we to the shield, Galdar?"

"The scouts report that we are within two days' march, Mina," he said.

Her amber eyes gazed past him, past the army, past the trees and the river, past the sky itself or so it seemed to him. "We are called, Galdar. I feel a great urgency. We must be at the border of Silvanesti by tonight."

Galdar gaped. He was loyal to his commander. He would have laid down his life for her and considered his death a privilege. Her strategies were unorthodox, but they had proven effective. But there were some things not even she could do. Or her god.

"We can't, Mina," Galdar said flatly. "The men have been

marching ten hours a day already. They're exhausted. Besides, the supply wagons can't move that fast. Look at them." He waved his hand. Acting under the direction of the quartermaster, his men were digging out one of the wagons, which had sunk in the mud during the night. "They won't be ready to set out for another hour, at least. What you ask is impossible, Mina."

"Nothing is impossible to the One God, Galdar," said Mina. "We will camp beside the shield this night. You will see. I— What is that noise?"

A frantic horn call split the air, coming from behind them.

The long line of troops stretched along the road that ran over a hill, around a bend, down a valley, and over another hill. The men stood up, hearing the horn call, and looked back down the ranks. Those digging out the wagon ceased their work.

A single scout, riding hard, crested the hill. The troops scrambled to move off the road, out of his way. It seemed he shouted a question as he rode, for many of the men pointed to the front. Putting his head down, he dug his spurs into his horse's flanks and urged his steed forward.

Mina stepped out into the road to wait for him. The scout, reaching her, pulled up so hard on his horse that the animal reared on its hind legs.

"Mina!" The scout was breathless. "Ogres! In the hills behind us! Coming fast!"

"How many?" she asked.

"It's hard to tell. They're spread out all over the place, not in column or in any sort of order. But there's a lot of them. One hundred. Maybe more. Coming down out of the hills."

"A raiding party, most likely." Galdar grunted. "Probably heard about the big battle in the south and they're off to claim their fair share of the loot."

"They'll come together quick enough when they pick up our trail," Captain Samuval predicted. "They'll do that the moment they strike the river."

"They've done that now, seemingly," Galdar said.

Grinding shouts of rage and glee bounded like boulders among the hills. The raucous blasts of ram horns split the air. A few ogres had spotted them and were calling their fellows to battle.

The scout's report spread with the swiftness of wildfire along the line of Mina's troops. The soldiers scrambled to their feet, weariness and fatigue vanishing like dry leaves in the flames. Ogres are terrible enemies. Hulking, fierce, and savage, an ogre army, led by ogre mages, operates with a good notion of strategy and tactics. An ogre raiding party does not.

Ogre raiding parties have no leaders. Outcasts from their own brutal society, these ogres are extremely dangerous, will prey even upon their own kind. They do not bother with formations but will attack whenever the enemy is in sight, trusting to their strength, brute force, and ferocity to overwhelm the foe.

Ogres are fearless in battle and, due to thick and hairy hides, are difficult to kill. Pain maddens them, goads them to greater ferocity. Ogre raiders have no word for "mercy," they scorn the word "surrender," either with regard to themselves or an opponent. Ogre raiders take only a few prisoners, and these are saved to provide the evening's entertainment.

A disciplined, heavily armed, and well-organized army can turn back an ogre assault. Leaderless ogres are led easily into traps and completely vanquished by clever stratagems. They are not good archers, having no patience for the practice required to develop skill with bow and arrow. They wield enormous swords and battles-axes that they use to hack the enemy to pieces, or throw spears, which their strong arms can hurl long distances with deadly effect.

Hearing the ogres' fierce yells and the sound of their horns, Mina's officers began shouting orders. Her Knights turned their horses, ready to gallop back to face the foe. The wagon masters plied the whip, the draft horses snorted and strained.

"Pull those wagons forward!" Galdar bellowed out commands. "Footmen, form a line across the trail, anchor on the river. Captain Samuval, your men take positions behind—"

"No," said Mina and though she did not raise her voice, her single word sounded like a clarion and brought all action to a halt. The clamor and uproar fell silent. The men turned to look at her. "We are not going to fight the ogres. We're going to flee them."

"The ogres will chase after us, Mina," Samuval protested. "We'll never be able to outrun them. We have to stand and fight!"

"Wagon masters," Mina called, ignoring him, "cut free the horses!"

"But, Mina!" Galdar added his own protest, "we can't leave the supplies!"

"The wagons slow us down," Mina replied. "Instead, we will allow the wagons to slow down the ogres."

Galdar stared. At first he didn't comprehend, and then he saw her plan.

"It just might work," he said, mulling over her strategy in his mind.

"It will work," said Samuval jubilantly. "We'll toss the wagons to the ogres like you toss food to a ravening wolf pack at your heels. An ogre raiding party will not be able to resist such a prize."

"Footmen, form a double line, march column. Prepare to move out. You will run," Mina told the men, "but not in a panic. You will run until you have no more strength left to run and then you will run faster."

"Perhaps the dragons will come to our aid," said Samuval, glancing skyward. "If they're even still up there."

"They're up there," Galdar growled, "but they won't come to our rescue. If we're wiped out at the hands of ogres,

Targonne will be spared the expense of executing us."

"We're not going to be wiped out," Mina said crisply. "Pass the word for Subcommander Paregin!"

"I am here, Mina!" The officer pushed his way forward through his men, who were hurriedly falling into position.

"Paregin, you are loyal to me?"

"Yes, Mina," he said firmly.

"You asked for a chance to prove that loyalty."

"Yes, Mina, I did," he said again, but this time his voice faltered.

"I saved your life," Mina said. The shouts and yells of the ogres were coming closer. The men glanced uneasily behind them. "That life is therefore mine."

"Yes, Mina," he replied.

"Subcommander Paregin, you and your men will remain here to defend the wagons. You will hold off the ogres as long as possible, thereby giving the rest of us the time we need to escape."

Paregin swallowed. "Yes, Mina," he said, but he said the words without a voice.

"I will pray for you, Paregin," Mina said softly. She extended her hand to him. "And for all those who stay behind. The One God blesses you and accepts your sacrifice. Take your positions."

Grasping her hand, Paregin reverently pressed her hand to his lips. He looked exalted, uplifted. When he returned to the lines, he spoke to his troops in excited tones as if she had conferred upon them a great reward. Galdar watched closely to see that Paregin's men obeyed him and did not try to skulk off in the face of orders that were essentially a death warrant. The men obeyed, some looking dazed, others grim, but all determined and resolved. They ranged themselves around the supply wagons that were filled with barrels of beef and ale, sacks of flour, the smith's equipment, swords, shields and armor, tents and rope.

"The ogres will think it is Yule come early," Samuval remarked.

Galdar nodded, but made no comment. He remembered back to Beckard's Cut, remembered Mina ordering him to pack extra supplies. A shiver ran along his spine, caused his fur to rise. Had she known all along? Had she been given knowledge that this would come to pass? Had she foreseen it all? Were their ends determined? Had she marked Paregin for death the day she saved his life? Galdar felt a moment's panic. He wanted suddenly to cut and run, just to prove to himself that he could. Prove that he was still the master of his own fate, that he was not trapped like a bug in her amber eyes.

"We will reach Silvanesti by nightfall," said Mina.

Galdar looked up at her, fear and awe constricting his heart.

"Give the order to move out, Galdar. I will set the pace."

She dismounted and handed the reins to one of her Knights. Taking her place at the front of the line, she raised her voice, and it was sweet and cold as the silver moonlight. "On to Silvanesti! On to victory!"

She began to march double-time, her strides long, starting out at swift but easy pace until her muscles warmed to the exercise. The men, hearing the ogres rampaging in the rear, needed no urging to keep up with her.

Galdar could escape into the hills. He could volunteer to remain with the doomed rear guard. He could follow her for as long as he lived. He fell into step beside her and was rewarded with her smile.

"For Mina," Subcommander Paregin shouted. He stood beside the loaded wagon, listening to the ogres raise their battle cry.

Gripping his sword, he waited for death.

Now that the troops no longer had the wagons to slow them, Mina's army made excellent time, especially with the howls and hoots of the ogres to spur them on. Each man could hear the sounds of the battle behind him, each man imagined what was happening, could tell the progress of the battle by the noise. Ogre shouts of rage, human death cries. Wild yelps of glee—the ogres discovered the wagons. Silence. The ogres were looting the wagons and hacking apart the bodies of those they had slaughtered.

The men ran as Mina had told them they would run. They ran until they were exhausted, and then she urged them to run faster. Those who fell were left behind. Mina permitted no one to assist them and this gave the men additional incentive for keeping their aching legs moving. Whenever a soldier thought he could no longer go on, he had only to look to the front of the line, to see the slender, fragile-looking girl, wearing plate and chain mail, leading the march, never flagging, never pausing to rest, never looking behind to see if anyone was following. Her gallant courage, her indomitable spirit, her faith was the standard that led her men on.

Mina permitted the soldiers only a brief rest, standing, to drink sparingly of water. She would not let them sit or lie down for fear their muscles would stiffen so that they would not be able to move. Those who collapsed were left where they fell, to straggle along behind when and if they recovered.

The sun's shadows grew longer. The men continued to run, officers setting the grueling pace with songs at first. Then no one had any breath left except for breathing. Yet with every step, they drew closer to their destination—the shield that protected the border of Silvanesti.

Galdar saw in growing alarm that Mina's own strength was flagging. She stumbled several times and then, at last, she fell.

Galdar leaped to her side.

"No," she gasped and shoved away his hand. She regained her feet, staggered forward several more steps and fell again.

"Mina," said Galdar, "your horse, Foxfire, is here, ready

and able to carry you. There is no shame in riding."

"My soldiers run," she told Galdar faintly. "I will run with them. I will not ask them to do what I cannot!"

She tried to rise. Her legs would not support her. Her face grim, she began to crawl on her hands and knees along the trail. Some of the soldiers cheered, but many others wept.

Galdar lifted her in his arms. She protested, she ordered him to set her back on her feet.

"If I do, you will only fall again. You will be the one to slow us down, Mina," Galdar said. "The men would never leave you. We will never make the Silvanesti border by nightfall. The choice is yours."

"Very well," she said, after a moment's bitter struggle against her own weakness. "I will ride."

He helped her onto Foxfire. She slumped over the saddle, so tired that he feared for a moment she could not even remain in the saddle. Then she set her jaw, straightened her back, sat upright.

Mina looked down, her amber eyes cool.

"Do not ever defy my orders again, Galdar," she said. "You can serve the One God just as well dead as alive."

"Yes, Mina," he answered quietly.

Gripping the reins in her hands, she urged the horse forward at a gallop.

Mina's prediction proved correct. Her army reached the forested lands outside the Shield before sundown.

"Our march ends here for the night," Mina said and climbed down from her exhausted horse.

"What ails this place?" Galdar asked, eyeing the dead and dying trees, the decaying plants, the corpses of animals found lying along the trail. "Is it cursed?"

"In a way, yes. We are near the shield," Mina said, looking intently at everything around her. "The devastation you see is the mark of its passing."

"The shield brings death?" Galdar asked, alarmed.

"To all it touches," she replied.

"And we must break through it?"

"We cannot break through it." Mina was calm. "No weapon can penetrate it. No force—not even the magical force of the most powerful dragon- –can shatter it. The elves under the leadership of their witch-queen have hurled themselves against it for months and it remains unyielding. The Legion of Steel has sent its knights to batter it to no effect.

"There." Mina pointed. "The shield lies directly before us. You can see it, Galdar. The shield and beyond the shield, Silvanesti and victory."

Galdar squinted against the glare. The water caught the setting sun's lurid red glow, turning the Thon-Thalas into a river of blood. He could see nothing at first, and then the trees in front of him rippled, as if they were reflected in the blood-tinged water. He rubbed his eyes, thinking fatigue was causing them to blur. He blinked and stared and saw the trees ripple again, and he realized then that what he was seeing was a distortion of the air created by the magic of the shield.

He drew closer, fascinated. Now that he knew where to look, he fancied he could see the shield itself. It was transparent, but its transparency had an oily quality to it, like a soap bubble. Everything inside it—trees and boulders, brush and grasses—looked wobbly and insubstantial.

Just like the elf army, he thought, and immediately took this as a good omen. But they still had to pass through the shield.

The officers brought the troops to a halt. Many of the men pitched forward face-first on the ground as soon as the order to cease march was given. Some lay sobbing for breath or sobbing from the pain of muscle spasms in their legs. Some lay quiet and still, as if the deadly curse that had touched the trees around them had claimed them as well.

"All in all," Galdar growled in an undertone to Captain Samuval, who stood gasping for breath beside him, "Given a choice between walking into that shield and facing ogres, I think I'd take the ogres. At least then you know what you're up against."

"You said a true word there, friend," Captain Samuval agreed when he had recaptured some of his breath and had enough left over to use for speech. "This place has an uncanny feel to it."

He nodded his head in the direction of the shimmering air. "Whatever we're going to do, we'd best be doing it soon. We may have slowed the ogres down a bit, but they'll catch up with us fast enough."

"By morning, I'd say," Galdar agreed, slumping to the ground. He lay on his back. He had never been so tired in all his life. "I know ogre raiding parties. Looting the wagons and butchering our men will occupy them for a while, but they'll be looking for more sport and more loot. They're on our trail right now. I'll bet money on it."

"And us too goddamn worn out to go anywhere, even if we had anywhere to go," Captain Samuval said, dropping wearily down alongside him. "I don't know about you, but I don't have energy enough to lift my hand to brush away a gnat, much less attack some blamed magical shield."

He cast a sidelong glance at Mina, who alone of all her army remained on her feet. She stood staring intently at the shield, or at least in the direction of the shield, for night was closing upon them fast, and its distortion could no longer be easily detected.

"I think this ends it, my friend," Captain Samuval said in a low voice to the minotaur. "We cannot get inside the magic of the shield. The ogres will catch us here in the morning. Ogres at our rear. The shield to our front. Us caught between. All that mad dash for naught."

Galdar didn't reply. He had not lost faith, though he was too tired to argue. Mina had a plan. She would not lead them into a blind alley to be caught and slaughtered by ogres. He didn't know what her plan might be, but he had seen enough of her and enough of the power of her God that he now believed her capable of doing the impossible.

Mina shoved her way through the gray and lifeless trees, walked toward the shield. Dead limbs fell around her. Dead, dry leaves crackled beneath her boots. Dust like ashes sifted down upon her shoulders and covered her shaved head with a pearl gray mantle. She walked until she could go no farther. She came up against an invisible wall.

Mina reached out her hand, pushed at the shield, and it seemed to Galdar that the insubstantial oily soap bubble must give way. She drew back her hand swiftly, as if she had touched a thistle and been stung. Galdar thought he saw a tiny ripple in the shield, but that might have been his imagination. Drawing her morning star, Mina struck it against the shield. The morning star fell from her hand, jarred out of her grasp by the blow. Shrugging, she bent down to pick up her weapon. Reports confirmed, she turned and made her way back through the forest of death to her command.

"What are your orders, Mina?" Galdar asked.

She looked around her army that lay scattered over the gray ground like so many corpses.

"The men have done well," she said. "They are exhausted. We will make camp here. This is close enough, I think," she added, looking back at the shield. "Yes, this should be close enough."

Galdar didn't ask, "Close enough for what?" He didn't have the energy. He staggered to his feet. "I'll go set the watch—"

"No," Mina countered. She laid her hand on his shoulder. "We will not set a watch this night. Everyone will sleep."

"Not set a watch!" Galdar protested. "But, Mina, the ogres are in pursuit—"

"They will be on us by morning," she said. "The men should eat if they are hungry and then they must sleep."

Eat what? Galdar wondered. Their food was now filling

the bellies of the ogres. Those who had started out on that mad run carrying packs had long ago dropped them by the side of the road. He knew better than to question her.

Assembling the officers, he relayed Mina's orders. To Galdar's surprise, there was little protest or argument. The men were too tired. They didn't care anymore. As one soldier said, setting a watch wouldn't do much good anyhow. They'd all wake soon enough when the ogres arrived. Wake up in time to die.

Galdar's stomach rumbled, but he was too tired to go searching for food. He would not eat anything from this accursed forest, that much was certain. He wondered if the magic that had sucked the life from the trees would do the same for them in the night. He pictured the ogres arriving tomorrow morning to find nothing but desiccated husks. The thought brought a smile to his lips.

The night was dark as death. Tangled in the black branches of the skeleton trees, the stars looked small and meager. Galdar was too stupid with fatigue to remember if the moon would rise this night or not. He hoped it wouldn't. The less he saw of this ghastly forest, the better. He stumbled over limp bodies as he walked. A few groaned, and a few cursed him, and that was the only way he knew they were alive.

He returned to the place he had left Mina, but she was not there. He could not find her in the darkness, and his heart spasmed with a nameless fear, the fear a child feels on finding himself lost and alone in the night. He dare not call. The silence was a temple silence, had an awful quality he did not want to disturb. But he had to find her.

"Mina!" he hissed in a penetrating whisper.

"Here, Galdar," she replied.

He circled around a stand of dead trees, found her cradled in a severed arm that had fallen from an enormous oak. Her face glimmered pale, more luminous than the moonlight, and he wondered that he could have missed her.

He made his report. "Four hundred and fifty men, Mina," he said. He staggered as he spoke.

"Sit down," she ordered.

"Thirty left behind with the wagons. Twenty more fallen on the road. Some of those may catch up, if the ogres don't find them first."

She nodded silently. Galdar eased himself to the ground. His muscles ached. He would be sore and stiff tomorrow, and he wouldn't be the only one.

"Everyone's bedded down." He gave a cavernous yawn.

"You should sleep, too, Galdar."

"What about you?"

"I am wakeful. I will sit up for awhile. Not long. Don't worry about me."

He settled himself at her feet, his head pillowed on a pile of dead leaves that crackled every time he moved. During that hellish run, all he had been able to think about had been the blessed night when he would be able to lie down, to rest, to sleep. He stretched his limbs, closed his eyes, and saw the trail at his feet. The trail went on and on into forever. He ran and ran, and forever moved farther away from him. The trail undulated, twisted, wrapped around his legs like a snake. Tripped him, sent him plunging head first into a river of blood.

Galdar woke with a hoarse cry and a start.

"What is it?" Mina was still seated on the log. She hadn't moved.

"That damned run!" Galdar swore. "I see the road in my dreams! I can't sleep. It's no use."

He wasn't the only one. All around him came the sounds of breathing—heavy, panting—restless shifting, groans and coughs and whispers of fear, loss, despair. Mina listened, shook her head, and sighed.

"Lie down, Galdar," she said. "Lie down and I will sing you a lullaby. Then you will sleep."

"Mina . . ." Embarrassed for her, Galdar cleared his throat. "There is no need for that. I'm not a child."

"You are a child, Galdar," she said softly. "We are all children. Children of the One God. Lie down. Close your eyes."

Galdar did as he was told. He lay down and closed his eyes, and the road was ahead of him, and he was running, running for his life . . .

Mina began to sing. Her voice was low, untrained, raw and yet there was a sweetness and a clarity that struck through to the soul.

> The day has passed beyond our power.
> The petals close upon the flower.
> The light is failing in this hour
> Of day's last waning breath.
>
> The blackness of the night surrounds
> The distant souls of stars now found.
> Far from this world to which we're bound,
> Of sorrow, fear and death.
>
> Sleep, love; forever sleep.
> Your soul the night will keep.
> Embrace the darkness deep.
> Sleep, love; forever sleep.
>
> The gathering darkness takes our souls,
> Embracing us in a chilling folds,
> Deep in a Mistress's void that holds
> Our fate within her hands.
>
> Dream, warriors, of the dark above,
> And feel the sweet redemption of
> The Night's Consort, and of her love
> For those within her bands.

Sleep, love; forever sleep.
Your soul the night will keep.
Embrace the darkness deep.
Sleep, love; forever sleep.

Galdar felt a lethargy steal over him, a languor similar to that experienced by those who bleed to death. His limbs grew heavy, his body was dead weight, so heavy that he was sinking into the ground. Sinking into the soft dirt and the ash of the dead plants and the leaves that drifted down upon him, settling over him like a blanket of dirt thrown into his grave.

He was at peace. He knew no fear. Consciousness drained away from him.

Gamashinoch, the dwarves called it. The Song of Death.

Targonne's dragon riders were up with the gray dawn, flying low over the forests of the ogre land of Blöde. They had watched from the heavens yesterday, watched the small army run before the ogre raiding party. The soldiers had fled before the ogres in near panic, so far as the dragon riders could see, abandoning their supply wagons, leaving them for the ogres. One of the riders noted grimly that Targonne would not be pleased to hear that several hundred steel worth of equipment was now adorning ogre bodies.

The ragtag army had run blindly, although they had managed to keep in formation. But their mad dash to safety had taken them nowhere. The army had run headlong into the magical shield surrounding Silvanesti. The army had come to a halt here at sundown. They were spent, they could go no farther, even if there had been any place for them to go, which there wasn't.

Looting the wagons had occupied the ogre raiding party for a couple of hours, but when there was nothing more to eat and they had stolen all there was to steal, the ogres moved south, following the trail of the humans, following their hated scent that drove them to fury and battle madness.

The dragon riders could have dealt with the ogres. The blues would have made short work of the raiding party. But the riders had their orders. They were to keep watch on this rebellious Knight and her army of fanatics. The dragon riders were not to interfere. Targonne could not be blamed if ogres destroyed the Silvanesti invasion force. He had told Malys many times that the ogres should be driven out of Blöde, exterminated like the kender. Maybe next time she would listen to him.

"There they are," said one of the riders, as his dragon circled low. "In the Dead Land. The same place where we left them last night. They haven't moved. Maybe they're dead themselves. They look it."

"If not, they soon will be," said his commander.

The ogres were a black mass, moving like sludge along the road that ran alongside what the Knight had termed the Dead Land, the gray zone of death that marked the edge of the shield, the border of Silvanesti.

The dragon riders watched with interest, looking forward with anticipation to the battle that would finally bring an end to this tiresome duty and allow them to return to their barracks in Khur.

The Knights settled themselves comfortably to watch.

"Do you see that?" said one suddenly, sitting forward.

"Circle lower," the commander ordered.

The dragons flew lower, wings making a gentle sweep, catching the pre-dawn breeze. The riders stared down at the astonishing sight below.

"I think, gentlemen," said the commander, after a moment spent watching in gaping wonder, "that we should fly to Jelek and report this to Targonne ourselves. Otherwise, we might not be believed."

A horn blast woke Galdar, brought him to his feet before he was fully conscious, fumbling for his sword.

"Ogres attacking! Fall in, men! Fall in!" Captain Samuval was shouting himself hoarse, kicking at the men of his company to rouse them from their slumbers.

"Mina!" Galdar searched for her, determined to protect her, or, if he could not do that, to kill her so that she should not fall alive into ogre hands. "Mina!"

He found her in the same place he had left her. Mina sat in the curl of the dead oak's arm. Her weapon, the morning star, lay across her lap.

"Mina," said Galdar, plunging through the gray ash and trampling the dead leaves, "hurry! There may yet be a chance for you to escape—"

Mina looked at him and began to laugh.

He stared, appalled. He had never heard her laugh. The laughter was sweet and merry, the laughter of a girl running to meet a lover. Mina climbed upon the stump of a dead tree.

"Put your weapons away, men!" she called out. "The ogres cannot touch us."

"She has gone mad!" Samuval said.

"No," said Galdar, staring, unbelieving. "Look."

Ogres had formed a battle line not ten feet away from them. The ogres danced along this line. They clamored, roared, gnashed their teeth, gibbered, and cursed. They were so close that their foul stench made his nostrils twitch. The ogres jumped up and down, kicked and hammered with their fists, wielded their weapons in murderous rage.

Murderous, frustrated rage. The enemy was in clear sight, yet he might as well have been playing among the stars in some distant part of the universe. The trees that stood between Galdar and the ogres shimmered in the half-light, rippled as Mina's laughter rippled through the gray dawn. The ogres beat their heads against a shield, an invisible shield, a magical shield. They could not pass.

Galdar watched the ogres, watched to make certain that they could not reach him or his comrades. It seemed impossible to him that they could not enter through this strange and unseen barrier, but at last he had to admit that what his mind at first disbelieved was true. Many of the ogres fell back away from the barrier, alarmed and frightened of the magic. A few seemed to have simply grown weary of beating their heads against nothing but air. One by the one, the ogres turned their hairy backs upon the human army that they could see, but could not reach. Their clamor began to die down. With threats and rude gestures, the ogres straggled off, disappeared into the forest.

"We are *inside* the shield, men!" Mina called out in triumph. "You stand safe within the borders of the Silvanesti! Witness the might and power of the One True God!"

The men stood staring, unable at first to comprehend the miracle that had befallen them. They blinked and gaped, reminding Galdar of prisoners who have been locked in dark cells for most of their lives, suddenly released to walk in the bright sunshine. A few exclaimed, but they did so softly, as if fearful to break the spell. Some rubbed their eyes, some doubted their own sanity, but there was the unmistakable sight of ogre backsides—ogres in retreat—to tell the soldiers that they were in their right minds, that they were not seeing things. One by one, the men fell to their knees before Mina and pressed their faces into the gray ash. They did not chant her name in triumph, not this time. This moment was too holy, too sacred. They paid Mina homage in silent awe and reverence.

"On your feet, men!" Mina shouted. "Take up your arms. This day we march to Silvanost. And there is no force in the world that can stop us!"

25

From Day to Night

aces.

Faces floating over him. Bobbing and receding on a rippling surface of pain. When Gerard rose to the surface, the faces were very close to him—strange faces, with no expression, corpses, drowned in the dark sea in which he floundered. The pain was worse closest to the surface, and he didn't like the faceless faces so near his own. He let himself sink back into the darkness, and there was some part of him that whispered he should cease struggling and give himself to the sea and become one of the faceless himself.

Gerard might have done so, but for a firm hand that gripped his when the pain was very bad and kept him from sinking. He might have done so but for a voice which was calm and commanding and ordered him to stay afloat. Accustomed to obedience, Gerard obeyed the voice. He did not drown but floundered in the dark water, clinging to the hand that held him fast. Finally, he made his way to the shore, pulled himself out of the pain and, collapsing on the banks of consciousness, he slept deeply and peacefully.

He woke hungry and pleasantly drowsy to wonder where he was, how he came to be here, what had happened to him. The faces that had bobbed around in his delirium were real faces now, but they were not much more comforting than the drowned faces in his dreams. The faces were cold and inexpressive, passionless faces of men and women, humans, dressed in long, black robes trimmed in silver.

"How are you feeling, sir?" one of these faces asked, bending over him and placing a chill hand upon his neck to feel his pulse. The woman's arm was covered with black cloth that fell over his face, and Gerard understood the image of the dark water in which he'd believed himself to be drowning.

"Better," said Gerard cautiously. "I'm hungry."

"A good sign. Your pulse is still weak. I will have one of the acolytes bring you some beef broth. You have lost blood, and the beef will help restore it."

Gerard looked at his surroundings. He lay in a bed in a large room filled with beds, most of which were empty. Other black-robed figures drifted about the room, moving silently on slippered feet. Pungent smells of herbs scented the air.

"Where am I?" Gerard asked, puzzled. "What happened?"

"You are in a hospital of our order, Sir Knight," the healer replied. "In Qualinesti. You were ambushed by elves, seemingly. I do not know much more than that." Nor did she care, by her cold expression. "Marshal Medan found you. He brought you here the day before yesterday. He saved your life."

Gerard was baffled. "Elves attacked me?"

"I know nothing more," the healer told him. "You are not my only patient. You must ask the marshal. He will be here shortly. He has been here every morning since he brought you in, sitting by your side."

Gerard remembered the firm hand, the strong, commanding voice and presence. He turned his body, slowly, painfully. His wounds were tightly bound, his muscles weak from lying in bed. He looked to see his armor—black armor, cleaned and polished—placed carefully on a stand near his bed.

Gerard closed his eyes with a groan that must have made the healer think he had suffered a relapse. He remembered all, or at least most, of what had happened. He remembered fighting two Neraka Knights. He remembered the arrow, remembered a third Knight, remembered challenging the Knight to fight. . . .

He did not remember being attacked by elves.

A young man came carrying a tray on which was a bowl of broth, a bit of bread, and a mug.

"Shall I help you, sir?" the young man asked politely.

Gerard imagined being spoon-fed like a child. "No," he said, and, though it cost him considerable pain, he struggled to a seated position.

The young man placed the tray on Gerard's lap and sat down on a chair at his side to watch him eat.

Gerard dunked his bread in the broth. He drank the clear, cool water from the mug and wondered how to find out the truth.

"I take it I am a prisoner here," he said to the young man.

"Why, no, sir!" The acolyte appeared astonished. "Why should you think that? You were ambushed by a band of elves, sir!" The acolyte was regarding Gerard with obvious admiration. "Marshal Medan told everyone the story when he brought you to us. He carried you in his arms himself, sir. He was covered with your blood. He said you were a true hero and that you were to receive the very best care, to spare no effort. We have had seven dark mystics working on you. You! A prisoner!" The young man laughed and shook his head.

Gerard shoved the bowl of soup away, uneaten. He had lost his appetite. Mumbling something to the effect that he was weaker than he'd supposed, he lay back among his pillows. The acolyte fussed over him, adjusting his bandages and checking to see if any of his wounds had ripped open. He said that they were all almost healed, then left, telling Gerard he should sleep.

Gerard closed his eyes, pretended to be asleep, but sleep was far from coming. He had no idea what was going on. He could only guess that this Medan was playing some sort of sadistic game that would end in Gerard's torture and death.

This decided, he was at peace, and he slept.

"No, don't wake him," said a voice, deep and familiar. "I just came to see how he was doing this morning."

Gerard opened his eyes. A man wearing the armor of a Knight of Neraka, with a marshal's sash, stood by the side of the bed. The man was in his fifties. His face was sun-darkened, heavily lined, stern, and grim, but it was not a cruel face. It was the face of a commander who could order men to their deaths but who took no pleasure in it.

Gerard knew him immediately. Marshal Medan.

Laurana had spoken of the marshal with a certain grudging respect, and Gerard could now understand why. Medan had governed a hostile race for thirty years, and there had been no death camps established, no gallows set up in the marketplace, no burning and looting and wanton destruction of elven households and business. Medan saw to it that the dragon's tribute was collected and paid. He had learned to play elven politics and, according to Laurana, he played it well. He had his spies and his informers. He dealt harshly with rebels, but he did so to maintain order and stability. He kept tight hold on his troops. No small feat in these days when the Knights of Neraka were recruited from the dregs of society.

Gerard was forced to abandon the notion that this man would use him for sport, would make a mockery of him and of his death. But if that were true, then what was Medan's game? What was the tale of elves attacking?

Gerard pushed himself to a sitting position, made his

salute as best he could with his chest and arm bound with bandages. The marshal might be the enemy, but he was a commander and Gerard was bound to give him the respect that was due his rank.

The marshal returned the salute and told Gerard to lie back, take care not to reopen his wounds. Gerard barely heard him. He was thinking of something else. He was thinking back to the attack.

Medan had ambushed them for a reason—to catch Palin and recover the artifact. That means Medan knew exactly where to find us, Gerard said to himself. Someone told him where we were going to be and when.

Someone had betrayed them, but who? Someone in Laurana's own household? That was hard to credit, yet Gerard thought of the elf who had left to go "hunting" and had not returned. Perhaps he had been killed by the Knights. Perhaps not.

His thoughts were in bubbling turmoil. What had happened to Palin and the kender? Had they managed to escape safely? Or were they being held prisoner, too?

"How do you feel, sir?" Medan asked, regarding Gerard with concern.

"I am much better, my lord, thank you," Gerard replied. "I want to tell you, sir, that there is no need to continue with this pretense, which, perhaps, you do out of concern for my health. I know I am your prisoner. There is no reason why you should believe me, but I want you to know that I am not a spy. I am—"

"—a Solamnic Knight." Medan finished, smiling. "Yes, I am aware of that, Sir—" He paused.

"Gerard uth Mondar, my lord," Gerard replied.

"And I am Marshal Alexius Medan. Yes, Sir Gerard, I know you are a Solamnic." Medan pulled up a chair, seated himself near Gerard's bed. "I know you are my prisoner. I want you to keep your voice down." He glanced at the dark mystics, who were moving about at the far end of the room. "These two pieces of information will be our little secret."

"My lord?" Gerard gaped. If the dragon Beryl had plummeted out of the skies and landed in his soup, he could not have been more astonished.

"Listen to me, Sir Gerard," Medan said, resting a firm hand on the Solaminc's arm. "You were captured wearing the armor of a Knight of Neraka. You claim that you are not a spy, but who will believe you, do you suppose? No one. Do you know the fate that would befall you, as a spy? You would be interrogated by men skilled in the art of making other men talk. We are quite modern and up to date here in Qualinesti. We have the rack, the wheel, red-hot pincers, bone-crackers. We have the iron maiden with her painful and deadly embrace. After a few weeks of such interrogation, you would, I think, be quite glad to tell your interrogators everything you know and a lot of things you didn't. Anything to end the torment."

Gerard opened his mouth, but Medan exerted painful pressure on his arm and Gerard kept silent.

"What would you tell them? You would tell them about the queen mother. You would tell them that Laurana was harboring a human mage who had discovered a valuable magical artifact. Because of Laurana's intervention, this mage and the artifact are now safely beyond Beryl's reach."

Gerard breathed an inward sigh. Medan was watching him closely. "Yes, I thought you might be glad to hear that," he said dryly. "The mage escaped. The dragon Beryl was thwarted in her desire for the magical artifact. You will die. You will be glad to die. Your death will not save Laurana."

Gerard was silent, taking this all in. He wriggled and squirmed in the grasp of Medan's logic. The Knight could see no way out. He would have liked to think he could withstand any torture, go to his death mute and silent, but he could not be certain. He'd heard of the effects of the rack—how it pulled the joints out of the socket, left a man crippled, for the injuries would never fully heal. He had heard stories of the other torments they could inflict on a man; he recalled Palin's twisted hands, deformed fingers. He pictured Laurana's hands, white, slender, marred with the calluses where she had once held a sword.

Gerard cast another glance at the black-robed mystics. The Knight looked back at Medan. "What do you want me to do, my lord?" he asked quietly.

"You will go along with the tale I have concocted about the battle with the elves. In return for your heroic actions, I will take you on as my aide. I need someone I can trust," Medan said wryly. "I believe that the life of the queen mother is in danger. I do what I can to shield her, but it may not be enough. I need an assistant who has the same regard for the queen mother as I have myself."

"Yet, my lord," said Gerard, bewildered, "you yourself spy upon her."

"For her own protection," Medan returned. "Believe me, I do not enjoy it."

Gerard shook his head, looked up at the marshal. "My lord, here is my answer. I ask that you draw your sword and kill me. Here, where I lie in this bed. I cannot offer any resistance. I absolve you in advance of the crime of murder. My death here and now will solve all our problems."

Medan's grim face relaxed into a smile. "Perhaps not as many as you might think. I refuse, of course. I have taken a liking to you, Solamnic. I would not have missed seeing that fight you put up for all the jewels in Qualinesti! Most other Knights I know would have flung down their weapons and taken to their heels."

Medan's expression darkened, his tone grew bitter. "The days of glory for our order are long dead. Once we were led by a man of honor, a man of courage. A man who was the son of a dragonlord and Zeboim, Goddess of the Sea. Who is our leader now?" Medan's lip curled. "An accountant. A man who wears a money belt instead of sword belt. Those he makes Knights no longer win their places through valor in battle or by deeds of bravery. They buy their rank with cold cash."

Gerard thought of his own father and felt his skin grow flushed and hot. He had not bought his way into the Knighthood, at least he could credit himself there. But his father had certainly bought his son's way into every soft-cushioned assignment that came along. "The Solamnics are no better," he muttered, lowering his gaze, smoothing out the wrinkles in the sweat-soaked sheet.

"Indeed? I am sorry to hear that," Medan said and he did sound genuinely disappointed. "Perhaps, in these last days, the final battle will be fought by men who choose honor instead of choosing sides. I hope so," he added quietly, "or else I believe that we are all lost."

"Last days?" Gerard asked, uneasily. "What do you mean, my lord?"

Medan looked about the room. The mystics had departed. They were alone, the two of them.

"Beryl is going to attack Qualinesti," Medan said. "I don't know when, but she is gathering her armies. When she does, I will have a bitter choice to make." He looked at Gerard intently. "I do not want the queen mother to be part of that choice. I will need someone I can trust to help her escape."

This man is in love with Laurana! Gerard realized, amazed. Not so surprising, he supposed. He was a little bit in love with her himself. One could not be around her without becoming enchanted by her beauty and grace. Still Gerard hesitated.

"Have I mistaken you, sir?" Medan asked, and his voice was cold. He rose to his feet. "Perhaps you are as devoid of honor as the rest."

"No, my lord," Gerard said emphatically. Strange as it seemed, he wanted the marshal to think well of him. "I worked to become a Knight. I read books on the art of warfare. I studied strategy and tactics. I have held my place in tourney and joust. I became a Knight to defend the helpless, to find honor and glory in battle and instead, because of my father's influence"—Gerard paused, a shame-filled pause— "I guarded a tomb in Solace."

Medan said nothing, looked down at him, waited for his decision.

"I accept your offer, my lord," Gerard said. "I do not understand you, but I will do what I can to help the Qualinesti," he said pointedly, "and the queen mother."

"Fair enough," said the marshal. With a curt nod, Medan turned, started to walk away. Halting, he glanced back over his shoulder.

"I joined the Knighthood for the same reasons you did, young man," he said, and then strode to the door, his footsteps loud, his cloak sweeping behind him. "If the healers pronounce you well, you will move into my house tomorrow."

Gerard settled back into his bed.

I do not trust him, Gerard reflected. I will not allow myself to trust him or admire him. He could be lying about the dragon. This could all be a trick. To what end, I do not know, but I will remain watchful and on my guard.

At least, he thought, feeling a strange sort of contentment wash through him, I'll be doing more than freeing some damn kender who manages to lock himself in a tomb.

Medan left the hospital, well pleased with his interview. He did not trust the Solamnic, of course. Medan trusted no one these days. The marshal would watch the man closely over the next few days, see how he acquitted himself. He could always take the Solamnic up on his offer and run his sword through him.

At least, I do not doubt his courage or his loyalty to his friends, the marshal reflected. He has proven these to me already.

The marshal turned his steps toward Laurana's house. He enjoyed the walk. Qualinesti was beautiful in all seasons, but summer was his favorite, the season of festivals, with its myriad flowers, the soft air filled with exquisite perfumes, the silvery green of the leaves and the wondrous bird song.

He took his time, pausing to lean over garden walls to admire a flaming display of day lilies lifting their orange heads to the sunshine. He lingered in the walkway to watch a shower of white blossoms shaken from a snow-ball bush by a fluttering robin. Coming upon an elf from House Woodshaper, Medan stopped the man to discuss a blight he feared had overtaken one of his rose bushes. The Woodshaper was hostile, made it clear he talked to Medan only because he was forced to do so. Medan was polite, respectful, his questions were intelligent. Gradually the elf warmed to his topic and, in the end, promised to come to the marshal's house to treat the ailing rose.

Arriving at Laurana's house, Medan rang the silver chimes and stood listening with pleasure to their sweet song as he waited for a response.

An elf answered the door, bowed politely. Medan looked at him intently.

"Kelevandros, isn't it?" he asked.

"Yes, Marshal," the elf returned.

"I came to see—"

"Who is it, Kelevandros?" Laurana appeared, walking down the hallway. "Ah, Marshal Medan. Welcome to my home. Please come in. Will you take some refreshment?"

"Thank you, madam, but I cannot stay," Medan said politely. "We have had reports that a band of rebels are operating in the wilderness not far from here. One of my own men was savagely attacked." He eyed her closely. "The rebels have no love for the royal family, considering them to be collaborators. If, as you say, you have no influence over these rebels—"

"I live a quiet and retired life, Marshal," Laurana said. "I go nowhere except to the palace to visit my son. Yet I find myself constantly under suspicion. My first love and loyalty are to my homeland and my people."

"I am aware of that fact, madam," Medan said with a cool smile. "Therefore, madam, until we have caught these rebels, it is not safe for you to leave the confines of your house. I must ask that you and those you care about remain close to home. You have permission to visit the palace, naturally, but I must prohibit trips to other places in the realm."

"Am I a prisoner in my house, then, Marshal?" Laurana demanded.

"I do this for your own protection, madam," Medan said. He reached out his hand to draw near one of the purple blossoms, inhaled its sweet fragrance. "My commendations on this beautiful lilac bush. I have never known one to bloom so long past spring. Good-day to you, Queen Mother."

"And to you, Marshal Medan," Laurana said.

"How I detest this game," said Medan to himself. Making his solitary way back to his own dwelling, he could smell the lilac's perfume.

"How I hate this game," Laurana said, shutting the door and leaning her head with its crown of golden hair against it.

The waterfall played sweet and gentle music and Laurana listened to its song, let the melody soothe her, restore her to her customary hopefulness. She was not one to give way to despair. She had walked in darkness, the greatest darkness the world had known. She had come face-to-face with the dread goddess Takhisis. She had seen love surmount the darkness, love triumph. She believed that even the darkest night must eventually give way to the dawn.

She held fast to that belief through all the sorrows and travails of her life, through the loss of her son to the political machinations of her own people, through the death of her beloved husband, Tanis, who had died defending the High

Clerist's Tower against the Dark Knights, died of a sword thrust in the back. She grieved his loss, she missed him sorely, she established a shrine to him in her heart, but his death did not bring about her own. She did not bury her heart in his grave. To do so would have been to deny his life, to undo all the good that he had done. She continued to fight for the causes both of them had championed.

Some people took exception to this. They thought she should have clothed herself in black and retired from the world. They took offense that she should laugh and smile, or listen with pleasure to the minstrel's song.

"It is so sad," they would say. "Your husband died such a senseless death."

"Tell me, sir," Laurana would reply, or, "Tell me, madam. Tell me what you consider to be a *sensible* death?"

Smiling to herself at their discomfiture, Laurana heard, in her heart, Tanis's laughter. There had been a time, shortly after his death, when she could hear his voice and sense his presence watching over her, not protectively, but supporting, reassuring. She had not felt his presence, however, in a long, long time. She could only assume that he had passed on to the next stage on life's journey. She was not saddened or sorrowful. She would meet him when it was time for her to depart this life. They would find each other, though all eternity might stand between them. Meanwhile, the dead did not need her. The living did.

"My lady," said Kelevandros softly, "do not let the marshal's threats upset you. We will outwit him. We have always done so."

Laurana lifted her head and smiled. "Yes, we will. How fortunate that you had returned from your mission, Kelevandros. Medan might have noted your absence, and that would have made things awkward. We must take extra precautions from now on. Gilthas reports that the dwarven tunnels are near completion. You will use that route now. It will take you out of your way, but it will be safer. Kalindas! You should not be out of bed!"

The elf stood swaying unsteadily in the doorway. His head was swathed in bandages, he was so pale that his skin had a translucent quality. Laurana could see the blue veins in his face. Kelevandros came to his brother's aide, put his arm around him, assisted him to a couch. He eased his brother down gently, all the while scolding Kalindas roundly for leaving his bed and causing their mistress concern.

"What happened to me?" Kalindas asked dazedly.

"You don't remember?" Laurana asked.

"Nothing!" He put his hand to his head.

"Kelevandros," Laurana said sharply, "go to the front door. Make certain that Marshal Medan remembered to leave."

"Birds sing in the trees," Kelevandros reported on his return. "The bees buzz among the flowers. No one is about."

"Now, Kalindas"—Laurana turned to him—"do you remember guiding Master Palin, Gerard, and the kender to the meeting with the griffon?"

Kalindas considered. "Vaguely, madam."

"You were attacked while you were in the wilderness," said Laurana, readjusting the bandages on the young elf's head. "We have been very worried about you. When you didn't return, I asked the Lioness to send her people to search for you. The rebels found you lying wounded in the forest. They brought you back yesterday. Why did you rise? Do you need anything?"

"No, madam, thank you," said Kalindas. "Forgive me for causing you alarm. I heard the marshal's voice and thought perhaps you might stand in need of me. I fancied myself well enough to leave my bed. I was mistaken, it seems."

Kelevandros eased his injured brother to a more comfortable position on the couch, while Laurana spread her own shawl over Kalindas to keep him warm.

"You have endured enough from Medan and his men," Laurana said, her voice cool with anger. "You are fortunate you weren't killed!"

"They had no need to kill me," Kalindas said bitterly. "They must have struck me from behind. Did Master Palin and the kender escape safely with the magical device?"

"We believe so. The rebels found no trace of them, and we have received no reports that they were captured."

"What about the Solamnic?"

"The Lioness reported signs of a fight. Two of the Neraka Knights were killed. They could not find Gerard's body and so they assume that he was made prisoner." Laurana sighed. "If that is true, I could almost wish him dead. The rebels have their spies in the army trying to discover information about him. He is not in prison, that much we know, and that is all we know.

"As for Palin, Kelevandros has just returned from a meeting with the griffons, who arrived bearing a message, which I hope is from Palin."

"I have it here, madam," said Kelevandros. He removed a roll of parchment from his boot, handed the roll to Laurana.

"Are you certain you are all right?" she asked Kalindas, accepting the scroll. "Shall I call for a glass of wine?"

"Please read your letter, Madam," Kalindas said. "Do not worry about me."

After another worried glance, Laurana went to her writing desk and sat down. Kelevandros lit a candle for her, brought it to her desk. She unrolled the parchment. It was covered with ink and smelled faintly of lemon. The words written in the letter were inconsequential. A former neighbor told Laurana of the crops that he had planted, how big his children were growing, how he'd recently purchased a fine horse at the Midyear Day's Fair. He inquired after her health, hoped she was well.

Laurana held the parchment above the candle's flame, taking care not to hold it too near, taking care not to burn the paper or singe it. Slowly, more writing began to appear on the parchment, words written in between the lines of words written in ink. She passed the paper back and forth above the flame until the hidden message written on the parchment was revealed.

Placing it on the desk, she read the missive silently, to herself. The handwriting was not Palin's. Laurana was puzzled as to who had written the letter, looked to see the signature on the bottom.

"Ah, Jenna," she murmured.

She read on, growing more amazed with each line.

"What is it, madam?" Kalindas asked, alarmed. "What has happened?"

"Strange," she murmured. "So very strange. I cannot believe this. Going back in time to find the past no longer exists. I don't understand."

She continued on. "Tasslehoff missing." She shook her head. "He did not come here."

She read on. The brothers exchanged glances. A dark line marred the smooth skin of her forehead. Her brows came together. She read to the end of the scroll, stared at it long moments, as if willing it to say something other than what it said, she slowly released the end. The scroll curled in upon itself, hung limply in her hand.

"We are being spied upon, it seems," Laurana said, and her tone was deliberately even and calm. "Palin and Tasslehoff were chased by a dragon, one of Beryl's minions. Palin believes that the dragon was after the artifact. That means Beryl knows of the artifact's existence and where it is to be found. The Neraka Knights did not stumble across the four of you by accident, Kalindas. You walked into an ambush."

"A spy! In your own house. Perhaps one of us? That is impossible, madam," Kelevandros stated heatedly.

"Indeed, it is," said Kalindas.

"I hope you are right," Laurana said gravely. "An elf who

would betray his own people . . ." She shook her head, her tone was sorrowful. "It is hard to believe that such evil could exist. Yet, it has happened before."

"You know that none of us would betray you," Kalindas reiterated, with emphasis.

Laurana sighed. "I don't know what to think. Mistress Jenna suggests that perhaps there is a mentalist among the Neraka Knights, one who has learned to see into our minds and gather our thoughts. What a bitter pass we are come to! We have to set a guard now upon what we think!"

She slipped the message into the girdle of gold she wore around her waist. "Kelevandros, bring me some lemon juice and then ready Brightwing to carry a message to the griffons."

The elf did as he was told, departing on his errands in silence. He exchanged a final glance with his brother before he left. Both noted that Laurana had not answered the question about Palin. She had taken care to change the subject. She did not trust even them, it seemed. A shadow had fallen over their peaceful dwelling place, a shadow that would not soon be lifted.

Laurana's answer to the letter was short.

Tasslehoff is not here. I will watch for him. Thank you for the warning about spies. I will be on my guard.

She rolled the message tightly so that it would fit in the small crystal tube that would be tied to the hawk's leg.

"Forgive me for disturbing you, madam," Kalindas said, "but the pain in my head has increased. Kelevandros told me that the healer spoke of poppy juice. I think that might help me, if my brother would bring it to me."

"I will send for the healer at once," Laurana said, concerned. "Lie here until your brother returns to fetch her for you."

Marshal Medan walked late in his garden. He enjoyed watching the miracle of the night-blooming flowers that shunned the sun and opened their blossoms to the pale moonlight. He was alone. He had dismissed his aide, ordered him to clear out his things. The Solamnic would arrive tomorrow, start upon his new duties.

Medan was pausing to admire a white orchid that seemed to glow in the moonlight, when he heard a voice hissing from the bushes.

"Marshal! It is I!"

"Indeed," said Medan, "and here I thought it was a snake. I am weary. Crawl back under your rock until morning."

"I have important information that cannot wait," the voice said. "Information Beryl will find most interesting. The mage Palin Majere has used the artifact to journey back in time. This is a powerful magical artifact, perhaps the most powerful yet discovered in this world."

"Perhaps." Medan was noncommittal. He had a very low opinion of mages and magic. "Where is this powerful artifact now?"

"I do not know for certain," said the elf. "His letter to my mistress said that the kender had run off with the artifact. Majere believes the kender has gone to the Citadel of Light. He travels there to attempt to recover it."

"At least he did not come back here," Medan said, breathing a sigh of relief. "Good riddance to him and the blasted artifact."

"This information is worth a great deal," the elf said.

"You will be paid. But in the morning," Medan said. "Now be gone before your mistress misses you."

"She will not." The elf sounded smug. "She sleeps soundly. Very soundly. I laced her evening tea with poppy juice."

"I told you to leave," Medan said coldly. "I will deduct a steel piece for every second you remain in my presence. You have lost one already."

He heard a scrabbling sound in the bushes. The marshal

waited a moment longer, to be certain the elf was gone. The moon disappeared behind a cloud. The garden was submerged in darkness. The pale glowing orchid vanished from his sight.

It seemed a sign. A portent.

"Only a matter of time," he said to himself. "Days, maybe. Not longer. This night I have made my decision. I have chosen my course. I can do nothing now but wait."

His pleasure in the night destroyed, the marshal returned to his house, forced to fumble his way through the darkness for he could no longer see the path.

26

Pawn to King's Knight Four

his day, Gerard would meet with Marshal Medan and be coerced into serving the commander of the Knights of Neraka. This day, Laurana would discover that she harbored a spy, perhaps in her own home. This day, Tasslehoff would discover that it is difficult to live up to what people say about you after you are dead. This day, Mina's army would march deeper into Silvanesti. This day, Silvanoshei was playing a game with his cousin.

Silvanoshei was king of the Silvanesti. He was king of his people, just like the bejeweled and ornately carved bit of alabaster who was king of the *xadrez* board. A silly, inefffectual king, who could only move a single square at a time. A king who had to be protected by his knights and his ministers. Even his pawns had more important work to do than the king.

"My queen takes your rook," said Kiryn, sliding an ornate game piece across the green-and-white marble board. "Your king is doomed. This gives me the game, I think."

"Blast! So it does!" Silvan gave the board an irritated

493

shove, scattering the pieces. "I used to be quite good at *xadrez*. My mother taught me to play. I could even beat Samar on occasion. You are a far worse player than he was. No offense, Cousin."

"None taken," said Kiryn, crawling on the floor to retrieve a foot soldier who had fled the field and taken refuge underneath the bed. "You are preoccupied, that is all. You're not giving the game your complete concentration."

"Here, let me do that," Silvan offered, remorseful. "I was the one who spilled them."

"I can manage—" Kiryn began.

"No, let me do something constructive, at least!" Silvan dived under the table to come up with a knight, a wizard and, after some searching, his beleaguered king, who had sought to escape defeat by hiding behind a curtain.

Silvan retrieved all the pieces, set the board up again.

"Do you want to play another?"

"No, I am sick to death of this game!" Silvan said irritably.

Leaving the gaming table, he walked to the window, stared out it for a few moments, then, restless, he turned away again. "You say I am preoccupied, Cousin. I don't know by what. I don't *do* anything."

He wandered over to a side table on which stood bowls of chilled fruit, nuts, cheese, and a decanter of wine. Cracking nuts, as if he had some grudge against them, he sorted through the shells to find the meats. "Want some?"

Kiryn shook his head. Silvan tossed the shells onto the table, wiped them from his hand.

"I hate nuts!" he said and walked back across the room to the window. "How long have I been king?" he asked.

"Some weeks, Cousin—"

"And during that time, what have I accomplished?"

"It is early days, yet, Cousin—"

"Nothing," Silvan said emphatically. "Not a damn thing. I am not allowed out of the palace for fear I will catch this wasting disease. I am not permitted to speak to my people for fear of assassins. I sign my name to orders and edicts, but I'm never permitted to read them for fear it will fatigue me. Your uncle does all the work."

"He will continue to do it so long as you let him," Kiryn said pointedly. "He and Glaucous."

"Glaucous!" Silvan repeated. Turning, he eyed his friend suspiciously. "You are always on me about Glaucous. I'll have you know that if it were not for Glaucous, I would not know the little I do know about what is happening in my very own kingdom. Look! Look there, now!" Silvan pointed out the window. "Here is an example of what I mean. Something is happening. Something is going on, and will I hear what it is? I will"—Silvan was bitter—"but only if I ask my servants!"

A man dressed in the garb of one of the kirath could be seen running pell-mell across the broad courtyard with its walkways and gardens that surrounded the palace. Once the elaborate gardens had been a favorite place for the citizens of Silvanost to walk, to meet, to have luncheons on the broad green swards beneath the willow trees. Lovers took boats fashioned in the shape of swans out upon the sparkling streams that ran through the garden. Students came with their masters to sit upon the grass and indulge in the philosophical discussions so dear to elves.

That was before the wasting sickness had come to Silvanost. Now many people were afraid to leave their homes, afraid to meet in groups, lest they catch the sickness. The gardens were almost empty, except for a few members of the military, who had just come off-duty and were returning to their barracks. The soldiers looked in astonishment at the racing kirath, stood aside to let him pass. He paid no heed to them but hurried onward. He ran up the broad marble stairs that led to the palace and vanished from sight.

"There! What did I tell you, Kiryn? Something important has happened," said Silvan, gnawing his lower lip. "And will the messenger come to me? No, he will go straight to your uncle. I am king, not General Konnal!"

Silvan turned from the window, his expression dark and grim. "I am becoming what I most detest. I am becoming my cousin Gilthas. A puppet dancing on another's strings!"

"If you are a puppet, Silvan, then that is because you want to be a puppet," Kiryn said boldly. "The fault is yours, not my uncle's! You have shown no interest in the day-to-day business of the kingdom. You could have read those edicts, but you were too busy learning the newest dance steps."

Silvan looked at him, anger flaring. "How dare you speak to me like that. I am your—" He checked himself. He had been about to say, "your king!" but realized that in view of the conversation, that would sound ridiculous.

Besides, he admitted, Kiryn had spoken nothing more than the truth. Silvan had enjoyed playing at being king. He wore the crown upon his head, but he would not take up the mantle of responsibility and drape it around his shoulders. He drew in a deep breath, let it out. He had behaved like a child, and so he had been treated like a child. But no more.

"You are right, Cousin," Silvan said, his tone calm and even. "If your uncle has no respect for me, why should he? What have I done since I came here but skulk about in my room playing games and eating sweets. Respect must be earned. It cannot be dictated. I have done nothing to earn his regard. I have done nothing to prove to him and to my people that I am king. That ends. Today."

Silvan threw open the huge double doors that led to his chambers, threw them open with such force that they banged back against the walls. The sound startled the guards, who had been dozing on their feet in the quiet, drowsy afternoon. They clattered to attention as Silvan strode out the door and walked right past them.

"Your Majesty!" cried one. "Where are you going? Your Majesty, you should not be leaving your room. General

Konnal has ordered . . . Your Majesty!" The guard found he was speaking to the king's back.

Silvan descended the long, broad marble staircase, walking rapidly, with Kiryn at his heels and the guards hastening along behind.

"Silvan!" Kiryn remonstrated, catching up, "I didn't intend that you should take charge this very moment. You have much to learn about Silvanesti and its people. You've never lived among us. You are very young."

Silvan had understood his cousin's intentions quite well. He paid him no heed, but kept walking.

"What I meant," Kiryn continued, dogging Silvan's footsteps, "was that you should take more interest in the daily business of the kingdom, ask questions. Visit the people in their homes. See how we live. There are many of the wise among our people who would be glad to help you learn. Rolan of the kirath is one. Why not seek his advice and counsel? You would find him far wiser than Glaucous, if less pleasing."

Silvan's lips tightened. He walked on. "I know what I am doing," he said.

"Yes, and so did your Grandfather Lorac. Listen to me, Silvan," Kiryn said earnestly. "Don't make the same mistake. Your grandfather's downfall was not the dragon Cyan Bloodbane. Pride and fear were Lorac's downfall. The dragon was the embodiment of his pride and his fear. Pride whispered to Lorac that he was wiser than the wise. Pride whispered that he could flout rules and laws. Fear urged him to act alone, to refuse help, to turn a deaf ear to advice and counsel."

Silvanoshei halted. "All my life, Cousin, I've heard that side of the story, and I have accepted it. I have been taught to be ashamed of my grandfather. But in recent days I've heard another side, a side no one mentions because they find it easy to blame my grandfather for their troubles. The Silvanesti people survived the War of the Lance. They are alive today *because* of my grandfather. If he had not sacrificed himself as he did, you and I would not be standing here discussing the matter. The welfare of the people was Lorac's responsibility. He accepted that responsibility. He saved them, and now instead of being blessed by them he is denigrated!"

"Who told you this, Cousin?" Kiryn asked.

Silvan saw no reason to answer this, and so he turned on his heel and continued walking. Glaucous had known his grandfather. He had been very close to Lorac. Who would know better the truth of the matter?

Kiryn guessed the name Silvan did not speak. He walked a few paces behind his king, said no more.

Silvan and his oddly assorted escort, consisting of his cousin and the clamoring guards, strode rapidly through the corridors of the palace. Silvan passed by magnificent paintings and wondrous tapestries without a glance. His boots rang loudly on the floor, expressive of his haste and his determination. Accustomed only to silence in this part of the palace, the servants came running to see what was amiss.

"Your Majesty, Your Majesty," they murmured, bowing in fluttered confusion and looking at each other askance when he had gone by, as much as to say, "The bird has flown the cage. The rabbit has escaped the warren. Well, well. Not surprising, considering that he is a Caladon."

The king left the royal quarters of the palace, entered the public areas, which were crowded with people: messengers coming and going, lords and ladies of House Royal standing in clusters talking among themselves, people bustling about with ledgers under their arms or scrolls in their hands. Here was the true heart of the kingdom. Here the business of the kingdom was accomplished. Here—on the side of the palace opposite the royal quarters where Silvan resided.

The courtiers heard the commotion, paused and turned to see what was going on, and when they saw it was their king, they were astonished. So astonished that some lords forgot to bow, remembered only belatedly and then because scandalized wives poked them in the ribs.

Silvan noted the difference between the two sides of the palace immediately. His lips tightened. He ignored the courtiers and brushed aside those who tried to speak. Rounding a corner, he approached another set of double doors. Guards stood here, but these guards were alert, not dozing. They came to attention when the king approached.

"Your Majesty," said one, moving as if to block his way. "Forgive me, Sire, but General Konnal has given orders that he is not to be disturbed."

Silvan gazed long at the man, then said, "Tell the general he will be disturbed. His king is here to disturb him."

Silvan enjoyed watching the struggle on the guard's face. The elf had his orders from Konnal, yet here stood his king before him. The guard had a choice to make. He looked at the pale eyes and set jaw of the young king and saw in them the blood line that had ruled Silvanesti for generations. This guard was an older man, perhaps he had served under Lorac. Perhaps he recognized that pale fire. The guard bowed with respect, and, throwing open the doors, announced in firm tones, "His Majesty, the King."

Konnal looked up in amazement. Glaucous's expression was one of astonishment at first, but that swiftly changed to secret pleasure. Perhaps he, too, had been waiting the day when the lion would tear free of his chains. Bowing, Glaucous cast a glance at Silvan that said plainly, "Forgive me, Your Majesty, but I am under the general's control."

"Your Majesty, to what do we owe this honor?" Konnal asked, highly irritated at the interruption. He had obviously received some unsettling news for his face was flushed, his brows contracted. He had to struggle to maintain a show of politeness, and then his voice was cold. Glaucous was disturbed by something as well. His face was grim, he seemed disturbed and anxious.

Silvan did not reply to the general's question. Instead, he turned to the elf of the kirath, who immediately bowed very low.

"You bring news, sir?" the king asked imperiously.

"I do, Your Majesty," said the kirath.

"News of importance to the kingdom?"

The kirath stole a glance at Konnal, who shrugged in response.

"Of the utmost importance, Your Majesty," the kirath replied.

"And you do not bring that news to your king!" Silvan was pale with anger.

The general intervened. "Your Majesty, I would have apprised you of the situation at the proper time. This matter is extremely serious. Immediate action must be taken—"

"So you thought you would tell me of the matter *after* you had taken the action," said Silvan. He looked back at the kirath. "What is your news, sir? No, don't look at him! Tell me! I am your king!"

"A force of Dark Knights has managed to penetrate the shield, Your Majesty. They are inside the borders of Silvanesti and marching toward Silvanost."

"Dark Knights?" Silvan repeated, astonished. "But how . . . ? Are you certain?"

"Yes, Your Majesty," the kirath replied. "I saw them myself. We had received reports of an army of ogres assembling outside the shield. We went to investigate these reports and it was then we discovered this force of about four hundred human soldiers *inside* the shield. The officers are those known to us as the Dark Knights of Takhisis. We recognized their armor. A company of archers, probably mercenaries, marches with them. They have among their number a minotaur, who is second in command."

"Who is their leader?" Silvan asked.

"There is not time for this—" Konnal began.

"I want to know all the details," Silvan stated coldly.

"The leader is very strange, Your Majesty," the kirath replied. "She is a human female. That in itself is not surprising, but this leader is a child, even among their kind. She cannot be more than eighteen human years, if she is that. Yet she is a Knight, and she is their commander. She wears the black armor, and the soldiers defer to her in everything."

"That is odd," said Silvan, frowning. "I can hardly believe it. I am familiar with the structure of the Dark Knights, who now call themselves Knights of Neraka. I have never heard of a person that young being made a Knight, much less an officer."

Silvan shifted his gaze to Konnal. "What do you plan to do about this threat, General?"

"We will mobilize the army, at once, Your Majesty," Konnal replied stiffly. "I have already given orders to do so. The kirath are following the enemy's progress through our land. We will march out to meet them, and we will repulse them and destroy them. Their force numbers only four hundred. They have no supplies, no means of acquiring supplies. They are cut off, isolated. The battle will not last long."

"Do you have any experience fighting against the Knights of Neraka, General Konnal?" Silvan asked.

Konnal's face darkened. He pursed his lips. "No, Your Majesty. I have not."

"Do you have any experience fighting against any foe other than a dream foe?" Silvan pursued.

Konnal was extremely angry. He went livid. Two bright flaring spots of red stained his cheeks. Jumping to his feet, he slammed his hands on the desk. "You young—"

"General!" Glaucous came back from wherever his thoughts had been wandering to hastily intervene. "He is your king."

Konnal muttered something that sounded like, "He is not *my* king . . ." but he said the words beneath his breath.

"I have fought against these Knights and their forces, General," Silvan continued. "My father and mother fought the Dark Knights in the forests around Qualinesti. I have fought ogres and human brigands. I have fought elves, as you may know, General."

The elves they had fought had been elven assassins sent out before the shield was put in place, sent to murder Porthios and Alhana, who had been declared dark elves, perhaps on the orders of General Konnal.

"Although I myself did not fight," Silvan said, bound to be truthful, "I have been witness to many of these battles. In addition, I have taken part in the meetings during which my father and mother and their officers planned their strategies."

"And yet, the Dark Knights managed to capture Qualinesti, despite your father's best efforts," Konnal said, with a slight curl of his lip.

"They did, sir," Silvan replied gravely, "and that is why I warn you not to underestimate them. I agree with your decision, General. We will send out a force to fight them. I would like to see a map of the area."

"Your Majesty—" Konnal began impatiently, but Silvanoshei was already spreading a map on the desk.

"Where are the Dark Knights, kirath?" Silvan asked.

The kirath stepped forward, indicated with his finger on the map the location of the troops. "As you can see, Your Majesty, by following the Thon-Thalas River, they entered the shield here at the Silvanesti border, where the two intersect. Our reports indicate that they are currently hugging the banks of the Thon-Thalas. We have no reason to believe that they will deviate from that course, which will lead them directly into Silvanost."

Silvan studied the map. "I agree with the kirath that they are not likely to abandon the road that runs alongside the river. To do so would be to risk losing themselves in unfamiliar wilderness. They know they have been seen. They have no reason to hide. They have every reason to move with haste. Their only hope is to attack us while we are presumably reeling from the shock of finding them inside our borders."

He glanced pointedly at Konnal as he said this. The general's face was stone hard, stone cold. He said nothing.

"I suggest that here"—Silvan placed his finger on the map— "would be an excellent location for us to engage them. The enemy will come down out of the hills to find our forces spread out in this valley. They will find themselves trapped between the river on one side and hills on the other, which will make it difficult for them to deploy their forces to best advantage. While the foot soldiers hit them from the front, a company of cavalry can circle around and hit them from the rear. We will gradually close the jaws of our army"—he moved his finger from the footmen in the front to the cavalry in the rear, forming a semicircle—"and swallow them."

Silvan looked up. Konnal stared down at the map, frowning, his hands clasped behind his back.

"That is a good plan, Your Majesty," Glaucous said, sounding impressed.

"General Konnal?" Silvan demanded.

"It might work," General Konnal conceded grudgingly.

"My only concern is that the Knights may hide in the wilderness," Silvan added. "If they do that, we will have a difficult time flushing them out."

"Bah! We will find them," Konnal stated.

"It seems your forces cannot find an immense green dragon, General," Silvan returned. "They've been searching for Cyan Bloodbane for thirty years. If this army of humans was to separate, scatter, we might search for them for a century."

Glaucous laughed, causing the general to cast him a baleful glance.

"I find nothing amusing in any of this," Konnal said. "How did this spawn of evil come through that precious shield of yours, Glaucous? Answer me that?"

"I assure you, General, I do not know," Glaucous said and his face was once again troubled, shadowed. "Not yet, at any rate. There is some fell magic at work here. I can smell it."

"All I smell is the stench of humans," Konnal said bitterly.

"I suggest that we try to capture alive this strange woman-child who leads them. I would like very much to speak to her. Very much indeed," Glaucous added, frowning.

"I agree with Glaucous, General." Silvanoshei turned to Konnal. "You will give the necessary orders. And you will arrange for me to join the army."

"Out of the question," Konnal said shortly.

"I *will* go," said Silvan imperiously, staring intently at the general, daring him to defiance. "You will make the arrangements, sir. Would you have me cower under the bed while my people ride to defend their homes?"

Konnal considered, then he made an ice-rimed bow to the king. "Very well. If your Majesty insists, I will see to it," he said.

Silvan turned on his heel. He left the room in a flurry of robes. Kiryn cast a thoughtful glance at Glaucous, then followed after the king. The guards closed the doors behind them, took up their posts.

"I would be interested to know why you changed your mind, General," Glaucous said quietly.

"Battles are chancy affairs," Konnal replied, shrugging. "No one knows how they will turn out. No one knows who may fall victim to the enemy. If His Majesty were to suffer some hurt—"

"—you would make him a martyr," said Glaucous, "as you made his parents martyrs. You will be blamed. Never doubt it. You should not permit him to go." The mage was grave, withdrawing into himself again. "I have a presentiment that, if he does, something awful will happen."

"Something awful has already happened, in case you hadn't noticed!" Konnal said angrily. "Your magic is failing, Glaucous! Like all the others! Admit it!"

"Your fear is talking, my friend," said Glaucous. "I understand that, and I forgive you for impugning my magical skills. I forgive you this time." His voice softened. "Consider well what I have said. I will endeavor to persuade His Majesty to reconsider riding to war. If I cannot do so, permit him to come, but keep him safe."

"Leave me!" Konnal said harshly. "I do not need a wizard telling me what to do."

"I will leave," said Glaucous, "but remember this, General. You need me. *I* stand between the Silvanesti and the world. Cast me aside, and you cast aside all hope. I am the only one who can save you."

Konnal spoke no word, did not look up.

27

The Touch of the Dead

his evening, while Silvanoshei prepared himself for his first battle, Goldmoon prepared herself as if for battle. For the first time in many long weeks, Goldmoon asked that a hand mirror be brought to her quarters. For the first time since the storm, she lifted the mirror and looked at her face.

Goldmoon had been vain as a girl. She was graced with a rare beauty, the only woman in her tribe to have hair that was like a shimmering tapestry woven of silken threads of sunshine and of moonlight. The chieftain's daughter, she was spoiled, pampered, brought up with an exalted opinion of herself. She spent long hours gazing into the water bowl just to see her own reflection. The young warriors of her tribe adored her. They came to blows for her smile. All except one.

One day, she looked into the eyes of a tall outcast, a young shepherd named Riverwind, and she saw herself in the mirror he held up to her. Looking into his eyes, she saw her vanity, her selfishness. She saw that she was ugly in his eyes, and she was shamed and despairing. For him, for Riverwind, Goldmoon wanted to be beautiful.

So she had come to be beautiful, but only after they had both gone through many trials and travails together, only after they had confronted death fearlessly, clasped in each other's arms. She had been given the blue crystal staff. She had been given the power of bringing the healing love of the gods back into the world.

Children were born to Goldmoon and Riverwind. They worked to unite the contentious tribes of the Plains people. They were happy in their lives and in their children and their friends, the companions of their journeying. They had looked forward to growing old together, to taking their final rest together, to leaving together this plane of existence and moving on to the next, whatever that might be. They were not afraid, for they would be together.

It had not happened that way.

When the gods left following the Chaos War, Goldmoon mourned their absence. She was not one who railed against them. She understood their sacrifice, or thought she did. The gods had left so that Chaos would leave, the world would be at peace. She did not understand, but she had faith in the gods, and so she did what she could to argue against the anger and bitterness that poisoned so many.

She believed in her heart that someday the gods would return. That belief dwindled with the coming of the monstrous dragons, who brought terror and death to Ansalon. Her belief vanished altogether when word came that her beloved Riverwind and one of her daughters had both been slain by the heinous dragon Malys. Goldmoon had longed to die herself. She had fully intended to end her life, but then Riverwind's spirit had come to her.

She must stay, he told her. She must continue her fight to keep hope alive in the world. If she left the world, the darkness would win.

She had not wanted to heed his words, but she had given way.

She had been rewarded. She had been given the gift of healing a second time. Not a blessing from the gods, but a mystical power of the heart which even she did not understand. She brought this gift to others and they had banded together to build the Citadel of Light in order to teach all people how to use the power.

Goldmoon had grown old in the Citadel. She had seen the spirit of her husband as a handsome youth once again. Though he curbed his impatience, she knew he was eager to be gone and that he waited only for her to complete her journey.

Goldmoon lifted the mirror and looked at her face.

Lines of age were gone. Her skin was smooth. Her once sunken cheeks were now plump, the pale skin rose colored. Her eyes had always been bright, shining with the indomitable courage and hope that had made her seem young to her devoted followers. Her lips, thin and gray, were full, tinged with coral. Her hair had remained her one vanity. Though her hair had turned silver white, it remained thick and luxuriant. She reached her hand to touch her hair, a hand that was young and smooth and strong again, and the fingers touched gold and silver strands. But her hair had an odd feel to it. Coarser than she remembered, not as fine.

She knew suddenly why she hated this unasked for, unlooked for, unwanted gift. The face in the mirror was not her face. The face was a memory of her face, and the memory was not her own. The memory was another's. The face was someone's idea of her face. This face was perfect, and her face had not been perfect.

The same was true of her body. Youthful, vigorous, strong, slender waist, full breasts, this body was not the body she remembered. This body was perfect. No aches, no pains, not so much as a torn nail or a blister on her heel.

Her old soul did not fit into this new young flesh. Her old

soul had been light and airy, ready to take wing and soar into eternity. That soul had been content to leave behind mundane cares and woes. Now her soul was caged in a prison of flesh and bone and blood, a prison that was making its own demands on her. She did not understand how or why. She could not give reasons. All she knew was that the face in the mirror terrified her.

She laid the mirror down, facedown on the dressing table, and, sighing deeply, prepared to leave the one prison she could leave, desperately wishing all the while that she could leave the other.

Wonder and amazement greeted Goldmoon's appearance in the hall of the Grand Lyceum that night. As she had feared, her transformation was taken for a miracle, a good miracle, a blessed miracle.

"Wait until word spreads!" her pupils whispered. "Wait until the people hear! Goldmoon has conquered age. She has vanquished death! The people will come flocking to our cause now!"

Pupils and masters clustered around her and reached out to touch her. They fell to their knees and kissed her hand. They begged her to grant them her blessing, and they rose to their feet exalted. Only a few looked closely at Goldmoon to see the pain and anguish on the youthful, beautiful face, a face they recognized more by the light in her eyes than by any resemblance to the face of contentment and wisdom they had come to know and revere. Even that light seemed unhealthy, a luster that was the luster of a fever.

The evening was a trial to Goldmoon. They held a banquet in her honor, forced her to sit in a place of honor at the head of the hall. She felt everyone was looking at her, and she was right. Few seemed able to take their eyes off her, and they stared at her until it occurred to them that they were being rude, then they shifted their gazes pointedly in another direction. Goldmoon couldn't decide which was worse. She ate well, much better than usual. Her strange body demanded large quantities of food, but she did not taste any of it. She was doing nothing more than fueling a fire, a fire she feared must consume her.

"In a few days, they will be used to me," she said to herself drearily. "They will cease to notice that I am so terribly altered. *I* will know, however. If I could just understand why this has been done to me."

Palin sat at her right hand, but he was grim and cheerless. He picked at his food and finally pushed most of the meal away uneaten. He paid no attention to conversation but was wrapped in his own thoughts. He was, she guessed, making that journey back through time over and over again in his mind, searching for some clue to its strange conclusion.

Tasslehoff was also out of spirits. The kender sat beside Palin, who kept close watch on him. He kicked the chair rungs and occasionally heaved a doleful sigh. Most of his eating utensils, a salt cellar, and a pepper pot made their way into his pockets, but the borrowing was halfhearted at best, a reflexive action. He was clearly not enjoying himself.

"Will you help me map the hedge maze tomorrow?" asked his neighbor, the gnome. "I have come up with a scientific solution to my problem. My solution requires another person, however, and a pair of socks."

"Tomorrow?" said Tas.

"Yes, tomorrow," repeated the gnome.

Tas looked at Palin. The mage looked at Tas.

"I'll be glad to help," Tas said. He slid off his chair. "Come on, Conundrum. You were going to show me your ship."

"Ah, yes, my ship." The gnome tucked some bread into his pocket for later. "The *Indestructible XVIII*. It's tied up at the dock. At least it was. I'll never forget the surprise I had when I went to board its predecessor, the *Indestructible XVII*, only to discover that it had been woefully misnamed. The committee made sweeping changes to the design, however, and I am quite confident—"

Palin watched Tasslehoff walk away.

"You must talk to him, Goldmoon," the mage said in a low voice. "Convince him he has to go back."

"Go back to his death? How can I ask that of Tas? How could I ask that of anyone?"

"I know," Palin said, sighing and rubbing his temples as if they ached. "Believe me, First Master, I wish there were some other way. All I know is that he's supposed to be dead, and he's not, and the world has gone awry."

"Yet you admit yourself you are not certain that Tasslehoff, either dead or alive, has anything to do with the world's problems."

"You don't understand, First Master—" Palin began wearily.

"You are right. I don't understand. And therefore what would you have me say to him?" she asked sharply. "How can I offer counsel when I do not comprehend what is happening?" She shook her head. "The decision is his alone to make. I will not interfere."

Goldmoon rested her hand on her smooth cheek. She could feel her fingers against her skin, but her skin could not sense the touch of her fingers. She might have been placing her fingers on a waxen image.

The banquet ended, finally. Goldmoon rose to her feet and the others rose in respect. One of the acolytes, an exuberant youngster, gave a cheer. Others picked it up. Soon they were applauding and yelling lustily.

The cheering frightened Goldmoon. The noise will draw attention to us, was her first panicked thought. She wondered at herself a moment later. She'd had the strangest feeling that they were trapped in a house and that something evil was searching for them. The feeling passed, but the cheering continued to jar on her nerves. She lifted her hands to halt the shouting.

"I thank you, my friends. My dear friends," Goldmoon said, moistening lips that were stiff and dry. "I . . . I ask you to keep me in your hearts, to surround me with your good thoughts. I feel I need them."

The people glanced at each other, troubled. This wasn't what any of them had expected to hear her say. They wanted to hear her tell them about the wondrous miracle that had been wrought upon her. How she would perform the same miracles for them. Goldmoon made a gesture of dismissal. People filed out, returning to their work or their studies, glancing back at her often and talking in low voices.

"I beg your pardon for disturbing you, First Master," Lady Camilla said, approaching. Her eyes were cast down. She was trying very hard not to look at Goldmoon's face. "The patients in the hospital have missed you. I was wondering, if you are not too tired, if you would come . . ."

"Yes, assuredly," said Goldmoon readily, glad to have something to do. She would forget herself in her work. She was not in the least fatigued. The strange body was not, that is.

"Palin, would you care to accompany us?" she asked.

"What for? Your healers can do nothing for me," he returned irritably. "I know. They have tried."

"You speak to the First Master, sir," Lady Camilla said in rebuke.

"I am sorry, First Master," Palin said with a slight bow. "Please forgive my rudeness. I am very tired. I have not slept in a long time. I must find the kender, then I plan to go straight to my bed. I bid you a good night."

He bowed and turned and walked away.

"Palin!" Goldmoon called after him, but either he didn't hear or he was ignoring her.

Goldmoon accompanied Lady Camilla to the hospital—a separate building located on the Citadel grounds. The night was cool, unusually cool for this time of year. Goldmoon gazed up at the stars, at the pale moon to which she had never grown truly accustomed but always saw with a sense of shock and unease. This night, she looked at the stars, but they seemed small and distant. For the first time, she looked beyond them, to the vast and empty darkness that surrounded them.

"As it surrounds us," she said, chilled.

"I beg your pardon, First Master," Lady Camilla said. "Were you speaking to me?"

The two women had been antagonists at one point in their lives. When Goldmoon made the decision to build the Citadel of Light on Schallsea, Lady Camilla had been opposed. The Solamnic was loyal to the old gods, the departed gods. She was suspicious and distrustful of this new "power of the heart." Then she had come to witness the tireless efforts of the Citadel's mystics to do good in the world, to bring light to the darkness. She had come to love and to admire Goldmoon. She would do anything for the First Master, Lady Camilla was wont to say, and she had proved that statement, spending an inordinate amount of time and money on a fruitless search for a lost child, a child who had been dear to Goldmoon, but who had gone missing three years earlier, a child whose name no one mentioned, to avoid causing the First Master grief.

Goldmoon often thought of the child, especially whenever she walked along the seashore.

"It wasn't important," Goldmoon said, adding, "You must forgive me, Lady Camilla. I am poor company, I know."

"Not at all, First Master," said Lady Camilla. "You have much on your mind."

The two continued their walk to the hospital in silence.

The hospital, located in one of the crystal domes that were the central structures of the Citadel of Light, consisted of a large room filled with beds that stood in straight rows up one side and down the other. Sweet herbs perfumed the air and sweet music added its own healing properties. The healers worked among the sick and injured, using the power of the heart to heal them, a power Goldmoon had discovered and first used to heal the dying dwarf, Jasper Fireforge.

She had performed many miracles since that time, or so people claimed. She had healed those thought to be past hope. She had mended broken bodies with the touch of her hands. She had restored life to paralyzed limbs, brought sight to the blind. Her miracles of healing were as wonderful as those she had performed as a cleric of Mishakal. She was glad and grateful to be able to ease the suffering of others. But the healing had not brought her the same joy she had experienced when the blessing of the healing art came to her as a gift from the god, when she and Mishakal worked in partnership.

A year or so ago, her healing powers had begun to wane. At first, she blamed the loss on her advancing age. But she was not the only one of her healers to experience the diminution of healing power.

"It is as if someone has hung a gauze curtain between me and my patient," one young healer had said in frustration. "I try to draw the curtain aside to reach the patient, but there is another and another. I don't feel as if I can come close to my patients anymore."

Reports had begun coming in from Citadel masters throughout Ansalon, all bearing witness to the same dread phenomenon. Some had blamed it on the dragons. Some had blamed it on the Knights of Neraka. Then they had heard rumors that the Knights' dark mystics were losing their powers, as well.

Goldmoon asked her counselor, Mirror, the silver dragon who was the Citadel's guardian, if he thought that Malys was responsible.

"No, First Master, I do not," Mirror replied. He was in his human form then, a handsome youth with silver hair. She saw sorrow and trouble in his eyes, eyes that held the wisdom of centuries in them. "I have felt my own magical powers start to wane. It is rumored among dragonkind that our enemies are also feeling their powers weaken."

"Then there is some good in this," Goldmoon said.

Mirror remained grave. "I fear not, First Master. The tyrant who feels power slipping away does not let loose. He tightens his grasp."

Goldmoon paused on the threshold of the hospital. The beds were filled with patients, some sleeping, some talking quietly, some reading. The atmosphere was restful, peaceful. Bereft of much of their mystical power, the healers had gone back to the herbal remedies once practiced by healers in the days following the Cataclysm. The smells of sage and rosemary, chamomille and mint spiced the air. Soft music played. Goldmoon felt the soothing influence of the restful solitude, and her heart was eased. Here, perhaps, the healer would herself be healed.

Catching sight of Goldmoon, one of the master healers came forward immediately to welcome her. The welcome was, of necessity, low-key, lest the patients be disturbed by undue commotion or excitement. The healer said how pleased she was that the First Master was returned to them and stared with all her might at Goldmoon's altered face.

Goldmoon said something pleasant and innocuous and turned her face from the amazed scrutiny to look around. She asked after the patients.

"The hospital is quiet this night, First Master," said the healer, leading the way into the ward. "We have many patients, but, fortunately, few who are really worrisome. We have a baby suffering from the croup, a Knight who received a broken leg during a joust, and a young fisherman who was rescued from drowning. The rest of our patients are convalescing."

"How is Sir Wilfer?" Lady Camilla asked.

"The leg is mended, my lady," the healer replied, "but it is still weak. He insists he is ready to be released, and I cannot convince him that he would do better to remain another few days to fully recover. I know that he finds it very dull here, but perhaps if you were to—"

"I will speak to him," said Lady Camilla.

She moved among the rows of beds. Most of the patients came from outside the Citadel, from villages and towns on Schallsea. They knew the elderly Goldmoon, for she often visited their homes. But they did not recognize this youthful Goldmoon. Most thought her a stranger and paid little attention to her, for which she was grateful. At the far end was the cradle with the baby, his watchful mother at his side. He coughed still and whimpered. His face was flushed with fever. The healers were preparing a bowl of herbs to which they would add boiling water. The steam would moisten the lungs and ease the child's cough. Goldmoon drew near, intending to say a few words of comfort to the mother.

As Goldmoon approached the cradle, she saw that another figure hovered over the fretful baby. At first, Goldmoon thought this to be one of the healers. She did not recognize the face, but then she had been absent from them for weeks. Probably this was a new student . . .

Goldmoon's steps slowed. She halted about three beds away from that of the sick child, put out a hand to steady herself upon the wooden bedpost.

The figure was not a healer. The figure was not a student. The figure was not alive. A ghost hovered over the child, the ghost of a young woman.

"If you will excuse me, First Master," said the healer, "I will go see what I can do for this sick child."

The healer walked over to the child. The healer laid her hands upon the baby, but at the same instant, the fleshless hands of the ghost intervened. The ghost grasped the healer's hands.

"Give me the blessed power," the ghost whispered. "I must have it, or I will be cast into oblivion!"

The baby's coughing grew worse. The mother hung over him worriedly. The healer, shaking her head, removed her hands. Her healing touch had failed the baby. The ghost had stolen the energy for herself.

"He should breathe in this steam," the healer said, sounding tired and defeated. "The steam will help keep his lungs clear."

The ghost of the woman drifted away. More insubstantial figures took her place, crowding around the sick baby, their burning eyes staring avidly at the healer. When the healer moved to another bed, they followed her, clinging to her like trailing cobweb. When she put out her hands to try to heal another patient, the dead grasped hold of her, crying and moaning.

"Mine! Mine! Give the power to me!"

Goldmoon staggered. If she had not been holding onto the bedpost, she would have fallen. She closed her eyes tightly shut, hoping the fearful apparitions would disappear. She opened her eyes to see more ghosts. Legions of the dead crowded and jostled each other as each sought to steal for his own the blessed life-giving power that flowed from the healers. Restless, the dead were in constant motion. They passed by Goldmoon like a vast and turbulent river, all flowing in the same direction—north. Those who gathered around the healers were not permitted to linger long. Some unheard voice ordered them away, some unseen hand pulled them back into the water.

The river of dead shifted course, swept around Goldmoon. The dead reached out to touch her, begged her to bless them in their hollow whisperings.

"No! Leave me alone!" she cried, cringing away. "I cannot help you!"

Some of the dead flowed past her, wailing in disappointment. Other ghosts pressed near her. Their breath was cold, their eyes burned. Their words were smoke, their touch like ashes falling on her skin.

Startled faces surrounded her. Faces of the living.

"Healer!" someone was calling. "Come quickly! The First Master!"

The healer was in a flutter. Had she done something to offend the First Master? She had not meant to.

Goldmoon recoiled from the healer in horror. The dead were all around her, pulling on her arm, tugging at her robes. Ghosts surged forward, rushing at her, trying to seize hold of her hands.

"Give us . . ." they pleaded in their terrible whisperings. "Give us what we crave . . . what we must have . . ."

"First Master!" Lady Camilla's voice boomed through the sibiliant hissings of the dead. She sounded panicked. "Please let us help you! Tell us what is wrong!"

"Can't you see them?" Goldmoon cried. "The dead!" She pointed. "There, with the baby! There, with the healer. Here, in front of me! The dead are draining us, stealing our power. Can't you see them?"

Voices clamored around Goldmoon, voices of the living. She could not understand them, they made no sense. Her own voice failed her. She felt herself falling and could do nothing to halt her fall.

She was lying in a bed in the hospital. The voices still clamored. Opening her eyes, she saw the faces of the dead surrounding her.

28

The Dragon's Edict

eneral Medan rarely visited his own headquarters in Qualinost. Constructed by humans, the fortress was ugly, purposefully ugly. Squat, square, made of gray sandstone, with barred windows and heavy, iron-bound doors, the fortress was intended to be ugly, intended as an insult to the elves, to impress upon them who was master. No elf would come near it of his own free will, though many had seen the inside of it, particularly the room located far below ground, the room to which they were taken when the order was given to "put them to the question."

Marshal Medan had developed an extreme dislike for this building, a dislike almost as great as that of the elves. He preferred to conduct most of his business from his home where his work area was a shady bower dappled with sunlight. He preferred listening to the song of the lark rather than to the sounds of screams of the tortured, preferred the scent of his roses to that of blood.

The infamous room was not much in use these days. Elves thought to be rebels or in league with the rebels vanished like shadows when the sun hides beneath a cloud before the Neraka Knights could arrest them. Medan knew very well that the elves were being spirited away somehow, probably through underground tunnels. In the old days, when he had first taken on the governing of an occupied land, he would have turned Qualinost upside down and inside out, excavated, probed, brought in Thorn Knights to look for magic, tortured hundreds. He did none of these things. He was just as glad that his Knights arrested so few. He had come to loathe the torturing, the death, as he had come to love Qualinesti.

Medan loved the land. He loved the beauty of the land, loved the peaceful serenity that meandered through Qualinesti as the stream wound its sparkling way through his garden. Alexius Medan did not love the elven people. Elves were beyond his ken, his understanding. He might as well have said that he loved the sun or the stars or the moon. He admired them, as he admired the beauty of an orchid, but he could not love them. He sometimes envied them their long life span and sometimes pitied them for it.

Medan did not love Laurana as a woman, Gerard had come to realize. He loved her as the embodiment of all that was beautiful in his adopted homeland.

Gerard was amazed, entranced, and astounded upon his first entrance into Marshal Medan's dwelling. His amazement increased when the marshal told him, proudly, that he had supervised the design of the house and had laid out the garden entirely to his own liking.

Elves would not have lived happily in the marshal's house, which was too ordered and structured for their tastes. He disliked the elven practice of using living trees as walls and trailing vines for curtains, nor did he want green grasses for his roof. Elves enjoy the murmur and whispers of living walls around them in the night. Medan preferred his walls to allow him to sleep. His house was built of rough-hewn stone.

He took care not to cut living trees, an act the elves considered a grievous crime.

Ivy and morning glories clung to the surfaces of the rock walls. The house itself was practically hidden by a profusion of flowers. Gerard could not believe that such beauty could live in the soul of this man, an avowed follower of the precepts of darkness.

Gerard had moved into the house yesterday afternoon. Acting on Medan's orders, the healers of the Nereka Knights had pooled their dwindling energies to restore the Solamnic to almost complete health. His wounds had knit with astonishing rapidity. Gerard smiled to himself, imagining their ire if they knew they were expending their limited energies to heal the enemy.

He occupied one wing, a wing that had been vacant until now, for the marshal had not permitted his aides to live in his dwelling, ever since the last man Medan had retained had been discovered urinating in the fish pond. Medan had transferred the man to the very farthest outpost on the elven border, an outpost built on the edge of the desolate wasteland known as the Plains of Dust. He hoped the man's brain exploded from the heat.

Gerard's quarters were comfortable, if small. His duties thus far—after two days on the job—had been light. Marshal Medan was an early riser. He took his breakfast in the garden on sunny days, dined on the porch that overlooked the garden on days when it rained. Gerard was on hand to stand behind the marshal's chair, pour the marshal's tea, and commiserate with the marshal's concerns over those he considered his most implacable foes: aphids, spider mites, and bagworms. He handled Medan's correspondence, introduced and screened visitors and carried orders from the marshal's dwelling to the detested headquarters building. Here he was looked upon with envy and jealousy by the other knights, who had made crude remarks about the "upstart," the "toady," the "ass-licker."

Gerard was ill-at-ease and tense, at first. So much had happened so suddenly. Five days ago, he had been a guest in Laurana's house. Now he was a prisoner of the Knights of Neraka, permitted to remain alive so long as Medan considered Gerard might be useful to him.

Gerard resolved to stay with the marshal only as long as it took to find out the identity of the person who was spying on the queen mother. When this was accomplished, he would pass the information on to Laurana and attempt to escape. After he had made this decision, he relaxed and felt better.

After Medan's supper, Gerard was dispatched to headquarters again to receive the daily reports and the prisoner list—the record of those who had escaped and who were now wanted criminals. Gerard would also be given any dispatches that had arrived for the marshal from other parts of the continent. Usually, few came, Medan told him. The marshal had no interest in other parts of the continent and those parts had very little interest in him. This evening there was a dispatch, carried in the clawed hands of Beryl's draconian messenger.

Gerard had heard of the draconians—the spawn born years ago of the magically corrupted eggs of good dragons. He had never seen one, however. He decided, on viewing this one—a large Baaz—that he could have gone all his life without seeing one and never missed it.

The draconian stood on two legs like a man, but his body was covered with scales. His hands were large, scaly, the fingers ending in sharp claws. His face was that of a lizard or a snake, with sharp fangs that he revealed in a gaping grin, and a long, lolling tongue. His short, stubby wings, sprouting from his back, were constantly in gentle motion, fanning the air around him.

The draconian was waiting for Gerard inside the headquarters building. Gerard saw this creature the moment he entered, and for the life of him he could not help hesitating, pausing in the doorway, overcome by revulsion. The other

Knights, lounging around the room, watched him with knowing smirks that broadened to smug grins when they saw his discomfiture.

Angry with himself, Gerard entered the headquarters building with firm strides. He marched past the draconian, who had risen to his feet with a scrape of his claws on the floor.

The officer in charge handed over the daily reports. Gerard took them and started to leave. The officer stopped him.

"That's for the marshal, too." He jerked a thumb at the draconian, who lifted his head with a leer. "Groul, here, has a dispatch for the marshal."

Gerard steeled himself. With an air of nonchalance, which he hoped didn't look as phony as it felt, he approached the foul creature.

"I am the marshal's aide. Give me the letter."

Groul snapped his teeth together with a disconcerting click and held up the scroll case but did not relinquish it to Gerard.

"My orders are to deliver it to the marshal in person," Groul stated.

Gerard had expected the reptile to be barely sentient, to speak gibberish or, at the best, a corrupt form of Common. He had not expected to find the creature so articulate and, therefore, intelligent. Gerard was forced to readjust his thinking about how to deal with the creature.

"I will give the dispatch to the marshal," Gerard replied. "There have been several attempts on the marshal's life. As a consequence, he does not permit strangers to enter his presence. You have my word of honor that I will deliver it directly into his hands."

"Honor! This is what I think of your honor." Groul's tongue slid out of his mouth, then slurped back, splashing Gerard with saliva. The draconian moved closer to Gerard, clawed feet scraping across the floor. "Listen, Knight," he hissed, "I am sent by the exalted Beryllinthranox. She has ordered me to hand this dispatch to Marshal Medan and to wait for his reply. The matter is one of utmost urgency. I will do as I am ordered. Take me to the marshal."

Gerard could have done as the draconian demanded and saved himself what was probably going to be a world of trouble. He had two reasons for not doing so. First, he fully intended to read the dispatch from the dragon before handing it over to Medan, and that would be difficult to manage with the dispatch clutched firmly in the draconian's claws. The second reason was more subtle. Gerard found this reason incomprehensible, but he felt oddly guided by it. He did not like the thought of the loathsome creature entering the marshal's beautiful house, his clawed feet ripping holes in the ground, tearing up the flower beds, trampling the plants, smashing furniture with his tail, leering and poking, sneering and slavering.

Groul held the scroll in his right hand. The creature wore his sword on his left hip. That meant the draco was right-handed, or so Gerard hoped, though there was always the possibility the creatures were ambidextrous. Resolving to himself that if he lived through this, he would take up a study of the draconian race, Gerard drew his sword with an overdone flourish and jumped at the draconian.

Startled, Groul reacted instinctively, dropping the scroll case to the floor and reaching with his right hand for his sword. Gerard pivoted, stooped down to the floor and snatched up the scroll case. Rising, he drove his shoulder and elbow, with the full weight of his armor, into the midriff of the draconian. Groul went down with a clatter of sword and sheath, his wings flapping wildly, his hands waving as he lost the struggle to retain his balance. He crashed into a bench, smashing it.

The sudden movement and attack on the draconian tore

open several of Gerard's wounds. Sucking in his breath against the pain, he glared a moment at the creature floundering on the floor, then turned and, resisting the impulse to see how badly he'd injured himself, started to leave.

Hearing clawed feet scrabbling and a vicious cursing, Gerard wheeled, sword in hand, intending to finish the fight if the creature pursued it. To Gerard's astonishment, three of the Knights of Neraka had drawn their swords and now blocked the draconian's path.

"The marshal's aide is right," said one, an older man, who had served in Qualinesti many years and had even taken an elven wife. "We've heard stories of you, Groul. Perhaps you carry a dispatch from Beryl as you say. Or perhaps the dragon has given orders that you are to 'dispatch' our marshal. I advise you to sit down on what you've left of our bench and wait. If the marshal wants to see you, he'll come himself."

Groul hesitated, eyeing the Knights balefully. Two of the guards drew their swords and joined their officers. The draconian cursed, and, with a snarl, sheathed his sword. Muttering something about needing fresh air, he stalked over to the window and stood staring out of it.

"Go along," said the Knight to Gerard. "We'll keep an eye on him."

"Yes, sir. Thank you, sir."

The Knight grunted and returned to his duties.

Gerard left the headquarters with haste. The street on which the building stood was empty. The elves never came anywhere near it voluntarily. Most of the soldiers were either on duty or had just come off duty and were now asleep.

Leaving the street on which the headquarters building was located, Gerard entered the city proper, or rather the city's outskirts. He walked among the city's inhabitants now, and he faced another danger. Medan had advised him to wear his breastplate and helm, make his trip to headquarters before darkness fell. He was conscious of beautiful faces, of almond eyes either staring at him with open, avowed hatred, or purposefully averting their gaze, so as not to disturb the loveliness of the midsummer's twilight by adding his ugly human visage to it.

Gerard was likewise conscious of his strangeness. His body seemed thick and clumsy in comparison to the slender, delicate elven frames; his straw-colored hair, a color not usually seen among elves, was probably regarded as freakish. His scarred and lumpish features, considered ugly by human standards, must be looked upon as hideous by the elves.

Gerard could understand why some humans had come to hate the elves. He felt himself inferior to them in every way—in appearance, in culture, in wisdom, in manner. The only way in which some humans could feel superior to elves was to conquer them, subjugate them, torture and kill them.

Gerard turned onto the road leading to Medan's house. Part of him sighed when he left the streets where the elves lived and worked behind, as if he had awakened from a lovely dream to dreary reality. Part of him was relieved. He did not keep looking constantly over his shoulder to see if someone was sneaking up on him with a knife.

He had a walk of about a mile to reach the marshal's secluded house. The path wound among shimmering aspens, poplars, and rustling willows, whose arms overstretched a bubbling brook. The day was fine, the temperature unusually cool for this time of year, bringing with it the hint of an early fall. Reaching the halfway point, Gerard looked carefully up the path and down the path. He listened intently for the sound of other footfalls. Hearing nothing, seeing nobody, he stepped off the trail and walked to the brook. He squatted down on his haunches as if to drink and examined the scroll case.

It was sealed with wax, but that was easily managed. Removing his knife, he laid the blade upon a flat rock still hot from the afternoon sun. When the metal had heated, Gerard edged the knife blade carefully beneath the wax seal. He removed the seal intact, placed it on a bit of bark to keep it safe. Gerard eyed the scroll case, started to open it, hesitated.

He was about to read a dispatch intended for his commander. True, Medan was the enemy, he was not really Gerard's commander, but the dispatch was private, meant for Medan only. No honorable man would read another's correspondence. Certainly no Solamnic Knight would stoop so low. The Measure did not countenance the use of spies upon the enemy, deeming them "dishonorable, treacherous." He recalled one paragraph in particular.

Some say that spies are useful, that the information they gather by low and sneaking means might lead us to victory. We knights answer that victory obtained by such means is no victory at all but the ultimate defeat, for if we abandon the principles of honor for which we fight, what makes us better than our enemy?

"What indeed?" Gerard asked himself, the scroll case unopened in his hand. "Nothing, I guess." With a quick twist, he opened the lid and, glancing about the forest one final time, he drew out the parchment, unrolled it, and began to read.

A weakness came over him. His body chilled. He sank down upon the bank, continued reading in disbelief. Completing his perusal, he considered what to do. His first thought was to burn the terrible missive so that it would never reach its destination. He dared not do that, however. Too many people had seen him take it. He thought of burning it and substituting another in its place, but he abandoned that wild idea immediately. He had no parchment, no pen, no ink. And perhaps Medan was familiar with the handwriting of the scribe who penned this message at the dragon's injunction.

No, Gerard reasoned, sick at heart, there was nothing he could do now but deliver the dispatch. To do otherwise would be to put himself in danger, and he might be the only means of thwarting the dragon's evil design.

Medan would be wondering what had become of him. Gerard had already been longer on his daily errand than usual. He hurriedly rolled up the dispatch, thrust it into the tube, carefully replaced the wax seal, and made sure that it was firmly stuck. Thrusting the foul thing in his belt, unwilling to touch it more than necessary, he continued on his way back to the marshal's at a run.

Gerard found the marshal strolling in his garden, taking his exercise after his evening meal. Hearing footsteps along the walkway, the marshal glanced around.

"Ah, Gerard. You are behind your time. I was starting to fear something might have happened to you." The marshal looked intently at Gerard's arm. "Something has happened to you. You are injured."

Gerard glanced down at his shirtsleeve, saw it wet with blood. In his distraction over the dispatch, he'd forgotten his wounds, forgotten the fight with the draconian.

"There was an altercation at headquarters," he said, knowing that Medan would come to hear what had happened. "Here are the daily reports." He placed those upon a table that stood beneath a trellis over which Medan had patiently trained grapevines to grow, forming a green and leafy bower. "And there is this dispatch, which comes from the dragon Beryl."

Medan took the dispatch with a grimace. He did not immediately open it. He was much more interested in hearing about the fight. "What was the altercation, Sir Gerard?"

"The draconian messenger insisted on bringing the dispatch to you himself. Your Knights did not think that this was necessary. They insisted he remain there to await your response."

"Your doing, I think, sir," said Medan with a smile. "You

acted rightly. I am wary of Groul. Who knows what he is thinking in that lizard brain of his? He is not to be trusted."

He turned his attention to the dispatch. Gerard saluted, started to leave.

"No, no. You might as well wait. I will have to draft an answer. . . ." He fell silent, reading.

Gerard, who knew every line because he felt each one burned on his brain, could follow Medan's progress through the dispatch by watching the expression on his face. Medan's lips tightened, his jaw set. If he had appeared happy, overjoyed, Gerard had determined to kill the marshal where he stood, regardless of the consequences.

Medan was not overjoyed, however. Far from it. His face lost its color, took on a sallow, grayish hue. He completed reading the dispatch and then, with studied deliberation, read it through again. Finished, he crushed it in his hand and, with a curse, hurled it to the walkway.

Arms folded across his chest, he turned his back, stared grimly at nothing until he had regained some measure of his composure. Gerard stood in silence. Now might have been a politic time to absent himself, but he was desperate to know what Medan intended to do.

At length, the marshal turned around. He glanced down at the crumpled piece of parchment, glanced up at Gerard. "Read it," he said.

"Sir." Gerard flushed. "It's not meant for—"

"Read it, damn you!" Medan shouted. Calming himself with an effort, he added, "You might as well. I must think what to do, what to say to the dragon in reply and how to say it. Carefully," he admonished himself softly. "I must proceed carefully, or all is lost!"

Gerard picked up the dispatch and smoothed it out.

"Read it aloud," Medan ordered. "Perhaps I misread it. Perhaps there was some part of it I misunderstood." His tone was ironic.

Gerard skipped through the formal address, came to the body of the text.

" 'It has come to my attention,' " he read, " 'through one who is in sympathy with my interests, that the outlawed sorcerer Palin Majere has discovered a most valuable and wondrous magical artifact while he was unlawfully in my territory. I consider that the artifact is therefore mine. I must and I will have it.

" 'Informants tell me that Palin Majere and the kender have fled with the artifact to the Citadel of Light. I give the elf king, Gilthas, three days to recover the device and the culprits who carry it and another three days to deliver them up to me.

" 'In addition, the elf king will also send me the head of the elf woman, Lauranalanthalas, who harbored the sorcerer and the kender in her home and who aided and abetted them in their escape.

" 'If, at the end of six days, I have not received the head of this traitor elf woman and if the artifact and those who stole it are not in my hands, I will order the destruction of Qualinesti to commence. Every man, woman, and child in that wretched nation shall be put to sword or flame. None shall survive. As for those in the Citadel of Light who dare harbor these criminals, I will destroy them, burn their Citadel to the ground, and recover the magical device from amidst the bones and ashes.' "

Gerard was thankful he'd read this once. Had he not been prepared, he would not have been able to read it as calmly as he managed. As it was, his voice caught in his throat and he was forced to cover his emotions with a harsh cough. He finished reading and looked up to find Medan observing him closely.

"Well, what do you think of this?" Medan demanded.

Gerard cleared his throat. "I believe that it is presumptuous of the dragon to give you orders, my lord. The Knights of Neraka are not her personal army."

Medan's grim expression relaxed. He almost smiled.

"That is an excellent argument, Gerard. Would it were true! Unfortunately, the High Command crawled on their bellies before the great dragons years ago."

"She can't mean this, my lord," Gerard said cautiously. "She wouldn't do this. Not an entire race of people—"

"She could and she will," Medan replied grimly. "Look what she did to Kenderhome. Slaughtered the little nuisances by the thousands. Not that kender are any great loss, but it goes to prove that she will do what she says."

Gerard had heard other Solamnic Knights say the same thing about the slaughter of the kender, and he recalled laughing with them. He knew some Solamnic Knights who would not be displeased to see the elves depart this world. We consider ourselves so much better, so much more moral and more honorable than the Dark Knights, Gerard said to himself. In reality, the only difference is the armor. Silver or black, it masks the same prejudices, the same intolerance, the same ignorance. Gerard felt suddenly, deeply ashamed.

Medan had begun to pace the walkway. "Damn the blasted elves! All these years I work to save them, and now it is for nothing! Damn the queen mother anyhow! If she had only listened to me! But, no. She must consort with rebels and the like, and now what comes of it? She has doomed herself and her people. Unless . . ."

He paused in his pacing, hands clasped behind his back, brooding, his thoughts turned inward. His robes, of elven make, elven cut, and elven design, fell loosely about his body. The hem, trimmed with silk ribbon, brushed his feet. Gerard remained silent, absorbed with his own thoughts—a confusion of sickening rage against the dragon for wanting to destroy the elves and rage at himself and his own kind for standing idly by and doing nothing all these years to stop her.

Medan raised his head. He had made a decision. "The day has arrived sooner than I anticipated. I will not be a party to genocide. I have no compunction about killing another warrior in battle, but I will not butcher helpless civilians who have no way to fight back. To do so is the height of cowardice, and such wanton slaughter would break the oath I swore when I became a Knight. Perhaps there is a way to stop the dragon. But I will require your help."

"You have it, my lord," said Gerard.

"You will have to trust me." Medan raised an eyebrow.

"And you will have to trust me, my lord," said Gerard, smiling.

Medan nodded. A man of quick and decisive actions, he did not waste breath in further talk but seated himself at the table. He reached for pen and ink. "We must stall for time," he said, writing rapidly. "You will deliver my answer to the draconian Groul, but he must never reach the dragon. Do you understand?"

"Yes, sir," said Gerard.

Medan completed his writing. He sprinkled sand on the paper, to help the ink dry, rolled it and handed it to Gerard. "Put that in the same scroll case. No need to seal it. The message states that I am the Exalted One's Obedient Servant and that I will do her bidding."

Medan rose to his feet. "When you have completed your task, go straight to the Royal Palace. I will leave orders that you are to be admitted. We must make haste. Beryl is a treacherous fiend, not to be trusted. She may have already decided to act on her own."

"Yes, my lord," Gerard said. "And where will you be, my lord? Where can I find you?"

Medan smiled grimly. "I will be arresting the queen mother."

Marshal Medan walked along the path that led through the garden to the main dwelling of Laurana's modest estate. Night had fallen. He had brought a torch to light his way. The flame singed the hanging flowers as he passed beneath them, caused leaves to blacken and curl. Bugs flew into the fire. He could hear them sizzle.

The marshal was not wearing his elven robes. He was accoutered in his full ceremonial armor. Kelevandros, who answered Medan's resounding knock upon the door, was quick to note the change. He eyed the marshal warily.

"Marshal Medan. Welcome. Please enter. I will inform madam that she has a visitor. She will see you in the arboretum, as usual."

"I prefer to remain where I am," said the marshal. "Tell your mistress to meet me here. Tell her," he added, his voice grating, "that she should be dressed for travel. She will need her cloak. The night air is chill. And tell her to make haste."

He looked intently and constantly about the garden, paying particular attention to the parts of the garden hidden in shadow.

"Madam will want to know why," Kelevandros said, hesitating.

Medan gave him a shove that sent him staggering across the room. "Go fetch your mistress," he ordered.

"Travel?" Laurana said, astonished. She had been sitting in the arboretum, pretending to listen to Kalindas read aloud from an ancient elven text. In reality, she had not heard a word. "Where am I going?"

Kelevandros shook his head. "The marshal will not tell me, Madam. He is acting very strangely."

"I don't like this, Madam," Kalindas stated, lowering the book. "First imprisonment in your house, now this. You should not go with the marshal."

"I agree with my brother, Madam," Kelevandros added. "I will tell him you are not well. We will do what we have talked about before. This night, we will smuggle you out in the tunnels."

"I will not," said Laurana determinedly. "Would you have

me flee to safety while the rest of my people are forced to stay behind? Bring my cloak."

"Madam," Kelevandros dared to argue, "please—"

"Fetch me my cloak," Laurana stated. Her tone was gentle but firm, brooked no further debate.

Kelevandros bowed silently.

Kalindas went to fetch the cloak. Kelevandros returned with Laurana to the front door, where Marshal Medan had remained standing.

Sighting her, he straightened. "Lauranalanthalas of the House of Solostaran," he said formally, "you are under arrest. You will surrender yourself peacefully to me as my prisoner."

"Indeed?" Laurana was quite calm. "What is the charge? Or is there a charge?" she asked. She turned so that Kalindas could place the cloak about her shoulders.

The elf started to do so, but Medan took the cloak himself. The marshal, his expression grave, settled the cloak around Laurana's shoulders.

"The charges are numerous, Madam. Harboring a human sorcerer who is wanted by the Gray Robes, concealing your knowledge of a valuable magical artifact, which the sorcerer had in his possession when, by law, all magical artifacts located in Qualinesti are to be handed over to the dragon. Aiding and abetting the outlaw sorcerer in his escape from Qualinesti with the artifact."

"I see," said Laurana.

"I tried to warn you, madam, but you would not heed me," Medan said.

"Yes, you did try to warn me, marshal, and for that I am grateful." Laurana fastened the cloak around her neck with a jeweled pin. Her hands were steady, did not tremble. "And what is to be done with me, Marshal Medan?"

"My orders are to execute you, madam," said Medan. "I am to send your head to the dragon."

Kalindas gasped. Kelevandros gave a hoarse shout and

lunged at Medan, grappling for his throat with his bare hands.

"Stop, Kelevandros!" Laurana ordered, throwing herself between the elf and the marshal. "This will not help! Stop this madness!"

Kelevandros fell back, panting, glaring at Medan with hatred. Kalindas took hold of his brother's arm, but Kelevandros angrily shook him off.

"Come, madam," said Marshal Medan. He offered Laurana his arm. The torch smoked and sputtered. Orchids, hanging over the door, shriveled in the heat.

Laurana rested her hand on the marshal's arm. She looked back at the two brothers, standing, white-faced with shadowed eyes, watching her being led away to her death.

Which one? she asked herself, sick at heart. Which one?

29

PRISON OF AMBER

he midsummer's morning dawned unusually cool in Silvanesti.

"A fine day for battle, gentlemen," said Mina to her assembled officers.

Galdar led the cheers, which shook the trees along the riverbank, caused the leaves of the aspens to tremble.

"So may our valor set the elves to trembling," said Captain Samuval. "A great victory will be ours this day, Mina! We cannot fail!"

"On the contrary," said Mina coolly. "This day we will be defeated."

Knights and officers stared at her blankly. They had seen her perform miracle after miracle, until the miracles were now stacked up one on top of the other like crockery in a neat housewife's cupboard. The idea that these miracles were to now come spilling out of the cupboard, come crashing down around their ears was a catastrophe not to be believed. So they did not believe it.

"She's joking," said Galdar, attempting to pass it off with a laugh.

Mina shook her head. "We will lose the battle this day. An army of a thousand elven warriors has come to test us. We are outnumbered over two to one. We cannot win this battle."

The Knights and officers looked at each other uneasily. They looked at Mina grimly, doubtfully.

"But though we lose the battle this day," Mina continued, smiling slightly, her amber eyes lit from behind with an eerie glow that made the faces captured in them glitter like tiny stars, "this day we will win the war. But only if you obey me without question. Only if you follow my orders exactly."

The men grinned, relaxed. "We will, Mina," several shouted, and the rest cheered.

Mina was no longer smiling. The amber of her eyes flowed over them, congealed around them, froze them where they stood. "You will obey my orders, though you do not understand them. You will obey my orders, though you do not like them. You will swear this to me on your knees, swear by the Nameless God who is witness to your oath and who will exact terrible revenge upon the oath breaker. Do you so swear?"

The Knights sank down on their knees in a semicircle around her. Removing their swords, they held them by the blade, beneath the hilt. They lifted their swords to Mina. Captain Samuval went down on his knees, bowed his head. Galdar remained standing. Mina turned her amber eyes on him.

"On you, Galdar, more than on anyone else rests the outcome of this battle. If you refuse to obey me, if you refuse to obey the God who gave you back your warrior's arm, we are lost. All of us. But you, most especially."

"What is your command, Mina?" Galdar asked harshly. "Tell me first, that I may know."

"No, Galdar," she said gently. "You either trust me or you do not. You put your faith in the God or you do not. Which will it be?"

Slowly, Galdar knelt down upon his knees before her. Slowly he drew his sword from its scabbard and slowly held it up as did the others. He held it in the hand the God had returned to him.

"I so swear, Mina!" he said.

The rest spoke as one.

"I so swear!"

The battleground was a large field located on the banks of the Thon-Thalas River. The elf soldiers trampled tender stalks of wheat beneath their soft leather boots. The elf archers took their places amid tall stands of green, tasseled corn. General Konnal set up his command tent in a peach orchard. The arms of a great windmill turned endlessly, creaking in the wind that had a taste of autumn's harvest in it.

There would be a harvest on this field, a dread harvest, a harvest of young lives. When it was over, the water that ran at the feet of the great windmill would run red.

The field stood between the approaching enemy army and the capital of Silvanost. The elves put themselves in harm's way, intending to stop the army of darkness before it could reach the heart of the elf kingdom. The Silvanesti were outraged, insulted, infuriated. In hundreds of years, no enemy had set foot on this sacred land. The only enemy they had fought had been one of their own making, the twisted dream of Lorac.

Their wonderful magical shield had failed them. They did not know how or why, but most of the elves were convinced that it had been penetrated by an evil machination of the Knights of Neraka.

"To that end, General," Glaucous was saying, "the capture of their leader is of the utmost importance. Bring this girl in for interrogation. She will tell me how she managed to thwart the shield's magic."

"What makes you think she will tell you?" Konnal asked,

annoyed at the wizard and his harping on this subject alone.

"She may refuse, General," Glaucous assured him, "but she will not have any choice in the matter. I will use the truth-seek on her."

The two were in the general's command tent. They had met early that morning with the elf officers. Silvan had explained his strategy. The officers had agreed that the tactics were sound. Konnal had then dismissed them to deploy their men. The enemy was reported to be about five miles away. According to the scouts, the Knights of Neraka had halted to arm themselves and put on their armor. They were obviously preparing for battle.

"I cannot spare the men who would be required to seize a single officer, Glaucous," the general added, recording his orders in a large book. "If the girl is captured in battle, fine. If not . . ." He shrugged, continued writing.

"I will undertake her capture, General," Silvan offered.

"Absolutely not, Your Majesty," Glaucous said hurriedly.

"Give me a small detachment of mounted warriors," Silvan urged, coming to stand before the general. "We will circle around their flank, come in from behind. We will wait until the battle is fairly joined and then we will drive through the lines in a wedge, strike down her bodyguard, capture this commander of theirs and carry her back to our lines."

Konnal looked up from his work.

"You said yourself, Glaucous, that discovering the means by which these evil fiends came through the shield would be useful. I think His Majesty's plan is sound."

"His Majesty puts himself in too much danger," Glaucous protested.

"I will order members of my own bodyguard to ride with the king," Konnal said. "No harm will come to him."

"It had better not," Glaucous said softly.

Ignoring his adviser, Konnal walked over to the map, stared down at it. He laid his finger on a certain point. "My guess is that the enemy commander will take up her position here, on this rise. That is where you should look for her and her bodyguard. You can circle around the battle by riding through this stand of trees, emerging at this point. You will be practically on top of them. You will have the element of surprise, and you should be able to strike before they are aware of you. Does Your Majesty agree?"

"The plan is an excellent one, General," said Silvan with enthusiasm.

He was to wear new armor, beautifully made, wonderfully designed. The breastplate bore the pattern of a twelve-pointed star, his helm was formed in the likeness of two swan's wings done in shining steel. He carried a new sword, and he now knew how to use one, having spent many hours each day since his arrival in Silvanost studying with an expert elf swordsman, who had been most complimentary on His Majesty's progress. Silvan felt invincible. Victory would belong to the elves this day, and he was determined to play a glorious part, a part that would be celebrated in story and song for generations to come.

He left, ecstatic, to go prepare for battle.

Glaucous lingered behind.

Konnal had returned to his work. Glaucous made no sound, but Konnal sensed his presence, as one senses hungry eyes watching one in a dark forest.

"Begone. I have work to do."

"I am going. I only want to emphasize what I said earlier. The king must be kept safe."

Konnal sighed, looked up. "If he comes to harm, it will not be through me. I am not an ogre, to kill one of my own kind. I spoke in haste yesterday, without thinking. I will give my guards orders to watch over him as if he were my own son."

"Excellent, General," said Glaucous with his beautiful smile. "I am much relieved. My hopes for this land and its people depend on him. Silvanoshei Caladon must live to rule

Silvanesti for many years. As did his grandfather before him."

"Are you certain you will not reconsider and ride with us, Kiryn? This will be a battle celebrated for generations to come!"

Silvan fidgeted under the ministrations of his squire, who was attempting to buckle the straps of the king's damascened armor and having a difficult time of it. The leather was stiff and new, the straps refused to ease into place. Silvan's constant shifting and moving did not help matters.

"If Your Majesty would please hold still!" the exasperated squire begged.

"Sorry," Silvan said and did as he was told, for a few seconds at any rate. Then he turned his head to look at Kiryn, who sat on a cot, watching the proceedings. "I could lend you some armor. I have another full suit."

Kiryn shook his head. "My uncle has given me my assignment. I am to carry dispatches and messages between the officers. No armor for me. I must travel light."

A trumpet call sounded, causing Silvan to give such a start of excitement that he undid a good quarter of an hour's worth of work. "The enemy is in sight! Hurry, you oaf!"

The squire sucked in a breath and held his tongue. Kiryn added his assistance, and between the two of them the king was readied for battle.

"I would embrace you for luck, Cousin," said Kiryn, "but I would be bruised for a week. I do wish you luck, though," he said more seriously as he clasped Silvan's hand in his, "though I hardly think you'll need it."

Silvan was grave, solemn for a moment. "Battles are chancy things, Samar used to say. One man's bravery may save the day. One man's cowardice may spoil it. That is what I fear most, Cousin. More than death. I fear that I will turn coward and flee the field. I've seen it happen. I've seen good men, brave men fall to their knees and tremble and weep like little children."

"Your mother's courage flows in your veins along with your father's fortitude," Kiryn reassured him. "You will not fail their memories. You will not fail your people. You will not fail yourself."

Silvan drew in a deep breath of the flower-scented air, let it out slowly. The sunshine was like warm honey spilling from the sky. All around him were familiar sounds and smells, sounds of battle and war, smells of leather and sweat, sounds and smells he had been born to, sounds and smells he had come to loathe but which, oddly, he had also come to miss. His playground had been a battlefield, a command tent his cradle. He was more at home here, he realized, than he was in his fine castle.

Smiling ruefully, he walked out of his tent, his armor of silver and gold gleaming brightly, to be greeted by the enthusiastic cheers of his people.

The battle plans for both sides were simple. The elves formed ranks across the field, with the archers in the rear. The army of the Knights of Neraka extended their thinner lines among the trees of the low hillside, hoping to tempt the elves into attacking rashly, attacking up hill.

Konnal was far too smart to fall for that. He was patient, if his troops were not, and he kept fast hold of them. He had time, all the time in the world. The army of the Knights of Neraka, running low on supplies, did not.

Toward midafternoon, a single braying trumpet sounded from the hills. The elves gripped their weapons. The army of darkness came out of the hills on the run, shouting insults and defiance to their foes. Arrows from both sides arced into the skies, forming a canopy of death above the heads of the armies, who came together with a resounding crash.

When battle was joined, Silvan and his mounted escort

galloped into the woods on the west side of the battlefield. Their small force screened by the trees, they rode around the flank of their own army, crossed over enemy lines, and rode around the enemy's flank. No one noticed them. No one shouted or called out. Those fighting saw only the foe before them. Arriving at a point near the edge of the field, Silvan called a halt, raising his hand. He rode cautiously to the edge of the forest, taking the commander of the general's guard with him. The two looked out upon the field of battle.

"Send out the scouting party," Silvan ordered. "Bring back word the moment they have located the enemy commanders."

The scouts proceeded ahead through the woods, edging closer to the field of battle. Silvan waited, watching the progress of the war.

Combat was hand to hand. The archers on both sides were now effectively useless, with the armies locked together in a bloody embrace. At first, Silvan could make nothing of the confusion he looked upon, but after watching several moments, it seemed to him that the elf army was gaining ground.

"A glorious victory already, Your Majesty," his commander said in triumph. "The vermin are falling back!"

"Yes, you are right," Silvan replied, and he frowned.

"Your Majesty does not seem pleased. We are crushing the human insects!"

"So it would seem," said Silvan. "But if you look closely, Commander, you will note that the enemy is not running in panic. They are falling back, certainly, but their movements are calculated, disciplined. See how they hold their line? See how one man steps in to take the place if another falls? Our troops, on the other hand," he added with disgust, "have gone completely berserk!"

The elves, seeing the enemy in retreat, had broken ranks and were flailing at the enemy in a murderous rage, heedless of the shouts and cries of their commanders. Competing trumpet calls sounded over the screams of the wounded and dying, fighting their own battle. Silvan noted that the Dark Knights listened closely for their trumpet calls and responded immediately to the brayed commands, while the maddened elves were deaf to all.

"Still," Silvan said, "we cannot help but win, seeing that we outnumber them so greatly. The only way could possibly lose would be to turn our swords on ourselves. I will have a few words with General Konnal on my return, however. Samar would never permit such a lack of discipline."

"Your Majesty!" One of the scouts returned, riding at a full gallop. "We have located the officers!"

Silvan turned his horse's head, rode after the scout. They had advanced only a short way through the forest, before they met up with another scout, who had been left to keep watch.

He pointed. "There, Your Majesty. On that rise. They're easy to see."

So they were. A huge minotaur, the first Silvan had ever seen, stood upon the rise. The minotaur wore the regalia of a Knight of Neraka. A massive sword was buckled at his side. He was watching the progress of the battle intently. Twelve more Knights, mounted on horses, were also observing the battle. Beside them stood the standard-bearer, holding a flag that might have once been white, but was now a dirty brownish red color, as if it had been soaked in blood. An aide stood nearby, holding the reins of a magnificent red horse.

"Surely the minotaur is their commander," Silvan said. "We were misinformed."

"No, Your Majesty," the scout replied. "See there, behind the minotaur. That is the commander, the one with the blood-red sash."

Silvan could not see her, at first, and then the minotaur stepped to one side to confer with another of the Knights.

Behind him, a slight, delicate human female stood on a knoll, her gaze fixed with rapt intensity upon the battle. She carried her helm beneath her arm. A morning star hung from a belt at her waist.

"*That* is their commander?" Silvan said, amazed. "She does not look old enough to be attending her first dance, much less leading seasoned troops into battle."

As if she had heard him, though that was impossible, for she was a good forty yards distant, she turned her face toward him. He felt himself suddenly exposed to her view, and he backed up hurriedly, keeping to the deep shadows of the dense woods.

She stared in his direction for long moments, and Silvan was certain that they had been seen. He was about to order his men forward, when she turned her head away. She said something to the minotaur, apparently, for he left his conference and walked over to her. Even from this distance, Silvan could see that the minotaur regarded the girl with the utmost respect, even reverence. He listened intently to her orders, looked over his shoulder at the battle and nodded his horned head.

He turned and, with a wave of his hand, summoned the mounted Knights. With a roar, the minotaur ran forward toward the rear of his own lines. The Knights galloped after him, with what purpose Silvan could not tell. A counter-charge, perhaps.

"Now is our chance, Your Majesty!" said the commander excitedly. "She stands alone."

This was beyond all possible luck, so far beyond that Silvan mistrusted his good fortune. He hesitated before ordering his men forward, fearing a trap.

"Your Majesty!" the commander urged. "What are you waiting for?"

Silvan looked and looked. He could see no troops lying in ambush. The mounted Knights of the enemy were riding away from their commander.

Silvan spurred his horse and galloped forward, the other soldiers streaming behind him. They rode with the swiftness of an arrow, with Silvan as the silver arrowhead, aiming straight at the enemy's heart. They were halfway to their destination before anyone was aware of them. The girl kept her gaze fixed on her forces. It was her standard-bearer who spotted them. He cried out and pointed. The red horse lifted its head, whinnied loud enough to rival the trumpets.

At the sound, the minotaur halted in his charge and turned around.

Silvan kept the minotaur in the corner of his eye as he rode, dug his spurs into his horse's flank, urging more speed. The mad race was exhilarating. A skilled rider, he outdistanced his bodyguard. He was not far from his objective now. She must have heard the pounding hooves, but still she did not turn her head.

A great and terrible roar sounded over the battlefield. A roar of grief and rage and fury. A roar so horrible that the sound caused Silvan's stomach to shrivel and brought beads of sweat to his forehead. He looked to see the minotaur rushing for him, a great sword raised to cleave him in twain. Silvan gritted his teeth and pressed the horse forward. If he could lay his hands on the girl, he would use her as both shield and hostage.

The minotaur was extraordinarily fast. Though he was on foot and Silvan was mounted, it seemed that the racing minotaur must reach Silvan before Silvan's horse could reach the enemy commander. Silvan looked from the minotaur to the girl. She had still taken no notice of him. She seemed completely unaware of her danger. Her gaze was fixed upon the minotaur.

"Galdar," she called, her voice beautifully clear, oddly deep. "Remember your oath."

Her voice resounded over the cries and screams and clashing steel. The call acted upon the minotaur like a spear to his heart. He ceased his furious rush. He stared at her, his gaze pleading.

She did not relent, or so it seemed. She shifted her gaze from him to the heavens. The minotaur gave another howl of rage and then plunged his sword into the ground, drove it into the cornfield with such force that he buried it halfway to the hilt.

Silvan galloped up the rise. At last the girl shifted her gaze from the heavens. She turned her eyes full upon Silvan.

Amber eyes. Silvan had never seen the like. Her eyes did not repel him but drew him forward. He rode toward her, and he could see nothing but her eyes. It seemed he was riding into them.

She clasped her morning star, hefted it in her hand, and stood awaiting him fearlessly.

Silvan dashed his horse up the small rise, came level with the girl. She struck at him with the morning star, a blow he deflected easily, kicking it aside with his foot. Another kick knocked the morning star from her hand and sent her staggering backward. She lost her balance, fell heavily to the ground. His guards surrounded her. The guards killed her standard-bearer and made an attempt to seize the horse, but the animal lashed out with its hooves. Breaking free of the holder, the horse charged straight for the rear lines, as if it would join the battle alone and riderless.

The girl lay stunned on the ground. She was covered with blood, but he could not tell if it was hers or that of her standard-bearer, who lay decapitated by her side.

Fearing she would be trampled, Silvan furiously ordered his guards to keep back. He slid from his horse, ran to the girl and lifted her in his arms. She moaned, her eyes fluttered. He breathed again. She was alive.

"I will take her, Your Majesty," offered his commander.

Silvan would not give her up. He placed her on his saddle, climbed up behind her. Clasping one arm around her tightly, he took hold of the reins in the other. Her head rested against his silver breastplate. He had never in his life seen any face so delicate, so perfectly formed, so beautiful. He cradled her tenderly, anxiously.

"Ride!" he ordered and he started for the woods, riding swiftly, but not so swiftly that he risked jarring her.

He rode past the minotaur, who was on his knees beside his buried sword, his horned head bowed in grief.

"What do you men think you are doing?" Silvan demanded. Several of the elves were starting to ride in the minotaur's direction, their swords raised. "He is not a threat to us. Leave him."

"He is a minotaur, Your Majesty. He is always a threat," protested the commander.

"Would you kill him unarmed and unresisting?" Silvan demanded sternly.

"He would have no compunction killing us, if the situation was reversed," the commander replied grimly.

"And so now we are reduced to the level of beasts," Silvan said coldly. "I said leave him, Commander. We have achieved our objective. Let us get out of here before we are overrun."

Indeed, that seemed likely. The army of the Knights of Neraka was falling back rapidly now. Their retreat was in good order, they were keeping their lines intact. Silvan and his Knights galloped from the field, Silvan bearing their prize proudly in his arms.

He reached the shadows of the trees. The girl stirred and moaned again and opened her eyes.

Silvan looked down into them, saw himself encased in amber.

The girl was a docile captive, causing no trouble, accepting her fate without complaint. When they arrived back in camp, she refused Silvan's offers of assistance. Sliding gracefully from Silvan's horse, she gave herself willingly into custody. The elves clapped iron manacles on her wrists and ankles and marched her into a tent that was furnished with nothing but a pallet of straw and a blanket.

Silvan followed her. He could not leave her.

"Are you wounded? Shall I send the healers to you?"

She shook her head. She had not spoken a word to him or to anyone. She refused his offer of food and drink.

He stood at the entrance to the prison tent, feeling helpless and foolish in his regal armor. She, by contrast, blood-covered and in chains, was calm and self-possessed. She sat down cross-legged on her blanket, stared unblinking into the darkness. Silvan left the tent with the uncomfortable feeling that he was the one who had been taken prisoner.

"Where is Glaucous?" Silvan demanded. "He wanted to question her."

But no one could say what had become of Glaucous. He had not been seen since the start of the battle.

"Let me know when he comes to interrogate her," Silvan commanded and went to his tent to remove his armor. He held still this time, still and unmoving, as his squire detached the buckles and lifted the armor from him piece by piece.

"Congratulations, Cousin!" Kiryn entered the tent, ducking through the tent flap. "You are a hero! I will not need to write your song, after all. Your people are already singing it!" He waited for a laughing response, and when it did not come, he looked at Silvan more closely. "Cousin? What is it? You don't look well. Are you wounded?"

"Did you see her, Kiryn?" Silvan asked. "Go away!" he shouted irritably at his squire. "Get out. I can finish this myself."

The squire bowed and left. Silvan sat down upon his cot, one boot on and one boot off.

"Did I see the prisoner? Only a glimpse," Kiryn said. "Why?"

"What did you think of her?"

"She is the first human I have ever seen, and I did not find her as ugly as I had been led to believe. Still, I thought her extremely strange. Bewitching. Uncanny." Kiryn grimaced. "And is it now the custom among human females to shave their heads?"

"What? Oh, no. Perhaps it is the custom of the Knights of Neraka." Silvan sat with his boot in his hand, staring at the darkness and seeing amber eyes. "I thought her beautiful. The most beautiful woman I have ever seen."

Kiryn sat down beside his cousin. "Silvan, she is the enemy. Because of her, hundreds of our people lie dead or dying in that blood-soaked field."

"I know. I know!" Silvan cried, standing up. He tossed the boot into the corner. Sitting down, he began to tug viciously on the other. "She wouldn't say a word to me. She wouldn't tell me her name. She just looked at me with those strange eyes."

"Your Majesty." An officer appeared at the entrance. "General Konnal has asked me to relate to you the news. The day is ours. We have won."

Silvan made no response. He had ceased to tug on the boot, was once again staring into the dark tent corner.

Kiryn rose, went outside. "His Majesty is fatigued," he said. "I'm certain he is overjoyed."

"Then he's the only one," said the officer wryly.

Victory belonged to the elves, but few in the elven camp that night rejoiced. They had halted the enemy's advance, driven him back, kept him from reaching Silvanost, but they had not destroyed him. They counted thirty human bodies upon the field of battle, not four hundred as they had anticipated. They laid the blame to a strange fog that had arisen from the river, a dank, chill, gray fog that hung low over the ground, a swirling, obfuscating fog that hid foe from foe, comrade from comrade. In this fog, the enemy had simply disappeared, vanished, as if the blood-soaked ground had opened up and swallowed him.

"Which is probably exactly what happened," said General Konnal to his officers. "They had their escape arranged in advance. They retreated, and when the fog came, they ran to their hideout. They are skulking about in the caves somewhere near here."

"To what purpose, General?" Silvan demanded impatiently.

The king was feeling irritable and out of sorts, restless and antsy. He left his tent that was suddenly cramped and confining, came to confer with the officers. Silvan's courage had been praised and lauded. He was undoubtedly the hero of the hour, as even General Konnal admitted. Silvan cared nothing for their praise. His gaze shifted constantly to the tent where the girl was being held prisoner.

"The humans have no food, no supplies," he continued, "and no way of obtaining any. They are cut off, isolated. They know that they can never take Silvanost now. Surely, if anything, they will attempt to retreat back to the borders."

"They know we would cut them down if they tried that," Konnal said. "Yet, you are right, Your Majesty, they cannot remain in hiding forever. Sooner or later they must come out, and then we will have them. I just wish I knew," he added, more to himself than to anyone else, "what they are planning. For there was a plan here as certain as I live and breathe."

His officers offered various theories: The humans had panicked and were now scattered to the four winds, the humans had descended below ground in hopes of finding tunnels that would lead them back north, and so on and so forth. Each theory had its opponents, and the elves argued among themselves. Growing weary of the debate, Silvan left abruptly, walked out into the night.

"There is one person who knows," he said to himself, "and she will tell me. She *will* talk to me!"

He strode purposefully toward her tent, past the bonfires where the elves sat disconsolately, reliving the battle. The soldiers were bitter and chagrined at their failure to annihilate the detested foe. They swore that when it was dawn they would search beneath every rock until they found the cowardly humans, who had run away to hide when it became clear defeat was imminent. The elves vowed to slay them, every one.

Silvan discovered that he wasn't the only one interested in the prisoner. Glaucous stood at the entrance to her tent, being cleared for admittance by the guard. Silvan was about to advance and make himself known when he realized that Glaucous had not seen him.

Silvan was suddenly interested to hear what Glaucous would ask her. He circled around to the rear of the prisoner's tent. The night was dark. No guard stood back here. Silvan crept close to the tent, being careful to make no sound. He quieted even his breathing.

A candle on the floor inside the tent flared, brought to life two dark silhouettes—the girl's with her smooth head and long, graceful neck and the elf, tall and straight, his white robes black against the light. The two stared at each other unspeaking for long moments and then, suddenly, Glaucous recoiled. He shrank back away from her, though she had done nothing to him, had not moved, had not raised her hand, had not said a word.

"Who *are* you?" he demanded and his voice was awed.

"I am called Mina," she replied.

"And I am—"

"No need to tell me," she said. "I know your name."

"How could you?" he asked, amazed. "You couldn't. You have never seen me before."

"But I know it," she replied calmly.

Glaucous had regained his self-possession. "Answer me one thing, witch. How did you pass through my shield? By what magic? What sorcery did you use?"

"No magic," she said. "No sorcery. The Hand of the God reached down and the shield was lifted."

"What hand?" Glaucous was angry, thinking she mocked him. "What god? There are no gods! Not anymore!"

"There is One God," Mina stated.

"And what is the name of this god?"

"The God has no name. The God needs no name. The God is the One God, the True God, the Only God."

"Lies! You will tell me what I want to know." Glaucous lifted his hand.

Silvanoshei expected Glaucous to use the truth-seek, as had been done to him.

"You feel your throat start to close," said Glaucous. "You gasp for air and find none. You begin to suffocate."

"This is not the truth-seek," Silvan said to himself. "What is he doing?"

"Your lungs burn and seem about to burst," Glaucous continued. "The magic tightens, tightens all the while until you lose consciousness. I will end the torment, when you agree to tell me the truth."

He began to chant strange words, words that Silvan did not understand, but which he guessed must be words to a magical spell. Alarmed for Mina's safety, Silvan was ready to rush to her rescue, to tear the fabric of the tent with his bare hands if need be to reach her.

Mina sat calmly on the cot. She did not gasp. She did not choke. She continued to breathe normally.

Glaucous ceased his chant. He stared at her in amazement. "You thwart me! How?"

"Your magic has no effect on me," Mina said, shrugging. The chains that bound her rang like silver bells. She looked up at him. "I know you. I know the truth."

Glaucous regarded her in silence, and though Silvan could see only Glaucous's silhouette, he could tell that the elf was enraged and, also, that he was afraid.

Glaucous left the tent abruptly.

Troubled, fascinated, Silvan came around to the front of

the tent. He waited in the darkness until he saw Glaucous enter General Konnal's tent, then approached the guard.

"I will speak with the prisoner," he said.

"Yes, Your Majesty." The guard bowed, started to accompany the king.

"Alone," Silvan said. "You have leave to go."

The guard did not move.

"I am in no danger. She is chained and manacled! Go fetch yourself some dinner. I will take over your watch."

"Your Majesty, I have my orders—"

"I countermand them!" Silvan said angrily, thinking he was cutting a very poor figure in the sight of those amber eyes. "Go and take the fellow of your watch with you."

The guard hesitated a moment longer, but his king had spoken. He dared not disobey. He and his companion walked off toward the cooking fires. Silvan entered the tent. He stood looking at the prisoner, stood inside the amber of her eyes, warm and liquid around him.

"I want to know . . . if . . . if they are treating you well. . . ." What a stupid thing to say! Silvan thought, even as the words fumbled their way out of his mouth.

"Thank you, Silvanoshei Caladon," the girl said. "I need nothing. I am in the care of my God."

"You know who I am?" Silvan asked.

"Of course, you are Silvanoshei, son of Alhana Starbreeze, daughter of Lorac Caladon and of Porthios of the House of Solostaran."

"And you are . . . ?"

"Mina."

"Just Mina?"

She shrugged and when she shrugged, the chains on her manacles chimed. "Just Mina."

The amber began to congeal around Silvan. He felt short of breath, as if he were the one to fall victim to Glaucous's suffocating spell. He came closer to her, knelt on one knee before her to bring those lovely eyes level with his own.

"You mention your god. I would ask you a question. If the Knights of Neraka follow this god, then I must assume that this god is evil. Why does someone so young and so beautiful walk the ways of darkness?"

Mina smiled at him, the kind and pitying smile one bestows upon the blind or the feebleminded.

"There is no good, there is no evil. There is no light, there is no darkness. There is only one. One truth. All the rest is falsehood."

"But this god must be evil," Silvan argued. "Otherwise why attack our nation? We are peace-loving. We have done nothing to provoke this war. Yet now my people lie dead at the hands of their enemy."

"I do not come to conquer," Mina said. "I come to free you, to save you and your people. If some die, it is only that count-less others may live. The dead understand their sacrifice."

"Perhaps *they* do," said Silvan with a wry shake of his head. "I confess that I do not. How could you—a human, single and alone—save the elven nation?"

Mina sat quite still for long moments, so still that her chains made no sound. Her amber eyes left him, shifted to stare into the candle's flame. He was content to sit and gaze at her. He could have been content to sit at her feet and gaze at her all night, perhaps all his life. He had never seen a human woman with such delicate features, such fine bone structure, such smooth skin. Every movement was graceful and fluid. He found his eyes drawn to her shaved head. The shape of the skull was perfect, the skin smooth with a faint shimmer-ing red down upon it, which must be like feathery down to touch . . .

"I am permitted to tell you a secret, Silvanoshei," said Mina.

Silvan, lost in her, started at the sound of her voice. "Who gives you this permission?"

"You must swear that you will tell no one else."

"I swear," said Silvan.

"Truly swear," said Mina.

"I swear," Silvan said slowly, "on my mother's grave."

"An oath I cannot accept," Mina returned. "Your mother is not dead."

"What?" Silvan sank back, amazed. "What are you saying?"

"Your mother lives, and so does your father. The ogres did not kill your mother or her followers, as you feared. They were rescued by the Legion of Steel. But your parents' story is ended, they are in the past. Your story is just begun, Silvanoshei Caladon."

Mina reached out her hand, the chains ringing like altar bells. She touched Silvan's cheek. Exerting a gentle pressure, she drew him near. "Swear to me by the One True God that you will not reveal what I am about to tell you to anyone."

"But I don't believe in this god," Silvan faltered. Her touch was like the lightning bolt that had struck so near him, raised the hair on his neck and arms, sent prickles of desire through his bloodstream.

"The One God believes in *you*, Silvanoshei," Mina told him. "That is all that matters. The One God will accept your oath."

"I swear, then, by the . . . One God." He felt uncomfortable, saying the word, felt uncomfortable swearing the vow. He did not believe, not at all, but he had the strange and uneasy impression that his vow had been recorded by some immortal hand and that he would be held to it.

"How did *you* enter the shield?" Mina asked.

"Glaucous raised the shield so that I could—" Silvan began, but he stopped when he saw her smile. "What? Did this God lift it for me, as you told Glaucous?"

"I told him what he wanted to hear. In effect, you did not enter the shield. The shield captured you while you were helpless."

"Yes, I see what you are saying." Silvan remembered back to the night of the storm. "I was unconscious. I collapsed on one side of the Shield and when I woke, I was on the other. *I* did not move. The shield moved to cover me! Of course, that is the explanation!"

"The shield will stand firm against an attack, but it will try to apprehend the helpless, or so I was given to know. My soldiers and I slept and while we slept, the shield moved over us."

"But if the shield protects the elves," Silvan argued. "How could it admit our enemies?"

"The shield does not protect you," Mina replied. "The Shield keeps out those who would help you. In truth, the shield is your prison. Not only your prison, it is also your executioner."

Silvan drew back, away from her touch. Her nearness confused him, made thinking difficult. "What do you mean?"

"Your people are dying of a wasting sickness," she said. "Every day, many more succumb. Some believe the shield is causing this illness. They are partly right. What they do not know is that the lives of the elves are being drained to provide energy to the shield. The lives of your people keep the shield in place. The shield is now a prison. Soon it will be your tomb."

Silvan sank back on his heels. "I don't believe you."

"I have proof," Mina said. "What I speak is true. I swear by my God."

"Then give your proof to me," Silvan urged. "Let me consider it."

"I will tell you, Silvanoshei, and gladly. My God sent me here with that purpose. Glaucous—"

"Your Majesty," said a stern voice outside the tent.

Silvan cursed softly, turned swiftly.

"Remember, not a word!" Mina warned.

His hand trembling, Silvan opened the tent flap to see General Konnal, flanked by the two guards.

"Your Majesty," General Konnal repeated and his voice held a patronizing tone that grated on Silvan, "not even a king may dismiss those who guard such an important and dangerous prisoner. Your Majesty places himself in peril, and that cannot be allowed. Take up your positions," the general ordered.

The elf guard moved to stand in front of the prison tent.

Words of explanation clustered thick on Silvan's tongue, but he couldn't articulate any of them. He might have said that he was there to interrogate the prisoner about the shield, but that was coming too close to her secret, and he feared he could not mention one without revealing the other.

"I will escort Your Majesty back to his tent," said Konnal. "Even heroes must sleep."

Silvan maintained a silence that he hoped was the silence of injured dignity and misunderstood intentions. He fell into step beside the general, walked past campfires that were being allowed to die down. Those elves not out on patrol, searching for the humans, had wrapped themselves in their blankets and were already asleep. Elf healers tended to the wounded, made them comfortable. The camp was quiet and still.

"Good night, General," said Silvan coldly. "I give you joy on your victory this day." He started to enter his tent.

"I advise Your Majesty to go straight to bed," the General said. "You will need to be rested for tomorrow. To preside over the execution."

"What?" Silvan gasped. He caught hold of the tent post to steady himself. "What execution? Whose?"

"Tomorrow at noon, when the glorious sun stands high in the sky to serve as our witness, we will execute the human," said Konnal. He did not look at the king as he spoke, but stared straight into the night. "Glaucous has recommended it, and in this I agree with him."

"Glaucous!" Silvan repeated.

He remembered Glaucous in the tent, remembered the

fear he had sensed in him. Mina had been about to tell Silvan something about Glaucous before they had been interrupted.

"You cannot kill her!" Silvan said firmly. "You will not. I forbid it."

"I am afraid that Your Majesty has no say in this matter," said Konnal. "The Heads of House have been apprised of the situation. They have voted, and their vote is unanimous."

"How will she be killed?" Silvan asked.

Konnal laid a kindly hand on the king's shoulder. "I know this is an onerous task, Your Majesty. You don't need to remain to watch. Just step out and say a few words, and then retire to your tent. No one will think the worse of you."

"Answer me, damn you!" Silvan cried, striking the man's hand away.

Konnal's face froze. "The human is to be taken to the field that is drenched in the blood of our people. She is to be tied to a stake. Seven of our best archers will be chosen. When the sun is directly overhead, when the human no longer casts a shadow, the archers will fire seven arrows into her body."

Silvan could not see the general for the blinding white rage that filled his being. He clenched his fist, dug his nails into his flesh. The pain helped him steady his voice. "Why does Glaucous say she must die?"

"His reasoning is sound. So long as she lives, the humans will remain in the area, hoping to rescue her. With her execution, they will lose all hope. They will be demoralized. Easier to locate, easier to destroy."

Silvan felt his gorge rise. He feared he would be sick, but he struggled to make one last argument. "We elves revere life. We do not by law take the life of any elf, no matter how terrible his or her crime. Elf assassins exist, but only outside the law."

"We do not take the life of an elf," Konnal answered. "We take the life of a human. Goodnight, Your Majesty. I will send a messenger to you before dawn."

Silvan entered his tent and shut the flap behind him. His servants awaited him.

"Leave me," Silvan ordered irritably, and the servants hurriedly departed.

Silvan threw himself on his bed, but he was up almost immediately. He flung himself into a chair and stared moodily into the darkness. He could not let this girl die. He loved her. Adored her. He had loved her from the moment he had seen her standing courageously, fearlessly, among her soldiers. He had stepped off the precipice of sanity and plummeted down on love's sharp rocks. They tore and mangled him. He gloried in the pain and wanted more.

A plan formed in his mind. What he was doing was wrong. He might well be placing his people in danger, but— he argued—what they were doing was wrong, and their wrong was greater than his. He was, in a way, saving them from themselves.

Silvan gave the general time to return to his tent, then wrapped himself in a dark cloak. He thrust a long, sharp knife into his boot. Peering out of the tent flap, he looked to see that no one was about. He left his tent, sneaked through the slumbering camp with quiet tread.

Two guards, alert and watchful, stood outside Mina's tent. Silvan did not go near them. He circled to the back of the tent where he had hidden to eavesdrop on Glaucous. Silvan looked carefully around. The woods were only a few paces away. They could reach them easily. They would find a cave. He would hide her there in safety, come to visit her in the night, bring her food, water, his love . . .

Removing the knife, Silvan placed its sharp point against the fabric of the tent and, working carefully and silently, cut a slit near the bottom. He crawled through the slit and inside the tent.

The candle still burned. Silvan was careful to keep his body from passing in front of it, afraid that the guards would see his shadow.

Mina had fallen asleep on her straw pallet. She slept on her side, her legs drawn up, her hands—still chained—curled up against her breast. She looked very fragile. Her slumbers were seemingly dreamless, and peaceful. Her breath came and went easily through her nose and her parted lips.

Silvan clapped his hand over her mouth to prevent any startled exclamation. "Mina!" he whispered urgently. "Mina."

Her eyes opened. She made no sound. The amber eyes gazed up at him, aware of him, cognizant of her surroundings.

"Don't be afraid," he said and realized as he said it that this girl had never known fear. She did not know fear now. "I've come to free you." He tried to speak calmly, but his voice and his hands trembled. "We can escape out the back of the tent into the woods. We have to get these manacles off."

He moved his hand away. "Call the guard. He has the key. Tell him you're ill. I'll wait in the shadows and—"

Mina put her fingers on his lips, stopped his words. "No," she said. "Thank you, but I will not leave."

"What was that?" one of the guards asked his fellow. "Did you hear something?"

"It came from inside the tent."

Silvan lifted his knife. Mina laid a restraining hand on his arm. She began to sing.

> Sleep, love; forever sleep.
> Your soul the night will keep.
> Embrace the darkness deep.
> Sleep, love; forever sleep.

The voices of the guards ceased.

"There," she said to Silvan. "The guards are asleep. We may talk without fear."

"Asleep . . ." Silvan lifted the tent flap. The guards remained standing at their posts, their heads bowed, their chins resting on their chests. Their eyes were closed.

"Are you a sorceress?" he asked, coming back to her.

"No, I am only a faithful follower," Mina replied. "The gifts I have are from my God."

"May your God keep you safe. Hurry, Mina! Out this way. We will find a path not far from here. The path runs through . . ." Silvan halted.

She was shaking her head.

"Mina," he said desperately, "we must escape! They're going to execute you at noon this very day. With the rising of the sun. Glaucous has convinced them. He fears you, Mina."

"He has good reason to fear me," she said sternly.

"Why, Mina?" Silvan asked. "You were going to tell me something about him. What is it?"

"Only that he is not what he appears and that by his magic, your people are dying. Tell me this"—she put her hand upon his cheek—"is it your desire to punish Glaucous? Reveal his intentions to your people and thereby reveal his murderous plan?"

"Yes, of course, but what—"

"Then do as I instruct you," Mina said. "Do exactly as I say. My life is in your keeping. If you fail me—"

"I will not fail you, Mina," Silvan whispered. Seizing her hand, he pressed it to his lips. "I am yours to command."

"You will attend my execution— Hush! Say nothing. You promised. Make certain that you are armed. Position yourself at Glaucous's side. Keep a large number of your bodyguards around you. Will you do that?"

"Yes, but what then? Must I watch you die?"

"You will know what to do and when to do it. Rest assured. The One God is with us. You must go now, Silvan. The general will send someone to your tent to check on you. He must not find you absent."

To leave her was to leave a part of himself. Silvan reached out his hand, ran his fingers over her head, felt the warmth of her skin, the softness of the downlike hair, the hardness of the bone beneath. She held perfectly still under his touch, did not warm to him, but did not move away from him either.

"What did your hair look like, Mina?" he asked.

"It was the color of flame, long and thick. The strands would curl around your finger and tug at your heart like a baby's hand."

"Your hair must have been beautiful," Silvan said. "Did you lose it in a fever?"

"I cut it," she told him. "I took a knife and I cut it off at the roots."

"Why?" He was aghast.

"My God required it of me. I cared too much for my looks," Mina replied. "I liked to be petted, admired, loved. My hair was my vanity, my pride. I sacrificed it to prove my faith. I have only one love, now. Only one loyalty. You must leave me now, Silvan."

Silvan stood up. Reluctantly, he moved to the back of the tent.

"You are my one love, Mina," he said softly.

"It is not me that you love," she said to him. "It is the God in me."

Silvan did not remember leaving her tent, but he found himself standing outside in the darkness.

30

To your health!

ight settled over the battlefield of Silvanesti, shrouding the bodies of the dead that were being ceremoniously prepared for burial. The same night wrapped like a winding cloth around the elven capital of Qualinost.

The night had a feel of doom about it, or so Gerard thought. He walked the streets of the elven capital with his hand on the hilt of his sword, his watchful gaze looking for the glint of steel in every shadowed corner, every dark doorway. He crossed the street to avoid passing in front of an alley. He scrutinized every second story window curtain to see if it fluttered, as it might if an archer stood behind it, ready with an assassin's arrow.

He was conscious, always, of eyes watching him, and once he felt so threatened that he whipped around, sword drawn, to defend against a knife in the back. He saw nothing, however, but he was certain someone had been there, someone who had perhaps been daunted by the Knight's heavy battle armor and his shining sword.

Gerard could not even breath a sigh of relief when he

reached safely the Headquarters of the Knights of Neraka. Danger was no longer sneaking stealthily behind him. Danger was front and center.

He entered the headquarters to find a single officer on duty, the draconian asleep the floor.

"Here's the answer for Beryl from Marshal Medan," said Gerard, saluting.

"About time!" The officer grunted. "You can't believe how loudly that thing snores!"

Gerard walked over to the draconian, who was twitching in his sleep and making strange, guttural sounds.

"Groul," Gerard said and reached out a hand to shake the slumbering draconian.

A hiss, a snarl, a flapping of wings and scrabbling of feet. Clawed hands grappled for Gerard's throat.

"Hey!" Gerard yelled, fending off the draconian's attack. "Calm down, will you?"

Groul glared at him with squint lizard eyes. His tongue flicked. Lowering his hand from Gerard's neck, the draconian drew back. "Sorry," he muttered. "You startled me."

The marks of Groul's claws stung and burned on Gerard's skin. "My fault," he said stiffly. "I shouldn't have wakened you so suddenly." He held out the scroll case. "Here is the marshal's answer."

Groul took it, eyed it to make certain the seal was intact. Satisfied, he thrust it into the belt of his harness, turned and, with a grunt, headed for the door. The creature wasn't wearing armor, Gerard noted, thinking glumly to himself that the draco didn't need to wear armor. The thick, scaly hide was protection enough.

Gerard drew in a deep breath, sighed it out, and followed the draconian.

Groul turned. "What are you doing, Nerakan?"

"You are in a hostile land after nightfall. My orders are to accompany you safely to the border," Gerard said.

"You are going to protect me?" Groul gave a gurgle that might have been a laugh. "Bah! Go back to your soft bed, Nerakan. I am in no danger. I know how to deal with elf scum."

"I have my orders," said Gerard stubbornly. "If anything happened to you, the marshal would do the same to me."

Groul's lizard eyes glittered in anger.

"I have something with me that might shorten the journey for both of us," Gerard added. Drawing aside his cloak, he revealed a flask he wore on his hip.

The glitter of anger brightened to a gleam of desire, a gleam swiftly hooded.

"What is in the flask, Nerakan?" Groul asked, his tongue darting out between his sharp teeth.

"Dwarf spirits," said Gerard. "A gift from the marshal. He asks that once we are safe across the border, we join him in drinking to the downfall of the elves."

Groul made no more protest about Gerard's accompanying him. The two trudged off through the silent streets of Qualinost. Again, Gerard felt eyes watching them, but no one attacked. Gerard was not surprised. The draconian was a fearsome opponent.

Reaching the wilderness, the draconian followed one of the main trails leading into the woods. Then, with a suddenness that took Gerard by surprise, Groul plunged into the forest, taking a route known only to the draconian, or so Gerard guessed. The draconian had excellent night vision, to judge by the rapidity with which he moved through the tangled forest. The moon was waning, but the stars provided light, as did the glow of the lights of Qualinost. The forest floor was a mass of brush and vines. Weighed down by his heavy armor, Gerard found the going hard. He had no need to feign fatigue when he called out for the draconian to halt.

"No need to kill ourselves," Gerard said, panting. "How about a moment's rest?"

"Humans!" Groul sneered. He was not even breathing hard, but he came to a halt, looked back at the Knight. To be more precise, the draconian looked at the flask. "Still, this walking is thirsty work. I could use a drink."

Gerard hesitated. "My orders—"

"To the Abyss with your orders!" Groul snarled.

"I don't suppose one little nip would hurt," Gerard said and removed the flask. He drew the cork, sniffed. The pungent, dark and musky odor of dwarf spirits burned his nostrils. Snorting, he held the flask at arm's length. "A good year," he said, his eyes tearing.

The draconian snatched the flask and brought it to his mouth. He took a long drink, then lowered the flask with a satisfied sigh. "Very good," he said in husky tones and burped.

"To your health," Gerard said and put the flask to his mouth. Keeping his tongue pressed against the opening, he pretended to swallow. "There," he said with seeming reluctance, putting the cork back in the flask, "that's enough. We should be on our way."

"Not so fast!" Groul seized the flask, drew out the cork and tossed it away. "Sit down, Nerakan."

"But your mission—"

"Beryl isn't going anywhere," Groul said, settling himself against the bole of a tree. "Whether she gets this message tomorrow or a year from tomorrow won't make any difference. Her plans for the elves are already in motion."

Gerard's heart lurched. "What do you mean?" he asked, trying to sound casual. He settled down beside the draconian and reached for the flask.

Groul handed it over with obvious reluctance. He kept his gaze fixed on Gerard, grudging every drop the Knight supposedly drank, and snatched it back the moment Gerard lowered it from his lips.

The liquid gurgled down the draconian's throat. Gerard

was alarmed by how much the creature could drink, wondered if one flask would be enough.

Groul sighed, belched and wiped his mouth with the back of a clawed hand.

"You were telling me about Beryl," Gerard said.

"Ah, yes!" Groul held the flask to the moonlight. "Here's to my lady dragon, the lovely Beryl. And to the death of the elves."

He drank. Gerard pretended to drink.

"Yes," said Gerard. "The marshal told me. She has given the elves six days—"

"Ha, ha! Six days!" Groul's laugh bubbled in his throat. "The elves do not have six minutes! Beryl's army is probably crossing the border as we speak! It is a huge army, the largest seen on Ansalon since the Chaos War. Draconians, goblins, hobgoblins, ogres, human conscripts. We attack Qualinost from without. You Neraka Knights attack the elves from within. The Qualinesti are caught between fire and water with nowhere to run. At last, I will see the day dawn when not one of the pointy-eared scum are left alive."

Gerard's stomach twisted. Beryl's army crossing the border! Perhaps within a day's march on Qualinost!

"Will Beryl herself come to ensure her victory?" he asked, hoping that the catch in his throat would be mistaken for an aftereffect of the fiery liquor.

"No, no." Groul chuckled. "She leaves the elves to us. Beryl is flying off to Schallsea, to destroy the so-called Citadel of Light. And to capture some wretched mage. Here, Nerakan, stop hogging that flask!"

Groul grabbed the flask, slid his tongue over the rim.

Gerard's hand closed over the hilt of his knife. Slowly, quietly, he drew it from its sheath on his belt. He waited until Groul had lifted the flask one more time. The flask was almost empty. The draconian tilted back his head to retrieve every last drop.

Gerard struck, driving his knife with all his strength into the draconian's ribs, hoping to hit the heart.

He would have hit the heart on a human, but apparently a draconian's heart was in a different place. Either that or the creatures didn't possess hearts, which would not have surprised Gerard.

Realizing that his blow had not killed, Gerard yanked free the bloody knife. He scrambled to his feet, drawing his sword in the same motion.

Groul was injured but not critically. His grunt of pain rising to a howl of rage, he jumped up out of the brush, roaring in fury, his clawed hand grappling for his sword. The draconian attacked with a hacking blow, meant to split open his opponent's head.

Gerard parried the blow and managed to knock the sword from Groul's hand. The weapon fell into the brush at Gerard's feet. Frantically, he kicked it away as Groul sought to recover it. Gerard drove his booted foot into Groul's chin, knocking him back, but not felling him.

Drawing a curved-bladed dagger, Groul leaped into the air, using his wings to lift him well above Gerard. Slashing with his dagger, Groul launched himself bodily at the Knight.

The draconian's weight and the force of his blow drove Gerard to the ground. He fell heavily, landing on his back, with Groul on top, slavering and snarling and trying to stab Gerard with the dagger. The draconian's wings beat frantically, flapping in Gerard's face, stirring up dust that stung Gerard's eyes. He fought in panicked desperation, striking at Groul with his knife while trying to seize hold of the draconian's dagger.

The two rolled in the dust. Gerard felt his dagger hit home more than once. He was covered with blood, but whether the blood was his or Groul's, he could not tell. Still, Groul would not die, and Gerard's strength was giving out. Fear-pumped adrenaline was all that was keeping him going, and that was starting to recede.

Suddenly Groul choked, gagged. Blood spewed from the draconian, splashed over Gerard's face, blinding him. Groul stiffened, snarled in fury. He raised himself up off Gerard, lifted his dagger. The blade fell from the draconian's hand. Groul fell back onto Gerard, but this time, the draconian did not move. He was dead.

Gerard paused to draw a shuddering breath of relief, a pause that was his undoing. Too late, he remembered Medan's warning. A dead draconian is just as dangerous as a draconian living. Before Gerard could heave the carcass off him, the body of the Baaz draconian had changed into solid stone. Gerard felt as if he had the weight of a tomb on top of him. The stone carcass pressed him into the ground. He could not breathe. He was slowly suffocating. He fought to heave it off him, but it was too heavy. He drew in a ragged breath, planning to exert every last ounce of energy.

The stone statue crumbled to dust.

Gerard staggered to his feet, sank back against a tree. He wiped Groul's blood from his eyes, spit and retched until he had cleared it out of his mouth. He rested a few moments, waiting for his heart to quit trying to beat its way out from beneath his armor, waited until the battle rage had cleared from his eyes. When he could see, he fumbled at the draconian's harness, found the scroll case, and retrieved it.

Gerard took one last look at the heap of dust that had been Groul. Then, still spitting, still trying to rid himself of the foul taste in his mouth, the Knight turned and wearily made his way back through the darkness, back toward the flickering lights of Qualinost. Lights that were just starting to pale with the coming of dawn.

Sunshine streamed in through the crystal windows of the Palace of the Speaker of the Sun. Gilthas sat bathed in the sunlight, absorbed in his work. He was writing another poem, this one about his father's adventures during the War of the Lance, a poem that also contained encoded messages for two families of elves who had come under suspicion of being rebel sympathizers.

He had nearly completed it and was planning to send Planchet out to deliver the poem to those who took an interest in the king's literary pursuits, when Gilthas suddenly visibly shuddered. His fingers holding the quill pen shook. He left a blot upon his manuscript and laid down the pen hurriedly. Cold sweat beaded his brow.

"Your Majesty!" Planchet asked, alarmed. "What is wrong? Are you unwell?" He left his task of sorting the king's papers and hastened to his side.

"Your Majesty?" he repeated anxiously.

"I just had the strangest feeling," Gilthas said in a low voice. "As though a goose had walked on my grave."

"A goose, Your Majesty!" Planchet was baffled.

"It is a human saying, my friend." Gilthas smiled. "Did you never hear it? My father used to use it. The saying describes that feeling you get when for no reason that you can explain a chill causes your flesh to raise and your hair to prickle. That's exactly how I felt a moment ago. What is even stranger is that for an instant I had a very strong impression of my cousin's face! Silvanoshei. I could see him quite clearly, as clearly as I see you."

"Silvanoshei is dead, Your Majesty," Planchet reminded him. "Slain by ogres. Perhaps the goose was walking on his grave."

"I wonder," said Gilthas, thoughtfully. "My cousin did not look dead, I assure you. He wore silver armor, the kind worn by Silvanesti warriors. I saw smoke and blood, battle raged around him, but he was not touched by it. He stood at the edge of a precipice. I reached out my hand, but whether it was to pull him back or push him over, I don't know."

"I trust you were going to pull him back, Your Majesty," said Planchet, looking slightly shocked.

"I trust so, too." Gilthas frowned, shook his head. "I remember being quite angry and afraid. Strange." He shrugged. "Whatever it was, the feeling's gone now."

"Your Majesty must have dozed off. You have not been getting much sleep—"

Planchet suddenly ceased speaking. Making a sign to Gilthas to keep silent, his servant crept across the room and put his ear to the door.

"Someone is coming, Your Majesty," Planchet reported, speaking Common.

"At this hour in the morning? I am expecting no one. I hope it's not Palthainon," said Gilthas. "I have to finish this poem. Tell him I am not to be disturbed."

"Let me pass!" An elven voice outside the door spoke to the guards. The voice was calm but held an underlying note of tension and strain. "I have a message to the king from his mother."

One of the guards knocked loudly. Planchet cast a warning glance at Gilthas, who subsided back into his chair and resumed his writing.

"Hide those clothes!" he whispered urgently, with a gesture.

Gilthas's traveling clothes lay neatly folded on top of a chest, in preparation for another nightly journey. Planchet whisked the clothes back into the chest, which he closed and locked. He dropped the key into the bottom of a large vase of fresh-cut roses. This done, he walked over to answer the knock.

Gilthas played with his pen and took up a pensive attitude. Lounging back in his chair, he propped his feet up on a cushion, ran the tip of the feather over his lips, and stared at the ceiling.

"The Runner Kelevandros," announced the guard, "to see His Majesty."

"Let him enter," said Gilthas languidly.

Kelevandros came into the room in a bound. He was hooded and cloaked, the hood covering his face. Planchet shut the door behind him. Kelevandros threw back his hood. His face was deathly pale.

Gilthas rose involuntarily to his feet.

"What—"

"Your Majesty must not excite himself," Planchet remonstrated with a glance at the door, reminding the king that the guards could hear him.

"What has happened, Kelevandros?" Gilthas asked indolently. "You look as if you had seen a ghost."

"Your Majesty!" Kelevandros said in a low, quivering voice. "The queen mother has been arrested!"

"Arrested?" Gilthas repeated in astonishment. "Who has done this? Who would dare? And why? What is the charge?"

"Marshal Medan. Your Majesty." Kelevandros gulped. "I don't know how to say this—"

"Out with it, man!" Gilthas said sharply.

"Last night, Marshal Medan placed your honored mother under arrest. He has orders from the dragon Beryl to put . . . to put the queen mother to death."

Gilthas stared wordlessly. The blood drained from his face, as if someone had taken a knife and drawn it across his throat. He was so pale and shaken that Planchet left the door and hastened to the king's side, placed a firm and comforting hand on Gilthas's shoulder.

"I attempted to stop him, Your Majesty," Kelevandros said miserably. "I failed."

"Last night!" Gilthas cried, anguished. "Why didn't you come to me at once?"

"I tried, Your Majesty," Kelevandros said, "but the guards would not let me inside without orders from Palthainon."

"Where has Medan taken the queen mother?" Planchet asked. "What is the charge against her?"

"The charge is harboring the sorcerer Palin and helping

him escape with the magical device brought by the kender. I don't know where Medan has taken my mistress. I went first to the Knight's headquarters, but if she is being held there, no one would tell me. I have had people searching for her all night. They are to report back to Kalindas, who has offered to remain in the house in case there is news. Finally, one of the guards who is a friend of our cause admitted me.

"I came next to you. You have heard nothing then?" Kelevandros looked anxiously at the king.

"No," said Gilthas. The word made no sound as it left his pallid lips.

"We are about to learn something more, I believe," said Planchet, his ear cocked. "That is Medan's heavy tread on the staircase. His footsteps shake the house. He comes quickly."

They could hear the stamp of the guards' feet as they came to attention, hear the thud of their spears strike the floor. One of the guards started to knock, but the knock was never finished. Medan, accompanied by one of his bodyguards—helmed and wearing black leather armor—thrust the door open, strode into the room.

"Your Majesty—"

Gilthas lunged from his chair. He covered the distance between himself and the marshal in two great bounds. Catching hold of the startled Medan by the throat, Gilthas slammed the human back against the wall, while Planchet accosted the bodyguard. Seizing hold of the man's arm, Planchet twisted it behind his back, held a knife to his ear.

"What have you done with my mother?" Gilthas demanded, his voice hard and grim. "Tell me!" He tightened his grip on Medan's throat. "Tell me!"

The marshal had been caught flat-footed by the king's sudden assault. Medan did not move. The young king's fingers were exceptionally strong, and he appeared to know precisely what he was doing.

The marshal was by no means afraid. He had his hand on

the handle of his dirk and could at any moment draw the weapon and plunge it into the king's belly. That was not, however, what Medan had come here to accomplish.

He stared at Gilthas long moments without speaking, then said, as best he could for being choked, "Either the pup has grown into a wolf, or I am in the presence of a consummate actor." Noting the fearless determination in the young elf's eyes, the resolution in the jaw, the firmness of the fingers and the expertness of the hold, Medan had his answer.

"I tend to think the latter," he gasped.

"My mother, sir!" Gilthas said through clenched teeth. "Where is she?"

"I am here, Gilthas," Laurana replied, her voice echoing inside the helm of the Neraka Knights.

"Queen Mother!" Planchet gasped. He dropped the knife he had been holding and fell to his knees. "Forgive me! I had no idea . . ."

"You weren't supposed to, Planchet," Laurana said, removing the helm. "Let the marshal go, Gilthas. I am safe. For the moment. As safe as any of us."

Gilthas let loose of Medan, who stepped away from the wall, massaging his bruised throat.

"Mother, are you hurt?" Gilthas demanded. "Did he harm you? If he did, I swear—"

"No, my son, no!" Laurana reassured him. "The marshal has treated me with all possible respect. With great kindness, even. He took me to his house last night. This morning, he provided me with this disguise. The marshal fears my life may be in peril. He took me into custody for my own safety."

Gilthas frowned as if he found all this difficult to believe. "Mother, sit down. You look exhausted. Planchet, bring my mother some wine."

While Planchet went to fetch the wine, the marshal walked over to the door. Flinging it open, he stepped out into the hallway. The guards scrambled to attention.

"Guards, the rebel force has been reported within the city limits. His Majesty's life is in danger. Clear the household. Send all the servants home. Everyone. No one is to remain within the palace. Is that understood? I want guards posted at all the entrances. Admit no one, with the exception of my aide. Send him to king's chambers directly upon his arrival. Go!"

The guards departed, and soon their voices could be heard loudly ordering everyone to leave the palace. The voices of the servants rose in perplexity or consternation. It was early morning, breakfast was prepared but had not been served, the floors had yet to be swept. The guards were firm. There was a hubbub of voices, the household staff exclaiming loudly and fearfully, the scream of an overexcited maid. The guards herded everyone out the doors and took up their positions outside as ordered.

Within a few moments, the palace was strangely, unnaturally quiet.

Medan reentered the room. "Where do you think you are going?" he demanded, finding Kelevandros about to depart.

"I must take this news to my brother, my lord," Kelevandros said. "He is frantic with worry—"

"You are not taking this news to him or to anyone. Go sit down and keep quiet."

Laurana glanced up swiftly at this, looked searchingly at Kelevandros. The elf glanced at her uncertainly and then did as he was told.

Medan left the door open behind him. "I want to be able to hear what is going on outside. Are you all right, madam?"

"Yes, thank you, Marshal. Will you join me in a glass of wine?"

"With His Majesty's permission." The marshal made a slight bow.

"Planchet," Gilthas said, "pour the marshal some wine." The king continued to stand protectively beside his mother, continued to glower at the marshal.

Medan raised his glass in a toast. "I congratulate you, Your Majesty. I have been duped for the first and only time in my life. That weak, vacillating, poetry-loving act of yours took me in completely. I have long wondered how and why so many of my best plans were thwarted. I believe that I now have the answer. Your health, Your Majesty."

Medan drank the wine. Gilthas turned his back on the man.

"Mother, what is going on?"

"Sit down, Gilthas, and I will tell you," Laurana said. "Or better yet, you may read for yourself."

She looked to Medan. He reached inside his armor, produced the scroll sent by the dragon, and handed it, with a new and marked show of respect, to the king.

Gilthas walked to the window, unrolled the parchment. He held it to the waning twilight and read it slowly and carefully.

"The dragon cannot mean this," he said, his voice strained.

"She means it," said Medan grimly. "Erase all doubt from your mind, Your Majesty. Beryl has long been seeking an excuse to destroy Qualinesti. The rebel attacks grow bolder. She suspects the elves of keeping the Tower of Wayreth from her. The unfortunate fact that Palin Majere was discovered hiding in the house of the queen mother merely confirms the dragon's suspicions that the elves and the sorcerers are in collusion to rob her of her magic."

"We pay her tribute—" Gilthas began.

"Bah! What is money to her? She demands tribute only because it pleases her to think she is inflicting a hardship on you. Magic is what she lusts after, magic of the old world, magic of the gods. It is a pity this blasted device ever came into his land. A pity you sought to keep it from me, madam." The marshal's voice was stern. "Had you turned it over to me, this tragedy might have been averted."

Laurana sipped her wine, made no answer.

Medan shrugged. "But, you didn't. Spilled ale, as they said. Now you must fetch the device back. You must, madam," he reiterated. "I have done what I can to stall for time, but I have bought us only a few days. Send your griffon messenger to the Citadel. Instruct Palin Majere to turn over the device and the kender who bears it. I will take them to the dragon personally. I may be able to stave off this doom that hangs over us—"

"Us!" Gilthas cried in anger. "*You* hold the executioner's axe, Marshal! The axe hangs poised over our heads, not yours!"

"Forgive me, Your Majesty," Medan replied with a low bow. "I have lived in this land for so long that it has come to seem like my home."

"You are our conqueror," said Gilthas, speaking the words distinctly, separately them with bitter emphasis on each. "You are our master. You are our jailer. Qualinesti can never be your home, sir."

"I suppose not, Your Majesty," said Medan, after a moment's pause. "I should like you to consider, however, that I escorted your mother to the palace, when I might have escorted her to the block. I have come to warn you of the dragon's intent, when I might have been marching prisoners to the market place to serve as targets for my archers."

"What is all this generosity to cost us?" Gilthas demanded, his voice cold. "What is the price you set on our lives, Marshal Medan?"

Medan smiled slightly. "I should like to die in my garden, Your Majesty. Of old age, if that is possible." He poured himself another glass of wine.

"Do not trust him, Your Majesty," Planchet said softly, coming to pour wine for the king.

"Don't worry," said Gilthas, twisting the fragile stem of the glass in his fingers.

"And now, madam, we do not have much time," the

Marshal said. "Here is paper and ink. Compose your letter to Majere."

"No, Marshal," Laurana said firmly. "I have been giving this matter a great deal of thought. Beryl must never come into possession of this device. I would die a hundred deaths first."

"You would die a hundred deaths, madam," said Medan grimly, "but what about thousands of deaths? What about your people? Will you sacrifice them to save some sorcerer's toy?"

Laurana was pale, resolute. "It is not a toy, Marshal Medan. If Palin is right, it is one of the most powerful magical artifacts ever made. Qualinesti could be burned to the ground before I would turn over the artifact to Beryl."

"Tell me the nature of this artifact, then," Medan said.

"I cannot, Marshal," Laurana replied. "It is bad enough that Beryl knows the artifact exists. I will not provide her with any more information." Calmly, she lifted her blue eyes to meet his irate gaze. "You see, sir, I have reason to believe that I am being spied upon."

Medan's face flushed. He seemed about to say something, changed his mind and turned abruptly to speak to the king.

"Your Majesty. What have you to say?"

"I agree with my mother. She told me of this device, described its powers to me. I will not give the device to the dragon. "

"Do you realize what you are doing? You sentence your nation to death! No magical artifact is worth this," Medan protested angrily.

"This one is, Marshal," Laurana said. "You must trust me."

Medan regarded her intently.

She met his gaze, held it, did not blink or flinch away.

"Hush!" Planchet warned. "Someone's coming."

They could hear footfalls on the stairs, taking them two at a time.

"My aide," Medan replied.

"Can he be trusted?" Laurana asked.

Medan gave a wry smile. "Judge for yourself, Madam."

A Knight entered the room. His black armor was covered in blood and gray dust. He stood still for some moments, breathing heavily, his head bowed, as if climbing those stairs had drained every last ounce of his energy. At length, he raised his head, lifted his hand, held out a scroll to the marshal.

"I have it, sir. Groul is dead."

"Well done, Sir Gerard," said the Marshal, accepting the scroll. He looked at the Knight, at the blood on his armor. "Are you wounded?" he asked.

"To be honest, my lord, I can't tell," Gerard said with a grimace. "There isn't one single part of me that doesn't hurt. But if I am, it's not serious, or else I'd be lying out there dead in the street."

Laurana was staring, amazed.

"Queen Mother," Gerard said, bowing.

Laurana seemed about to speak, but, glancing at Medan, she caught herself.

"I do not believe that we have met, sir," she said coolly.

Gerard's blood-masked face relaxed into a faint smile. "Thank you, madam, for trying to protect me, but the marshal knows I am a Solamnic Knight. I am the marshal's prisoner, in fact."

"A Solamnic?" Gilthas was startled.

"The one I told you about," Laurana said. "The Knight who accompanied Palin and the kender."

"I see. And so you are the marshal's prisoner. Did he do this to you?" Gilthas demanded angrily.

"No, Your Majesty," said Gerard. "A draconian did this to me. Beryl's messenger. Or rather, Beryl's former messenger." He sank down in a chair, sighed, and closed his eyes.

"Some wine here," Medan ordered. "The dragon won't be

receiving any more information from Qualinesti," he added with satisfaction. "Beryl will wait at least a day to hear from me. When she does not, she will be forced to send another messenger. We have gained some time, at least."

He handed Gerard a glass of wine.

"No, my lord," said Gerard, accepting the wine, but not drinking it. "We haven't. The dragon deceived us. Beryl's forces are on the march. Groul figured that they might already be crossing the border. The largest army assembled since the Chaos War is marching on Qualinesti."

A silence as of death settled over the room. Each person listened unmoving, absorbing the news. No one's eyes sought another's. No one wanted to see the reflection of his own fear.

Marshal Medan smiled ruefully, shook his head.

"I am not to die of old age, after all, it seems," he said, and poured himself another glass of wine.

31

The Pale River of the Dead

hat night, Goldmoon left the hospital, ignoring the pleas of the Healers and Lady Camilla.

"I am well," Goldmoon said, fending off their attempts to keep her in bed. "I need rest, that is all, and I will not find rest here!"

Not with the dead.

She walked swiftly through the gardens and courtyards of the citadel complex, bright with lights. She looked neither to the left nor the right. She did not answer greetings. She kept her gaze fixed upon the path before her. If she looked anywhere else, she would see them. They were following her.

She heard their whispered beggings. She felt their touch, soft as milkweed, upon her hands, her face. They wrapped around her like silken scarves. She was afraid, if she looked at them, she would see Riverwind. Then she thought, perhaps this is why his spirit has not come to me. He is lost and foundering in this river, swept away. I will never find him.

Reaching the Grand Lyceum, she ran swiftly up the many stairs leading to her chambers. For the first time, she blessed this strange, young body, which was not only quick but was eager to meet the physical demands she now placed upon it. Brought to bay, Goldmoon turned to face them.

"Be gone. I have nothing for you."

The dead drew near, an old, old man, a thief, a warrior, a crippled child. Beggars all, their hands extended. Then, quite suddenly, they left—as if a voice had ordered them gone. But not her voice.

Goldmoon shut the door behind.

In her chamber, she was alone, truly alone. The dead were not here. Perhaps when she had refused to grant them what they sought, they had left her to seek other prey. She sank back against the door, overwhelmed by her vision. Standing in the darkness, she could see again, in her mind's eye, the dead draining the life-giving power from her followers. This was the reason healing was failing in the world. The dead were robbing the living. But why? What need had the dead for mystical power? What force constrained them? Where were they bound with such urgency?

"And why has it been given to me to see them?" Goldmoon murmured.

A knock sounded on her door. She ignored it and felt to make certain the door was locked. The knock was repeated several times. Voices—living voices—called to her. When she did not answer, they were perplexed. She could hear them wondering aloud what to do.

"Go away!" she ordered finally, wearily. "Go away, and leave me in peace."

And eventually, like the dead, the living also departed and left her alone.

Crossing her chambers, Goldmoon stood before the large windows that overlooked the sea and flung open the casement.

The waning moon cast a pallid light upon the ocean. The sea had a strange look to it. An oily film covered the water, and beneath this film, the water was smooth, still. No breeze stirred, not a breath. The air had a foul smell to it, tainted by the oil upon the water, perhaps. The night was clear. The stars bright. The sky empty.

Ships were putting out to sea, black against the moonlight waters. There was a smell of thunder in the air. Seasoned mariners were reading the signs and heading for the open waters, far safer for them than lying close to shore, where crashing waves could send them smashing up against the docks or the rocks of the island's coast. Goldmoon watched them from her window, looking like toy boats gliding across a dark mirror.

There, moving over the ocean, were the dead.

Goldmoon sank to her knees at the window. She placed her hands upon the window frame, rested her chin upon her hands, and watched the dead cross the sea. The moon sank beneath the horizon, drowned in dark water. The stars shone cold and bleak in the sky, and they also shone in the water, which was so still that Goldmoon could not perceive where the sky ended and the sea began. Small waves lapped gently upon the shore with a forlorn urgency, like a sick and fretful child trying to capture someone's attention. The dead were traveling north, a pallid stream, paying no attention to anything except to that call they alone could hear.

Yet not quite alone.

Goldmoon heard the song. The voice that sang the song was compelling, stirred Goldmoon to the depths of her soul.

"You will find him," said the voice. "He serves me. You will be together."

Goldmoon crouched at the window, head bowed, and shivered in awe and fear and an exaltation that made her cry out in longing, reach her hands out in longing for the singer of that song as the dead had reached out their hands to her in longing. She spent the night on her knees, her soul listening to the song with a thrill that was both pain and pleasure, watching the dead travel north, heeding the call, while the wavelets of the still sea clung as long as they could to the shore, then receded, leaving the sand smooth and empty in their going.

Day dawned. The sun slid out of the oily water. Its light seemed covered with the same film of oil, for it had a greenish sheen smeared across the yellow. The air was tainted, hot, and unsatisfying to breathe. Not a cloud marred the sky.

Goldmoon rose from kneeling. Her muscles were stiff and sore from the uncomfortable position, but usage warmed and limbered them. She picked up a cloak, thick and heavy, and wrapped it around her, though the early morning was already hot.

Opening her door, she found Palin standing outside, his hand raised to knock.

"First Master," he said. "We have all been worried . . ."

The dead were all around him. They plucked at the sleeves of his robes. Their lips pressed against his broken fingers, their ragged hands clutched at the magical ring he wore, trying to pull it loose, but not succeeding, to judge by their wails of frustration.

"What?" Palin halted in the middle of his speech of concern, alarmed by the expression on her face. "What is it, First Master? Why do you stare at me like that?"

She pushed past him, shoving him out of her way with such force that he staggered backward. Goldmoon caught up the skirts of her white robes and ran down the stairs, her cloak billowing behind her. She arrived in the hall, startling masters and students. They called after her, some ran after her. The guards stood staring and helpless. Goldmoon ignored them all and kept running.

Past the crystal domes, past the gardens and the fountains, past the hedge maze and the silver stair, past Knights and guards, visitors and pupils, past the dead. She ran down to the harbor. She ran down to the still, smooth sea.

Tas and the gnome were mapping the hedge maze—successfully mapping the hedge maze, which must be considered a first in the long and inglorious history of gnomish science.

"Are we getting close, do you think?" Tasslehoff asked the gnome. "Because I think I'm losing all the feeling in my left foot."

"Hold still!" Conundrum ordered. "Don't move. I've almost got it. Drat this wind," he added irritably. "I wish it would stop. It keeps blowing away my map."

Tasslehoff endeavored to do as he was ordered, although not moving was extremely difficult. He stood on the path in the middle of the hedge maze, balanced precariously on his left foot. He held his right leg hoisted in a most uncomfortable position in the air, his foot attached to a branch of the hedge maze by the end of the thread of the unraveled right stocking. The stocking was considerably reduced in size, its cream-colored thread trailing along the path through the hedge maze.

The gnome's plan to use the socks had proved a brilliant success, though Conundrum sighed inwardly over the fact that the means by which he was going to finally succeed in mapping the hedge maze lacked the buttons, the gears, the pulleys, the spindles and the wheels, which are such a comfort to the scientific mind.

To have to describe the wondrous mechanism by which he had achieved his Life Quest as "two socks, wool" was a terrible blow. He had spent the night trying to think of some way to add steam power, with the result that he developed plans for snowshoes that not only went extremely fast but kept the feet warm as well. But that did nothing to advance his Life Quest.

At length Conundrum was forced to proceed with the simple plan he'd originally developed. He could always, he reflected, embellish the proceedings during the final report.

They began early in the morning, up before the dawn. Conundrum posted Tasslehoff at the entry of the hedge maze, tied one end of the kender's sock to a branch, and marched Tasslehoff forward. The sock unraveled nicely, leaving a cream-colored track behind. Whenever Tasslehoff took a wrong turn and came to a dead end, he reversed direction, rolling up the thread, and proceeded down the path until he came to the right turn in the path, which was leading them deeper into the middle of the hedge maze.

Whenever they struck a correct turning, Conundrum would fall flat on his belly and mark the route on his map. By this means, he advanced farther than he'd ever been able to go. So long as Tasslehoff's supply of hosiery held out, the gnome felt certain that he would have the entire hedge maze well and truly mapped by day's end.

As for Tasslehoff, he was not feeling quite as cheery and pleased as one might expect for someone who was on the verge of wondrous scientific breakthrough. Every time he put his hand in a pocket he felt the prickly jewels and the cold, hard surface of the Device of Time Journeying. He more than half suspected the device of deliberately making a nuisance of itself by turning up in places and pockets where he knew for a fact it had not been ten minutes earlier. No matter where he put his hands, the Device was jabbing him or poking him.

Every time the device jabbed him or poked him, it was like Fizban's bony finger jabbing him or poking him, reminding him of his promise to come right back.

Of course, kender have traditionally considered promises to be about as binding as a silken strand of gossamer—good for holding butterflies, but not much more. Normally anyone relying on a kender's promise would be considered loony, unstable, incompetent and just plain daft, all of which descriptions fit Fizban to a tee. Tasslehoff would not have worried at all about breaking a promise he had really never intended to keep in the first place and that he had assumed

Fizban knew he never meant to keep, but for what Palin had said about his—Tasslehoff's—funeral.

That funeral speech seemed to indicate that Fizban expected Tasslehoff to keep his promise. Fizban expected it because Tas was not an ordinary kender. He was a brave kender, a courageous kender, and—that dreadful word—an *honorable* kender.

Tasslehoff looked honor up and he looked it down. He looked it inside out and sideways, and there were just no two ways about it. Honorable people kept promises. Even promises that were terrible promises, promises that meant one had to go back in time to be stepped on by a giant and squashed flat and killed dead.

"Right! That's got it!" said the gnome briskly. "You can put your foot down. Now, just hop along around that corner. To your right. No, left. No, right . . ."

Tasslehoff hopped, feeling the sock unravel from around his leg. Rounding the corner, he came upon a staircase. A spiral staircase. A spiral staircase made all of silver. A silver spiral staircase in the middle of the hedge maze.

"We've done it!" The gnome shouted ecstatically.

"We have?" asked Tasslehoff, staring at the stair. "What have we done?"

"We've reached the very center of the hedge maze!" The gnome was capering about, flinging ink to the four winds.

"How beautiful!" said Tasslehoff and walked toward the silver stair.

"Stop! You're unraveling too fast!" the gnome cried. "We still have to map the exit."

At that moment, Tasslehoff's sock gave out. He barely noticed, he was so interested in the staircase. The stair seemed to rise up out of nothing. The stair had no supports, but hung suspended in the air, shining and fluid as quicksilver. The stair turned round and round upon itself, leading ever upward. Arriving at the bottom, he looked up to see the top.

He looked up and up and all he saw was sky, blue sky that seemed to go on and on like a bright and lovely summer's day, which is so bright and so lovely that you never want the day to end. You want it to go on and on forever. Yet you know, the sky seemed to say, that night must come, or else there will be no day tomorrow. And the night has its own blessing, its own beauty.

Tasslehoff began to climb the silver stair.

A few steps below, Conundrum was also starting to climb. "Strange construction," he remarked. "No pylons, no struts, no rivets, no balusters, no hand railings—safety hazard. Someone should be reported." The gnome paused about twenty steps up to look around. "My what a view. I can see the harbor—"

The gnome let out a shriek that might have been mistaken for the Mt. Nevermind noon whistle, which generally goes off at about three in the morning.

"My ship!"

Conundrum dropped his maps, he spilled his ink. He dashed down the stair, his wispy hair flying in the wind, tripped over Tasslehoff's stocking, which was tied to the end of the hedge, picked himself up and ran toward the harbor with a speed that the makers of the steam-powered, piston-driven snowshoes might have tried hard to emulate.

"Stop thief!" the gnome bellowed. "That's my ship!"

Tasslehoff glanced down to see what all the excitement was about, saw it was the gnome, and thought nothing more about it. Gnomes were always excitable.

Tasslehoff sat down on the stairs, put his small pointed chin in his hand and thought about promises.

Palin tried to catch up with Goldmoon, but a cramp in his leg had brought him up, gasping in pain. He massaged the leg and then, when he could walk, he limped down the stairs to find the hall in an uproar. Goldmoon had come running through like a madwoman. She had run out before any could stop her. The masters and healers had been taken by such surprise that only belatedly had some thought to chase after her. By that time, she had vanished. The entire Citadel was being turned upside down, searching for her.

Palin kept to himself what Goldmoon had said to him. The others were already speaking of her in tense whispers. Her wild talk about the dead feeding off him would only convince them—as it had convinced him—that the poor woman had been driven insane by her amazing transformation. He could still see her look of horror, still feel the powerful blow that had sent him falling back against the wall. He offered to search for her, but Lady Camilla told him curtly that both her Knights and the citadel guards had been sent to locate the First Master and that they were quite capable of handling the situation.

Not knowing what else to do, he returned to his rooms, telling Lady Camilla to be certain to notify him upon the First Master's return.

"In the meantime," he said to himself, sighing, "the best I can do is to leave Schallsea. I've made a mess of things. Tas won't come near me, and I can't blame him. I am only adding to Goldmoon's burdens. Perhaps I am the one responsible for her madness!"

His guest room in the Citadel was a spacious one, located on the second floor. He had a small bedroom, a study, and a parlor. One wall of the parlor was crystal, facing west, providing a magnificent view of sea and sky. Restless, exhausted, but too tense to sleep, he wandered into the parlor and stood gazing out across the sea. The water was like green glass, mirroring the sky. Except for a gray-green line on the horizon, he could not tell where one left off and the other began. The sight was strangely disquieting.

Leaving the parlor, Palin entered his study and sat down at his desk, thinking he would write a letter to Jenna. He picked up the pen, but the words scrambled in his head, made no sense. He rubbed his burning eyes. He had not been able to sleep all night. Every time he drifted off, he thought he heard a voice calling to him and he woke with a start to find that no one was there.

His head sank down, pillowed on his arms. He closed his eyes. The smooth crystal sea stole over him, the water warm and dark.

"Palin!" a voice cried, a hollow, whispering voice. "Palin! Wake up!"

"Just a moment more, father," Palin said, lost in a dream that he was a child again. "I'll be down—"

Caramon stood over him. Big of body, big of heart as when Palin had last seen him, except that he was wavering and insubstantial as the smoke from dying embers. His father was not alone. He was surrounded by ghosts, who reached out grasping hands to Palin.

"Father!" Palin cried. His head jerked up. He stared in amazement. He could say nothing more, only stare, gaping, at the phantasmic shapes that had gathered around him and seemed to be trying to seize hold of him.

"Get back!" Caramon shouted in that dreadful whisper. He glared around, and the ghosts shrank back, but they did not go far. They stared at Palin with hungry eyes.

"Father," Palin said—or tried to say. His throat was so dry that the words seemed to shred his flesh. "Father, what—"

"I've been searching for you!" Caramon said desperately. "Listen to me! Raistlin's not here! I can't find him! Something's wrong. . . ."

More ghosts appeared in the study. The ghosts surged past Caramon, over him and around him. They could not rest, could not remain long in one place. They seized Caramon and tried to carry him away, like a panicked mob that bears its members to destruction.

Exerting all his effort, Caramon broke free of the raging current and flung himself at Palin.

"Palin!" he shouted, a shout that made no sound. "Don't kill Tas! He's the—"

Caramon vanished suddenly. The ephemeral forms swirled a moment and then separated into ragged wisps, as if a hand had brushed through smoke. The wisps were wafted away on a soul-chilling wind.

"Father? I don't understand! Father!"

The sound of his own voice woke Palin. He sat upright with a start, gasping, as if he'd been splashed with cold water. He stared about wildly. "Father!"

The room was empty. Sunlight streamed in through the open window. The air was hot and fetid.

"A dream," Palin said, dazedly.

But a very real dream. Remembering the dead clustering around him, Palin felt horror thrilling through him, raising the hair on his arms and his neck. He still seemed to feel the clutching hands of the dead, plucking at his clothes, whispering and pleading. He brushed at his face, as if he'd run into a spider's web in the dark.

Just as Goldmoon had said. . . .

"Nonsense," he said to himself out loud, needing to hear a living voice after those terrible whispers. "She put the thought into my mind, that is all. No wonder I'm having nightmares. Tonight, I will take a sleeping potion."

Someone rattled the doorknob, trying to open the door, only to find that it was locked. Palin's heart was in his throat.

Then came the sound of metal—a lockpick—clicking and snicking in the door lock.

Not ghosts. Just a kender.

Palin, sighing, stood up and walked to the door, opened it.

"Good morning, Tas," said Palin.

"Oh, hullo," said Tasslehoff. The kender was bent double, a lockpick in his hand, peering intently at the place where the lock had been before the door swung open. Tas straightened, tucked the lockpick back in a front pocket.

"I thought you might be asleep. I didn't want to bother you. Do you have anything to eat?" The kender entered the room, making himself at home.

"Look, Tas," Palin said, trying hard to be patient, "this isn't a good time. I am very tired. I didn't sleep well—"

"Me neither," said Tas, marching into the parlor and plunking himself down on a chair. "I guess you don't have anything to eat. That's all right. I'm not really hungry."

He sat in silence, swinging his feet back and forth, looking out at the sky and the sea. The kender was silent for several whole minutes put together.

Palin, recognizing this as an extraordinarily unusual phenomenon, drew up another chair and sat down beside him.

"What is it, Tas?" he asked gently.

"I've decided to go back," Tas said, not looking at Palin, but still looking out at the empty sky. "I made a promise. I never thought about it before, but a promise isn't something you make with your mouth. You make a promise with your heart. Every time you break a promise, your heart breaks a little until pretty soon you have cracks running all through it. I think, all in all, it's better to be squished by a giant."

"You are very wise, Tas," said Palin, feeling ashamed of himself. "You are far wiser than I am."

He paused a moment. He could hear again his father's voice. *Don't kill Tas!* The vision was real, much more real than any dream. A mage learns to trust his instincts, to listen to the inner voices of heart and soul, for those are the voices that speak the language of magic. He wondered if, perhaps, this dream wasn't that inner voice cautioning him to slow down, take no drastic actions, do further study.

"Tas," said Palin slowly. "I've changed my mind. I don't want you to go back. At least not yet."

Tas leaped to his feet. "What? I don't have to die? Is that true? Do you mean it?"

"I said only that you didn't have to go back yet," Palin admonished. "Of course, you have to go back sometime."

His words were lost on the excited kender. Tas was skipping around the room, scattering the contents of his pouches every which way. "This is wonderful! Can we go sailing off in a boat like Goldmoon?"

"Goldmoon went off in a boat?" Palin repeated, amazed.

"Yes," said Tas cheerfully. "With the gnome. At least I guess Conundrum caught up with her. He was swimming awfully fast. I didn't know gnomes could swim so well."

"She has gone mad," Palin said to himself. He headed for the door. "We must alert the guards. Someone will have to go rescue her."

"Oh, they've gone after them," Tas said casually, "but I don't think they'll find them. You see, Conundrum told me that the *Destructible* can dive down under the water just like a dolphin. It's a sub—sup—soop—whatchamacallit. A boat that travels under water. Conundrum showed it to me last night. It looks exactly like a gigantic steel fish. Say, I wonder if we could see them from here?"

Tasslehoff ran to the window. Pressing his nose against the crystal, he peered out, searching for some sight of the boat. Palin forgot the strange vision in his amazement and consternation. He hoped very much that this was just another of Tasslehoff's tales and that Goldmoon had not sailed away in a gnomish contraption.

He was about to go downstairs, to find out the truth of the matter, and was heading for the door when the morning stillness was split by a trumpet blast. Bells rang out, loudly, insistently. In the hallway voices could be heard demanding to know what was going on. Other voices answered, sounding panicked.

"What's that?" Tas asked, still peering out the window.

"They're sounding the call to arms," Palin said. "I wonder why—"

"Maybe it has something to do with those dragons," Tasslehoff said, pointing.

Winged shapes, black against the morning sky, flew toward the citadel. One shape, flying in the center, was larger than the rest, so large that it seemed the green tinge in the sky was a reflection of the sunlight on the dragon's scales. Palin took one good look. Appalled, he drew back into the center of the room, into the shadows, as if, even at that distance, the dragon's red eyes might find him.

"That is Beryl!" he said, his throat constricting. "Beryl and her minions!"

Tas's eyes were round. "I thought it was finding out that I didn't have to go back to die that was making me feel all squirmy inside. It's the curse, isn't it?" He gazed at Palin. "Why is she coming here?"

A good question. Of course, Beryl might have decided to attack the citadel on a whim, but Palin doubted it. The Citadel of Light was in the territory of Khellendros, the blue dragon who ruled this part of the world. Beryl would not encroach on the Blue's territory unless she had desperate need. And he guessed what that need was.

"She wants the device," Palin said.

"The magical device?" Tasslehoff reached into a pocket and drew forth the magical artifact.

"Ugh!" He brushed his hand over his face. "You must have spiders in here. I feel all cobwebby." He clutched the device protectively. "Can the dragon sniff it out, Palin? How does she know we're here?"

"I don't know," Palin said grimly. He could see it all quite clearly. "It doesn't matter." He held out his hand. "Give me the device."

"What are we going to do?" Tas asked, hesitating. He was still a bit mistrustful.

"We're going to get out of here," Palin said. "The magical device must not come into her possession."

Palin could only imagine what the dragon might do with it. The magic of the device would make the dragon the undisputed ruler of Ansalon. Even if there was no longer past, she could go back to the point after the Chaos War when the great dragons had first come to Ansalon. She could go back to any point in time and change events so that she emerged victorious from any battle. At the very least, she could use the device to transport her great bloated body to circumnavigate the world. No place would be safe from her ravages.

"Give me the device," Palin repeated urgently, reaching for it. "We have to leave. Hurry, Tas!"

"Am I coming with you?" Tas asked, still hanging onto the device.

"Yes!" Palin almost shouted. He started to add that they didn't have much time—but time was the one thing they did have. "Just . . . give me the device."

Tas handed it over. "Where are we going?" he asked eagerly.

A good question. In all the turmoil, Palin had not given that important matter any thought.

"Solace," he said. "We will go back to Solace. We'll alert the Knights. The Solamnic Knights in the garrison ride silver dragons. They can come to the aid of the people here."

The dragons were closer now, much closer. The sun shone on green scales and red. Their broad wings cast shadows that glided over the oily water. Outside the door the bells clamored, urging people to seek shelter, to flee to the hills and forests. Trumpets sounded, blaring the call to arms. Feet pounded, steel clashed, voices shouted terse orders and commands.

He held the device in his hands. The magic warmed him, calmed him like a draught of fine brandy. He closed his eyes, called to mind the words of the spell, the manipulation of the device.

"Keep close to me!" he ordered Tas.

The kender obediently clamped his hand firmly onto the sleeve of Palin's robes.

Palin began to recite the spell.

" 'Thy time is thy own . . .' "

He tried to turn the jeweled face of the pendant upward. Something was not quite right. There was a catch in the mechanism. Palin applied a bit more force, and the face plate shifted.

" 'Though across it you travel . . .' "

Palin adjusted the face plate right to left. He felt something scrape, but the face plate moved.

" 'Its expanses you see . . .' "

Now the back plate was supposed to drop to form two spheres connected by rods. But quite astonishingly, the back plate dropped completely off. It fell to the floor with a clatter.

"Oops," said Tas, looking down at the spherical plate that lay rolling like a crazed top on the floor. "Did you mean for that to happen?"

"No!" Palin gasped. He stood holding in his hands a single sphere with a rod protruding from one end, staring down at the plate in horror.

"Here, I'll fix it!" Tas helpfully picked up the broken piece.

"Give it to me!" Palin snatched the plate. He stared helplessly at the plate, tried to fit the rod into it, but there was no place for the rod to go. A misty film of fear and frustration swam before his eyes, blinding him.

He spoke the verse again, terse, panicked. " 'Its expanses you see!' " He shook the sphere and the rod, shook the plate. "Work!" he commanded in anger and desperation. "Work, damn you!"

The chain dropped down, slithered out of Palin's grasping fingers to lie like a glittering silver snake on the floor. The rod separated from the sphere. Jewels winked and sparkled in the sunlight. And then the room went dark, the light of the jewels vanished. The dragons' wings blotted out the sun.

Palin Majere stood in the Citadel of Light holding the shattered remnants of the Device of Time Journeying in his crippled hands.

The dead! Goldmoon had told him. They are feeding off you!

He saw his father, saw the river of dead pouring around him. A dream. No, not a dream. Reality was the dream. Goldmoon had tried to tell him.

"This is what is wrong with the magic! This is why my spells go awry. The dead are leeching the magical power from me. They are all around me. Touching me with their hands, their lips. . . ."

He could feel them. Their touch was like cobwebs brushing across his skin. Or insect wings, such as he had felt at Laurana's home. So much was made clear now. The loss of the magic. It wasn't that he had lost his power. It was that the dead had sucked it from him.

"Well," said Tas, "at least the dragon won't have the artifact."

"No," said Palin quietly, "she'll have us."

Though he could not see them, he could feel the dead all around him, feeding.

32

The Execution

he candle that kept count of the hours stood beside Silvan's bed. He lay on his belly, watching the hours melt with the wax. One by one, the lines that marked the hours vanished until only a single line was left. The candle had been crafted to burn for twelve hours. Silvan had lit it at midnight. Eleven hours had been devoured by the flame. The time was nearly noon, the time set for Mina's execution.

Silvan extinguished the candle with a breath. He rose and dressed himself in his finest clothes, clothes he had brought to wear on the return march—the victory march—into Silvanost. Fashioned of soft pearl gray, the doublet was stitched with silver that had been twisted and spun into thread. His hose were gray, his boots gray. Touches of white lace were at his wrist and neck.

"Your Majesty?" a voice called from outside his tent, "it is Kiryn. May I come in?"

"If you want," said Silvan shortly, "but no one else."

"I was here earlier," Kiryn said, upon entering. "You didn't answer. You must have been asleep."

"I have not closed my eyes," Silvan said coldly, adjusting his collar.

Kiryn was silent a moment, an uncomfortable silence. "Have you had breakfast?" he asked.

Silvan cast a him a look that would have been a blow to anyone else. He did not even bother to respond.

"Cousin, I know how you feel," Kiryn said. "This act they contemplate is monstrous. Truly monstrous. I have argued with my uncle and the others until my throat is raw from talking, and nothing I say makes any difference. Glaucous feeds their fear. They are all gorging themselves on terror."

"Aren't you dining with them?" Silvan asked, half-turning.

"No, Cousin! Of course not!" Kiryn was astonished. "Could you imagine that I would? This is murder. Plain and simple. They may call it an 'execution' and try to dress it up so that it looks respectable, but they cannot hide the ugly truth. I do not care if this human is the worst, most reprehensible, most dangerous human who ever lived. Her blood will forever stain the ground upon which it falls, a stain that will spread like a blight among us."

Kiryn's voice dropped. He cast an apprehensive glance out the tent. "Already, Cousin, Glaucous speaks of traitors among our people, of meting out the same punishment to elves. My uncle and the Heads of House were all horrified and utterly opposed to the idea, but I fear that they will cease to feed on fear and start to feed on each other."

"Glaucous," Silvan repeated softly. He might have said more, but he remembered his promise to Mina. "Fetch my breastplate, will you, Cousin? And my sword. Help me on with them, will you?"

"I can call your attendants," Kiryn offered.

"No, I want no one." Silvan clenched his fist. "If one of my servants said something insulting about her I might . . . I might do something I would regret."

Kiryn helped with the leather buckles.

"I have heard that she is quite lovely. For a human," he remarked.

Silvan cast his cousin a sharp, suspicious glance.

Kiryn did not look up from his work. Muttering under his breath, he pretended to be preoccupied with a recalcitrant strap.

Reassured, Silvan relaxed. "She is the most beautiful woman I ever saw, Kiryn! So fragile and delicate. And her eyes! I have never seen such eyes!"

"And yet, Cousin," Kiryn rebuked gently, "she is a Knight of Neraka. One of those who have pledged our destruction."

"A mistake!" Silvan cried, going from ice to fire in a flash. "I am certain of it! She has been bewitched by the Knights or . . . or they hold her family hostage . . . or any number of reasons! In truth, she came here to save us."

"Bringing with her a troop of armed soldiers," Kiryn said dryly.

"You will see, Cousin," Silvan predicted. "You will see that I am right. I'll prove it to you." He rounded on Kiryn. "Do you know what I did? I went last night to set her free. I did! I cut a hole in her tent. I was going to unlock her chains. She refused to leave."

"You did what?" Kiryn gasped, appalled. "Cousin—"

"Never mind," said Silvan, turning away, the flame flaring out, the ice reforming. "I don't want to discuss it. I shouldn't have told you. You're as bad as the rest. Get out! Leave me alone."

Kiryn thought it best to obey. He put his hand on the tent flap and was halfway out when Silvan caught hold of him by the shoulder, gripped him hard.

"Are you going to run to tell Konnal what I told you? Because if you are—"

"I am not, Cousin," Kiryn said quietly. "I will keep what you have said in confidence. You need not threaten me."

Silvan appeared ashamed. Mumbling something, he let loose of Kiryn's sleeve, turned his back on him.

Grieved, worried, afraid, both for his people and for his cousin, Kiryn stood outside the king's tent and tried to think what to do. He did not trust the human girl. He did not know much about the Knights of Neraka, but he had to believe that they would not promote someone who served them reluctantly or unwillingly to the rank of commander. And though no elf could ever speak well of a human, the elven soldiers had talked grudgingly of the enemy's tenacity in battle, their discipline. Even General Konnal, who detested all humans, had admitted that these soldiers had fought well, and though they had retreated, they had done so in good order. They had followed the girl through the shield and into a well-defended realm, where surely they must have known they would march to their deaths. No, these men did not serve an unwilling, treacherous commander.

It was not the girl who was bewitched. It was the girl who had done the bewitching. Silvan was clearly enamored of her. He was of an age when elven men first begin to feel the stirrings of passion, the age when a man falls in love with love itself. An age when he may become drunk with adoration. "I love to love my love," was the first line of a chorus of a popular elven song. A pity that fortune had thrown the two of them together, had literally tossed the exotic and beautiful human girl into the young king's arms.

Silvan was plotting something. Kiryn could not imagine what, but he was sick at heart. Kiryn liked his cousin. He considered that Silvanoshei had the makings of a good king. This folly could ruin him. The fact that he had tried to free this girl, their mortal enemy, was enough to brand him a traitor if anyone came to know of it. The Heads of House would never forgive Silvan. They would declare him a "dark elf" and would exile him as they had exiled his mother and his father. General Konnal only wanted an excuse.

Kiryn did not for a moment consider breaking his vow to the king. He would not tell anyone what Silvan had told him.

He wished very much that Silvan had never spoken of it. Kiryn wondered unhappily what his cousin planned, wondered what he could do to prevent Silvan from acting in some foolish, hotheaded, impulsive manner that would end in his ruin. The best, the only thing he could do would be to keep close to his cousin and be ready to try to stop him.

The sun hung directly overhead, its single eye glaring down through the gauzy curtain of the shield as if frustrated that it could not gain a clearer view. The watery eye shown upon the bloody field being readied for yet another wetting. The sun gazed unwinking upon the sowers of death, who were planting bodies in the ground, not seeds. The Thon-Thalas had run red with blood yesterday. None could drink of it.

The elves had searched the woodlands to find a fallen tree that would be suitable for use as a stake. The Woodshapers crafted it so that it was smooth and sturdy and straight. They thrust the stake deep into the ground, hammered it into the soil, drove it deeply so that it was stable and would not fall.

General Konnal, accompanied by Glaucous, took the field. He wore his armor, carried his sword. The general's face was stern and set. Glaucous was pleased, triumphant. Officers formed the elven army into ranks in the field, brought them to attention. Elf soldiers surrounded the field, forming a protective barrier, keeping a lookout for the humans, who might take it into their heads to try to rescue their leader. The Heads of House assembled. The wounded who could drag themselves from their beds lined up to watch.

Kiryn took his place beside his uncle. The young man looked so unwell that Konnal advised him in a low voice to return to his tent. Kiryn shook his head and remained where he was.

Seven archers had been chosen to make up the death squad. They formed a single line about twenty paces from the stake. They nocked their arrows, held their bows ready.

A trumpet sounded announcing the arrival of His Majesty the Speaker of the Stars. Silvanoshei walked alone, without escort, onto the field. He was extremely pale, so pale that the whispered rumor ran among the Heads of House that his majesty had suffered a wound in the battle, a wound that had drained his heart's blood.

Silvan halted at the edge of the field. He looked around at the disposition of the troops, looked at the stake, looked at the Heads of House, looked at Konnal and at Glaucous. A chair had been placed for the king on one side of the field, at a safe distance from where the prisoner must make her final walk. Silvan glanced at the chair, strode past it. He took up his place beside General Konnal, standing between Konnal and Glaucous.

Konnal was not pleased. "We have a chair for Your Majesty. In a place of safety."

"I stand at your side, General," Silvan said, turning his gaze full upon Konnal. "I can think of nowhere I would be safer. Can you?"

The general flushed, flustered. He cast a sidelong glance at Glaucous, who shrugged as much as to say, "Don't waste time arguing. What does it matter?"

"Let the prisoner be brought forth!" Konnal ordered.

Silvan held himself rigid, his hand on his sword hilt. His expression was fixed, set, gave away nothing of his inner thoughts or feelings.

Six elven guards with swords drawn, their blades flashing white in the sunlight, marched the prisoner onto the field. The guards were tall and accoutered in plate mail. The girl wore a white shift, a plain gown, unadorned, like a child's nightclothes. Her hands and feet were manacled. She looked small and frail, fragile and delicate, a waif surrounded by adults. Cruel adults.

A murmur swept among some of the Heads of House, a murmur of pity and dismay, a murmur of doubt. This was the dread commander! This girl! This child! The murmur was answered with an angry growl from the soldiers. She is human. She is our enemy.

Konnal turned his head, silenced the dismay and the anger with a single baleful glance.

"Bring the prisoner to me," Konnal called, "so that she may know the charges for which her life is forfeit."

The guards escorted the prisoner, who walked slowly, due to the manacles on her ankles, but who walked with regal bearing—straight back and lifted head and a strange, calm smile upon her lips. Her guards, by contrast, looked exceedingly uncomfortable. She stepped lightly over the ground, seemed to barely touch it. The guards slogged across the churned-up dirt as if it were rough going. They were winded and exhausted by the time they escorted their charge to stand before the general. The guards cast watchful, nervous glances at their prisoner, who never once looked at them.

Mina did not look at Silvanoshei, who was looking at her with all his heart and all his soul, willing her to give him the sign, ready to battle the entire elven army if she but said the word. Mina's amber-eyed gaze took in General Konnal, and though he appeared to struggle against it for a moment, he could not help himself. He joined the other insects, trapped inside the golden resin.

Konnal launched into a speech, explaining why it was necessary to go against elven custom and belief and rob this person of her most precious gift—her life. He was an effective speaker and produced many salient points. The speech would have gone over well if he had given it earlier, before the people were allowed to see the prisoner. As it was, he had now the look of a brutal father inflicting abusive punishment on a helpless child. He understood that he was losing his audience; many in the crowd were growing restless and uneasy, reconsidering their verdict. Konnal brought his speech to a swift, if somewhat abrupt, end.

"Prisoner, what is your name?" he barked, speaking Common. His voice, unnaturally loud, bounded back at him from the mountains.

"Mina," she replied, her voice cool as the blood-tinged Thon-Thalas and with the same hint of iron.

"Surname?" he asked. "For the record."

"Mina is the only name I bear," she said.

"Prisoner Mina," said General Konnal sternly, "you led an armed force into our lands without cause, for we are a peace-loving people. Because there exists no formal declaration of war between our peoples, we consider you to be nothing but a brigand, an outlaw, a murderer. You are therefore sentenced to death. Do you have aught to say in answer to these charges?"

"I do," Mina replied, serious and earnest. "I did not come here to make war upon the Qualinesti people. I came to save them."

Konnal gave a bitter, angry laugh. "We know full well that to the Knights of Neraka 'salvation' is another word for conquering and enslavement."

"I came to save your people," said Mina quietly, gently, "and I will do so."

"She makes a mockery of you, General," Glaucous whispered urgently into Konnal's left ear. "Get this over with!"

Konnal paid no attention to his adviser, except to shrug him off and move a step away from him.

"I have one more question, Prisoner," the General continued in portentous tones. "Your answer will not save you from death, but the arrows might fly a little straighter and hit their target a little quicker if you cooperate. How did you manage to enter the shield?"

"I will tell you and gladly," Mina said at once. "The hand of the God I follow, the Hand of the One True God of the world and all peoples in the world reached down from the heavens and raised the shield so that I and those who accompany me could enter."

A whisper like an icy wind blowing unexpectedly on a summer's day passed from elf to elf, repeating her words, though that was not necessary. All had heard her clearly.

"You speak falsely, Prisoner!" said Konnal in a hollow, furious voice. "The gods are gone and will not return."

"I warned you," Glaucous said, sighing. He eyed Mina uneasily. "Put her to death! Now!"

"I am not the one who speaks falsely," Mina said. "I am not the one who will die this day. I am not the one whose life is forfeit. Hear the words of the One True God."

She turned and looked directly at Glaucous. "Greedy, ambitious, you colluded with my enemies to rob me of what is rightfully mine. The penalty for faithlessness is death."

Mina raised her hands to the heavens. No cloud marred the sky, but the manacles that bound her wrists split apart as if struck by lightning and fell, ringing, to the ground. The chains that bound her melted, dissolved. Freed of her restraints, she pointed at Glaucous, pointed at his breast.

"Your spell is broken! The illusion ended! You can no longer hide your body on the plane of enchantment while your soul walks about in another form. Let them see you, Cyan Bloodbane. Let the elves see their 'savior.'"

A flash of light flared from the breast of the elf known as Glaucous. He cried out in pain, grappled for the magical amulet, but the silver rope that held it around his neck was broken, and with it broke the spell the amulet had cast.

The elves beheld an astonishing sight. The form of Glaucous grew and expanded so that for the span of a heartbeat his elven body was immense, hideous, contorted. The elf sprouted green wings. Green scales slid over the mouth that was twisted in hatred. Green scales rippled across the rapidly elongating nose. Fangs thrust up from the lengthening jaws, impeding the flow of vile curses that were spewing from his mouth, transforming the words into poisonous fumes. His arms became legs that ended in jabbing claws. His legs were now hind legs, strong and muscular. His great tail coiled, prepared to lash out with the deadly power of a whip or a striking snake.

"Cyan!" the elves cried in terror. "Cyan! Cyan!"

No one moved. No one could move. The dragonfear paralyzed their limbs, froze hands and hearts, seized them and shook them like a wolf shakes a rabbit to break its spine.

Yet Cyan Bloodbane was not yet truly among them. His soul and body were still joining, still coming together. He was in mid-transformation, vulnerable, and he knew it. He required seconds only to become one, but he had to have those few precious seconds.

He used the dragonfear to buy himself the time he needed, rendering the elves helpless, sending some of them wild with fear and despair. General Konnal, dazed by the overwhelming horror of the destruction he had brought down upon his own people, was like a man struck by a thunderbolt. He made a feeble attempt to draw his sword, but his right hand refused to obey his command.

Cyan ignored the general. He would deal with that wretch later. The dragon concentrated his fury and his ire upon the one, true danger—the creature who had unmasked him. The creature who had somehow managed to break the powerful spell of the amulet, an amulet that permitted body and soul to live apart, an amulet given to the dragon as a gift from his former master, the infamous wizard Raistlin Majere.

Mina shivered with the dragonfear. Not even her faith could guard her against it. She was unarmed, helpless. Cyan breathed his poisonous fumes, fumes that were weak, just as his crushing jaws were still weak. The lethal gas would immobilize this puny mortal, and then his jaws would be strong enough to tear the human's heart from her breast and rip her head from her body.

Silvan was also consumed with dragonfear—fear and astonishment, horror and a terrifying realization: Cyan

Bloodbane, the dragon who had been the curse of the grandfather, was now the curse of the grandson. Silvan shuddered to think what he might have done at Glaucous's bidding if Mina had not opened his eyes to the truth.

Mina! He turned to find her, saw her stagger, clasp her throat, and fall backward to lie senseless on the ground in front of the dragon, whose slavering jaws were opening wide.

Fear for Mina, stronger and more powerful than the dragonfear, ran through Silvan's veins. Drawing his sword, he leaped to stand over her, placing his body between her and the striking dragon.

Cyan had not wanted this Caladon to die so swiftly. He had looked forward to years of tormenting him as he had tormented his grandfather. Such a disappointment, but it could not be helped. Cyan breathed his poisoned gas on the elf.

Silvan coughed and gagged. The fumes sickened him, he felt himself drowning in them. Weakening, he yet managed a single wild sword swipe at the hideous head.

The blade sank into the soft flesh beneath the jaw, doing little true damage but causing the dragon pain. Cyan reared his head, the sword still embedded in the jaw, jerking the blade from Silvan's limp hand. A shake of the dragon's head sent blood spattering and the sword flying across the field

The dragon was whole. He was powerful. He was furious. His hatred for the elves bubbled in his gut. He intended to unleash his poison upon them, watch them die in writhing, choking agony. Cyan spread his wings and bounded into the air.

"Look upon me!" the dragon roared. "Look upon me, Silvanesti! Look upon my might and my power, and look upon your own doom!"

General Konnal saw suddenly the full extent of Glaucous's deception. He had been duped by the dragon. He had been as much Cyan Bloodbane's pawn as the man Konnal had despised, Lorac Caladon. In those last moments, Konnal saw the truth. The shield was not protecting them. It was killing them. Horror-stricken at the thought of the terrible fate he had unwittingly brought down upon his people, Konnal stared up at the green dragon that had been his bane. He opened his mouth to give the order to attack, but at that moment, his heart, filled with fury and guilt, burst in his chest. He pitched forward on his face.

Kiryn ran to his uncle, but Konnal was dead.

The dragon soared higher, circling, beating the air with his great wings, letting the dragonfear settle over the elves like a thick, blinding fog.

Silvan, his vision dimming, sank to the ground beside Mina. He tried, even as he fell dying, to shield her body with his own.

"Mina," he whispered, the last words he would ever speak, "I love you!"

He collapsed. Darkness closed over him.

Mina heard his words. Her amber eyes opened. She looked to see Silvan lying beside her. His own eyes were closed. He was not breathing. She looked about and saw the dragon above the battlefield, preparing to launch his attack. The elves were helpless, paralzyed by the dragonfear that twisted inside them, squeezing their hearts until they could not breathe or move or think of anything except the coming pain and horror. The elven archers stood staring up at death, their arrows nocked and ready to fire, but their shaking hands were limp on the bow strings, barely able to hold the weapons.

Their general lay dead on the ground.

Mina bent over Silvanoshei. Kissing him, she whispered, "You must not die! I need you!"

He began to breathe, but he did not move.

"The archers, Silvanoshei!" she cried. "Tell them to fire! You are their king! They will obey you."

She shook him. "Silvanoshei!"

He stirred, groaned. His eyes flickered, but Mina was running out of time.

She leaped to her feet. "Archers!" she shouted in flawless Silvanesti Elvish. "*Sagasto!* Fire! Fire!"

Her clarion call penetrated the dragonfear of a single archer. He did not know who spoke. He heard only the one word that seemed to have been pounded into his brain with the force of an iron spike. He lifted his bow and aimed at the dragon.

"*Sagasto!*" Mina cried. "Slay him! He betrayed you!"

Another archer heard her words and obeyed, and then another and another after that. They let fly their arrows and, as they did so, they overcame the dragonfear within themselves. The elves saw only an enemy now, one who was mortal, and they reached swiftly to nock their arrows. The first shafts fired from fingers that still trembled flew none too straight, but their target was so immense that even the worst shot must hit its mark, though perhaps not the mark at which it had been aimed. Two arrows tore holes in the dragon's wings. One stuck in his lashing tail. One struck the green scales on his chest and bounced off, fell harmlessly to the ground.

Once the dragonfear was overcome, the elves would not be affected by it again. Now the archers aimed for the vulnerable parts of the dragon's body, aimed for the tender flesh the scales did not cover, under the front legs, so near the heart. They aimed for the joints where the wings attached to the dragon's main body. They aimed for the dragon's eyes.

The other elves lifted their heads now. Dozens at first, then hundreds shook off the dragonfear and grabbed up bow and arrow, spear and lance, and joined the battle. Cries of horror changed to fierce exultation. At last, they were able to face in combat the foe who had brought despair and ruin and death to their land and their people. The sky was dark with arrows and with the dragon's falling blood.

Maddened by the pain, Cyan Bloodbane made a mistake. He did not retreat from the fight. He could have withdrawn, even now, grievously hurt as he was, and flown away to one of his many lairs to nurse his wounds. But he could not believe that the puny people who had been subject to his will for so long could possibly do him mortal harm. One enormous breath of poison would settle them. One breath would end it.

Cyan sucked in that breath and let it out. But the breath that should have been a killing cloud came out a gasp. The poisonous gas was little more than a mist that dissipated in the morning's soft breeze. His next breath rattled in his chest. He felt the arrows sink deep into his bowels. He felt their points perilously close to his heart. He felt them puncture his lungs. Too late, he tried to break off the battle. Too late, he sought to flee his tormentors. His torn and broken wings would not hold the air. He could not maintain his altitude.

Cyan rolled over on his back. He was falling, and he could not stop his fall. Plummeting to the ground, he realized in a final moment of bitter despair that his last wrenching moves had carried him away from the battlefield, where his body crashing down on top of the elves might have taken many of his enemies with him. He was over the forest, above the trees.

With a last defiant roar of fury, Cyan Bloodbane fell onto the trees of Silvanesti, the trees that he had twisted and tormented during the dream. The trees were waiting to receive him. The aspens and the oaks, the cypress and the pines stood firm, like bold pikeman. They did not break beneath his weight but held strong and true as their enemy smashed into them. The trees punched through Cyan Bloodbane's scales, pierced his flesh, impaled him on their splintered limbs. The trees of Silvanesti took their own full measure of revenge.

Silvanoshei opened his eyes to see Mina standing protectively over him. He staggered to his feet, dazed and unsteady, but improving with each passing moment. Mina was watching the battle against the dragon. Her face held no expression, as she watched the arrows meant to pierce her own body penetrate the body of her foe.

Silvan barely noticed the battle. He could see and think only of Mina.

"You brought me back from death," Silvan whispered, his throat raw from the gas. "I was dying, dead. I felt my soul slipping away. I saw my own body lying on the ground. I saw you kiss me. You kissed me, and I could not leave you! And so I live!"

"The One God brought you back, Silvanoshei," said Mina calmly. "The One God has a purpose for you yet in this life."

"No, you!" he insisted. "You gave me life! Because you love me! My life is yours, now, Mina. My life and my heart."

Mina smiled, but she was intent on the fight. "Look there, Silvanoshei," she said, pointing, "This day you have defeated your most terrible enemy, Cyan Bloodbane, who put you on the throne, thinking you as weak as your grandfather. You have proved him wrong."

"We owe our victory to you, Mina," Silvan said, exultant. "You gave the order to fire. I heard your voice through the darkness."

"We have not achieved victory yet," she said, and her gaze was farseeing, abstracted. "Not yet. The battle has not ended. Your people remain in mortal danger. Cyan Bloodbane will die, but the shield he placed over you remains."

Silvan could barely hear her voice over the cheers of his people and the furious howls of the mortally wounded dragon. Putting his arm around her slender waist, he drew her near to him, to hear her words better.

"Tell me again, Mina," he said. "Tell me again what you told me earlier about the shield."

"I tell you nothing more than what Cyan Bloodbane told you," Mina replied. "He used the elves' fear of the world against them. They imagine the shield protects them, but in

reality it is killing them. The magic of the shield draws upon
the life-force of the elves to maintain its life. So long as it
remains in place, your people will slowly die until at last
there will be no one left for the shield to protect. Thus did
Cyan Bloodbane mean to destroy every one of you, laughing
all the while because your people imagined themselves to be
safe and protected when, in reality, they were the means of
their own destruction."

"If this is true, the shield must be destroyed," said Silvan.
"But I doubt if even our strongest sorcerers could shatter its
powerful magic."

"You don't need sorcerers, Silvan. You are the grandson of
Lorac Caladon. You can end what your grandfather began.
You have the power to bring down the shield. Come with
me." Mina held out her hand to him. "I will show you what
you must do."

Silvan took hold of her hand, small-boned, fine. He drew
close to her, looked down into her eyes. He saw himself, shining in the amber.

"You must kiss me," she said and she lifted her lips.

Silvan was quick to obey. His lips touched hers, tasted the
sweetness for which he hungered.

Not far distant, Kiryn kept watch beside the body of his
uncle. He had seen Silvanoshei fall. He had known that his
cousin was dead, for no one could survive the dragon's poisoned breath. Kiryn grieved for them both, for his cousin, for
his uncle. Both had been deluded by Glaucous. Both had paid
the price. Kiryn had knelt beside his uncle to wait for his own
death, wait for the dragon to slay them.

Kiryn watched, astonished, to see the human girl, Mina,
lift her head and regain her feet. She was strong, alert, seemingly untouched by the poison. She looked down at Silvanoshei, lying at her side. She kissed the lifeless lips, and to
Kiryn's amazement and unease, his cousin drew in a breath.

Kiryn saw Mina act to rally the flagging spirits of the elven archers. He heard her voice, crying out the order to fire in Elvish. He watched his people rally, watched them battle back against their foe. He watched the dragon die.

He watched all with boundless gladness, a gladness that brought tears to his eyes, but with a sense of unease in his heart.

Why had the human done this? What was her reason? Why had she watched her army kill elves one day and acted to save elves the next?

He watched her embrace Silvan. Kiryn wanted to run to them, to snatch his cousin away from the girl's touch. He wanted to shake him, shake some sense into him. But Silvan would not listen.

And why should he? Kiryn thought.

He himself was confused, stunned by the day's awful events. Why should his cousin listen to Kiryn's words of warning when the only proof he could offer of their veracity was a dark shadow that passed over his soul every time he looked upon the girl, Mina.

Kiryn turned away from them. Reaching down, he closed his uncle's staring eyes with a gentle touch. His duty, as a nephew, was to the dead.

"Come with me, Silvan," Mina urged him, her lips soft against his cheek. "Do this for your people."

"I do this for you, Mina," Silvan whispered. Closing his eyes, he placed his lips on hers.

Her kiss was honey, yet it stung him. He drank in the sweetness, flinched from the searing pain. She drew him into darkness, a darkness that was like the darkness of the storm cloud. Her kiss was like the lightning bolt, blinded him, sent him tumbling over the edge of a precipice. He could not stop his fall. He crashed against rocks, felt his bones breaking, his body bruised and aching. The pain was excruciating, and the pain was ecstasy. He wanted it to end so badly that he would have been glad for death. He wanted the pain to last beyond forever.

Her lips drew away from his, the spell was broken.

As though he had come back from the dead, Silvan opened his eyes and was amazed to see the sun, the blood-red sun of twilight. Yet it had been noontime when he had kissed her. Hours had passed, seemingly, but where had they gone? Lost in her, forgotten in her. All around him was still and quiet. The dragon had vanished. The armies were nowhere in sight. His cousin was gone. Silvan slowly realized that he no longer stood on the field of battle. He was in a garden, a garden he dimly recognized by the fading light of the waning sun.

I know this place, he thought dazedly. It seems familiar. Yet where am I? And how do I come to be here? Mina! Mina! He was momentarily panicked, thinking he had lost her.

He felt her hand close over his, and he sighed deeply and clasped his hand over hers.

I stand in the Garden of Astarin, he realized. The palace garden. A garden I can see from my bedroom window. I came here once, and I hated it. The place made my flesh crawl. There—a dead plant. And another and another. A tree dying as I watch, its leaves curling and twisting as if in pain, turning gray, falling off. The only reason there are any living plants at all in this garden is because the palace gardeners and the Woodshapers replace the dead plants with living plants from their own personal gardens. Yet, to bring anything living into this garden is to sentence it to death.

Only one tree survives in this garden. The tree in the very heart of the garden. The tree they call the Shield Tree, because it was once surrounded by a luminous shield nothing could penetrate. Glaucous claimed the magic of the tree kept the shield in place. So it does, but the tree's roots do not draw nourishment from the soil. The tree's roots extend into the heart of every elf in Silvanesti.

He felt the tree's roots coiling inside him.

Taking hold of Mina by the hand, Silvanoshei led her through the dying garden to the tree that grew in the center. The Shield Tree lived. The Shield Tree thrived. The Shield tree's leaves were green and healthy, green as the scales of the green dragon. The Shield Tree's trunk was blood-colored, seemed to ooze blood, as they looked at it. Its limbs contorted, wriggled like snakes.

I must uproot the tree. I am the Grandson of Lorac. I must tear the tree's roots from the hearts of my people, and so I will free them. Yet I am loathe to touch the evil thing. I'll find an axe, chop it down.

Though you were to chop it down a hundred times, a voice whispered to him, *a hundred times it would grow back.*

It will die, now that Cyan Bloodbane is dead. He was the one who kept it alive.

You are the one keeping it alive. Mina spoke no word, but she laid her hand on his heart. *You and your people. Can't you feel its roots twisting and turning inside you, sapping your strength, sucking the very life from you?*

Silvan could feel something wringing his heart, but whether it was the evil of the tree or the touch of her hand, he could not tell.

He caught up her hand and kissed it. Leaving her standing on the path, among the dying plants, he walked toward the living tree. The tree sensed its danger. Gray vines twined around his ankles. Dead branches fell on him, struck him on the back and on his shoulder. He kicked at the vines and tossed the branches away from him.

As he drew near the tree, he felt the weakness. He felt it grow on him the closer he came. The tree sought to kill him as it had killed so many before him. Its sap ran red with the blood of his people. Every shining leaf was the soul of a murdered elf.

The tree was tall, but its trunk was spindly. Silvan could

easily place his hands around it. He was weak and wobbly from the aftereffects of the poison and wondered if he would have the strength to pull it from the ground.

You have the strength. You alone.

Silvan wrapped his hands around the tree trunk. The trunk writhed in his grasp like a snake, and he shuddered at the horrible feeling.

He let loose, fell back. If the shield falls, he thought, suddenly assailed by doubt, our land will lie unprotected.

The Silvanesti nation has stood proudly for centuries protected by the courage and skill of its warriors. Those days of glory will return. The days when the world respected the elves and honored them and feared them. You will be king of a powerful nation, a powerful people.

I will be king, Silvan repeated to himself. She will see me puissant, noble, and she will love me.

He planted his feet on the ground. He took firm hold of the slithering tree trunk and, summoning strength from his excitement, his love, his ambition, his dreams, he gave a great heave.

A single root snapped. Perhaps it was the root that had tapped into his own heart for when it released, his strength and his will increased. He pulled and tugged, his shoulders straining. He felt more roots give, and he redoubled his efforts.

"For Mina!" he said beneath his breath.

The roots let go their hold so suddenly that Silvan toppled over backward. The tree came crashing down on top of him. He was unhurt, but he could see nothing for the leaves and twigs and branches that covered him.

Angry, feeling that he must look a fool, he crawled out from under. His face flushed with triumph and embarrassment, he wiped the dirt and the muck from his hands.

The sun shone hot on his face. Looking up, Silvan saw the sun, saw it shining with an angry red fire. No gauzy curtain obscured its rays, no shimmering aura filtered its light. He found he could not look directly at the blazing sun, could not look anywhere near it. The sight was painful, hurt his eyes. Blinking away tears, he could see nothing except a black spot where the sun had been.

"Mina!" he cried, shading his eyes, trying to see her. "Look, Mina! Your God was right. The shield is down!"

Silvan stumbled out onto the path. He could not yet see clearly. "Mina?" he cried. "Mina?"

Silvan called and called. He called long after the sun had fallen from the sky, called long into the darkness. He called her name until he had no voice left, and then he whispered it.

"Mina!"

No answer came.

33

For Love of Mina

aldar had not slept since the day of the battle. He kept watch all the long night, standing just inside the shadows of the caves where what remained of the forces of her Knights had taken refuge. He refused to relinquish his post to anyone, although several had offered to relieve him of his self-imposed duty. He shook his horned head to all proposals, sent the men away, and eventually they quit coming.

The men who had survived the battle lay in the caves, tired and frightened, speaking little. The wounded did their best to stifle their groans and cries, afraid that the noise would draw down the enemy upon them. Mostly they whispered a name, her name and wondered why she did not come to comfort them. Those who died did so with her name on their lips.

Galdar was not watching for the enemy. That duty was being handled by others. Pickets crouched in the thick foliage on watch for any elven scout who might happen to stumble upon their hiding place. Two elves did so, early this morning.

The pickets dealt with them swiftly and silently, breaking their necks and throwing the bodies into the deep and swift-flowing Thon-Thalas.

Galdar was furious when he found out that his men had actually captured the two elves alive before killing them.

"I wanted to question them, you dolts!" he cried in a rage, raising his hand to strike one of the scouts.

"Relax, Galdar," Samuval admonished, placing his hand on the minotaur's fur-covered arm. "What good would torturing them have done? The elves would only refuse to talk, and their screams would be heard for miles."

"They would tell me what they have done with her," Galdar said, lowering his arm, but glowering viciously at the scouts, who beat a hasty retreat. "They would tell me where she was being held. I would see to that." He clenched and unclenched his fist.

"Mina left orders that no prisoners were to be taken, Galdar. She ordered that any elf we found was to be put immediately to death. You vowed to obey her orders. Would you be foresworn?" Samuval asked.

"I'll keep my vow." Galdar growled and took up his post again. "I promised her, and I will keep my promise. Didn't I keep it yesterday? I stood there and watched her taken captive by that bastard elven king. Captured alive by her most bitter enemy. Carried off in triumph to what terrible fate? To be made sport of, to be made a slave, to be tormented, killed. I promised her I would not interfere, and I kept my word. But I am sorry now that I did so," he added with a bitter oath.

"Remember what she said, my friend," Samuval said quietly. "Remember her words. 'They think they will make me their captive. But in so doing I will capture them, every single one.' Remember that, and do not lose your faith."

Galdar stood at the entrance to the cave all that morning. He saw the sun rise to its zenith, saw its angry eye glare through the shield, and he envied it fiercely, for the sun could see Mina and he could not.

He watched in wonder the fight with the green dragon, saw the sky rain blood and green scales. Galdar had no love for dragons, even those who fought on his side. An old minotaur adage, dating back from the time of their great hero, Kaz, maintained that dragons had only one side: their own. Galdar heard the dragon's death roar, felt the ground shake from the beast's fall, and wondered only what portent this held for them. For Mina.

Captain Samuval joined Galdar to watch the fight. He brought the minotaur food—rat, caught in the cave—and drink. Galdar drank the water, but he refused the rat meat. The men had little enough to eat as it was. Others needed it more than he did. Captain Samuval shrugged and ate the rat himself. Galdar continued his watch.

The hours passed. The wounded groaned quietly, died quietly. The sun started to fall, a blood-red sun, dropping behind its curtain of gauze. The sun was distorted and misshapen, looking like no sun Galdar had ever before seen. He shifted his gaze away. He did not like seeing the sun through the shield, wondered how the elves could stand it.

His eyes closed in spite of himself. He was nodding off, drowsing on his feet, when Captain Samuval's voice sounded right next to him, seemed to explode over the minotaur like a fireball.

"Would you look at that!"

Galdar's eyes flared open. He fumbled for his sword. "What? Where?"

"The sun!" Captain Samuval said. "No, don't look at it directly. It will blind you!" He shaded his eyes with his hand, peered out from beneath the shadow. "Damn!"

Galdar looked heavenward. The light was so bright it made his eyes water, and he had to look hurriedly away. He wiped the tears from his muzzle and squinted. The sun had burned away the gauze. It shone bright and fierce upon the world as if it were a new-made sun and was exulting in its power. He lowered his gaze, half-blinded.

Mina stood before him, bathed in the blood-red light of the new-born sun.

Galdar was about to raise a shout of joy, but she laid a finger on her lips, counseling silence. The minotaur settled for a huge grin. He did not tell her he was thankful to see her. She had promised she would return to them, and he did not want her to think he doubted. In truth, he had not doubted. Not in his heart. He jerked a thumb toward the horizon.

"What does it mean?" he asked.

"The shield is lowered," Mina replied. She was pale and weary to the point of falling. She reached out her hand, and Galdar was honored and proud to support her with his arm, his right arm. "The spell is broken. As we speak, the forces of General Dogah, many thousands strong, are marching across the border of Silvanesti."

Leaning on Galdar's strong arm, Mina entered the cave. The men would have cheered, but she cautioned them to silence.

The men gathered around her, reached out their hands to touch her. Tired as she was, she said a word to each one of them, calling each by name. She would not eat or drink or rest until she had visited the wounded and asked the God to heal them. She prayed over every one of the dead, as well, holding the cold hands in her own, her head bowed.

Then and only then would she drink water and sit down to rest. She summoned her Knights and officers to a council of war.

"We have only to continue a little while longer in hiding," she told them. "My plan is to meet up with the armies of General Dogah and join them in the capture of Silvanost."

"How soon can he be here?" Samuval asked.

"Dogah and his forces will be able to march rapidly," Mina

replied. "He will meet no resistance. The elven border patrol was pulled back to deal with us. Their army is in disarray. Their general is dead. The shield has fallen."

"How, Mina?" Galdar asked and others echoed his wonder. "Tell us how you brought down the shield?"

"I told the king the truth," Mina said. "I told him that the shield was killing his people. Their king himself brought down the shield."

The Knights laughed, enjoying the fine irony. They were in excellent spirits, cheered and heartened by Mina's return and the miraculous lowering of the magical shield, which had for so long kept them from striking at their enemy.

Turning to ask Mina a question, Galdar saw that she had fallen asleep. Gently, he lifted her in his arms and carried her—she was a light as a child—to the bed he had made for her himself, a blanket spread over dried pine needles in a niche in the rock wall. He eased her down, covered her with a blanket. She never opened her eyes.

The minotaur settled himself near her, seated with his broad back against the rocky wall to guard her sleep.

Captain Samuval came to keep watch beside Galdar. The captain offered the minotaur more rat meat, and this time Galdar did not refuse.

"Why would the king lower the shield?" Galdar wondered, crunching the rat, bones and all. "Why would he bring down the elves' only defense? It doesn't make any sense. Elves are sneaky. Perhaps it is a trap."

"No trap," said Samuval. Bunching up a blanket, he shoved it beneath his head and stretched himself out on the cold cavern floor. "You will see, my friend. In a week's time, we'll be walking arm and arm down the streets of Silvanost."

"But why would he do such a thing?" Galdar persisted.

"Why else?" Samuval said, yawning until his jaws cracked. "You saw the way he looked at her. You saw her take him captive. He did it for love of her, of course."

Galdar settled himself. He considered the answer, decided that his comrade was right. Before he slept, he whispered the words softly to the night.

"For love of Mina."

Epilogue

ar from where Mina slept, guarded by her troops, Gilthas watched from a window of the Tower of the Speaker of the Sun as the sun lifted higher into the sky. He imagined its rays gilding the spears of the armies of Beryl as that army marched across the border into Qualinesti. The Solamnic, Gerard, had suggested a plan, a desperate plan, and now he and Marshal Medan waited for Gilthas to make a decision, a decision that would either mean salvation for his people or would end in their ultimate destruction. Gilthas would make that decision. He would make it because he was their king. But he would put off the decision for the moment. He would spend this moment watching the sun shimmer on the green leaves of the trees of his homeland.

On Schallsea, Tasslehoff and Palin watched Beryl and her minions fly closer and closer. They heard the trumpets blasting, heard people crying out in terror. They heard them cry for Goldmoon, but she was gone. The broken bits of the magical Device of Time Journeying lay scattered on the floor, the light of the jewels dimmed by the shadows of the wings of dragons.

Goldmoon did not see the sun. She did not see the dragons. She was far beneath the ocean, wrapped in its darkness. The gnome expostulated and sweated and raced here and dashed there, mopping up water, sopping up oil, cranking cranks and pumping bellows. Goldmoon paid no attention to him. She had been absorbed by the darkness. She traveled northward with the river of the dead.

Silvanoshei stood alone in the Garden of Astarin, beside the dying Shield Tree, and watched the new-made blazing sun wither the tree's roots.

Poised on the borders of Silvanesti, General Dogah of the Knights of Neraka watched the sun emerge from the crysallis of the fallen shield. The next morning, when the sun had mounted into the sky, when it shone clear and bright, General Dogah gave his army the order to march.

AN EXCERPT

THE MINOTAUR WARS
VOLUME ONE
NIGHT OF BLOOD

Richard A. Knaak

Chapter 1
Night of Blood

 okun Es-Kalin, first cousin of the emperor, Ship Master of the House of Kalin's merchant fleet . . .

They found Zokun at his estate on the wooded, northern edge of the imperial capital of Nethosak. He was fast asleep in his plush, down-filled bed. Although in command of a mighty fleet of some two hundred ships, he himself had not gone to sea for years and had no desire to do so. Zokun preferred the rewards of power to the work, and many of his tasks were handled by well-trained subordinates who knew their proper place in the imperium.

A bottle of rich and heady briarberry wine, one of the finest produced in the empire and coveted even by the lesser races beyond, stood empty next to three others previously drained. A slim, brown form beside the fat, snoring minotaur turned over in her sleep. This was not his mate, Hila, but a younger female who hoped soon to take Hila's place.

And so she did, dying along with the Ship Master. The helmed assassins dispatched her with one stroke—compared to the four needed to gut her drunken lover. Both perished swiftly.

No servants heard them cry out. None of Zokun's family came to his aid. Most of the former had been rounded up and taken away. The latter, including Hila, had been slain at exactly the same time as the venerable Ship Master and his mistress.

* * * * *

The feminine hand took the long quill pen, dipped it in a rich, red ink, and drew a line through Zokun's name. The wielder of the quill took care not to spill any of the ink on her silky gold and sable robes. She moved the pen to another name—

Grisov Es-Neros, councilor to the emperor and patriarch of the house most closely allied with that of Kalin . . .

Grisov was a scarred, thin minotaur whose fur was almost snow white. His snout had a wrinkled, deflated appearance, and over the years his brow had enveloped his eyes. Despite his grizzled countenance, the patriarch was hardly infirm. His reflexes were still those of the young champion of the Great Circus he had been years before the bloody war against the aquatic Magori. His well-schooled, well-paid healers encouraged him to sleep at a proper hour, but Grisov continued to take his late-night walks, a cherished tradition to him and others in this area of Nethosak. Grisov liked to survey his fiefdom, reminding himself that, as long as Chot was kept in power, the children of Neros would profit. He had no qualms about what part he had played over the years in propping up the emperor; the strongest and most cunning always triumphed.

The street did not seem as well tended as when he was young. Grisov recalled immaculate streets of white marble with nary a sign of refuse. These days, all sorts of trash littered the avenues. Bits and pieces of old food, broken ale bottles, and rotting vegetation offended the patriarch's sensibility. One large piece of trash, a snoring, drunken sailor, snuggled against the high, spiked wall of the abode of one Grisov's nephews, a wastrel who lived off the hard work of his uncle.

It was all the fault of the young generation. The young could be blamed for everything. They had never learned the discipline of their elders.

Two able warriors clad in thigh-length, leather-padded metal kilts, colored sea-blue and green—the official clan colors—accompanied the robed minotaur. Each carried a long, double-edged axe shined to a mirror finish and etched with the Neros symbol—a savage wave washing over rocks—in the center of the head. Grisov thought the guards a nuisance, but at least this pair knew not to speak unless spoken to. The guards knew his routine well, knew what stops their master would make, knew what comments he would murmur and how they ought to respond.

Yet, there was one change in the routine this night. Grisov had no intention of letting drunkards invade his domain.

"Kelto, see that piece of garbage on his way. I'll not have him sully this street!"

"Aye, patriarch." With a look of resignation, the young warrior headed toward the snoring sailor.

A whistling sound made the patriarch's ears stiffen. Recognition of what that sound presaged dawned just a second later—a second too late.

A gurgling noise made the elder warrior turn to see his guard transfixed, a wooden shaft piercing his throat.

As the hapless warrior fell, Grisov turned to Kelto—only to find him sprawled on the ground, his blood already pooling on the street.

Peering around, the elder minotaur discovered that the drunken sailor had vanished.

A decoy.

Grisov reached for his sword and cried, "Villains! Cowards! Come to me, you dishonorable—"

Two bolts struck him from opposite directions, one piercing a lung, the other sinking deep into his back. Blood spilled over his luxurious blue robe, overwhelming the green Neros symbol on his chest.

With a short gasp, the patriarch dropped his blade and collapsed beside his guards.

* * * * *

A young minotaur, clad in plain, ankle-length robes of white trimmed with red, approached the senior priestess, bringing a silver flask of wine for the empty chalice sitting next to the pile of parchments. The priestess looked up briefly, then flicked her eyes toward the half-melted candle by which she checked her lists. The servant glanced that way but saw nothing. The servant finished refilling the goblet then quickly backed away.

"Tyra de-Proul?" asked the senior priestess. She was a chestnut-colored female, still attractive in the eyes of her kind. Her words were whispered to the open air. She fixed her gaze in the general direction of a lengthy silk tapestry depicting a white, almost ghostlike bird ascending to the starry heavens. "You are certain?" the priestess asked the emptiness.

A moment later, her ears twitched in clear satisfaction. She nodded, then looked over the lists. Many lines were already crossed out, but she soon located the one she desired.

A smile crossed her visage as she brought the quill down. "Another page complete."

* * * * *

On the island of Kothas, sister realm to Mithas and a two-day journey from the capital, Tyra de-Proul stirred from sleep.

Her mate had been due to return this evening from his voyage to Sargonath, a minor minotaur colony located on the northeastern peninsula of Ansalon, but he had not yet arrived. Feeling pensive, Tyra pushed back her thick, gray mane and rose.

Jolar's ship might just be late. That shouldn't bother her at all, yet some vague dread insisted on disturbing her asleep.

The tall, athletic female poured some water. As appointed administrator of the emperor's interests, Tyra made constant sea trips between the imperial capital and this island's principal city of Morthosak. Jolar's lateness could readily be attributed to any number of innocent causes, even foul weather.

A muffled sound beyond her door brought her to full attention. At this hour, no one in the house other than the sentries should be awake, and the sentries knew to make their rounds without causing clamor of any sort.

Tyra seized her sword and scabbard, then headed toward the door. Weapon drawn, she opened it—

And was stunned to see a frantic struggle taking place between Jolar and three helmed minotaurs at the foot of the steps.

One of the intruders had a hand over her mate's muzzle, but Jolar twisted free and shouted, "Flee, Tyra! The house is under siege! There is no—"

He gasped, a dagger in his side. Jolar fell to the floor.

Like all minotaurs, Tyra had been trained from childhood first and foremost as a warrior. As a young female, she had helped fight back the vile Magori when the crustaceans rose from the sand and surf, the destruction of all minotaurs their sole desire. Never in her life had she turned from a battle, whether on the field or in the political arena.

With a savage cry, Tyra threw herself down the steps, her sword cutting the air as she descended.

The nearest foe stumbled against her mate's corpse. Tyra thrust the blade through the helmed assassin's unprotected throat. Before he had even dropped to the floor, she did battle with the second, a young female who moved with the haughtiness of one who thought that before her stood merely a decrepit elder. Tyra caught the intruder's blade and twisted it to the side. She kicked at her opponent and watched with satisfaction as the latter went flying back into a nearby wall, knocked unconscious.

In the dim illumination, she made out two dead bodies in the lower hall. One also wore a helm, but the other Tyra recognized even though he lay muzzle down.

Mykos. Her eldest son. In three days he would have become the newest addition to the Imperial Guard. General Rahm Es-Hestos, the commander of the emperor's elite, had personally recommended Mykos, a moment of great pride for his mother.

An axe had done him in. His blood still pooled beside his hacked torso.

Tyra screamed, swinging anew at the last of her attackers. He continued to back away from her.

"Stand still so I can smite the head from your body, you dishonorable dog! My mate—my children!—demand your blood!"

Still edging away, her opponent said nothing.

Too late did the obvious occur to the outraged minotaur. Tyra de-Proul wheeled quickly, but not quickly enough.

The female assassin who she thought had been knocked unconscious stabbed Tyra through the heart.

"Stupid old cow," the assassin muttered.

Tyra slipped to the floor and joined her mate in death.

* * * * *

So many names crossed out. So few remaining.

She looked over the pages, noting the survivors. Some looked to be of no major consequence, but a handful tugged at her, urgently.

A chill wind suddenly coursed through the stone chamber that served as her private sanctum. She quickly protected the candle.

My Lady Nephera . . . came a voice in her head, a voice rasping and striving for breath.

Nephera glanced beyond the candle, seeing only glimpses of a shadowy figure at the edge of her vision. At times, she could make out details—such as a hooded cloak—and within the cloak a minotaur unusually gaunt of form. Of the eyes that stared back at her, she sometimes made out the whites, but this monstrous phantasm had no pupils.

The cloak hung in damp tatters with glimpses of pale flesh beneath. Whenever this particular visitor appeared, the smell of the sea always seemed to accompany him—the sea as the eternal graveyard.

As she reached for a grape from the bowl set by her side—the only sustenance she would permit herself this glorious night—the elegantly clad High Priestess of the Temple of the Forerunners waited for the ominous figure to speak again.

The shade's decaying mouth did not move, but once more Lady Nephera heard a grating voice. *Four of the Supreme Circle now join me in death.*

She knew three names already, but the addition of a fourth pleased her. "Who? Name all four so that I can be certain!"

General Tohma, Boril, General Astos . . .

All names she had. "Who else?"

Kesk the Elder.

"Ah, excellent." Pulling free one of the parchments, Nephera located the name and gave it a swift, inky stroke—as lethal to the council member in question as the axes and swords that had actually killed him. The elimination of the highest-ranking members of the Supreme Circle, the august governing body under the emperor, gave her immense satisfaction. They, more than most, she held responsible for all that had happened to her and her husband—and to the empire.

Thinking of her mate, the Forerunner priestess scowled. "My husband's hand-picked warriors move quick, but not quick enough. This should be finished by now!"

Send out your own, responded the gaunt shadow. *Your trusted Protectors, mistress?*

She would have dearly loved to do so, but Hotak had insisted otherwise. This had to be done without the temple. The military would not look with favor on her husband if it appeared that the Forerunners influenced his actions.

"No. We shall leave this to my husband. The triumph must be his and his alone." Lady Nephera picked up the stack of parchments, her intense black gaze burning into each name. "Still, the temple will have its say."

* * * * *

Throughout the length and span of the empire, the Night of Blood continued relentlessly.

On Mito, three days' journey east of the imperial capital, the governor of the most populated island colony rushed forth to greet two massive vessels that had sailed into port. An honor guard had quickly been arranged, for who but an important dignitary would arrive without warning and with such a show of force? The captain of the first vessel marched a squad of helmed warriors down to salute the assembled well-wishers—and executed the governor where he stood.

On the island of Duma, the home of General Kroj, commander of the empire's southern forces and hero of the battles of Turak Major and Selees, became the scene of a pitched battle. The fight went on until dawn, when the barriers of the general's estate were finally broken down by his own troops, who joined the attackers. Kroj committed ritual suicide with a dagger even as helmed fighters burst down the door to his study. They would find his family already dead, their throats slit by Kroj just prior to his own demise.

In Mithas, Edan Es-Brog, the high priest of the Temple of Sargonnas, would be discovered dead in his sleep, a mixture of poisons in his evening potion.

Veria de-Goltyn, Chief Captain of the eastern fleet, drowned as she sought to escape her burning ship. Her own captains had been paid to turn on her.

Konac, imperial taxmaster, was stabbed more than a dozen times at the door of the emperor's coffers. A stronger figure than his rotund appearance indicated, Konac would outlast his guards and two assassins, making it to just within a few yards of the Imperial Guard's headquarters before dying. No one within heard his final choked warning.

A massive fleet, organized quickly and secretly over the course of weeks and combining the might of over three dozen turncoat generals and captains, spread out over the expanse of minotaur interests. Some of them had been on their journeys for days already. Before the night would conclude, twenty-two colonial governors, their principal officers, and hundreds of loyal subordinates would be executed. All but a handful of the major territories and settlements within a week's reach of the main island would be under the iron control of Hotak's followers.

All of this, Lady Nephera saw as it happened. She had eyes everywhere. She knew more than her husband's lackeys. Even the emperor, with his complex and far-reaching network of messengers and spies, knew but a fraction of what the high priestess knew.

Thinking of the emperor, Nephera turned her brooding eyes to one particular page, reading the only name still listed. No furious stain of ink expunged this name's existence, yet by her estimate, only minutes remained before she would have the ultimate pleasure.

The high priestess read the name over and over, picturing the puffy, overfed countenance, the vain, ambitious, clownish visage.

Chot Es-Kalin.

In his younger days, the massive, graying minotaur had been the scourge of the Circus, the unbeatable champion to whom all had deferred in admiration. Chot the Terrible, he was called. Chot the Invincible! Over the span of his life and decades-long rule, scores of would-be rivals had fallen to his bloody battle-axe. No minotaur had ever held the title of emperor for so many years.

"More wine, my lord?"

Chot studied the slim, dark-brown female lounging next to him on the vast silk-sheeted bed. She had not only the energy of youth, but the beauty as well. Chot's last mate had died over a decade ago, and since that time he had preferred enticing visitors to a regular companion. The much-scarred emperor knew that this added to the list of grievances his political foes spouted about him, but he did not care. His foes could do nothing so long as he accepted the imperial challenges and faced down his opponents in the Great Circus.

They could do nothing so long as each of their champions fell dead at his feet.

He shifted his great girth and handed his mistress the empty goblet. Years of living the glory of an emperor had taken some toll on his body, but Chot still considered himself the ultimate warrior, the envy of other males and the desire of all females.

"Is that enough, my lord?" his companion said as she topped off his drink.

"Enough, Maritia." Chot took a gulp of the rich, red liquid, then looked the female warrior over, savoring the curve of her lithe form. Some female minotaurs looked too much like males. Chot preferred curves. A female should look like a female, especially when she had been granted the glorious company of her emperor.

His bed companion replaced the squat wine bottle on the carved, marble table. The well-cleaned remains of a roasted goat sat atop a silver tray next to the bottle, and beside that stood a wooden bowl filled with exotic fruit shipped to the capital from one of the farthest and most tropical colonies.

Maritia leaned forward, rubbing the soft tip of her muzzle against him. Curiously, the image of her father flashed into his mind. Chot had recently solved the problem of her insufficiently loyal and increasingly irritating father by sending him far, far away on a mission of some import—and some danger as well. If he succeeded, his glory would reflect on Chot. If he died in combat—a more likely outcome—so much the better.

Chot belched, and the world briefly swam around him. The emperor rolled onto his back, snorting. Enough entertainment for tonight. Time he got some sleep.

There was a fuzzy sound in the distance.

"What's that?" he rumbled, trying to rise.

"I heard nothing, my lord," replied Maritia. She rubbed her graceful hand over his matted brown and gray fur.

Chot relaxed again. It would be a shame when he had to banish her, but she would never forgive him once she found out what he had done to her father.

"Sleep, my lord," Maritia cooed. "Sleep forever."

He jarred awake—in time to see the dagger poised above his head.

Drunken, tired, and out of shape, Chot nonetheless reacted with swiftness. He caught her wrist and managed to twist the blade free. The dagger clattered on the marble floor.

"What in the name of Argon's Chain do you think you're doing?" he roared, his head pounding.

In response, she raked her long, sharp nails across the side of his muzzle.

Roaring, Chot released the fool. Maritia scrambled away from the bed as the emperor put a hand to his bloody face.

"Vixen!" Legs protesting, the immense minotaur rose. "You little cow!"

She glared at the last insult, one of the worst things anyone could call a minotaur. Chot stood a head taller and still carried much muscle under his portly girth, but the female seemed strangely unafraid.

The emperor snorted. Maritia would learn fear.

Then he heard the same fuzzy noise as earlier, only closer. "What's that?" he mumbled, forgetting her for the moment. "Who's fighting out there?"

"That would be your Imperial Guard, my lord," Maritia said, pronouncing his title as if it were excrement. "They are busy falling to the swords and axes of your enemies."

"What's that?" Chot struggled to think clearly. His guards. He had to call his guards. "Sentries! Attend me!"

Maritia smirked. "They are otherwise detained, my lord."

The emperor's stomach suddenly churned. Too much wine, too much goat. Chot put one hand on the bed. "I must think. I must think."

"Think all you like, but my father should be here shortly."

"Your . . . father?" Battling against the nausea and the pounding headache, Chot froze. "Hotak's here? Impossible. I sent him to the mainland weeks ago!"

"And despite your treachery, he's returned. Returned to demand the justice due to him, due the entire imperium!"

With a roar, Chot lunged for her. Maritia eluded his grasp. The emperor turned, seized his favorite axe, and swung wildly. He came nowhere near the treacherous female, though he did drive her back.

"Assassin! Traitor! Traitors!"

Maritia attempted to retrieve her dagger, but Chot swung again. The heavy blade of the twin-edged axe buried itself in his bed, cutting through expensive sheets, through the rich, down padding, and even through the oak frame.

As the bed collapsed in a heap, the emperor stumbled back. Through bleary eyes he glared at Hotak's daughter.

"Slay me if you can," Maritia sneered. "But you'll not live more than a few minutes longer." Her ears twitched toward the window behind Chot. "You hear that?"

Keeping his gaze on the female at all times, Chot stepped back to the balcony. He glanced over his shoulder just long enough to see that the palace grounds swarmed with dark figures heading toward the building.

"Father will be here very soon now," Maritia called to him.

"Then he'll find you begging him to save your life . . . cow!"

Chot stumbled toward her, reaching clumsily with one hand while with the other he threatened her with the axe. Maritia dodged readily, leading Chot a merry chase through the room, mocking his growing rage and taunting him with her derision.

He swung wildly. Rounded crystalline vases, minotaur statuettes of emerald, tapestries of spun gold, marble icons of dragons and other fearsome beasts—the treasures he had accumulated through his lengthy reign—scattered in shards.

His own body finally rebelled. Even as fists began to pound upon the door, Chot the Invincible fell against the broken bed, his head spinning, his insides a maelstrom.

"Chot the Magnificent," he heard Maritia mutter. "Rather you should be called Chot the Pathetic."

"I'll . . . I'll . . ." The emperor could say no more.

He heard her open the door, heard the sounds of armed and armored figures marching into his chamber.

"And this is supposed to be the supreme warrior, the epitome of what our people seek to be?"

The emperor fought to raise his head.

They wore the traditional silver helms. Nose guards ran along their muzzles. Their breastplates were also silver, with the ancient symbol of the condor clutching the ax emblazoned on the chest in deep crimson. Well-worn, padded-metal kilts with red tips at the bottom completed their outfits.

These were his soldiers, warriors of the legions—and they had dared such treachery!

In the forefront of the traitorous band stood their leader. Although otherwise clad as his companions, he also wore the richly crested helmet reserved for the highest generals of the empire. The crest, made of thick, excellent horse hair, hung far back. Over his shoulders hung a long, flowing crimson cape.

Dark brown of fur, slightly over seven feet, well-muscled, and with very angular features for one of his race, the leader glared down at his lord with distaste. A pommel-handled sword hung in the scabbard at his side; a large battle-axe was in his grip.

"Chot Es-Kalin," announced the newcomer, nearly spitting out the name.

"Hotak de-Droka," responded the emperor. The de- before the clan name indicated House Droka had its roots on the island of Kothas, considered, especially by those who bore the more regal Es-, the lesser of the two kingdoms making up the heart of the empire.

Hotak looked to his daughter. His expression turned even grimmer. "You've sacrificed far too much, daughter."

"But it wasn't so terrible a sacrifice, father," she responded, turning back to smile coldly at Chot. "Only passing minutes."

"You . . . damned vixen!" Chot struggled to rise. If he could just get his hands around her throat —

The emperor fell to his hands and knees again. "I feel sick," he murmured.

General Hotak kicked at Chot's side. The immense, graying minotaur dropped flat, moaning.

Hotak snorted. He took a step toward his emperor. "Chot Es-Kalin. Chot the Invincible. Chot the Terrible." The one-eyed commander raised his weapon high. In the light cast by the torches of his followers, the symbol of the rearing horse etched into the axe head seemed to flare to life. "Chot the *Fool*. Chot the *Lying*. Chot the *Treacherous*. Time to put your misery and our shame to an end."

Chot could not think. He could not stand. He could no longer even raise a finger. This had to be a mistake! How could this happen?

"I am Chot," he mumbled, looking down in utter bewilderment. He felt the contents of his stomach finally coming up. "I am your *emperor*."

"No more," said Hotak. "No more."

The axe came down.

When it was over, the general handed the bloody weapon to one of his aides then removed his helmet. Dark brown hair with a touch of gray flowed behind his head. Nodding toward the body, Hotak commanded, "Remove that blubbery carcass for burning. Make sure nothing remains. As for the head . . . see to it that there's a high pole set up at the very entrance to the palace grounds. Make certain that anyone who passes by will be able to see it from some distance. Understood?"

"Aye, General—aye, my lord!" the warrior said, correcting himself.

General Hotak de-Droka looked at the soldier, then at his daughter. Maritia smiled and went down on one knee.

One by one, the rest of those who followed him knelt before he who had slain Chot the Terrible, knelt before the new emperor of the minotaur race.

MARGARET WEIS
&
TRACY HICKMAN

The co-creators of the DRAGONLANCE® world return to the
epic tale that introduced Krynn to a generation of fans!

THE LOST CHRONICLES

VOLUME ONE
DRAGONS OF THE DWARVEN DEPTHS

As Tanis and Flint bargain for refuge in Thorbardin, Raistlin
and Caramon go to Neraka to search for one of the spellbooks of
Fistandantilus. The refugees in Thorbardin are trapped when the
draconian army marches, and Flint undertakes a quest to find the
Hammer of Kharas to free them all, while Sturm becomes a key of a
different sort.
Now Available in Paperback!

VOLUME TWO
DRAGONS OF THE HIGHLORD SKIES

Dragon Highlord Ariakas assigns the recovery of the dragon orb taken to
Ice Wall to Kitiara Uth-Matar, who is rising up the ranks of both the dark
forces and of Ariakas's esteem. Finding the orb proves easy, but getting
it from Laurana proves more difficult. Difficult enough to attract the
attention of Lord Soth.
Now Available in Hardcover!

VOLUME THREE
DRAGONS OF THE HOURGLASS MAGE

The wizard Raistlin Majere takes the black robes and travels to the
capital city of the evil empire, Neraka, to serve the Queen of Darkness.
July 2008

RICHARD A. KNAAK

THE OGRE TITANS

The Grand Lord Golgren has been savagely crushing all opposition to his control of the harsh ogre lands of Kern and Blöde, first sweeping away rival chieftains, then rebuilding the capital in his image. For this he has had to deal with the ogre titans, dark, sorcerous giants who have contempt for his leadership.

VOLUME ONE
THE BLACK TALON

Among the ogres, where every ritual demands blood and every ally can become a deadly foe, Golgren seeks whatever advantage he can obtain, even if it means a possible alliance with the Knights of Solamnia, a questionable pact with a mysterious wizard, and trusting an elven slave who might wish him dead.

December 2007

VOLUME TWO
THE FIRE ROSE

With his other enemies beginning to converge on him from all sides, Golgren, now Grand Khan of all his kind, must battle with the Ogre Titans for mastery of a mysterious artifact capable of ultimate transformation and power.

December 2008

VOLUME THREE
THE GARGOYLE KING

Forced from the throne he has so long coveted, Golgren makes a final stand for control of the ogre lands against the Titans . . . against an enemy as ancient and powerful as a god.

December 2009

TRACY HICKMAN

PRESENTS
THE BRIDGES OF TIME

With the power of the Anvil of Time, the Journeyman can travel
the river of time as simply as walking upstream, visiting the
ancient past of Krynn with ease.

VOLUME ONE
THE SELLSWORD
Cam Banks

Vanderjack, a mercenary with a price on his head, agrees out of
desperation to retrieve a priceless treasure for a displaced noble. The
treasure is deep within enemy territory, and he must survive an army of
old foes, a chorus of unhappy ghosts, and the questionable assistance of
a mad gnome to find it.

April 2008

VOLUME TWO
THE SURVIVORS
Dan Willis

A goodhearted dwarf is warned of an apocalyptic flood by the god
Reorx, and he and his motley followers must decide whether the
warning is real—and then survive the disaster that sweeps
through their part of Krynn.

November 2008